PETER CAREY
The Tax Inspector

faber and faber
LONDON · BOSTON

First published in 1991
by Faber and Faber Limited
3 Queen Square London WC1N 3AU
This open market paperback edition first published in 1992

Printed in England by Clays Ltd, St Ives plc

The lines on p. 110 from 'Beds are Burning' by
Midnight Oil, from the album *Diesel and Dust*,
CBS/Sony, 1987, 1990, are quoted by permission of
Midnight Oil

A CIP record for this book is
available from the British Library

ISBN 0-571-16683-0

For Alison

Monday

In the morning Cathy McPherson put three soft-boiled eggs outside Benny Catchprice's door and in the afternoon she fired him from the Spare Parts Department. That's who she was – his father's sister. They were both the same – big ones for kissing and cuddling, but you could not predict them. You could not rely on them for anything important. They had great soft lips and they had a family smell, like almost-rancid butter which came from deep in their skin, from the thick shafts of their wiry hair; they smelt of this, from within them, but also of things they had touched or swallowed – motor oil, radiator hoses, Life Savers, different sorts of alcohol – beer, Benedictine, altar wine on Sundays. She was the one who stroked his ear with her small guitar-calloused fingers and whispered, 'I love you little Ben-Ben,' but she was still a Catchprice and it was not a contradiction that she fired him.

Cathy was married to Howie who had a pencil-line moustache, a ducktail, and a secret rash which stopped in a clean line at his collar and the cuffs of his shirt. He had the ducktail because he was a Rock-a-Billy throwback: Sleepy La Beef, Charlie Feathers, Mickey Gilley, all the losers of Rock 'n' Roll, they were his heroes. He had this rash because he hated Catchprice Motors but no one ever said that. Cathy and Howie sat behind the counter of the Spare Parts Department as if they were Shire engineers or pharmacists. They had a Waiting Room. They set it up with ferns and pots and pans so it smelled of damp and chemical fertilizer and rotting sawdust. In the places on the wall where any normal car business had charts of K.L.G. spark plugs and colour calendars from Turtle Wax, they had the photograph of Cathy shaking hands with Cowboy Jack Clement, the framed letter from Ernest Tubb, the photograph of the band on stage at the Tamworth Festival: Craig on bass guitar, Kevin on drums, Steve Putzel on piano, and Cathy herself out front with a bright red Fender and huge, snake-skin boots she got mail order from *Music City News*. The band was called Big Mack. If they had paid as much attention to Catchprice Motors as they paid to it, there would have been no crisis ever.

Until the Friday afternoon they fired him, Benny worked on the long bench which ran at right angles to the front counter where Cath and Howie sat like Tweedledum and Tweedledee. Behind him were the deep rows of grey metal bins, above his head was the steel mesh floor of the body panel racks. In front of him was a sweaty white brick wall and a single turquoise G.E. fan which swung back and forth but which was never pointed the right way at the right time.

He was sixteen years old. He had unwashed brown hair which curled up behind his ears and fell lankly over his left eye. He had slender arms and a collar-bone which formed a deep well between his neck and shoulder. He worked with a Marlboro in his mouth, a Walkman on his head, a Judas Priest T-shirt with vents cut out and the sleeves slashed so you could see the small shiny scar on his upper right arm. There was a blue mark around the scar like ink on blotting paper – he had tried to make a tattoo around it but the scratches got seriously infected and whatever words were written there were lost. He had a dark blurry fuzz on his sweaty lip, and bright blue cat's eyes full of things he could not tell you.

Those eyes were like gas jets in a rust-flaked pipe. They informed everything you felt about him, that he might, at any second, be ringed with heat – a peacock, something creepy.

Benny rode the length of the counter on a six-wheeled brown swivel chair, from computer to microfiche, from black phone to green phone. He slid, sashayed, did 360° turns, kicking the concrete floor with his size ten Doc Martens combat boots. He had long legs. He was fast and almost perfect. He ordered in parts ex-stock, entered the inventory for monthly delivery and daily delivery and special runs. He made phone quotations to ten different panel shops, to Steve-oh, Stumpy, Mr Fish. He was expert and familiar with them and they gave him a respect he could never get in Catchprice Motors which benefited most from his professionalism.

He hunted by phone and by computer for – to give a for instance – a Jackaroo brake calliper which General Motors at Dandenong said was a definite N/A and est. 12 weeks ex-Japan. It was hot and sweaty back there, with no air but the fan, and dust falling from the steel mesh floor above his head. It was also stressful, no one said it wasn't, and he was good at most of it, but she fired him.

He was shocked and humiliated, but she was the one doing the

4

crying. She offered him a job in the front office – serving petrol! Serving petrol! Her chin was crumpled and her wide nose was creased. You could smell the butter in her hair and the Benedictine on her breath.

She knew what being fired meant to him. They had sat together at her kitchen table at three and four in the morning, he smoking dope, she drinking Benedictine and Coke, while her old man was snoring in the bedroom. She was the forty-five-year-old who was still planning her escape. Not him. He wanted this life. It was all he ever wanted.

But now she was saying he was 'not sufficiently involved'. He was too stunned to say anything back, not even a threat. But when she was back at the front counter, he thought he understood – she imagined he made mistakes because he listened to comedy tapes on the Walkman. She saw him laughing and thought he was not serious.

The truth was: he wore the Walkman to block out the dumb things she and Howie said. They were so loud and confident. They went on and on in some kind of croaking harmony – her bar-smoke voice and his bass mumble. They were like two old birds who had been in one shitty cage all their lives.

He liked his aunt. She was more his mate than his aunt, but her ignorance could be embarrassing. She was frightened of bank-ruptcy and her fear destroyed what little judgement she had. He turned up the volume on 'Derek and Clive Live' and laughed at the lobsters up Jayne Mansfield's arse. Cathy and Howie were killing the business one dumb little bit at a time and Benny could not bear to listen to them do it.

He did not deny his own mistakes, but they were truly minor in comparison. Every part he dealt with had at least 7 digits. What anyone else would call a Camira engine mount was a 5434432 to Benny. These digits jumped places, transposed themselves, leap-frogged. They were like mercury in his fingers as he tried to keep them still: 6's rolled over, 2's and 5's leap-frogged and 4's turned into 7's. Benny's wrists were covered in numbers. Numbers stretched along his long fingers like tattoos, across his palms like knitting, but he still made errors.

He was asked to put in an order for three dozen 2965736 electrical connectors. The next day the truck turned up with thirty-six

2695736 Bedford bumper bars, all non-returnable. He put in an express order for a body shell of a 92029932S Commodore Station Wagon but he typed 92029933S instead so they delivered a sedan body and an invoice for $3,985-00.

These were serious mistakes. They saw him laughing at 'Derek and Clive Live' and thought he did not care. The opposite was true: every mistake made him hot with shame. It was his business. He was the one who was going to have to rescue Catchprice Motors from the mess they had made and carry it into the twenty-first century. He was the one who was going to find the cash to pay for their old people's home, who would buy them their little pastel blue tellies to put beside their beds. He would care for them the way they never cared for him – even Mort, his father – he would shame them.

So when he was fired from Spare Parts by his sole protector he was not only humiliated in front of the mechanics – who hated him for his mistakes and went out at night to the pub to celebrate – he was also pushed into a crisis, and the light in his eyes looked to be blown right out. He was dog shit. He had no other plan for life. He was a car dealer.

Of course the Catchprices were all car dealers, or they were known in Franklin as car dealers, but Benny was alone in wishing to describe himself that way. The others accepted the label even while they dreamed of losing it. They were Catchprices, *temporarily* G.M. dealers from Franklin near Sydney in the State of New South Wales.

The family had been in Franklin when it had been a country town with a population of 3,000 people and limited commercial potential. Then it was twenty miles from Sydney and in the bush. Now it was twenty miles from Sydney and almost in the city and there was no Sydney Road any more – there was the F4 instead, and when it left Franklin it passed through two miles of deserted farm land and then the suburbs started.

Franklin was no longer a town. It was a region. The population was 160,000 and they had bulldozed the old Shire Hall to make municipal offices six storeys high. Benny could tell you the value of the rates the Shire collected each year: $26 million. There was drug addiction and unemployment it is true, but there were airline pilots and dentists out along the Gorge. They came tooling down the F4 in Porsches and Volvos.

All of this should have been good for business, but Catchprice

Motors, a collection of soiled and flaking white stucco buildings with barley-sugar columns and arched windows, had somehow got itself isolated from the action. It was stranded out on the north end of Loftus Street opposite the abandoned boot-maker's and bakery. Loftus Street fed the stream of the F4, but the commercial centre had shifted to a mall half a mile to the south and there were now many people, newcomers to the area, to whom the name Catchprice had no meaning at all. They did not know there was a G.M. dealership tucked away between A.S.P. Building Supplies and the Franklin District Ambulance Centre.

There was a sign, of course, which said CATCHPRICE MOTORS and most of the Catchprices lived right behind it. Gran Catchprice's windows looked out through the holes in the letters 'A' and 'P'. Her grown-up son, Benny's father, lived in a red-brick bungalow which fitted itself against the back wall of the workshop like a shelf fungus against a eucalyptus trunk and her married daughter, Cathy, had taken over the old place above the lube bay.

The Catchprices clustered around the quartz-gravel heart of the business. Time-switched neon lights lay at their centre. The odours of sump oil and gasoline sometimes penetrated as far as their linen closets. They were in debt to the General Motors Acceptance Corporation for $567,000.

That Sunday night following Benny's dismissal, two members of the family kept him company. They sat above the showroom where the late Albert ('Cacka') Catchprice had sold his first 1946 Dodge to Jack Iggulden. In those days the rooms above the showroom had been Cacka's offices, but now they were his widow's home. The glass display case which had once displayed bottled snakes and sporting trophies now held Frieda Catchprice's famous collection of bride dolls. There were eighty-nine of them. They were all frizzy, frilly, with red lips and big eyes. They occupied the entire back wall of her living-room.

Granny Catchprice was eighty-six years old. She liked to smoke Salem cigarettes. When she put one in her mouth, her lower lip stretched out towards it like a horse will put out its lip towards a lump of sugar. She was not especially self-critical, but she knew how she looked when she did this – an old tough thing. She was not a tough thing. She made jokes about her leaking roof but she was frightened there was no money to fix it. She made jokes, also,

7

about the state of the bride dolls behind the glass display case. She liked to say, 'Us girls are getting on,' but the truth was she could not even look at the dolls, their condition upset her so. She would walk into the room and look up towards the neon tubes, or down towards the white-flecked carpet. She ducked, dodged, avoided. She always sat at the one place at her dining table, with her back hard against the case of dolls. The glass on the case was smeared. Sometimes it became all clouded up with condensation and the dolls had streaks of mould and mildew which, at a distance, looked like facial hair.

When she sat with her back to the dolls on Sunday night she had to face her youngest grandson. She would have preferred not to see how his spine was curved over and how his animated eyes had gone quite dead. He was not bright, had never been bright, could still not spell 'vehicle' or 'chassis' but he had a shining will she had always thought was like her own. She did not necessarily like him, but he was like a stringy weed that could get slashed and trampled on and only come back stronger because of it. Of all the things she had ever expected of him, this was the last – that he should allow himself to be destroyed.

She gave him a big white-dentured smile. 'Well,' she told him. 'The worst accidents happen at sea.'

He did not seem to hear her.

She looked across at his brother for support. She had dragged that one out here all the way from the Hare Krishna temple in Kings Cross but now he was here she could see that he was more frightened by his brother's collapse than she was. His name was Johnny but now he was a Hare Krishna he would not answer to it. He was Vishnabarnu – Vish – he looked at her and gave a little shrug. He had his grandfather's big knobbly chin and wide nose, and when he shrugged he squinched up his eyes just like Cacka used to do and she thought he would be no use to anyone.

He had the same neck as his grandfather as well, and those sloping strong shoulders and the huge calves which knotted and unknotted when he walked. He would be no real use, but she liked to have him near her and she had to stop herself reaching out to touch his saffron kurta with her nicotine-stained fingers. He was so clean – she could smell washed cotton, soap, shaving cream.

8

'It's not worth being upset about,' Vish was telling Benny. 'It's a dream. Think of it as a dream.'

Benny looked at Vish and blinked. It was the first thing to actually engage his attention.

'That's right,' Vish said, speaking in the way you coax a baby's arms into its sleeves, or a nervous horse into its bridle. 'That's right.'

Benny opened his mouth wide – ah.

Vish leaned across the table on his elbows, squinting and frowning. He peered right into the darkness of Benny's open mouth. Then he turned to his grandmother who was in her big chair with her back to the dolls' case.

'Gran,' he said. 'I think you're wanted in the kitchen.'

She went meekly. It was not characteristic of her.

2

The rain was so bad that summer that the plastic-painted walls of the ashram developed water bubbles which ballooned like condoms. You had to puncture them with a pin and catch the water in a cup. The quilts which the devotees threw on top of the rusty-hinged wardrobes at four each morning became sticky with damp and sour with mildew. The walls of the staircase they flip-flopped down on their way to chant *japa* at the temple were marbled with pink mould, but Ghopal's, the restaurant owned by I.S.K.O.N. (the International Society of Krishna Consciousness), was in a new building with a good damp course and all through that wet summer it stayed dry and cool. The devotees kept the tables and floors as clean as their dhotis.

Govinda-dasa oversaw them. He had been a devotee since the early years when Prabhupada was still alive and nothing that had happened since his death had shaken him, not the corruption of the Australian guru whose name he would never pronounce, not the expulsion of Jayatirtha who was accused of taking drugs and sleeping with female devotees, not the murders at the temple in California. He was now forty-one. He had a sharp, intelligent face with dark, combative eyes and small, white, slightly crooked teeth. He said 'deities' not 'deetes'. He was educated and ironic, a slight, olive-skinned man with a scholarly stoop.

Govinda-dasa was not an easy man to work for. He was too often disappointed or irritated with the human material that was given him. He was kind and generous but these qualities lay like milk-skin on the surface of his impatience, wrinkling and shivering at the smallest disturbance. He could not believe that young men whose only concern in life was the service of Krishna could be so complacent.

He found spots on tables which had seemed perfectly clean before his eyes had rested on them. He liked the *Bhagavad Gita* and *The Science of Self-Realization* to be placed on the table in a certain way which was at once casual and exact. He liked the glass jars on each table to hold nasturtiums and daisies which the young *brahmacharis* had to go and beg from the women who cared for the temple decorations. They did not like the women having power over them.

Govinda-dasa had such a passion for bleach that you could smell it still amid the ghee and cardamom and turmeric at ten o'clock on a busy night. He made it so strong that Vishnabarnu wore rubber gloves to stop the rash on his thick, farmer's arms. Vishnabarnu did not mind the bleach. Being inside Ghopal's was the opposite of Catchprice Motors – it was like being inside an egg. The Formica tables shone like pearly shells under neon light.

It was Govinda-dasa who took Gran Catchprice's call the night after the day when Benny got fired. He recognized the old woman's voice. She was an *attachment*. All devotees vowed to shed attachments. He put his hand over the receiver and looked at Vishnabarnu, who was arranging sprouts and orange slices on a plate of dhal. There was, even in that simple activity, such kindness evident in his big square face. You really did gain something just from looking at him.

He had such a big body, wide across the shoulders and chest, but his voice was high and raspy and his eyes lacked confidence. Now the phone call had produced a deep frown mark just to the right of his wide nose. He placed the dish of dhal and salad on the bench. He picked up a cloth and slowly wiped his big hands which were covered with nicks and cuts and stained yellow with turmeric. Then he picked up the plate and carried it to table no. 2.

Then he came back to the call.

'Who is it?' he asked.

'Don't dissemble,' said Govinda-dasa. There was no other devotee he could have used the word to, no one who would have understood it.

Vishnabarnu picked up the towel and gazed at his stained hands. For a moment it seemed as if he might actually refuse the call, but then he looked up at Govinda-dasa, grinned self-consciously, and held out his hand for the receiver.

'Hi-ya Gran,' he said.

The lightness of his tone was outrageous, as if he had never made a vow to anyone. Govinda-dasa's nostrils pinched. He leaned against the counter, folding and unfolding the urgent order for table no. 7, straining to hear both sides of the conversation.

Vish turned his back. His Grandma said: 'Benny needs you here at home.'

'Can't do that, Gran.'

'It's not good,' she said.

In the privacy of the shadowed wall, Vish smiled and frowned at once. There had been so many 'not good' things that had happened to Vish and Benny. Their grandmother had never seemed to notice any of them before.

'How is it not good?'

'Can't say right now,' she said.

Above the phone was an image of a half man, half lion – Krishna's fourth incarnation, Lord Nara Sinha – ripping the guts from a man in his lap.

Vish humped his body around the phone. 'I'm needed here,' he said.

'This is your home,' she said. 'You're needed here too.'

Vish looked at Govinda-dasa. Then he turned back to the wall and rested his forehead against it. When you were a *brahmacharis*, living in an ashram, it was hard to imagine that Catchprice Motors still existed. It was hard to remember the currents of anger and fear which made life normal there.

He tried to think what could be so bad that Granny Catchprice would actually notice. Probably something not very bad at all. 'O.K.,' he said at last. 'Put him on.'

'He can't talk,' she said. 'He's lost his voice. They fired him from Spare Parts.'

The inside world of the temple was calm and beautiful. It had marble floors and eggshell calm. When they said you knew God through chanting his name, they were not being poetic.

'Did you hear me?' she said.

'Yes.'

There was a long silence on the phone while Vishnabarnu felt the cool dry wall against his cheek.

'I'm not talking to my father, if that's what you want.'

'You don't have to talk to your father.'

Vish shut his eyes and sighed. 'I'll try for the 9.35,' he said at last. 'I'm going to have to borrow some money.'

He turned to see that Govinda-dasa was holding out ten dollars between thumb and double-jointed finger.

'Table 7 is in a hurry,' Vish said.

'Is this how you serve Krishna?' Govinda-dasa asked, pushing the money at Vishnabarnu like it was a lump of carrion.

One sharp tooth rested on his lower lip and he looked straight into Vish's eyes until Vish had to look down.

'You have no reason to feel superior to Janardan,' Govinda-dasa said.

Vishnabarnu respected Govinda-dasa more than anyone else except his guru, but now he felt impatient and disrespectful. He was shocked to recognize his feelings.

'If Janardan puts on a wig and smokes grass and talks about sex-pleasure, he's no more wedded to Maya than you are.'

'I know, Govinda-dasa.'

'But you don't know, or you wouldn't act like this. What is the greatest fear of any intelligent human being?'

Vishnabarnu closed his eyes. 'To spend their life as a lower animal.' He had fifteen minutes to make the train. 'Govinda-dasa, I have to go.'

'Will your attachment to your family bring you closer to God?'

This meant that you did not move closer to God by associating with Bad Karma. You associated with God by abandoning attachments, by chanting his name, by eating *prasadum*. Through good association you became a better person and took on His qualities of Compassion, Cleanliness, Austerity and Truthfulness.

Vish removed the damp note from between Govinda-dasa's fingers.

'I'm sorry,' he said. He looked briefly into Govinda-dasa's

12

blazing eyes and then walked out on to the landing and down the stairs towards the street.

In the dark shelter of the doorway he paused. He looked out through the rain at the traffic and the hooker in the red bunny suit standing in the white light of the BMW showroom across the street. He looked back up the white-walled stairway towards the restaurant. He looked out into the dark-bright street. He did not want to go to Catchprice Motors. He did not want to go through this silent anger with his father or walk back into that spongy mess of bad things that was his childhood.

He took the four steps down on to the street and chanted God's name once each step. And then he ran. He pounded through the rain-puddled streets – Darlinghurst Road, Oxford Street, Taylor Square – splashing his robes. He ran strongly, but without grace. His shaven head rolled from side to side and he bunched his forearms up near his broad chest like parcels he didn't want to get wet. He came down the dark part of the hill at Campbell Street and emerged on to the bright stage of Elizabeth Street like a bundle of rags and legs. His braided pigtail of remaining hair, his Sikha, glistened with drops of rain like sequins.

He ran against the Don't Walk sign: a mess of yellow illuminated by three sets of headlights. At the ticket counter he slipped and fell. He grazed his knees.

He burst into the carriage on the 9.35. His heart was banging in his ears. His breath worked his throat like a rat-tail file.

He collapsed in his seat opposite a man in shorts and a woman in a tight red dress. They did not see him. The man's hairy leg was between the woman's resisting knees and he was kissing her while he massaged her big backside.

Vish was coming home.

3

Granny Catchprice had her tastes formed up on the Dorrigo Plateau of Central New South Wales – she liked plenty of fat on her lamb chops and she liked them cut thick, two inches was not too much for her. She liked them cooked black on the outside and pink inside and when she grilled them in her narrow galley up above the car yard the fat spurted and flared and ignited in long liquid spills which left a sooty spoor on the glossy walls of her kitchen and a fatty smell which impregnated the bride dolls in the display case and the flock velvet upholstery on the chairs in the room where Vish sat opposite his expressionless brother. He knew whatever had gone wrong with Benny was his fault. This was something which was always understood between them – that Vish had abandoned his little brother too easily.

It was eleven o'clock on Sunday night and the griller was cold and the chop fat lay thick and white as candle wax in the bottom of the grill pan in the kitchen sink. Granny Catchprice was on her knees, her head deep in the kitchen cupboard, trying to find the implements for making cocktails. She was busying herself, just as she had busied herself through Cacka's emphysema. Then she had run ahead of her feelings with brooms and dusters. Now she was going to make her grandson's aerated brandy crusters but first she had to find the Semak Vitamiser in among the pressure cooker and the automatic egg poacher and all the aluminium saucepans she had cast aside when Benny told her that aluminium drove you crazy in old age.

People were used to thinking of Granny Catchprice as a tall woman although she was no more than five foot six and now, kneeling on the kitchen floor in a blue Crimplene pant suit which emphasized the slimness of her shoulders and the losses of mastectomy, she looked small and frail, too frail to be kneeling on a hard floor. The bright neon light revealed the eggshell scalp beneath her grey hair. Her lower lip protruded in her concentration and she frowned into the darkness of the cupboard.

'Drat,' she said. She pulled saucepans from the cupboard and dropped them on to the torn vinyl floor in order to make her search less complicated. She forgot Vish did not drink alcohol and he was too engrossed in his fearful diagnosis of his brother's condition to pay any attention to what she was doing.

The word *Schizophrenia* had come into his mind when he looked into Benny's ulcerated mouth and now he was wondering how he could find out what Schizophrenia really was. A saucepan clattered. His grandmother's red setter yelped and skittered across the slippery kitchen floor.

Benny winked at him.

Vish narrowed his eyes.

14

Benny pursed his lips mischievously and looked over his high bony shoulder towards the kitchen, then back at his older brother.

'Bah-bah-bah,' he said. 'Bah-Barbara-ann.'

Vish did not normally even think profanity. But when this quoted line from their father's favourite song told him that Benny's lost voice, his curved spine, his dead eyes, his whole emotional collapse had been an act, he thought *fuck*. He felt angry enough to break something, but as he watched his grinning brother take a pack of Marlboro from the rolled-up sleeve of his T-shirt, all he actually did was squinch up his eyes a little.

Benny lit a cigarette and placed the pack carefully in front of him on the table. He rolled his T-shirt up high to where you could see the first mark life had made on him – a pale ghost of a scar like a blue-ringed smallpox vaccination. He leaned back and, having checked his Grandma again, put his long legs and combat boots on the table and tilted back on the chair.

'No, seriously . . .' he said.

'Seriously!'

For a moment it looked as if Benny was going to mimic his brother's outraged squeak, but then he seemed to change his mind. 'No, seriously,' he said, 'I've got something great for you.'

There was a long silence.

'An opportunity,' said Benny.

Vish was breathing through his nose and shaking his head very slowly. He brought his hands up on the table and rubbed at the cuts on his knuckles. 'Do you know what it takes for me to come out here? Do you know what it costs me?' His eyes were so squinched-up they were almost shut with the result that his face appeared simultaneously puzzled and fatigued.

'I got *fired* from my own business,' Benny reminded him. 'I need you more than ever in my life. Isn't that enough of a reason to come?'

For a Hare Krishna the answer was no. Vish did not have the stamina to explain that again, nor did he want to hear what the 'opportunity' was.

'Sure,' he said.

Benny leaned across the dining-table to pat him on his shaven head. 'I wanted my brother . . . he's here. I needed a cocktail . . . she's making it. Relax . . . calm down. You going to have a Brandy

Cruster? A little Sense Grat-if-ication? Put a wig on.'

Benny's eyes were like their father's – the same store-house of energy. Humour and malice lay twisted together in the black centre of the pupil. 'Put on your wig,' he said. 'God won't see you if you have a wig on.'

'Don't be ignorant.'

'Fuck yourself,' Benny hissed.

Vish had a hold of his younger brother's grimy little wrist before Benny knew what was happening. Benny was a sparrow. He had light, fine bones like chicken wings. He yelped, but he was not being held hard enough to really hurt him.

'Please let me go,' he said. 'You shouldn't have called me that. You know you shouldn't call me that.'

'You shouldn't have said what you said.'

'About the wig?'

Vish tightened his grip.

'Let me go,' Benny said. He bowed his head until the burning end of his cigarette was half an inch from Vish's hand. He never could stand being held down. His chin quivered. The cigarette shook. 'Let me go or I'll burn your fucking hand.'

'I came here to *see* you,' Vish said, but he let go.

'Oh sure,' Benny said. 'You thought I'd flipped out, right?'

'I was worried about you.'

'Sure,' said Benny. 'You've been worrying about me for years. Thanks. Your worry has really helped my life a lot.'

'You want me here or not, Ben? Just say.'

Benny was messing with the butts in the yellow glass ashtray, pulling the skin off the cigarette and shredding the filter. 'I'm not joining the Krishnas,' he said. 'Forget it.'

'Listen Ben, you give this up, I'll give up the temple. I'll get a straight job. We'll get a place together. We'll get jobs.'

'Get it into your head,' Benny said. 'We don't need to get jobs. We've got jobs. We've got our own business. This is what you've got to understand.'

'They fired you.'

'They think they fired me.' Benny had these eyes. When he smiled like this, the eyes looked scary – they danced, they dared you, they did not trust you. The eyes pushed you away and made you enemy. 'They can't fire me,' he said.

16

'Cathy fired you. That's why I'm here. She fired you and you went down in a heap.'

Benny took out a fresh Marlboro and lit it. 'The situation keeps changing,' he said.

Vish groaned.

'No, look,' Benny said. 'Think about it. This is the best thing that could have happened.'

'Then why am I here? Why did I get this call from Gran?'

'Just listen to me. Think about what I'm saying. Cathy fired me, but she's a dead duck. She's got an unemployed carpenter for a drummer and a lead guitarist with a fucked-up marriage and they've actually got a record on the Country charts. They're charting! Nothing's going to stop these guys going on the road. This is *it* for them. What I'm saying is, they're entitled – it's their name too and if she wants to keep it, she'll have to leave the business and go on the road with them. She fired me but she doesn't count.'

'Benny, I don't know what you're talking about.'

'Then listen to me. She always thought she was Big Mack, right? She thought the Mack was hers because McPherson is her name, but Mickey Wright got a lawyer and the lawyer says the name is for the whole band. She's *got* to go on tour with them or they'll go and tour without her. She's got to go. She's out of here. She doesn't count. You leave the Krishnas, fine,' Benny said. 'But you stay here with me. We can run this show together. I can go through the details for you any time you like.'

'Did you work this out before Gran phoned me?'

'They feed you at the temple,' Benny said. 'I know – you've got no worries, well you've got no worries here. I'll guarantee a living. Don't shake your fucking head at me. You can make two hundred grand a year in this dump, really. You can walk on fucking water if you want. We can set this town on fire.'

The dog came and pushed his nose up between Benny's legs. Benny kicked him away and he went back to the kitchen, slipping and scratching across the floor to where Gran Catchprice was hunched over her defective Semak Vitamiser.

'This is our inheritance,' Benny said. 'I'm not walking away from that and neither are you.'

Vish shook his head and rearranged his yellow robe. In the

kitchen his grandmother was turning the single switch of the blender on and off, on and off.

'Did you talk to Him?'

'Who's Him?'

'You know who I mean . . . our father.'

'He's irrelevant.'

'Oh yes? Really?'

'His only relevance is these.' He held up a bottle of pills – Serepax prescribed for Mr Mort Catchprice.

'Benny, Benny. I thought you quit that.'

'Benny, Benny, I'm not selling them. I'm trading them.'

'For what?'

'Personal transformation,' Benny said.

Vish sighed. 'Benny, he's not going to let you do any of this. What do you think you're going to do?'

'Tonight,' Benny rattled the Serepax and pushed them down into the grubby depths of his jeans pocket, 'I'm swapping these with Bridget Plodder for a haircut. Tomorrow, I'm personally moving some of that stock off the floor.'

'You're selling *cars*?' Benny was coated with dirt. He had grimy wrists, dull hair, this film across his skin, but there was, once again, this luminous intensity in his eyes. 'You don't even have a driving licence.'

'He can't stop me,' Benny said. 'I've turned the tables. I've got him over a barrel.'

'Stay away from him, Ben.'

'Vish, you don't even know who I am. I've changed.'

'You're sixteen. He can do what he likes with you.'

'I've *changed*.'

For the second time that evening, Benny opened his mouth wide for Vish and pushed his face forward. Vish looked into his brother's mouth. Whatever it was he was meant to see in there, he couldn't see it.

4

At three-thirty on Monday morning Vish performed his ablutions, chanted *japa*, and made *prasadum* – a stack of lentil pancakes which he laid in front of the guru's picture before beginning to eat.

At five-thirty Granny Catchprice had her Maxwell House standing up at the kitchen sink. She politely ate some of the cold pancakes her grandson offered her.

At six-thirty the pair of them, she in an aqua-coloured, quilted dressing-gown, he in his yellow dhoti and kurta, opened the heavy cyclone gates to the car yard and locked the Yale padlock back on its bolt.

Just after the seven o'clock news there was a short, heavy thunderstorm.

At seven-thirty Mort Catchprice, unaware that his elder son had spent the night in his grandmother's apartment, gingerly nursed a newly registered vehicle through the yellow puddles of the service road and out on to the wet highway which was already heavy with city-bound traffic.

At eight-fifteen Cathy and Howie came down from their apartment and crossed the gravel to unlock first the showroom and then the Spare Parts Department. She wore her snake-skin boots. He wore pointy-toed suede shoes. He walked with the weight on his heels to keep the toes from spoiling in the wet.

At eight-twenty the air compressor thumped into life.

At eight-thirty-three a high racketing noise cut across the yard from the workshop – an air-driven power wrench spun the wheel nuts off the right-hand rear wheel of an HQ Holden.

At eight-thirty-five Benny Catchprice rose from the cellar one step at a time, feeling the actual weight of himself in his own calf muscles as he came up the steep stairs without touching the grimy handrail. He rose up through the cracked, oil-stained, concrete floor of the old lube bay and stood in the thick syrupy air, breathing through his mouth, blinking at the light, his stomach full of butterflies.

He was transformed.

His rat-tailed hair was now a pure or poisonous white, cut spiky short, but – above the little shell-flat ears – swept upwards with clear sculpted brush strokes, like atrophied angel wings. The eyes, which had always alarmed teachers and social workers and were probably responsible, more than any other factor, for his being prescribed Ritalin when eight years old, were so much at home in their new colouring that no one would think to mention them – no longer contradictory, they seemed merely nervous as they flicked from one side of the car yard to the other, from the long side wall of the workshop to the high louvre windows of his grandmother's kitchen.

His brow seemed broader and his round chin more perfectly defined, although this may have been the result of nothing more than Phisohex, soap, petroleum jelly, all of which had helped produce his present cleanliness.

His lips, however, were the most remarkable aspect of his new look. What was clear here now in the reflected quartz-gravel light underneath the cobwebbed rafters had not been clear yesterday: they were almost embarrassingly sensual.

Benny was fully aware of this, and he carried with him a sense of his new power together with an equally new shyness. He was waiting to be looked at. He lined up the toes of his shoes with the crumbling concrete shore of the old lube bay floor. He knew he was on the very edge of his life and he balked, hesitating before the moment when he would change for ever.

The old lube was directly beneath the cobwebbed underfloor of Cathy and Howie's apartment, at the back end of the car yard farthest from the big sliding cyclone gates. He looked out at the glittering white gravel of his inheritance.

The Camiras and Commodores were laid out like fish on a bed of crushed ice. They were metallic blue and grey. There was a dust silver Statesman fitted with black upholstery. On the left-hand side near the front office was a Commodore S.S. with spunky alloy wheels in the shape of a spinning sun. The G.M. cars were angled towards the road, like arrows which suggested but did not quite point towards the creature the family seemed so frightened of – the Audi Quattro 90 with leather trim. A $75,000 motor car they had traded from a bankrupt estate.

The compressor cut off, revealing the high whine of a drill press which had been going all the time. In a moment one of the mechanics would look out over his bench top and see him. Benny could imagine himself from their point of view. They would see the suit, the hair, and they would whistle. They would think he was effeminate and stupid, and maybe he was stupid, in a way. But in other ways he was not stupid at all. He had redevelopment plans for that workshop, and he knew exactly how to finance it.

When Vish had abandoned him five years ago, had run off to leave him unprotected, he had drawn Vish on his cellar wall, being fucked by a donkey with a dunce's hat. He had drawn his father tied to a chair. He had drawn a black eagle but it would not go black enough. That was a long time ago, on the day he had moved into the cellar. He did not draw these dumb things any more. The donkey and dunce's cap were now covered with a dense knitted blanket of red and blue handwriting. Among these words, one set repeated.

I cannot be what I am.

He was stupid, maybe, but he would not continue to be what he was, and when Cathy fired him he had already spent $400 on a Finance and Insurance course at the Zebra Motor Inn and he had passed it – no problems with the numbers.

He had also spent $495 on the 'Self-Actualization' cassettes, $300 on the suit, $150 on sundries and, as for where the money came from, that was no one's business and totally untraceable. So when his father began by saying, no way was he going to sell cars, all he did was ask himself 'How do I attain the thing that I desire?'

Then he followed the instructions of the 'Self-Actualization' cassettes, descending the imaginary coloured stairways to the mental image on the imaginary Sony Trinitron which showed the object of his desire. His father was finally irrelevant.

The rain which had been falling all summer began to fall again. Summer used not to be like this. This was all the summer he had inherited. The raindrops were soft and fat. They made three large polka dots on the padded shoulders of his 80 per cent silk suit. He would not run. It was not in his new character to run. He walked out across the crunching gravel. His legs felt a little odd to him – as if he had just risen from his sick-bed. Rain ricocheted off the metallic roofs and bonnets of the Holdens and flecked his shining cheekbones with glittering beads of water. He passed beside the Audi 90. It was jet black. Very sexy. He could see himself reflected in it, held in it. When he came in the door of the Front Office he was blushing crimson.

This was where Cathy thought he was going to sell petrol. The Front Office was at the front of the left-hand arm of the 'U' which made up Catchprice Motors. There were a couple of old Esso pumps out front and sometimes the apprentice would bring a car around to get a litre or two for a road test, but petrol was cheaper – and cleaner – at a regular service station. The underground petrol tanks at Catchprice Motors had been there nearly forty years. They were rusting on the inside, and the outside was under pressure from the water table. The petrol tanks Grandpa Catchprice had installed were now rising like whales and the concrete on the forecourt cracked a little more each summer. You would have to be mentally deficient to stand on the forecourt at Catchprice Motors.

When Benny took up his station in the Front Office, the two old Esso petrol pumps were in the very centre of the big glass window in front of him. Behind his back was a white door with a grubby smudged area around its rattly metal handle. Across the road, through the giant trunks of camphor laurels which he was going to cut down the minute Cathy was on the road, he could see the abandoned boot-maker's and bakery.

Benny stood in the centre of the office with his legs apart and his hands folded behind his back. His skin smelt of soap. Rain sat on his cheekbones. In an ideal world, his brother would be beside him, might be beside him yet.

He was going to sell his first car.

When the rain stopped again, Benny planned to move out into the yard. He wanted them to *see* him. He wanted to see himself in the mirror of their faces.

It was still raining when the first 'prospect' appeared. A woman in a white Mitsubishi Colt pulled up under the trees on the other side of the petrol pumps. The rain was heavy now, far too heavy to walk out into, and Benny did not see the red 'Z' plates which would have told him the Colt was a government car.

He was the first member of the Catchprice family to see the Tax Inspector. He did not know there was anything to be frightened of. He adjusted his shirt cuffs. All he thought was: watch me.

5

The Tax Inspector parked the Colt on a small island of weeds which was more closely associated with the Building Supplies Store than with Catchprice Motors. This was an old Taxation Office courtesy which Maria Takis, alone of all the auditors in her section, continued to observe – you did not humiliate your clients by parking a Taxation Officer car right on their doorstep, not even in the rain.

A wall beside a pot-holed laneway bore flaking signwriting with arrows pointing towards SERVICE DEPT and SPARE PARTS DEPT but there was no mention of an OFFICE or ALL ENQUIRIES. Rainwater spilled over the blocked guttering and ran down the wall, rippling across the signs, and flooded back across the cracked concrete forecourt towards the car yard itself.

Maria Takis walked carefully through the shallow edges of the puddle in the direction of the petrol pumps. Behind the petrol pumps she found an oddly beautiful boy standing like a mannequin in an empty neon-lit office.

He came to the doorway to give her directions. When she thanked him, he reached his hand out through the open door so he could shake her hand.

As she walked through the rain across the car yard towards the old wooden fire-escape he had pointed out, she could feel the skin of his hand still lying like a shadow on her own. Had she not been eight months pregnant she might have thought about this differently, but she felt so full of baby, of fluid, such a net of bulging veins and distended skin (she would have drawn herself, had you asked her, like an orange with twig legs) she did not expect to be the object of anybody's sexual attentions.

In any case: she had more serious things to think about.

She could hear shouting, even here at the bottom of the storm-bright fire-escape, above the din of the rain which fell like gravel on the iron roofs of Catchprice Motors and cascaded over the gutter and splashed her shoes. The rain cooled her legs. It made patterns on her support stockings, as cool as diamond necklaces.

The treads of the stairs were veined with moss and the walls needed painting. The door she knocked on was hollow, ply-wood, with its outer layer peeling away like an old field mushroom. The Tax Inspector knocked reluctantly. She was accustomed to adversaries with marble foyers and Miele dishwashers. She was used to skilful duels involving millions of dollars. To be sent to this decaying door in Franklin was not only humiliating, but also upsetting on another level – after twelve years with the Taxation Office she was being turned into something as hateful as a parking cop.

No one heard her knock. They were shouting at each other. She knocked again, more loudly.

Maria Takis was thirty-four years old. She had black, tangled hair and a very dark olive-skinned face which her mother always said was 'Turkish' (i.e. not like her mother) and which Maria began, in her teenage years, to accentuate perversely with gold rings and embroidered blouses so that even now, coming to a door as a tax auditor, she had that look that her mother was so upset by.

'Pop po, fenese san tsingana.' (You look like a gypsy.)

There was nothing gypsy about the briefcase in her hand – it was standard Taxation Office – two gold combination locks with three numbers on each side, two large pockets, two small pockets, three pen-holders on the inside lid, a Tandy solar- and battery-powered 8-inch calculator, three pads of lined writing paper, six public service Biros, and a wad of account analysis forms with columns for the date, the cheque number, the cheque particulars and columns to denote capital, business, or personal. She had a book of receipt forms for any documents she removed from the premises, a stand-ard issue Collins No. 181 day-a-page diary, a tube of handcream, a jar of calcium tablets, two packets of thirst Life Savers, and her father's electricity bill.

Her identification warrant was in her handbag and she was already removing it as she waited for the door to open. It was a black plastic folder with the Australian Taxation Office Crest in gold on the front and her photograph and authorization on the inside. In the photograph she looked as if she had been crying, as if she had somehow been forced to pose for it, but this was her job. She had chosen it freely.

'Yes?'

A plump woman in a chamois leather cowgirl suit stood behind the flyscreen door. Her hips and thighs pushed against her skirt and the chamois rucked and gathered across her stomach. Her bare upper arms fought with the sleeve holes of the waistcoat top. Everything about her body and her clothes spoke of tension. Her plump face reinforced the impression, but it did so as if she was someone sweet-tempered just woken from her sleep, irritable, yes, frowning, sure, but with a creamy complexion and pale, well-shaped, sensuous lips, and a natural calm that would return after her first cup of coffee. She had dense, natural straw-blonde hair set in a soft curl, and small intelligent eyes which stared out at Maria from behind the flyscreen door.

Maria wondered if this was Mrs F. Catchprice. The abrupt way she opened the door and took Maria's I.D. told her this was unlikely to be the taxpayer's accountant.

'I'm Maria Takis . . .' She was interrupted by an old woman's voice which came out of the darkness behind the flyscreen.

'Is that Mortimer?'

'It's not Mort,' said the big woman, shifting her gaze from the I.D. to Maria's belly. She said it wearily, too quietly for anyone but Maria to hear.

'Mortimer come in.' The voice was distressed. 'Let Mortimer come in. I need him here.'

Rain drummed on the iron roof, spilled out of gutters, splashed out on to the landing around Maria's feet. There was a noise like furniture falling over. The woman in cowboy boots turned her head and shouted back into the room behind her: 'It's not Mortimer . . . It . . . is . . . *not* Mort.' She turned back to Maria and blew out some air and raised her eyebrows. 'Sorry,' she said. She scrutinized the I.D. card again. When she had read the front she opened it up and read the authorization. When she looked up her face had changed.

'Look,' she said, coming out into the rain, and partly closing the door behind her. Maria held out her umbrella.

'Jack,' the old woman called.

'Look, Mrs Catchprice is very sick.'

'Jack . . . '

'I'm Cathy McPherson. I'm her daughter.'

'Jack, Mort, help me.'

Cathy McPherson turned and flung the door wide open. Maria had a view of a dog's bowl, of a 2-metre-high stack of yellowing newspapers.

'It's not Jack,' shrieked Cathy McPherson. 'Look, look. Can you see? You stupid old woman. It's the bloody Tax Department.'

Maria could smell something sweet and alcoholic on Cathy McPherson's breath. She could see the texture of her skin, which was not as good as it had looked through the flyscreen. She thought: if I was forty-five and I could afford boots like those, I'd be saving money for a facelift.

'This is ugly,' Cathy McPherson said. 'I know it's ugly. I'm sorry. You really have to talk to her?'

'I have an appointment with her for ten o'clock.'

'You'll need someone to interpret.' Cathy McPherson said. 'If this involves me, I want to be there. Does it involve me?'

'I really do need to talk to her. She is the public officer.'

'She's senile. Jack hasn't lived here for twenty years.'

Maria released the catch on her umbrella. 'None the less she's the public officer.'

'She pisses in her bed.'

Maria collapsed her umbrella and stood in front of Cathy McPherson with the rain falling on her head.

'Suit yourself.' Cathy McPherson opened the door. Maria followed her into a little annexe no bigger than a toilet. Dry dog food and Kitty Litter crunched beneath their feet. The air was spongy, wet with unpleasant smells.

The door to the left led to a galley kitchen with hot-pink Laminex cupboards. There was a flagon of wine sitting on top of a washing machine. There were louvre windows with a view of the car yard. Ahead was the sitting-room. They reached it through a full length glass door with yellowed Venetian blinds. For a moment all Maria could see were rows of dolls in lacy dresses. They were ranked in spotlit shelves along one end of the room.

'Who is it?' Granny Catchprice asked from a position mid-way between Maria and the dolls.

'My name is Maria Takis. I'm from the Taxation Office.'

'And you're going to have a baby,' said Mrs Catchprice. 'How wonderful.'

Maria could see her now. She was at least eighty years old. She was frail and petite. She had chemical white hair pulled back tightly from a broad forehead which was mottled brown. Her eyes were watery, perhaps from distress, but perhaps they were watery anyway. She had a small but very determined jaw, a wide mouth and very white, bright (false) teeth which gave her face the liveliness her eyes could not. But it was not just the teeth – it was the way she leaned, strained forward, the degree of simple attention she brought to the visitor, and in this her white, bright teeth were merely the leading edge, the clear indicator of the degree of her interest. She did not look in the least senile. She was flat-chested and neatly dressed in a paisley blouse with a large opal pendant clasped to the high neck. It was impossible to believe she had ever given birth to the woman in the cowgirl suit.

There was a very blond young man in a slightly higher chair beside her. Maria held out her hand, imagining that this was her accountant. This seemed to confuse him – Australian men did not normally shake hands with women – but he took what was offered him.

'Dr Taylor will give you his chair,' said Mrs Catchprice.

Not the accountant. The doctor. He looked at his watch and sighed, but he did give up his chair and Maria took it more gratefully than she might have imagined.

Mrs Catchprice put her hand on Maria's forearm. 'I'd never have a man for a doctor,' she said. 'Unless there was no choice, which is often the case.'

'I was hoping your accountant would be here.'

'Let me ask you this,' Granny Catchprice said. 'Do I *look* sick?'

Cathy McPherson groaned. A young male laughed softly from somewhere in the deep shadows beside the bride dolls.

'No,' said Maria, 'but I'm not a doctor.'

'What are you?' said Mrs Catchprice.

'I'm with the Taxation Office. We have an appointment today at ten.' Maria passed Mrs Catchprice her I.D. Mrs Catchprice looked at it carefully and then gave it back.

'Well that's an *interesting* job. You must be very highly qualified.'

'I have a degree.'

'In what?' Mrs Catchprice leaned forward. 'You have a lovely face. What is your name again?'

'Maria Takis.'

'Italian?'

'My mother and father came from Greece.'

'And slaved their fingers to the bone, I bet.'

'Mrs Takis,' the doctor said. 'I'm sorry to interrupt you, but I was conducting an examination.'

'Oh,' said Mrs Catchprice, 'you can go now, Doctor.' She patted Maria's hand. 'We women stick together. Most of us,' said Mrs Catchprice. 'Not all of us.'

Cathy McPherson took two fast steps towards her mother with her hand raised as if to slap her.

'See!' said Mrs Catchprice.

Maria saw: Cathy McPherson, her hand arrested in mid-air, her face red and her eyes far too small to hold such a load of guilt and self-righteousness.

'See,' said Mrs Catchprice. She turned to Maria. 'My house-keeping has deteriorated, so they want to commit me. Not Jack – the others. If Jack knew he'd be here to stop them.'

'No one's committing you,' Cathy McPherson said.

'That's right,' Mrs Catchprice said. 'You can't. You thought you could, but you can't. They can't do it with one doctor.' She patted Maria's wrist. 'They need two doctors. I am correct, am I not? But you don't know – why would you? You're from Taxation.'

'Yes.'

'Well you can't see me if I'm committed.' Mrs Catchprice folded her fine-boned, liver-spotted hands in her lap and smiled around the room. 'Q.E.D.', she said.

'The situation,' said Dr Taylor, with the blunt, blond certainties that come from being born 'a real aussie' in Dee Why, New South Wales. 'The situation . . .' He wrote two more words on the form and underlined a third.

'Put a magazine under that,' said Mrs Catchprice. 'I don't want to read my death warrant gouged into the cedar table.'

A Hare Krishna emerged from the gloom with some newspaper which he slid under the doctor's papers.

'The situation,' said the doctor, 'is that you are incapable of looking after yourself.'

'This is my *home*,' said Mrs Catchprice, and began to cry. She clung on to Maria's arm. 'I own this business.'

Cathy sighed loudly, 'No you don't, Frieda,' she said. 'You are a shareholder just like me.'

'I will not be locked up,' said Mrs Catchprice. She dug her hands into Maria's arm and looked her in the face.

Maria patted the old woman's shoulder. She had joined the Taxation Office for bigger, grander, truer things than this. She knew already what she would find if she audited this business: little bits of crookedness, amateurish, easily found. The unpaid tax and the fines would then bankrupt the business.

The kindest thing she could do for this old woman would be to let her be committed. Two doctors attesting to the informant's senility might be enough to persuade Sally Ho to stop this investigation. Sally could then use her ASO 7 status to find something equally humiliating for Maria to do, and this particular business could be left to limp along and support this old woman in her old age.

But Mrs Catchprice was digging her (very sharp) nails into Maria's forearm and her face was folding in on itself, and her shoulders were rounding, and an unbearable sound was emerging from her lips.

'Oh don't,' Maria whispered to the old woman. 'Oh don't, please, don't.'

The Hare Krishna knelt on Mrs Catchprice's other side. He had great thick arms. He smelt of carrots and patchouli oil.

'What will happen to you when you're too old to be productive?' he asked the doctor. His voice was high and breathless, trembling with emotion.

'For Christ's sake,' Cathy McPherson said. 'For Christ's sake, just keep out of this, Johnny.'

'Christ?' the boy said. 'Would Christ want this?'

Cathy McPherson groaned. She closed her eyes and patted the air with the palms of her hands. 'I can't handle this . . .'

'Krishna wouldn't want this.'

'Johnny, please, this is very hard for me.'

'In the Vedic age the old people were the most respected.'

'Fuck you.' Cathy McPherson slapped the Hare Krishna across his naked head. The Hare Krishna did not move except to squeeze shut his eyes.

'Stop it,' said Maria. She struggled to her feet.

'I think *you* should stop it,' the doctor said, pointing a pen at Maria. 'I think you should just make your appointment for another time, Mrs . . .'

'Ms,' Maria told the doctor.

The doctor rolled his eyes and went back to his form.

'Ms Takis,' said Maria, who had determined that Mrs Catchprice would not be committed, not today at least. 'Perhaps you did not hear where I am from.'

'You are a little Hitler from the Tax Department.'

'Then you are a Jew,' said Maria.

'I am a *what*?' said the doctor, rising from his seat, so affronted that Maria burst out laughing. The Hare Krishna had begun chanting softly.

'Oh dear,' she laughed. 'Oh dear, I really *have* offended you.'

The doctor's face was now burning. Freckles showed in the red.

'What exactly do you mean by that?'

'I meant no offence to Jews.'

'But I am not a Jew, obviously.'

'Oh, obviously,' she smiled.

'Hare Krishna, Hare Krishna.'

'Shush darling,' said Mrs Catchprice, who was straining towards the doctor so that she might miss none of this.

'I meant that if I were a doctor with a good practice I would be very careful of attracting the attention of the Taxation Officer.'

'Hell and Tommy,' exclaimed Mrs Catchprice and blew her nose loudly.

'I have an accountant.'

Mrs Catchprice snorted.

'I bet you do,' said Maria. 'Do you know how many accountants were investigated by the Taxation Office last year?'

'Hare Krishna, Hare Krishna.'

'I'll report you for this,' said Cathy McPherson to Maria Takis.

'And what will you "report" me for?'

'For interfering in our family, for threatening our doctor.'

'Mrs McPherson . . .'

'Ms,' hissed Cathy McPherson.

Maria shrugged. 'Report me,' she said. If Sally Ho ever heard what Maria had just done, she would be not just reprimanded – she would be drummed out. 'They'll be pleased to talk to you, believe me.'

The doctor was packing his bag. He slowly put away his papers and clipped his case shut.

'I'll phone you later, Mrs McPherson.'

'Would you like one of my dolls?' Mrs Catchprice asked Maria. 'Choose any one you like.'

'No, no,' Maria said. 'I couldn't break up the collection . . .'

'Jonathon,' said Mrs Catchprice imperiously, 'Jonathon, fetch this young lady a doll.'

'Could I have a word with you?' Cathy McPherson said.

'Of course,' said Maria, but Mrs Catchprice's nails were suddenly digging into her arm again.

Cathy McPherson obviously wished to talk to her away from her mother, and Maria would have liked to have complied with her

30

wishes but Mrs Catchprice's nails made it impossible.

Maria did not feel comfortable with what she had just done. She did not think it right that she should interfere in another family's life. She had been a bully, had misused her power. The child in her belly was made with a man whose great and simple vision it was that tax should be an agent for equity and care, and if this man was imperfect in many respects, even if he was a shit, that was not the issue, merely a source of pain.

Cathy McPherson stood before her with her damaged dream complexion and her cowboy boots. Maria would have liked to speak to her, but Mrs Catchprice had her by the arm.

'Not here,' said Cathy McPherson.

Mrs Catchprice's nails released their pressure. Jonathon had placed a Japanese doll on her lap.

'It's a doll bride,' said Mrs Catchprice, 'Bernie Phillips brought it back from Japan. Do you know Bernie Phillips?'

'This is my *mother*,' said Cathy McPherson, her eyes welling up with tears. 'Do you have the time to look after her? Are you going to come back and wash her sheets and cook her meals?'

'No one needs to look after me,' said Mrs Catchprice. 'You are the one who needs looking after, Cathleen, and you've never been any different.'

'Mother, I am forty-five years old. The cars I sell pay for everything you spend.'

'I don't eat any more,' Mrs Catchprice said to Maria. 'I just pick at things. I like party pies. Do you like party pies?'

'I've got a whole band about to walk out on me and steal my name because I'm trying to care for you,' Cathy said. 'You want me to go on the road? You really want me to leave you to starve?'

'Bernie Phillips brought it back from Japan,' said Mrs Catchprice, placing the doll in Maria's hand. 'Now isn't that something.'

'Fuck you,' screamed Cathy McPherson. 'I hope you die.'

There was silence in the room for a moment. The noise came from outside – the rain on the tin roof, Cathy McPherson running down the fire-escape in her white cowboy boots.

31

6

When she was twenty, after she had run away from both her marriage and her mother, Maria Takis went back to the island of Letkos to the house she was born in and stayed for six weeks with her mother's uncle, Petros, a stern-looking old man who bicycled ten miles along the dirt road to Agios Constantinos for no other reason than to buy his great-niece an expensive tin of Nescafé which he believed would please her more than the gritty little thimblefuls of *metries kafe* he made on his single gas burner.

Petros was the worldly one. He had worked on ships to New York and Shanghai, Cape Town and Rio and to have questioned or refused the Nescafé would have been somehow to undercut who he was. Maria had not come all this way to make her life fit the expectations of others, but just the same she could no more tell him she hated Nescafé than she could confess that she was already married and separated.

Instead she said, 'It is too hot today,' and held the handles of his bicycle as if this might prevent him buying it.

'It is always hot,' he said. He had to wrench the bicycle away from her and his dark eyebrows pressed down on eyes that suddenly revealed a glittering temper.

'No, no,' she said. 'It is hotter than it used to be.'

That made him laugh. He mounted his bicycle and rattled down the chalky road towards the square still laughing out loud and when her parents' friends and relations came to meet her he would tell them, 'When Maria lived here the summers used to be cooler.'

Everyone in Letkos found this very funny and Maria found them very irritating.

'I didn't remember the heat,' Maria said, too many times. 'Only the air. We left in the autumn and arrived in Sydney in the summer.' She told them about how hot it had been walking the streets of Newtown looking for work with her mother – like hell, like a heat so hot and poisonous you could not breathe – but she could see their eyes glaze over as they stopped listening to her. It was not their way of thinking about Australia and they did not want to hear. Australians were all rich, all drank Nescafé. That was why Nikkos refused to apologize for the state of her parents' house. He was meant to look after it but he had stolen the furniture and let the goats eat the pomegranate tree and he could not see that this would matter to Maria or her family. But she had grown up mourning for this beautiful little house which Nikkos had filled with goat shit. It was the place her mother meant when she said, 'Let's go home,' whispering to her husband in bed in a shared house in Sydney where you could hear the people in the next room doing everything.

On the ground floor of the house in Letkos her mother had cooked preserves, fried eggplant, *keftethes* – the room was always sweet with spices and oil. In the house which Nikkos had wrecked they kept almonds and walnuts and dry rustling bundles of beans. Maria had sat on the wooden doorstep in a great parallelogram of sunshine, eating pomegranate from the tree in the garden.

The first house in Sydney was a painful contrast. They rented a room from a friend of an uncle in Agios Constantinos. His name was Dimitri Papandreou. He smelt of sweat and old rags and was stingy. He used newspaper instead of toilet paper. He turned off the hot water when he left the house each morning. He had a secret tap no one else could find, not even Helen, who was smaller than Maria, and who was sent climbing under the floor boards to search for it. Dimitri Papandreou's wife worked at Glo-weave. The family therefore expected Maria's mother to look after all of the Papandreous. Dimitri Papandreou would cook lentils or beans and keep them in an aluminium pot in the fridge for weeks. It was his way of criticizing Maria's mother.

'Let's go home,' Maria's mother said whenever she imagined they were alone, but she never had a chance – fifteen men from the village had come to Australia and they were all working on the production line at the British Motor Corporation in Zetland. They were like men in a team.

Helen would ask their father if they could go home, but Maria was less principled. She sat on his lap and he stroked her hair.

'O Pateras son ine trellos,' ('Your father is crazy') her mother would say as she and Maria and Helen looked for work in the merciless heat (so endlessly hot, inescapably hot) of the Newtown streets. She had no English and Maria would walk with her to interpret and to help push Helen's stroller.

'What does that sign say?'

'Just a room to let.'

'It looks like a factory.'

'No, Mama.'

'It's a factory,' she said half-heartedly. 'No, Helen, no, no wee-wee yet. He's crazy. His life was better. He had a house – better oil, better fruit. Look what we had to carry out here – oil, ouzo – in our bags – he asks me to carry oil to him. Now he sends me out here to be humiliated.'

'Please, Mama, don't.'

'Don't don't.' Her mother's eyes were more and more shrunken, like *throubes*, shrunken in on themselves around the small hard pip. 'Don't you say "don't" to me. You think he is happy? Listen to them all when they sit around. What are they talking about?'

They came to the house. They sat in a circle in the kitchen. They were all from Agios Constantinos. They said, remember the year this happened. Remember the time that happened. They never talked about Australia.

'What is better here?' her mother asked. 'Help her. Help her. She has to wee-wee.' She was ashamed to have Helen pee in the street and turned her back even as she said, 'Help her.'

'The future,' Maria said, holding her little sister suspended over a gutter between two parked cars.

'That's what he says, but you never wanted to go. You were only four and you didn't want to go.'

'I know, Mama,' Maria said bustling her sister back into the stroller.

'You lost the use of your legs.'

'I know, I know.'

'He went to Athens for his immigration tests and when he came back and we told you we were going to Australia, you lost the use of your legs. The doctor had to come all the way to Agios Constantinos in an ambulance.'

Her father always said there was no ambulance.

'An ambulance,' her mother said. 'He couldn't find anything the matter.'

'I know.'

'You can't remember. Do you remember your father held out the *loukoumia* to you and you ran to get them. It was a trick to make you walk but if he hadn't offered you sweets you wouldn't have walked – you didn't want to go. We had a house. For what did we come? So

34

I can walk the streets and be a beggar for work? Did you ever see anyone in Agios Constantinos do their wee-wee in the street?'

The newspapers, of course, had their columns of employment ads, but the Letkos women could not read the letters of the alien alphabet. The newspapers were closed to them. They walked. They worked an area – Enmore, Alexandria, Surry Hills – going from factory to factory, following up the rumours their relations brought to the house. It was all piece-work, and her mother hated piece-work. Childhood friends competed against each other to see who would get the bonus, who would get fired.

Once a week they called on Switch-Electrics Pty Ltd in Camperdown. The women would converge on the footpath, swelling out around the Mercedes-Benzes which were never booked for parking on the footpath, pushing towards the door marked OFFICE. They would be there from seven in the morning. At eight o'clock the son would emerge. He had three folds of fat on his neck above his shirt collar. He had thick arms covered in pale hair. He had three pens in his shirt pocket.

He would point his thick finger into the crowd and say, 'You, you.'

He was like God. He did not have to explain his choices.

'You and you.'

One time he might choose you and another time he might not.

'No more. Vamoose.'

The women would beg in Greek, in Italian, in Spanish, in Catalan. They would do anything – kneel, weep – it was acting, but sincere at the same time.

The man with the pens in his shirt pocket would flap his arms at them as though they were hens.

'Piss off. Go home.'

Sometimes the man's mother would come out. She was nearly sixty but she dressed like a filmstar with tight belts and high heels. She had bright yellow blonde hair and pink arms and red lips and dark glasses. She would come out of a side door carrying a mop bucket filled with water. She would swing it back and then hurl it towards the women, who were already running backwards and tripping over themselves, spilling back through the white Mercedes-Benzes into the path of the timber trucks from the yard next door. As the trucks blasted their horns and as the women

35

screamed, a fat tongue of grey water would splat on to the foot-path and the son and daughter would stand in the doorway, laughing.

Maria's mother lost 85 per cent of her hearing in one ear in a Surry Hills sweat-shop where she made national brand-name shirts. She would say, this machine is deafening me. The owner was Greek, from Salonika. He would say, if you don't like it, leave.

Later she worked at Polaroid, polishing lenses. Then she got arthritis in her fingers and could not do it any more.

It was not a coincidence that, after the Tax Office began checking the returns of Mercedes-Benz owners, Maria was one of the two auditors who sat in the office of Switch-Electrics Pty Ltd opposite this same man with the fat neck and the three pens in his shirt pocket. He was now sixty years old. When he squeezed behind the wheel of his car, air came out of his nose and mouth like out of a puffball. He was a sad and stupid man, and his business was riddled with corruption and evasions which cost him nearly one million dollars in fines and back taxes.

Maria was not above feelings of revenge on behalf of all those women he had humiliated. She was pleased to get him, pleased to make him pay, and when he wept at the table she felt only a vague, distanced pity for him. She looked at him and thought: I must tell Mama.

Her mother was battling with cancer in the George V Hospital at Missenden Road in Camperdown and Maria brought flowers and Greek magazines and gossip that would cheer her up. It was for this reason – certainly not for her own pleasure – that she finally revealed what she had previously thought she could never reveal – her pregnancy.

The approaching death had changed Maria, had made her softer with her mother, more tolerant, less angry. She sat with her for ten, twelve hours at a stretch. She bathed her to spare her the humili-ation of being washed by strangers. She fed her honey and water in a teaspoon. She watched her sleep. Death had changed the rules between them. The love she felt for her mother seemed, at last, without reserve.

As it turned out, the emotions Maria Takis felt were hers, not her mother's. She had hoped that the idea of a birth might somehow make the death less bleak. She had imagined that they had moved, at last, to a place which was beyond the customs and morality of Agios Constantinos. But death was not making her mother's centre soft and when Maria said she was going to have a baby, the eyes that looked back at her were made of steely grey stuff, ball-bearings, pips of compressed matter. Her mother was a village woman, standing in a dusty street. She did not lack confidence. Fear had not shifted her.

'We'll kill you,' she said.

It was a hard death and the story of Switch-Electrics Pty Ltd never did get told.

7

'Yes, but do we have milk?' Mrs Catchprice used her walking stick to flick a magazine out of her path. 'It's very clever,' she told Maria. She hit the magazine so hard the pages tore. 'The roof leaks right into the kitchen sink. It washes my dishes for me.'

'Mrs Catchprice,' Maria smiled. 'It's nearly eleven.'

'Are you hungry?'

'I really need to start our meeting.'

'You sit down,' Mrs Catchprice said.

'There are questions I have to ask you, or your accountant.'

'Vish will get you a glass of milk.'

Mrs Catchprice struck the magazine again. Vish crossed from the kitchen to the plastic and paper confusion of the annexe, holding out a carton of milk at arm's length. He gently lowered the milk carton into a green plastic bag.

'You take my chair,' Mrs Catchprice told Maria. 'It's too low for me.' She pushed the magazine with the rubber tip of her stick and slid it underneath a bookcase.

'Gran, the milk was off.'

'Be a dear,' said Mrs Catchprice. 'Go and see Cathy. They've got milk in Spare Parts for the staff teas.'

'I can't ask Cathy. Cathy won't give me milk.'

'You don't understand Cathy,' said Mrs Catchprice. She pulled free a dining chair, turned it on one leg so it faced away from the bride dolls, and then sat down on it hard. 'Ask her for milk,' she said. 'She won't kill you.'

Maria thought: she 'plonks' herself down. She is pretty, but not

37

graceful. She is full of sharp, abrupt movements which you can admire for their energy, their decisiveness.

She looked to see what the Hare Krishna was going to do about his orders. He had already gone.

'Bad milk!' said Mrs Catchprice. 'I've got old.'

'We all get old,' Maria said, but really she was being polite. She had an audit to begin. She wanted to make it fast and clean – a one-day job if possible.

'One minute you're a young girl falling in love and the next you look at your hand and it's like this.' She held it up. It was old and blotched, almost transparent in places.

Maria looked at the hand. It was papery dry. She thought of bits of broken china underneath a house.

'I can see it like you see it,' Mrs Catchprice said. 'I can see an old woman's hand. It has nothing to do with me. I think I'll have brandy in my milk. Did he take an umbrella?'

'I guess so.'

'I know he looks peculiar but he's very kind. He looks like such a dreadful bully, don't you think?' She leaned forward, frowning.

Maria had worked in the Tax Office twelve years and had never begun an audit in such a homey atmosphere. She opened her briefcase, removed a pad and laid it on her lap. 'He's got a nice smile,' she said.

'Yes, he has.' Mrs Catchprice fitted a Salem into her mouth and lit it without taking her eyes off Maria Takis's face. 'The Catchprices all have kissing lips. Actually,' she said, as if the thought was new to her, 'he's the spitting image of my late husband. Did you meet his younger brother, Benny? Vish's been looking after Benny since he could stand. They told you about their mother?'

'I haven't talked to anyone,' Maria said. 'I thought my colleague had talked to you to set up this interview. I . . .'

'Did you talk to Jack? Jack Catchprice, my youngest son.' She nodded to a colour photograph hanging on the wall beside the doorway to the kitchen. It was of a good-looking man in an expensive suit shaking hands with the Premier of the State of New South Wales. 'Jack's the property developer. He tells everyone about his funny family. He tells people at lunch – Benny's mother tried to shoot her little boy.'

Maria closed the pad.

'It's no secret,' Mrs Catchprice said. 'Benny's mother tried to shoot him. What sort of mother is that? Nice, pretty-looking girl and then, bang, bang, shoots her little boy in the arm. Benny was three years old. I'm not making it up. Shot him, with a rifle.'

'Why?'

'Why? God knows. Who would ever know a thing like that?'

'What was she charged with?'

'Oh no,' Mrs Catchprice said. 'We wouldn't report it. What would be the point? She went away, that's what matters. We wouldn't want the family put through a court case as well. Everyone in Franklin gossips about it anyway. They all know the story – on the Sunday Sophie Catchprice was confirmed an Anglican, on the Monday she did this . . . thing. *Confirmed*,' said Mrs Catchprice, responding to the confusion on Maria's face. 'You're a Christian aren't you? Your mother still goes to church I bet? Is she a Catholic?'

The Tax Inspector's mother was dead, but she said, 'Greek Orthodox.'

'How fascinating,' said Mrs Catchprice. 'How lovely.'

It was not the last time Maria would wonder if Mrs Catchprice was sincere and yet she could not dismiss this enthusiastic brightness as false. Mrs Catchprice might really find it fascinating – she brought her Salem to her lips, inhaled and released the smoke untidily. 'I always told them here in Franklin,' she said, 'that if they went in with the Presbyterians I'd switch over to the Catholics. We never had a Greek Orthodox. I never thought about Greeks. But now I suppose we have. We have all types here now. The Greek Orthodox is like the Catholic I think, is it not?'

'The service is very beautiful.'

'Oh I *do* like this,' said Mrs Catchprice. 'It's so *lovely* you are here. Has Johnny gone for the milk?'

'Mrs Catchprice, do you know why I'm here?'

'You mean, am I really ga-ga?' said Mrs Catchprice, butting her Salem out in an ugly yellow Venetian glass ashtray.

'No,' Maria said, 'I did not mean that at all.'

'You are a Tax Inspector?'

'Yes. And I'll need an office to begin doing my audit.'

'They're up to something, all right.'

Maria cocked her head, not understanding.

'You met her?' Mrs Catchprice said.

'Your daughter?'

'And her husband. I don't like him but I've only got myself to blame for the fact she even met him.'

'And you feel they are up to something?'

'There's something fishy going on there. You'll see in a moment. They'll have to give you access to the books. They won't let me look but they can't stop you. I think you'll find the tax all paid,' said Mrs Catchprice, folding her hands in her lap. 'We've always paid our tax. It's not the tax I'm worried about.'

Maria felt tired.

'People always expect car dealers to be crooks, but you try buying a car from a classified ad and you'll see where the crooks are. When my husband was alive, we always worked in with the law. We always supported the police. We always gave them presents at Christmas. A bottle of sparkling burgundy for the sergeant and beer for the constables. I would wrap up the bottles for him. He'd take them down to the police. They thought he was the ant's pants.'

'Mrs Catchprice,' Maria said, patting the old woman's hand to ease the sharp point she was making, 'you weren't *bribing* the police?'

'It was a small town. We always supported the police.'

'And now you're supporting the Taxation Office.'

'I wonder where that boy is with the milk.'

'Mrs Catchprice. Are you Mrs F. Catchprice?'

'Frieda,' said Mrs Catchprice. 'I've got the same name as the woman who was involved with D. H. Lawrence. She was a nasty piece of work.'

'There's no other Mrs F. Catchprice in your family?'

'One's enough,' she laughed. 'You ask the kids .'

'So you are the public officer and also the one with the anomalies to report?'

'Me? Oh no, I don't think so.' Mrs Catchprice folded her arms across her chest and shook her head.

'You didn't telephone the Taxation Office to say you were worried that your business had filed a false tax return?'

'You should talk to Cath and Howie. They're the ones with all the tricks up their sleeves. All this talk about being a professional musician is just bluff. She's an amateur. She couldn't make a living at it. No, no – what they want is to set up a motor business of their own, in competition to us. That's their plan – you mark my words. But when you look at the books, you take my word, you're going to find some hanky-panky. I won't lay charges, but they're going to have to pay it back.'

'Mrs Catchprice, you do understand – I'm a *tax* auditor. I'm here to investigate tax, nothing else. You phoned the Taxation Office. Your call is on record.'

Mrs Catchprice looked alarmed.

'They recorded me? Is that what you say?'

'They recorded your name.'

Mrs Catchprice was looking at Maria, but it was a moment before Maria saw that there were tears flooding down her ruined cheeks.

'The terrible thing is,' said Mrs Catchprice, 'the terrible thing is that I just can't remember.'

8

At twelve o'clock Mort Catchprice returned from the coast with a Volvo trade-in and saw Benny standing in front of the Audi Quattro. He did not recognize him. He knew his son intimately, of course, had held his little body, bathed it, cleaned it, cared for it from the year his wife had run away. He had seen his body change like a subject in slow-motion photography, seen its arms thicken and its shoulders broaden, its hooded little penis grow longer and wider, its toenails change texture and thickness, insect bites appear and fade, cuts open like flowers and close up with scabs the colour of dead rose petals. He knew what his son was like – a teenager with pimples, razor rash, pubic hair – someone who treated his skin as if he wished to make himself repulsive – left it smeared with dirt, ingrained with the residue of sumps and gearboxes. He had rank-smelling hair and lurid T-shirts in whose murky painted images his father could see only violence and danger.

What Mort saw as he drove slowly down the lane-way to the workshop, was not his son but a salesman, hired without his knowledge, against his wishes, a slick car salesman like Jack, neater than Jack, someone they could not, in any case, afford to pay.

He was mad already when he drove in beneath the open roller doors into the large grey steel-trussed space that was the workshop. He parked the Volvo on a vacant Tecalemit two-poster hoist.

He moved an oxy gas stand and began to push a battered yellow jack back against the wall when Arthur Dermott came shuffling over from his workbench rubbing his hands with a rag and grinning under his wire-framed spectacles.

'They tell you?' he asked, reaching for the crumpled pack of Camels in his back pocket.

Mort felt hot around the neck. *He saw the salesman. He knows I'm weak.*

'They tell me what?'

'Tax office is raiding you,' Arthur said, lighting the cigarette with satisfaction.

He saw the salesman.

'What?'

'Tax Office is raiding you. The way we heard, it was serious. The boys are a bit stirred up, job-security-wise.'

'Bullshit, Arthur. Who told you that?'

Arthur nodded towards Spare Parts. 'Howie come and took Jesse off the fuel pumps to carry all the books up to your Mum's apartment. They're doing their raid up there.'

'All right, Arthur, how about the Camira?'

'A Welsh plug and some coolant.'

'You road test it?'

'It's an R.T., yep.'

'O.K., now you can pre-delivery the blue Commodore.'

'I thought I was going to do the brakes on the Big Mack truck?'

'Forget the fucking Big Mack truck, just do what the fuck I tell you.'

It was true what Granny Catchprice said – the Catchprices had kissy lips. Mort had the best set of all of them. And although he was a wide and burly man, spilling with body hair, and with a rough, wide nose which had been broken twice on the football field, it was the lips which were remarkable not just for their fullness but also – in that bed of blue-black stubble – their delicacy.

Yet had you seen him emerge from under the roller doors of the workshop you would have seen a fighter, not a kisser. He came up the concrete lane-way beside the Spare Parts Department like a front row forward, occupying the centre of the road. He wore a clean white boiler suit, cut short at the arms and open for two or three press studs so the hairy mat of his wide chest was visible. He walked with a roll to his shoulders and his lips had gone thin and his eyes were looking at nothing they could see.

He knew there was no way he could have been told about the Tax Inspector, but he was still mad about not being told. When he passed the fern-filled window of Spare Parts he was giving them a chance to tell him, but they did not tap on the window or come out to tell him.

Also: they had hired a salesman without consultation.

In any case, fuck them, they made him angry almost every day of his life. Now he was going to piss the salesman off. He did not want to fight. He was sick of fight, sick of his body being a mass of stretching ropes. All he wanted was to be someone with a Garage, not a Service Station, not a Dealership, not a Franchise, but a Garage with deep, wide, oil stains on the floor and a stack of forty-four-gallon drums along his back fence, a Garage in a country town. There was one in the paper this week, at Blainey – $42,000, vendor finance. Blainey would be good enough. You could be the guy who drives the school bus, delivers the kerosene and fuel oil, cuts the rust spots out of the school teacher's old car, fixes the butcher's brakes with used parts, is handy with a lathe, is a good shot, a good bloke, a scout master, the coach of the football team, someone who, when looking for a screw or bolt, upturns a drum full of old saved screws and bolts on to the workshop floor and can find – there it is – a ⅜ inch Whitworth thread with a Philips head.

Instead he had one kid lost to a cult, the other with severe learning difficulties and the belief he was a genius. He had a $567,000 debt to G.M.A.C. and a tax audit which, maybe, who knows, would put the lot of them in jail.

He stepped around the puddle on the end of the lane-way and crossed by the petrol pumps. There, twenty metres ahead of him, standing in front of the Audi Quattro, was the striking blond-haired young man in a glistening grey suit, the salesman. He was flexing his knees, holding his yellow-covered guide to auction prices behind his back. When he turned and looked him straight in the eye, Mort felt a sexual shiver which made him speak more harshly than he had planned.

'Get your arse out of here,' he said.

'You promised,' the salesman said, but he turned and walked away, swinging his shoulders and wiggling his butt like a frigging tom cat. My God, it was an embarrassment, the way he moved.

'And don't come back,' he said. Even as he said it he recognized his son. He wanted to cry out, to protest. He felt the blood rise hot in his neck and take possession of his face. He stood in his overalls in the middle of the yard, bright red.

His phone was ringing – loud as a fire bell. He walked towards it, shaking his head. In any other business of this size, one where the sales director was not wasting half her time trying to be a Country singer, there would be a service manager to answer the phone and soothe the customers. There would also be a workshop manager to co-ordinate the work flow, and a foreman to diagnose the major problems, work on the difficult jobs, do the final road tests and then tick them off on the spread sheet. Mort did all of these jobs. So even while he worried what the hell he would do about his embarrassing son, he also knew that three Commodores on the spread sheet were in for a fuel pump recall. General Motors graded this job as 4.2 which meant they would pay Catchprice Motors for forty-two minutes' labour, but they made no allowance for the time it took to drain the tank. He tried to cover himself by using Jesse, the first-year apprentice, but each recall still cost the business fifty dollars. That was Howie's calculation. He had said to Howie: 'What you want me to do about it?'

Howie said: 'Just help us keep Benny out of Spare Parts, Mort. Benny loses us more in a day than you could in a week.'

Mort walked into the Spare Parts Department to ask Cathy would she hold his calls for half an hour so he could help out on the fuel pumps. She should be standing in the showroom, but she never would. She had a handwritten sign there, saying please come over to Spare Parts, and now she was on the phone making a parts order, doing Benny's job in fact, probably fucking up as well.

Howie was on the phone too. He was meant to look like Elvis's original drummer, D. J. Fontana. This was bullshit. He looked like what he would have been if Granny Catchprice had never hired him – a country butcher. He had a tattoo on his forearm and a ducktail haircut, always four weeks too long. He had his pointy shoes up on the desk, and the phone wedged underneath his chin. He had smoke curling round his hair, and clinging to his face. He stank of it.

'Listen, Barry, no: *I* went in there personally and asked them for it. They haven't got the record in stock. It's not even on their damn computer.' He paused. 'I know.' He paused again and nodded to Mort to sit down. He lived his life surrounded by radiator hoses and shock-absorbers but he acted like he was in show business. It was pathetic. He wore *suits*, probably the only spare parts manager in Australia to do it. The suits all came mail order – with extra long jackets and padded shoulders.

'We *were* number eight. That was two days ago. If you can't keep the record in the shops, we're dead meat.'

He took his feet off the desk but only to flick ash off his trousers.

'I'm sympathetic, of course I am.' He was a slime. He was dark-haired and pale-skinned and he closed his heavy-lidded eyes when he spoke to you. That made you think he was shy, but he was a slime. Before he came into their lives, Cathy never fought with anyone.

When Howie put the phone down, Mort said: 'They tell me the Tax Department is upstairs with Mum.' He was pleased with how he said it – calm, not shaky.

'It's an audit,' Howie said. He had the desk covered with papers. Mort saw the record company logo – nothing to do with Catchprice Motors.

'So what's that mean?' Mort asked. 'An audit?'

Howie opened his drawer and pulled out a pink and black pamphlet. He stood up and brought it over to the counter. Mort took it from him. It was titled *Desk Audits & You*. 'They tell me Benny's gone blond.'

'What's it mean?' Mort tapped the brochure on the counter.

'It means ooh-la-la,' Howie said.

'What's it mean?' Mort could feel himself blushing. 'Are we in the shit or aren't we?'

'Mort, you're blushing,' Howie said.

He could not walk out. He had to stay there, enduring whatever it was that Howie knew, or thought he knew, about his son.

You did not need to like a car to sell it. A car was a pipe, a pump for sucking money from the 'Prospect' before you maximized it. You did not need to feel nothing, but Benny loved that fucking Audi. It looked so polite. It had its suit on, its hair cut, but it could take you to hell with your dick hard, and it would be no big deal to sell it. It could sell itself to anyone who liked to drive.

Of course seventy-five grand was a lot of money. So what? There were plenty of different ways to skin the cat, cut that cake, parcel it, package it, make it affordable for the 'Prospect' and profitable to the business, and he – dumb Benny – knew these ways.

He had, right now, the missing spare key in his pocket and the first 'prospect' who came his way, he was going to demo it, licence or no licence. This would surprise the Catchprice family, who were so worried about scratching it they would not even let him *wash* it. What would they do when he handed them the paper work – the sale made, the finance pre-approved by ESANDA? What would they say? *No please, don't sell the Audi, Benny? No please, you're only sixteen and we'd rather pay four hundred bucks a week?* They had dropped their bundle. Lost it. They had a jet black Audi Quattro sitting in the star position in the yard and instead of thanking God for giving them such a beautiful opportunity, they blamed each other for having it and worried that the floor plan payments were going to send them broke.

He could see Bozzer Mazoni across the road checking for change in the public phone box which held up the boot-maker's collapsed veranda. Bozzer had orange, red and yellow hair, a huge star ear-ring, maroon boots with black straps and a fence chain wrapped around his ankle. He looked across and saw Benny standing there. Benny raised his hand in a formal wave. Bozzer squinted and ducked his brilliant head. You could see him thinking *fucking yuppy*. He did not have a clue who Benny was.

Then the woman from the 7-Eleven came out of the drive-way with her Commodore. She knew Benny, too, from the time she tried to get him and Squeaker Davis done for shop-lifting in 4th year. As she came along the service road, she slowed down, and Benny waved at her. She frowned, and waved back, but you could see it – he was transformed – she had no more idea who he was than Bozzer had.

He waited for Vish, but Vish would not come down from Gran's flat. He was hiding, praying like a spider in a web. He was scared of that fucking car yard, but if he would only look out of the window, he would see – Benny had the *power*, Vish could have it too. They could stop being nerds. They could be millionaires, together.

Benny could feel this power, physically, in his body, in his finger tips. He was so full of light, of Voodoo. He could feel it itching on the inside of his veins. If he opened his mouth it would just pour out of him. He straightened his hard penis so it lay flat against his stomach. He felt so incredible, waxed all over, free of body-hair, full of clean-skinned possibility, that he did not even know what to think about what he thought.

But nothing would stay constant. The power ebbed and flowed as it had all morning while the rain had kept him locked in the front office. You looked at the feeling, it went. You thought about the plan, you got scared. When he heard his father's feet on the gravel the hair on the nape of his neck bristled and he wanted to put his hand across his navel and hold it. It was so hard to keep his hand behind his back. His body was already doing all the things it did when it was scared. It was sweating at the hands, and the arsehole. The heart was squittering in its cage. He made himself turn and look his father in the eye.

'Get your arse out of here,' his father said. He had what the boys used to call 'the look' – bright blue peas, crazy lasers. If you were a dog you would back away.

Benny lost it.

'Get out of here,' Mort said, 'before I throw you out.'

Benny walked back to the front office, and shut the door. When his father walked back down the lane-way to the workshop, Benny sat behind the grey metal desk and shut his eyes, trying to get his power back. He did the exercises he had learned from 'Visualizing, Actualizing'. He exhaled very slowly and he laid his pretty, long-fingered hands flat on the desk.

He could see his own reflection in the glass in front of him and once again he was astonished by himself. *I look incredible.* He had moved so far beyond the point where Spare Parts could be an issue in his life.

He wondered how he looked to someone who had never seen him before, someone walking past the petrol pumps on the way to A.S.P. Building Supplies. He imagined himself seen framed by the arched windows and barley-sugar columns. He thought he would look religious or scientific. He was pleased to think he was a most unusual-looking person to be in the office of a car dealership.

He unlocked his desk drawer and removed a magazine. The viewer would have no idea what this religious or scientific person was looking at. It was unimaginable. When Benny had first looked at it, he had felt a numbness, a dizziness, like a new piece of music that he must somehow own or name. It was shiny and thrilling, as if something that had always been a part of him was now being revealed.

It was a women being fucked up the arse. She had short, blonde hair. She had a thin waist and a plump arse that was as smooth and round as something in a dream.

Whoever looked in the window would not know this. They would not know how clean he felt, so clean that he could feel the thin, shiny scar-skin on his arm as it brushed his poplin shirt. He smelt of Pears shampoo. He had no hair on his arms, his legs, not even the crack of his arse.

The woman's legs were bound with woven metal straps. They looked like battery straps from a fifties Holden, but where the terminal points would be, they disappeared into some fabric – it was unclear how they were attached.

The woman was held at the shoulders and arms. She was held at the top of the calves and the ankles. The base was made of moulded fibreglass. It was more or less in the shape of a shallow 'n', not a hard thing to make, really easy. You could do it in your back yard, your cellar. The end result was that her arse stuck up in the air and she could not move. She could not fucking *move*.

You could not see the man's face, just his torso and cock. There was a pic of him putting Vaseline on his cock. They showed it close and it was good quality printing – you could feel the coolness of grease on the knob.

Benny thought: this is not nothing.

It was now sunny. Steam lay along the borders of Loftus Street. The traffic continued between these hedges of steam, unaware of the lives inside Catchprice Motors.

48

Benny thought: they could not imagine me.

When he heard a boot scrape on the concrete floor of the Spare Parts bays, he slipped the magazine into the drawer and locked it. He turned in his chair (only his tumescent lips could have betrayed him) and as he turned he saw Jesse.

Jesse was only five foot five inches tall. He was fifteen years old and had a freckled, scrunched-up little face, but he was fast and graceful. He was the wicket-keeper in the Franklin XI. He was Mort's little mate. He had carrot-coloured, springy straight hair. He got his job because Benny failed his apprenticeship, and he thought – they all thought, Cathy, Howie, Granny Catchprice, the men, the cleaners – they all thought it was because Benny was dumb. They thought they were above him.

Jesse had been fitting new fuel pumps to the recalled Commodores. He had been standing in the pit, soaking himself in petrol. He feinted a light punch to Benny's shoulder and then tried to grab his nuts with his grease-black hands.

Benny jumped back from the greasy hands as if they were 240 live. He stood in front of the window. He put his legs astride and held his Aloe-Vera'd hands behind his back and looked Jesse in the eye.

Benny was older. Benny's family were Jesse's employers. Benny was taller. None of this counted. The first thing Jesse said, he tried to put Benny down.

'You reckon you're a salesman, that it?'

Benny smiled. 'You got no future, Jesse.'

This was new territory for both of them. Jesse blinked three times, quickly, before he spoke. 'You got fired, not me.'

'Fired?' Benny said. 'Do I look like I am fucking fired?'

It was then he saw Mort coming back up the lane-way from the workshop, swinging his arms. Jesse said something but Benny did not hear him. He folded his arms behind his back and stood right in his father's path. The heavy aluminium door swung and hit his shoe, but Mort did not even look at him. He walked straight to the bookshelf behind the desk where young Jesse was looking through the dusty spares catalogues for old Fords and Chevrolets. He did not ask Jesse what he was doing there and why the fuck he was not getting the fuel pumps changed. He put his big hand on the apprentice's shoulder. It fitted round it like a 'U' bolt. 'How's tricks, titch?' he said, and stood beside him, right against him, looking at the old Chevrolet catalogue.

'Stephen Wall done another oil seal,' Jesse said.

Mort was red and blotchy on his neck. He didn't seem to hear what Jesse said. When he looked up at Benny his eyes were frightened and angry and his trunk was already twisting towards the door. 'Who in the fuck do you think *you* are?' he said.

Benny looked at his father with his mouth open.

Mort walked out the back door, into the Spare Parts bays.

He came back in a second later.

'You look like a poof,' he said and banged out of the office and into the yard.

Benny felt like crying. He wanted to tie his father up and pour water over his face until he said he was sorry. He felt like a snail with its shell taken off. He was pink and slimy and glistening. Even the air hurt him. He felt like dying. It was not just his father. It was everything. He could feel depression come down on him like mould, like bad milk, like the damp twisted dirty sheets in the cellar. He wanted to go to the cellar and lock the door.

'If anyone's a poof,' he said to Jesse, 'it's him.'

But Jesse was so dumb. He looked at Benny and grinned. 'That'll be the day,' he said.

'You're a fucking baby,' Benny said.

'You got mousse on your hair?'

'No I haven't.'

Jesse considered this a moment. 'You look pretty weird, you know that? You looked better before. How do you get it to stand up like that if you don't use mousse?'

'Gel.'

'You're going to do that every day now? It must take you an hour to get ready to come to work to sell petrol.'

'Listen, little bubby,' Benny said, 'you're going to remember me, I'm going to be famous and you're going to remember that all you could do was worry about my fucking hair.' He knew already he would be sorry he had said that. Jesse would tell the others and they'd fart and hee-haw like about Bozzer and his bullshit story of his father who was meant to be a yuppy with a 7 Series BMW.

But if he had to be sorry, he was fucked anyway. *I cannot be what I am.* In the corner of his eye he saw something. He turned. It was

Maria Takis, walking slowly back to her car. She waved at him. Benny liked her face. He liked her wide, soft mouth particularly. He waved back, smiling.

'Christ,' he said, 'that's all woman.'

'That's all woman,' Jesse mimicked. 'You're a poof, Benny, admit you're a poof.'

Benny heard himself say: 'She's mine.' He meant it too. He committed himself to it as he said it.

He watched the Tax Inspector getting into her car. He had a very nice feeling about her. He had had a nice feeling about her this morning, the way she spoke, the way she looked at him. He took an Aloe-Vera facelette and wiped his cheeks.

Jesse said: 'You want to fuck a whale?'

Benny looked at Jesse and saw that he was very young, and very short. He had soft, fair, fluffy hair in a line from his ears down to his chin. Benny felt his power come back. He felt it itch inside his skin.

He said, 'When you're grown up you'll like their bellies like that.'

'You don't like girls, Benny.'

'Their tits get big,' Benny said. 'Their nipples too. They like you to drink their milk while you fuck them.' He was smiling while he spoke. He felt his skin stretch. His face was full of teeth.

Jesse frowned.

Benny thought: you dwarf. He thought: I am going to rise up from the cellar and stand in the fucking sky.

'She's from the Tax Department,' Jesse said. 'I had to carry all the ledgers and that up to your Granny's flat for her. She's going to go through your old man like a dose of salts.'

This was the first time that Benny had heard about the Tax Department. He was travelling too fast to notice it. 'I don't care where she's from.' He looked down at Jesse and smiled as he checked his tie. 'I am going to fuck her.'

Jesse was going to say something. He opened his mouth but then he just made a little breathy laugh through his nose and teeth.

Finally he said, 'You?'

'Yes.' Benny's chest and shoulders felt good inside his suit. His posture was good. He was suffused with a feeling of warmth.

'We can realise our dreams,' he told Jesse.

Jesse blushed bright red.

'Also,' Benny said. He held up a single, pink-nailed forefinger and waited.

'Also what?'

'Also I am selling five vehicles a week, starting now.'

Benny smiled. Then he picked up the 'Petrol Sales' invoice book and went to read the meters on the pumps.

10

Mrs Catchprice sat in her apartment above the car yard in Franklin, and was angry about what happened in Dorrigo nearly sixty-five years before.

Her grandson chanted. It did her no particular good, although she liked the company. He chanted on and on and on, and she smiled and nodded, watching him, but she was Frieda McClusky and she was eighteen years old and she would never have the flower farm she had been promised.

In Franklin she narrowed her cloudy eyes and lit a Salem cigarette.

In Dorrigo she lost her temper. She emptied her mother's 'Tonic' across the veranda. She threw a potato through the kitchen window and watched it bounce out into the debris of the storm. She would never have a flower farm in Dorrigo. Then she would have her flower farm somewhere else.

She walked out down the long straight drive. She was eighteen. She had curly fair hair which fell across her cheek and had to be shaken back every ten yards or so.

I was pretty.

She was tall and slender and there was a slight strictness in her walk, a precision not quite in keeping with the muddy circumstances. The drive ran straight down the middle of their ten-acre block. The gutters on each side of it were now little creeks running high with yellow water from the storm. Occasional lightning continued to strike the distant transmitter at Mount Moomball, but the thunder now arrived a whole fifty seconds later. It was six o'clock in the evening. Steam was already beginning to rise from the warm earth.

There was a dense forest of dead, ring-barked trees on either side of the slippery, yellow-mud road. They were rain-wet, green-white. They were as still as coral, fossils, bones. There was a beauty in them, but Frieda McClusky did not care to see it.

There were three trees fallen across the road. She had to pick her way between the thickets of their fallen branches. She was fastidious in the way she touched the twigs. She kept her back straight and her pretty face contorted – her chin tucked into her neck, her nose wrinkled, her eyes screwed up. When a branch caught in her coat, she brushed and panicked against the restriction as though it were a spider's web.

She wore a pleated tartan skirt and a white cotton blouse with a Peter Pan collar. On her feet she had black Wellingtons. She carried a tartan umbrella, a small hat-case, a navy blue waterproof over-coat, and – for her own protection – a stick of AN 60 gelignite which had been purchased four and a half years ago in order to blow these dead trees from the earth.

In a year when no one had ever heard the term 'hobby farm', the McCluskys had sold their family home in Melbourne and moved here to Dorrigo a thousand miles away. There was, of course, no airport in Dorrigo, but there was no railway either. From the point of view of Glenferrie Road, Malvern, Victoria, it was like going to Africa.

Frieda's father was fifty-eight years old. He had energy in the beginning. He had blue poplin work-shirts and moleskin trousers which went slowly white. He set out to ring-bark every large tree on the ten-acre block. When the trees were dead he was going to blast their roots out of the earth with gelignite. The ten acres he chose were surrounded by giant trees, by dramatic ravines, escarp-ments, waterfalls. It was as romantic a landscape as something in a book of old engravings. Within his own land he planned rolling lawns, formal borders, roses, carnations, dahlias, hollyhocks, pan-sies, and a small ornamental lake.

He had notebooks, rulers, pens in different colours. He had plans headed 'Dorrigo Springs Guest-house' which he drew to scale. He listed his children on a page marked 'Personnel'. Daniel McClusky – vegetable gardener. Graham McClusky – carpenter, mechanic. Frieda McClusky – flower gardener. It did not seem crazy at the time. He wrote a letter to the Technical Correspondence School so he might 'qualify in the use of handling of explosives to a standard acceptable to the chief Inspector of Explosives of New South Wales'. He bought Frieda *Large Scale Plantings* by A. C. Reade. She learned to push the soil auger hard enough to take samples from the land. She parcelled up each sample in separate brown paper bags and sent them by train to C.S.I.R.O.

Frieda's mother was not listed as 'Personnel', but the move had a positive effect upon her temper. She bought a horse and wore jodhpurs which made her skittish and showed off her good legs and her small waist. She brushed Frieda's hair at night, and stopped going to bed straight after dinner. She was less critical of Frieda's appearance. Sometimes she walked down the drive-way with her husband, hand in hand. You could see them pointing out the future to each other. Frieda watched them and felt a great weight removed from her.

Frieda loved the feel of the soil between her fingers, the smell of earth at night in deep, damp gullies, chicken and horse manure, rich reeking blood and bone from the Dorrigo abattoirs. She liked the smell of rotting grass as it slowly became earth. She liked to dig her garden fork down deep and see the pink-grey bodies of worms, lying still and silent, hiding from the air.

She was stupid enough to be grateful for the life she was given. She did not see what her brothers saw – that they were stuck with mad people. They did not have the decency to share their thoughts with her. They left an envelope propped against the ugly little butter dish Aunt Mae had given them. The letter said they could not have expressed their feelings because 'we would have been talked out of it'. They said they were now men and had to choose their own lives and would write later. They left their shirts and sweaters folded neatly in their drawers.

Marcia McClusky blamed her husband, although, typically, she never did say this clearly. By noon on the day they opened the envelope, Stan and Marcia McClusky had stopped speaking to each other. By the following evening Marcia was sleeping in the boys' room. The next morning neither of them got up.

It was grief of course, but grief does not stay grief for ever. It changes, and in this case it also must have changed, although into what is by no means certain. It could not be grief, it was something drier and harder than grief, a knot, a lump. They lay all day, cocooned in their beds in their own rooms, like grubs locked out of metamorphosis. They read second-hand romances and detective novels – three, sometimes four a day – while the ring-barked trees outside slowly died and grew white and were left to crash and fall around the house in storms.

Frieda worked cheerfully around her parents, cooking, cleaning, dusting, as if she could, by the sheer force of her goodwill, effect their recovery. She carried the vision for them. Not a guest-house any more. She pared it down to the thing she had been promised – the flowers. She would have a flower farm. For three years – an impossible time in retrospect – she ran to and fro, trying to make them cheerful again. She paid for the *Horticulturalist* from housekeeping. She began a correspondence with the Horticultural Society. She grew flowers – Gerberas particularly – and exhibited them at local shows.

Only in the midst of the violent storms of summer did she express her anger. With giant trees crashing in the night, she hated her parents for putting her in terror of her life. In the clear white flash of lightning, she said things so extreme that their remembrance, at morning, was shameful to her.

But when the giant red cedar finally hit the house it was after-noon, and there was no sleep to take the edge off her rage or make her forget the extremity of her terror.

The cedar wiped out the south-west corner of the veranda and pushed its way into the kitchen. The noise was so great that her parents actually rose from their beds, both at the same time.

The sky to the east was still black. But the sun came from the west and as they came out on to the shattered veranda it shone upon them. They stood staring at the receding storm and squinted as the unexpected sunlight took them from the side. In the light of the sun they looked spoiled and sickly, like things left too long in the bath. Frieda saw the toes sticking from the slippers, the string where the dressing cord should be, the yellow, dog-eared pages of a musty John Buchan in her father's hand, and felt all her unper-mitted anger well up in her. She opened her mouth to release some word bigger than a pumpkin. She could do nothing but hold her hands apart and shake her head. They put their hands across their brows to shade their eyes from glare.

She fetched her mother's tonic and poured it away in front of her.

She took the bread and butter pudding from the oven and threw it off the edge of the veranda.

'Maggots,' she said. 'You nearly killed me.'

No one said anything, but by the time she reached the front gate her mother was on the phone to the police.

Percy Donaldson was the Sergeant. He was half-shickered when he got the call and he dropped the car keys down between the slats on the veranda and had to take his son's bicycle to get Frieda back. Mrs McClusky, who had seen her daughter walk up towards the Ebor Road, hadn't troubled to tell him that the runaway had a stick of AN 60 and a bag of detonators in a little lilac whats-oh hanging round her neck.

He found her up at the beginning of the gravel road where the town's macadam stopped. It was dark by then, although not pitch black. She waved the gelly at him: 'You grab me and you're minced meat.' He could see her pale face in the light of his bicycle lantern. 'I've got the detonators,' she said in a trembling voice. 'I know what to do with them.'

'Whoa,' he said. 'Easy girl.' He peered into the poor, pale-yellow nimbus of light which was all the flat battery was able to bring to bear on the girl. She sure was pretty.

'It's real,' she said. 'I'm Stan McClusky's daughter.'

'I know who you are, Frieda.'

'Good,' she said.

She did not even have the detonators wrapped up. They clinked next to each other in their little bag next to her breast.

'You want to wrap them things up,' he said. 'They'll blow your little titties off.'

It was because of that remark she refused to speak to him all night. And it was all night they were to spend together – because she would not return with him, and he would not leave her alone, and so they walked together over the pot-holed road – Percy hearing those damned detonators clinking round her neck while they walked for ten hours with their stomachs rumbling – neither of them had eaten before they left – until at piccaninny dawn they were on the outskirts of Wollombi. Fifty-two miles. Ten hours. Over five miles an hour!

As they walked on to the mile-long stretch of macadam which was Wollombi, Frieda burst into tears. Her face was caked with dust and the tears made smudgy mud and she bowed her head and howled. Percy felt sorry for her. He lent her his handkerchief and watched helplessly as her pretty little shoulders shook. The milkman was stopped a little up the road. He was ladling milk from his bucket, but staring at the policeman and the crying girl.

'You've got guts,' Percy said, motioning the milkman to piss off. 'I'll say that for you.'

He guessed she was frightened of what trouble she had got herself into, which was true, but he had no idea how empowered she was. Under the mud of her despair and misery ran this hard bedrock of certainty – the fact that gelignite was as light as a feather. Until that day she had thought it was a thing for men.

She and Percy got a lift with a fellow who was a traveller in Manchester and Millinery. His car was filled with samples but they wrapped the bicycle in hessian bags and strapped it to the roof with twine. They travelled home together in the dickey seat, silently, but companionably, like soldiers who have fought beside each other in the same trench. The only charges ever laid were against her father for not keeping his gelignite locked up.

Everyone in Dorrigo heard the story, of course, Freddy Sparks the butcher knew it, told it to people who had already heard it. But he never did connect it with the sweet cloying smell that rose from Frieda McCluskey's handbag when she opened it to pay the bill. The source of the smell was nothing to look at – like a cheap sausage, or some cold porridge wrapped in brown paper. It was a stick of AN 60 gelignite.

This was the year Frieda did her mines exams and got a permit herself. No one wanted to let her have it – her parents least of all – but she wanted to make a flower farm and they were too frightened to say no.

11

She was carrying gelignite in her white leather clutch-bag when she first danced with 'Cacka' Catchprice. He arrived in August as official scorer for the touring Franklin 'Magpies'.

All that time I was pretty and did not know it.

This thought could still make her rheumy eyes water – she had been brought up to think herself so goddam plain, such a collection of faults – wide mouth, small bosom, thin legs – which would all be clear for all the world to snicker at if she did not listen to her mother's advice about her shoes, her skirt, her lipstick colour.

I could have married anyone I damn well pleased.

When she walked into town in gum boots, holding gelignite in her clutch-bag, her dancing shoes in a paper bag, she had decided to get married, to anyone, she did not care – anything would be better than staying in that house another year – but when she opened the wire gate in the fence around the C.W.A. rooms, she almost lost her resolve and her legs went weak and rubbery and she really thought she was going to faint.

She saw men in blazers leaning against the ugly concrete veranda posts. There was a string of coloured lights in a necklace underneath the veranda guttering. Under the wash of blue and red there were girls she recognized, people she had 'dealt with' in the shops who were now powerful and pretty in scallops of peach organza. They did not try to speak to her. The smell of beer came out to meet her, as alien as sweat, hair oil, pipe tobacco. She had to make herself continue up the path in her gum boots.

Inside it was no better. She sat beneath the crepe paper streamers, on a chair in a corner by the tea urn, and removed her muddy gum boots. She kept her head down, convinced that everyone was looking at her. When she saw that the gum boots were too big to fit in her paper bag, she did not know what to do with them.

If it had not been for the gum boots Cacka might never have spoken to her. If she had come in with shiny black high heels, he would almost certainly have found her beyond his reach. But he came from a red clay farm where you had to wear gum boots to go to take a shit at night. His mother wore gum boots to get from the back door to the hire car which took them to their father's funeral.

'Tell you what,' he said. 'I'm going to put these out the back. You tell me when you want them. I'll get them for you.'

'You're most kind,' she said.

'How about a dance when I get back?'

'Oh,' she said.

'I know I'm not an oil painting.'

'Thank you,' she said. 'That would be lovely.'

He had this bulk, this thick neck and sloping shoulders, so all his strength seemed centred in his chest, which occasionally touched

58

her breasts when he danced with her, formally, apologetically. He held her as if she were somehow fragile, and she let herself be held this way. She had spent three years being 'strong' and now she was so tensed and wound up that when, by the fifth dance, she allowed herself to give her weight to him, she could not give a part of it, but laid the full load on his shoulders which she dampened with a tear or two.

His nose had a big bump in it just beneath the eye, and his left ear was slightly squashed and the skin around his left eye was blue and yellow, but he was also very gentle, and it was not that opportunistic gentleness the roughest man will adopt around a woman – it was written permanently on his lips which were soft and well-shaped and formed little cooing words she felt like warm oil-drops in her ears. This was a man whose secret passion was the Opera, who had the complete HMV recording of *Die Zauberflöte* hidden beneath his bed – eight 78 rpm records with a cast most of whose names he could not pronounce – Tiana Lemnitz, Erna Berger, Helge Rosvaenge, Gerhard Hüsch, and the Berlin Philharmonic conducted by Sir Thomas Beecham.

Die Zauberflöte, however, meant nothing to Frieda. She was thirsty for what was practical, and when she drew him out she was the daughter of a man with little coloured pens and pretty pencils and paper plans on flimsy sheets of tracing paper. She loved to hear him talk about post-hole digging, barbed wire, white ants, concrete fencing posts, poultry sheds.

'You really want to hear this stuff?' he asked.

'Oh yes,' she said.

'Truly?'

'Truly and really.'

And when the band played 'Begin the Beguine' she held him tightly and sang the words softly in his ear. It was that which put the little wet spot on his Jockey shorts – that voice she did not even know she had. He told his mate, Billy Johnston, with whom he shared a room at the Dorrigo Court House Hotel, 'I didn't even kiss her, mate. I didn't even touch her. She's got these little tits, you know. I think I love her.'

At ten o'clock in the morning on the day after the dance, he came to call on her. She met him in her gum boots – halfway up the muddy drive – and told him she was going to have a flower farm there. She was going to blast those trees herself if no one would do it for her.

She said this almost angrily, for she had to say it and she expected that saying it would drive him from her, but Cacka was too shocked to laugh – he thought he never saw a sadder bit of country in his life.

'If it's flowers you want,' he said, 'I could show you land more suitable.'

All her life she would accuse him of lying about this, but even she knew this was not quite fair. Cacka withheld things and had secrets but he rarely told an outright lie. This land did exist, forty-five minutes from the central markets just the way he said it did. He was happy and in love. He really saw the land. He really saw Gerberas on it. It was the opposite of lying.

What he omitted was that it was part of a deceased estate and held up for probate.

It was ten years before Frieda and Albert Catchprice finally got possession of that land, and then she was the one who showed him how he could put a motor business on it. The only thing she had ever wanted was a flower farm, but what she got instead was the smell of rubber radiator hoses, fan belts, oil, grease, petrol vapour, cash flows, overdrafts and customers whose bills ran 90, 120 days past due. It was this she could not stand – she did it to herself.

12

It was the day they had tried to put her in a nursing home, but it would be the same on any other day – when Mrs Catchprice went to lock the big cyclone gates of Catchprice Motors, she would look up at Cathy and Howie's apartment window. The look would say: just try and stop me.

At six o'clock exactly – in two minutes' time – Howie would look through the Venetian blinds and see her apartment door open, like a tricky clock in a Victorian arcade. First, the old woman would put her nose out and sniff the air. Then she would look down at the cars. Then she would come out on to the landing and stare at the window where she thought her enemy was waiting for her to die.

She thought it was Howie who conspired to commit her. She needed no proof. It was obvious. He was fiddling with the books, renting other premises, preparing to set up as a Honda dealer, in opposition.

He was plotting, certainly, continually, every moment of the day, but what he was plotting to do was to have a life like Ernest Tubb, The Gold Chain Troubadour. He was plotting to have his wife run away with him.

It was only Cathy who kept him locked inside those cyclone gates. She had an entire band trying to drag her out on to the road. She had 'Drunk as a Lord' with a *bullet* on the Country charts. She had fans who wrote to her. She had a life to go to, but she was a Catchprice, and she was tangled in all that mad Catchprice shit that had her shouting at her mother while she fed her, at war with her brother while she fretted about his loneliness, firing her nephew while she went running to his cellar door, knocking and crying and leaving presents for him – she bought him *dope*, for Chrissakes, *dope*, in a pub, to cheer him up. You would not want to know about that kid's life, his brother either. They were like institution kids with old men's eyes in their young faces, but she loved them, unconditionally, with an intensity that she tried to hide even from her husband. Howie could not trust those boys, either of them, but he had learned not to speak against them in his wife's presence.

Indeed, Howie had become as calculating and secretive as Granny Catchprice thought he was, but he did not covet Catchprice money or the Catchprice Goodwill Factor and he did not want to set up in competition to the family firm. His 'happy thought' was of long tendrils of vines snaking through brick walls of Catchprice Motors, collapsed fire escapes, high walls covered by bearded mosses and flaking lichens, rusting cyclone fence collapsing under a load of Lantana and wild passionfruit. He was not counting on Granny Catchprice's death to free him – he judged it would be too long in coming.

Mrs Catchprice had the only authorized keys to the cyclone gates, and she would not give them up. Every morning at half-past six she opened them, and every night she locked them up again. They were not light or easy. You could see her lean her brittle little shoulders into the hard steel and guess what it might take her to get those big galvanized rollers moving. But she would not give up those keys to anyone. If you wanted to get a car out of the yard outside the 'hours' you were meant to go up the fire escape and ask her, please, if it was not too much trouble.

Granny did not have guests and neither did Mort. When they shut the gates at night it was as if they were severing connection with 'The General Public' until the morning.

It was only Howie and Cathy who were 'social'. Their guests had to drive down the workshop lane-way and park outside the entrance to the Spare Parts Department. They then honked once or twice and Howie went down to let them in. This was never any problem with musicians. But Howie was sometimes embarrassed to have their visitors first approach their apartment along a steel-shelved avenue stacked with leaf springs and shock absorbers.

At six o'clock, on the dot, Gran Catchprice came out on to her landing. She not only looked across at him, she bowed, and gave a mocking little curtsy.

'You old chook,' he said. He frowned and fitted a cigarette into the corner of his smile.

Cathy came in from the kitchen with two cans of Resch's Pilsener. She was wearing a gingham skirt which showed off her strong, well-shaped legs, and white socks and black shoes like a school kid. She gave him one can and sat on the rickety ping-pong table.

It was two and a half hours before their meeting with the band but already she had that high nervous look she had in the fifteen minutes before she did a show. He loved that look. You could not say she was beautiful, but he sat night after night in bars for a hundred miles around Franklin and watched men change their opinion of her as she sang.

She had a good band, but it was nothing special. She had a good voice, but there were better. It was her words, and it was her feelings. She could turn the shit of her life into jewels. She had plump arms and maybe a little too much weight under the chin and her belly pushed out against her clothes, but she was sexy. You had to say, whatever problems she had in bed, she was a sexy woman. You could watch men see it in her, but never straightaway.

'Big night,' he said. He stood up so she could take the bar stool and he sat instead on the ping-pong table.

'Sure,' she said. She was bright and tight, could barely talk. Tonight she was going to have her meeting with the band and with the lawyer. She drank her beer. He leaned across to rub her neck, but you could not touch her neck or shoulders unless she had been drinking.

'Don't, hon.' She took his hand and held it. Something had happened with the neck and shoulders. Sentimental Cacka had dragged her out of bed at two in the morning to sing 'Batti, batti' from *Don Giovanni* to his visitors. It happened then, he guessed. She never said exactly, but he saw it exactly, in his mind's eye. You could see the shadows of it. You could draw a map from them.

'What you think?' she said.

'About what?'

'Will I do it?'

'You've got to decide,' he said. 'I can't tell you what to do.'

'I'm just hurt, I guess. I'm pissed off with them for talking to a lawyer.'

'Sure,' he said. 'I know.' He patted her thigh sympathetically – he was the one who had persuaded Craig and Steve Putzel that they could pull Cathy out on the road if they did what he said. He was the one who found them this so-called Entertainment Lawyer. He had manoeuvred them all to this point where they were an inch away from having the lives they wanted, all of them. He brushed some ash off his suede shoe. He buttoned his suit jacket and unbuttoned it.

'Big night,' he said again. Through the Venetian blinds he could see Mort walking down the fire escape from his mother's apartment. This time next year, all this was going to seem like a bad dream.

Cathy saw Mort too. 'They've been talking about the doctor,' she said. 'You can bet on it. He's been telling her it was all my idea, the coward.'

Howie always thought Mort was a dangerous man, but he doubted he would be dishonest in the way Cathy imagined. He watched Mort as he bent over the whitewashed sign Howie had written on the windscreen of the red Toyota truck. He scratched at it with his fingernail.

'He doesn't like my sign,' he said.

Cathy lifted the Venetian blind a fraction so it pinged.

Mrs Catchprice had walked back from the gates and joined her son. She also scratched at the whitewash with one of her keys.

'You know he thinks "As-new" is sleazy,' Cathy said. 'You must have known they'd wipe it off.'

'Ah,' said Howie, 'who cares.'

That surprised her. She looked at him with her head on one side and then, silently, drew aside his jacket, undid a shirt button, and looked at the colour of his rash.

She said: 'You really think I'm going to take the leap, don't you?'

He wasn't counting on anything until it happened. She had been this close four years before, and once again, two years before that. Each time Granny Catchprice pulled her strings. You would not believe the tricks the old woman could pull to keep her workhorse working.

'If we're done for tax I can't go on the road. You know that. I can't just desert them.'

'Yes you can,' he said. He did up his shirt button. 'This time you've got to.'

'Yes,' she said. 'I've got to.'

She had that tightness in her bones, a flushed luminous look, as if she was about to do a show. He watched her drain her beer.

'You look beautiful,' he said.

'This time I'm going to do it.'

'When you look like that I want to fuck you.' He came and held her from behind and began to kiss her neck. She accepted his kisses. They lay on her skin like unresolved puzzles.

'He's coming up here,' she said.

She meant Mort. He could see why she said it. Mort was walking across the yard this way, but he was probably on his way to hammer and yell at Benny's cellar door. Mort's house shared a hot water service with their apartment, but Mort had not visited them for nine years.

'He's coming *here*,' she said. 'This is it. It's starting.'

She had such amazing skin – very white and soft.

'Don't!' She broke free from his hands, suddenly irritated.

'It's nothing,' he said. 'It'll be about the nursing home.'

'They're going to try and make me stay.'

'Cathy, Cathy . . . they don't even believe you're leaving them.'

'She's sending him to say something to me.'

'Honey, calm down. Think. What could they say to you at this stage?'

Cathy's eyes began to water. 'She's so unfair.'

Howie stroked her neck. 'You're forty-six years old,' he said. 'You're entitled to your own life.'

'She makes him say it for her. He's going to say how much she needs me.' She put her hand on his sleeve. 'He's coming up the stairs.'

'Let me lock the door,' Howie said.

Mort had not visited their apartment since he argued with Howie about the ping-pong table.

'This is the living room,' he said. 'There's no room for a ping-pong table.'

'With all respect,' Howie had answered, 'that's not your business.'

'Respect is something you wouldn't know about,' Mort said. 'It's the Family Home. You're turning it into a joke.'

Even allowing for the fact his father had just died, this was a crazy thing to say. Howie could not think of how to answer him.

'Respect!' Mort said.

Then he slammed his fist into the brick wall behind Howie's head. It came so close it grazed his ear.

'I'll lock the door,' Howie said, not moving.

Cathy poured some Benedictine into a tumbler. Then the door opened and she looked up and there was Mort and his lost wife, side by side. But it couldn't be Sophie. Sophie had left thirteen years ago.

13

It wasn't Sophie. It was Benny. He had made himself into the spitting image of the woman who had shot him. Whether he had meant to do it, or if it was an accident of bright white hair, the effect was most disturbing, to Cathy anyway.

All through the day the men from the workshop had come and gone with their grubby job cards, cracking their jokes about her nephew's 'look', but not one of them had said – how could they have known, they were all too young – how like his mother it made him seem. His hair was the same colour, the *exact* same colour, and it gave his features a luminous, fresh-steamed look. Sophie had grown her hair long in the end but at the beginning she had it short like this and now you could see he had the cheekbones. He was like his mother, but he had a damaged, dangerous look his mother never had. No matter what shit she put up with from the Catch-prices she kept her surface as fresh and clean as a pair of freshly whitened tennis shoes right up to the day she shot her son.

Cathy said: 'Benny, you look nice.'

The person he made her think of was Elvis – not that he looked like Elvis, but he *felt* how Elvis must have felt when he walked into Sam Phillips's recording studio in Memphis – a shy boy, who maybe never played but in his bedroom, with the mirror. Sam Phillips must have seen his sexy lips, but the thing that struck him was how inferior Elvis felt, how *markedly* inferior. He said this in an interview on more than one occasion.

Benny had already phoned her once today to say he was going to 'hurt' her, and she knew he had a temper which you can only describe as violent, but she knew him with his little arms tight around her neck at three in the morning, and when she compli-mented him he blushed and lowered his eyes because he knew she meant it and would never lie to him.

It was only when Mort heard his son's name that he actually realized Benny had come up the stairs behind him.

'Oh, shit,' he said.

Cathy looked at Mort and wondered now if he even saw the similarity.

Benny raised his eyebrows at his father and shrugged apolo-getically. He put out his hand as if to take his sleeve or his hand, but the sleeves on Mort's overall were cut off and there was nothing to hold on to except a hand he would not take. Cathy would have taken his hand, but it was not offered her.

Benny had been in trouble with almost everything, lying, cheating, truancy, shop-lifting, selling bottled petrol for inhalation, trying to buy Camira parts from the little crooks who hung about in Franklin Mall; but now he just looked very young and frightened of being laughed at. He walked lightly on his feet, holding his back straight. You could hear his new shoes squeaking as he crossed the room to the yellow vinyl armchair which had once belonged to Cacka. When he sat and crossed his long legs, he revealed socks as long as a clergyman's – no skin showed. Benny folded his clean hands in his lap and looked directly at his father, blushing.

Mort's colour was also high and his lips had a loose embarrassed look. He shook his head and shut his eyes.

'Ignore your father,' Cathy said. 'You look wonderful, better than your uncle Jack.'

'Thanks Cath,' Mort said. He leaned against the window-sill opposite her and stared critically at the stupid ping-pong table. It was not properly joined in the middle. It was marked with stains from their 'Social Ambitions' – ring marks from glasses and bottles, sticky circles of Benedictine stuck with dust.

'You singing tonight?' he asked. 'You got a jig-jig?'

'Very funny,' she said. 'What do you want?'

Mort shook his head as if in disappointment at this hostility. He looked down at his boots a moment as if he was considering a riposte, but then he looked up, spoke in what was, for him, in the circumstances, a calm voice: 'Why does this Tax Inspector have her office in Mum's apartment?'

'You come up here to ask about that?' Cathy crossed her arms below her breasts and shook her head.

'Mort . . .' Howie said.

'I don't believe you,' Cathy said.

'Tough,' said Mort.

'The auditor needs a desk,' Howie said, 'that's all. She could have taken any vacant desk. She could have had your office.'

'You wouldn't want me near a Tax Inspector,' Mort said. 'You couldn't trust me not to give the game away.'

Cathy looked into his eyes and he held hers. He was her brother in a way that Jack had never been. She and Mort were the ones who had sung opera together, killed chooks, sold cars, but now she had no idea what he thought about anything.

'There is no game,' Cathy said.

'I wouldn't know.'

'No,' Cathy said. 'You wouldn't, but you'd better find out. If I was you I'd be finding out what makes this business tick pretty damn fast.'

'You going to try and run away again, Cathy?' Mort grinned. 'Did you get another letter from The Gold Chain Troubadour?'

There was silence which was broken by the sound of Benedictine being poured into Cathy's tumbler. Benny crossed his legs and laid his left palm softly on the back of the right hand.

'Look,' Mort said. 'What I came up here to say was that I've had a talk to Mum.'

Cathy poured herself some extra Benedictine, but then she didn't drink it.

'I talked with Mum and we both decided that if you want to sell the back paddock to cover us with any back taxes, we'll vote in favour. That's why I'm here, to tell you that.'

'Do you remember,' Howie said, smiling sideways at Cathy, 'that we wrote your mother in as head salesman?'

'Sure.'

'And we claimed tax deductions for what we said we paid her?'

'Sure, I remember that. We had Jack's smart-arse accountant. You all got excited about how you were going to keep the trade-ins off the books. But do you remember what I said then?'

'Tell me.'

'I said that I didn't want to do business like Jack. I said we've gone off the rails. We shouldn't be playing tricks with tax. We should be running the business by its original principles . . .'

'Mort,' Howie said. 'I'm trying to explain that if this audit goes through we are going to need *twenty* back paddocks to pay the bill.'

'And I'm trying to tell you, Mr Rock 'n' Roll,' said Mort, suddenly shouting and jabbing his finger at Howie, 'that this business will run itself just fine if we stop listening to crooks and stick to Cacka's philosophy.'

It was very quiet. Then there was a squeaking noise. The ping-pong table started to move in front of Benny's nose. It pushed towards him, then withdrew. It was Cathy pushing with her big thighs. She had a bright little smile on her face.

'Philosophy?' she said. Her mouth was small in her big face and she had two hot spots on her pale cheeks. 'What sort of philosophy would that be, Mort? Like Socrates? Like Mussolini? What sort of philosophy did you have in mind exactly?'

Mort said: 'He was one of the greats.' Benny looked down at the floor: He thought: don't, please don't.

'Mort,' Cathy said, 'say he was a creep. Admit it. It's not your fault.'

'He was human, but he was one of the greats.'

'Look at us,' Cathy said. There was a bang as she slammed her glass down on the table. Benedictine spilled. (Howie went to the

68

kitchen to get a Wettex. Benny despised him for doing it.) 'Look at us,' Cathy said, watching Howie wipe the table. 'We don't know how to be happy. Look out of the window. We're car dealers. That's all we do. You cannot be a *great* car dealer.'

'You can be a great *boot-maker*,' Mort said.

Benny agreed. He took a facelette of Aloe-Vera and wiped the back of his hands. He thought: *I* will be a great car dealer.

Cathy took the Wettex from Howie and folded it and placed it on the table. Howie picked it up and took it out to the kitchen.

'You want to talk about *great*,' Cathy said. 'Elvis was great.'

Mort laughed.

'Hank Williams was great, but Christ, Morty, even if you could be a *great* car dealer, you could not be great and bankrupt at the same time.'

'Spend some time with the books, Mort. I'd be happy to take you through them.'

'Listen.' Mort said. 'I don't like this business. I don't think you like it either, but we're stuck with it. If we want to save our arse, we should go back to Cacka's principles.'

'And what principles were you thinking of?' Howie asked.

'You remember Catchprice Motors, Cathy?' Mort asked his sister. 'We didn't wind our speedos back. We paid our taxes. We told the truth.'

'Why do you mime the words of the hymns in Church?' Howie asked.

Mort looked at him, his mouth loose.

'I just meant to ask you,' Howie said. 'I wondered why you won't sing out loud. Barry Peterson asked me why someone with such a good voice wouldn't sing out loud. I wondered if this had something to do with Cacka's philosophy.'

'Shut up, Howie,' Cathy said.

'What I'm getting to,' Mort said, his neck now blazing red above his white overall collar, 'is Cacka paid his taxes. He'd have shut the doors if he couldn't pay his taxes.'

'Mort,' said Cathy, more gently than before, 'Franklin has changed.'

'If it's changed so much we have to be cheats, I'd rather run some little garage up at Woop-woop. I'd rather be on the dole.'

'You might get your wish,' Cathy said.

'How?' asked Benny.

They all looked at him. For a moment the only noise came from the rattling air-conditioner.

'What?' Cathy said, frowning at him.

'How will my father get his wish?'

'What this conversation is about, Benjamin, is that we are being investigated by the Taxation Department.'

'I know that.'

'And by the time they have finished with us, we'll have to sell the business to pay them back.'

'So, what are you going to do, Cathy?' Benny asked.

'Don't speak to your auntie like that.'

'No,' Benny insisted, 'what are you going to do to protect us? *What positive steps can be taken towards realizing our desires?*' He blushed and stood up. They were all staring at him. Not one of them had any idea of who he was and what it was he had quoted to them. Howie was smirking, but none of them had any plan appropriate to their situation. In their shiny suits and frills and oily overalls, they were creatures at the end of an epoch. The climate had changed and they were puzzled to find the familiar crops would no longer grow. He stood up. He was full of light. They saw him, but did not see him, for the best and most vital part of him was already walking down the path towards the actualization of his desires. *I am new. I am born now.* Even while they stared at him across the bottle-stained emptiness of the ping-pong table, he was descending the staircase, not the one that led to his physical actual cellar – not the metal staircase with its perforated treads, the oil-stained ladder with the banister he must not touch – but the other staircases which are described in seven audio cassettes *Actualizations and Affirmations 1–14.*

He was descending the blue staircase (its treads shimmering like oil on water, its banisters clear, clean, stainless steel) and all they could think was that he had no right to wear a suit.

At the bottom of the blue staircase he found the yellow staircase.

At the bottom of the yellow staircase, the pink.

At the bottom of the pink, the ebony.

At the end of the ebony, the Golden Door.

Beyond the Golden Door was the Circular Room of Black Marble.

In the centre of the Circular Room of Black Marble he visualized a Sony Trinitron.

Benny turned on the Sony Trinitron and saw there the vivid picture of what it was he desired: all the books and ledgers of Catchprice Motors, wrapped in orange garbage bags and sealed with silver tape.

'Leave it to me,' he said out loud.

By then he was already walking across the crushed gravel of the car yard. His father was a yard ahead of him.

'What?' he said.

14

Maria's image of herself was made in all the years before 15 July, the day she finally discovered that she was pregnant. No matter what kicks the baby gave her, no matter how it squirmed and rolled and pushed and made her lumpy and off-centre, no matter how her legs ached, her back hurt, irrespective of the constipation, haemorrhoids and insomnia, the fine webs of spider veins and stretch marks that threatened to make her old and ugly overnight, she could still forget what her body had actually become. She could look in the mirrors as she entered the birth class and be surprised to see a short, big-bellied woman.

There were also other times when she knew exactly what she looked like and then she felt that she had been that way for ever, and then it was almost impossible to remember that it had only been on 15 July last year that she had discovered she was pregnant.

On 15 July she still had beer and wine in her refrigerator, no milk. She made her last cup of strong black coffee, not even bothering to taste it properly, and slipped into her quilted 'Afghan' skirt and embroidered black silk blouse not guessing that before five weeks had passed the $220 skirt would be unwearable.

Her period was late, but her period was often late, or early. She stopped in Darling Street, Balmain and spent $15 on a pregnancy test kit and drove over the Harbour Bridge to Crows Nest where she was auditing a property developer. It wasn't until after lunch she found the pregnancy test kit in her handbag.

In the property developer's white bathroom she saw a slender phial of her urine turn a pretty violet colour.

She sat it on the window ledge and shook her head at it. Such was her capacity for denial that she assumed the kit was faulty and at three o'clock she spent another $15 on a second kit and got the same result.

She tried to phone her best friend at the Tax Office. Gia Katalanis had an office with a view and an answer machine on her desk. Maria left a message: 'Extraordinary news.'

As for Alistair, she put it off. She knew where he was, in an office two floors above Gia's. Even when she phoned him, on his direct line, at five o'clock, she did not know quite what she was going to say.

'I want to buy you dinner,' she told him, looking out of the property developer's spare office to where $80,000 yachts heeled over in the Nor'-easter.

'I can't,' he said.

She understood exactly what he meant – his wife.

'Oh, yes you can,' she said. She laughed, but it did not soften the effect – she had already crossed a line. 'It's something good,' she said. 'Not bad. It's worth it.'

She knew how false this was even when she said it – that what she was to present him with was something totally unacceptable, something that could not fit into the odd shapes they had made of their lives.

'I'm going to have to tell such dreadful lies,' he said.

'That's life,' she said.

But when she hung up she knew that was exactly what she did not want life to be. She dropped her half-finished can of Diet Coke into the rubbish bin. That night when she met Alistair at the Blue Moon Brasserie the first thing he noticed was that she had taken all the silver rings off her hands.

'What happened?' he asked as they sat down. It was her hands he was talking about.

But she was already telling him that she was pregnant and she would have the child.

She had rehearsed a more reasoned, gradual, diplomatic speech, but in the end the words came out gracelessly, sounding more angry than she thought she felt. 'You're going to have to choose,' she said. It was amazing. It was just like saying 'pass the bread' – only words, gone already, disappeared into that loud river of talk that bounced off the hard tiled floor of the Brasserie.

Alistair nodded as he nodded with men when arguing on

television, absorbing their points, holding his counsel, the picture of reasonableness. He was holding her newly naked hand, massaging her wrist, but he suddenly looked very far away and she was frightened by what she had begun.

He was almost fifty. He had a craggy, handsome face and curly grey hair. She had watched that face so closely for so many years she could no more describe him than she could, as a child, have described her mother or father. The shape of his face corresponded to some shape in her mind, a place to lie down and sleep and be safe.

'I don't care if we don't get married,' she said, although this was different from what she had planned to say. 'But you're going to have to choose.'

He sat looking at her, nodding his head. Without his face seeming to change, he began to cry.

She watched the frightening fat drops run down the creases of his tanned and ruined face. They dropped like blobs of jelly and splashed into his Cabernet Sauvignon.

'You wouldn't stop me seeing our child?'

'Of course not,' she said. 'You'll always be its father.' She saw her whole adult life dissolving as she spoke. She saw what she was embarked on. Alistair could not leave his drunk, unhappy wife. He was not sufficiently strong, or cruel, and she was suddenly, as the Blue Swimmer Crabs were placed in front of her, not at all sure she wanted a child. She was cut through with fear. It pierced her like an iceberg.

Alistair did not see this fear, that she should not have a baby, that she was not suited. She never let anyone but Gia see it, but it was almost always there, and it had been present all that Monday at Catchprice Motors. At the birth class that evening there was no avoiding it. They rubbed her nose in 'reality' and would not let her look away.

She sat on a bean bag, surrounded by couples, and watched the videotape called 'Belinda's Labour'.

After thirty minutes of film time – thirty hours of real time – the baby's head emerged. The husband's mouth was open, staring at it. The midwife's green-gloved hands delivered the baby. The wife saw the husband's face and could only have read it as a banner headline shouting GRIEF. The baby was blue. Its head flopped, as if it were broken or rotten. There was a silence as if something unexpectedly, horribly wrong had happened. It was like a home movie of an assassination.

But this videotape had been *selected* to show the birth class. There could be nothing 'unexpected' in this respect. This birth happened over and over, like the hellish mechanical creatures in Disneyland who are condemned to repeat the same action eighty times a day. Someone had planned to show them this record of thirty hours of pain.

In a moment, of course, the class would criticize the husband. He was not supporting his wife. He was looking at the distressed baby. At that second, he thought the child was dead.

But all Maria could think was: I don't want it.

She was angry and frightened, although none of the women in the room could have guessed these feelings. It was not, as they say, how she 'presented', which was strong and confident and often funny.

If Gia had been there, as she normally was, they would have stayed for herbal tea at the end. But Gia was not there, and although she could hardly be angry at Gia for this, it occurred to her now that Gia might, on the very night she went into labour, not be in her own bed when Maria rang for her.

Maria left the birth class without saying goodnight to anyone. The lifts were prone to jamming and there was a hand-written sign advising birth class members to use the stairs. The stairs were like Hong Kong: concrete, sweaty-smelling, guarded by heavy metal fire doors. Maria Takis clattered down them alone, like a victim in a movie.

Who will care for me?

The street was empty of people, lined with parked cars. There was a derelict man peeing in the middle of the vacant block which had once been the Crown Street Maternity Hospital. The destruction of this hospital felt both cruel and personal. She thought: I am becoming neurotic.

Her car was parked round the corner, not her car, the Tax Department's car. She should not be driving it for private use. Once she would have thought this an important principle. Now she did not give a damn. She looked in the back seat before she unlocked the car, and then she turned on the light and looked again. Mrs

Catchprice's Japanese Bride sat propped up against a Sister Brown Baby Bath.

'*Dear God, please save me.*'

15

The Blue Moon Brasserie was loud, full of clatter and shouting. Glasses broke, were swept up. The air was rich with olive oil and garlic. The Tax Inspector threaded her way through the chrome-legged chairs towards her table. She was wearing a red deco blouse and a black skirt with a red bandanna which sat above her bulging stomach. She wore a peasant print scarf around her head and silver bracelets and a necklace. In the privacy of her bedroom mirror, she had thought all of this looked fine, but now she saw how she was stared at, she felt she had made an error of judgement – she was a blimp with bangles.

The grey-aproned waiter was eighteen years old and had nicked himself shaving. He was new that day and had no idea that this pregnant woman's emotional life was deeply enmeshed with the place he worked at. He sat her in the corner, next to the table where she had told Alistair that she was having a baby. All around her there were couples, lovers, husbands, wives. They touched each other's sleeves, arms, hands, and were pleased with each other's company. It was a perfectly ordinary table – square, varnished, wooden, as devoid of obvious history as a hotel bed. Then it had seen the death of an affair. Now it celebrated a birthday. Maria craned her neck towards the blackboard menu but she was really watching that table – a man with a thick neck and pouched, melancholy eyes took a small gold-wrapped box from his wife – whose face Maria could not see – and passed it to his daughter. The daughter was sixteen or so, very pretty with long dark hair.

'Happy birthday, angel,' her father said. He gave her a kiss and a crumpled rag of a smile. He rubbed at the table surface, dragging bread crumbs into his cupped hand.

'I've been flirting with stockbrokers,' said Gia Katalanis, sitting down opposite Maria.

Gia was crisp and yellow in a linen suit. She dumped her files and briefcase on the floor and papers from the files spilled out towards the wall. She looked down at the papers, wrinkled her nose and shrugged.

'I've been flirting with stockbrokers,' she said again, leaning forward and taking Maria's hands. She was small and blonde with a dusting of golden hairs along her slim, tanned arms. She smelt of shampoo and red wine. She had straight hair she always cut in a neat fringe. She had fine features, a fine chin which clearly suggested both frailty and determination. 'Well they *think* they are stockbrokers,' she said, 'but they are used car dealers in their secret hearts. One of them is from Hale & Hennesey. We hit them for three-forty thou in back taxes, plus the fines, and I think he fell in love with me.' She laughed. 'Ask me is he cute.'

'Is he cute?'

'He's cute.'

A champagne cork popped at the next table and they both turned to watch the champagne being poured into the sixteen-year-old's birthday glass, then laughed at their own Pavlovian response to the cork pop.

'These days,' Maria said, 'when they drink champagne in movies, I always look at the label.'

'Me too,' Gia said. 'Exactly.' She lit a St Moritz and put lipstick on its gold filter tip. 'Heidsieck,' she said. 'Krug, Taittinger, Bollinger, Moët, Piper-Heidsieck . . .'

'Pol Roger . . .'

'Veuve Clicquot.'

'I used to think anything with bubbles was champagne,' Maria said. 'When I told my mother I had drunk champagne she said, "Po po anaxyi yineka" – no one will want to marry you now.'

'Your mother always said that.'

'She was right, poor Mama. This would kill her if she wasn't dead, really. Even my father. I visit him at night and I always ring first and say, "Papa I'm going to come over." I don't want to shame him with someone . . .'

'But, Maria, come on – the street knows . . .'

'The street knows? Don't be nice to me.'

'O.K., all Newtown.'

'Newtown? Mrs *Hellos* knows. She was in Balmain inspecting real estate. I always felt safe in Balmain . . .'

'Oh God, Mrs Hellos. I saw her in D.J.'s with that buck-toothed

76

nephew.'

'Tassos.'

'Tassos, that's right. She said, poor Mr Takis, such a good man – first his wife, now his daughter. I said, but Mrs Hellos, Maria is not dead. No, said Mrs Hellos – so melodramatic, you know – no! So I said – Mrs Hellos, are you saying it is better that Maria is dead? I'm not saying nothing, said Mrs Hellos, I'm just thinking about Mr Takis and his kidneys.'

'Oh God, Mrs Hellos. Oh shit,' Maria said laughing. 'Dear Gia, you always make me laugh. The birth class was so miserable without you.'

Gia took Maria's hand. 'Did they show one of those horror tapes again?' Maria's skin was so moist and supple and her fingers so long that it made her own hands seem dry and neurotic.

'Uh-huh.' There was a veiled, weary look around her eyes.

'Are you mad at me?'

'Of course not. Really. Not even a tiny bit.'

'Oh Maria, I'm sorry. Did you have a shitty day as well?'

'Well, I wasn't flirting with stockbrokers.'

'But I thought they finally sent you out to catch some rats?'

'They sent me to Franklin. Can you believe that?'

'*Franklin*. My God. Who's in Franklin?'

'No one's in Franklin. It was some shitty little GM dealer.'

'Maria, you've got to just tell them "no".'

'That's what they want. They're going to keep giving me these insulting little audits until I blow up. I'm like the emperor's wife. They have to kill me too.'

'The emperor's ex-wife.'

'I cooked dinners for the creeps when Alistair was director. They came to my house and drank *my* Heemskerk Cabernet. They were meant to be my friends. Billy Huxtable, Sally Ho. It was Sally who sent me to Franklin. I said, "What if I go into labour in Franklin?" She said, "There are very good medical facilities." What a bitch! Plus, the clients – really – they were mice! They looked like they were Social Welfare clients, not ours. They were trying to commit her – this is an old woman, eighty-six – to a mental home when I arrived. Her children were trying to lock her up, and she seemed more sane than they did. If I hadn't arrived she'd be locked up right now.'

'Good for you, Maria.'

'Well, maybe – I'm investigating her, and I'm sitting here, talking about champagne, surrounded by people drinking vintage Bollinger.'

'Well, let's go somewhere else. I don't like all this either.'

Maria chose not to hear that. 'It makes me feel sleazy,' she said.

'What? The clients or the restaurant?'

'Both, together. The juxtaposition.'

'Maria, you're not sleazy. You're the least sleazy person I know.'

'I'm going to pull this investigation. I can stop it.'

'You can't stop it, and you're being really dumb. Listen, my dear, you are the least sleazy person I know. You never spend more than twenty bucks here. You've got a village mentality. Remember when you told me Alex was wealthy . . . He had a new 1976 Holden and went to Surfers Paradise for his holidays. You know what you said to me . . . You said, "Typical Athens Greek." And you wouldn't go out with him.'

'I was a little prig,' Maria said. 'All I'm thinking is how I can cancel the investigation.'

'So you're going to break into the computer, right?' When she was anxious Gia had a tendency to shout.

'Shush,' said Maria. 'I think that is what I am going to do. Yes.'

'You don't know how to.'

'Shush, please, but yes I do. I'm not going to be made into a bully.'

Gia picked up Maria's bread roll and began to tear it up. 'O.K. Maria . . . O.K. . . . If you're really upset by crooks drinking vintage Bollinger, we'll just go somewhere else.'

Maria saw the stoop-shouldered man at the next table flinch as he heard himself labelled a crook. He looked up sharply.

Maria said, 'All the poor guy is doing is giving his daughter a birthday party.'

Gia leaned across the table and spoke in her idea of a whisper. 'That "poor guy" is Wally Fischer.'

'Oh.'

'Oh. That's right. Oh. We're going to get him. He's an inch away from jail. He can get away with dealing smack and organizing murder but he's not going to get away with tax. He didn't hear me.'

'I thought he was an accountant being sweet to his wife and

daughter,' Maria whispered. 'He heard us. He knows we're talking about him now.'

'This restaurant makes me sick,' Gia said. 'Let's go somewhere else.'

'No,' Maria said. 'I like it here.'

Gia started giggling.

'I do,' Maria said.

'I know you do.'

'When the baby's born I won't be able to afford to come here, but it's very cheap for the sort of place it is.'

'I know,' Gia said. 'You can get *focaccia* for $7.50 and wine for $3 a glass and once you sat next to Joan Collins, right over there.'

'Right,' Maria said. 'And you always give me the best scandal here.'

'I'm less interesting elsewhere?'

'There are artists and celebrities here. The atmosphere is good,' Maria said. 'It promotes gossip. It's the only corner of my life where gossip is acceptable. It stops me being a total prig.' She seemed to have abandoned her thoughts about breaking into her client's tax file. 'Also, I have a history here. Alistair and I used to sit there, it was our table.'

'Don't do this to yourself.'

'He's a part of me,' Maria said. 'Don't make me pretend he isn't.'

'Maria, he's a creep – he dumped you.'

'He didn't dump me. I dumped me. What did he do?'

'Even now, you can't see who he is.'

'I know who he is,' Maria said quietly. 'Please. Gia, allow me to know him a little better than you.'

'O.K.' said Gia, grinning like a cat. 'So allow me to tell you where Paulo wants to kiss me.'

She was gifted with perfect recall. She recited a whole phone conversation with her 'love interest'. He wanted to kiss her armpit. He had said to her, 'Guess where I want to kiss you?' She had guessed everywhere but armpit. She had shocked him with her guesses. This sort of talk was making Maria look alive and happy again. The headscarf showed off her beautiful face, her dark olive skin and white, perfect teeth. She could have any man she liked, even now, this pregnant.

Gia spoke very quietly, so quietly no one could have heard them, but they laughed so much they could hardly see. Through her tear-streamed vision Maria saw Wally Fischer speaking to Tom, one of the owners of the Brasserie.

Tom was a small, solemn man of thirty who had made himself look forty with a belly and a pair of round, wire-framed glasses. He leaned across the table and put a hand on the back of their chairs.

'Gia, Maria, I'm sorry . . . would you mind, you know, a little *cleaner*.'

'All we're doing is laughing,' Gia said. 'It's not as if we're murdering anyone.'

The words fell into the silence like stones into an aquarium. Maria could see Gia's eyes widening as she heard what she had said. She looked at Maria and made a grimace, and up to Tom and shrugged, and across to Wally Fischer who had heard this very clearly – his thick neck was beginning to puff up and turn a deep plum colour.

Gia was pale. She sat with her palms flat on the table. She looked helplessly in Wally Fischer's direction and smiled.

'Hey,' she said. Her voice was so loud and scratchy, Maria knew she was very frightened. 'I'm sorry, really.'

Wally Fischer moved his chair back and stood up. You could feel his physical strength. He had bright, shining, freshly shaven cheeks and you could smell his talcum.

'One,' he said to Maria, 'I don't like my daughter having to listen to smut.' He turned to Gia: 'Number two: I like even less for her to hear people say untrue and insulting things about her father.'

'All I . . .' Gia began.

'Sssh,' said Wally Fischer. He was no longer plum-coloured. He was quite pale except for the red in his thick lips. 'You've done enough hurt for one night.' He blinked his heavy-lidded eyes once, and turned to take his daugher by the arm.

'Sheet,' said Gia as they walked out of the door. She leaned across to the abandoned table and retrieved the Bollinger from the bucket.

'Gia, don't.' Maria looked down, ashamed.

Gia was pale and nervous, but she was already holding her trophy high and pouring Wally Fischer's Bollinger into her empty water glass. 'Have some. Don't be such a goody-goody.' Maria looked up to see Wally Fischer looking in the window from the street. He made a pistol with his finger and pointed it at Gia. Gia did not see him but she looked pale and sick anyway, and there seemed no point in making her more distressed. 'Have some,' she said to Maria.

Maria took the champagne, not to drink, as an act of solidarity. It frothed up and spilled on to the wooden table. Gia drank without waiting for the froth to settle. Her hand shook.

'You all right?' Maria asked.

'Yeah, I'm O.K. But I don't want to come here any more.'

Maria took her hand. Gia shut it into a fist, self-conscious about her bitten nails.

'We don't have to come here,' said Maria.

'It stinks,' Gia said. 'I can smell the dirty money at the door.' Gia pushed away the champagne. 'I don't even like the taste of this.'

'It isn't the restaurant that's the problem. It's us.'

'For instance?'

'We keep doing things we don't believe in. I didn't join the department to be an anal authoritarian. I'm not going to bankrupt these poor people out at Franklin.' Maria soaked up the spilled champagne with a paper napkin. 'I'm going to pull their file,' she said.

'Maria, what's happened to you?'

'Nothing's happened.'

'You've had a character transplant.' Gia took back the champagne and drank it.

Maria smiled. 'Sorry to disappoint you.'

'A complete character transplant.'

'Goody two-shoes?' Maria asked, her eyebrows arched.

'That was a long time ago I said that . . .'

'Fourteen years . . .'

'I was angry with you. You made me feel bad about cheating on my car mileage. But there are people in the department who would drop dead if they thought you were going to pull a file.'

'And you?'

'I think it's very therapeutic, Maria. I think it's exactly what you should do.' Gia reached over and emptied the last of Wally Fischer's champagne into her glass. 'You know the computer codes? That's the important thing. You'll need old Maxy's access code.'

Maria smiled.

'And you need a corrupt ASO 7 to open doors for you at night?'

81

'Just lend me the keys.'

'You're kidding,' said Gia, draining the champagne and standing a little unsteadily. 'You think I'd miss this?'

'It's an offence under the Crimes Act.'

'Come on,' Gia said, making scribbling Amex signs at Tom. 'Don't be so melodramatic. All we're going to do is work late at the office.'

16

Sarkis Alaverdian was depressed and unemployed, and when he came to sit on his back step, he saw Mrs Catchprice standing at the bottom of the back yard, below the culvert under the Sydney Road. He saw a still, pink figure, like a ghost. It just stood there, looking back at him.

Sarkis stood directly under the light of the back porch. He was not tall, but he was broad. He had a weight-lifter's build, although when he walked he did not walk like a gym-ape, but lightly, more like a tennis-player. He had not had a pay cheque in ten weeks but he wore, even at home, at night, a black rayon shirt with featured mother-of-pearl buttons on the collar points. He wore grey cotton trousers shot with a slight iridescence, and soft grey slip-ons from the Gucci shop. He had curly black hair, not tight, not short, but tidy just the same. He had a broad strong nose, and a small tuft of hair, a little squiff on his lower lip.

He was twenty years old and he had been forced to come and stand out here while his mother made love with the Ariel Taxi driver. He was ashamed, not ashamed of his mother, but ashamed on her behalf, not that she would make love, not exactly, although a little bit. He had known something like this would happen when they moved from Chatswood. When she wanted to be away from Armenians, he had both sympathized with her and suspected her. He had readied himself for it and prepared himself so he would behave correctly, but he could not have imagined this taxi-driver. It was the taxi-driver who made him feel ashamed.

The taxi-driver was 'out of area'. He was not even meant to drive in Franklin, but he came down here and cruised around, mostly up at Emerald and Sapphire where the women were abandoned and lonely and often just getting used to the idea that they would now be poor for ever. Before Sarkis lost his job, he had been in this particular taxi a number of times. He had once taken it from Cabramatta Leagues Club to Franklin. The taxi-driver did not recognize Sarkis, but Sarkis recognized him.

Sarkis liked women. He liked their skin, their smells, and he liked the things they talked about. When you are a hairdresser you talk with women all day long. At apprentice school they will call this 'chatter', but ultimately it is more important than finger-waving or working on plastic models with wobbly heads, both of which are things that are very important in apprentice school but don't exist in salon life. If you have talent and you can chatter, you will end up being a Mr Simon or Mr Claude, i.e. you will own your own salon and you can have the pleasure of hiring and firing the ones who topped the class at tech.

The tragedy was that it was chatter that ruined him. He had put Mrs Gladd in the No.2 cubicle with her dryer on extra low. This was at half-past four. He did this so he could talk with this little blonde – Leone – who had almost perfect hair – naturally blonde, and so dense and strong you could do almost anything you liked with it. He was giving her his 'Sculptured' look. It was a dumb word, but reassuring. It was a tangled, curled sort of look, that looked like you just got out of bed until you noticed just how 'deliberate' it was. He talked her into it because it was going to suit her, but also because it was the sort of job you could pick and fuss over, and he was picking and fussing while he talk-talk-talked and he knew how nice it felt to have someone doing this, all these little pick-pick-cut-snips to your hair, and he had checked Mrs Gladd at ten to five and then gone back to pick-pick-cut-snip. Leone was getting this honey glaze around her eyes. He talked to her about skiing. He worked out she went with her girlfriend. He talked on and on. When he asked her to the Foresters for a drink he was holding up the mirror for her and she just nodded.

She was beautiful.

'Yes,' she said, 'I'd love to.'

He had made her incredible, like a film star, and he had (*fuck it*) forgotten, completely, that Mrs Gladd was still under the slow dryer. He went off to the Foresters and locked her in. The cleaners found her at half-past ten – pissed off beyond belief.

Mrs Gladd got it in her head she had been 'traumatized'. She got herself on television with Mike Willesee and they took a film crew round to Mr Simon's one Friday morning at ten o'clock. Sarkis held his coat up so they could not see his face on camera, but the show made him famous anyway and once Mr Simon had fired him live on camera he could not find another salon to employ him, not even as a washer.

That was why he had to stand in the back garden. Everyone he knew was in Chatswood or Willoughby. He no longer had a car to drive there in. When he heard the mattress squeaking, he could not even take a stroll around Franklin – it was not safe at night.

Sarkis knew this taxi-driver did not like women. He made the boys laugh, saying things like, 'If they didn't have cunts you wouldn't talk to them'. His mother did not know this. She was still celebrating her independence from the Armenian community. She was wearing short skirts and smoking in the street. Ready-snap Peas had closed their doors and she had lost her job as well, but it still seemed, to Sarkis, that she was having a good time. She had come all the way to Franklin because she had convinced herself that there were no Armenians here. But the first people they met were Tahleen and Raffi who ran the corner store in Campbell Street. The first thing they did was offer to drive Sarkis and his mother to the Armenian Church on Sundays. Sarkis thought it wouldn't hurt – if only from the employment point of view. But he could not budge his mother. She said: thank you. She thought: no way, José. From there on she walked an extra mile to buy her ciggies from another shop.

His mother's feeling about the Armenian community made her judgement bad. She might have hated them, but she was one of them. When she met someone who was not Armenian, she got herself into a drama. No way she was going to serve *Gargandak*. She was reinventing herself as Australian. But if not *Gargandak*, what cakes were right? She did not know what to call the people, even. But she was so happy she did not care. The taxi-driver was a Yugoslav. She called him 'Doll'. She was thawing out the Sara Lee Cherry Cheese Cake. She opened all her miniature bottles of liquor. She called the taxi-driver Doll even though he was lean and balding, with a slight stoop and nicotine stains on his fingers. The only thing like a doll was his eyes, which were very blue. They were doll eyes only in colour. They stared at you. No matter how

84

you might smile, he never smiled back. Even when Sarkis's mother offered the tiny bottles of Gilbey's gin and Bond 7 whisky which she had kept from the time they had shared a house in Willoughby with Anna from East-West Airlines, even when she laughed, and showed him how to do the twist, he never once smiled.

For a while Sarkis sat at the kitchen table and cut out more fabric for ties. The fabric he was cutting was 100 per cent French silk. It was dark green with hard-edge motifs in silver and black. He concentrated hard on the cutting because the fabric was beautiful, because it had been expensive, and because he was angry and did not want to see what was happening on the other side of the servery door where the taxi-driver was adjusting his pants. It made him ill to think of that thing being put inside his mother.

The taxi-driver smelled of unwashed sweat. His mother did not know shit about men. She took the taxi-driver to show him her wedding pictures. They were in the bedroom. He could hear her light young voice – she was still only thirty-six – as it named the members of the wedding party. The names were of Armenians who had once lived in the suburbs of Teheran. She talked about them as if they were certainly alive.

Tomorrow she would tell Sarkis all the good things she had found out about the taxi-driver – he was kind, he supported his sick father or he was a bad dancer but had read her palm 'sensitively'. She would not learn that the taxi-driver cruised the Franklin streets which were named after jewels putting his dick wherever there was isolation and desperation. He could have AIDS. His mother did not even think of this possibility. Instead she opened up her miniatures. She showed him wedding pictures. She pointed out Sarkis's father to the taxi-driver. She said how handsome he was, like Paul McCartney.

Earlier, in the living-room, she told the taxi-driver he looked like George Harrison. This made the taxi-driver smile. It was extraordinary to see. It was impossible to know why he smiled, whether from pleasure or because he could see how ridiculous it was.

Sarkis put down his scissors and folded the fabric. Then he went out to sit on the back steps which were farthest from the bedroom and where the noise of the trucks on the Sydney road drowned out the various noises of the night. Sarkis was normally optimistic. He could lose three jobs and not be beaten. He could be angry and irritable, but he always had a way forward. He was a member of a race which could not be destroyed. He had energy, intelligence, resilience, enthusiasm.

But tonight he was oppressed by his circumstances: he could not get a job, a girl-friend or even a sewing machine. He could not even telephone his friends in Chatswood.

It was in this mental state that he saw Mrs Catchprice standing at the bottom of the yard. He thought it might be someone from the Commonwealth Employment Service come to take his dole away because they were already paying benefits to his mother.

'Hey,' he said.

The figure waved, a tinkly little wave from the wrist. Did not look like the C.E.S.

'Who's that?' He picked up a Sidchrome spanner for protection.

'I'm a ghost.'

Sarkis felt prickly on the neck. Then a match flared and he saw an old woman with a cigarette stuck to her pouting lower lip. She had a big black leather handbag in the crook of her arm, a pink floral dress and a transparent plastic raincoat. 'We had a poultry farm for twenty years,' she said. He could smell the meat-fat smell then, from that far away, the Aussie smell, as distinctive as their back yard clothes-lines with their frivolous flags of T-shirts, board shorts and frilly underwear, so different from Armenian washing which was big and practical – sheets, rugs, blankets, grey work trousers and cotton twill shirts.

'You're not a very good ghost,' he told her. He stood, and stepped down into the yard.

'I'm damned near old enough,' said Mrs Catchprice, dropping the lit match on to the sodden ground where it sizzled and went out. 'I'll be eighty-six in March. You might find it hard to imagine, but we had two thousand birds and this was just the bottom of the property. There was a little natural pond here and a stand of Gymea Lilies. I was going to have a flower farm, but there was better money in poultry then, so it ended up being poultry. You had some here yourself, I think . . . last week?'

'The Health Department made us kill them.'

'You're better off without them. There is nothing nice about poultry. The smell of plucked feathers makes me nauseous now. Who washed the chook-poo off the eggs? Your mother I suppose. I

86

always washed the eggs. I sat at the kitchen table with a bucket and a bowl. You never forget the smell of it on your fingers.'

'I've found your cigarettes here,' said Sarkis. 'You smoke Salem. You just take a few drags and throw them away. Do you come from the nursing home?'

'I'm Mrs Catchprice.'

'Where do you live?'

'Are you local?' asked Mrs Catchprice, coming forward to peer at the good-looking young man by the light of the kitchen window. 'You must know Catchprice Motors.'

He did. He had bought a fuel pump there once from a woman in a cowgirl suit. 'And that's where you live?'

'And where needs be I must wearily return,' said Mrs Catchprice, throwing her Salem in among the Hydrangeas. 'Don't you find the nights are sad?'

'I'll walk you to your car,' said Sarkis.

'Car!' said Mrs Catchprice, straightening her back and tilting her chin. 'Car. I have no car. I walk.'

Walk? Sarkis was young and strong, but he would never walk at night alone in Franklin. There were homeless kids wandering around with beer cans full of petrol. They saw fiery worms and faces spewing blood. They did not know what they were doing.

'I think I'll walk with you a bit of the way,' Sarkis said.

'How lovely,' said Mrs Catchprice. 'I didn't catch your name?'

'Sarkis Alaverdian.' He was scared. He slipped the Sidchrome spanner into his back pocket. He thought: her family should be ashamed.

17

Mrs Catchprice did not stand in Sarkis's back yard in order to employ him. Yet if she had set out that night with no other purpose than to rescue a life from the asbestos sheet houses in the real estate development she had once planned, this would have been consistent with her character.

In the days when Catchprice Motors had sold combine harvesters and baling twine, she had taken boys from the Armvale Homes, girls in trouble with the police. She had given them positions of trust, placed a shoplifter in charge of petty cash, for instance. She was erratic – loud in her trust on the one hand but vigilant and even suspicious on the other. She was ready to ascribe to her protégés schemes and deceptions too complex and Machiavellian for anyone but her to conceive of, and yet she could manage, in the same breath, to think of them as 'good kids'. She was sentimental and often patronizing (she spoke loudly of her beneficiaries in their presence) and what is amazing is not that a few of them never forgave her for it, but that most of them were so grateful for her patronage that they did not even notice.

Mrs Catchprice was their lucky break. Some of them even loved her. And Howie, who had been one, could – despite the complications of his Catchprice-weary heart – still say, 'You old chook,' and smile. The first time he ever saw a T-bone steak was at Mrs Catchprice's table. The first time he took a shit where you could lock the door was in that apartment which was now his home. He was an orphan from Armvale Boys' Farm. He was given Mort's Hornby 'OO' train set when Mrs Catchprice decided Mort had grown out of it. That was her style. She gave away Cathy's teddy bear without asking her, not to Howie, to someone else.

Even now, when she no longer had either an executive position or a majority shareholding, it did not take a lot to tip Frieda Catchprice into charity, and when she stood in Sarkis's backyard on that red loam earth which should have been her flower farm but which had supported instead two thousand laying hens in twenty-three separate electrically heated sheds, charity was the emollient she automatically applied to the sadness she felt. She reached for it, almost without thinking, much as she always pecked at her honey and Saltana crackers in the hope that one more smear of Leatherwood honey might finally remove that metallic taste in her stomach which she secretly and wrongly believed was caused by cancer.

She was a ghost. She told him she was a ghost as a joke, but she meant all her jokes. This is how it was with ghosts – you stood in one life, but you could see another. You were in one world, but not part of it. You visited your past mistakes and tried to undo them. You held your babies to your breasts and suckled them. You sponged them through their fevered nights. You petted them and wept, knowing you were doing something wrong that would result in them growing up without properly loving you.

Sarkis's backyard was a corner of the second piece of land she had wanted to grow flowers on. It had been within her grasp but what had she done? First she had turned it into a poultry farm, and then she had turned it into a housing development. These things had made her 'Mrs Catchprice' but she had wanted neither of them. It was Cacka who wanted them. He aspired to poultry farming like other people dreamed of a beach house or an imported Chevrolet Bel-aire. No one aspired to poultry farms. It was something poor battlers did in the rough scrub outside town, a desperate part-time occupation. It was never clear how the passion for it entered Cacka's head, but if you went to live at his family's orange-primed bungalow out at Donvale and listened to the never-ending argument, you would get an education in egg marketing, and one of the first things Frieda learned (after discovering which was Old Mrs Catchprice's seat) was that the Egg Marketing Board were a pack of little Hitlers who wanted you to pay them fourpence a dozen and wouldn't let you sell direct to shops without a special permit.

She also learned, pretty damn smart, that Cacka's mother had no time for chooks.

'I hope you ain't an Oprey singer,' she said to Frieda. 'I told him already, we won't have Oprey or the chooks.'

Her boys thought this was very funny, everyone except for Cacka who sat beside his fiancée at the kitchen table, blushing bright red.

Poultry was one of the few species of livestock Old Mrs Catchprice had no time for, and even at sixty-five she was plotting new ways to make a living from her 50 acres and her three strong boys. She had Romney Marsh, some Border Cross, ten Jerseys with some odd scars where you might expect a brand to be, poll Herefords, and half-a-dozen sows she thought Frieda might like to take an interest in. She had the resprayed Ferguson tractor Hughie brought home one night without explaining. She had Cacka and the youngest brother, Billie, advertised in the *Gazette* as fencing contractors. Also, the family had a few acres given over to wheat and had traded cases of apples with de Kok's grocery until there were complaints about their codlin-moth infestation.

The Catchprices were in the habit of listening to the Country Hour each day at lunch. They came in across the treeless, car-littered Home Paddock to the bungalow and sat around the electric-blue Laminex table brushing the flies off their serious faces, drinking black tea – they had no midday meal – and listening to the market prices delivered in a proper English accent.

It didn't matter what the prices were – they were always broke. That was Cacka's point to them, and he never let up no matter how they spoke to him. He was not thick-skinned, but he was persistent. When he wanted something he talked about it in that 'cooing' way, talk and talk, on and on, rubbing his big dirt-dry hands together and smiling sadly and looking at you with his brown eyes, talking on and on until you would give him anything he wanted. He sat at the table in that depressing bright-orange weatherboard bungalow propped on its 'temporary' concrete blocks in the middle of the barren paddock and he folded his arms across his big chest and tilted back on a battered chrome chair and talked on and on about the future in a way that would have seemed almost insane were it not for the fact that he had been smart enough to have Frieda McClusky there to listen to him.

And while it is true that Frieda did not want chooks any more than the old lady did, she loved him, and loved him in a more tender and protective way than she would have imagined possible. She could not bear to see him want a thing like that and just not have it. All her instinct warned her about poultry, even then, before she heard of battery farming. But she had needs even stronger than her instincts and she pressed her little breasts against his big back each night and put her arms around him and squeezed her thigh up in around his furry backside and knew that it was up to her to get him his chook farm.

She would spend all her life going over these events, thinking of how it might have been otherwise. She thought it self-deceiving to give herself too much credit for love. What she remembered was how much she had wanted to escape that musty confinement of one more family, that sour, closed smell like a mouse nest in a bush-hut wall. She gave this prominence in her memory, and it was true, of course, but she was wrong to discount the effects of love.

Also, she wanted Cacka to admire her, and sometimes she made this need for admiration the only reason she had sacrificed the perfect flower farm to wire netting and chook shit and the Egg Marketing Board of New South Wales.

Also: there was gelignite. She had a passion to let it off with her mother-in-law watching. She wanted to split wood and shatter earth and frighten her and make her go away.

Also: to hurt herself, to fill herself brimful of blame and rage. She wanted to make the damned earth bleed. *See. See. See what you made me go and do.*

It was old Huey Dawson who showed her the land – eight o'clock in the morning and all the dew so heavy they were drenched just walking through it: grass, Watsonias, wild roses drifted there from God knows where, stands of spotted gums with pale, pale green trunks so slippery they would make you cry. It was 5 acres cut off from the bottom of old Doctor Andes' property and it had never seen a cow on it. There were tiny bush orchids and native grasses with seeds like yellow tear drops – it had probably been that way for ever. It was lot 5, folio 14534 being parcel 54 of the parish of Franklin. It had vendor finance of 5 per cent and no deposit and she had to take Cacka to it (along the straight, soft, sandy road where the overgrown acacias brushed the edges of the ute and made him anxious about the powdery duco) and when he resisted because he was actually frightened of the financial commitment and was ready to run back to the bungalow and listen to stock prices on the radio, she showed him how he could make a good business on this piece of land: three acres for chooks, one acre for the lucerne, maize and oats. She had the idea – it was original, she read it nowhere – of building the brick building where they cooled down the hens in heat waves. She did not mean to insist that she was smarter than he was, but when she saw his scheme about to flounder, she panicked. It must happen, it had to happen, she would not let him fail.

It was the beginning of a pattern – every time she helped him get something he wanted, a poultry farm, a car dealership, she drove him further from her. She was the one who talked him into that damn poultry farm when it was the last thing on earth she wanted.

This was the site of Catchprice Poultry – Cacka and Frieda Catchprice were to be the first ones west of Sydney with battery farming. And although she entered into the business as a full partner with her husband she had no idea what battery farming was and had not appreciated the consequences.

Now she knew. Men can do this sort of thing and not think about it. They can cut the chickens' beaks, and amputate their legs if necessary. They can walk out into the shed every day for ten years and see and smell those rows of caged birds and not think about it any more than how nicely the eggs roll into the conveyor belt and how clean they are. Nothing wrong with this – Frieda did not feel censorious about men's ability to disconnect their feelings. She thought it useful. God had planned it so one half of humanity could kill the food, the other half could nurture the young.

But what she was too young to know, what she learned later, was that it was damned silly for a woman to do men's work, by which she meant work that entailed a denial of female feelings – killing people in war, working in slaughter houses, putting chooks in rows in cages. This was something men can do and it will have no harmful effects for them.

But it sends a woman's chemicals into conflict. This was how she got breast cancer – that poultry farm. She never told anyone this, but shocked Cacka and the doctor on the eve of her mastectomy by saying, 'Take them both off.'

She could see the idiots thought she was unnatural, that she had got so used to ordering Cacka around that she now wanted to be a man. Did they think she *wanted* to lose breasts? To spend the rest of her life with these huge scars like plastic sandwich wrapper?

Cacka could be weepy and sentimental about her breasts, but Frieda Catchprice was an animal caught in a trap, eating through its own limbs. She was poisoned and wanted to be free from the parts that would kill her. And sure enough, there was a second mastectomy – the one they so confidently told her she didn't need to have – another five years later.

When Frieda Catchprice stood in Sarkis Alaverdian's back yard, she ran over and over all these events, looking for a crack in the story, a place where she might have acted differently and have come to a different place. She worked up and down the events, like a fly trying to find its way through glass to air.

The trucks thundered over the Sydney Road overpass above the 60×120ft blocks which had been sold thirty years before as Catchprice Heights. The streets were named Albert, Frieda, Cathleen, Mortimer, Jack. It was the Catchprice Estate that Sarkis Alaverdian was now a prisoner of. And it was now Mrs Catchprice, walking with him back to Catchprice Motors, who determined to set him free.

'Do you have a suit?' she asked.

It was only after they had escaped from Vernon Street (where the twelve-year-olds were ripping the insignia off a Turbo Saab) that Mrs Catchprice offered Sarkis a job as a salesman. Sarkis had seen the twelve-year-olds too late to avoid them and he did not wish to turn round or even cross the street because it was like running, like blood in the water, and he had no choice but to continue walking. Three of them were sitting on a white-railed garden fence. Two were perched on the Saab's hood. The space they left to walk through was bordered by the bright white stones of their naked kneecaps.

The Saab's alarm started. Sarkis took Mrs Catchprice's bird-wing arm, and Mrs Catchprice, who must have seen what was happening, just kept on talking. She was telling him stories about the disadvantaged people she had employed at Catchprice Motors.

'But I am boring you,' she said.

He was frightened, not bored. He guided the old woman under the dark umbrella of mould-sweet street trees, between the gauntlet of twelve-year-old knees – stolen commando boots, lighter-fluid breath. Even in the midst of it, he could not hurry her. He felt the bones through the wrapping of her plastic coat. Old women needed extra calcium. He had his own mother on 800 mg a day, and she was young. Without calcium they became hunch-backed and fragile. And although Mrs Catchprice was not hunch-backed, she had that dried, neglected feeling in his hand, like shoes no one has bothered to oil. She was someone's grandmother, or mother – they should treasure her. She should eat with them, sleep in their house. They should listen to her papery breathing in the night and it should give them a sense of completeness they would never have without her. If not for her, they would not exist.

Sarkis could press 140 kg. He could split a shirt by flexing his deltoids, but the twelve-year-olds were like dogs in a pack. Their breath stank like service stations and their nails scratched. They were feral animals. He was scared of them, even now, twenty metres past the Saab. There was a dull thudding noise. They were running over the roof of the Saab and jumping on its hood and if the owners were smart they would stay in their house and wait for the cops to come. A breeze brought a flower scent he could not name. A rock bounced off a low paling fence and rolled along the footpath past his feet. The car alarm stopped for a moment and everything was suddenly very quiet.

He steered her off the street, and on to a rough clay path across the burnt-out K Mart lot. This was maybe dumb. How could he tell? He hoped that the buskers from Victoria had not come back to live in the concrete pipes. He could see the pipes glistening nastily in the centre of the site. He could smell them from here: piss like a subway tunnel. She stumbled and gripped his arm. It was then she asked: 'Do you have a suit?'

Maybe she said other things and he missed it. He was worrying about her bones, the buskers.

'Yes,' he said.

'Well, you'd better come to the garage at eight-thirty tomorrow morning and we'll see how we go.' Sarkis was thinking how could he tell her to shut up, not to talk so loud. The piss-smelling pipes might hide Nasties, people without a human heart. They might beat you because they thought you had money, or a job, or a handsome face you did not deserve.

She held out her hand. He shook it. Just a little thing – a Chinese dish – bones and rice paper.

'It's a deal?' she asked.

What?

'Yes,' he said.

They passed the concrete pipes and no one tried to hurt them, although Sarkis muddied his slip-ons and his socks. *Did we shake hands about what I thought we shook hands about?*

They came out on to Loftus Street. Sarkis saw the Esso sign illuminated in the sky above Catchprice Motors. *Am I employed?*

'Do you walk at night very often?' he said, but his mind was trying to figure out a way to check on what had happened to him.

'Always,' said Mrs Catchprice.

'Actually,' said Sarkis, 'it's very dangerous.' They had come to a bench which the Franklin Council had bolted to a concrete block beneath the collapsing veranda of an old store. Mrs Catchprice sat down on the seat and began looking for a cigarette in her handbag.

'Really very dangerous,' Sarkis said. He sat beside her, with his arms resting on his knees. He peered across the road, through the trees, at Catchprice Motors.

'You don't want your new employer bumped off, eh?' said Mrs

94

Catchprice, and flashed her big white teeth at him.

He could have kissed her wrinkled-up old face.

'If these louts give me trouble,' she said, 'I'll blow them up.' She opened her handbag wide and held up what Sarkis thought at first was a piece of salami. He took it from her. It was about fifteen centimetres long and very sticky.

'Gelignite. You know what that is? Smell your fingers.'

Sarkis sniffed. It was musty and aromatic, like amyl nitrate.

'Nitroglycerine,' she said.

The street lights were an orange/yellow and made everything look like a colour negative. You had to think about the most ordinary things to work out what they really were and even when they had been pigeon-holed and labelled, read and understood, they kept some of their spooky double-self. So when Mrs Catchprice said, 'I'm a lot more dangerous than they are,' she had orange lips and a yellow face and copper hair, and she was very scary looking.

'You know how to let it off?'

'Oh yes,' Mrs Catchprice said. 'I know how to "let it off" just fine.' Her teeth were huge and gold in her orange mouth. She was standing in Loftus Street, but she was walking through the grass, trees and wild roses while the Catchprice boys were standing with their hands on their hips and their great dusty legs were sticking out of their little blue shorts. She walked from stump to stump in her straw hat and summer dress with her crimping pliers and her gelly in an old Gladstone bag. She used a torch battery to do the detonators. She beefed up the gelly with some 'Nitron' fertilizer which sure did lift the stumps out of the soil and made Cacka wince and squinch up his face and push his great dusty hands across his battered ears.

Broken earth was like any fresh killed thing – a rabbit, a fish – alive with colour. When you fractured it, the smell poured out, like from a peeled orange, and the hedgerows were made from long pale blue trunks and giant yellow flowers with the bees still feeding off them.

Mrs Catchprice held up the handbag by her forefinger and let it swing there. 'You know how old this gelignite is?' she asked Sarkis. 'You can see it's old by how it sweats. When it's like this you can let it off just by throwing it.'

Sarkis's previous employer had pierced nipples with metal rings in them. He showed Sarkis the photo. He had a metal stud which went through the end of his penis. Sarkis did not ask what the metal rings were for. He smiled and nodded. Likewise with this gelignite – smile. Later he would tell her that the twelve-year-olds were too stupid and doped-up to even understand what a stick of gelignite was. Now he would get her home. He would make her a cup of tea. After work one day he would even cut her frail, old, over-treated hair. It had lost its elasticity but you could still do something with hair like that. He could give her oil with hot towels. She would enjoy that. It was more personal than a steaming machine.

'So,' she said, taking back her stick of gelignite and putting it in her handbag where Sarkis could see a great number of crumpled twenty-dollar bills. 'You were out of work, and now you have a chance again.'

'Thank you,' Sarkis said.

'This is lovely,' said Mrs Catchprice. 'This is what I always liked best about having a business. I liked giving young people a chance.'

'I won't disappoint you,' Sarkis said. 'You won't be sorry.'

'This is lovely,' Mrs Catchprice said. 'This is such a nice town, even now.'

'I'm Armenian,' said Sarkis. 'We are famous for being salesmen.'

'Armenian?' said Mrs Catchprice brightly. 'How fascinating. Have you lived in Franklin long?'

'Six months.'

It was this answer that seemed to make Mrs Catchprice step out on to the road, straight in front of an on-coming car. Sarkis grabbed for her but she was gone. She was bright pink and silver in the car's headlights and it was only when it stopped that Sarkis realized it was a taxi and she had hailed it. She did not seem capable. She seemed too old and frail to be capable of making sudden movements and yet that was what particularly distinguished her – she leaped, jolted, slammed, and – right now, she jumped into the taxi and banged the door hard behind her.

'Come on,' she called as she wound down the window. 'Don't dawdle.'

When Sarkis entered the back seat of the cab, Mrs Catchprice was telling the driver: 'You cannot call yourself a taxi-driver and not know about the Wool Wash. You wait,' she said to Sarkis. 'You'll like this.'

Sarkis recognized the driver – whatever he had done with his mother had not taken very long. The driver sat there with his meter on, staring into the rear vision mirror. He did nothing to acknowledge that he knew who Sarkis was. Mrs Catchprice continued to talk about the Wool Wash. Sarkis could not listen. He looked at the back of the man's little shoulders and pink shell ears. He looked at the fleck of dandruff sticking to the stringy hair below his bald spot.

'If you don't know where the Wool Wash is,' Mrs Catchpole said loudly, tapping the driver on the shoulder, 'it might be polite to turn off your meter while you find out.'

The taxi-driver flinched from the touch and spoke into the mirror. 'Please,' he said. 'In my taxi, control your mouth.'

'It is my eyes you should worry about, not my mouth,' said Mrs Catchprice, fiddling with her handbag. 'I have a cataract on one eye,' she said, producing a crumpled pack of Salems, 'but I can still see your name is Pavlovic and you are plying for trade out of area.'

Pavlovic's shoulders stiffened. Then he turned the meter off. 'Wullwas?' he asked.

'W-o-o-l W-a-s-h.'

When the driver could not find the Wool Wash in his street directory, Mrs Catchprice took it from him.

'Everyone knows the Wool Wash,' she told her new employee. 'It is the most lovely part of Franklin.' But it was not listed in the driver's street directory. Mrs Catchprice stared at the map page, looking at the bend in the river where she thought the Wool Wash was.

'I never heard of it,' said Pavlovic.

'I never heard of it either,' said Sarkis.

To the taxi-driver she said: 'Just head south. I'll direct you,' but she was stricken with that horrible feeling that sometimes came to her on her night-time walks. It was as if all her past had been paved over and she could not reach it, as if she was a snake whose nest had been blocked while she was out and could only go backwards and forwards in front of the place where the hole had been, finding only cold hard concrete where she had expected life.

While Maria sat in the Blue Moon Brasserie, discussing Catchprice Motors, Benny Catchprice was playing Tape 7 of *Affirmations and Actualizations*. Tape 7 was not to be played unless or until you experienced 'Blockage'.

'You are not transformed,' Tape 7 now said to Benny. 'So whose fault do you think that is?'

Benny had come back from work feeling powerful and confident and he had undressed to do the mirror exercise and then suddenly – zap – he lost it. As he faced himself in the mirror he felt 'the fear'. It was hard to stand straight. He put his hand across his navel. His balls went tight in his newly hairless scrotum and he sweated around his arsehole. Five minutes ago he felt fantastic to be so clean and smooth, like a fucking statue. It had been just a blast to look at himself in the mirror and see his power. Then suddenly the thing that made him feel great – how he looked – marble white skin, wide shoulders, slim waist – made him feel like shit.

He turned to Tape 7 and pressed the 'Play' button.

'You paid us $495,' Tape 7 said, 'so if you're cheating, who are you cheating? Can't be us, we've got our money. If you're cheating, you're cheating yourself.'

'Fuck you,' Benny said and pushed at the cassette player with his foot. There was a grease mark on the foot, dust on his hands as well. That was the old Benny – he drew dirt on to himself like iron filings on to a magnet. Snot, sleep, grease, blackheads, he made neglect so much a part of him that no one, not even Mort Catchprice, wished to touch him and everything he made contact with became tarnished, mildewy, mouldy, ruined in some way. Something that had been shining clear silver in its polythene-wrapped box, became 'used' the minute Benny touched it. Even his Christmas presents had been unpleasant to receive – rammed shut at the corners and torn and gummed up with glue and sticky tape so they felt like an oil-skinned table on which jam has been spilled and not properly cleaned.

'You're so used to cheating,' the tape said.

'Shut up.'

'What story do you tell yourself? Nobody loves you? You're too stupid? These are just stories you use to cheat yourself.'

'What do you fucking know?'

'That's why you're the way you are. You have no authenticity. You are unable to separate the bullshit you tell yourself from the truth. You've paid your $495 so now you can see – you either do the job properly or you see how you cheat yourself.'

The step he had omitted was no big deal. It was embarrassing, but he would do it if it was important – he had to fold his clothes carefully in separate parcels and then float them down the river. 'This does not mean flush them down the toilet,' the tape said. 'And if you are asking, is it O.K. if I put them in the sea, it is not. It means a river, not the sea, not a lake, not a drain. If you have any doubts as to whether it is a river or not, you can assume you're trying to cheat yourself out of your life and it is not a river.'

To wrap a shoe in black paper and tie it with gold ribbon seemed like an easy thing to do when you heard it on the tape. Benny swept nails and pins and cake crumbs from the bench with the flat of his hand and wiped the surface with a 'Fiery Avenger' T-shirt.

'You are going to wrap your old clothes to do honour to yourself. If you cannot do honour to your past, how are you going to do honour to your future? Each one of these parcels is you and I want you to dress it like you are dressing it for the funeral of a King or Queen.'

It sounded easy. It sounded inspiring, until you tried it and all of your old self kept soaking out of you, crumpling the paper, tangling the ribbon. When it was done, and wrapped, he saw the parcel had no 'Integrity'. It was a lumpy shitty thing. This was why the transformation could not be complete.

Slowly he unwrapped the shoes on the table and then he tried to flatten the paper with his hands. The paper would not go flat. It was Benny-ised.

'Shut up,' he told the tape. 'I'm going to fucking *iron* them.'

He dressed in his suit again. He took his time dressing properly, and when he remembered that he had not cleaned the smudge on his foot, he unlaced his shoes, took off his trousers, rubbed off the smudge with a wet washer, and dressed once more. Then he walked up the stairs.

He knew Granny Catchprice was out walking and he knew that Vish was up there in her apartment, skulking, waiting like some kind of missionary. He had been up there all day long, hiding. If you asked him why he was hiding he would deny it, but Benny knew he was hiding, from Mort, from Benny, from the cars themselves. He had been cooking curry and now he was standing in front of the bride doll cabinet doing stuff in front of the picture of his guru. There was a bowl of yellow food beside the picture and there was a sprig of jasmine in a Vegemite jar. Vish believed the picture could taste the food with its eyes.

Benny said: 'Whatcher doing?'

Vish turned and saw him.

'Hi,' he said. He looked wide awake, alert, without that dumb, blissed-out look he normally got from chanting.

'You should have come and seen me,' said Benny, and patted the wings of his platinum hair flat on the side of his head. 'History is being made round here.' *I look like her.*

'I'm pleased you came,' Vish said. He was pleased too. He walked towards Benny as if he was going to hug him, but then he stopped, a foot in front of him, grinning. He made no acknowledgement that his brother had undergone a total transformation.

'You should have come down.' Benny said. 'I was expecting you.'

'I didn't want to hassle you.' Vish smiled. It was impossible to know what he was thinking.

'You shoulda dropped in, you know.' Benny said. He was standing in front of his brother in a $300 suit and his brother was saying nothing about it. He had never owned a suit before, neither of them had. 'I've been thinking about you all day. About all that stuff we talked about . . .'

'Now we can talk,' Vish nodded to the dining table and pulled out a chair.

'I was just hanging out down in the cellar after work,' Benny said. 'You should have come down.'

Vish sat down and patted the chair beside him.

'I've *changed*,' Benny said. 'For Chrissakes, look at me.'

Vish looked up and squinted his eyes at Benny. 'Your appearance?'

'Oh Vish,' Benny said, grabbing his brother by his meaty upper arm. 'Don't be a pain in the arse. Come on, come and help me iron some stuff. Will you do that? Remember when you used to iron my school shirts? Come down to the cellar and help me iron my shirts.'

'You want me to come to your cellar?'

Benny sighed.

'It's just that you never wanted me to be there before.'

'There's stuff I want you to see,' Benny said, patting his brother softly on the cheek. 'You'll never understand if you don't come.'

20

'Welcome to the Bunker,' Benny said.

It was worse than anything Vish could have imagined. The air was as thick as a laundry. The concrete floor was half an inch deep in water. It was criss-crossed with planks supported by broken housebricks. A brown-striped couch stood against one end, its legs on bricks. The bricks were wrapped in green plastic garbage bags. Electric flex was everywhere, wrapped in Glad Wrap and bits of plastic bag with torn ends like rag; it crossed the planks and ran through the water. Two electric radiators stood on a chipped green chest of drawers, facing not into the room but towards the walls where you could see the red glow of two bars reflected in what Vish, at first, thought was wet floral wallpaper. It was not wallpaper. It was handwriting, red, blue, green, black, webs of it, layer on layer. In the corner to the left of the door was a white fibreglass object, like a melted surfboard in the shape of a shallow 'n'.

'What's that?'

'Wigwam for a goose's bridle.' Benny pushed him towards the striped couch which stood against the end wall.

The melted surfboard had straps on it like safety belts.

'Sit down, come on.'

Vish looked at the couch he was being offered. 'I came to iron for you,' he said, stepping gingerly away from the couch and looking for a clean flat surface to place the iron on.

'What's the matter?' Pride and blame jostled each other in Benny's voice. He jutted his round smooth chin a little and checked his tie. 'You don't want to look at me? Am I ugly?'

'Benny, you can't stay here. You deserve better than this.'

'You're my brother, right? You're the guy who came up on the train to see me because I was in the shit? That's you?'

'I won't let you stay here.'

'We're family, right?'

101

'Yes, we're family. That's what we're going to talk about.'

'Then don't patronize me, O.K.? I know I deserve better than this. I'm not going to live here for ever. I'm going to buy a double block at Franklin Heights. There's some great places up there now. They got tennis courts and everything. Vish, we could do so fucking *well*.'

Vish put the steam-iron down on the work bench. 'I won't let you live like this . . .'

'You're scared of money. I understand. Don't worry. I'll look after the money.' Benny smoothed a green garbage bag on the regency couch and sat on it. 'I've changed, just like you changed once. I've made a transformation.'

Vish looked up at Benny and was about to say something before he changed his mind.

'What?' Benny prompted.

'It's not the time.'

'Say it – it's O.K. You think I can't handle money?'

'No one can change.'

'You can fucking *see* I changed. You're not the only one who's spiritual.'

'You dyed your hair.'

'Is that all you can fucking see . . .'

'You cleaned your face. You got a suit. You know what that makes me feel? It just makes me feel depressed. Even if you had plastic surgery, you couldn't change. I couldn't either. We're both going to be the same thing for all eternity. Even when we die and get born again, even if we get reborn a dog . . . we're the same thing. Everything has a Sanatana Dharma,' Vish said. 'It means Eternal Occupation. It doesn't matter what form we take, this is like our essence – it stays the same.'

Benny sighed and crossed his legs. 'The way I see it,' he said at last, 'is that there are white ants breeding underneath their feet, but they can't see it.'

Vish nodded, waiting to see how this connected.

'They think they're on a rock,' Benny said. 'Howie, Cathy, Mort. They think they're on a rock, but they're on ice. They don't know what's beneath them. Down here,' he gestured at the walls – blue, red, green, words written over each other so they looked like ancient blotting paper. 'Down here I make the future, our future.

I've prepared myself for a completely new life. For you too. We can do this thing together.'

'What about Mort?'

'No, no, I won't hurt him. I'll look after him. I'll look after all of them. Go ahead,' Benny said, seeing Vish trying to read the writing on the wall. 'Please . . . you're my brother, partner . . . It's not a secret from you.'

Vish could read: 'Let a virgin girl weave a white wool carpet . . .' Some foreign names: 'Kushiel, Lahatiel, Zagzagel . . .'

'There's nothing to be frightened of. I'm going to run this business effectively, that's all. I'm transforming myself,' Benny said. 'By various methods, not just that.'

'Into what?'

Benny grinned. He nodded his head and looked selfconscious. 'I can show you a new layout for the whole place. A proper workshop, a modern showroom. If we put all the insurance work through British Union, we can finance it all through them.'

'Into what?' Vish insisted with his forehead all creased and his eyes squinting at his brother. 'Into what are you transforming yourself?'

'Many things.'

'For instance.'

'Angel.'

'Angel?'

'I have changed myself into an angel.'

Vish was suddenly back in that odd dreamy world you enter when you hear someone has died, or you see someone shot in the street in front of you. He heard himself say: 'What sort of angel?'

Benny hesitated. 'There's angels for all of us,' he said, standing up and brushing at his trousers. 'Like you found out at the temple, right? Angels they never told us about in Sunday School.' He smiled and folded his hands behind his back like a salesman on the lot and Vish, seeing the clear confidence in his eyes, thought, once again, that his brother was mentally unwell.

'Benny,' Vish said, 'you've got to get out of here. Whatever's bad, this place only makes it worse.'

'You ask me, then you don't want to listen to my answers. I already told you. I'm going to buy a block at Franklin Heights.'

'It stinks in here. I won't let you live like this.'

'Let's be honest. It's because of you I'm here. You put me here, Vish. And that's why you're here now.'

'Oh no. Let's be clear about this. I took you to the ashram. I would have got you in.'

'I was a runaway minor. They shat themselves when they knew that.'

'I would have got you in. You ran away before they had a chance.'

'Bullshit, Vish, you kissed their arses. Where else could I come except down here? You think I was going to stay with Old Kissy Lips alone? Is that how you were looking after me?'

Vish bowed his head.

'Hey,' Benny said.

Vish had his eyes squinched up tight.

'Come on,' Benny said.

Vish felt his brother's arm around his shoulder.

'I'm not mad at you,' Benny said. 'I was never mad at you. We each got out of home, in different ways. All I want is you fucking listen to me, eh?' He paused, and smiled. 'O.K.?'

'O.K.' said Vish, also smiling. 'Fair enough.'

'Ask me what angel I am.' He pushed his brother in the ribs, 'Go on.'

'What angel are you?'

'Fallen angel,' Benny said, 'Angel of Plagues, Angel of Ice, Angel of Lightning.'

Vish shook his head.

'Hey, it's not for you to say yes or no. You think I made this up?' Benny held up a book – *A Dictionary of Angels*. 'This is not bullshit. Look up Krishna. He's there, and all his atvars.'

'Avatars.'

'Atavars, yes. If I'm wrong, you're wrong too.' He opened the front of the book and let Vish read the inscription: 'I cannot be what I am – A.V.'

'Who is A.V.?' Vish asked. 'You've become an angel? Is that it? You've become an angel from this book?'

The truth was that Benny did not know. He had made himself into an angel, and he came out looking like his mother. But he was not his mother, he was an angel. The angels were his creation. By writing their names he made them come true.

He made Saboeth with a dragon's face and the power of destruction. He made Adonein, a mischievous angel with the face of a monkey. They were his masters. They were his victims. He smoked dope and took their power. He broke their spines and crushed them as he tore them out of books. He played Judas Priest with the volume turned up full. He had a real blue tattoo wing which ran from his right shoulder blade to his round, white, muscled buttock. The angels had feet with five toes and toenails and heavy white callouses round their heels.

'You've become an angel?' Vish asked.

'Hey,' said Benny, 'relax . . . I was just kidding you.'

'Really?'

'I was just scaring you. We don't need to do anything extreme.'

21

When Benny was three years old, his mother was only twenty-three. Her name was Sophie Catchprice. She had bell-bottomed jeans and long blonde hair like Mary in Peter Paul and Mary. She had bare feet and chipped red nail-polish on her toenails. She stood at the door of her bedroom one Saturday afternoon and saw her husband sucking her younger son's penis.

There was a Demolition Derby in progress in the paddock behind the house. The car engines were screaming, hitting that high dangerous pitch that tells you they are way past the red line, and you could smell the methyl benzine racing fuel right here in the bedroom. Sun poured through the lace curtains with the rucked hems. All around her were signs of her incompetence: the bed unmade; the curtains still stained; an FJ generator-coil on the dressing table; Mort's .22 still leaning in the corner next to the broken standard lamp. She had told him for two years – pick up that rifle.

She saw her husband, the father of her children, with his hand inside his unzipped trousers. Neither Mort nor Benny knew she was there. She was a fly on the wall, a speck, a nothing. She felt like her own dream – where she scratched her stomach and found her innards – her life – green and slippery and falling through her fingers. She picked up the rifle. What else was she to do?

'Give him to me,' she said. But she could not look at Benny. She was frightened of what she would see. He was three years old. He had a white Disney T-shirt with Minnie kissing Mickey: SMACK it said. Johnny had one the same, but Johnny was safe with his Grandma in Spare Parts.

'You evil slime,' she said.

'Hey come on,' Mort said. His trousers were undone, but Benny was not reaching for his mother. He clung tight to his father's neck. Sophie felt like her chest was full of puke.

She had to do something. She heard the shell 'snick' into the firing chamber as if someone else put it there. She was not even angry, or if she was angry then the anger was covered with something rumpled and dirty and she could not recognize it. What she felt was sourer and sadder than anger, more serious than anger. Her fingers felt heavy, and spongy. She looked at Benny. His little eyes seemed alien and poisoned. He balanced on his father's hip staring back at her.

'Come to Mummy,' she said.

But Benny was looking at the rifle. He shook his head.

'Give him to me,' she said to Mort, 'and I won't hurt you, I swear.'

'Put that rifle down,' he said. 'You don't know how to use it.'

Sure, she knew how to. She could not see what else to do but what she did. But even as she did it, as she took one action after the other, she expected something would happen that would stop her travelling all the way to the logical conclusion. She walked a little closer to Mort, frowning, and then there was nothing left to do but fire. Even as she did it, she thought she lacked the courage.

She fired from less than a metre. The bullet missed her husband and caused a red flower to blossom on the arm of her son's Mickey Mouse T-shirt.

It was Sophie who called out, not Benny. Benny looked as if he'd fallen playing – his lip pouted and his big eyes swelled with tears.

Sophie held out a hand towards him, but Mort crouched on the floor, holding his corduroy trousers together, shielding the wounded child with his big body. Benny clung to his father. He had his arms around his neck. Blood was smeared all round Mort's ears and collar.

Sophie reached out towards her son but he flinched from her.

'Go *way*,' he screamed. He was three years old, alive with rage towards her. She could not bear to be the focus of it. 'Go way.'

The windows were filthy. The sunlight illuminated the small balls of fluff which drifted across the uncarpeted floor. Their child's blood was a bright, bright red, like newly opened paint. It flooded the chest of Benny's shirt. Sophie felt soaked with shame. It was unendurable.

'What did you do that for?' Mort was crying, stroking Benny's head.

She felt the first flicker of doubt.

'You know what you were doing, slime.'

'Tell me,' Mort screamed. 'Tell me what we've done.'

She brought another shell into the chamber, but everything she thought so definitely was now dissolving in the acid of her chronic uncertainty. What she had seen was already like a thing she might have feared or dreamed or even, yes, imagined.

'I was kissing his tummy,' he said. He had blood on his fingers. He was streaking blood through his son's fair hair.

'Kissing!'

'I was fucking *kissing* him,' he said. 'For Chrissake, Sophie. Why do you want to kill our little boy?'

She looked at his big swollen lips and his bright blaming eyes and saw the way the terrified child held him around the neck, and she believed him.

It was like you pour water on a fire that is burning you. Sophie just put the barrel of the rifle in her mouth and fired. She messed that up as well. The bullet passed beside her spinal column, and out through the back of her neck.

She ran from the house, across the car yard. She waited for a wall, a barrier, but nothing stopped her flight. Her father-in-law was selling a Ford Customline to a man in a leather jacket. He held up his hand and waved to her. She ran down Loftus Street, splashing blood behind her. She had not planned to leave, not leave her little boys, not leave by train, but she was at the railway station and she had twenty dollars in her slacks and she had done a crime and she bought a ticket and boarded the 6.25 train to Sydney which was just departing from the platform next to the booth. She was dripping blood and nearly fainting but no one looked at her particularly. No one tried to stop her. She just kept on going. She just kept on going on and on, and as the train pulled out she could see the Demolition Derby in the back paddock behind Catchprice Motors.

When his little brother was being bashed up by Matty Evans behind the boys' lavatories, Vish came running into the school yard from the hole in the fence next to the milk factory. He had a housebrick. He was not yet Vish – he was still John. He was nine years old. He was bigger than Benny but he still had to carry the brick in both hands. He pushed his way through the circle of yelling boys and threw the brick, point blank. It hit Matty Evans on the side of the head and he dropped so fast and lay so still that the little kids started crying, thinking he was dead. There was a dark red pool of blood glistening on the hot asphalt playground, and teachers were yelling and making everyone stand in line even though it was the magpie season and two kids were swooped just standing there. Johnny Catchprice vomited up his sandwiches, just as the ambulance arrived. It drove straight into the school yard and left deep ruts in the grass in front of 'Paddles' Rogers's rose garden.

Matty Evans got six stitches and they clipped his hair like he was a dog with mange. Paddles paddled Johnny Catchprice for every one of those stitches. Johnny's hand puffed up so much he had to be excused from English Composition and this was why Mort put on his suit and came up to the school to talk to Paddles during the double Algebra on Thursday afternoon.

Everyone thought he had come to threaten law suits, but Mort was not shocked by either the crime or the punishment. What panicked Mort was that he maybe had a 'disturbed child' on his hands, that a whiff of his home life could be detected in the open air. He put on his grey suit and went up to school, not to sue, but to plug the leak somehow. He was not sure how he would do it, not even when he opened his mouth.

Paddles was a little bald-headed man with a swagger and a hairy chest which grew up under his shirt collar. He felt himself an inch away from litigation and so he was chatty and pleasant and over-eager. He looked across at Johnny and winked.

Johnny laid his bandaged hand on his lap and looked out of the window at the ruts the ambulance had left on the green lawn.

'No matter who bullied whom,' Mort said. 'I never saw him do anything like this in all his life. And when I say all his life, I mean, all his life. I don't know if you know it, but his mother left us when he was five . . .'

'Noo-na,' said Paddles sympathetically. He was confused about what Mort Catchprice was up to. This gave him an odd 'hanging-on-every-word' look.

'She just pissed off.'

Johnny shut his eyes.

'At that time I couldn't cook, I couldn't sew, and I wasn't seeing my kids as much as I should have. I was coaching the Under-fifteens in the football and the cricket. I was setting up the panel shop. But suddenly there were all these fucking bureaucrats – pardon my French – wanted to take my boys away, because I was a man.'

'Isn't that typical,' said Paddles. 'Sure. I can imagine . . .'

'You can imagine,' Mort said. 'You can imagine I soon found out how to cook and how to sew. I was there for them in the morning and I was there for them at night, so when I say Johnny doesn't do this sort of thing,' Mort kicked Johnny underneath the desk, 'hitting a boy with a *brick*. When I say this is not him, I know what I'm talking about. You understand me?'

'Yes,' Paddles said. 'Sure. Hell, yes.' The minute he said yes he thought he had made a legal mistake.

'Good,' Mort said, kicking Johnny again. 'So you understand why I'm upset – I work for years of my life to give you a sweet, gentle kid, you give me back a kid who hits another kid with a brick.'

It was only then that Johnny got the joke – his dad was *lying*.

'It's not in his character. I hope you agree?'

Paddles thought he could see Mort assembling evidence for court. 'Without prejudice?' He saw the kid trying to hide his grin. 'Look,' he said. 'It will never happen again.' He meant the strapping.

Mort meant brick-throwing. 'That's your decision,' he said, 'totally, but if I hear of any more behaviour like this, you're the man I'll be holding responsible.'

Johnny and his father walked out of the school, making odd little noises up behind their noses, holding their laughter in like you keep water in a garden hose with your thumb. They walked out across the lawn, biting their lips and creasing their eyes.

They left a screech of rubber on Vernon Street that stayed there for two months. Mort was wailing with laughter, banging the wheel. Thump, thump, thump with the fat heel of his hand, and his lips now all big and loose with pleasure at the lie he had told. He grabbed Johnny's thigh – a horse bite – and squeezed him till he yelped, and then Johnny laughed too, not at the lie, but at their shared experience, their complicity.

'Not in his character!'

It was 100 per cent his character. That was the joke – this mild, sweet-faced boy could attack his father with a tyre lever.

'You little bastard,' his father said, admiringly it seemed.

They were like each other, twins, they had the same chin, the same ears, the same temper too.

He knew that when the time came, he would never be able to explain about his father – how you could want to crush him like an insect, how he was also almost perfect.

He'd drive them to wherever the Balmain Tigers were playing – 40, 60 K's – no wuckers. He played Rock 'n' Roll really loud – AC/DC, Judas Priest. He was the one who bought the Midnight Oil tape.

> *How can we sleep when our beds are burning*
> *How can we sleep while our world is turning*

He sang the words out loud. He was as good as Peter Garrett – he could have been a Rock 'n' Roller. They ate potato crisps, hot dogs, twisties, minties, pies. At the game he did not abandon them for the bar. He was their mate. They argued and farted all the way home to Franklin. He cooked pancakes and served them up with butter and sugar and fresh-squeezed lemon juice.

He was a good father. He got up at six each morning so he could cook them a proper breakfast. He brushed their hair. He fussed over their clothes. He gave them expensive fizzy vitamins and did not over-cook the vegetables.

He was affectionate. He was never shy to kiss them on the cheek or hold them. He liked to kiss. He had soft kissing lips. And it was the lips which were the trouble, the lips that showed when things were going bad again.

Johnny looked like his Dad. Naturally this was not so interesting for their Dad to look at. Benny looked like the other person, the one they were not allowed to ask about and the bad nights always began with their father staring at Benny and looking sad. Then he would cuddle in to him and stroke his hair and kiss him on the neck. He was not ashamed of it. He said: 'You see those other fathers, too scared to even touch their kids. They're just terrified of natural feelings.' He kissed them both, often, like you saw mothers kissing babies. Kissing their necks and backs.

Once he started kissing Benny's neck, he would not stay soulful and doggy-eyed for long. Johnny could watch the mood-change coming like wind across a paddock full of wheat. His dad's eyes would turn snaky. He'd start to talk sarcastic, spiky. He would laugh and say mean things about the shape of Johnny's head or how fat his legs were. He did not mean them really – nasty and nice were all the same to him when his mood changed. He had only one objective: to get Johnny to leave the room so he could be alone with Benny.

Johnny slammed the door to counterfeit his exit from the house. He sat outside the blessed circle of affection, outside the blue centre of the flame, safer but more lonely, excluded but responsible. He became the ugly one. He became a peek, a sneak. He watched his father stroke Benny's hair, waited for the moment when the mustard velvet cushion would be placed across his brother's lap. It was then he would come in throwing darts or pillows.

Sometimes Benny just looked at him with wet open lips and a smile on his face, sometimes he needed him bad. Sometimes Mort and Benny both shouted at him, told him to piss off out of there.

The day they saw Paddles it was still seven whole years away from the night when he would smash his father's bedroom window with a cast-iron casserole and cut him with the Stay-sharp knife.

He was not Vish yet.

He was still Johnny and when Mort said, 'Come on, killer, I'll buy you a quarter pounder,' he looked at the big face and in spite of everything, was still proud to be just like his Daddy.

23

At 10.15 on Monday night, while Maria and Gia drove from the Blue Moon Brasserie towards the Taxation Office, Cathy stood at her open refrigerator door wondering what she could be bothered cooking; Mrs Catchprice walked along Vernon Street, Franklin, and offered to employ Sarkis Alaverdian; Vishnabarnu finished ironing Benny's wrapping paper and began to iron his jeans.

'I'm going to get you out of here,' he said.

'You never did listen to anyone but yourself, Vish.' Benny straightened the orange plastic sheet beneath his suit and adjusted his socks once again. 'I'm asking you to be my partner.'

'I'll take you out of here,' Vish smiled. 'If I have to pick you up and carry you out.'

'Only problem,' Benny lit a Marlboro and blew a long thin line towards his brother, 'I *want* to be here. You want to help me, stay here with me.'

Vish put the iron on its end and folded the jeans one more time.

'You're a stubborn fucker, aren't you?' Benny said.

Vish looked up and smiled.

'We know the truth though,' Benny blew a fat and formless cloud of smoke. 'You've got the business and the personal mixed up. The problem is you were always jealous.'

'Oh really? Of what?'

'Of me and Him.'

'Benny, you hated him. You used to cry in your *sleep*. We were plotting to poison him with heart tablets.'

'You were jealous of us. That's why you went crazy. It wasn't the business. If you want him to retire, we can do that. We can look after him. We can get him out of here.'

'This is nothing to do with Mort.'

'You smashed the window. You stabbed him. You have to admit you've got a problem with him, not with the business.'

'I was protecting you.'

'You want to protect me – be my partner.'

Vish had that red-brown colour in his cheeks. His neck and shoulders were set so tight – if you touched him he would feel like rock.

'Benny, I'm not coming back. O.K.? Never, ever.'

Benny laughed but he felt the sadness, like snot, running down his throat. He did not say anything. He could not think of anything to say.

Vish folded the jeans and laid them carefully beside the bottled brown snakes Benny had rescued from his Grandpa's personal effects. He took the AC/DC T-shirt and smoothed it against his broad chest. 'You should have washed them first,' he said.

'I'm never going to wear them again,' Benny said.

He waited for Vish to ask him why. But Vish was a Catchprice – he was never going to ask. He just kept on ironing, with his big square face all wrinkled up against the steam.

After a while, Benny said: 'Aren't you even curious?'

Vish jabbed at the T-shirt with the point of the iron.

Benny asked: 'Do you think I look like her?'

'Like who?'

'Like who?' Benny mimicked the high scratchy voice. He pulled the photograph out of the silky pocket of his suit and pushed it at his brother. Vish took it and held it up to the light.

'Oh, yeah.' He looked up at Benny but made no comment on his dazzling similarity.

Benny took the photo back. He put it in his pocket.

Vish said: 'Remember the night you saw her?' He folded the T-shirt arms over so they made a 45° with the shoulder, then he pressed them flat. He was grinning.

'You saw her too,' Benny smiled as well. 'Who else would stand like that at the front gate at two in the morning.'

'It could have been anyone.' Vish folded the T-shirt so its trunk was exactly in half. When the hot iron hit it, the shirt gave off a smell like Bathurst – oil, maybe some methyl benzine.

'It must have been her,' Benny said. 'Anyone gets shot with an air rifle – if they're innocent they call the cops.'

Vish smiled.

'Admit it – you think about her too.'

'All I try to think about is Krishna.'

'Bullshit, Johnny. What total bullshit.' Benny said. 'You should learn to ask questions, it's amazing what you find out. Did you know how long it took you to get born? Ask me.'

'You don't know.'

'Ten hours. You know how long it took me? It took me thirty hours. You don't believe me, ask Cathy. The second baby should be faster but I was lying back to front. They cut our mother open to get me out. It fucked up all her stomach muscles. She got a stomach like an old woman when she was twenty, all wrinkled like a prune.'

'And that's why she shot you? Come on, Benny. Give up. Get on with your life.'

'Hey,' Benny rose from the couch, his finger pointing. 'Forget all this shit you tell yourself about me. Forget all the bullshit stories you carry in your head.' He straightened his trouser legs and ran his palms along his jacket sleeves. 'What did I tell you?'

'When?'

'Any time.' He held his palms out. The gesture made no sense. 'Ever. I told you we could do this thing together. I told you I was changed. Angel. Look.' He walked carefully along the plank to reach his brother. Then he opened his mouth for his brother to look in.

What he meant was: light. I have light pouring out of me.

'Benny you need help.'

'You don't believe me,' Benny hit his forehead with his palm. 'You jerk-off – you're walking away from two hundred thou a year. You don't know what you're doing. You don't know where you are. Where are you?' Benny helped him. He pointed. He pointed to the walls, the writing. He invited him to look, to read, to understand all this – the very centre of his life – but all Vish did was shrug and unplug the iron. He stood the iron end up on the bench beside the clothes and the snakes. Right behind him was the fibreglass 'thing' in the shape of a flattened 'n'.

'Where are you?' Benny asked. 'Answer me that.'

'I'm in your cellar, Benny.'

'No,' said Benny. 'You are inside my fucking head and I have got the key.'

All around Vishnabarnu were the names of angels. They hung over him like a woven web, a net, like a map of the human brain drawn across the walls and ceilings of the world. He knew himself a long way from God.

24

Benny greased the Monaro out of the back paddock with its lights off. He was not licensed, and the car was not meant to be driven on the road, but his father was watching a video in his bedroom and he took the Monaro out on the far side, on to the little gravel lane which ran right beside the railway tracks.

There was a path direct to the Wool Wash, and for a moment he had toyed with the idea of walking there. The path led out through the hole in the paling fence at the back of Mort's house.

This was the path they had walked with old Cacka down to see the frogmouth owl, the path they walked together each day to go swimming down at the Wool Wash. The path went (more or less) straight across the back paddock, crossed the railway line, curved round the council depot where a huge cyclone fence protected nothing more than a pile of blue gravel and two battered yellow 44-gallon drums, cut round the edge of the brickworks clay pit and then went straight across those little hills which had once been known as 'Thistle Paddocks' but were now a housing estate known as Franklin Heights. The path then ran beside the eroded drive-way to the 105-room house, down into the dry bush gullies, and then out on to the escarpment where a path was hacked into the cliff wall like something in a comic strip. The path led finally to the clear waters of the Wool Wash pool.

The truth was: it was not like that any more. The path was fucked. It was cut like a worm by a garden spade – new yellow fences, subdivisions, prohibitions, walls, new dogs, shitty owners with psychotic ideas about their territorial rights, frightened lonely women who would press the panic button on their Tandy burglar alarms at the sight of a stranger climbing over their fence.

Once it had been the best thing in Benny's life. Now it was just an imaginary line cutting through suburbia. Once he had been able to sit above the Wool Wash for hours on hot still days in summer doing Buddha grass and feeling the wind bend the trees and show the silver colour in the Casuarinas and watching the old eels making their sand-nest in the river. When everything was so bad he thought he had to die, his mind went there, to the Wool Wash, and when Tape 7 said find a river, there was only one river.

He considered the path but it was not a serious option. When his brother went off to bed, he carried his gift-wrapped clothes and his sawn-off shotgun down to the Monaro. Fifteen minutes later he came down the S's to the Wool Wash with the tacho needle almost on the red line. He put the nose too close into the corner on the second last bend and he nearly lost it in the fucking gravel. He changed down even as he knew he shouldn't. The tail kicked out. Fuck it. He flicked the wheels into line and and saved it. He cut a clean line across the next curve and came down into the car park at 150Ks but he was prickling hot with shame. It was such a shitty gear change.

He did two slow circuits with his quartzes on, blasting a pure white light through the cloud of clay dust his arrival had created. His four headlight beams cut like knives through the dust, illuminating the bullet-scarred, yellow garbage bins, the POLLUTED WATER signs, and twisted galvanized pipe boom gates (NO 4-WHEEL DRIVE ACCESS).

He had a 1:3 ratio first gear and he just walked the Monaro like a dog on a leash, torqued it round the perimeters of the parking area, checking to make sure there was no one here to mock what he was going to do.

The Franklin Redevelopment Region now had a hundred thousand school kids. The banks of the Wool Wash were littered with beer cans and condoms and paper cups. Petrol-heads came here to do one dusty spin-turn before screaming up through the S's for the race back to the skid pan at the Industrial Estate. Stolen cars were abandoned here, virginities were lost, although not his. At weekends you could buy speed and crack by the gas barbecues. It was the sort of place you might find someone with their face shot away and bits of brain hanging on the bushes.

Benny drove round the edge of a metal boom gate. It bottomed out on some grass tussocks, and then he just slid it – you could feel the grass brushing along the floor beneath his feet – out of sight behind some ti-tree scrub.

When he had shut off the engine and the lights, he tucked the shot-gun underneath his seat. Then he carefully removed his suit trousers and his shirt. He folded them loosely and placed them on the lambswool seat cover. He put on a T-shirt and a pair of swimming trunks and then he put on his shoes as a protection against AIDS.

Even though it was warm, the rain clouds made the night dark and his flash-light was weak and yellow. He walked warily out across the empty car park to the river, carrying the ironed clothes in a red Grace Bros plastic shopping bag. The bank just here was flat and wide and treeless. When he got to where the round boulders started, he took off his good leather shoes and placed them in the shopping bag.

Benny failed every science subject he ever took, but he knew this water in Deep Creek now contained lead, dioxin and methyl mercury from the paper factory on Lantana Road. It was surprisingly cold on his feet. He could feel the poisons clinging like invisible odour-free oil slicks. They rode through the water like spiders' webs, air through air, sticking to everything they touched. Benny moved quickly, but carefully.

He heard the sound of the approaching car when it was up on the turn off from Long Gully Road. It was a Holden. He recognized the distinctive sound of the water pump, that high hiss in the night. He hesitated, wondering whether he should go back to the car and wait but he did not want to have to walk into the poisons twice.

There was a light wind, a cool wash of air that pushed up the river like a wave and the big Casuarinas on the shore bent and made a soft whooshing noise. No matter what had changed, it still smelt like the Wool Wash – moss, rotting leaves, something like blackcurrants that was not blackcurrants, and the slightly muddy tannin smell of the water which you could once drink, puddles full, from Cacka's old slouch hat.

The first package was the sneakers. He had them in a shoebox now, wrapped in ironed black paper and tied with a gold ribbon. He pushed the package out into the current, following it for a metre or two with the weak beam of his torch until it was lost.

He whispered: 'When my past is dead, I am as free as air.'

Then he squatted and pushed out the blue parcel which contained his T-shirt. It was flat and neat like a twelve-inch L.P. For a moment it seemed to mould itself like a Kraft cheese slice on to a rock, but then it was picked up and although it was lost to sight Benny thought he could hear the sound of its paper skin brushing over the shallow rapids downstream.

He said: 'When my past is cleared, there is only blue sky.'

The Holden was coming through the S bends above the river. He could see its lights as they cut out into the air. The car was burning oil and the lights cut back and shone white in the smoke of its own exhaust.

He hurriedly launched the gold parcel, throwing it a little carelessly so that it landed thin edge in and sank a little before it surfaced.

He spoke quickly: 'My past is gone and I am new – born again – my future will be wrapped with gold.'

He stepped off the rock. He tried to put a shoe on, but he could not get his foot into it. The leather stuck on his wet skin. He leaned over to fix it. Then his ankle twisted and he stumbled. The Holden was through the last bend. Benny picked up the shoe and ran barefoot. Death was everywhere, but no way was anyone going to see him doing rituals in his underwear. The earth was alive with organisms which wished to make a host of his blood. He felt cuts, nicks, toxins, viruses. The car – a fucking taxi! – was driving right down to the water's edge. He fled the beam of its lights and ran to his car. He got in, locked the doors, sat the shotgun across his lap.

The taxi did not stay long. As soon as it began its ascent through the S's he dressed, and backed the Monaro out into the centre of the car park. When he turned to head back to Franklin, he saw, in the halogen-white glare of the headlights – Granny Catchprice. Her legs were apart. Her left hand was shading her eyes.

25

'You pay me now,' Pavlovic said. 'Or I leave you here, dead-set. You walk all the way back to Franklin, wouldn't worry me.' He leaned back, opened the door on Mrs Catchprice's side, and smiled.

Sarkis was smiling too. He had that hot burning sensation down the back of his throat. He sat on the edge of the back seat of the taxi with his broad white hands on his knees. He was baring his teeth and narrowing his eyes – 'smiling' – but Pavlovic wasn't even aware of him. He was turned almost completely round in his seat with his hawk nose pointed at Mrs Catchprice.

'Might give you nicer manners,' he said.

'You'll be paid later,' said Mrs Catchprice. 'I don't carry cash on me.'

'You pay me now,' said Pavlovic.

'You heard her,' Sarkis said, but he was the one no one seemed to hear.

'Or you get out of my cab. That simple,' he smiled again. His mouth was prissy and pinched as if he could smell something nasty on his upper lip.

Sarkis did not want to have a brawl in these trousers and this shirt but he could feel anger like curry in his throat. His eyes were narrowed almost to slits in his incredulous, smiling face. Pavlovic was so *thin*. Sarkis smoothed the $199 grey moire trousers against his muscled thighs. He looked at Mrs Catchprice to see what it was she wanted him to do.

Mrs Catchprice, it seemed, needed nothing from him. Whatever Pavlovic said to her did not matter. Indeed she was concerned with her cigarette lighter, which had fallen down the back of the seat.

'I did not come to the Wool Wash to sit in the car. Ah,' she held up her Ronson. 'I cannot bear it when I see people sitting in their car to look at the scenery.'

Pavlovic sighed loudly and Sarkis – he couldn't help himself – slapped him on the side of the head, fast, sharp.

'You stop that,' Mrs Catchprice said. 'Right now.'

Sarkis opened his mouth to protest.

'I don't hire louts,' said Mrs Catchprice.

Pavlovic said something too but Sarkis did not hear what it was. Pavlovic was holding a clenched fist in the air and Sarkis kept an eye on it, but all his real attention was on Mrs Catchprice – what did she want him to do?

'Maybe you should pay him,' he said.

Mrs Catchprice 'acted' her response. She smiled a large 'nice' smile that made her white teeth look as big as an old Buick grille. 'I always pay my suppliers when they have *completed* the job.'

'I could have the police here,' Pavlovic smirked and rubbed his bright red ear. 'Or I could leave you here. I like both ideas.'

Sarkis did not actually have a police record, but he had experience of the police in Chatswood. To Mrs Catchprice, he said: 'Maybe you should look in your handbag.'

Mrs Catchprice's smile became even bigger. 'You must not equate age with stupidity,' she said. 'You'd have to be senile to walk around at night with money in your bag.'

She made him ashamed he had suggested such a cowardly course but he had seen the twenty-dollar notes very clearly in the jumble under the street lights before they caught the taxi. He did not wish to insult or anger her, but he tapped her very playfully on the back of the hand. 'I think I may have seen some there.'

Mrs Catchprice looked at him briefly, frowned, and addressed herself to the balding, hawk-nosed driver. 'What will the police think,' she asked, 'of a taxi-driver operating outside the correct area?'

'They do not give a fuck. Excuse my language, but if you were

119

nice, I would care. You are not nice, so I could not give a fuck. The police got no bloody interest in what area I'm in. Most of the young constables don't even know what an area is. But I tell you this – they got plenty of interest in assault, and they got plenty of interest in robbery. That's their business.'

'Maybe you should check your handbag,' said Sarkis.

'I can see I'm going to have to train you,' said Mrs Catchprice. 'When I say I have no money it is because I have no money.' To the taxi-driver she said: 'You wait.' Then she slid out of the door and disappeared into the night.

The taxi-driver leaned back and shut the door. Mrs Catchprice appeared in the headlights of the car walking towards the river. Then – so suddenly it whipped Sarkis's head forwards and backwards – Pavlovic reversed, made a U-turn, and before his passenger could do anything he was bouncing up the pot-holed track with the red electric figures on the meter showing $28.50.

They were half way through the first S bend when Sarkis leant forward and hooked his forearm round the taxi-driver's long thin neck. He pulled it back so hard he could feel the jaw bone grating against his ulna. All he said was: 'Turn back.' The driver's stubble was rubbing against his forearm. He hated to think of this against his mother.

'Road,' Pavlovic gasped. 'Too narrow.'

'O.K.'

'Can't breathe.'

'Shut up.'

'Breathe.'

Sarkis released his arm a little. The taxi-driver screamed. He screamed so loud he made the taxi like a nightmare, a mad place: 'You a dead man, Jack.' Sarkis could feel the wet on his arm. Not sweat. Pavlovic was crying. 'I hit my panic button, they get you, cunt. They get you in the cells, they fuck you with their baton, you wait.' The car slowed and slowed until it was juddering and kangaroo-hopping up the road. As the car leaped and jerked, Pavlovic was flailing around with his arm, trying to grab first Sarkis's ear or eye but also – the panic button. Sarkis grabbed Pavlovic's hand and held it. He held it easy, but he was now scared, as scared as Pavlovic. Pavlovic was crying but it was not simple scared-crying, it was mad-crying too.

'You pull up here,' Sarkis said.

'You get twenty years for this. You're dead.'

'She gets murdered or something,' Sarkis said. '*She*'s dead.' The car shuddered and stalled.

'You,' yelled the taxi-driver, his face glowing green in the light of his instruments, but he didn't finish the sentence.

'What you think I'm going to do to you?' Sarkis asked. 'Did I hurt you?'

'Just pay me,' Pavlovic said, glaring at him from streaming eyes.

'O.K.,' Sarkis said, relieved. 'You go back and get her, I'll pay you.'

'O.K. You take your arm away now.'

Sarkis unhooked his arm from under the driver's chin.

'O.K.,' said Pavlovic, blowing his nose. 'You got money on you?'

'At home.'

'Then I'll take you home for the money, then we come back here and get her.' He was hunched over the wheel. He did not need to tell Sarkis he had his finger an inch away from the panic button.

'We get her first.'

'You want me press this fucking button?'

That button was enough to get Sarkis put in jail. Pavlovic used it like a pistol. First he forced him to abandon Mrs Catchprice. Then he drove him to his house where his mother had $52 hidden under the lino in the sitting-room.

While Sarkis stole his mother's money, Pavlovic sat in the cab with the engine running. He stayed hunched over the wheel, his finger on that button.

'Come on,' Sarkis said when he got back in the cab. 'I've got the money.'

'Hold it up. Hold the notes.'

Sarkis showed him – five tens, one two.

Pavlovic twisted his neck to see the money. He had to keep his finger on that button. Even when he backed out of the drive-way he had to sit twisted sideways in his seat, and he drove back to the Wool Wash one handed, all the way, in silence.

When the meter showed $52 they were almost there, on the main road up above the Wool Wash Picnic Area. Pavlovic stopped the car.

'You pay me,' he said, 'or I hit this fucking button now. I charge you with fucking assault, at least. You understand me.'

'Relax,' said Sarkis. 'No one's going to hurt you.'

'Shut up, Jack. Just pay me.'

'I need a lift back. O.K. Can you hear me? I'll pay you more money when we get back.'

'Give me the fucking money or you're a dead man.'

'You don't want to make more money?' Sarkis held out the $52 and Pavlovic snatched the notes. 'I need a lift back,' Sarkis said. 'I'll pay you.'

'Not in this cab, Jack.'

'Just calm down, relax a little.'

'Get out,' screamed Pavlovic.

Sarkis shrugged and got out of the car.

Pavlovic locked the car doors.

'Listen,' Sarkis began, but the taxi was already driving away, leaving him to stand in pitch darkness.

It was now five minutes to eleven o'clock on Monday night. Mrs Catchprice was already back in Franklin, walking back across the gravel towards her apartment.

26

The Australian Tax Office was in Hunter Street. The glassed, marble-columned foyer remained brightly lit and unlocked and, apart from video cameras and an hourly M.S.S. patrol, the security for the building depended on deceptively ordinary blue plastic Security Access Keys which were granted only to ASO 7's and above. This was why Gia now had a key and Maria did not.

In the six months she had had the key, Gia had never used it. It sat in its original envelope in the bottom of her handbag, together with its crumpled instruction sheet. Now, standing before the blank eyes of video cameras which were connected to she knew not what, Gia read the instructions to Maria.

'O.K. Hold the key firmly between thumb and forefinger. Ensure blade is unobstructed.'

'We should have read this in the car,' Maria said. 'I can't see where the shitty thing goes.' She jabbed the key at the button.

'First you've got to step into the elevator, Señora.' Gia took Maria's arm. 'Then you put it in the Security/Air-conditioning slot.'

A red light came on. A buzzer sounded. Maria started.

'Calm down,' Gia said. 'No one's going to shoot you. All we're doing is working late.'

The lift ascended and the liquid display panel above the door wished someone called Alex a happy birthday. Maria seemed pale and unhappy. Gia took her arm and squeezed it.

'Relax,' she said.

'You know,' Maria said, 'that's exactly the wrong thing to say to me. If you're dealing with an agitated person, a maniac, you never say "relax". Relax means what you feel is not important to me. I read that in the *Sydney Morning Herald* yesterday.' She took Gia's hand and held it: 'You're very brave to come with me. Thank you.'

'I think this is going to be very therapeutic,' Gia said. 'I only wish Alistair could see you do it.'

'This is nothing to do with Alistair . . .'

Gia thought: Sure! It was the first real sign she'd seen that Maria would let herself be angry with him.

The door opened on to the rat-maze partitioned world of the eighteenth floor which now housed the file clerks and section heads and auditors who concerned themselves with returns from small businesses like Catchprice Motors.

When Alistair's star had been in the ascendant they had all worked here – although not on small businesses. During those years, no one on the eighteenth floor would have wasted their genius on Catchprice Motors.

They went to big-game fishing conventions in Port Stephens and photographed the people with the big boats and then investigated them to see if their income correlated with their assets. They spotted Rolls-Royces on the way to work and, on that chance encounter, began investigations that brought millions into the public purse. It is true that they were occasionally obsessive (Sally Ho started fifteen investigations on people with stone lion statues in their gardens) but mostly they were not vindictive. They investigated major corporations, multi-nationals with transfer pricing arrangements and off-shore tax havens. They went hunting for Slutzkin schemes, Currans, and sham charities. This is the work for which Alistair recruited Maria Takis and her best friend Gia Katalanis.

It had not been a rat-maze then. Alistair had had all the

partitioning ripped out. There had been no careful grading of offices and desks but a clamorous paddock of excitable men and women who lived and breathed taxation. They worked long hours and drank too much red wine and smoked too many cigarettes and had affairs or ruined their marriages or did both at the same time. More than half of them came from within the Taxation Office but many – those with new degrees like Gia and Maria – came from outside it, and thereby leap-frogged several positions on the promotion ladder without sensing that the old Taxation Office was a resilient and unforgiving organism. Had they realized what enemies they were making it is unlikely they would have acted any differently – they were not cautious people. They were sometimes intolerant, always impatient, but they were also idealists and all of them were proud of their work and they were not reluctant to identify themselves at dinner parties as Tax Officers.

It was Alistair who created this climate, and for a long time everyone in the Taxation Office – even those who later revealed themselves to be his enemies – must have been grateful to him. It was something to be able to reveal your profession carelessly.

It was Alistair who said, on national television, that being a Tax Officer was the most pleasant work imaginable, like turning a tap to bring water to parched country. It felt wonderful to bring money flowing out of multi-national reservoirs into child-care centres and hospitals and social services. He grinned when he said it and his creased-up handsome face creased up some more and he cupped his hands as if cool river water were flowing over his big, farmer's fingers and it was hard to watch him and not smile yourself. This was one half of Alistair's great genius – that he was good on television. He sold taxation as a public good.

The Taxation Office had never had a television star before, so it was not surprising that Alistair would be envied and resented because of it nor – when the political forces against him succeeded – that he would be treated spitefully in defeat. What was less expected was that the bureaucracy would punish his lover almost as severely, more severely in one way, for Alistair's office, although much smaller and no longer in the power corner, was at least properly carpeted and had all of its shelving and wiring correctly installed.

'Oh, the *bastards*,' said Gia when she stood at the doorway of

Maria's office. 'The unmitigated petty little bastards.'

There was still wiring running across the floor from the computer to the black skirting board which was meant to hide it. There were no shelves. There were books and papers stacked on the floor. The only filing cabinet was grey and it was littered with sawdust, aluminium off-cuts, a hammer and a chisel.

'They fixed the modem,' Maria said. 'Gia, I don't care. I'm never here.'

Gia picked up a tradesman's dustpan and began to sweep the floor.

'It's not the point,' she said. She picked up metal shavings and a little block of hardwood and dropped them in the pan. 'What I can't believe is that anyone would hate you. It's not as if you were arrogant. It's not as if you were ever anything but lovely to everyone. Whatever fix Alistair is in, it's nothing to do with you.'

'It's to do with all of us,' Maria said. 'We should all be ashamed that he should be treated the way he is.'

Gia did not comment. She thought the great man of principle was a coward and a creep. He spent his days behind his ASO 9 desk in a poky little office across the hall. He now had nothing to do, except administer a division which no longer existed. All he was doing was reading nineteenth-century novels and waiting for his $500,000 superannuation while Maria and her child faced a hostile future you could optimistically call uncertain.

'Does he talk to you now?' Gia began to sweep the little coloured pieces of electrician's cable into the dustpan.

'He never didn't talk to me,' Maria said, 'and don't start that.' She wanted to leave the office and get on with it.

'Is he nice to you?' Gia asked, sweeping stubbornly.

'Gia, I don't just want to stand here. Let's just do it, quickly. Please.'

'You think I want to hang around here?' Gia emptied the dustpan into the wastebin and started wiping the dust off the books with a Kleenex tissue. 'Is he paying for anything?'

'This baby is my mistake, not his. If you want to be mad at someone, be mad at me. Now I need to get into Max Hoskins's office.'

'Sure.'

'You said you could unlock the doors.'

'Only the front door, only the lift to the floor.'

'O.K.'

Maria picked up the hammer from the top of the filing cabinet and walked off down the hall. By the time Gia found her she had fitted the claw beneath Max Hoskins's door and was levering upwards. 'Kick it,' she said.

'No,' said Gia, out of breath. 'We can't do this.'

'You hold the hammer. Push it down.'

Gia sighed and held the hammer and Maria slammed her shoulder hard against the door.

'Careful. I don't want you to go into labour.'

'Again.'

This time the door ripped open.

'This is break and entry,' Gia said, rubbing at the splintered wood at the base of the door. 'This is not some prank. This is like a violation . . . If you want to punish Alistair, you should do something to hurt him, not you. You need this job.'

'*This is nothing to do with Alistair.* I'm just damned if I'm going to let the department make me into someone I'm not. Gia . . . please . . . I need to get at Max's terminal and then we'll go back to the Brasserie and I'll buy you a glass of champagne. If you want to wait for me there, that's fine, really.'

'Just hurry, O.K.'

Gia watched from the doorway as Maria took out Max Hoskins's Day Book and flipped it open. He had a standard ASO 7 office with a green-topped desk, a leather-bound desk diary, a view to the north, two visitor's chairs. Only a tortoiseshell comb left on top of the computer terminal was non-standard and it had an unpleasant personal appearance like something found on the bedside table of someone who had died.

'I got stuck with him,' Maria said, 'at that barbecue at Sally Ho's place. He complained to me about all the terrible problems of running a department. You know, the way they changed his access code each week and he could never remember it. You know what he does? He writes it down. He writes his access number in his day book, back to front or something.'

Maria flipped on the computer terminal and punched the numbers into it.

The terminal stayed closed.

'Well,' Gia said, 'I guess that's it.'

'You go,' Maria said. 'I'll get it. It'll be these digits plus one, or the entire sequence back to front.'

Gia could see the reflection of the screen on the polished wall behind Maria's back. She could see the flashing panel on the screen which read *Access Denied*.

'It can't be too hard,' Maria said. 'He's so dull.'

'Dull but *exceptionally* secretive. Come on, please. Don't do this to me, Maria. We can go to jail for this. You don't even care who these Catchprices are. I mean, what's the principle? I don't get it.'

'We'd both be a lot happier if you went back to doing what you believed in. I'm subtracting 1 from each digit.'

'Maria, damn you, don't torture me – I'm your *friend*.'

'I'm subtracting 2.'

'Don't do a poker machine on me,' wailed Gia. 'I'll never forgive you for that club in Gosford. Two hours with the creep breathing over your shoulder.'

'We're in.'

Maria rose from the keyboard with her hands held high above her head. 'See! See! *Access Records. Add New Records. Edit Records.* We're in. We can edit.'

Maria was the worst typist in the world. This was why Gia made herself walk into the office. She only sat at the keyboard because she wanted to get out quickly. She called up *Edit Records*. 'How do you spell it?'

'C a-t-c-h-li-p-r-i-c-e.'

'File number?'

'Left it in the car. Call them all up. There. That one. Catchprice Motors.'

The last two entries were a record of Mrs Catchprice's call alerting the department to irregularities and a File Active designation dated for this morning when Maria had left to begin her audit in Franklin.

Gia went through the file deletion procedure. She took it to the penultimate step where the screen was flashing *Delete Record Y/N*.

'They'll see the broken door,' Gia said.

'If there's no file, there's no job. Hit it.'

Maria leaned across Gia and hit the Y key herself. The screen lost all its type. It turned solid green. A single cursor began to flash and the terminal began to emit a loud, high-pitched buzz.

'Run,' said Gia.

Maria did not argue. She ran as well as she could run with the weight of her pregnancy. The air was dull and hot and the corridors were heavy with a dull, plastic smell like the inside of a new electrical appliance. Gia tried to go down the stairs. ('They'll get us. Jam the elevator.') Maria pulled her into the lift. 'I don't want to use my key,' said Gia, her little chin set hard and her eyes wide.

'Use it,' said Maria, panting. 'The keys can't be coded.'

'Are you sure?'

'Of course not.'

The lift doors opened. The foyer was empty. Gia walked briskly from the building with her head down. Maria waddled just behind her, red in the face and out of breath. Did they imagine themselves being filmed? Yes, they did. They walked up the hill in Hunter Street to the car. They did not say a word. They drove back to the Brasserie and parked behind Gia's car.

'We're in a lot of trouble,' Gia said.

'No we're not,' Maria insisted. 'We're not in any trouble at all.'

'You're going to tell me why, aren't you?' Gia blew her nose.

'Yes,' Maria grinned. 'I am.'

It was midnight. It was summer. The windows were down. You could smell jasmine among the exhaust fumes of the Darlinghurst bus. Maria wondered what she was going to say next.

27

Maria's father was angry at the street she lived in. He spat at it and scuffed at its paspalum weeds with his half-laced boots. He hit the stone retaining wall outside Elizabeth Hindmath's with his aluminium stick and lost the rubber stopper off the end. The rubber stopper rolled down the street, bouncing off the cobblestones, and finally lost itself in the morning-glory tangle opposite Maria's cottage.

'See, see,' George Takis cried triumphantly, pointing his stick. 'See.'

He meant the street was too steep for a woman with a baby.

'Forty-five degrees,' he said, 'at least.'

It was nothing like forty-five degrees, but she did not contradict him. She did not point out that the streets of Letkos were far steeper and rougher than this one where she now lived in Sydney, that she herself had been pushed in an ancient German pram up streets steeper and rougher than the one that caused her father this upset – it was not the street he was upset with – it was the pregnancy. If he had articulated his anger honestly, he would have lost her. He was newly widowed and already had one daughter who would not speak to him, so he was angry with the street instead. It was too narrow, too steep. The drainage was bad and the cobbles were slippery. If she needed an ambulance they could never get it down there.

'You live here, you need good brakes. What sort of brakes it got?' He meant the pram. He wiped some dry white spittle from the corner of his lips and looked at her accusingly, his dark eyebrows pressed down hard upon his black eyes.

'I don't have one,' she said. She did not want to think about the pram. She did not want to think about what life was going to be like.

He sighed.

'I work,' she said. 'Remember.'

'You're not going to know what's hit you, you know that? You don't know what will happen to you. You get in trouble, you just stay in trouble. Always. Forever.'

'Shut up, Ba-ba.'

'You come home from the hospital, how are you going to buy a pram then? You need to have everything bought beforehand.'

'Who told you that? Mrs Hellos?'

'No one,' he said, hitting at the Williamsons' overgrown jasmine with his stick. 'I talk to no one.' He paused. 'I was reading the magazines at the barber's.'

'About babies, Ba-Ba? In a barber's shop magazine?'

'I bought it,' he said, fiddling with the button on his braces.

'Ba-Ba, this doesn't help me. Really. I know I must seem terrible to you, but it doesn't help.'

'Maria, come with me, I'll buy you a nice one. Come on. I'll buy it for you.' She could not really be angry with him. She did not need to be told how her pregnancy hurt him and excited him, how he struggled with it, how he loved her. They went shopping for a pram at Leichhardt Market Town and he got angry about prices instead, and afterwards she cooked him the noodles and keftethes which his wife had made for him three times a week for forty years, and afterwards, when it was dark, Maria drove him home to his house in Newtown, slipping into Greek territory like a spy in a midget submarine.

At midnight on the night she had failed to delete the Catchprice file from the computer, Maria felt George Takis's anger at the street might have some basis outside of his own shame. She parked her car up on Darling Street and then began the long walk down the steep lane.

She was tired already. She was heavy and sore and this was a street for a single woman with a flat stomach and healthy back. It was a street you walked down arm in arm with a lover, stumbling, laughing after too much wine, your vagina moist and warm and your legs smooth from waxing. This was so unsexy, and difficult. So endless.

She walked past the fallen stone wall at Elizabeth Hindmath's house. The rocks had tumbled out on to the street just as George Takis had said they would. The path was slippery with moss and lichen and Maria stepped very carefully. There was a movement in her womb like a great bubble rising and rolling – but not breaking – and it made her exclaim softly and put her hand on her rising stomach.

Sometimes at night she would lie on her back and watch the baby move around her stomach, watch its ripples, and guess its limbs, and although she would always try to do this fondly, with wonder, she would often end up in tears. She knew her fondness was a fake.

The moon was full and the air was heavy with honeysuckle and jasmine. Someone was playing Country music in a house down the street. There was a smell of oil in the air – at least she thought it was oil – which seemed to come from the container ships at the bottom of the hill.

She did not realize that the Country music was coming from her house until she was right outside it. Then she saw the small red light – the ghetto blaster – in the centre of her own front steps. The hair stood on her neck.

'Don't you recognize a tax-payer when you see one?' a male voice said.

Maria walked straight on.

Every Tax Inspector knows these stories: the mad 'client', whose

130

business you have destroyed, who seeks you out and beats you or puts dog-shit in your letter box. She kept on walking with her breath held hard in her throat. The cassette player turned off with a heavy thunk.

A woman called: 'We didn't think you'd be out so late. Being pregnant.'

Maria stopped a little distance off and stared into the shadow of her own veranda. She could see the axe she had left leaning against the stack of firewood.

'Are you going to ask us in?' the woman said. Her voice sounded thin, stretched tight between apology and belligerence.

'Maybe', Maria said, 'we could all meet for a cup of coffee in the morning.'

There was a light on at number 95, but it was twenty metres away down hill and the lane was so slippery with moss it would be dangerous to run.

'We've got to work tomorrow.' It was a teenage boy. She could see his hair – shining white as a knife in the night. 'We've got customers to attend to.'

A cowboy boot shifted out of the shadow into the white spill from the street light.

'Mrs McPherson?' she asked.

The boy with the blond hair stood and walked down off the concrete steps.

'Benjamin Catchprice,' he said, extending his hand. 'We've been waiting two hours.'

'Fuck you.'

'Woooo,' said Benny, dancing back, grinning, fanning his hands, 'language.'

'You scared me shitless, you little creep,' Maria said. 'Who gave you my address? What right do you think you have to come here in the middle of the night?'

'We're sorry about that,' said Cathy McPherson. She was holding a goddam guitar – standing like a giantess blocking the access to the veranda, holding a guitar, wearing a cowgirl suit, her great strong legs apart as if it was her house, not Maria's. 'Really, we're sorry. We really didn't mean to frighten you. It wasn't the middle of the night when we got here.'

'Mrs McPherson,' said Maria. 'Don't you realize how prejudicial it is for you to be here?'

Cathy McPherson stepped down off the step. 'I'd be obliged,' she said, 'if I could use your toilet.'

28

Cathy was in this ridiculous position because she had done what *Benny* had said. She could not stand being told what to do by anyone, and she was here because *Benny* told her to be there – little frightened, crying Benny whom she used to take into bed and soothe to sleep – Benny who ground his teeth – Benny who wet his bed – Benny who did so badly at school she had to take him to Special Needs to have his I.Q. tested.

Now the alcohol had worn off and she was following the Tax Inspector into her house holding her guitar. She knew right away this woman had no personal connection with Benny. He had dreamed it. He had manufactured it inside his head.

Benny came behind her carrying his cassette player. He was smiling, not *at* anything or *for* anything, but smiling like an evangelist on television. He had been like this already when he had appeared in front of her. That was at ten o'clock and she had had a row with Howie about all the songs he had copyrighted 'Big Mack', and she had been sitting up drinking Scotch and Coke by herself because she was upset – about her mother, about the tax audit, about the ownership of songs she had written but now might not own, about the shambles she had made of her life – and Benny crept up the stairs – she had The Judds' version of 'Mr Pain' playing really loud – and gave her such a fright. He just appeared in the kitchen in front of her and spoke. She nearly shat herself.

He said, 'What are you doing to control your destiny?'

As if he read her mind.

He stood before her in his fancy suit and folded his hands in front of his crotch. The hands were even more amazing than the suit. She could not help staring at them – so white and clean like they had been peeled of history.

His hair shone like polyester in the neon light and when he spoke, it was in a language not his own – his mother's perhaps (although who could remember after all this time how Sophie spoke?). In any case, it was not the language of a problem child, not someone whose I.Q. you worry about.

He said: 'I can take you to talk to the Tax Inspector.'

Normally she would have poured him a drink and tried to talk him out of it, whatever the latest 'it' was. But she was dazzled, no other word for the experience. She turned off The Judds.

He said: 'Her name is Takis. There are only three in the phone book and I've ruled out the other two. She's not back yet because I've been ringing her every twenty minutes to check.' He wiped some perspiration from his lip with a handkerchief with a small gold brand-name still stuck in the corner.

She had sipped some more of her Scotch. Howie always said the Coke killed the Scotch but she could taste it. 'Ben, what's happened to you?'

'Getting fired was the best thing ever happened to me,' he said. She started to say sorry – and she was sorry – it was the worst thing she'd ever had to do – but he held up his hand to stop her. 'I've come to repay the favour,' he said.

She pushed out a chair for him but he would not sit. He grasped the back of the chair with his hands and rocked it back and forth.

'You can see I've changed?'

'You could have been your Mum,' she said.

He nodded his head and smiled at her. His eyes held hers. They were as clear as things washed in river water. 'We all possess great power,' he said. Jesus Christ – he gave her goose-bumps.

'Get your guitar,' he said. Not 'please' or 'would you mind', just 'get your guitar'.

Later she told Howie: 'It was like your dog stood up and talked to you. If the dog said get your guitar, you would. Just to see what happened next.' She lied about dog. She did not think dog at all. What she was thinking of was that holy picture where the angel appears to Mary. Only later she said dog.

She sneaked into the bedroom where Howie was asleep, straight up and down on his back – taught himself to do it in a narrow bed. She got down the Gibson. She brought it back into the kitchen and he was trying to unplug the ghetto blaster from over the sink. He had all the power cords tangled – toaster, kettle, blender.

'Benny, I don't know this is smart,' she said.

'What's smart? Waiting here so you get busted?' He pulled the ghetto blaster cord clear of the mess and wound it round his wrist.

133

'Spending the rest of your life stuck here paying off the tax bill? You want to stay here till you die?'

She saw it. She felt it. Some tight band clamped around her stomach.

'The Tax Inspector *likes* me,' he said. 'That's the key to everything.'

'You talked to her?'

'It's personal. We're going to call on her in a personal capacity. Come on Cathy – she's kind. She's a very kind person.'

'She sure doesn't feel kind about me.'

'You have the power,' Benny insisted. 'I'll introduce you properly. She is going to see who you are. We are going to show her your life.'

'My life?'

'Our lives have power,' he said. 'You're an artist. What was it Ernest Tubb wrote to you?'

'Oh, Ernest Tubb . . .'

'You have the talent to . . .?'

'The *ability* to change the rhythms of the human heart.'

'Right. Ability. Plus: she's pregnant. She's full of milk.'

'Benny,' Cathy smiled, 'there's no milk till there's a baby.'

'O.K.' Benny said impatiently. 'Forget that bit. Once she understands the consequences of her actions, she'll go easy on you. Sing her a song. Show her who you are. You've got to sell her. You've got to demonstrate what's at stake here. Come with me,' he said.

And she did.

But now the alcohol had worn off and she felt sour and dehydrated and she just wanted to apologize. She stood on one side of the Tax Inspector's neat white kitchen, filled with shame. Maria Takis was holding a shining metal kettle. Cathy admired 'nice things' although she did not own many and the obvious quality of the kettle, its good taste, its refinement, the sort of shop it must have come from, all this somehow made the intrusion worse. Cathy felt coarse and vulgar. She had not even washed her hair before she left.

'Ms Takis,' she said, although she hated to hear herself say 'Ms'. 'I think I've made a big mistake. I'm sorry. But I was really horrible to you this morning and it's been on my mind and I just wanted to say how sorry I was. I know you've got your job to do.'

134

She said she was sorry. She made herself small. But there was no relief. All it did was make the woman look at her as if she was a frigging ant.

Cathy McPherson came back from the bathroom smelling of Elizabeth Arden and whisky. She wore her chamois leather cowgirl suit with high-heel boots with spurs. Her waistcoat cut into her big fleshy arms. She stood in the kitchen doorway with her huge guitar and her little white hands and sent confusing signals with her eyes.

The guitar was a big instrument – too big to take visiting, but presumably too valuable to leave in a parked car. Cathy McPherson leaned against the doorway, on the hallway side, fiddling with the little mother-of-pearl guitar picks which were wedged in beside the tuning pegs like ticks on a cattle dog's ear.

If this had been an investigation Maria had wanted to pursue, this would have been the turning point. Someone was about to divulge some information or to try to cut a deal, but Maria did not want more information about the Catchprices. She wanted them out of her house, out of her life and if this was a confession, she did not want to hear it.

She said: 'You didn't need to drive all this way to say sorry.'

'But we didn't come to say we were *sorry*.' It was the boy again, back from wherever he had been in her house. He slid around the edge of the guitar and stood with his back to the refrigerator. His hair looked as hard and white as spun polymer.

'Would you mind staying right here?' she said. She shifted her kettle on to the hottest and fastest of her gas jets. When she looked up, his eyes were on hers.

'Mrs McPherson is going to sing to you,' he said.

Maria looked at the woman.

'I'm really a singer,' she said. Her face was burning red.

The boy came into the kitchen and plugged the ghetto blaster into the power point next to the kettle.

'We're people, not numbers,' he said. He would not take his eyes off her eyes. She thought: this is the sort of thing that happens in Muslim countries – these dangerous doe-eyed boys with their heads filled with images of western whores in negligees. She looked away from him to his aunt.

'So you would like to sing to me in the hope it will affect your tax assessment?'

Cathy McPherson had the good grace to look embarrassed, but her nephew buttoned the jacket of his suit without taking his eyes away from Maria's. 'We think you're human,' he said in that nasal accent as sharp and cold as metal. He moistened his lips and smiled. For Chrissakes – he was coming on to her. 'We want to talk to you like humans.'

'O.K.,' said Maria. 'I'm going to make one cup of tea, then you're going to sing, and then you're going to get out of here because I've really had enough for one day.'

'Fair enough,' he said. 'We're going to present two songs.'

'You can have one.'

'One is fine.' Benny unbuttoned his suit coat. 'You can have recorded or live.'

'I don't care what it is. Just do it.'

'You'd like live?'

'Sure, live.'

'O.K., that will be live, then.'

He was one of those people whose personal space was too large, who could be too close to you when you were a metre from them.

She waited for the kettle to boil, staring at it like she might have stared at the floor numbers in an elevator. When the kettle boiled she gave them tea bags of English Breakfast tea but, for herself, an infuser filled with the foul-tasting Raspberry Leaf which Gia's naturopath said would strengthen the uterine muscles and promote a quick labour.

The Catchprices jiggled their tea bags in silence and dropped them into the kitchen tidy she held open for them and then she shepherded them into the living-room.

Maria sat down on the rocking chair her father had bought for her and put her feet up on the foot stool. She began to see the comic aspect of her 'information' and began to observe details of the Catchprices' dress in order to tell the story properly to Gia.

'Is this going to be too loud?' she asked.

'If you're worried about noise,' Benny said, 'we can play you the demo tape.'

136

'It's just acoustic,' Cathy was trying to fit her bottom on the window-ledge opposite. She strummed a few chords, stopped, started again, and then stood up. 'Ms Takis,' she said, 'it would be more polite if I sang sitting down, but I'm damned if I can get myself comfortable.'

'Fine,' Maria said.

'Thank you.' Cathy tapped her boot three times. The floor shook. It was an old wooden Balmain cottage which was badly built even in 1849.

You were a married man I know, she sang. The voice got Maria in the belly. It was raw, almost croaky, and way too loud for this street, this time of the morning.

I shouldn't have begun.

Cathy McPherson changed physically. She became taller, straighter. The athletic armature of her body revealed itself and she rocked and rolled and showed a sexual confidence which was previously unimaginable. There was something happening in those belligerent little eyes which made her as soft as a cat rubbing itself against your leg.

> *You told me you'd always love your wife*
> *I shouldn't have begun.*

Thirty seconds ago she was big and blowzy like a farmer's wife, or someone with fat burns on their sallow skin, working in a fish 'n' chip shop at 2 o'clock in the morning. Her arms were still plump. Her belly still pressed against her leather skirt, but now you could not look at her without believing that this was someone who made love passionately – she was a sexual animal.

> *But it was late at night and I was lonely*
> *I didn't know I'd fall in love*
> *and now you've gone and left me baby*
> *with a freeway through my heart.*

She occupied Maria's living room like a compressor unit or some yellow-cased engine so loud and powerful that it demanded you accommodate yourself to it. This was what Maria did not like about it – she felt bullied on the one hand and seduced on the other. Also: the subject matter was discomforting. It seemed too close for coincidence.

> *Trucks are running*
> *through the freeway in my heart*
> *Twisting sheets*
> *All this noise and pain*
> *Ten retreads hissing*
> *through the driving rain.*

Just as the second verse was about to start, the singer saw Maria's face and stopped.

Maria said: 'Thank you.'

Cathy shrugged.

Maria said: 'How do you think this could affect my work?'

Cathy opened her mouth, then shut it, frowned, rubbed her bedraggled hair. 'This doesn't make a pinch of difference to anything does it?'

'No, it can't.'

'Fine.'

'What the hell could I do?' said Maria, angrily. 'What sort of corrupt person do you want me to be? Are you going to try to bribe me now?'

'I'm sorry.' And Cathy was sorry; at the same time she was angry. She was sorry she had placed herself in such a foolish position.

'If I cared more for Country music I could say something intelligent about your song.'

'You don't like Country music?'

'Not a lot, no.'

'I think you do,' Cathy said. 'But you're like your sort of person.'

Maria did not ask what her sort of person was.

'You are moved by it. Allow me to know that. Allow me to judge what an audience is feeling. I saw you: you were moved by it. What did you tell yourself about it? *Oh I mustn't be moved. This is masochistic*? Women like you always say "masochistic" when they feel things.'

'O.K., I was moved.'

'You're saying that but what you're trying to *tell* me is that you weren't moved at all.' Cathy said, sitting down. She sat on the edge of the sofa where Alistair and Maria used to make love. He used to kneel on the carpet there and she put her legs around his neck and opened up to him full of juice – she would get so wet all her thighs would be shining in the firelight and now there was a damn Catch-price sitting there holding a Gibson by the neck and another one watching and they were like burglars in her life.

'It doesn't matter,' Cathy said. 'I'm a real banana to be here but I'll tell you something for your future reference – Country music is about those places people like you drive past and patronize. You come to Franklin and you've decided, before you even get off the F4, that we are all retards and losers – unemployed, unemployable. Then you find we have an art gallery and some of us actually read books and you are *very impressed*. What you've just been listening to is poetry, but all you could hear was, oh, Country & Western. What I like about Country music is that it never patronizes anyone, not even single mothers.'

'We're not numbers,' Benny said.

Cathy looked up at Benny as if she had forgotten he was there. She sighed, but said nothing. She needed something stronger than a cup of tea.

'We're people,' said Benny.

Cathy looked at him again. He was not wilted or defeated. He was standing upright in the corner. Good for you, she thought. 'You go ahead with this audit of yours,' she told the Tax Inspector, 'and I'll be stuck in that shit-heap for the rest of my damn life just keeping them all alive. You go ahead, I'll never get to sing except in pubs within a 100 kilometre radius. I should have just walked out when I had the business healthy. "Guilt-free". That's a song I wrote. "Guilt-free", but if we get in strife with the tax, then I'm lumbered with the responsibility of a mother who hates me and a brother who refuses to sell a motor car because he wants to punish his Daddy for being a creep.'

'Don't,' Maria said. 'It doesn't help.'

'I'm going to lose my band and my damn name,' said Cathy, her lower lip quivering.

Maria stood up. She hoped the woman would not cry. 'Catch-price Motors is in the computer with an "active" designation,' she said gently. 'Even if I wanted to, I couldn't take it out.'

'I believe you,' Cathy stood up. 'Come on, Benny. Enough's enough.'

Now they were really going, Maria let herself look at the boy again. He caught her eye and did up his suit jacket and smiled. He did have an extraordinary face. If you saw it in a magazine you would pause to admire it – its mixture of innocence and decadence was very sexy – in a magazine.

'I'll see you around,' he said.

'You'll see her in the morning,' said his aunt. 'Which is now.'

'Yes, which is now.' Maria stood.

She shepherded the singer along the corridor to the front door. In a moment they would be gone. The boy was behind her. Maria was so convinced that he was about to put a guiding hand on the small of her back that she put her own hand there to push it off.

At the front door, Cathy McPherson turned, and stopped. She was solid, immovable. She looked at Maria with her little blue eyes which somehow connected to the heart that had written the words of that song. Not 'small' eyes or 'mean' eyes, but certainly demanding and needful of something she could not have expressed. Her breath smelt of alcohol. She said: 'When I was thirty-two I was ready to go out on the road. I mean, I wasn't a baby any more. Then my father died, and my mother sort of made it impossible for me to leave.'

Maria could feel the boy behind. She could feel him like a shadow that lay across her back. She was too tired to listen to this confession but the eyes demanded that she must. They monitored her response.

'I can't tell you how my mother did it, but she made me stay. I was the one who was going to save the business. And I did save it and then my mother decided I was getting too big for my boots and she turned on me, and I would have gone then, except I could not walk away and see it crash. I'm a real fool, Ms Takis, a prize number one specimen fool. If you fine us, I'll be stuck there. I won't be able to leave them.'

It would have seemed false to be her comforter and her tormentor as well. So even when she began to cry all Maria did was offer her a Kleenex and pat her alien shoulder. She wanted her to leave the house. She took the guitar from her and together the three of them walked up Datchett Street.

At Darling Street she shook hands first with Cathy McPherson and then she turned to the boy. He said: 'You can't just abandon us, you know.'

Cathy said: 'Come on, Benny.'

'No, she understands me. She's got a heart. She understands what I'm saying.'

'I'm sorry,' Cathy McPherson said. She grabbed his arm, and pulled him up the street. Maria could hear them hissing at each other as she walked back to her front door.

Tuesday

At Catchprice Motors they called a potential customer a 'Prospect', and as the big black cumulus clouds rolled in from the west and the first thunder of the day made itself heard above the pot-hole thump of the Fast-Mix Concrete trucks heading north towards the F4, Benny hooked a live one. It was a Tuesday, the second day of Benny's new life.

He found the Prospect there at eight-thirty, crunching around in the gravel beside the Audi Quattro. Benny made no sudden movements, but when the Prospect found the Quattro's door was locked, Benny was able to come forward and unlock it for him.

'Thank you,' the Prospect said.

'No worries,' Benny said, holding the black-trimmed door open and releasing a heady perfume of paint and leather. The driver's seat made a small expensive squeak as it took the Prospect's weight. The white paper carpet-protector rumpled beneath grey slip-ons whose little gold chains made Benny take them for Guccis. The guy folded his hands in his lap and asked to be given 'the selling points'. Benny had not slept all night – he had been working on one more angle in his campaign to seduce the Tax Inspector – but now all of his gritty-eyed tiredness went away and the fibreglass splinters in his arms stopped itching and he squatted on the gravel beside the open door and talked about the Quattro for five minutes without lying once. He watched the Prospect as he spoke. He waited for signs of boredom, some indication that he should shift the venue, alter the approach, but the guy was treating this like information he just had to have. After twenty minutes, Benny's knees were hurting and he had run out of stuff to say.

Then the Prospect got out of the Quattro. Then he and Benny stood side by side and looked at it together. The Prospect was five foot six, maybe five foot seven – shorter than Benny, but broader in the shoulders. He played sport, you could see it in the way he balanced on the balls of his feet. He had a broad nose, almost like a boxer's, but you could not call him ugly. He was good-looking,

in fact. He had a dark velvet suit and a small tuft of black hair –
you could not call it a beard – sitting underneath his lower lip.
He was twenty-two, maybe twenty-five years old, and he had
Guccis on his feet and he was looking up at Benny – what a wood
duck!

'So,' he said. 'When do we do the test drive?'

'Hey,' said Benny, 'don't panic.' The truth was: he was
unlicensed. They would kill him if they saw him demo this unit.
He was going to do it none the less, but gentlee gentlee catchee
monkey – he had to wait for Mort who was sitting in a
Commodore by the front office. He was hunched over in the seat
reading out the engine functions on the computerized diagnostic
device – the Compu-tech.

'The thing you've got to appreciate about an Audi,' Benny said,
'is nothing is rushed. They rush to make all this G.M. shit, but not
an Audi.'

'I have something for you,' the Prospect said.

Benny did not notice what he had. He was watching Mort
unplug the Tech II and put it in his back pocket.

The Prospect was occupied with a separate matter – withdrawing a sleek silver envelope from his inside jacket pocket.

'Here,' he said.

He held it out to Benny.

Benny took the envelope. *What do you want?*

The Prospect smiled. Benny was spooked by his black eyes.

'You have good taste in ties,' the Prospect said. 'I'm sure you
will like this one.'

The envelope held a black and silver and green tie.

Benny felt a tingling at the back of his neck.

'Silk,' said Sarkis.

Benny looked up at the eyes and then down at the tie.

'I'll buy it,' he said. He had a boner. He did not want a boner.
He did not want a gift or come in his mouth, but the man's eyes
were like a sore tooth he could not keep from touching.

'No, it's a sample,' said Sarkis. 'I made it.'

Benny smiled at the Prospect. He wet his lips and smiled.

'You make ties?' he asked.

'There are no good ties in Australia,' said Sarkis, who was as
impressed with Benny's haircut as Benny had been with Sarkis's

146

shoes. You needed to be making big money to maintain a cut like that. 'There's a big market waiting for these ties. What I need is the capital to do it in a bigger way. Here . . . have it . . . It's a gift.'

The man held the packet out with one hand. The other hand he kept behind his back. He flexed his knees and looked out at the street trees with their pretty red-dotted lichen-encrusted leaves and their hairy, mossy trunks. They were side by side. Benny could feel the space between them.

'A present? Just for nothing?'

'For good luck,' said Sarkis, 'on my first day here.'

'First *day*?'

'I'm sorry . . .' Sarkis said, suddenly confused.

'First day? Come on, what are you saying to me. What are you proposing?'

'Working here,' said Sarkis. 'I'm sorry. I was hired to work here. She said someone would come and fill me in.'

'Got it,' said Benny. He felt a pain in his stomach. He watched his father nurse the Commodore slowly out along the brown-puddled service road. All the fibre-glass splinters in his arms began to itch. 'Who hired you? Mrs McPherson?'

'The owner hired me,' said Sarkis. 'The old lady.'

This was exactly how Howie got into Catchprice Motors and it made Benny get a freezing feeling behind his eyes. 'Oh shit,' he laughed. 'You got hired by *Grandma*.' He tapped his forehead and rolled his eyes.

'She's got the keys,' Sarkis said. 'I saw her.'

'She's got the keys because she's got the keys – she doesn't own the business.'

'She told me that she did.'

'Well she doesn't. It's owned by my auntie and my Dad and me. Not even my uncle Jack has got shares. He's a property developer in town, but he doesn't work here so he can't have shares. Even my brother', Benny said, 'could have had a future here . . .'

Then he saw the Tax Inspector's Colt making a right-hand turn across the traffic to come into Catchprice Motors.

'I've got to tell you,' Sarkis said, 'I never sold cars before.'

Benny groaned.

'So if you can help me . . .' Sarkis rubbed his fingers together, indicating money passing hands . . .

'What do you mean?'

'You help me, I'll split my commission.'

'We don't have commissions,' Benny said. 'This is a family business.' But he was mollified by the offer. 'This is a fucking minefield,' he said. 'It's a snake-pit. They all hate each other. None of them can sell a car. If you work here, you'd have to work for me.'

'Sure,' said Sarkis. 'Sure, O.K.'

'We've got a lot of stock to move,' Benny explained. 'We've got a fucking enormous tax bill.' He looked at Sarkis. 'What makes you think you can sell cars . . . what's your name?'

'Sarkis.' He hesitated. 'They call me Sam,' he told this kid. He hated how it sounded. The kid must be seven years younger and he was saying, 'Call me Sam'.

'Sam? Listen Sam. The first thing you've got to know is that the car is not the issue. The car is only the excuse. It's the F&I you make the money from. No one understands that. The kings of this business are the F&I men. There's no one in Catchprice Motors knows an F&I man from their arsehole. Someone says to my old man, "I need insurance," he picks up the fucking phone and dials the fucking insurance company for them and it costs us thirty cents and makes us nothing. You want to work here, you got to go away for five days and learn about F&I . . .'

'Sorry . . . what's F&I?'

'I've been telling you,' said Benny. 'Finance and Insurance. F&I. You stay here now, all this week, but next Monday you get on an F&I course. You learn how to use the computer, how to do the paper work. You don't need to know shit about cars. You don't need to know the difference between an Audi Quattro and a washing machine. A week from now you'll know how to sell them comprehensive insurance, disability cover, extended warranty. If that's impossible . . .'

'I'm Armenian,' said Sarkis. 'We're the best salesmen in the world.'

'Yeah, well don't go round giving people silk ties. You get people mad with you. Forget it now. Listen to me – I've got a hundred bucks and I want to buy a car from you, how are you going to do it? I mean, I come in here with a blue mohawk and a leopard-skin vest and a ring through my nose and when I've finished jerking off all I can get together is a hundred bucks . . .'

148

'You can't afford a car, sorry . . .'

'You know as much as the directors of this business.' Benny could see Cathy standing at the top of Grandma Catchprice's landing. She was waving her arms around and waving at Benny and Sarkis. 'You want to sell a car, you've got to understand finance, O.K. Listen to me,' Benny said, 'not her. You've got a hundred bucks, you want a nice car. I say to you, see that old F. J. Holden over there. I'll sell you that for a hundred bucks.'

'You call that a nice car?'

'No, I don't. Just be patient. O.K. You buy it from me for a hundred. O.K.?'

'O.K.' said Sarkis.

'O.K., now I buy it back from you at five hundred. Car hasn't even moved. What's happened?'

'You've lost money.'

'No, now you have five hundred bucks – you can afford to do business with me. You've got enough money for a deposit on a $3,500 car. I can finance it to you. I'll make good money on the sale, I'll keep on making money on the F&I. You understand me?'

'I think so,' said Sarkis.

'It takes time, don't worry,' Benny said. 'They think I'm dumb round here, I'll tell you now.' He could see Cathy lurching awkwardly down the stairs. 'But none of them appreciates this. You're getting it faster than they are. You can make two hundred grand a year in this dump, really. You believe me.'

'You want to know? I think it's a great opportunity.'

'You get this F&I under your belt, we can set this town on fire.' He turned to face Cathy who was weaving towards them. 'Just ignore this,' he told Sarkis. 'This doesn't count.'

31

Sarkis watched the chunky blonde woman in the gingham dress walk down the staircase. Her eyes were on him, he knew, and he was optimistic about the effect her presence would have on the conversation she was so obviously about to enter. At a certain distance – from the top of the fire escape to the bottom, and a metre or two onwards from there – she gave an impression of a bright blonde Kellogg's kind of normality and he hoped that she might, somehow, save him from this sleaze. But then she passed the point where there could be conjecture and he saw, even before he smelt her, that her face was puffy and her mascara was running. The smell was not the smell, as subtle as the aroma of Holy Communion, you get from a drink or two, but the deep, sour aura that comes from a long night of drinking, and it explained more readily than her high-heeled knee-high boots, the careful way she walked across the gravel.

'Who are you?' she asked Sarkis. She looked both hurt and hostile and Sarkis's strongest desire was to turn away from all this poison and walk to the sane, cloves-sweet environment of his home.

Instead he said something he had promised never to say again: 'Hi, I'm Sam Alaverdian.'

The 'Sam' did not make her like him any better. She sighed, and put her finger on the small crease at the top of her nose. 'So you're the latest candidate,' she said. 'Tell me, honey, what experience do you have?'

'He's Armenian.'

'What's that got to do with it, Benny?'

'They're the best salesmen in the world.'

'Oh shit, Benny, spare us, please. Tell me . . . what's an Armenian? Where's Armenia? You tell me.'

Obviously, Benny did not know. He stared at her as if he could vaporize her. His eyes got narrower and narrower and she stared right back at him. Sarkis did not want to work for either of them. They both stared at each other for a long time until finally, the woman shifted her ground. You could see her surrender in her shoulders before she spoke.

'I'm sorry,' she said. She put out her little white hand towards him and he stepped away from it.

'Don't give me shit about this,' he said. 'I'm saving you.'

The woman's face screwed up. She wiped her eyes and made a big black horizontal streak that went from the corner of her eye into her permed curly hair.

'I'm saving you,' Benny said again. He put out his hand to her and she took it and held it, and began to stroke the back of it. Sarkis was embarrassed but they were oblivious to him. 'I'm making it possible.'

'Honey, it was a nice try, but we can't stop the Tax Office. She's back.'

'I know she's back,' Benny said defensively. 'I *saw*. Maybe she just came to get her things . . . you won't know until you talk to her.'

'Forget it, Ben.'

'Try being positive, just for once.'

Cathy smiled and shook her head. 'Honey, you're *sixteen*.'

Sarkis did not want to interrupt. He waited until whatever process they were engaged in – Benny stroking her hand, she touching Benny's cheek – was completed. But when they brought their attention back to Sarkis, he said: 'I can sell.'

The Catchprices took their hands back from each other.

'What can you sell, Sam?'

'F&I,' Sarkis told her. From the corner of his eye he saw Benny smile. 'I'm an F&I man,' he said.

She frowned and scratched her hair. The hair was good and thick but dry and brittle from home perming. She took a Lifesaver packet from the pocket of her gingham dress, and bit off the top one.

'Please,' Benny said. 'I can use him.'

She squinted at Sarkis and frowned. 'We can't afford an F&I man.'

'You can't afford not to have one,' said Sarkis, wanting to be definite but having no idea how to be really definite, rushing her towards the idea of an F&I man while, at the same time, he dragged his own heels, anxious lest he be forced to talk any more about the alien subject.

'I'm very sorry, Sam, but my mother had no authority to hire you.'

'Don't worry about him. He's mine.'

'She made a verbal contract with me,' said Sarkis, remembering his father's argument with a builder when they first arrived in Northwood.

This made the woman stare at him very hard.

'Did she get the chance to tell you about her gelignite?'

'Yes.'

'You don't want to get involved with us, Sam.'

'I need a job.'

151

'How long you been living in Franklin?'

'Six months.'

'You better just forget it, Sam. You don't want this work. Please go away.'

'You're the one who should go away,' Benny said, very gently. 'You've got a reason to go away. We've got a reason to stay here.'

The woman looked at Benny and clenched her smudged eyes shut and opened her mouth and suffered a small convulsion or a shiver as if she might be about to weep. Then she turned and walked away across the gravel, holding out her hand to steady herself among the cars as she passed them.

32

In the gauzy rain-streaked light of Tuesday morning, Mort Catchprice became aware that there was an angel standing beside his bed. It had its back to him. It had broad shoulders and a narrow waist and on the cool white canvas of its back were wings of ball-point blue and crimson which seemed to lie like luminous silk across the skin.

In his dream he had been a river. It had been a rare and wonderful dream, to be water, to watch the light reflecting off his skin and so he came from sleep to meet the angel feeling unusually tranquil, and in the minute or so it took before he was really properly awake, he studied the wings and saw how they followed the form of the body, incorporating the collar bone, for instance, into what was clearly a tattooist's *trompe l'œil*, one which gave perfect attention to each individual feather, dissolving sensuously from crimson into blue, always quite clear, not at all ambiguous until the upper reaches of the marble-white buttocks where the feathers became very small and might be read as scales.

As he stirred and stretched, the angel turned towards him and was recognized. Then all the heavy weight of the past and present flooded back into his limbs.

He quickly saw that the tattooed wings were not the only thing his son had done to himself – he had also used a depilatory to remove any trace of body hair. His chest, his legs, his penis all had that shiny slippery look of a child just out of the bath.

It was the lack of hair that woke him properly. He understood its intention perfectly and as the blood engorged his own penis, he picked up the blue water jug beside his bed and threw it at the creature. The water spilled yet stayed suspended in mid-air like a great crystal tongue-lick – dripping diamonds suspended above the angel's dazzling white head.

The angel stepped, slowly, to one side and the jug hit the soft plaster wall and its handle penetrated the plasterboard. It did not bounce or break, but stuck there, like a trophy.

Benny gave his father a rather bruised and blaming smile. 'You're so predictable,' he said.

The crystal transformed itself into water and fell – splat – on to the floor. The alarm clock began to ring.

'Please,' Mort said. 'Please don't do this.' But even as he did say, 'please don't,' the other cunning part of his brain was saying, please, yes, one more helping.

'Well sure,' Benny sat down in the rocking-chair beside the bed and began rubbing his hands along his long shiny thighs. 'We've got some dirty habits.'

His father sat up in bed with the sheet gathered around his hairy midriff. 'Not any more we don't.'

'You know I could have you put in jail,' Benny said. 'I wish I'd known that before. Did you see that on 'Hinch at Seven' last week? They take you to the Haversham clinic and they put you in a chair and they strap this thing around your dick and show you pictures of men doing it to little boys. You get a hard-on, you're done. They call you a rock spider and chuck away the key.'

Mort threw the alarm clock. He was not play-acting. It was a heavy silver clock from Bangkok Duty-Free and it hit the boy on the chest so hard it made him rock back in the chair. The confidence left his eyes and was replaced by a baleful, burning look.

'You shouldn't have done that,' he said. 'I'm going to have to do something if you hurt me.'

Mort was already sorry, sorry because he had been brutal, sorry because he was now even more vulnerable. He could see a large red half moon showing on the boy's chest. Anybody could examine it and see what he had done. 'I'm sorry.'

'Sorry isn't enough.' Benny said, rubbing at the mark. 'You're always sorry.'

Mort knew he had to get out of there before something bad happened. He slipped out of bed with his back to Benny. He bent down by the muslin curtains looking for his underpants.

'Christ,' said Benny. 'Look at the boner.'

Mort tripped and staggered with his toes caught in his underpants. 'God help me, shut up.'

Benny was standing, grinning. 'You can't say shut up to me now. I'm an angel. You like it?' He stood and turned and wiggled his butt a little.

'You'll never get them off,' Mort said. He did not ask how much the tattoos cost. 'Where did you get the money, are you thieving again?'

Benny said: 'It's the hair, isn't it? That's what you get off on.'

Mort was trying to find the shirt and trousers he had dropped on the floor at bedtime. They were tangled with a towel and dressing gown.

'It's the hair got you stiff again? You stopped liking me when you got that stuff stuck between your teeth.'

Mort sat on the bed. 'I'm not listening to this shit. We're beyond all this now. We left it behind.'

'Oh, I'm a bad boy.' Benny made his eyes go wide. 'I made it up. It never happened.'

Mort zipped the trousers and pulled a T-shirt over his head. When his face emerged he felt all his weakness showing. 'What do you want?'

'Who was it who made me like this?'

'It's finished. We've got to get over it.'

'It's not over,' said Benny taking down his shirt from the coat hanger behind the door. 'It's never over. I think about it every day.'

'It's over for me. Benny, I've changed. I swear.'

'I've changed too,' Benny said. 'I'm an angel.'

'I'm not buying you a motor bike, forget it.'

'You don't listen. I didn't say Hell's Angel. I said, angel!'

'What the fuck does that mean?'

'Means I say to one man go and he goeth, say to another man come and he cometh.'

'That's the centurion.'

'I don't give a fuck what you call it,' said Benny.

'Don't talk to me like that.'

'I am talking to you like this. I want you to go to the Tax woman and show her your life.'

'Look,' said Mort. He sat down on the bed. 'My father did it to me. His father did it to him. You think I like being like this?'

'Just listen to me. Listen to what I say. She's a nice lady. Talk to her. That's all you've got to do. Tell her about Cacka's philosophy. Just make her responsible for you. She can't destroy us if she thinks we're decent people.'

'Benny, don't be simple.'

'Listen, I know who she is. I'm going out with her.'

'You're what?'

'I'm going *out* with her. Believe me. She's a human. She responds.'

He unbuttoned his slippery cool white shirt and returned it to the coat hanger. He hung the hanger behind the door again. He slipped off his underpants and ran his hands down his flawless hairless chest and between his thighs. 'You can't help yourself can you, Kissy? You're responding. You know I think you're shit, but you don't care.'

'I am shit,' Mort said.

'You are shit.' He hooked his finger into the top of Mort's underpants and tugged at the elastic. 'I went to her house last night. She's pregnant. Her tits are full of milk.' He let the elastic go and lay on the bed on his stomach. 'When I came back here I took the books off Granny's desk,' he rolled on his back, smiling. 'I wrapped them in a plastic bag and buried them.'

'You really think that's smart?' Mort said, but he had already stopped caring if it was smart or not.

'You want to argue with me, or you want to have some fun?'

'Benny, what's happened to you?'

'I'm an angel,' Benny said.

'What does that mean?' Mort put out a finger to feel the boy's smooth thigh.

'It means I am in control. It means everyone does what I say.'

33

He would 'show his life', sure, silly as this was. He would be a monkey for his son. You know what was weird? What was weird was he was finally an inch away from happiness.

Show his life? Bare his arse? Sure, but not like the little black-mailer imagined.

He would talk to her, sure he would. What's more: he was busting to do it. He had the day's job sheets spread out across his desk, but he could not concentrate on them. They had finally become irrelevant.

He knew nothing about tax. He could not even read the balance sheets he signed each year, but he knew enough, by Christ he did, to show his life to the Tax Inspector. He would embrace her. He would draw her towards him like a dagger, have her drive some official stake into the business, right into its rubbery, resisting heart.

Howie and Cathy were always full of blame, always had been. They could blame him for not selling. They could blame him for fuck-ups in the workshop. They presumably blamed him for Benny turning out a poof, and Johnny going to the cults, but they could not blame him for the tax investigation. They were the ones – Mr and Mrs Rock 'n' Roll – who played funny buggers with the tax.

Mort took three Codis tablets and stacked the work sheets in a pile and threw them in his filing cabinet. He came and stood in the cavernous doorway, pacing up and down just inside the drip line of the roof. When he saw the Tax Department's Mitsubishi Colt park at the end of the lane-way he put up his umbrella and walked right towards it. He filled his wide chest with air and came down the oil-stained concrete with a light-footed athlete's stride.

I'll show her my life.

The Tax Inspector was already erecting her umbrella, juggling with her papers and her case. When he saw her age, how pregnant she was, he laughed. The little bullshitter was going *out* with her?

This Tax Inspector was very, very pretty – a lovely soft wide mouth, and stern and handsome nose. He saw straightaway that she would want to walk quickly through the rain and that he was going to have to stop her. He was going to talk to her in front of the Front Office. This was what he had agreed with Benny.

You would think it would be humiliating, to be a prancing bear for your disturbed son. But actually, no. He was dancing on the edge of freedom.

'Mort Catchprice,' he said.

He had the workshop courtesy umbrella, big enough to take to the beach. He held it over her and her umbrella. She put her own umbrella down, but the rain was bouncing around their ankles. He guessed it was worse for the woman with stockings on.

Benny stood behind the glass with a strange-looking young man in a light-coloured suit. He grinned and pointed his finger at his father.

You want me to show her my life?

O.K., I touched you.

Not touched.

O.K., fucked, sucked. I made you stutter and wet your bed. Made you a liar too, quite likely. My skin responded. It's physiology. The male skin – you touch it, you get a response. Like jellyfish – you touch them, they fire out darts. The jellyfish cannot control it. There are men more sensitive than others. Is that unnatural? You hold their hand, they get a hard-on. Whose fault is that? When does that happen? If there is no reason then there is no God.

If there is a God I am not a monster.

In my great slimy shape, in my two great eyes, my dark slimy heart, I am not a monster. Was I the sort of creep who hangs round scout troops, molesting strangers?

'It must have occurred to you,' he said to the Tax Inspector, when he had introduced himself, 'that what you decide affects our whole life.'

She took a step away and put up her own umbrella again.

'Yes,' she said. 'All the time.'

Behind her back, he could see Benny winking and grinning. Benny could not hear a damn word he said.

'Does it look bad for us?' he asked.

'It looks nothing much yet,' she said. 'I'm sure you'll just be fine.'

'Oh no,' he said. 'It won't be fine.'

'Maybe you should let me discover that.'

'I don't need to. I can tell you,' he said. He was a little out of breath, but he felt great. 'Look at the salary claims for our sales manager. I'd look at that one closely.' There was thunder all around them now. The traffic on Loftus Street was driving with its headlights on. 'Plus the trade-ins. You're going to find the lack of trade-ins interesting.'

The Tax Inspector was shaking her head and frowning.

'Mr Catchprice, please . . . don't do this.'

Mort looked at Benny and saw that he was frowning too. He thought: maybe he can read my lips. He said: 'No one set out to be crooked. Not even Cathy.'

'Mr Catchprice, please.' She put out her hand as if to touch him and then something about him, some stiffness, stopped her. 'Please just relax.'

He laughed. It was a stupid laugh, a snort. He could not help it.

She looked at him oddly.

'He wants me to show you our life,' he said.

The Tax Inspector frowned at him. She had such a pretty face. Benny was right – it was a kind face, but she would kill him with a rock if she could see his soul. Every time you turn on the television, someone is saying: child sexual *abuse*. But they don't see how Benny comes to me, crawling into my bed and rubbing my dick, threatening me with jail. Is this abuse?

'Maybe I should show you the true Catchprice life?' he said. He felt half dizzy.

I am the one trying to stop this stuff and he is crawling into bed and rubbing my dick and he will have a kid and do it to his kid, and he will be the monster and they'll want to kill him. Today he is the victim, tomorrow he is the monster. They do not let you be the two at once. They do not see: it is common because it is natural. No, I am not saying it is natural, but if it is so common how come it is not natural?

The rain was pouring down now. It was spilling across the front office guttering and running down the windows like a fish shop window.

Maria Takis looked at Mort Catchprice. He was staring her directly in the eyes and his own eyes were too alive, too excited for the context. His lips trembled a little. It occurred to her he was having a mental breakdown.

34

Cathy, at ten years old, you should have seen her – a prodigy. She'd never heard of Sleepy La Beef or Boogie or Rock-a-Billy. She listened to a Frankie Laine record once and laughed at it like everybody else. She knew *Don Giovanni, Isolde, Madame Butterfly*. Her teacher was Sister Stoughton at the Catholic School. There was no yodelling there. She sang 'Kyrie eleison' at St John's at Christmas before an audience which included the Governor General. There were no 'Hound Dogs' or 'Blue Suede Shoes'. The nearest she came to that sort of thing was the jeans with rolled-up cuffs she wore to square dancing classes at the Mechanics' Institute. She did not like square dancing either, said it was like going fencing with a wireless turned up loud. She was nine years old when she said that.

But she was not spoiled, or precious. Frieda thought how lucky she was, to have this girl, not a silly girl, or a flighty girl, but a girl like her Mummy, a practical girl – pretty as all get out, with tangled curls like a blonde Shirley Temple. She did not have her mother's build. No one would ever tell her she had sparrow legs. They were sturdy, smooth-skinned. Frieda could not help touching them, feeling the solidity of them. She *was* her legs – sturdy and reliable.

At ten years old she was up before the alarm clock to make the wet mash for the chooks – wheat, pollard, bran mash and warm water, all mixed up in the same tub they took their baths in. Cathy always knew she was important in the family. She counted the eggs and helped clean them for market. Frieda encouraged her to see what she was achieving.

Mort at twelve was dreamy and difficult, had moods, would want to help one day and then not the next, wet his bed, got head lice ten times for Cathy's two. He was weepy and clingy one day and gruff and angry and would not even let you touch him the next. He was the one you could love best when he was asleep. You could not guess that he would be the one to care for her when she was old, that he would cook her stew to eat, make sure she had her rum and Coke, sit with her into the night playing cribbage.

Cathy and her Frieda had matching yellow gum boots and they would stomp around the chook yard together, before dawn. They used old kitchen forks to break the ice on the cement troughs so the hens could drink.

It was Cathy who discovered that the light they left on to keep away the foxes also made the hens lay more. She counted the eggs. She was a smart girl, not a difficult girl – you did not need to fear she was plotting some scheme against her family.

And when they moved to the car business in town it was no

different. At fourteen she knew how to record the day's petrol sales, enter the mechanics' cards on to the job cards, even reconcile the till.

Then Frieda gave Howie a job in Spare Parts, and it was as though she had brought a virus into their healthy lives. Cathy had never even heard of Rock-a-Billy. She did not know what it was. She only knew the very best sort of music, and suddenly there he was playing her this trash, and she was wearing tight skirts which did not suit her build and writing songs about things she could not possibly understand. She paid ten dollars a time to register them in the United States. Australia was not good enough. Everything Yankee was the bee's knees. She began to argue with everyone. She broke her father's heart and then she decided *she* was not happy. She decided it to win the contest. Something came into her eyes, some anger so deep you could not even hope to touch it.

Howie wore pink shirts and charcoal grey suits. He was always so meek-seeming, yes Ma-am, no Ma-am. He could fool you at first. He fooled Frieda. She defended him against Mort and Cacka – his bodgie hair cut, his 'brothel creeper' shoes. But they were right and she was wrong – Howie was really a nothing, a little throw-away with no loyalty to anyone.

But he got his way – he married Cathy and a month later he took her to inspect the old Ford Dealership and enquire about renting the premises. Frieda heard that for a fact, from Herbert Beckett down at Beckett's Real Estate – Cathy Catchprice was ready to go into competition against her own flesh and blood. Frieda never trusted the pair of them after that, never, ever.

When Cathy came up the stairs on Tuesday morning berating her for hiring a new salesman and accusing her of stealing the company books, Frieda Catchprice saw her daughter as you see into a lighted window from a speeding train, saw the pretty little girl helping her paint wood oil on the roosts, screwing her eyes up against the fumes.

Next thing she was a demon, some piece of wickedness with small blue eyes and teeth bared right up to the gum line.

'The Tax Office doesn't need the ledgers to lock you up in jail,' she said.

Frieda hugged her arms across her flat chest. She was wearing brown leather slippers and an aqua quilted dressing-gown. She had a tough look on her face – her little jaw set, her lower lip protruding, but she was scared of what Cathy would do to her, and her hand, when she brought the Salem to her lips, was trembling.

'I hired the salesman,' she said. 'That's my right, but if you think I pinched the ledgers – you've got a fertile imagination.'

But the ledgers were gone and she would not invite Cathy into her living-room to give her the pleasure of seeing this was so. So they stayed all crushed in that little annexe – Frieda, Cathy, Vish – like Leghorns in a wire cage for the train.

'You've got no right to hire an *ant*,' Cathy said, tossing her head down towards where Sam the Armenian was making friends with Benny. 'When Takis sees the books are gone she's going to go through this business like a dose of salts.'

'*I'm* not the one who should be worried,' Frieda said.

'Mum, what are you imagining?'

Frieda knew she was at a disadvantage – age – the brain losing its way, forgetting names, losing a thought sometimes in the middle of its journey. She had looked at the ledgers herself and the truth was, she could no longer follow them. She hid her weakness from her daughter, cloaking herself in sarcasm.

'I can imagine you might find the prospect of an audit frightening.'

'But you're the public officer,' Cathy said. 'You're the one who goes to jail.'

Jail! Good God. She sucked on her Salem so hard that she had nearly an inch of glowing tobacco on the end of the white paper. '*I've* never cheated anyone.'

'Would you happen to recall the renovation we claimed on the showroom?' Cathy said.

'I don't know what lies you've been telling.'

'Oh come on!'

Frieda could feel her chin begin to tremble. 'All they'll find when they investigate is who is fiddling whom.'

'It wasn't the showroom. It was your new bathroom.'

'I asked Mrs Takis to keep an eye out for me. I'll be very interested to hear what she finds out.'

'Please,' Vish said.

'You might think this Takis is cute,' Cathy said.

Frieda did not think Maria Takis was cute at all. She imagined she would turn out to be an officious bitch. That was why she took so much trouble to be nice to her.

Cathy said: 'She's a killer.'

'Good,' said Frieda. 'That's just what I want.' She jabbed out her cigarette into the plastic garbage can – it made a smell like an electrical fire. 'I want a killer.'

'You look at her eyes and nose – that'll tell you. She's one of those people who can't forgive anyone. Mummy,' Cathy said, 'she's going to destroy everything you spent your life making.'

The 'Mummy' took Frieda by surprise. Cathy was smart. She saw that. She saw how it affected her. She pushed her advantage. 'You might not be able to believe this, but I'm trying to help you.'

'It's true,' Vish said, nodding his head up and down. He was acting as though she was a horse he had to calm.

Cathy was the same. She held out her hand towards Frieda. She might have had a damn sugar lump in it, but Frieda whacked the hand away.

'Why did you do that?'

The answer was – because you think I'm simple. She did not say it. She was not entering into any arguments. You could lose an argument but it did not affect the truth. She folded her arms across her chest.

'There's something you think I did,' Cathy said. 'That's it isn't it?'

Frieda gave Cathy an icy smile.

'Why do we keep *hurting* each other?' Vish said. It was the scratchy broken voice that made his grandmother turn towards him. His mouth was loose, glistening wet and mortified. Tears were oozing from his squeezed-shut eyes, washing down his broad cheeks. 'All we ever do,' he bawled, 'is hurt each other.'

Cathy put her hand on his shoulder. 'Johnny,' she said, 'you're better staying in your ashram. You're happy there, you should just stay there.'

'He came to see me,' Frieda said. 'If you don't like it here, Cathy, why don't you go?'

'I want to go,' Cathy said. 'I want to go away and have my own life, but I have to help you first. I have to get it straight between us.'

'You've helped enough already,' Frieda said. 'Vish will help me back inside.'

As Cathy ran down the fire escape, Vish walked his grandmother

162

back into the decaying darkness of the living-room. He sat her at the table and brought her ashtray and a glass of Diet Coke with Bundaberg rum in it. He blew his nose on a tight wet ball of Kleenex.

'You don't want to let Cathy upset you,' his grandmother said.

'Everybody is miserable here, Gran. There's no one who's happy.'

She brought the full focus of her attention to him and he had the feeling that she was, finally, 'seeing' him. 'You think we should all be Hare Krishnas?' she asked.

Vish hesitated. He looked at his grandmother's face and did not know what things he was permitted to say to it.

'You want me to say what I really think?'

She made an impatient gesture with her hand.

'Let the business go to hell,' he said.

He waited but he could read no more of her reaction than had he been staring out of a window at the night.

'It's making Benny very sick,' he said. 'If you let the business go . . . I know this will sound extreme . . . I really do think you'd save his life.'

'I never wanted this business,' she said. 'Did you know that? I wanted little babies, and a farm. I wanted to grow things.' She had a slight sing-song cadence in her voice. It was like the voice she used when praying out loud in church and he could not tell if what she was saying was true or merely sentimental. 'It was your grandfather who wanted the business. I never liked the smell of a motor business. He worshipped Nellie Melba and Henry Ford. They were the two for him, Nellie & Henry. I never liked the music, I admit it, and I never gave a damn about Henry Ford, but he was my husband, for better or for worse. It was Henry Ford this, and Henry Ford that, and now I look out of the windows and I see these cars, you know what I see?'

'It's a prison,' Vish said, then blushed.

'I was perfectly right not to like the smell. My nose had more sense than a hundred Henry Fords. They're pumping out poison,' she said. 'Our noses told us that, like they tell you if a fish is bad or fresh. Who ever liked the smell of exhaust smoke?'

'Benny.'

'Do you know we put concrete over perfectly good soil when we made this car yard? There's concrete underneath all the gravel in the car yard. Your grandfather liked concrete. He liked to hose it down. But there's good soil under there, and that's what upsets me. It's like a smothered baby.'

'Then let them have it,' Vish said, 'Let them take it . . .'

'I'd rather blow it up,' she said. 'With her and Howie in it.'

'No, no . . .'

'I mean it.'

'I meant the tax. If the Tax Department wants to fine us . . .'

'I didn't work all my life to let the Tax Department take everything I'd built up.'

The telephone began ringing in the kitchen.

'You've got to,' Vish said.

'I don't "got to" anything.' His Granny did not seem to hear the telephone. She looked at him in a way she had never looked at him before, more in the way she looked at Cathy, but never at Vish. It produced an equivalent change in him, a toughening of his stance, a stubbornness in the muscles of his thick neck that made his grandmother (so used to thinking of his gentleness, of seeing him chant, light his incense, say his Krishnas, bless his *prasadam*) see his physical bulk, his great muscled forearm, his squashed nose and the big fists he was now clenching stubbornly upon her dining-table.

Someone began knocking on the door.

35

The first thing Maria noticed was that the Catchprice Motors books were not on Mrs Catchprice's table where she had left them. There was an ashtray and a glass of some black liquid and when she sat down at the central dining chair on the long side and opened her briefcase she found the surface of the table unpleasantly sticky.

The Hare Krishna was called Fish. He plugged the telephone in beside the bride dolls' cabinet and Maria began to create the correct emotional distance between herself and her client who now sat down on a yellow vinyl chair some three metres away and arranged her ashtray and cigarettes on its stuffed arm.

Maria looked across the room, frowning. If pregnancy had not prevented her, she would have chosen this as the day to wear her black suit.

She had not been aware there was a call on the line until Fish handed her the telephone and said, without any other preamble, 'Your office.' So just as she was steeling herself to threaten Mrs Catchprice, she heard Gia's voice: 'I just had a death threat.'

When Maria heard 'death threat' she thought it meant a threat of dismissal because of their activities last night.

'What will they do?'

'What do you think they'll do? They're watching my house.'

'They're watching your *house*?'

'It was eight o'clock in the damn morning. In the morning. How could he find my name, by eight in the morning, let alone my number? How could he even know who I am?'

'Who is "he"?'

'Wally Fischer.'

Mrs Catchprice was holding her ashtray, a small replica of a Uniroyal tyre with a glass centre. She was craning her withered neck towards the conversation.

'He called you on the telephone?'

'Not him personally.'

'Gia, darling, please, tell me what happened.'

'The phone rang. I was still in bed. I picked it up. It was a man. He said: "This is Dial-a-Death, you insolent little slag." He said, "Which day would you like to meet your death? Today? We could just burn your car today. Then you could wait while we decided which day you were going to meet your death." '

'They're just scaring you,' said Maria, but her throat was dry. She had read about Dial-a-Death in a tabloid paper.

'You're not listening, Maria. They were watching the house.'

'They wouldn't dare. For God's sake, you're a Tax Officer.'

'He said, your slut friend has left. You are alone in the house. It was true: Janet had just left.'

'Have you called the police?'

'The police? Don't be naïve, Maria. You don't ring the police about Wally Fischer. He pays the police. He lives up the road from the Rose Bay police station. I've got to ring Wally Fischer. I've got to apologize.'

'Christ,' Maria said. 'I hate Sydney.'

'Maria, I called you for *help*.'

'I'm sorry.'

'I've got to go.'

The phone went dead. Maria closed her eyes.

'Everything all right?' said Mrs Catchprice.

'No,' said Maria. 'It's not.'

She sat for a moment trying to steady herself. She had failed her friend completely.

'I need those books,' she told Mrs Catchprice. 'I need them here right now.'

'I need them too,' said Mrs Catchprice. 'Are you all right?'

'I'll be a lot better when I have the books. Please,' she said. 'I want to wind up this job today.'

'How nice,' said Mrs Catchprice. 'I'm so pleased. There are so many important things I need to ask you.'

Maria heard herself saying, 'Mrs Catchprice, my best friend has just received a death threat.'

36

Jack Catchprice loved smart women, although to say he 'loved' them is to give the impression of hyperbole whereas it understates the matter. He had an obsession with smart women. He had a confusion of the senses, an imbalance in his judgement where smart women were concerned. Their intelligence aroused his sexual interest to a degree that his business associates, men admittedly, found comic as they watched him – slim, athletic, strikingly handsome, with a tanned, golfer's face and just-in-control curly blond hair, good enough looking to be a film-star – go trotting off to Darcy's or Beppi's with some clumpy, big-arsed, fat-ankled woman whom he had just met at some seminar and on whom he was lavishing an amusing amount of puppy-dog attention. If he had been a whale he would have beached himself.

And indeed his sexual radar was somehow confused and his private life was always in chaos as he flip-flopped between these two most obvious types – the bimbos whom he treated badly, and the mostly unattractive geniuses whom he seemed to select from the ranks of those who would despise him – academics, socialists, leaders of consumer action groups.

It never occurred to him that it might be his own mother who had implanted this passion in him. The parallel was there for him to see if he wished to – in the privacy of the Catchprice home there was never any doubt about who the smart one was meant to be: not Cacka, that was for sure, no matter how many 'prospects' he shepherded across the gravel, cooing all the time into their ears. It was Frieda who read books and had opinions. She was the one who was the church-goer, the charity organiser, and – for one brief period – Shire Councillor. These things had more weight – even Cacka gave them more weight – than selling cars to dairy farmers, and yet it would have been repugnant for Jack to imagine that the women he fell in love with were in any way like his mother. He imagined he felt no affection for her, and whether this was true or not, there were betrayals he could not forgive her for. She had been the smart one, the one who read the front page of the papers, but she had let Cacka poison her children while she pretended it was not happening.

Jack had driven out from the city in an odd, agitated mood – bored, tense, but feeling the sadness that the various roads to Franklin – the F4, the old Route 81, or the earlier Franklin Road – had always brought with them. These roads, on top of each other, beside each other, followed almost exactly the same course. They made the spine of his life and he had driven up and down them for nearly forty years. It was an increasingly drab second-rate land-scape – service stations, car yards, drive-in bottle shops and, now, three lanes each way. It was the path he had taken from childhood to adulthood and it always forced some review of his life on him. Its physical desolation, its lack of a single building or street, even one glimpsed in passing, that might suggest beauty or happiness, became like a mould into which his emotions were pressed and he would always arrive in Franklin feeling bleak and empty.

He would drive back to Sydney very fast, surrounded by the smell of genuine leather, with the Mozart clarinet concerto playing loudly. He left as if Catchprice Motors were a badly tended family grave and he were responsible for its neglect, its crumbling sur-faces, its damp mouldy smell, its general decrepitude. And it was true – he was responsible. He had a gift – he could sell, and he had applied it to his own ends, not the family's. No one ever said a thing about this, but as Jack became richer, the family business sank deeper and deeper into the mud. They could see his betrayal in his expensive cars – which he did not buy from them – and his suits which cost as much as his brother made in a month.

When his mother called for help, he gave it, instantly, ostentatiously. She called him at nine-thirty on Tuesday morning, in the midst of her second meeting with the Tax Inspector. Even while she whispered into the telephone, Jack was mapping pencilled changes in his appointment book and by a quarter to ten he was on the road. He was meant to somehow 'send away this Tax woman' who his mother imagined was going to jail her.

It was impossible, of course. He could not do it. Indeed, driving out to Franklin was less useful than staying in his office and talking to some good professionals, but Jack was like a politician who must be seen at the site of a disaster – he felt he must be seen to care.

As for whether he did care or did not care he would have found it hard to know what was the honest answer. He thought his mother dangerous, manipulative, almost paranoid, but he was also the one who sent her the photograph of himself shaking hands with the Premier of the State. He would say he no longer felt affection for her, but he phoned her once or twice a week to tell her what building he had bought or sold and whom he had lunch with. If it was true he felt no affection for her, it was equally true that he craved her admiration.

He was her favourite. He knew it, and he carried a sense of the unjustness of his own favouritism. He thought Mort was more decent, and Cathy certainly more gifted, but he was physically lighter, blond-haired, pretty – a McClusky, not a Catchprice.

The Jaguar had an intermittent fault in the electrics and was, because of this, missing under load. He came down to Franklin more slowly than usual – in forty-five minutes.

He saw the two salesmen standing under yellow umbrellas in the yard, but did not recognize the blond one as his nephew. He crossed the gravel, self-conscious in his Comme des Garçons suit. He climbed the fire escape which had rotted further since his previous visit.

In his mother's living room, beneath the photograph of himself shaking hands with the Premier of the State, he met the Tax Inspector.

She was handsome beyond belief. She had a straight back, lovely legs, big black frightened hurt eyes, a chiselled proud nose, and a luxuriant tangle of curling jet-black hair. She was no more than five foot five and she had a great curved belly which he realized, with surprise, he would have loved to hold in both hands.

'You tell Jack,' his mother told the Tax Inspector. 'Jack will know what to do.'

The Tax Inspector told him about the death threat. She sat opposite him at the table. She was upset but she was articulate and considered in the way she assembled the information for him, telling him neither too much nor too little. This impressed him as much as anything else – he was impatient, he demanded that his executives say everything they had to say in documents of one page only.

He sat opposite her, frowning to hide his happiness. She was a jewel. Here, among the smell of dog pee and damp.

'O.K.' he said, when she had finished. 'There are three ways to fix this. One: your friend does nothing. She'll get a few more calls and that will probably be that. The crappy part is she has to listen to this creep. It's upsetting.'

'It's terrorism,' said Maria, who was pleasantly surprised to find a Catchprice who was not angry and threatened and who seemed, more importantly, to be in control of his life. In the way he talked he reminded her of a good lawyer.

'Exactly,' he said. 'So we rule that out as an option. The second option would be to get some help. Someone – I could do it if she liked – would go and find out how to contact Wally Fischer. And then we could arrange for your friend to apologize. Maybe we could get away with a phone call.'

The Tax Inspector was drawing on the table with her finger.

'It sounds pretty bad, I know, but you can be sure it would work. She doesn't want to apologize?' Jack guessed.

'In a flash. I'm the one who thinks she shouldn't.'

'And she'll take your advice?'

'Let's see what the third option is.'

In fact Jack had no third option to offer her. He had been making it up as he went along. It was a bad habit to specify a number of points. It was a salesman's habit. Politicians did it too. You said: there are five points. It made you seem in control when you were winging it. People rarely remembered when you only got to four.

But this one demanded a third option and he had to find her one. If the friend wouldn't apologize, he would arrange to have someone telephone Wally Fischer and grovel on the friend's behalf, impersonate her even – why the hell not? He saw himself drifting into the fuzzy territory on the edge of honesty, but he could not see where else to go. He must fix this for her.

'I have some friends in the police,' he said. 'I can maybe arrange for one of them to have a quiet talk to Mr Fischer.' Actually this was better. He could talk to Moose Chanley in the Gaming Squad. Moose Chanley owed him one. If Moose couldn't make it sweet with Fischer, he would know someone with whom he had a working relationship. It was no big deal – networking – 98 per cent of property development was networking. He would need to have Moose phone the friend to tell her Dial-a-Death had been called off. Maybe it would be possible to get whichever of Fischer's thugs who was currently playing the role of Dial-a-Death to phone her and tell her it was off. *No, no, no. Take the simplest course.*

'Why did you pull that face?'

'I was thinking of Wally Fischer,' he said.

He had got himself off the main straight road and on to the boggy side-roads of lies and he had to get back on the hard surface again. This was a woman with a clear and simple sense of right and wrong. You could see this in the nose. It was a damn fine nose. It was chiselled, almost arrogant, but very certain. This was apparent when she rejected the thought of her friend's apology. She was a moralist. She had guts. She was one of those people whom Jack had always loved, people with such a clear sense of the moral imperatives that they would never find themselves in that grey land where 'almost right' fades into the rat-flesh-coloured zone of 'nearly wrong', people with a clear sight, sharp white with edges like diamonds, people whom Jack would always be in awe of, would follow a little way, more of a way than his profession or what might appear to be his 'character' would allow, people in whom he had always been disappointed and then relieved to discover small personal flaws, lacks, unhappinesses that proved to him that their moral rectitude had not been purchased without a certain human price – this one is lonely, that one impractical, this one poor, that one incapable of a happy sex life.

He could imagine none of these flaws in Maria, nor did he seek any. The only flaw he could see was that evidence which suggested there could be no intimate relationship between them, not that she was pregnant, but that because she was pregnant she was, although she wore no ring, married.

One step at a time.

He said: 'Let me make some phone calls.'

Once he had the death threats cancelled it was only a very small step to having her agree to have dinner with him. He knew this was an achievable goal.

37

Gino Massaro was a greengrocer from Lakemba. He had a large, hooked nose and little hands. He had soft, lined, yellowish-olive skin which was creased around his eyes and cheeks. In his own shop, he was a funny man. He spun like a bottom-heavy top with a black belt above his bulging stomach. He would shadow-box with the men (duck, weave, biff), have sweets for the children, flirt with the women ('How you goin' darling, when you going to marry me?') in a way his exquisite ugliness made quite permissible. In his shop he showed confidence, competence – hell – success. He had two kids at university. He spoke Italian, Australian, a little Egyptian. He had his name painted on the side of a new Red Toyota Hi-Lux ute – G. Massaro, Lakemba, Tare 1 tonne.

No one knew the Toyota was financed on four years at $620 per month. He also had a serious overdraft, and a weakening trade situation caused mainly by competition from the Lebanese – not one shop, three, and all the bastards related to each other – who were staying open until nine at night and all day Sunday as well. He also had a ten-year-old white Commodore with flaky paint and black carbon deposits above the exhaust pipe. On the Tuesday afternoon when he parked this vehicle in front of Catchprice Motors he had just spent $375 on the transmission and there was a folded piece of yellow paper on the passenger seat – a $935 quote for redoing the big end. He also carried – not on paper, in his head – four separate valuations for the Commodore from yards between here and Lakemba, every one of which told him that the car was not worth what he owed on it.

He parked on the service road, behind a yellow Cherry-picker crane. He touched the St Christopher on his dashboard, closed his eyes, and turned off the engine. Sometimes it worked, sometimes it didn't and today it didn't – the engine knocked and farted violently before it became still. Two salesmen in the yard stood watching him. Behind them was a red Holden Barina. He did not like the red or the flashy mag wheels. He did not like it that his son would say it was a woman's car, but it was the right price range.

He was not a fool. He knew he should prepare the Commodore, have it wax-polished, detailed, present it as well as if it were apples at five dollars a kilo. But who had time? Every second he was away from the shop he lost money. He picked the pieces of paper off the seat, and the ice-cream carton off the floor and thrust them into the side pocket.

Then he got out of the car, locked it, and walked into the car yard. With fruit he was a different man, not like this.

He was already on the gravel when he saw the face. He would have retraced his steps, but somehow he couldn't. The blond salesman was smiling at him in a weird kind of way, and Gino was smiling back.

Gino knew that his angelic smiling face was a lie, that he secretly and silently mocked his big nose, his fat arse, his car blowing too much smoke. But now he had come this far and he was somehow caught and caressed by the smile which made him feel that he did not care if he was despised and he had no will or even desire to turn back. It was the feeling you had with a whore. You knew it was not true, but you pretended it was. He thought: this kid with the yellow umbrella would rob me if I let him. But he could not turn back and so he walked across the gravel towards him. Lines of plastic bunting hung across the yard. They made a noise like wings flapping in a cage.

38

'I'll tell you what I'll do,' the one called Benny said. 'First thing, I'm going to give you five grand for your old car, smoke or no smoke.'

They were all sitting in the red Barina with the engine on and the air conditioner running. The one called Benny was in the front seat, with his hand resting on Gino's headrest. The other one, Sam, was in the back. This one didn't say too much.

Gino sat with his hands on the wheel feeling the cool quiet air blasting on his face. He liked it in there. He liked the smell, the dark green digits glowing out of the black leather dark. He had that feeling, of surrender and luxury, like when you were in an expensive barber's shop. As long as they cut and snipped and combed he did not care what sort of haircut he was getting, only how it felt, like in that whore house in Surry Hills when he paid them to rub his toes afterwards – $100 an hour to have your toes rubbed. Those were the days – a crazy man.

'Five grand for the old one, smoke or no smoke, I don't care.'

Gino leaned down to undo the hood release – clunk – in order to hide his excitement.

'What do you say to that, Mr Massaro – from square one, you're out of trouble. Your credit rating is out of danger. You have an almost new car.'

It was true. He could pay out the loan on the Commodore. He stroked the hood release button, reading its embossed hieroglyphic symbol with the tip of his finger. 'O.K.,' he said. 'So where's the catch?'

'We've got a big tax bill to pay.'

Gino Massaro looked at the kid and grinned. 'Come on . . .' he said. 'I wasn't born yesterday.' He tried to get himself back into the sort of fellow he was in his shop. 'Come on,' he said, and boxed the kid's arm. 'Don't shit me.'

'Mr Massaro, if I tell you lies I'll go to hell for it.' He smiled. 'They'll torture me down there. They'll pull my toenails out for fucking ever.'

The kid made you smile. He could say this, maybe even mocking – who could say – but make you smile.

'Look over there,' the kid said.

There was a line of giant camphor laurels, their trunks covered with parasites, their leaves dotted red from lichen. In front of them, by a faded sign reading PARTS/WORKSHOP, a white Mitsubishi Colt with Z plates was parked on a patch of weeds. Gino had been audited. He knew the feeling.

'There's the Tax Department car, O.K.? I'll tell you what I'll do,' he smiled. 'I'll put in a word for you with the Tax Inspector . . .'

'Whoa, no get *away*,' Gino said. 'You keep those boys away from me.'

'But it's a girl,' Benny grinned. 'She's pretty too. She's very nice. You'd like her.'

'Let's stick to the car, O.K.,' he said. He got out of the car so he could think responsibly, but the air was muggy and unpleasantly heavy. He took out a handkerchief and wiped his forehead. He heard the two doors open and heard the salesmen walk across the gravel towards him. They lined up beside him and then the three of them stood in a line with their hands behind their back and stared at the Barina.

'Now I'm going to "load" you up,' Benny smiled pleasantly. 'Load up your trade in an effort to get your business.'

Gino smiled too, even as he thought he was being mocked. 'Loading up' was car dealer slang for whatever it was they were doing to him.

'I wasn't born yesterday,' he said. He punched Benny's shoulder again. This time the boy didn't like his suit touched. His brows came down hard against his eyes and he withdrew an inch, looking pointedly at Gino's hand. Gino took it away.

'We got to take enough shit from the Tax Department,' the boy said. 'We don't have to take shit from you. Come on Sam . . .' He turned to walk away.

'Christ,' Gino said. 'Don't be so sensitive.'

He looked up and saw the one called Sam shaking his head at him.

The one called Benny turned and said, 'Look, I'm trying to be straight with you, but this is losing us money and it really gives me the shits, excuse me – it makes me "sensitive" – when I am not believed. This is a family business, we're in a lot of trouble here and you're the one who'll benefit. That's O.K. with me, but it really pisses me off to be called a liar as well.'

The other salesman looked Gino straight in the eye and slowly shook his head.

'I didn't mean to offend you,' Gino said to the first boy, all the time puzzling about the other one shaking his head.

'I know you didn't,' Benny said. 'Forget it. It's over.'

'I've been audited myself. They're bastards.'

'You could drive it away,' Benny Catchprice said. 'We could do the paperwork in ten minutes and you could be on the road in fifteen. You don't have to ever touch your old car again.'

It was an attractive thought.

'So what do you want for this one?' Gino asked.

Benny said: 'Eleven. Do we have a deal?'

The second salesman made a cut-throat sign and rolled his eyes.

'So what do you say, Mr Massaro?'

The blond salesman was smiling at him in a weird kind of way, and Gino was smiling back. It was impossible not to. He had that quality – he was not a man, he was a boy, like an altar boy in Verona.

That was when Sarkis Alaverdian, who knew the car was valued at eight thousand, stood on Benny Catchprice's foot.

The altar boy's face changed, its brows contracted, its lips curled. Gino Massaro began to back away.

'That's very expensive,' he said.

'Don't go,' Benny said. 'I gave you a big trade-in. You only have to finance seven.'

'I'll tell you what I'm going to do,' Gino Massaro said. 'I'm going to think about it. I'll be back on Saturday morning with my wife.'

39

'I'm sorry,' Sarkis said. 'I guess I was nervous.'

Benny sucked in his breath. 'You arsehole,' he said. His jaw was drawn tight. His neck was all tendons and sinews. 'I am in control of my own life. I am in control of you as well.'

'Hey, come on – what sort of talk is that?'

'English,' said Benny, watching Gino Massaro drive away down the service road in a cloud of white smoke – his first damn sale – $3,000 clear profit plus the finance plus the insurance minus a drop of say five hundred on the shitty trade-in. 'English,' he said, as the Commodore entered Loftus Street. 'You better learn it. You better shave that hair off your lip you want to work here tomorrow.' He was kneeling, tenderly exploring the toe region of his shoe. 'What sort of fucking nut case are you? For Chrissakes I had him eating out of my fucking hand. I could have dumped the fucking Commodore at the auctions and got seven and a half for it, tomorrow, cash.'

'Look,' said Sarkis.

'Hey, don't "look" me,' the pretty boy said. '"Look" me and you're on your arse in the fucking street without a job. I had him. I had his little dago heart in the palm of my fucking hand.' He held out his hands. Sarkis saw them wet with viscera. He did not need this. He'd rather eat eggplant soup all summer.

'Goodbye,' he said. He held out his hand. 'Nice knowing you.'

The boy took his hand, and held it. 'What do you mean?'

'I mean, goodbye.'

Benny kept a hold of his hand, smiling.

A man in a XJ6 Jaguar was pulling up in front. The man had curly blond hair and a tanned face. He wore a beautiful grey silk suit. He walked across in front of Benny and Sarkis. Benny still had Sarkis by the hand.

'Hi-ya, Jack,' Benny said to the man.

'Hi-ya,' the man said. He walked on up the same fire escape Cathy McPherson had come down.

'So,' Sarkis said, taking his hand back. 'I'm off.'

'Calm down, O.K.' Benny said.

'Listen,' Sarkis said. 'I get more courtesy at the dole office.'

'Yeah, yeah,' Benny laughed. 'But the pay is not nearly so good. O.K., O.K., I know, I was excited. I'm sorry. O.K.?' He smiled. It was actually a nice smile. He touched Sarkis on the back. 'I was a creep, I'm sorry.'

'O.K.,' Sarkis said.

'It's my inexperience,' the boy said. 'I'm learning too.'

Sarkis thought: it is not fair. A person like this gets property and a business and all these cars and expensive suits and he doesn't have the first idea how to talk to people decently, and no matter what was old-fashioned and dumb about the Armenian School at Willoughby, at least there was this behind it – that you had some dignity about yourself and you spoke to others decently.

'Look,' the boy said. 'Let's take a break, O.K. Put our feet up, relax. What d'you say?'

Sarkis's mother thought he was arrogant and vain and this was why he had lost three jobs in a year. His father would have understood better. His father never bought a newspaper because the

Australians he worked with only read the sports pages and gave him the news section. When the horse races were on the radio his father would say: 'There go the donkeys.'

'O.K.,' said Sarkis, 'let's take a break.' He did not want a break. He wanted to sell every one of these cars they walked past. He was an Armenian. It was in his blood. Thousands of years of buying and selling.

He followed his boy-employer into the lube bay instead, and climbed down some metal stairs. In the dark he heard him fiddling with chains and keys and then they walked into something which stank like the inside of a rubbish bin and a laundry basket.

'Someone lives down here?' he asked, his voice dead flat.

'Sort of.'

Not sort of at all. The poor little sucker lived here. He had lived here a long time. He had new food, old food, bad-smelling clothes and oils and chemicals. The cellar would be enough to make you sorry for the boy, to wonder what drove him down here and why he could not live in a place with windows.

They were standing side by side now, shoulder to shoulder. There were cans of epoxy resin on a messy, muddled, low bench on which there were also school books, empty ice-cream containers, scrunched-up paper, ancient hurricane lamps with rusty metal bases, and several snakes, preserved in tea-coloured liquid in tall, wide-mouthed, screw-topped bottles like the ones in which Sarkis's mother still sometimes preserved lemons.

'You work with fibreglass?' he asked, responding partly to his own embarrassment but also to his sense of Benny Catchprice's prickly pride.

'My Grand-dad killed them,' Benny said. 'It was a different world, eh? Every one of them snakes was killed on a property where my Grand-dad sold a car.'

Sarkis nodded.

'We used to sell to farmers,' Benny said. 'That's why the business is like it is now. They were brought up to sell to farmers.' He picked up one of the bottles and handed it to Sarkis, who hefted its weight and gave it back. 'V. Jenkins,' Benny read from a small white label with spidery brown writing, 'F.J. Special sold September 1952.' He looked up at Sarkis as he put it down. 'The farmers were all flush with money. They would have all their cheques from the Milk

Board . . . never bothered to even put them in the bank. My Grand-dad would write out the order and they'd count out Milk Board cheques until they had enough to pay for it.'

'If you're going to work with fibreglass you should ventilate better.'

'S&L Unger,' Benny read from a second jar. 'Vauxhall Cresta 1956.'

'Tell me it's none of my business,' Sarkis said, 'but you'll poison yourself working with fibreglass down here.'

Benny put the bottle down, and Sarkis could see he had offended him.

Sarkis said. 'When I was your age I wouldn't have read the can either.'

Benny looked around the room a little, Sarkis too. The walls were covered in mould like orange crushed velvet. Benny pulled a blan-ket off what Sarkis had taken for a chair.

'You ever seen one of these?'

What it was was hard to say. It looked like a melted surf board with buckles. The buckles were a little like the clips of skis. The whole thing was pale and white and a little lumpy. It was ugly, like something from a sex shop.

'What is it?'

'What do you think?'

Benny was grinning. He stood in front of Sarkis with his hands in his pockets. He looked excited, conspiratorial, uncertain – he was colouring above his collar.

'You want to try it out then?'

'What is it?'

'Try it out,' said Benny. He unfolded a sheet and flung it across the melted surf board and then indicated with his open-palmed hand that the older man should 'try it out'.

'Give me your jacket.'

Sarkis was trying to make peace with Benny Catchprice, whose eyes were now bright and whose lower lip had seemed to grow swollen in anticipation. He gave up his jacket. Benny checked the label before he hung it, not on the new wooden hanger, but on a thin wire one. He suspended it from a water pipe above their heads where it partly blocked out the light.

Sarkis sat on the surf board. It made no sense to him. It had a

178

profile like an 'n' but flatter and it was not of even width.

'Wrong way,' said Benny. 'Face down.'

Sarkis hesitated.

'Come on, what's going to happen to you?'

What can happen?

Sarkis lay face down on the sheet. To get half comfortable you had to have your head down and your arse in the air.

'More up,' said Benny.

Sarkis squirmed upwards. The sheet was rumpled beneath him. He felt Benny adjusting something around his legs and then he felt a snap, and a pain. His legs were held, strapped by metal. His skin was pinched.

'Hey,' he said.

Benny got a strap to his right arm before Sarkis realized what was happening. He kept his left hand free but it did him no good. He was pinioned. Benny was giggling. He smelt of peppermint.

'Let me go,' said Sarkis Alaverdian. 'My pants are getting crushed.'

But Benny had him by the left hand, trying to pinion that one too. And all the time – this giggling, this weird luminous excitement on his face.

Benny was smooth and white, a stranger to the sports field and the gym, but he had two arms and he used them to slowly press Sarkis's stronger arm flat against the rubbery-looking epoxy. He snapped the clip around it with his teeth and chin.

He knelt for a moment, and brought his face close to Sarkis. 'Don't think you can walk out on me,' he said. His expression had changed completely. No smile – just small pink hot spots on his cheeks. His breath was cold and antiseptic.

Sarkis felt a prickle of fear run down his spine. 'O.K.,' he said. 'Very funny.'

Benny stood. 'Funny?' he said. 'You just stole my first sale. You cost me three thousand fucking dollars. Then you think you can walk away from me.'

Sarkis acted as normal as he could be with his backside in the air and his head full of blood. He tried to look his captor in the eye, but could not twist his neck enough. 'You admitted yourself, Benny,' (he was talking to the buckle of his belt) 'it was your fault too.'

'You don't get it, do you? Why did I say it was my fault? How could it have been my fault? Why do you think I'd say it was?'

'You were going to do this to me?'

'Sure.'

'You made this thing? What's it really for?'

'For this,' said Benny.

'O.K.,' it hurt to twist his neck up, it hurt to leave his head down. 'Now let me go.'

'Let me go, let me go,' Benny mocked. He took a step away to a place where Sarkis could not even see his shoes. He was somewhere behind him, near his back. 'You don't know what you're asking – I gave you a family position. Do you appreciate that? I gave you my brother's position. You are some slime off the street. You are no one. I offer you a ground-floor position. You could make two hundred thou a *year*. And all you can do is fuck up my sale, and *then* you try and walk out on me.'

'Hey relax.'

'Oh no, you relax, mate. You relax a lot. You should have listened to my aunt,' Benny said. 'This is a serious business you have got yourself involved with.'

'What do you want me to do? Stay or go?'

Sarkis twisted his head sideways and this time, found him – the little spider was arranging a sheet of orange plastic on the sofa.

'Stay or go?' Benny laughed through his nose. 'You're going to have to be more clever than that.' He was fussing with the sheet of plastic – wiping it with a rag, smoothing it with his hand – so he could sit down without dirtying his suit. When he sat he made a crumpling noise.

'Stay or go,' he said. He arranged himself with his legs crossed and his manicured hands folded in his lap. He smiled at Sarkis just as he had smiled at Gino Massaro.

40

Vish knocked on the cellar door, not once, but many times. When he opened the door, still uninvited, Benny was sitting on the rumpled orange sheet on the couch and staring at him. He was the only neat thing in the middle of this stinking mess and he had laid himself out, so to speak, with his hands folded on his lap, as pale and perfect as a wax effigy.

He had changed the lighting since last night. He had altered the direction of those little reading lights which had originally been above the beds in the family home. He had rigged them up so they shone on the webs of handwriting on the distempered wall, on the green concrete ceiling, on anything but where you'd want a light to be. The room was criss-crossed with the shadows of electric wires.

Vish stepped forward on to an empty ice-cream container. He stumbled and put his hand down to stop him falling.

He put his hand on to a living thing. His heart whammed in his chest.

'Shit,' he said.

It was a human being, he saw that. He got such a fright he could hardly breathe. He had his hand on a man's buttocks.

The man was lying on his stomach and had to crane his neck so he could grimace up at the yellow-robed figure to whom he looked like a gypsy at a country show. He had a little wisp of beard under his lip and trousers made from some velvety material. He showed a lot of teeth, like someone about to be cut in half on stage.

'You left it too late,' Benny said. 'I found another brother.'

Vish held his kurta close to his chest and peered down at the poor fellow who had been pinioned in position like a butterfly. The man stretched up his head again and rolled his eyes at Vish. He had white dry stuff in a rim around the edges of his lips. Vish observed this and accepted it like he might have accepted the presence of a goat or a policeman.

'Anything you want to say to me,' Benny said, 'you can say to Sam. He's my brother.'

'Help me,' Sarkis said.

'He's only joking. No one needs you.'

'Please,' said Sarkis. 'My legs are hurting.'

'Is this what you call being an angel?' Vish said.

'Do I look like an angel?' Benny sneered. 'You think I'd live down here if I was a fucking angel? No, I'm not an angel – I'm an *attachment*. Isn't that it? Isn't that what they call me at the temple?'

Vish smiled and smoothed the air as if he was patting the roof of a sand castle. 'Even if they do say that . . .'

'No, you said that – your guru doesn't want you to have *attachments*. So now you're free.'

'Who is this bloke?'

'This is Sam. He's my brother. He's going to make two hundred grand a year. He's going to do an F&I course next week . . .'

'Don't hurt him,' Vish said. 'He hasn't done anything to you.'

'Don't side with him. That's fucking typical. You don't know what he's done to me.'

'You're an accessory,' Sarkis said to Vish, twisting his head upwards. 'Why don't you phone the cops, before you both get in a lot of trouble?'

'Listen to him,' said Benny. 'He's smart.'

'You want me to call the cops?'

'Don't ask me. Ask him. I'd like to know myself.'

'You want me to call the cops?' Vish asked the man. He came closer to him so he could see the dried white stuff around his mouth and his slightly yellow blood-shot eyes.

The man was quiet for a moment. It looked as though he was trying to swallow. 'Just let me go,' he said. 'I'm losing circulation.'

'See,' said Benny. 'I'm just calming him down. He got excited.'

'You're right,' Vish said. 'You're not an angel, you're an insect. You'll live and die an insect, a million times over. I'm sorry I ever listened to your stupid story. I'm really sorry I came back down here.'

Benny's lips opened and he went soft around the chin. He stood up, but he put out his hand towards his brother as if he meant to stroke his sleeve. He took the fabric between thumb and forefinger and held it. 'You give me dog shit to eat,' he said softly, 'I'll still grow wings. It's my nature. It's who I am. I'll tell you, Vishy, they burn us, they shoot us, they pour shit on us and lock us in boxes, but you cannot trap us in our pasts.'

Vish shook his head again.

'We could be lying around lighting our farts, or doing Ice or M.D.A.'

'Help me.'

'One more peep out of you and you're in deep shit,' said Benny. To his brother he said: 'I need you.' He held out his hand.

'I need you too,' said Vish. He took the hand and held it.

Benny looked at him and blinked.

'We're brothers,' Vish said. 'It is an attachment, but I've got it. I put you here, that's right. It's my responsibility. So now,' he grinned, putting his hand around his brother's neck, 'I'm going to get you out of here, tonight.' He made a move on Benny, trying to get a half-nelson on him, but Benny slipped out and started shouting and flailing with his bony hands. Vish stepped backwards and fell off the plank, twisting his leg and falling backwards into the pool of water. A glass fell and shattered. As Vish rose, his yellow robes clinging wet against his barrel chest, Benny came at him with the power cord from the toaster, twirling it like a propeller. The plug smashed a light globe, and bounced against the back of Vish's hand, and head. He retreated, holding his hand round an injured ear from which fat drops of blood fell, tracing a dripping line up the perforated metal steps to the world outside.

41

Maria waited for Gia in the Brasserie garden near the dripping ferns, sipping mint tea. There was an office love affair being conducted in the bar, and the waiters were eating at the long table by the kitchen, but apart from this the Brasserie was empty.

Maria had planned to tell Gia about Jack Catchprice but Gia was late, and by the time she had arrived, found a dry place to put her briefcase, and begun to deal with the Brasserie's celebrated cocktail menu, it was after six-thirty.

'What I am really looking for,' Gia said, 'is something very silly and alcoholic.'

'The Hula-Hula,' said Peter, taking his order pad out of his grey apron.

'Does it have an umbrella?' said Gia skittishly.

'Trust me. It's very kitsch. It's exactly what you're looking for.'

'But it tastes nice?'

'You want silly or you want nice?'

Gia considered.

'What's a Mai Tai again? I never had a Mai Tai.'

If you did not know her and saw her do this – run her newly painted fingernails down the cocktail list, fiddle with her gold choker chain – you would think she was vain and indulged, a political conservative from the Eastern suburbs. In fact she was a liberal who worried (excessively) about the waiters and their work and, in Peter's case, his music as well. In a town where 10 per cent was meant to be the norm, Gia tipped an arithmetically difficult 12.5 per cent.

'Have a glass of champagne,' Peter said. 'You love champagne.'

'Maybe I should. Should I, Maria? It would have a certain symmetry.'

'It would be bad luck,' Maria said. 'Have the Hula-Hula. Have anything. She has news to tell me,' she told Peter. 'She is withholding. She is driving me crazy.'

'She's the one who hoards her news,' Gia said. 'I'm normally the one who blurts it out. This is her own treatment. She has to wait for everything to be perfect.'

'If you want perfect, have the Hula-Hula,' said Peter. 'If you don't like it, I'll drink it for you.'

'I'll have the Hula-Hula then.'

'I'll have a fresh squeezed orange juice,' Maria said.

'It doesn't have coconut milk does it?'

'No,' said Peter. 'It's definitely Lo-Chol.'

'Good,' said Gia.

'Tell me,' said Maria. It was twenty minutes to seven.

Gia hunched down over the table. 'Well . . .' she said.

'Yes, yes.'

'Your fellow rang me first . . .'

'Jack . . .'

'Jack Catchprice. What he hoped was he could just get it stopped.'

'He couldn't?'

'I'm sure he could have but the cop he had in mind just had a major heart attack, but he was really amazing. He was very sweet to me. He got someone else, I don't know who it was, to talk to Fischer. This took like three hours. They were going back and forth until two-thirty.'

'Back and forth about what?'

'About calling it off. Anyway, at two-thirty this very prissy-sounding woman phoned me. I don't know who she was. Like a real bitch of a private secretary. She gives me two phone numbers. One of them was for his car phone. That's where I got him.'

'It makes my flesh creep.'

'It just rang, you know, like anyone's phone and then this man answered and then I asked was that Mr Fischer and he said who wants to know and then I said my name, and he said, yes, it was him, and I said, I believe you know who I am.'

'What did he say?'

'He said yes,' Gia shivered. 'It was so creepy and frightening. I can't tell you how frightening it was. It sounds like nothing . . .'

'No, no. I can imagine.'

'Maria, you *can't* imagine.'

Peter brought the drinks. Gia's cocktail was full of fruit and had curling blue and green glass straws sticking out of it. It looked like something in an art gallery whose level of irony you might puzzle over. Gia put her lips to the blue glass straw and sucked.

'So I said I just wanted to apologize for my behaviour at the Brasserie.'

'But I thought that's what you didn't have to do. I thought that's what he was fixing for you.'

'Maria, I'll kill you. The cop had a fucking heart attack. What else did you want him to do? He was sweet.'

'I know he's *sweet* . . .'

'Christ, I don't think you can imagine this. I was so frightened, I would have said anything. I'm sure you would have been dignified, but I wasn't. I would have said anything. It just poured out of me.'

Maria squeezed her hand. 'Poor Gia.'

'Then he *interrupted* my grovelling. That was *really* humiliating. He just cut across me and said, give me your number – I'll have to ring you back. By then I was back in at the office and I didn't want him to know I worked for the Taxation Office but I didn't have any choice. And then I just sat by the phone for an entire hour. I won't tell you all the things I thought, but it was like torture. Ken tried to ring me up to have a chat, and I really fancy him, and I had to say, Ken I can't talk to you, and he got really offended. Then Fischer finally rang back and said yes he would accept my apology. He made me promise I wouldn't ever say anything like that again, and I did. It was so pathetic.'

'God, it's so creepy. It's as though you had to talk to something with scales. It's like some slimy thing you think is mythical. You think it doesn't really exist and then there it is and you're touching it. You talked to him about your execution while he was just sitting in his car. It makes me hate this city.'

'Don't hate Sydney, Maria. It makes me really anxious when you hate Sydney.'

'It's Sydney I hate, not you.'

'All cities are like this. Where could you go that would be different?'

'This city is really special.'

'When you say that I think you're going to go away. But where could you go that would be any different?'

'This is the only big city in the world that was established by convicts on the one side and bent soldiers on the other. I'm sorry. I'll shut up. You must be feeling terrible.'

Gia's straw made a loud sucking noise at the bottom of her glass.

'Only when you talk like that.'

'I've stopped. I didn't know it made you anxious.'

Gia picked the maraschino cherry from her drink and ate it. 'Maria, I feel great. I'm alive and no one wants to kill me. I'm going to take a week off and just go to the theatre and the art galleries and have lunch with my friends.' She picked up the orange-slice umbrella and ate the flesh from it. She looked around for a waiter but they were all – Peter too – eating. 'You saved my life,' she said.

Maria shook her head: 'No.'

'But you did.'

'They weren't really going to kill you,' Maria said.

Gia narrowed her eyes.

'Oh Gia, I'm sorry. I didn't mean that.'

'I know that's what you think.' Gia drained her glass for the second time and waved her hand.

'I think it's horrible. I think it's really frightening.' Maria said. She held her friend's forearm and stroked its pale soft underside. 'Who can ever know if they would have or not?'

'I'm sure you would have behaved quite differently.'

'No. I think you were amazing. I wouldn't have known what to do. You were very brave.'

'What's your fellow's name?'

Maria Takis bit her lip and raised her eyebrow and coloured. She dabbed her wide mouth with a paper napkin. 'Which fellow?'

'Maria!'

'What?'

'Stop blushing.'

'Jack Catchprice? He's actually a classic investigation target.'

'Is he nice looking?'

Maria smiled, a tight pleased smile that made her cheekbones look even more remarkable.

'Is he married?'

Maria looked up and saw Jack Catchprice walk into the Brasserie. He was ten minutes early. Jack was talking to Peter. Peter was pointing out towards the garden. Maria shook her head at Gia.

'Is this what I think it is? Maria what have you been *doing*?'

'Shush. Don't look. I've been trying to tell you. Don't look, but he's here.'

It was not a good idea to say 'Don't look' to Gia. She turned immediately, and looked straight back, grinning.

'Maria,' she said in that same whisper that had started the trouble with Wally Fischer, 'he's a doll.'

42

Jack had asked her out while they stood in the kitchen of his mother's apartment. Rain fell from the overhang above the rusting little steel-framed window behind the sink. The rain was loud and heavy. It fell from the corrugated roof like strings of glass beads. Water trickled through the plaster-sheeted ceiling and fell in fat discoloured drops on to a bed of soggy toast and dirty dishes. A red setter tried to mount Jack's leg.

'Listen,' she said, 'I can't go out with clients.'

'I'm not your client.'

'But you have an interest, you know.'

'I have *no* interest, I swear.' He looked around and screwed his face up. 'I got out of this family a long, long time ago. Their problems are their problems.'

'Really?'

'Really,' he said. 'Cross my heart. Check the share register.'

'Well,' she said, but the truth was that she had already clearly communicated, through a series of well-placed 'I's', her single status, and she would like to be taken out to dinner more than anything else she could think of. 'I leave Franklin at three. It's a little too early for dinner.'

'God, no, not Franklin. I didn't mean Franklin.'

'I have drinks with a friend at the Blue Moon Brasserie at six.' She did not say it was the attractive friend Jack had already talked to.

'The Blue Moon Brasserie?' he asked. 'In Macleay Street? I could meet you there. We could eat there. Or we could walk over to Chez Oz. I was thinking of Chez Oz. It's round the corner.' And when she hesitated, 'It doesn't matter. We can decide later.'

'Oh, I can't . . .' Maria's face betrayed herself – she would dearly love to be taken to Chez Oz.

'Jack,' Mrs Catchprice was calling him from the other room. 'I hope you're behaving yourself.'

'I have to drop in on my father at half-past seven. He's certainly not round the corner. Nowhere near Chez Oz.'

'Then I can meet you at the Brasserie and we could have a drink and then I could drive you to your father's. You like Wagner? You could put your feet up. I could play you some nice Wagner. It doesn't have to be Wagner. I have the Brahms Double Concerto that is very appropriate to this weather. I have a nice car. I would wait for you while you visited your father. I won't be bored.'

She did not prickle at the 'nice car' although she knew he had a Jaguar from John Sewell's. She had sat in John Sewell's herself, two years before, copying down the names of Jaguar owners as starting points for tax investigations.

'I'll be driving my own car to the Brasserie.'

'I'll drive you back to it after dinner.'

'My father lives in Newtown.'

'That's O.K., I can find Newtown.'

'I mean it's not a very exciting place to sit in a parked car for half an hour.'

'Oh,' he smiled. His whole face crinkled. She liked the way he did that. He had nice lines around his mouth and eyes and his face, tilted a little, had a very intent, listening sort of quality which she found immensely attractive. 'I think I can manage half an hour in Newtown.'

She was in the middle of an investigation of his family business. She might be the one who made his mother homeless, but he was flirting with her, more than flirting and she was reciprocating. He was the first man to treat her as a sexual being since she began to 'show'.

'Listen,' she said. 'It is an odd situation in Newtown. I have to sneak into Newtown sort of incognito. I might have to ask you not to park outside the house.'

He pursed his lips and raised his eyebrows comically.

'It's ridiculous,' she said, 'I know.'

'I used to go out with a Jewish woman called Layla. She was twenty-four and I was nearly thirty but I could never take her home. I had to sit outside in the car.'

'Yes, but you're not "going out" with me,' Maria smiled.

'No, of course not.' He coloured.

What was weird was that this embarrassment was pleasing. Indeed, the prospect of this 'date' gave everything that happened for the rest of the day – including her second serious chat with Mrs Catchprice about the company books, and her unpleasant phone conversation with her section leader where she requested one more day on the job – a pleasant secret corner, this thing to look forward to.

She had never planned to introduce him to her father, or have him sit in that little kitchen drinking brandy. That only happened because they were a little late and because, even after two circuits, the only parking spot in Ann Street was right in front of George Takis's house where he was – in spite of all the rain – hosing down the green concrete of his small front garden. It was the mark of his widowed state – it was the woman who normally hosed the concrete.

Maria got out of the Jaguar in front of him but he was so taken by the car he did not recognize her.

'Ba-Ba.'

'Maria?'

Maria started to walk towards the house but George was drawn towards the Jaguar. When she called to him he did not even turn but patted the air by his thigh, as though he was bouncing a ball.

'Ba-Ba, please.'

But he knew there was a man in that sleek, rain-jewelled car and he became very still and concentrated, a little hunched and poke-necked, as he stalked round the front of it, not like a poor man in braces and wet carpet slippers who is shamed in the face of wealth, but like a man coming to open a present.

George Takis opened the door of Jack Catchprice's Jaguar and solemnly invited him out into the street.

It was not yet dark in Ann Street. You could still see the flaking paint sign of the 'Perfect Chocolate' factory which made the cul de sac. You could see the expressions on the neighbours' faces. They were out enjoying the break from the rain, sitting on the verandas of the narrow cottages which gave the street its chequered individuality – white weather-board, pale blue aluminium cladding, red brick with white-painted mortar, etc., etc. The Katakises and the Papandreous were sitting out, and the Lebanese family were in their front-room sitting down to dinner in the bright light of a monster television. Stanley Dargour, who had married Daphne Katakis's tall daughter, was redoing the brake linings on his Holden Kingswood but he was watching what was happening in front of George Takis's house, they all were, and George Takis not only did not seem to care, but seemed to revel in it.

It was not yet dark, only gloomy, but the street lights came on. George Takis left his daughter alone on the street next to the mail box with the silhouetted palm tree stencilled on it. The light was really weak and still rather orange but Maria suffered a terrible and unexpected feeling of abandonment. There was nothing to protect her from the judgement of the street. She could not run back into the house, she could not come forward, and yet she had to. Stanley Dargour had put down his tools – she heard them clink – and was standing so that he could get a better view of her over the top of the Jaguar.

Jack Catchprice had stayed in the car with the door shut even while the Tax Inspector's father had come directly towards him. He had blackened windows and thought he knew what Maria Takis wanted of him, but then the door was opened and he had no choice but to turn the music off and get out.

They shook hands under the gaze of the street.

Then George Takis put his hand up on Jack's shoulder and guided him into the house. Sissy Katakis called out something to Ortansia Papandreou but Maria did not catch it properly.

In the painfully tidy neon-lit kitchen George Takis made Maria and Jack Catchprice sit on chromium chairs while he fussed around in cupboards finding preserves to put out in little flat glass dishes and then he poured brandy into little tumblers which bore sand-blasted images of vine leaves – the Easter glasses. He watched the stranger all the time, casting him shy looks. He was small and shrunken as an olive, his eyebrows angrily black and his hair grey and his whiskers too, in the pits and folds of his shrunken, fierce face.

'So,' he said at last. 'You got a British car, Mr Catchprice.'

'Yes.'

'I used to make them cars,' said George Takis. 'When the British Motor Corporation became Leyland, we made some of these in Sydney. They are a good motor car, eh? They got a smell to them? That leather?'

'Yes.'

'No rattles. Tight as a drum. You could float it on the harbour, it wouldn't sink.'

Maria frowned. She knew they had made a grand total of ten Jaguars in Australia and that the men had been mortified to be told that the production was ceasing because the production quality was too low.

'She don't like them,' George said. 'You have one of them cars, you're a real crook. That's what she told me, mate. Now she's changed her mind, eh, mori?'

'Ba-Ba, lay off.'

'Ha-ha,' said George, so eager to make a pact with the new 'intended' that he could not worry about the feelings of the daughter he was so afraid of alienating. 'I always tell her, there are nice people have these cars. Some bastards, but not all. You know what? You know the trouble? You never met one, mori. You never had a chance to discover the truth.'

Maria said, 'That is about half true.'

'No, no,' George said, waving his finger at her in an imitation of a patriarch, topping up his glass with brandy and then Jack's. 'Completely true.'

'Half true,' said Maria. 'We never did like people with money in this house. We mostly grew up thinking they were crooks, or smart people.'

Jack smiled and nodded, but Maria thought there were strain marks on his face.

'We didn't like Athens Greeks, did we Ba-Ba? That was about the worst thing to be in our view.' She was irritated with her father.

'You've got to be careful with this brandy,' George said, adding a little to Jack's glass. 'You ever drink Greek brandy before?'

191

'Once or twice.'

'You've been to Greece?'

'Ba-Ba, we've got to go. I just came round to see you were O.K.'

Her father ignored her. 'So,' he asked Jack Catchprice, 'you single? Would you like to marry my daughter?'

'Ba-Ba!'

'She looks after me real good,' George Takis said. 'Here.' He tugged on Jack's lapel and led him to where his dinner stood, in the brown casserole dish on the bare stove. 'Keftethes,' George said. He lifted the lid. Jack looked in. 'Meat balls. You want to taste? She can cook.'

'Ba-Ba,' Maria said. She was trying to laugh. She knew she was blushing. 'Mr Catchprice is a client of mine. There's nothing going on here, Ba-Ba. He just gave me a lift, O.K.' She rearranged the knife and fork and place mat he had set for himself at the table. She could not even look at Jack. She felt him sit down again at the table. She heard him scrape the preserves from his little glass plate.

George was spooning cold keftethes on to a dish. 'Every night she comes, or if she can't come, she calls.' He fossicked in the cutlery drawer and found a knife and fork. 'I know people have to pay some service so if they get a heart attack there is someone will know. I said to the fellow, mate, I don't need one. I'm a Greek.'

He placed the cold keftethes in front of Jack who sat looking back at him with an odd, shining, smiling face.

'You interested?' George asked.

Jack picked up the fork. Maria put her hand out and took it from him.

'Sige apo ti zoemou,' she said.

She stood up. Her ears were hot. She carried the fork, not the knife, back to the cutlery drawer. She picked up her handbag and put it over her shoulder. Her father – standing alone in the middle of the lonely neat kitchen where her mother's eyes had once burned so brightly – she was sorry, already, for what she had said: *keep out of my life*.

In English she said: 'You're very naughty, Ba-Ba.'

'She works too hard,' George said.

She should not have said it. It was wrong to see him take this from a daughter. She was shocked to see his eyes, not angry at all, a grate with the fire gone out. 'I'll be back tomorrow,' she said. 'O.K., Ba-Ba?'

Jack was standing, buttoning his suit jacket, tucking in his tie.

'You come again,' George said to him. 'We'll drink brandy together.'

Jack smiled this shining, bright smile. You could not guess what it might mean.

George detained them a fraction too long in the harsh light of the front door and then again, at the open door of the Jaguar he made a fuss of retracting the seat belt and making some suggestions about the best seat position. Jack Catchprice watched tolerantly while George Takis adjusted and readjusted the rake of the seat while the street looked on.

'O.K.' he said, crouching by the window when they were leaving. 'Now just relax, O.K.?'

He stepped back, still crouching, with his hand held palm upwards in a wave. *Sige apo ti zoemou*. She should never have said it.

The Jaguar window slid up silkily without Maria touching the handle. The car slowly rolled out of Ann Street.

'Oh God,' said Maria. 'I'm sorry.'

'Don't be sorry. I liked him. It was fine.'

Jack braked at the corner beside the cut glass and gilt jumble of fittings of PLAKA LIGHTING and nosed the car into the eight o'clock congestion of King Street. He pressed a button and the Brahms double concerto engulfed her in a deep and satisfying melancholy so alien to Ann Street in Newtown.

'Greeks!' she said.

'It must be hard for him.'

'Yes, it's hard for him,' Maria said.

'But he doesn't have to have the baby, right?'

She laughed.

'There's a sleeping bag down there,' Jack said. 'You might like to rest your legs on it.'

She accepted gratefully. She shifted her legs up on to the top of the feather-soft cylinder and kicked her shoes off. The seat was absolutely perfect. She shut her eyes. The music in his car sounded better than the music in her house. The smell of leather engulfed her.

She said: 'I hope you weren't too embarrassed.'

He turned the music down a little in order to hear her better.

'He is so obviously smitten with you. It was very touching. It's impossible to be embarrassed by that.'

'I would have thought we were at our most embarrassing when we were smitten.'

'Oh no,' said Jack, turning right into Broadway. He turned to her and smiled. 'Never,' he said. 'How are the legs?'

Maria was silent for a moment. 'Do you entertain a lot of pregnant women?' she asked.

'Sorry?' he asked, discomforted.

He passed his hand over his mouth as if hiding his expression and she had the sense that she had touched an 'issue'. He was too good-looking, too solicitous. His interest in her legs suddenly seemed so unnatural as to be almost creepy.

'Not a lot of men would think about the legs.'

'My partner's wife is due next week. I just drove her home before I picked up you.'

It was not the last time Maria would judge herself to be too tense, too critical with Jack Catchprice, to feel herself too full of prejudices and preconceptions that would not let her accept what was pleasant and generous in his character. She sought somehow to make recompense for her negativity.

She said: 'It's a lovely car. Do you get a lot of pleasure from it?'

'Well it's a sort of addiction.'

'A pleasant addiction?'

'I never had one you could say was pleasant. It's an addiction – it's something I think I can't do without, but every now and then I "feel" it – just like you're feeling it now. Not often.'

'I don't think I'd ever get used to it.'

'Oh you would.'

'And it wouldn't make me any happier?'

'No. Make you worse. Make you a *bad* person, an Athens Greek.'

'Oh,' Maria said. 'I thought my father made me seem like a vindictive person, full of envy. I'm sure that it all fitted so neatly together – how I would obviously end up being a Tax Officer.'

'He didn't make you seem like that at all.'

'No?'

'Not at all. You came out of it very well – calling every night, cooking his meals. A little moralistic perhaps,' he raised his eyebrows, 'but that's no bad thing,' he smiled. 'It's actually attractive.'

He was coming on to her, and she was excited, and suspicious.

'I do have a moralistic streak, but I do like this car. I'm surprised how much I like being in it.' She didn't say how surprised she was to be having dinner with a property developer.

'You shouldn't be surprised. None of these addictive things would be addictive if they didn't make you feel wonderful. Do you think crack is unpleasant?'

'I bet it's wonderful.'

'How about Chez Oz?'

'I bet that's wonderful too.'

'Have you ever been there?'

'Hey,' Maria said, 'I'm a Tax Officer. I'm doing very well on $36,000 a year. You work it out. How am I going to get to Chez Oz? I don't know anyone who could afford Chez Oz. I was thinking about this last night, and you know – almost everyone I know works for the Australian Tax Office, or did. That's how it is in the Tax Office. We divide the world up into the people who work there and the people who don't. Tax Office people socialize with Tax Office people. They marry each other. They have affairs with each other. When I was younger I used to be critical of that, but now I sympathize with them. Now I usually lie about what I do, because I can't bear the thought of the jokes. You know?'

'I can imagine. It must be horrible.'

'It's rotten. And people, mostly, are not well informed about tax. So I live in a ghetto. Something like Chez Oz I read about in the paper and I see on American Express bills when I audit.'

'What does that do?'

'Well, let's say it makes me pay attention.'

'Good,' said Jack. 'That's perfect. I want you to pay attention.'

43

Maria dressed well. On the one hand, she knew she dressed well, but on the other she feared she did not understand things about clothes that other women knew instinctively. She had invented her own appearance, part of which was based in a romantic, 'artistic' idea about herself, part in defiance of her mother (an embrace of

'Turkishness'), part in the Afghan-hippy look of the early seventies which had never ceased to influence her choices. She collected red, black, gold, chunky silver jewellery with such a particular taste that she was, as Gia said, beyond fashion. She had herself so firmly into a look that she could not choose anything that did not, in some way, fit within its eccentric borders. She did not know how to dress differently, and whenever she tried – her black suit, for instance – she felt inauthentic. She was as inextricably linked with her wardrobe as men often were with their motor car.

In her parents' house there had been no money for female fashion. Her mother wore black as she had in Letkos and fashion was something you made over a noisy sewing machine in Surry Hills. Maria had grown up in a house without clothes just as someone would grow up in a house without books or music. It had affected her sister Helen in the way you could see – she bought clothes at Grace Bros at sale times, and so even though she and Con now owned five electrical discount stores Helen still dressed like a piece-goods worker from Surry Hills.

As Maria entered the very small foyer at Chez Oz, pressed in behind the bare tanned shoulders of women with blonde coifed hair and little black dresses, she suddenly felt herself to be vulgar and inelegant, and not in the right place.

'Am I dressed well enough?' she asked her partner who, although she had not even thought about it in Franklin, so obviously was. Now she saw the insouciant crumpled look was 100 per cent silk.

'Perfectly.'

She was thirty-four years old and thought herself at ease with herself, but now she was selfconscious, and on edge. Through a gap between the bodies in front of her she saw a famous crumpled face – Daniel Makeveitch – a celebrated artist whose work she much admired. She was shocked, not merely to see him in the flesh for the first time, but by the juxtaposition of this old Cassandra with these black-dressed women with expensive hair. *He comes here?* He was their enemy, surely?

They were guided through the restaurant. Maria hardly saw anything. She felt herself being stared at. They sat beside the glass brick wall she had seen glowing from the street.

'The clones are looking at you,' Jack said, breaking his bread roll immediately and spilling crumbs across the cloth. Maria saw she was indeed being looked at.

'They're anxious,' Jack said. 'They're thinking – what if this is the new look? How will I know?'

'Is it too extreme?' said Maria who realized slowly she was the only person, of either sex, whose clothes were not predominantly black or grey. Many of the men, like Jack, wore black shirts. 'I suppose I look like a circus to them.'

'You expose them as the bores they are.'

'You know them?'

'A few. Now,' he picked up the wine list, 'I take it we have to throw this away.'

'I'm permitted one glass.'

'Then we'll both limit ourselves to one glass of something wonderful.'

Alistair would never have done that, not even Alistair at his charming best. He would have confidently gone on doing exactly what he wanted to do and assume that this was why you would like him, which was mostly true. He was gentle and loyal but he also had a will of iron, and when she felt Jack Catchprice bend his will to hers she felt a gooeyness at her centre which surprised her.

He guided her through the menu and she was amused to find herself enjoying the experience of being pampered until he said: 'You should have protein, am I right?'

'Yes,' she said, 'you're right.' But it made her distrust him and he saw this, she thought, because his smile faltered a second and his mouth seemed momentarily weak and vulnerable. She was immediately sorry.

'This restaurant is perfect for protein,' he said, looking at his menu. 'It is famous for protein.'

If she had known him better she would have laid her hand on his arm and said, 'sorry'. Instead she did something she had never done in her life – encouraged him to order for her. He chose oysters from Nelson Bay and, for their main course, duck breast with a half bottle of 1966 Haut Brion. It was, admittedly, a little more than one glass each.

Maria sipped the Haut Brion and smiled. 'I can't believe this.'

'The wine?'

'You,' she said.

'What about me?'

'From Catchprice Motors in Franklin.'

'From that terrible place, you mean?'

'I didn't mean that at all. Although,' she paused, not quite sure if she should smile or even if she should continue, 'you seem so totally unconnected with them. You're Cathy McPherson's brother. It seems impossible.'

'I'm like my mother, physically.'

'But you're not *like* any of them.'

'Well they got stuck there. They didn't want to be stuck there, but by the time they realized it they had no other choices. The environment affects you. If I'm different it was because I had to get out. If I hadn't got out, I would have been just like them, different of course, but the same too.'

'But you got out. That makes you different.'

'You know why I am sitting here tonight?' Jack said, wiping the corners of his very nice mouth with the crisp white napkin. 'It wasn't discontent. It was because I couldn't sing.'

She laughed expectantly.

'If I was musical, I'd still be there. Mort and me, side by side.'

'But you love music. You have great taste in music.'

'I love it, but I listen to it like an animal,' he said. 'If you want to picture how I listen, think of the dog on the H.M.V. label. Intelligent, attentive, and ultimately – puzzled.'

'Oh dear.'

'Oh dear, exactly. No matter how many times I listen to that Wagner, I never know what's going to happen next. Every second is a surprise to me.'

'Well I guess we're all the product of little tragedies,' Maria said. 'This wine is amazing. I have never tasted wine like this in my life.'

'Mort and Cathy have really very good voices,' he said. 'Our father loved music, so he loved them. He had them up in the middle of the night to sing, not rubbish – opera. He had them singing Mozart to drunken farmers. He couldn't help himself. He'd come into the room and shake them and shake them until they were awake. He was like me though – he couldn't sing. No one ever knew this, but I found him once, in the back paddock, trying to sing. I watched him for an hour. He had sheet music. It was really terrible. One of the worst things I ever saw, like an animal trying to talk. You could not believe all the effort in the face and the terrible noise.'

'The poor man.'

'Well it's worse than what I'm saying, obviously.'

'I hear lots of bad things,' she said.

'You'll tell me your bad things, too?'

She thought: surely he doesn't want to go to bed with me. 'Yes,' she said, 'if you want.'

He cut a piece of perfect white potato and joined it to a piece of duck which he had already neatly dissected. 'He messed around with them,' he said.

'Oh.'

He tore his bread and mopped up a little gravy.

She drank from her water glass. 'How horrible.'

'He was always at them in the night. I don't really know what happened. Sometimes I think I invented it, or dreamed it. I stood beside Mort in church last Christmas and he was miming the words. He wouldn't sing out loud.'

'He told me your father was a wonderful man '

Jack shrugged.

'And your mother?'

'Who would have any idea what goes on in that head? Who would guess what she knew or understood? But it was definitely my father who decided there was no room for me in the business. I was very hurt, at the time. Can you believe it – I cried. I really wept. All the things I'm lucky about, they hurt me at the time.' He hid his eyes in the depths of his wine glass. 'Your turn.'

'I sort of lived with a man for a long time and he had a wife and I wanted a baby and I made a choice and this is it.'

'You were happy with him?'

'Yes,' Maria said, then: 'No.' She smiled. 'I think I was rather depressed for rather a long time. I'm just noticing it. I think I must have got used to it.'

'Now?'

'Well, yes, now.'

'Now you're what?''

'I'm not depressed right now,' she laughed, and then looked down, unable to hold his eyes, aware of the movement of his knee an inch or two away from hers.

'Do you know who Daniel Makeveitch is?' she asked.

'A painter sitting two tables to your right.'

'You know him?'

'You mustn't seem so surprised,' he said. 'I know I'm a property developer and I even used to be a second-hand car salesman . . .'

He was smiling, but his eyes were hurt and Maria was embarrassed at what she had said.

'I'm sorry. I thought you would have mentioned it.' She put out her hand and touched his sleeve. 'When we sat down.'

'Oh,' he said, 'I used to spend a lot of time being offended, but I'm not any more.' None the less his face had closed over and showed, in the candlelight, a waxy sort of imperviousness. 'When I was a car salesman in the Parramatta Road – I worked for Janus Binder and I started buying paintings because he collected them. People were always amazed – gallery owners, people who should have known better. It was as if there was something ludicrous about car dealers having any sensitivity or feeling. But once I was a property developer, no one was surprised at all. They expect it of me. There's a great relief, socially, in not being a car dealer.'

'Like being a Tax Officer.'

'You don't even half-believe that, Maria.'

She blushed. 'In its social isolation, I meant.'

He paused and looked at her and she felt herself seen as dishonest. She blushed.

'Do you like Daniel Makeveitch's work?'

He allowed enough space to register the change of subject, but when he spoke his eyes were soft again and his manner as charming as before. 'Would I seem too *nouveau* to you if I said I owned one?'

'Oh please, Jack, do I really seem that bad? Which one?'

' "Daisy's place",' he said.

'I'm impressed,' she said.

His lower lip made an almost prim little 'v' as he tried not to smile. 'It's only tiny.'

'What I hate,' she told him, 'is how impressed I am.' She laughed and shook her head in a way she knew, had known, since she was sixteen, made her curling black hair look wonderful. 'I hate being happy here with all these people.'

'With me too?' he smiled.

'With you too,' she said and allowed him to hold her hand a moment before she reached towards her glass of water.

44

At half-past ten on Tuesday night, Maria Takis left Chez Oz to see the Daniel Makeveitch painting at Jack Catchprice's beach house.

As Chez Oz was on Craigend Street, and as the Brahmacari ashram was around the corner, it was not astonishing that they should, in hurrying out into the night, bump into Vishnabarnu on the pavement, but Maria was astonished none the less.

'Hi,' she said, with an exuberance and a familiarity totally new in her relationship with Vish. 'Small world.'

'Not really,' said Vish, and nodded at Jack.

He was with another Hare Krishna, a soft, olive-skinned man of forty or so who had noticeably crooked teeth and a scholarly stoop.

'The ashram is here,' Vishnabarnu pointed to the grey stucco block of flats. 'The temple is round the corner from the fire station. I walk past here six times a day.'

'That's an ashram?' Maria smiled. She was excited and happy. 'I always imagined something more exotic.'

The other Hare Krishna took a step away and stared off into the night.

'I could have given you a lift to town,' she said.

'Yes.'

'Well, I guess I'll see you tomorrow?'

Vishnabarnu looked at his friend. Something passed between them. When Vish looked back to Maria he was almost laughing.

'No,' he said.

The older Hare Krishna began to walk towards the ashram.

'This is goodbye.' Vish shook Maria's hand. 'Excuse me.'

And then, without saying a word to his uncle, he followed his friend, who was already in the dark, arched doorway of the grey stuccoed building.

'He thinks I'm the devil,' Jack said as he let her into the Jaguar.

'I don't like them generally,' Maria said. 'The way they treat their women . . .'

'It's about what you'd expect from people trying to duplicate life in a sixteenth-century Indian village . . .'

'But they do feed the street kids in the Cross and also when your sister was trying to have your mother committed. Yes, that happened on Monday. He was very good then. You get the feeling he's capable of doing what's needed.'

'What was needed?'

'Well not much as it turned out. But you get the feeling from him that he is timid but that he would go to the wall with you. That's a very impressive quality.' She paused. 'Even if he does think you're the devil.'

They drove down past the lighted car showrooms in William Street with their back-lit, bunny-suited, teenage prostitutes and the long, slow line of cruising traffic in the kerbside lane. They turned right down into Woolloomooloo beneath the Eastern Suburbs railway bridge and up beside the art gallery and on to the Cahill Expressway which cut like a prison wall across the tiny mouth of Port Jackson.

'If you look at the Cahill Expressway,' Jack said, 'you can understand almost all of this city. I had an investor here from Strasbourg last week. It was his observation. That you can see how corrupt the city is from looking at it.'

'Because of the Expressway?'

'Things like the Expressway.'

'Was this a good thing or a bad thing, from an investor's point of view?'

He looked at her, bristling a little. 'A disappointing thing,' he said at last. He was silent for a minute as they came up the rock cutting and on to Sydney Harbour Bridge, but then he went on more softly. 'You can read a city. You can see who's winning and who's losing. In this city,' he said, 'the angels are not winning.'

'I'm sorry,' she said. 'Did I sound offensive?'

'No,' he said, but she was sure he was sulking and she had, as they drove beneath the high, bright windows of insurance companies and advertising agencies in North Sydney, one of those brief periods of estrangement that marked her feelings for Jack Catchprice.

'It's true I go to work in the swamp each day,' he said, 'but I do try to wipe my boots when I come into decent people's homes.'

'Oh relax,' Maria said. 'Please.'

'I am relaxed,' he smiled. 'Well, no, I'm not relaxed. I probably want you to like me too much.'

'I like you,' she said uneasily.

At the top of the hill above The Spit, he took the long, lonely road which cuts across the back of French's Forest.

'I never came this way,' she said.

'You normally go through Dee Why? This is much nicer.'

Maria did not like the countryside particularly. She did not like the lonely gravel roads she saw disappearing into the bush on either side of the road. The signposts to places like Oxford Falls did not sound romantic to her, but reminded her how foolish she was being taking this drive with a single man who kept special pillows for pregnant women's legs.

He was a Catchprice, for Chrissakes. He came from a disturbed and difficult home. Anything could have happened to him. It was stupid to place herself in this situation to see a painting she had already seen in the Makeveitch retrospective at the art gallery of New South Wales.

He began to play Miles Davis, 'Kind of Blue'. She imagined his father holding his sheet music, roaring like a beast in a fairy tale. She loved this music, but now she knew he was tone deaf it suggested a sort of inauthenticity and forced an unfavourable comparison with Alistair, who was musically gifted and whom she saw, in the soft green glow of the Jaguar's instrument lights, Jack Catchprice rather resembled.

'It's farther than I remembered,' she said, a little later as they emerged from the bush into the brightly lit coastal strip at Narrabeen.

'Are you tired?'

'A little, I guess.'

'You could sleep there if you wanted. There's a guest room.'

'Oh no,' she said.

'Or I could take you back.'

'I'll just stay a moment and look at the painting.'

But it was not the painting but the house that captivated her, and when she was standing there at last, she could not fear a man who lived in a house whose main living room had an arched roof which opened like an eyelid to the night sky, whose side walls were of pleated canvas, a house whose strong, rammed-earth back wall promised all the solidity of a castle but whose substance then evaporated before her eyes as Jack, clambering first on to the roof, and then round the walls, opened the house to the cabbage tree palms which filled the garden and in whose rustling hearts one could hear brush-tailed possums.

It was a night of clouds and moon, of dark and light, and as Maria sat in a rocking chair in the middle of the teak-floored living-room she felt as she had previously felt one late summer afternoon in the Duomo in Milan, a feeling of such serendipitous peace that she felt she could, if she would let herself, just weep. She sat there rocking gently, looking up at the moon-edged clouds scudding across the belt of Orion and all the dense bright dust of the Milky Way while Jack Catchprice made camomile in a small raku teapot.

'You should develop Sydney like this,' she said when he came back, kneeling beside her in a sarong and bare feet. She rocked back and forth. 'I didn't know that places like this even existed on the earth.' A moment later she asked: 'Is the architect famous?'

'Only with architects. Watch the tea. I'm putting it just here. When you've finished it, we can look at the painting.'

He was standing at the back of the rocking chair and she stood, to be able to talk to him properly.

'Look,' he said, 'there goes the possum family.'

She turned. Along the top of the wall, at the place where the eyelid of roof opened to the sky, she could make out a brush-tailed possum.

'See,' he said, 'the baby is on her back.'

He was standing behind her, with his two hands holding her swollen belly and nuzzling her neck. 'It's very beautiful,' he said.

In another situation the sentimentality of this observation might have made her hostile, but now it actually touched her. She began to do exactly what she had planned she would not do and as she, now, turned and kissed him, she felt not the weight of her pregnancy but the quite overwhelming ache of desire.

'Oh,' she said. 'Aren't you a surprise.'

He had a very beautiful mouth. Up close he smelt of apples. She kissed him hungrily but insistently, hanging on his neck and feeling him take her whole weight in his shoulders and in his arms. She was not willing to be parted, made a small humming sound of pleasure in the back of her throat while mosquitoes drew blood from her shoulder and the back of his hands.

He noticed first. He held up his thumb and forefinger to show her a crumpled wing and bent proboscis, a smear of blood.

'Normally I light coils,' he said, 'but I think they may be too toxic . . . for this fellow.'

'Oh yes,' she said. He made her feel negligent.

'I have mosquito netting,' he said. And before she understood what he meant he had led her along the galley-like kitchen and down into a bedroom which was hung with a cobalt blue silk net.

'Hey, hey,' she said when she realized his intention. 'Whoa, Jack, stop now.'

But he was already inside the net. He sat cross-legged, smiling at her.

'There are no mosquitoes in here.'

'I'm not going in there,' she said.

'Just a cuddle,' he said.

She laughed. There were mosquitoes in the air around her hair. She could feel them more than hear them.

He grinned. He flicked on a switch at the bed head. A light illuminated the cabbage tree palms in the garden. Then he lit three fat yellow candles above the bed head. Their flames were reflected in the pool immediately outside the bedroom window.

'Jack, I'm too old for this bachelor pad stuff.'

'I never bring strangers here,' he said.

'I bet,' she said, but then she thought, what the hell. She got in under the net but now she was there the spell was broken. She had been so happy kissing him but now she was inside the net she was lumpy and graceless. She was too big. There was nowhere to put her feet.

'Look, Jack,' she said. 'Look at me.' She snapped at the support stockings which had hitherto been hidden under her long dress. 'Do you really wish to seduce this? You're a nice man. Why don't we wait a few months?'

'You look beautiful.'

'My back hurts. I can't even see my feet when I stand up. Even while I'm kissing you I've got this thing inside me kicking and nudging me for attention. I can't concentrate.'

'We could try. We could just lie here.'

'I don't know you.' She put her arm around him, but she felt the wrong shape to kiss sitting down. 'You don't know me. It's not smart for people to just jump into bed any more.'

'Is this a discussion about the Unmentionable?'

'I don't want to offend you.'

'You don't offend me at all. We could play it safe.'

'Safer, not actually safe,' she smiled. While still involved in her monogamous adulterous relationship with Alistair, she had complacently pitied those who must go through this. She had never thought that the tone of the conversation might be quite so tender.

He touched her on the forehead between her eyes and ran his finger down the line of her nose. 'I'll make love to you 100 per cent safe.'

She had never imagined you could say these words and still feel tender, but now she was lying on her side and he was lying on his and he had those clear blue Catchprice eyes and such sweet crease marks around his eyes. She touched them. These were what women called 'crow's feet'. They were beautiful.

'Is there 100 per cent?' she asked.

'Is this safe?'

'Mmm?'

'Does this feel safe?'

'Jack, don't.'

'Don't worry. I'll keep my word. Is this safe?'

'Of course.'

She let him undress her and caress her swollen body. God, she thought – this is how people die.

'Is this beautiful to you?'

'Oh yes,' he said. 'You glisten.'

He cradled her stomach in his hands and kissed her back and then he turned her and kissed her stomach, not once but slowly, as if he was following the points on a star map that only he could see.

Maria unbuttoned his shirt.

'Oh,' she said, 'you're very beautiful.' He had a tanned chest covered with tight curled golden hairs. He was already releasing his sarong. She began to kiss him, to kiss his chest, to nuzzle her face among the soft apple-sweet hairs, discovering as she did so a hunger for the scents and textures of male skin.

'Get the condom,' she heard herself say.

'You sure?'

'Mmm.'

'I've got it.'

'I'm crazy,' she said.

It was the second night she had stayed up late with members of the Catchprice family.

45

'Why would you ruin your life?' Benny said, smiling, holding the sawn-off shot gun an inch or two above his expensively tailored knees.

Sarkis took down his velvet jacket from the wire coat hanger with arms that trembled and twitched so much he could not fully control them. His legs were not as unreliable, but they hurt more and the pains in the legs were deeper, hotter, more specific – the left ankle would turn out to be gashed like a knife wound.

He looked at the ugly jagged cut across the barrels of the gun. 'I don't care about my life,' he said.

He had thought of all the things he would do to this juvenile delinquent for all the time he was held captive on that humiliating board. He had thought it through the terror of the dark, through the drum-beat of his headache. In just eight hours he had turned into someone no decent person could understand. He was the Vietnamese man who had gone crazy with the meat cleaver. He was the Turk who had thrown petrol over the children in the day care centre. He did not care what he did or what happened to him because of it. He looked at the sawn-off end of the gun. It was cut so badly that there was a sliver of metal bent over like a fish hook.

The pale and pretty Benny took a plastic shopping bag and laid it across his knees so he could rest the oil-slick gun there for a moment. He had pale blue cat's eyes, as full of odd lights as an opal.

'You're my F&I man,' he said.

'I'm going to kill you,' Sarkis said, rubbing his wrists and opening and closing his hands which were still very white and puffy, like things left too long in water. They did not have the strength to squeeze an orange.

'You're my F&I man.'

Benny held the shot gun up with the right hand and pulled something out from under the couch with his left. He threw it out towards Sarkis so that it fell half on the wooden planks and half in the iridescent water beneath them – a bright blue collapsible umbrella. 'You'll need your suit dry in the morning.'

Sarkis stooped and picked up the umbrella. It was cheap and flimsy and was useless as a weapon.

'You're going to jail, you silly prick.'

'I'm going to jail – you're going to kill me – make up your mind,' Benny smiled. If he was afraid or nervous about the consequences of what he had done, the only thing that showed it was his lack of colour, his pale, clammy glow. 'You've got a job,' he said. 'You think about that for a moment, Sam. You're off the street. You're going to be an F&I man. Do you understand that? Your life has just changed completely.'

Sarkis bit his pale forefinger to make it feel something. 'You're going to have to carry that gun a long time, junior.'

'Oh come on, give it up. It's *over*.'

'It's not over,' said Sarkis. 'You don't understand me. You don't have the brains to know who I am.'

'Hey . . .'

'You do this to me, it can't just be "over". You think this is "over", you're retarded.'

'Hey,' the boy said and did something with the gun which made it click-clack. 'My stupid teachers told me I was stupid. My stupid father thinks I'm stupid. But I'll tell you two things you can rely on. Number one: I'm going to run this business. Number two: you're going to be my F&I man.' Maybe he saw what he had done. His voice rose, it changed its tone, although you could not say it was anything as strong as pleading. 'You'll be able to drive a car,' Benny said, 'eat at restaurants, order any fucking thing you want.'

Sarkis tried to spit but his mouth was dry and all that came out were a few white bits. 'I'm going to kill you,' he said. 'I won't need a gun.'

'You're going to kill two hundred thou a year?' Benny stood, and smiled. 'Jesus, Sam, if I'd known you were going to get this upset . . .'

'You'd what?' he said.

Benny frowned. 'You don't get it, do you? I'm going to transform your life.' He looked very young and not very bright. There was perspiration on his upper lip and forehead.

Sarkis groaned.

Benny's brow contracted further: 'I could have chosen anyone . . .'

Sarkis did not bother to remind him it was Mrs Catchprice who had chosen him. The gun was so close. The thought he could grab it and twist it away was very tempting, but also stupid.

'All you need to remember,' Benny was saying, 'you just learned – I'm the boss, and you never contradict me on the job.'

'How can you be the boss?' Sarkis said. 'How old are you? Sixteen? I bet you don't even have a driving licence.'

Benny held the gun out with his right hand while he moved a step towards the wall. Sarkis thought: he's an actor: if he fires that now he'll break his wrist. With his left hand (smiling all the time) Benny unscrewed the wide-necked jar where a fat king brown snake lay coiled on itself in a sea of tea-coloured liquid. He took a black plastic cap from an aerosol can and dipped it into the liquid which he then raised to his red, perfect lips, and drank.

'That's my licence,' Benny said, 'I live and breathe it. Comprendo?'

Sarkis comprendoed nothing. He watched Benny smirk and wipe his lips and walk towards the cellar door, backwards, across the planks, never once seeming to look down. When he was at the door he transferred the gun to both hands and held it hard against his shoulder.

'Say you're my F&I man,' he said.

Sarkis looked at his eyes and saw his brows contract and knew: he's going to murder me.

'Say it,' Benny's chin trembled.

'I'm your F&I man.'

'We start fresh tomorrow. O.K. You understand me? Eight-thirty.'

'I'll be here,' Sarkis said. 'I promise.'

Benny unlocked the bolts on the rusty metal door and swung it open. Sarkis felt the cool, clear chill of the normal world. He limped up the steps towards the rain, but all the time he felt the dull heat of the gun across his shoulder blades and not until he was finally through the labyrinth of the Spare Parts Department, in the dark lane-way leading to the workshop, did he realize he was too badly hurt to run. He limped slowly home through the orange-lighted rain, ashamed.

Wednesday

46

Jack Catchprice woke with his prize beside him in the bed, her mouth open, her chin a little slack, her leg around the spare pillow he had fetched for her just before dawn. He put his hand out to touch her belly, and then withdrew it.

He knew then he was going to keep her, and the child too, of course, the child particularly – another man's child did not create an obstacle – it had almost the opposite effect. She had arrived complete. She was as he would have dreamed her to be – with a child that was not, in any way, a reproduction of himself.

It was all he could do not to touch her, wake her, talk to her and he slid sideways out of the bed as if fleeing his own selfish happiness. He lifted the veil of mosquito netting and put his feet on the floor.

The walls were open to the garden and he could almost have touched the cabbage tree palms dripping dry after the night of rain. The new pattern of wet summers had depressed him, but now he found in the rotting smells of his jungle garden such deep calm, such intimations of life and death, of fecundity and purpose that he knew he could, had it been necessary, have extracted happiness from hailstones.

The sun was shining, at least for now. He could roll back the roof and wear his faded silk Javanese sarong and pad across the teak floor in bare feet and watch the tiny skinks slither across the floor in front of him and see the red-tailed cockatoos and listen to the high chatter of the lorikeets as they pursued their neurotic, fluttering, complaining lives in the higher branches of his neighbour's eucalyptus.

He made coffee, he looked at the garden, he let the Tax Inspector sleep past seven, eight, nine o'clock. When it came to nine, he phoned his office.

The woman's voice which answered his office phone was deep and rather dry.

'Bea,' he said, 'we're going to have to cancel Lend Lease this morning.'

A long silence.

'Bea . . .'

'I hear you,' she said.

'So could you please tell the others . . .'

'What do you want me to tell them? That they worked two months for nothing?'

'Sure,' Jack smiled. 'That's perfect. Also, if you could call Michael McGorgan at Lend Lease.'

'I suppose I tell him you've fallen in love?'

Jack's lips pressed into the same almost prim little 'v' they had made last night, when he told her about Makeveitch's painting. How could he tell Bea – he had been given the impossible thing.

'All I hope,' Bea said, 'is this one doesn't have a PhD.'

Jack finished his call with his face and eyes creased up from smiling. He walked barefoot through the garden to borrow bacon and eggs from the peevish widow of the famous broadcaster who lived next door.

When the bacon was almost done and the eggs were sitting, broken, each one in its own white china cup, he went to the Tax Inspector and kissed her on her splendid lips, and wrapped her shining body in a kimono and brought her, half-webbed in sleep, to wait for her breakfast in the garden. She smelled of almond oil and apricots.

'You know what time it is?' she said as he brought her the bacon and eggs.

'Yes,' he said. 'I hope you like your eggs like this.'

'You really should have woken me.'

He sat opposite her and passed her salt and pepper. 'Pregnant women need their sleep.'

She looked at him a long time, and he felt himself not necessarily loved, but rather weighed up, as if she knew his secrets and did not care for them.

'Are you sorry?' he asked her.

'Of course not,' she said, but drank from her orange juice immediately, and he saw it was all less certain between them than he had hoped or believed and he had a premonition of a loss he felt he could not bear.

'Should I have woken you early?'

'Oh,' she smiled. 'Probably not. These are lovely eggs.'

He watched her eat. 'Today I'll get a blood test,' he said, a little experimentally. 'I don't know how long they take but I'll send the results to you by courier the moment they are in. I don't want you to worry about last night.'

'Oh,' she said, but her tone was positive. 'O.K., I'll do the same for you.'

'You don't need to. They've been running HIV tests on you since you were pregnant.'

'Can they do that?'

'No, but they do.'

He had no idea if what he said was true or not. He was not worried about HIV. He was concerned only with somehow establishing the presence of those qualities – scrupulousness, integrity – the lack of which he was sure went so much against him.

She leaned across and rubbed some dried shaving cream from behind his ear. 'And what else will you do?'

He took her hand and held it in both of his. 'What else are you worried by? Let me fix it for you. It's what I like most about business. Everyone is always brought down by all the obstacles and difficulties, but there's almost nothing you can't fix.'

'Not the money?'

'Not the money what?'

'Not the money you like about business. I would have thought that was very attractive?'

'Well money is important of course, in so far as it can provide.' He used this word carefully, suggesting, he hoped, ever so tangentially, accidentally almost, his credentials as *provider*. 'But after a certain stage, it's not why people work. Do you doubt that?'

'Uh-uh,' Maria said, her mouth full of bacon. 'But there's nothing you can fix for me. I tried to fix mine myself.'

'Maybe I could succeed where you've failed.'

'This is very specialized.'

'Just the same . . .'

'Jack, this is my *work*.'

'I'm a generalist,' he smiled. 'Tell me your problem.'

He could see her deciding whether to be offended by him or not. She hesitated, frowned.

'Will you tell me the truth if I ask you a direct question?'

'Yes,' he said.

215

'Did your family call you up to somehow "nobble" me?'

'My mother called me, yes. But I came to calm her down, not to nobble you.'

'Would you believe me if I told you I had already actually tried to stop their audit myself, and that my problem is I couldn't – can't?'

'Sure . . . yes, of course, if you said so.'

'Jack, this is a big secret I'm telling you . . .'

'I'm very good with secrets.'

'I'm telling you something I could be sent to jail for. I tried to stop it.'

'Why would you do that for Catchprice Motors? I wouldn't.'

'It's nothing to do with your family. It's between me and the Tax Office.'

'You don't seem a very Tax Office sort of person.'

'Well I am.' Maria reddened. 'I'm a very Tax Office sort of person. I hate all this criminal wealth. This state is full of it. It makes me sick. I see all these skunks with their car phones and champagne and I see all this homelessness and poverty. Do you know that one child in three in Australia grows up under the poverty line? You know how much tax is evaded every year? You don't need socialism to fix that, you just need a good Taxation Office and a Treasury with guts. And for a while we had both. For five years. I didn't join to piddle around rotten inefficient businesses like your family's. I never did anything so insignificant in my life. I won't do that sort of work. It fixes nothing. I'm crazy enough to think the world can change, but not like that.'

Without taking her eyes off him she put three spoons of sugar in her tea and stirred it.

'Maria,' Jack said, 'I'm on your side.'

'I'm sorry . . .'

'I know I have a car phone . . .'

'I'm sorry . . . I was offensive . . .'

'No, no, I know you don't know me very well, but I would do anything to help you.'

'Jack, you're very sweet. You were sweet last night.' She touched his face again, and traced the shape of his lips with her forefinger.

'You need someone to come and pick up your laundry in hospital . . . do you have someone who will do that for you?'

'Jack,' she started laughing, 'please . . .'

'No, really. Who's going to do that for you?'

'Jack, you are sweet. You were very sweet last night and today, I'm sorry, I was irritable with you when you didn't wake me. You wanted me to rest and I read it as a control thing. I was wrong. I'm sorry.'

'Will you have dinner with me again?' he asked her.

He could see in her eyes that it was by no means certain. She took his hand and stroked it as if to diminish the pain she was about to cause him.

'It could be early,' he said, 'I love to eat early.'

'Jack, I really do need to sleep. I'm thirty-two weeks pregnant.'

'Sure. How about tomorrow night then?'

She frowned. 'You really want to see me so soon?'

'I think the world can change too,' he said, and Maria Takis knew he was in love with her and if she was going to be honest with herself she must admit it: she was relieved to have him present in her life.

47

Sarkis could not know that he was limping back and forth across the Catchprice family history. He did not connect the names of the streets he walked along on Wednesday morning – Frieda Crescent, Mortimer Street, Cathleen Drive. He carried Benny's broken blue umbrella along their footpaths, not to reach anywhere – they did not go anywhere, they were criss-crosses on the map of an old poultry farm – but to save his pride by wasting time.

He was going back to Catchprice Motors to stop his mother going crazy, but he was damned if he would get there at eight-thirty. The air was soupy. His fresh shirt was already sticky on his skin. He walked in squares and rectangles. He passed along the line of the hall-way in the old yellow Catchprice house which was bulldozed flat after Frieda and Cacka's poultry farm was sub-divided. He crossed the fence line where Cathy had set up noose-traps for foxes. He passed over the spot – once the base of a peppercorn tree, now a concrete culvert on Cathleen Drive – where Cacka, following doctor's orders, first began to stretch the skin of his son's foreskin.

He walked diagonally across the floor of the yellow-brick shed where Frieda and Cathy used to cool the sick hens down in heat waves, trod on two of the three graves in the cats' cemetery, and, at the top of the hill where Mortimer Street met Boundary Road, walked clean through the ghost of the bright silver 10,000 gallon water tank in whose shadow Frieda Catchprice let Squadron Leader Everette put his weeping face between her legs.

Sarkis had pressed his suit trousers three times but they were still damp with last night's rain. His jacket was pulled very slightly out of shape by the weight of the Swiss army knife.

His mother had always been smiling, optimistic. Even in the worst of the time when his father disappeared, she never cried or despaired. When she lost her job she did not cry. She began a vegetable garden. Through the summer she fed them on pumpkin, zucchini, eggplant. She triumphed in the face of difficulties. She made friends with the stony-faced clerks in the dole office. When the car was repossessed, she spent twenty dollars on a feast to celebrate the savings they would make because of it. When Sarkis was on television, she pretended she had never seen the programme.

But on the night he was captured and tortured by Benny Catchprice, she had cooked him a special lamb dinner on the strength of a pay cheque he had no intention of receiving. She had been waiting for him six hours. He came in the door without thinking about her, only of himself – the wound in his leg, his fear, his humiliation and when he spoke, it was – he saw this later – insensitive, unimaginative.

He should have had room in his heart to imagine the pressure she lived under. It did not even occur to him.

He should also have spoken clearly about what had happened. He should have said, 'I was captured and tortured.' So she would know, immediately.

Instead he said, 'I'm not going back there.'

She began sobbing.

He tried to tell her what had happened to him, but he had said things in the wrong order and she could no longer hear anything. He tried to embrace her. She slapped his face.

He behaved like a child, he saw that later. He was not like a man, he was a baby, full of his own hurt, his own rights, his own needs. And when she slapped his face he was full of self-righteousness and anger.

He shouted at her. He said he would go away and leave her to be a whore for taxi-drivers.

The neighbours complained about the shouting as they complained about her Beatles records – by throwing potatoes on the roof. Who they were to waste food like this, who could say – they were Italians. The potatoes rolled down the tiles and bounced off the guttering.

In response she fetched a plastic basin and gave it to him.

'Here,' she said. Her eyes were loveless. 'Get food.'

He saw that she meant pick up the potatotes – that they should eat them.

'Mum. Don't be ridiculous.'

'You're embarrassed!'

'I am not embarrassed.'

'You coward,' she said. 'All you care about is your suit and your hair. You coward, you leave me starving. Zorig, Zorig,' tears began running down her face. She had never cried for her husband like this Sarkis had watched her comforting weeping neighbours who hardly knew Zorig Alaveidian, but she herself had not wept for him.

Sarkis could not bear it. 'Don't, please.'

He followed her to the back porch where she began struggling with her gum boots. 'If he was here we would not have to pick up potatoes,' she said. 'We would be eating beef, lamb, whatever I wrote on the shopping list I would buy. Fish, a whole schnapper, anything I wanted . . . where is the flashlight?'

'We don't need to pick up potatoes. Never. Mum, I promise, you won't go hungry.'

'Promise!' she said. She found the flashlight. He struggled to take it from her. 'You promised me a job,' she said.

He took the basin and followed her out into the rain with the flashlight and umbrella. He said nothing about the wound in his leg. He helped her pick up potatoes.

Then she sat at the table under the portrait of Mesrop Mushdotz. He helped her clean up the damaged potatoes. They peeled them, cut out the gashes, and sliced them thin to be cooked in milk.

'What is the matter with this job, Sar?' she said, more gently, but with her eyes still removed from him. 'What is not perfect?'

'It is not a question of "perfect" . . .'

219

'What do you think – a man to come home to his wife with no food because the job was not perfect. You think it was ever perfect for any of us? You think it is perfect for your father, right now?'

Sarkis Alaverdian left for work at ten past eight next morning. He could not bring himself to arrive at Catchprice Motors at the hour Benny had instructed him to. He walked up Frieda Crescent, Mortimer Street, Cathleen Drive. It was not until half-past ten that he finally carried the blue umbrella across the gravel car yard towards Benny Catchprice.

Even as he walked towards him he was not certain of what he would do. The smallest trace of triumph on Benny's pretty face would probably have set him off, but there was none. In fact, when Benny put out his hand to shake he seemed shy. His hand was delicate, something you could snap with thumb and finger.

'Hey,' the blond boy said, 'relax.'

Sarkis could only nod.

There was a young apprentice fitting a car radio to a Bedford van. He was squatting on the wet gravel, frowning over the instruction sheet. Benny and Sarkis stood side by side and stared at him.

Then Benny said, 'You were a hairdresser.'

Sarkis thought: he saw me on television.

'My Gran says you were a hairdresser,' Benny said.

'You got a problem with that?'

'No,' Benny said, 'no problem.' He took a few steps towards the fire escape and then turned back. 'You coming or what?'

'Depends where it is.' When he saw how Benny's gaze slid away from his, Sarkis wondered if he might actually be ashamed of what he'd done.

'Look,' Benny said, 'all that stuff is over. It's O.K.' He nodded to the fire escape. 'It's my Gran's apartment.'

'I'm not cutting your hair,' Sarkis said, 'if that's what you think.'

'No, no,' Benny said. 'My Gran wants to see you, that's all. O.K.?'

'O.K.' Sarkis put his hand into his jacket pocket and clasped the Swiss army knife and transferred it, hidden in his fist, to his trouser pocket.

48

The first thing Sarkis saw was the dolls lined up in a way you might expect, in an Australian house, to find the sporting trophies. They occupied the entire back wall of the apartment, in a deep windowless dining alcove. They were lit like in a shop.

Only when Benny turned the neon light on, did Sarkis notice Mrs Catchprice sitting, rather formally, in the dining chair in front of them. She looked like an old woman ready for bed or for the asylum. Her long grey hair was undone and spread across the shoulders of a rather severe and slightly old-fashioned black suit. An ornate silver brooch was pinned to her artificial bosom. The skirt was a little too big for her. Her slip showed.

Sarkis clasped his knife in his fist. The air was close.

'You like my dolls?' she said.

He smiled politely.

'I never cared for them,' she said. 'Someone gives you one because they do not know you. Someone else gives you a second one because you have the first. It's so like life, don't you think?'

'I hope not.'

'I do too,' she said, and winked at him. 'That's why I like to have young people working for me.'

'It's Granny needs a hair-do,' Benny said.

Sarkis tightened his jaw.

'Not me,' Benny said. 'I said it wasn't me.'

When Sarkis lived in Chatswood, his mother's friends would sit around beneath the picture of Mesrop Mushdotz and pat their hair a certain way and curl their fringe around their fingers. When they asked outright, he said to them what he now said to Mrs Catchprice.

'I don't have my scissors.'

'She's got to have a hair-do,' Benny said. 'It's an occasion.'

'All my gear's at home,' Sarkis said. 'You should go to a salon. They have the basins and sprays and all the treatments.'

'But you're a hairdresser,' Mrs Catchprice said, 'and you work for me.'

'I thought I was going to be a salesman.'

'You will be,' said Mrs Catchprice. 'When you've cut my hair.'

No one offered to drive him – Sarkis walked, first to his home for his plastic case, then to Franklin Mall to buy the Redken Hot Oil Treatment. The air was hot and heavy, and the low grey clouds gave the low red-brick houses a closed, depressed look.

When he returned to Catchprice Motors he washed the disgusting dishes in Mrs Catchprice's kitchen sink and scrubbed the draining board and set up basins and saucepans for the water. He could see Benny Catchprice in the car yard below him. Benny stood in the front of the exact centre of the yard and he never shifted his position from the time Sarkis began to wash Mrs Catchprice's hair until he'd done the eye-shadow.

There were people, old people particularly, so hungry for touch they would press their head into the washer's fingers like a cat will rub past your legs. Mrs Catchprice revealed herself to be one of them. You could feel her loneliness in another way too, in her concentration as you ran the comb through her wet hair, her intense stillness while you cut.

Sarkis stripped the yellow colour from her grey hair with L'Oréal Spontanée 832. When he applied the Hot Oil and wrapped her in a towel she made a little moan of pleasure, a private noise she seemed unaware of having made, one he was embarrassed to have heard.

He did not ask her how she wanted her hair done. He styled it with a part and a french bun set a little to one side. It did nothing to soften the set of her jaw or the effects of age, but it gave her, in this refusal to hide or apologize, a look of pride and confidence. It was the same approach as you might take with a kid with ear-rings in her nose – you gave her a close shave up one side of her head, declared her ugly ears, did nothing to soften the features, and therefore made her sexy on the street.

He softened Mrs Catchprice a little with her make-up – some very pale blue eye-shadow and, from among all the grubby, ground-down Cutex reds she brought him, one Petal Pink.

'How's that?' he asked, but only because he had finished and she had said nothing.

'I look like a tough old bird,' she said.

He was offended.

'It's just what the doctor ordered,' she said. She opened her handbag and uncrumpled a $20 bill which she pushed into his hand.

'Thank you,' he said, although it was not enough to cover the cost of the Redken and the Spontanée 832. He brushed off her shoulders and swept up the floor and swept her hair on to a sheet of newspaper and put it in the rubbish. He folded the sheet he had used for a cape and placed it on top of the yellow newspapers on top of the washing machine. Then he let the dog out of the bathroom.

He came back into the living-room with the dog skeltering and slipping around his feet and found a pregnant woman with a briefcase, Benny Catchprice and Cathy McPherson all pushing their way into the living-room.

'It is true?' Cathy's voice was tremulous. 'Just tell me?'

Haircuts can alter people and this one seemed to have altered Mrs Catchprice. She led the way to the dining-room table and sat with her back to the row of brightly illuminated dolls. She looked almost presidential.

'What are you dressed up for?' Cathy asked.

The pregnant woman with the briefcase sat next to Mrs Catchprice. Benny sat opposite the pregnant woman.

Cathy took the big chair facing the dolls' case, but would not sit in it. She grasped its back.

'What are you dressed up for? Is it true?' she asked her mother. 'Because if it is, you really should tell me.'

'The investigation,' Mrs Catchprice said, 'has been stopped.'

Sarkis did not know what investigation she was talking about but when he saw her speak he saw her power and thought he had created it.

'Mrs Catchprice . . .' the pregnant woman said.

'How come you're dressed up?' Cathy asked. 'How come you know?'

'She doesn't know,' the pregnant woman said. 'There's nothing to know. Mrs Catchprice, Mrs McPherson, you can all calm down. The investigation has not been stopped. Once a Tax Office investigation starts, it has to go on until the end. Not even I could stop it.'

'It's been stopped all right,' said Benny in a thin nasal voice that cut across the others' like steel wire. He was trying to smile at the pregnant woman. 'I'm sorry,' he said. He used her first name, 'Maria.'

Maria was pushing at the pressure points beside her eyes.

'We like you,' Benny said. He used her first name again. 'We don't blame you for what you did . . .'

'Maria' coloured and tapped on the table with her pencil.

Mrs Catchprice held the edge of the table with her hands. She seemed to spread herself physically. Sarkis thought of Bali, of Rangda the Witch. She had that sort of power. The whole room gave it to her and she threw it back at them. It was not the haircut. It was her.

'Can I remind you all,' Maria said, 'that I'm the one who's from the Tax Office.'

Mrs Catchprice gave her a smile so large you could think that all her teeth were made from carved and painted wood. 'You'd better phone your office,' she said. 'Use the extension in the kitchen. It's more private.'

The Tax Inspector hesitated, smiled wanly, then left the room. Mrs Catchprice turned to her daughter.

'So now you can go, Cathy,' Mrs Catchprice said. 'You want to go square dancing, you go. I'm taking the business back for safe-keeping.'

'It's not yours to take back.'

'That's irrelevant, Cathy,' said Benny. 'You get what you want. We get what we want.'

'The business isn't hers. It's not her decision. She's a minority shareholder.'

But Mrs Catchprice did not look like a minority of anything. Her jaw was set firmly. Her face was blotched with liver spots and one large red mark along her high forehead below her hairline. She looked scary.

The Tax Inspector, by contrast, looked white and waxy and depressed. She had not come all the way back into the room, but stood leaning against the door jamb with her hand held across her ballooning belly. Her hands were puffed up, ringless, naked.

'I've been called back to the office,' she said.

'How lovely,' said Mrs Catchprice. 'You'll be closer to the hospital. What hospital was it? I forget.'

'George V,' said Maria Takis. All the colour had gone from her wide mouth.

'It's a lovely hospital.'

'My mother died there.' The Tax Inspector clicked shut her briefcase.

'Let me,' Benny said. He took the briefcase from her, smiling charmingly. 'I'd like to walk you to your car.'

49

At the bottom of the fire escape, Benny took the car keys from the Tax Inspector's hand. She let him take her briefcase, imagining he would carry it to her car, but he immediately set off across the gravel towards the back of the yard where a faded red sign read LUBRITORIUM.

'Wrong way,' she said.

He turned, and his lower lip, in trying not to smile, made a little 'v' that was disturbingly familiar. 'You can't go,' he said. He threw her car keys in the air and caught them. 'It isn't over yet.'

'It's over. Believe me.' She did not know how the audit could possibly be over, and she was confused, and mostly bad-tempered that it was. It was not logical that she should feel this, but she felt it. She held out her hand for the keys.

Benny grinned, then frowned and held the keys behind his back. 'I've got stuff I want to show you.'

'Come on, I've got work to do.' She was going to the Tax Office to shout at Sally Ho. That was her 'work'.

Benny pouted and dangled the keys between his thumb and forefinger. She snatched them from him, irritated. The minute she had done it and she saw the hurt in his face, she was sorry.

'You should be happy,' she said. 'Isn't this what you wanted when you came to my house? Isn't this exactly what you wanted to achieve?'

'Yes,' he said. 'Sort of.'

She began to walk slowly, purposefully, towards her car. 'So?' she said.

He was close beside her – a little ahead. She could feel his eyes demanding a contact she did not have the energy to give him.

He said, 'I thought we might be, sort of, friends.'

She began to laugh, and stopped herself, but when she looked up she saw it was not in time to stop her hurting him. By the time they reached the car he had a small red spot on each of his cheeks.

'I don't see why not,' he said. He held out his hand for the keys and she gave them to him, in compensation for her laughter. He

unlocked her door and held it open for her. She squeezed herself in
behind the wheel. He passed her the briefcase. She held out her
hand for the keys. He wagged his finger and danced round the
minefield of puddles to the passenger side. She watched him,
wearily, as he unlocked the passenger side door and got in. He
locked the door behind him.

'O.K.' she said. 'But now I've got to go.'

She held out her hand for the keys. He placed them in her open
palm. She inserted the keys in the ignition switch then turned it far
enough to make the instrument lights, the three of them, shine red.

'I came to talk to you last night,' he said. 'I thought we could, you
know . . . I came by myself.'

'Why?'

'Why not?'

She moved the gear stick into neutral.

'I got the company books for you,' he said. 'I brought them to your
house. I was going to leave them on the veranda, but you didn't
come home all night.'

She felt her hair prickle on the nape of her neck. 'I was at my
father's,' she said.

'That's who you had dinner with?'

'Yes. It is absolutely who I had dinner with.'

'But you went out to dinner with uncle Jack.'

She turned to look at him. He was smirking.

'You don't want to waste your time with him,' he said. 'He's a creep.'

'Benny, what do you want from me? What is it?'

Benny shrugged and looked out of the window at a pair of men at
ASP Building Supplies loading roofing iron on to the roof-rack of an
old Ford Falcon. 'How old are you?' he asked, still not looking at her.

Maria started the engine.

'How *old* are you?'

He turned. He looked as if he was going to cry.

'I'm thirty-four.'

'I like you,' he said. 'I never liked anyone like that before.'

'Benny, that's enough.'

'This is serious,' he said.

'Enough.'

But he was unbuttoning his shirt.

Maria opened her door. 'I'm going to get your father.'

'My father is a joke,' said Benny. He pulled down his jacket and his shirt to show her his upper arm. 'Just look, that's all. Please don't turn away from me.'

Maria Takis looked. She saw a smooth white scar the size of a two-cent piece surrounded by a soft blue stain.

Benny looked at her with large tear-lensed eyes. 'My mother did this to me. Can you imagine that? My own mother tried to kill me.'

'Benny,' Maria said. 'Please don't do this to me. I am an auditor from the Australian Taxation Office.'

'I was three years old.'

'What is this serving?'

'For Chrissake,' Benny kicked out and smashed the glove box. It flipped off and fell on to the floor. 'I'm trying to show you my fucking life.' He looked at her. His eyes were big and filled with tears. 'You wouldn't come with me. I wanted you to come with me. I can't *stand* that.'

'Benny, what can I do? I'm a stranger to your family.'

'You're kind,' he said. He rubbed his nose with the back of his hand. He picked up the glove box lid and tried to fit it back on. 'I know you're kind.'

'Benny,' she gave him a tissue from her bag, 'just take my word for it – I'm very selfish.'

He wiped his eyes and blew his nose. 'You care about other people, I know you do. You live all by yourself and you're having this baby. That's not selfish.'

Maria looked forward out the window, not wanting to hurt him, fearing his anger, wishing it would end.

'You could have had an abortion.' He persisted with the glove box lid. Every time he closed it, it dropped to the floor.

'I often wish I had.'

'No, you don't.'

'You want to know the truth? I wanted to hurt the baby's father. That's why I'm having a baby – to make him feel sorry for the rest of his life.'

Benny took the glove box lid and squinted at it, as if trying to read a part number.

'You're kind,' he said. 'You can't put me off by lying to me. I can replace this glove box,' he said. 'If you come back tomorrow I'll replace it free.'

'Benny I'm not coming back. I'm sorry.'

'You come out here, you try to screw my life. I'm interested in you. I'm interested in your baby, everything. I like you, but you don't even take the trouble to see how I live. You know how I live? I live in a fucking hole in the ground. You wouldn't even use it for a toilet. Come and look at it. I'll show you now.'

The Tax Inspector shook her head. She looked down at her skirt and saw it rucked above her knees. They looked like someone else's knees – old, puffy, filled with retained fluid. In the middle of the anxiety about Benny she had time to register that she had developed œdema.

'You can't just dump me. You think you can go away and leave me to rot in my cellar, just let me rot in hell, and nothing will ever happen to you because of it.' He was folding his jacket. He was opening the car door. He was leaving her life.

Maria Takis waited for the door to slam. It did not seem smart to start the engine until it did.

50

Granny Catchprice had made her life, invented it. When it was not what she wanted, she changed it. In Dorrigo, she called them maggots and walked away. She had gelignite in her handbag and Cacka was nervous, stumbling, too shy to even touch her breasts with his chest.

There was no poultry farm, she made one. There was no car business, she gave it to him, out of her head, where there had been nothing previously. She freed him from his mother. She gave him a yard which he paved with concrete so he could hose it down each morning like a publican, a big man in his apron and gum boots. He was Mr Catchprice. She was Mrs Catchprice. She hired boys and girls in trouble and showed them how they could invent themselves. Little Harry Van Der Hoose – she tore up his birth certificate in front of him. He watched her with his mouth so wide open you could pop a tennis ball inside.

'Now,' she said. 'What are you?'

Years later he wrote a letter from Broome where he had a drive-in liquor store. He said: 'Before I had the good fortune to be employed by yours truly, I was what you would call a dead-end kid. Whatever life I enjoy here today, I have you to thank for.'

Mrs Catchprice stood in the annexe on Wednesday afternoon and watched them bring the horrid-looking 'Big Mack' tour truck right into the yard. It belonged to Steven Putzel, the pianist – a nasty little effort with sideburns and a tartan shirt. They had to move the Holdens and that black foreign car to one side. They made a mess of the gravel doing it.

Her daughter ran out from under the LUBRITORIUM sign, carrying guitar cases.

'That's a joke,' Frieda said. She lit a Salem and folded her arms across her prosthetic chest. It was a bumpy, silly thing and she was sorry she had put it on.

'What is?'

She looked and saw Mort was standing next to her. This sort of thing happened more and more. She damn well could not remember if she had known he was there or if he had sneaked up on her. She said nothing, gave nothing away. She held out the Salem pack to him. He shook his head.

'What's a joke?' he said. She remembered then – he gave up smoking when he married Sophie.

She looked out of the window at her daughter who was now struggling out into the sunlight carrying a big amplifier.

'Where's she think she's going?' she said.

'You know exactly what she's doing,' Mort said.

She guessed she did know. 'She can't sing.'

'Jesus, Mum. Give up, will you?' Mort grinned. She was a tough old thing, that's who she was.

'She *used* to sing as well as you. She used to sing the "Jewel Song" for your father. People would pay to hear that.'

'Come on, lay off – you know she's popular.'

'Is she?' said Granny Catchprice. 'Truthfully?'

Mort folded his arms across his chest and looked down at her with a thin, wry grin on his face. 'You're not going to get a rise out of me.'

She was not sure if she was taking a rise out of him or not. She knew, of course, that Cathy sang in halls. She was popular enough to sing at a dance in a hall. She could sing for shearers, plumbers, that sort of thing.

'She'd do anything to get herself written up,' she said.

'Our Cath always did like attention,' he said. 'It's true.'

'And you were always so bashful.' Cathy was trying to climb into the truck and Frieda felt nervous that she had somehow allowed this thing to get this far. 'She could be a bit more bashful with that backside.'

At ten years old, you should have seen her – a prodigy. She never knew what Country & Western was. She knew *Don Giovanni*, *Isolde*, *Madame Butterfly*. Her teacher was Sister Stoughton at the Catholic School. She sang 'Kyrie Eleison' at St John's at Christmas before an audience which included the Governor General. There was no 'Hound Dogs' or 'Blue Suede Shoes'. The nearest she came to Hill-Billy or Rock-a-Billy, she had a checked shirt and jeans with rolled-up cuffs to go and learn square dancing at the Mechanics' Institute. She did not know anyone with duck-tailed hair or Canadian jackets. She did not like square dancing either, said it was like going fencing with a wireless playing. She was nine years old when she said that.

Frieda said: 'I suppose she's got our money entered in her bank book.'

She was trying to enlist him, but he took her shoulder and made her turn towards him.

'Look at me,' he said. He held her too hard. It hurt but she did not tell him. 'Listen to what I'm saying – whatever Cathy is, she's not a criminal. Now come on, be a good stick, eh? You've pushed her this far. You let her go ahead and jump.'

'I'm not any sort of stick.'

'Let her do what she wants to do.'

'I'm going down to talk to her.'

'You've already talked to her.' He stood in front of her and for a moment she thought he was going to block her way. He was frightening – big, and emotional, like a horse that might do anything.

'Come with me, Morty.'

He shook his head, but he stepped aside and held the door open. 'You told her you didn't need her. That was the message you gave her. If you want my opinion, you are incorrect . . .'

'If I'm incorrect, then help me talk to her.'

'No, Mum.' He shook his head with those big teary eyes, like his father.

'You don't know anything about Cathy and me. You never did understand.'

'You've got her like a monkey on a stick.'

'Rot and rubbish.'

'You're very cruel, Mum.'

That hurt her, hurt her more than she could imagine being hurt but she did not show it.

'You always panic,' she said. 'You're like your father.'

That made him sniff and put his mouth into a slit. 'You're the one who should be panicking,' he said.

She let that pass.

'Walk me down the stairs?'

'No,' he shook his head.

So she walked by herself and left him sulking.

She met her daughter in the old lube bay, carrying a big cardboard box of papers. Cathy brushed past, saying nothing. She passed the box to Steven Putzel and then hurried back across the cracked, oil-stained lube bay floor where Benny had painted the skull and cross bones and the Day-glo no admittance sign. Frieda remembered when that concrete floor was wet and new. You could have written anything in it. Cathy began to go up the metal stairs to the flat. Frieda followed her.

Half way up, Cathleen stopped and turned.

'Just leave me alone,' she said.

'I'm not stopping you,' Frieda said, but she saw then – in the way Cathy was standing – that it was not too late to stop her. She started feeling better than she had.

'You'll fall and break your hip.'

'I've every right to see my house.'

'It is not your house any more.'

But she had invented it. There had been nothing there before she started. She had chosen that red marbled Laminex, that lemon wall paint. The floors were strewn with newspaper, record covers, sheet music. In the middle of the room was the yellow vinyl chair she had covered for Cacka. He used to sit in that to listen to his records. She loved to watch him listen. His big eyes would fill with moisture – glistening like in the movies when people were in love. Now it was his daughter who stood before her, red faced, her hands on her hips, her lips parted.

'You know I won't live too much longer,' Frieda said.

'Don't start that . . .'

'We got through this far . . .'

'Just don't, O.K.?'

Howie came into the living-room. He stood back in the corner as if none of this was to do with him.

'You never had children, Cathy,' Frieda said. This was not exactly aimed at Howie. She did not mean it this way, but she glared at him when she said it. 'Unless you've been through labour you couldn't understand.'

Cathy began to give that nervous laugh and shake her head like she had water in her ear. 'Listen, Ma – it's not going to work . . .'

She got that 'Ma' from Howie. It was common. Frieda hated it. 'You're going to be alive a long time yet, Cathy. You're the one that'll have to live with the guilty conscience.'

'Mrs Catchprice,' Howie said. He was leaning against the door frame with his arms folded. 'You've got no right to say these things to her.'

He was a no one. She had made him, invented him. He came into her shop with his greasy hair and brothel creepers and a note from the police sergeant.

'I'm her mother, Howie.'

Cathy said: 'You never did what a mother should have done.'

'You mean that business with Mr Heywood's cat?'

'You know I don't mean that. Don't make me say it. Just don't make it hard for me to go.'

Howie spoke out of the shadow near the bedroom door frame. It was so dull there you could not even see his eyes. 'He used to rub her tits,' he said.

Frieda felt she had missed something.

She looked up. Steven Putzel was there at the doorway next to Howie, listening.

'How dare you speak to me like that,' she said, but she was confused by the circumstances and did not speak with her full force.

'He used to rub her tits.'

'You little filth.' She could not believe the *language*.

'He's not a filth,' Cathy said. 'He's a decent man.'

Decent?

'He is a filth, all right,' she said. 'I knew he was a filth when I saw him. I thought I could change him but look how wrong I was.'

'He used to lie on top of me so I could not breathe.'

'You were the one who wanted to marry him.'

'Your husband. My father. He used to lie on top of me so I could not breathe.'

'He loved to tease you,' Frieda said.

'For Christ's sake, Mother, our father was a creep. He used to touch my tits. He used to lie on top of me. You saw him do it. You used to watch him do it.'

'I did not.'

'You did, you old fool. You used to sit there, in the same room. He used to do things to me while you were *knitting*.'

Cathy had her by the arm, squeezing her, pulling at her, shouting about ten hours of labour, but Frieda had already slipped away. She was running through the ring-barked trees, down the wet clay road. Walking towards her was Cacka, smiling, in his Magpies jacket.

She had the gelignite in her handbag when she met him. She had it in the butcher's. The detonators clinking around her neck. She had it there from the beginning.

51

Ghopal's was hot and busy when Govinda-dasa took the call. When he heard the old woman's voice he had a mental picture of a demon with tusks, one of the servants of Yamaraja, the lord of death, who came to claim the soul of Ajamila.

'O.K.' he said to Vishnabarnu, 'It's her.'

Vish picked up the phone and cradled it between his big smooth chin and yellow cotton shoulder.

'Hi, Gran.' He continued to ladle out the Sweet and Sour tofu. He passed the plate to Ramesvara and then began to fill a blender with banana and milk, yoghurt, cinnamon, honey.

'Vish,' Gran Catchprice said, 'I need you out here.'

'Oh no, Gran,' Vish said. 'I'm sorry. One sec.' He turned on the blender and mouthed to Govinda-dasa: 'It's O.K.'

'I don't think there's too much I can do about Benny any more,

Gran,' he said as he poured the smoothies into their tall green glasses. 'I think he needs to see a doctor.'

'I'm the doctor,' Gran said.

'Good luck, Gran.' He smiled. He handed the glasses to Govinda-dasa who added the mint sprig and placed them on the counter top for Ramesvara.

'You're the doctor,' she corrected.

'No way, José.'

'But I'm going to follow your prescription – let the business go to hell, wasn't that it?'

'Gran I can't come back now. I've gone now. I've gone for ever. I'm sorry.'

Govinda-dasa turned his back and began to dish some stuffed eggplant. But if Govinda-dasa understood Vish perfectly, Granny Catchprice would not.

'Isn't that what you told me?' she said. 'Let the business go to hell?'

'It is hell,' Vish said. 'That's the truth.'

'I think so too,' she said.

Vish shut his eyes, puffed up his cheeks, blew out air.

Govinda-dasa made a sign with his finger, like a record going round. He meant: don't enter into argument or discussion, just keep repeating it – I – AM – NOT – COMING – BACK.

'Gran, I'm not coming back.'

'Not even to get your brother out of his hole?'

'I'm not coming back.'

'You don't care what happens to your brother?'

'Gran,' Vish turned back towards the wall and the painting of Lord Nara Sinha, 'he's sawn off Grandad's shot gun. He's suffering from delusions. The best thing you can do is keep away from him. Don't go down there.'

'I'm not going to go down there. I'm not going to even talk to him.'

'Well, I'm not either. Gran, there's nothing anyone can do.'

'Oh yes there is.'

'What?'

'I can't say on the phone.'

Vish grinned and turned back to look at Govinda-dasa who was making the record sign – I – AM – NOT – COMING – BACK. 'This is not Dorrigo,' he said. 'There's no operator listening to the call.'

'I know it's not Dorrigo,' she said. 'Do you really think I don't know that? I'm going to wind this business up. It makes me sick myself.'

He said nothing.

'It makes me ill in my stomach just looking out of the window. I feel like such a fool . . .'

He did not ask her what she felt a fool about. He smiled at Govinda-dasa and played the record: 'Just the same, Gran – I can't come.'

'You never want to see it again?' She was persistent, like a salesman. 'As long as you live?'

'Gran. I can't come.'

'You don't want to see it, but it's always there. It won't go away. It just goes on and on like some bad dream . . .'

He did not answer her. He nodded.

'If you could wave a magic wand and make it go . . .'

'A magic wand . . .' he laughed. 'Sure, Gran.'

'Well, yes or no?'

Govinda-dasa was all the way over at table 14 but he saw what was happening. He walked rapidly back towards the counter, making circular motions with his index finger.

'Did you hear me?' she said.

'Yes I heard.'

There was a long silence on the phone while Vishnabarnu felt the cool dry wall against his cheek.

'I'm not talking to my father,' he said.

52

Jack Catchprice was scared and amazed by what he had brought off. The thing happened so fast. Really, he was just enquiring – could he do it? He was testing his strength – did he know the guy who knew the guy? Did he have the clout with the first guy to get him to use his clout with the second guy? Did he have enough in the favour bank to get this investigation stopped? The truth was – he was flirting with it. But then he was in the deep end and suddenly he was in a very dark place and it was, like, you want it or not, yes or no, shit or get off the can. 'Sure,' he said. What the fuck else could he say?

Thirty minutes after she left the Bilgola house, without her knowing anything had changed, Catchprice Motors was no longer a part of Maria Takis's profesional life.

Jack had not been able to achieve it in two steps, but in three, and the steps were dirty and the connections dangerous. He was now joined to things he would rather not be joined to.

He wanted to ring Maria, straightaway, and tell her what he had done. But it was like ringing to check that a dozen long-stemmed roses had arrived – you could not do it. You had to wait to be thanked.

For Jack who had made his impatience into something like a professional virtue, waiting was difficult. But he did it. He had no choice. He told Bea he would take any calls from Maria Takis, and any call from any female who did not seem inclined to give a name.

He had a meeting with the dopey architect who had wilfully ignored his brief and now wanted to give the Circular Quay land to the city for a park in return for the right to put two towers in the water where the ferries came in. It was like a giant π, a gateway to the city with a ballroom, a fucking *ballroom*, across the top. It was wrong to call him dopey. The guy was right in everything he said. He was trying to make a proper gateway for the city. He said the Cahill Expressway was like the Berlin Wall. He was a fucking genius, but he did not see that Jack could not *sell* a ballroom, and he did not have the resources to fight ten years to build in the water at Circular Quay. But he could not bear a gifted man like this to dislike him – he asked him to take his drawings to another stage.

After that, he called all the troops in for the Lend Lease meeting – three hours later than scheduled but Lend Lease still bought the whole Woolloomooloo package and when they went out of the door he opened a couple of magnums of Moët for the staff to celebrate.

There was still no call. He started to worry the connection had fucked up, that the case had not been stopped. He went back into his office. He picked up the phone, put it down, picked it up, put it down again.

Then he buzzed Bea and had her book a table for two at Darcy's for that evening, just in case.

'You're not going to Darcy's,' Bea said. 'You've got dinner at Corky Missenden's.'

'Then I'll cancel Corky. Get me Corky.'

'Good luck,' Bea said.

But of course there was no way Corky was going to excuse him.

'All right,' Jack said. 'Well, if I have to come, I'm going to have to bring someone.'

'Jack, don't do this to me.'

'Corky, I don't want to. I have to.'

'You're a shit, Jack. This dinner has been planned for weeks. You don't know what a tricky placement this is. Who is this person? Is she anyone I know? Does she *do* anything?'

Jack thought it best not to reveal her occupation. 'You'll like her,' he said, 'she's a friend of Daniel Makeveitch. You'll love her.'

But there was still no call from Maria.

Jack was tight and twitchy in the legs and at the back of his fingers. He had lunch at Beppi's with Larry Auerbach and took his cellular phone to the table like some nerd from the Parramatta Road. When Larry went for a piss, he rang Catchprice Motors, but the phone wasn't even answered.

At three he got the Taxation Office but her number did not answer either, and the switchboard said she was unavailable.

At four, now in his office, he telephoned Maria's home and got the answerphone.

'Hey, Maria. You there? It's Jack . . . Catchprice . . . I just had a crazy idea,' he said. 'It might be fun.'

She picked up.

He stood up and pulled the phone off his desk. 'You're there.'

'If it's fun, I'm up for it.'

'Are you O.K.? I worried you had gone into labour.'

'My fingers look like sausages,' she said, 'and I've had my worst day all year . . .'

'Nothing good happen at all? All day?'

'Not a thing.'

'Are you absolutely sure?'

'Did my legs look sort of funny last night? Were my knees puffy?'

'No!'

'Are you sure? Because if they looked like they do right now, I'm going to die of embarrassment.'

'Maria, you've got great legs. What happened that was so bad?'

'Something very shitty. I don't want to even think about it.'

'But your investigation stopped, right?' *He had done the fucking impossible. He had fixed what she had failed to fix.* 'You got called back to your office? Catchprice Motors is out of your life?'

Remember me? The generalist?

There was a pause. 'Jack, how do you know this?'

'How do you think?' he said. *I did the fucking impossible for you. I crawled down sewers. I shook hands with rats.* 'How would you reckon?'

'Oh, your mother told you.'

He made a silent face.

'Well,' Maria said. 'She's pleased.'

'Sure,' he said, 'you can rely on that, but I'm sorry you're not happier.'

'Oh, I want to have fun *now*.'

He felt anxious that now she would not like him, angry that she did not appreciate what he had done for her, indignant at what he suspected were her double standards, relieved she would probably come out to dinner with him, even if it was at Corky Missenden's.

'You might say no when you hear – but there's a dinner party at Rose Bay I thought you could have a good laugh at.'

'I like the laugh part.'

'You know this fellow Terry Digby – Lord Digby – who just paid $23 million for the de Kooning? He's in Sydney, and there's a dinner. It's Corky Missenden – she's good at this sort of thing. There'll be money and art, mostly, but the Attorney General will be there so that might be amusing. In any case, the food should be very good and we could leave early if you were bored – you'd be a perfect excuse for me to leave.'

'What would I wear?' she said.

He persuaded her she could wear exactly what she wore the night before, that it would be perfect. He said it because he figured that was who she was, but also because he was not going to lose her because she had nothing suitable to wear, and when they arrived out at Rose Bay, it made Corky Missenden raise a questioning eyebrow in his direction.

He had too much on his mind to be offended by Corky's eyebrow. He had seen that she was setting up her dinner party with two tables in two rooms, and, as he and Maria passed through the house, even as he pointed out the less embarrassing choices in Corky's erratic art collection, Jack's mind was racing, thinking what he could offer Corky, what he could trade her, how he could *make* her have Maria Takis sit at his table. He had Maria drink champagne. He looked at the harbour and pointed out a school of leather-jackets swimming up against the sea wall, but he had none of the lightness of heart his creased-up eyes and loose curly hair suggested – he knew that he would be sent, in a moment, to be charming to the Attorney General and Maria would be bumped into the second room with the rich and reactionary George Grissenden and the snobbish Betty Finch. He had fucked-up. It was the wrong way for her to see his life.

53

At four o'clock Maria Takis had been in her one-bedroom cottage in Balmain with her puffy feet elevated, staring at the discolouration on her freshly painted ceiling. At eight-fifteen she was standing beside Sydney Harbour with a long glass flute from which very small bubbles rose slowly through straw-coloured Dom Perignon. At four o'clock she had had red eyes and a headache. At eight-fifteen waiters with black shirts and pony tails brought hors d'oeuvres to the sea wall where she sat with a man with curly blond hair and a tanned face. The light was mellow, the water of the harbour pearly, touched with pink and blue and green. It was like nothing so much as a television commercial.

That she should like the too-good-looking man, that the setting itself – terra-cotta tiled terrace, flapping striped awnings, elegant men and women in black dresses – should be actually *pleasant* was disturbing for her.

She had been in homes like this before, often, professionally, but she had never allowed herself to think of wealth as attractive, was so accustomed to seeing it as a form of theft that it was shocking for her to feel herself responding to it at all, as if she were allowing herself to be sexually excited by a criminal.

The harbour licked and lapped against the wall she sat on. It slapped against the sandstone and smelt of sea-weed. She wondered if people in these houses bothered to fish. If ever she had a house like this, she would fish. She saw her mother on the sea wall

239

casting out towards where the water boiled with tailor.

'I thought about you all day,' he said.

But she was suddenly so uncomfortable with his attractiveness, his straight, perfect teeth – he was a 'type' she would once have labelled superficial or yuppy – that she could not bring herself to say she had thought of him – although she had, often – or even that she was pleased and excited to be here.

'Should we be mingling?'

'We don't have to do anything we don't want to do,' he said.

But then it turned out that they must sit, not merely apart, not merely at separate tables, but at tables in rooms separated by french doors.

'Surely we can sit together?' she said.

'I'll fix it,' Jack said, and disappeared into the house.

She stayed alone on the wall, looking out at the harbour where a long, low, wooden boat slowly putted past, no more than five metres away. A little girl, no more than ten, sat alone at the tiller. The girl waved. Maria waved back. She thought: I could handle this. That's the truth. I would actually love to live in a house like this.

When Jack came back to admit he could not change the seating she was disappointed, but not greatly.

'I've decided to enjoy myself,' she said. She held his hand.

'Are you sure? I'm sorry. We can leave straight after the pudding.'

When he put his hand against her stomach, she did not mind – the opposite.

'I like it here.' She kissed him softly on his expensive-smelling cheek and went to sit at the long dining-table in the room closest to the harbour. She found her name card, seated herself, permitted herself to take pleasure from the white linen, the Lalique bowl – she peered around the base and found the signature – even the heavy chandeliers above their heads. She was here to enjoy, not cross-examine.

A tall blond Englishman on her left introduced himself as 'Terry'. His hair fell over his forehead in a stiff lick. He had a black cotton shirt with overlapping double collars which she noticed straightaway. Later she intended to ask him where he bought it.

'Are you the de Kooning man?' she asked.

240

'Well, not the de Kooning woman,' he said, smiling.

'Well, I'm grateful for that,' Maria said, also smiling.

'Oh,' he said, pushing his lick of hair away, 'you're not fond of them?'

'He's such an extraordinary painter,' she said. She was pleased to be here. Tax Department people never talked about painting. Alistair was an educated man, but he would barely have known who de Kooning was. 'I love his work, but the women always frighten me.'

This made the man smile at the edges of his mouth. His eyes became thoughtful.

'Seen the butter?' he asked.

Maria looked for the butter, but could see none. 'He's so lyrical and beautiful,' she said. 'I mean, it's like I'm giving my heart to him and then I walk into the next room and feel I'm in the power of a serial killer. I mean, is he Ted Bundy?'

The man turned towards a puffy-faced dark-haired woman on the other side of the table. Maria imagined he was going to ask for butter. Instead he said: 'Janice, I was very impressed by your piece on our mutual friend, although I really do think you could have taken the matter even further.'

Maria saw she had been cut. She thought: how could you be so unkind to someone who was a stranger and not at home?

She looked across the table towards a man and woman engaged in conversation. The table was very wide. The conversation seemed too far away to enter. The woman was in her early fifties with large eyes and a way of listening that must have been most flattering to the man, who was short and smooth and shaved so close his red cheeks shone like soup bones.

'The thing I object to,' the man said, 'is to pay my taxes, fine, but not to subsidize some bored housewife so she can be pleasured by a doctor.'

It was a moment before she understood his use of 'pleasured'. He meant a vaginal examination. Maria looked at his listener who was studiously brushing toast crumbs off the table cloth. *You hate him surely. You are nodding your head while you despise him.*

'I agree, I agree,' she said. 'I like the American system.'

'No-one ever goes to the doctor in the States just because they're bored.'

'My God, no.'

'But these women are bored,' the man with glistening cheeks said. 'Probably hubby is ignoring them. So they go along to good old Doctor-of-your-choice with their little green and yellow Medicare card.'

When Alistair was running the department it had been flexible enough to accommodate the passions Maria Takis now felt. (You wrote down a Rolls-Royce number plate and checked it out. You saw a lot of marble on a building site, it was enough.) She would have taken pleasure wringing the tax out of the complacent little gynophobe. Indeed, she might yet do it, or have someone do it for her. She looked across the table trying to read his place card upside down.

'I think you're absolutely correct about the de Kooning women,' the man on her right said. 'I never knew how to take them either.'

He introduced himself, but she already knew who he was. She knew his paintings and admired them. She responded to their spareness, their austerity, their refusal ever to be pretty. They did not mesh with the face, which was rather pudgy, and pasty, but rather with the flinty light in his small grey eyes. The colour clung to the canvas like crushed gravel, and it was through them that Maria had learned to love the Australian landscape which she still saw, everywhere, in their terms. It was exhilarating to be in agreement with Phillip Passos about de Kooning.

'Did he buy a "Woman"?' she whispered. 'I feel such a fool. I've insulted him.'

'Him? He's not Digby.' Passos was breaking his bread roll with his shockingly small white hands.

'Then who is it?'

'No one to worry about. Digby's in there, at the Big Table. He bought a rather nice abstract piece from the early fifties. Not "pivotal",' he smiled, 'but "major". He paid 23 million for it.'

'I heard.'

'Well, he thought he had a bargain, because the market is so soft, but now he's in a panic because maybe the market is still falling and he's got to decide whether he has to bid for the next de Kooning. And that's a "pivotal" one. Sotheby's auction it in New York next week. He'll have to be over there to prop up his own investment.'

'I wonder what de Kooning thinks of all this.'

'Not much. He has Alzheimer's, I believe.'

'Well he should be benefiting somehow.'

'Mmmm,' said Passos, looking a little vague.

'Doesn't France have something like this? A Droit de Suite? Don't French artists now get a cut on all future sales of their work?'

Passos cut his smoked salmon carefully. 'What do you do?' he asked.

'Oh, just a public servant,' she said, and was disappointed and relieved to see she had satisfied his curiosity.

'You know what this dinner party is about, do you?'

'The de Kooning man.'

'Nah,' said Passos. 'He's just a bowl of fruit on the table. He's a *nature morte*. He's a thing you arrange other things around. The hidden agenda is Droit de Suite.'

'Oh, you're lobbying? Now?'

'The Attorney General wants artists to love him, and so he introduced this Droit de Suite legislation. Now he's hurt because we don't want it.'

'I would have thought it was great for artists.'

'So did he. So did I. But if it's going to work the art galleries have to keep honest records on how much people paid for paintings.'

Maria was already acting like a spy. 'Oh,' she said, 'so is that a problem?'

'Not if you pay tax. But they don't. They pay cash. Over half of it is funny money. So what the commercial galleries are saying to the government is Droit de Suite is too complicated to administer, and what they're saying to their artists is that over half our collectors will just stop collecting once the Tax Department can check on what is really going on. I can see I've disappointed you.'

'No, really. It's fascinating. Really.'

'Well, you know, we took dirty money from the Medicis, so I guess we'll take it from Jack Catchprice too.'

The smoked salmon on Maria's plate was subtle and flavoursome, and it became, as she separated it from itself on her plate, not like a fish, but something at once alive and abstract, which

243

had been bred for the pleasure of the connoisseur and about whose death she would be wise not to enquire too closely.

54

Frieda's son was now a big man with whorls of tight hair across his chest like a black man. He had soft, teary eyes and his father's lips. 'What did he do to you?' she asked him.

Mort had his big male hand around her arm, above the elbow. He had found her walking up the street towards the highway. He was propelling her back across a gravel car lot in Franklin. She lost one shoe. She kicked off the other. It fell between the treads down on to the gravel.

The annexe smelled like her father's bedroom in Dorrigo.

In her living-room, he pulled out her chair for her and she sat in it. Her stockinged feet were wet. She looked at the room, surprised by its disrepair. He pulled out a dining chair and did not seem to know what to do with it.

'Don't panic, Mort,' she said.

He said: 'I'm really sorry you had to hear this smut.'

'What did he do?'

'He was a good man,' Mort said, holding the back of the chair and lowering his big square stubborn head, his father's head. 'You can rely on that.'

'She says he touched her bosom.'

He sat on the chair. He leaned across and took her hand. 'He was widely liked. I could draw a map for you Mum, and show you where he was liked, all the way over to Warrakup, right over as far as Kiama even,' he smiled. 'I find old codgers who remember him. They hear my name and they say, "You Cacka's son?" I met one old man last week in the Railway Hotel at Warrakup, a Mr Gross.'

'Hector,' she said, but she was not thinking about Hector.

'His wife is called Maisie.'

'Minnie. She had bandy legs.'

He said, "Your old man sold me a Holden and when I complained about the rattle he bought it back from me, cash, in the pub." He said, "I respected him for that."'

'He always had cash. We did a lot of cash business at the

auctions.'

'Probably not a good idea to mention this with the Tax Office snooping around.'

'What did he do to you?'

'He didn't do anything.'

'He touched her bosom.'

'So she says.'

'He did something to you too. That's what she was suggesting.'

'Did WHAT?' he bellowed. It made her jump, the sheer noise of it. That was like him – the father – great rushes of rage coming out of nowhere, not always, not even often, but when you got close to things he wouldn't let you touch.

'Don't panic,' she said.

He had his arms bent around his chest and his forehead lowered and his brows down and his eyes were brimming with enough hate – no other word for it – to burn you.

A moment later he put his hands on his knees and said, 'Sorry.'

A moment more: 'You like me to make a cup of tea?'

Frieda said, 'She's quite correct when she said I knew it was happening.'

'Don't say that.'

'I didn't believe a man would do that, but I knew. I *knew* but I didn't believe.'

'He loved us,' Mort said. 'Whatever he was, he loved us. I know that. I rely on that, to look at him and know he loved us.'

'It's why she hates me, isn't it?'

'It's not for us to judge him. What would they have done to him if it had all come out? How could they understand he loved us?'

'It's why you won't sell cars.'

'What?' Mort screwed up his eyes and pushed his head at her. 'What are you saying?'

'Is that why you won't sell cars . . . because you won't do that for him? You're angry with him still.'

'For Chrissakes, he's dead.'

'But it's what he always wanted for you. He always wanted you to be a salesman.'

'You silly old woman . . .' Mort yelled. 'Someone takes that fucking workshop off my hands, someone hires a service manager and a foreman, I'll sell cars like you never saw them sold.'

'Do you think it's going to rain?' said Mrs Catchprice, looking up towards the ceiling.

'Just lay off,' he said.

'I really think it's going to rain.'

'Get off my back, Frieda. I've got enough problems without this.'

'Good for the gardens,' she said.

They were both silent for a while then, although she could hear him breathing through his mouth. After a while she leaned over and patted his knee. 'There's a boy,' she said.

Mort looked up at her. 'I'm sorry,' he said.

She took his hand and stroked it. 'You know I never wanted this business for myself?'

'Yes, I knew that.'

'You knew?'

'Jesus, Mum,' he took his hand back, 'you told me a hundred times. You wanted a flower farm.' He stood up.

'You think I'm a silly old woman.'

'No I don't.' He sat down. He took her hand in his. 'You know I don't. It would have been a very profitable business. You would have been well situated here.'

'But he still would have been who he was . . .'

'By the railway,' Mort said. 'Right on the railway.'

'He wanted the motor cars so much, I made sure he had them. He loved that first Holden as much as Dame Nellie herself. I must have loved him, don't you think?'

'Of course you did.'

'I don't know I did.' She paused. 'I thought he wasn't very interested in s-e-x. I thought it was the music he had, instead. I couldn't have loved a man who was doing that to my children. I never worried about him playing around. I saw his face listening to the opera. I can't explain the feeling, but I thought – he isn't going to play around. What did he actually do?'

'It's too late now, Mum.' He took his hands back and held them on his knees and rocked a little.

'I'm not dead yet,' she said. 'I have a right to know.'

Mort laughed and shook his head.

'What's so funny?'

He rubbed his hand across his face. 'You're incredible.'

'I said I have a right.'

'Oh no, you have no right.' She had set him off again. He had his arms wrapped around his chest. His eyes were staring at her – hate again – a different person. 'You have no damn right to anything. You are lucky I am still here. You are lucky I don't hate you. You're lucky to have anyone left who'll tolerate you, so don't say you didn't love him, because that would just be . . . I couldn't stand it.'

'Tell me,' Mrs Catchprice said. 'I'm not a child.'

'Jack pisses off. He doesn't care. Cathy pisses off. She doesn't care. I'm the one who's stayed to look after you. So listen to me: don't say you didn't love him, because I couldn't bear it.'

He was breathing hard. She was frightened of him.

'You want to know what he did?' he said at last.

Frieda thought it best to stay quiet.

'DO YOU WANT TO KNOW WHAT HE DID?'

He stood up. He had 'Mort Catchprice' embroidered in blue on his overall pocket.

'I'll tell you. I'm going to tell you. You're old enough to know,' he laughed, an ugly loose-mouthed laugh. 'He had a book, a dictionary of angels, with pictures. Did he ever show it to you? Of course he bloody didn't. He made me dress up like an angel and sing the "Jewel Song". Is that enough?'

It was enough. She nodded.

'You wouldn't want to know what else he did. You wouldn't want to even imagine it.' He was crying. He was ruined, wrecked, a human being with nothing.

She had made this, invented it. She knew she was 100 per cent responsible.

'What would that have done to you?' he said. 'What sort of person would you have become?' He had tears running down his big squashed nose. He was all crumpled up like rubbish in the bin.

Frieda went to the kitchen to phone the Hare Krishna temple.

55

'What's that film?' the Attorney General said. 'I forget its name . . .'

'*Jean d'Aboire*,' Jack said.

'That's the one,' the Attorney General said. 'It was pure Louis Quatorze. Most of them stuff it up, you know, the Yanks all the time, but the Frogs too – they put Empire and even Chippendale in with Louis Quatorze, but this *Jean d'Aboire* was spot on. They got the clothes right, everything. They got the little bodices,' he made small pinching gestures with his big fingers, holding them up near his tailored lapels. 'Just right,' the Attorney General said, before returning to his smoked salmon. 'They got everything right, it was just immaculate.'

Jack was worried about Maria. His view of her was obscured by the return wall with the doubtful Tiepolo on it. All he could see was her shoulder and George Grissenden. Grissenden could be very funny, if he wanted to be.

Across the table Digby was complaining loudly about Sotheby's who were offering to finance his bid on the New York de Kooning. To his left, Betty Finch had her eyes glued on the Attorney General and Jack had, occasionally, to head off her graceless attempts to bring the conversation directly to the matter of Droit de Suite. Nobody had bothered to brief her on the manners of lobbying.

He saw Maria stand and leave the room. He smiled in her direction, but she did not seem to see him. Then, through the open archway to his right, he saw her use the hall phone.

'So when you see a movie,' Jack said to the Attorney General, 'you're really more interested in the spoons than the drama.'

It was intended as a joke, but the Attorney General took it seriously. 'Absolutely,' he said. 'This *Jean d'Aboire* got it spot on.'

Jack looked towards the hall. Maria had gone. He looked towards her place – George Grissenden was removing smoked salmon from the plate in front of her empty chair.

From the street he heard electronic beeps and a hissing, high-pitched Holden water pump. *Maria.* He excused himself and walked out on to the street still carrying his damask napkin. The taxi's tail lights were speeding away in the direction of the cul de sac. He was so confident it was Maria, that he stood in the middle of road, waving the taxi down with his napkin.

He shaded his eyes, moving round the car towards a window which was already rolling down.

'Enjoy your dinner,' Maria said. 'We can talk tomorrow.'

'What happened?'

'Nothing happened.'

'It was George Grissenden. He's such a fascist. What happened?'

'Jack, I'm eight months pregnant. I'm very tired.'

'I'm driving you home.' He opened the door.

'Please, no, *please*.'

But he coaxed her from the cab, paid off the driver, escorted her to his car, and ran back into the house with his white napkin. He was back at the Jaguar in a moment.

'I told them you were going into labour.'

She did not smile.

He started the engine. 'I told them your family all had short labours.'

He could see her in the corner of his eye with her hands across her belly and the high fine nose and curly hair silhouetted against the window. He felt the silence like a screw turning in his throat. He drove quickly, but with excessive care, as if there was some fragile thing in the trunk he was fearful of breaking.

He turned right and headed down the hill towards Double Bay where Maria had left her car parked in front of his house.

'They're creeps, I guess,' he said at last.

'Yes,' she said.

He was frightened by the bluntness of her answer. He waited for her to say something else but nothing else was forthcoming.

'Were they terrible creeps?' he asked at last.

'Oh no,' Maria sighed. 'Probably not,' but there was a weariness in her voice that suggested to him that he had already lost her. 'I've admired Phillip Passos for years. It was great to meet him.'

'What happened then?'

'Oh, it's nothing new.'

'Were they rude to you?'

'I'm always shocked to hear wealthy people complaining about tax. I should be used to it. I should be very thick-skinned. In fact, I thought I was thick-skinned, but I watch them eating with their Georg Jensen cutlery and I want to stand up and shout and make speeches about poverty and homelessness.'

They had to stop for a red light at O'Sullivan Road. Across the road there were yachts bobbing at their moorings in the moonlight.

'I knew this was a bad idea,' Jack said. 'But I wanted to see you so badly and I was impatient. I was being expedient again.'

'Is expediency a problem with you?'

She had that edge in her voice, the same as when she asked him about working for money.

'Not normally,' he said curtly.

He did not need her to tell him – expediency ruled his life and made it shallow and unsatisfying. He could analyse all this a hundred times better than she could, more harshly too. He was a Catchprice – damaged, compromised, expedient – full of it.

'Know a man's friends and you know the man,' he said, bitterly.

'You are different?'

'Don't I seem different?'

'Yes, you do seem different.' It was the first time her voice had softened. When he looked across she was, finally, looking at him.

'Have you heard me complain about taxes?'

'Jack, tonight I listened to a very distinguished artist argue against Droit de Suite. In fact, I discovered, that's what we were there to do.'

'No,' he said. 'We were there because I've fallen in love with you and I had to go to dinner.'

She gave no sign of what this declaration meant to her.

'He was against it,' she said, 'because he believed the "funny money" would not go into art if investors had to pay tax on that money first.'

'You mean I'm taking bread out of the mouths of children.'

He was embarrassed and humiliated. He turned right into Cross Street, swinging the wheel and accelerating so that the Michelins screamed and smoked.

'I'm *pregnant*. Slow down.'

He slowed down, until the car was barely moving and then slid into the kerb.

'That was *stupid*.'

He turned off the engine and turned in his seat.

'I'm sorry,' he said. 'That was reckless. I love you both.'

He felt it himself – it was a false note, but God damn it, it was true. 'So now,' he said, 'you don't like me.'

'I don't doubt you have these feelings,' she put her hand on his. 'I just feel odd about you. Jack, I've only just met you and I'm very tired.'

'I want to look after you, and the baby too. It's all I want.'

She did not answer him. When he looked across he was shocked to see that she had begun to cry. She said: 'Do you want a baby? Is that it?' He tried to hold her but she pulled away from him, her face distorted.

'Maria, please . . .'

'I wish you could have it. Jack. I really do.' She looked like a Francis Bacon smeared with neon light. 'I don't want the fucking thing. I don't want to give birth to anything.'

'It'll be O.K.,' he said, shocked by her language.

'Don't you dare say it's O.K. *Christ.*'

'I'm with you.' He gave her tissues from the glove box.

'No, Jack, I'm sorry.' She blew her nose.

'What if I let you audit me?'

She looked at him with her mouth open, her cheeks wet. Then she started laughing and shaking her head. She blew her nose again, loudly.

'Is that so funny?'

'Yes, it's very funny.'

'Why?'

'Oh Jack . . .'

'Why?'

'Jack, please, if you care for me, just drive me to my car so I can go home and sleep.'

'You can sleep at my house, not the Bilgola house, the one here. You could be in bed in five minutes.'

'Jack, I'm tired, I'm not interested.'

'Maria, please, I'm not talking about sex.'

'No,' she said. 'I'm not coming to your house.'

He put his hands on the wheel and his head on his hands. 'I'm getting angry because I feel I'm ruining something very important in my life. We are just getting to know each other and I'm ruining it.'

'Jack,' she said. She unclasped a hand from the steering wheel and held it. 'You're very sweet and gentle, but you belong to an alien culture.'

He took his other hand from the steering wheel and put both his hands around hers. 'I can change. Don't roll your eyes.'

'I'm sorry. I'm tired.'

'If no one can change,' he said, 'what point is there in anything? If we cannot affect each other's lives, we might as well call it a day.

251

The world is just going to slide further and further into the sewer.'

She turned away from him. He saw her staring into the brightly lit shop where they advertised Comme des Garçons and Issey Miyake at 50 per cent off.

'You don't believe that we can change?' he asked. 'We can.'

'You should have said these things to me when I was twenty. How would you change, Jack? What would you do?'

'I could become a person you could trust, whom you could rely on totally.'

'Are you that now?'

'Not totally, not at all really.'

'Why me? Why am I so important to the Catchprices?'

He hit the steering wheel with his fist. He did not know his nephew had done a similar thing with a glove box lid. 'I'll drive you to the hospital when you go into labour. I'll come round and do the laundry for you. I'll make the formula. O.K., you'll probably be breast feeding, but I'll do what you need. I've got money. I'll hire help. Maria, please, I've done some rotten things, but the only reason I'm sitting here with you is that I'm not going to be like that any more.'

'You're going to be transformed through love?'

'Yes I am.'

She shook her head.

'Parents die to save their babies through love,' he said. 'There's nothing romantic about it. It's a mechanism. It's built into us whether we like it or not. It's how the species saves itself.'

She was listening to him. She was frowning, but her lips were parted, had in fact been parted so long that now she moistened them.

'If we can't change,' he said, 'we're dead.'

He leaned forward to kiss her. The Tax Inspector took his lips in hers and found herself, to her surprise, feeding on them.

56

At half-past eleven, standing in her kitchen, Maria Takis drank the bitter infusion of raspberry leaf tea and worried, as usual, if she had made it strong enough, if it would really work, if the muscles of her uterus were being really aided by this unpleasant treatment, or if it was some hippy mumbo jumbo that would – if it was too strong – give her liver cancer instead.

She removed her make up, put on her moisturiser in the bathroom and then lay on the living-room floor to do her pelvic floor exercises. In bed she massaged her perineum, swallowed three 200 mg calcium tablets and a multi-vitamin pill. By the time she could begin her 'Visualizing, Actualizing' exercise it was already half-past twelve. She turned off the overhead light and flicked on the reading light. She propped herself up on two pillows and closed her eyes.

She descended the blue staircase (its treads shimmering like oil on water, its bannisters clear, clean, stainless steel).

At the bottom of the blue staircase she found the yellow staircase.

At the bottom of the yellow staircase, the pink.

At the bottom of the pink, the ebony.

And the end of the ebony, the Golden Door.

Beyond the Golden Door was the Circular Room of Black Marble.

In the centre of the Circular Room of Black Marble, she visualized a Sony Trinitron.

She had found a picture of the Sony. She could visualize it exactly, right down to the three small dots beneath the screen: one red, one blue, one yellow.

She imagined turning on the Sony Trinitron. She imagined the picture emerging: Maria and her baby, sitting up in bed. She had done this almost every night for three months now, but still she could not get the mental picture clear. It was a little girl she tried to visualize. She made her pink. This was corny, but achievable. She could visualize the colour but not her face. The face shifted, dissolved, shivered, like an image on a bed of mercury. She held the shawl against her. She held it to her breast. She pressed her eyes tight, trying to stop thinking about Jack Catchprice. The picture of her baby would not come clearly. It never would. The baby cried and pushed at her. She could feel anxiety and impatience, but not the things she wanted to. Love was not visual. It did not work.

At twenty-past eleven, Cathy McPherson was still celebrating with the band. It was her last night inside the enclosure at Catchprice Motors. She poured a Resch's Pilsener for Mickey Wright. On stage he would wear the glittery black shirt Cathy had chosen for him, but now he was his own man and he wore blue stubby shorts, a 'Rip Curl' T-shirt, and rubber thongs. He had sturdy white legs and heavy muscled forearms. As she poured the beer he tapped the glass with a ballpoint pen. He was a drummer. He couldn't stop drumming. As the beer rose, the pitch changed. It was not a joke, not an anything. He could not help himself. With his right hand he paddled a table tennis bat upon his knee. He was the drummer. Drrrrrrrrrr. He was the one who had to take the drummer jokes. *Q: What do you call someone who hangs around with a band? A: A drummer. Q: Why should Mickey go to the Baltic States? A: He might get independence too.*

The truth was: Mickey was the best musician of the lot of them, and as for independence (the ability to keep different rhythms going simultaneously) he had it in bags. There were drummers making records, famous drummers on hit records, who could barely keep two patterns going. Buddy Rich could do two. Mickey could do four.

He was the ambitious one. The others would settle for a living, but Mickey was always pushing towards places it was bad luck even to dream about.

'I'll tell you what you want to do, Cathy, you want to get "Drunk as a Lord" to Emmylou Harris. No, no, not her agent.' He had a squashed-up Irish face, a boxer's nose. His whole manner was dry, dead-pan. 'Not her agent. Agents never know. You get it to her, direct.'

'The truth is,' said Howie, who was playing poker with Stevie Putzel, 'Emmylou Harris wouldn't do it half as well, you want to know the truth.'

'Sure,' said Mickey. He made a paradiddle with the tennis ball against the table: drrrrrrrrr. 'We'd all get rich listening to her fuck it up.' He looked up at Howie, blank-faced. Who could say if he would be trouble or not.

Howie was playing poker with Steve Putzel. The two of them were standing up, using the ping-pong table for the deck. Howie was watching Cathy more than his cards and was losing badly because of it. Cathy was mad at Mickey for calling in the lawyers.

'Come on, come on,' Steve said to Howie. 'You chucking out or what?'

'We're going to make it, Cath,' said Mickey. He drummed the bat, table, knee: Drrrrrrrrrrrrrrrr. Mickey could talk about success like other guys could talk about sex. He was never sick of it.

Cathy smiled. The apartment did not feel like a home any more, but like a clean-up room in a country motel. There were peanut husks and empty beer cans on the floor. It had never looked so good to her.

'This time, no shit,' Mickey said. Drrrrrrrr. 'We're the right age for it. You read your history books. We're the right age to make the break, believe me.'

'You're a fucking megalomaniac,' said Johnno Renvoise.

The lead guitarist was stretched out to his entire six foot three inches beneath the ping-pong table with his hand-tooled boots folded underneath his head.

'You know what a gentleman is, Johnno?' Mickey asked.

'Ha-ha.'

'A gentleman is someone who can play the accordion and doesn't.'

'Ha-ha,' Johnno Renvoise was happy. He kept *saying* he was happy. Everyone knew he had lost his wife and kids but he was happy because Big Mack were on the road. He held out his empty beer glass with one hand; with the other he threw crackers against the bottom of the table top and tried to catch the fragments in his mouth.

'Christ, Howie,' said Steve, 'you're so fucking impulsive.'

'Never rush,' Howie smiled and lowered his heavy lids.

Howie laid down his hand on the table where he had filled in the PA forms for each and every one of Cathy's songs and copyrighted them at $10 U.S. a time with the Library of Congress. He had made her use Albert's for her demos. Sometimes they paid two thousand bucks just for a demo. It was investment. He did not want to count the dollars. Now she had 'Drunk as a Lord' on the Country charts but even now – while everyone celebrated – he knew he would have to deal with some new tactic from Frieda. She would not let her daughter go so easily.

Mort Catchprice walked round the edge of the Big Mack truck feeling its chalky duco. It was a shitty vehicle for a Catchprice to have, an offence to anyone who cared about how a car yard should be laid out – its wheels were crooked, it dropped oil on the gravel, its front tyres were half scrubbed, and it was parked bang smack beneath the rear spotlight.

Mort's shoulders were rounded and his hands hung by his sides. He walked round the side of the old lube into the dark alleyway which led to his empty house.

Sarkis Alaverdian lay on his back in his bedroom with his arm flung out and an open copy of *Guide to Vehicle Sales at Auction This Week* on his broad bare chest. His mother tried to remove the book but he began to wake. She turned off the overhead light and knelt at the foot of the bed. Dalida Alaverdian prayed that Zorig might still be alive. She prayed that she would get a job. She prayed for Mrs Catchprice and the prosperity of Catchprice Motors.

A little after midnight Vish let himself into the Spare Parts Department, cut off the burglar alarm, and walked through the tall racks of spare parts through the car yard and up the stairs to his grandmother's apartment. She was waiting for him in the annexe, dressed formally in the suit she had worn to her husband's funeral.

'Are you game?' she asked him.

'I'm game,' he said, but he was frightened, by the suit, by the manner, but more by the realization that she had probably been standing alone in the dark here for an hour or more.

'I don't want your life ruined by this,' she said. He did not ask what 'this' was. He followed her across the creaking floors to her bedroom. 'You can go back on the milk train when it's done.'

In the half-dark bedroom she knelt in front of her old mirrored armoire.

'Gran what are we doing?' he said.

From the armoire floor she produced shoes, slippers and a pair of men's pyjamas.

'Do I have to explain it to you?' Granny Catchprice asked. Her mood was odd, more hostile than her words suggested. She threw the slippers and pyjamas into the corner. She pulled out a roll of something like electrical wire, striped red and white.

'Well yes,' he said, 'I think you do.'

The dog took the slippers and brought them back. It jumped up on Vish's back. He slapped its snout. The dog snarled and then retreated under the bed with the striped pyjamas. When Vish looked up he found his Granny looking at him. Her mouth was sort of slack.

'It's Vish,' he said.

'For God's sake,' she said. 'I do know who you are.'

'You said you were closing down the business if I came.'

'I know I'm just a stupid old woman, but why don't you look in front of your nose.' She nodded her head towards the open armoire door. Vish could smell camphor but all he could see inside the armoire was some item of pink underwear. 'It's at the end of your nose,' she said. She gave him an odd triumphant smirk that did not sit well with her cloudy eyes. It was the first time he ever thought her senile.

She winked at him. It felt lewd, somehow related to the ancient underwear which she now – smiling at him all the time – lifted. Underneath was a beautiful wooden crate with dovetail joints.

'I'm just a silly old woman,' she said. 'I know.'

If he had been able to pretend he did not know what he was up to, that time had passed. The word was on the box: Nobel.

'Well,' she grunted and stood, indicating that he should lift it out.

Vish had always imagined gelignite would be heavy, but when he picked up the box its lightness took him by surprise. Sawdust leaked from it like sand and gathered in the folds of his kurta.

They opened the box on Granny Catchprice's unmade bed. Its contents smelt like over-ripe papaya.

At half-past two Maria, who had dozed off in the middle of her Visualizations exercise, opened her eyes and saw Benny Catchprice standing at the foot of her bed.

At two-thirty-three, Vishnabarnu and Granny Catchprice began to lay the first charges in the structural walls of the showroom beneath her apartment. They had the main overhead lights turned off, but the lights in the yard cast a bright blue glow over their work. Granny Catchprice was on her knees at the east wall. She had a chisel and a hammer and she was looking for the place where the electrician had brought through the power cable thirty years before. Later there was a rat hole there – she remembered it.

'How are we going to get them out?' Vish said. 'I don't want to murder anyone.'

'There'll be no trouble getting them out. By jove,' she laughed. 'You'll see them running. Here give me that stick.'

The rat hole had been plugged with mortar and paper. A bodgey job, but now it made a perfect place to pack the gelly.

'You'll get the blame,' he said. 'They'll know it's you.'

Of course – he looked like Cacka. She always knew that. It struck her in a different way tonight – when he repeated back to her things she had already told him. That was Cacka all over.

'Blame me,' she said. She cleared the mess from the hole with the chisel and jammed the gelignite without any concern for the ancient material's stability. 'Blame me. It's mine, that's what they forget. It was my idea. It's mine to do with what I like.'

'Gran, I think you sold your shares.'

'One thing I learnt in life, you'll always find people to tell you you can't do what you want to do.' She wiped her sticky hands on her suit jacket. 'Help me up. My knees hurt.'

She found another hole against the skirting board but it was not substantial. The gelly would have done nothing more than blow the skirting board off.

'You're going to have to go down under the floor,' she told him. He had that square head and those lips. 'The bricks are old hand-made ones, so they're soft,' she said.

'Gran, do you really mean to be this drastic?'

'It's not hard, you can knock a brick out with a hammer. What you've got to do is pack it tight.'

'How do you know they won't get hurt?'

'They won't be there,' his Gran said. 'We'll tell them and they'll leave.'

'They'll call the police,' Vish said.

'Police!' she said, and clipped him around the ears.

She was thinking of Cacka.

'Please, no,' Vish said. 'Maybe this is not such a great idea.'

'You coward,' she said, hitting him again. She shocked herself with the strength of her blow, the pleasure of it. She pulled up the trap door beside the salesman's office. She gave him the flashlight. 'You leave the police to me. I never have a problem with police,' she said. 'You get down there, filth. I want a stick every three feet, and when you've done that you come back to me and I'll teach you how to use the crimping pliers.'

She sat down then in the swivel chair behind the Commodore brochures. She lit a Salem and drew a long rasping line of smoke down deep into her lungs. She closed her eyes and opened her mouth and let the smoke just waft away. *The dragon lady.* She grinned. Perhaps she was too angry to be actually happy and yet a certain amount of anger or irritation had never been incompatible with Frieda McClusky's happiness. Revenge, retribution – these were pepper, curry. She smoked her Salem in long deep drafts and enjoyed the slow abrasive feeling. *I'm not dead yet.* She had been duped, yes, but she was alive and he was dead. She had a plan. She was always the one with the plan.

I know I'm just a stupid old lady . . .

To call it a 'plan' was to diminish it. Once she would have done that. *I'm just a silly woman.* This was not a plan. It was a vision, the same one, the only one – a flower farm on the site of Catchprice Motors. *Do you think that it's impractical?* Irises, roses, petunias, long rows running parallel to the railway line and right across to Loftus Street. Propane trucks and concrete trucks bounced beside them, but in the centre of the farm there was just the smell of humus, of roses and the rich over-ripe smell of blood and bone.

In this garden Cacka did not exist. Her children had not been born.

57

As Maria Takis entered the cellar, Benny Catchprice remained behind her with his shot gun pushing into the base of her spine. He had already cut her cheek with it, and it did not even occur to her to plead with him.

It was like a subway tunnel in here. She could smell her death in the stink of the water. Even while she had fought to stop his grandmother being committed, all this – the innards of Catchprice Motors – had been here, underneath her feet. She did not see her name written on the wall, but in any case she did not understand the parts or what they did – the snakes in bottles, the cords tied with plastic, the writing on the wall, the ugly white fibreglass board with its straps and buckles. How could you ever understand it? It was like some creature run over on the road. The rough-sawn barrel grabbed and tore at her dress.

Benny saw the thing he had made: belts, buckles, trusses. He knew already that it was wrong. He had built it for her but he had not thought of how she was. He said he was going to fuck her. He did not want to fuck her, not at all. On the other hand: this was his course. He had visualized it, committed to it. He was going down this road at 200Ks. No way could he turn around.

Maria felt the beginning of another period pain. It was only now she realized these must be contractions. They were coming every five minutes or so. The pain tightened in her gut – this one made it hard to breathe. Through the pain she heard Benny Catchprice: 'This is where I come from,' he said. 'This is where I live.' He was whining. When he whined, he seemed softer, blond and pink-cheeked, baby-skinned, but he was not softer. The whining was joined to the anger, the anger was joined to the gas-jet eyes that threatened her and tore at her with the barbed steel of the shot gun barrel. 'I know you wouldn't ask a human being to live here. But you just walked away and left me here.'

The pain in her womb was like a great fist clenching. If it had been within her power she would have squashed him like a cockroach.

As the pain began to leave her, he moved round her and sat in front of her on the sofa. He balanced the gun on his knee while he began to take his shoes off.

'I like you,' Benny said, looking up from unlacing. He was taking one step at a time. He should tell her get her clothes off, but he did not want to. He did not have a fucking hard-on yet. He took his shoes off slowly, as slowly as he could manage it. 'You tried to run away from me, but I still like you.'

Maria thought he had pretty, slippery lips and dangerous, senti-mental eyes. She saw a teenage boy beset with lust and shyness – they were squashed in together like buckshot into chewing gum. He probably did not even know himself what cruelty he was cap-able of.

'I won't run away,' she said.

'Bullshit,' he shouted. He liked to shout. He liked to feel his voice fill up the room. He scared himself at the thought of what crazy thing he might next do. When he shouted at Cathy she always, finally, collapsed before him. Her face would turn from hard to sorry.

Maria flinched when he shouted, but then the face just hardened. You could see it set into place. He saw her eyes becoming dark and hostile. He could not let her stay like this.

'You don't like me,' he said. He wanted to be friends with her. He wanted her to stroke his hair, maybe, kiss him on his eyes, that sort of thing. Not fuck, not unless she made him. Most of all he wanted her to smile at him. He was trying to find a way back to the place where that might just be possible.

She watched him pout. She watched in chilly fascination as he pulled off his thin black socks, and rolled them up one-handed.

'It's dirty here,' he said. 'I'm sorry about that part of it.' She noticed that his hands were trembling. He rubbed his heels and soles with his hands. He gave the impression of being fine and pretty, but his feet were big, netted with the red chain-mail imprint of his socks. 'I didn't want it to be dirty.'

Her mouth was dry. She thought of all the 'useful tips' in birth class, how you should take a spray pack of Evian water and a sponge to suck.

'I wanted it to be clean.'

Now he was removing the trousers, with one hand, holding the shot gun with the other. He had shiny hairless legs like a girl.

'This isn't what you want,' she said. 'You don't do this to someone you like.'

'Shut *up*,' he said. 'You don't even know what I'm going to do to you.'

'This isn't what you want,' she repeated.

'Shut up,' he screamed. 'I'm the one in charge.'

Her eyes just seemed to narrow. When he saw her go like this, he knew he would have to make her cry.

'Don't tell me what I want,' he said. 'I know what I want.'

He would have to make her soft.

She said it again: 'This isn't what you want.'

'You don't get it,' he said. 'I *visualized* what is happening now. I *committed*. With a witness. Everything I commit to, I do. This is why I am a success.'

'You committed? You made an affirmation, is that what you mean? You sent away for the tape?' She stepped towards him. He pushed back at her with the gun. 'You paid five hundred dollars?' she said.

'You think I can't afford it?'

Oh dear God, I am part of Benny Catchprice's affirmation.

'Benny, am I your objective?'

'Mind your own business. How do you know about this stuff?'

'What was your Desire?'

'You bitch. Don't you do this. Don't you steal my stuff.'

'I was your Desire?'

'I am an angel. I'm a fucking angel now.' He was standing and shouting. She had all her clothes on. He was almost fucking starkers. 'I am an angel.' He screamed at her. It was his mad act. He was a demon. He made himself dribble. 'Ask me what angel I am.'

He had the gun up, pointed at her head.

Maria Takis knew she would have to die. Another contraction was here already, so soon. She felt the pain coming into the dark cloud of her present terror.

Benny Catchprice was still yelling: 'Ask me! Ask me!'

She managed to say: 'What angel are you?'

'Angel of lust,' he said. He licked his lips. 'Angel of fire.'

'You're going to have to kill me,' she said. 'You know that. If you think you're going to put me on that thing, you're going to have to kill me. That means you'll kill my baby too.'

'No.' He exploded. He was a spider, a lethal creature with his long shapely hairless legs protruding from a black silk carapace. He shoved his gun forward at her face. She screwed up her face against the darkness of the barrel, but then she saw him change his mind. He lowered the gun, and slapped her face. Her head jolted sideways and she felt a searing pain down her side. He did it again, so lights exploded against the screen of her retina. She stumbled and fell. 'Don't you ever, don't you *ever* even think of it.'

On the floor, she scraped her arm across a board and found her hand in tepid water. It touched something – a bar, a rod. She grasped it. He took a step back and she clambered to her feet, holding out her weapon: a tyre lever, slimy with rust. She hardly recognized the voice that came from her throat. 'You come near me,' she shouted, 'I'll break your arm.'

She was breathing hard. The pain came again. It was a tight hard pain, so hard she could not have talked if she had wanted to.

'You don't like me,' he said. 'I like you but you don't like me. What's the matter? What's the matter?'

The matter was the pain. 'Shut up.'

'I am my word,' Benny said. 'You've got to understand that – I committed.'

Behind her she heard the door handle rattle, a light tap on the cellar door.

Thank God. Dear God please save me.

'It's me, Vish,' a voice said. 'Can I come in?'

'Piss off.'

'Benny, you got to get out.'

'I'm not getting out.'

Maria screamed through the middle of her contraction. Benny lifted the gun towards her and she swung the bar hard at him. She missed.

'You got to get out. This place is going to go sky-high.'

Maria screamed again. 'Help me!'

Benny waved the sawn-off gun at Maria Takis while he shouted at the door. 'I don't need you, you fucking sell-out, you Jesus creep.'

'I'm coming in,' said Vish.

There was no warning: the shot gun exploded and blew a splintered hole in the wooden door. Shot rattled and ricocheted around the cellar. Maria felt a hot stinging in her upper arm, her waist, her thigh, her calf.

She looked at Benny Catchprice as he walked towards the door, bleeding from the cheek. He opened the door, but there was no one there. He turned back to her.

'What do you think I am?' he said.

She did not understand the question.

'I don't want to hurt the baby,' he said.

'Shut up.' She panted. She did not want to pant. She did not want to let him know what was happening to her. But now the pain was so bad she had no choice but to pant through it. She had the iron bar. He took the gun into his right hand, but then he put it back.

'You think I'm an animal, because I live here. I wouldn't hurt your baby.'

The pain was going.

'You're doing it now,' she said. She saw it frightened him. 'You're hurting the baby right now, this minute. You're killing it.'

'No,' he shouted.

'I'm having the baby now,' she said. 'It's coming.'

She saw his face. He was a child again, undecided. His mouth opened.

'This is very serious,' she said.

'Shut up, I know.'

Maria lowered the iron bar. 'You get me out of here right now,' she said. 'You can save this baby if you want to.'

Thursday

58

Vish's arm was like a run-over cat. It did not hurt. He could see pieces of white among the red. He thought: bone. The red ran through the yellow robe like paint on unsized canvas. He felt the blood drip on to his foot. It felt warm, oddly pleasant.

He walked up the steps from Benny's cellar, crossed the old lube bay and went straight on up the stairs to Cathy's flat. He banged on the door and walked right on in. He was hollering even going across the kitchen. 'Get out,' he said. 'She's going to do it.'

He turned on the lights in their bedroom. They had no air conditioning on account of Howie's asthma. They were lying on top of the sheets. Howie was bright purple across his chest. He had a fat ugly penis with a ragged uncircumcised foreskin. Cathy was wearing an outsize T-shirt with "Cotton Country" written on it.

'Come on,' he said. 'Sorry.' He meant there was blood dripping on their shag pile carpet.

'What's happened?' Howie asked. He was fishing in the drawer for his underpants. His back was white. He had no arse to talk of.

'Hurry,' Vish said.

He shepherded them through their kitchen. There were big splashes from his arm across the floor. 'She's crazy. She's blowing us all up.'

'What did she do to you?' Cathy said. She was looking at his arm. She thought Gran had hurt his arm. She wanted to tie a bandage but he pushed her away with his good arm.

'Run,' he said. 'The fuses are burning.'

This was not true.

Howie had underpants on. Cathy's shirt came to her knees. They came down the stairs to the lube bay and hippety hopped across the bright-lit gravel like people walking bare-foot from their car to a beach.

Granny was at the bottom of her fire-escape still holding the roll of safety fuse.

'There she is,' he shouted.

He shouted not for them, but for her. He was trying to signal

Granny Catchprice that the plan had got to change now. Howie and Cathy ran towards her. Then Howie was holding Gran. He was taking the safety fuse from her. Cathy and Howie had already stepped over a two-metre length of it at the bottom of their stairs without noticing. It was bright red and white and striped like a barber's pole but they did not see it. There were other pieces, one, two, three metres, sticking out from the air vents at the base of the workshop and the showroom walls. Each one ran into the cob-webbed underfloor, where it was crimped tight inside a detonator. Each detonator, in turn, was jammed into a clammy half stick of gelignite. The gelignite was wedged in among the crumbling brick piers which supported the building.

While Cathy and Howie shouted at Granny Catchprice, Vish stooped to light a fuse. He had not been able to get gelignite below the ground at the old lube bay. There was no sub-floor – only cellar. He had to pack it into the drainpipes which ran beneath the con-crete slab. He lit the fuse the way his Grandma had taught him, holding the match tight against the fuse and scraping the box across it. He chanted as he scraped. Hare Krishna, Hare Krishna. The fuse did not sparkle like a fuse in a cartoon. You could hardly see a flame at all. The fire slipped down into the tunnel of fuse casing. It made an occasional spark, a fart of blue smoke, a tiny heat bubble. It sneaked off like a spy, travelling 30 cm every ten seconds.

Vish thought he might die. He thought about God. Hare Krishna, Hare Krishna, running through this gravel-floored hell of bright painted things.

Howie and Cathy were pushing Granny back towards the fire escape. He hollered to them, 'No, she lit them off already,' and then he remembered he was not thinking of God, he must think of God, that all that was necessary was to think of God.

He prayed Benny would be safe. He was in the cellar with some woman. He did not know he would be safe. How could he know?

Cathy and Howie were now walking towards him. They had left Granny Catchprice standing alone at the bottom of the fire escape. Cathy had seen the plume of blue smoke coming from a fuse. She was pointing at it, stamping at it.

'It was her,' he pointed back at Granny Catchprice. *Hare Krishna, Hare Krishna.* 'She's crazy.'

Behind Cathy and Howie's shouting faces he could see his grandmother in her severe black suit. She had walked across the car yard to the workshop wall. She was working her way along the side of the wall, stooping, like a gardener weeding. She was lighting fuses. She had damp matches from her kitchen. Sometimes, he could see, these slowed her down.

Howie was panting and shouting at him. It was a moment before he saw what he wanted – the matches.

He pointed across the yard at Granny Catchprice. 'It's her,' he said. He handed Howie the matches. 'I took them off her, the crazy bitch. There she goes again.'

Hare Krishna, Hare Krishna. Not die. Not go to jail.

'Where's Benny?' Cathy yelled.

'You can't go down there,' he said. 'You'll get blown up.'

She tried to. She ran for the steps.

Howie grabbed Cathy. She had no underpants. He picked her up and carried her bare-arsed across the yard. She struggled and hit his head.

'Mort,' she called. 'What about Mort?'

'He's O.K.,' Vish said. He did not know he was O.K. He had fucked it up. He had changed the plan. It was Benny's fault. He had tried to murder him. It was Krishna who came to punish the people who hurt the followers of Krishna.

Vish walked slowly across the yard. He felt heat like a furnace in his wounded arm. He did not hurry. The Lord would decide when it ignited.

He had reached the front gate when the first explosion came. It spat out bricks and showered them over the cars. They rained down, bang, bang, bang.

He turned and saw a hole, like a tunnel, in the wall of Spare Parts. Nothing more. Granny Catchprice was fumbling with her matches at the Front Office. Then the next one went. It made a deeper 'crump' you could feel in your feet, in the earth. When Vish turned to look, he found the wall of the workshop was missing. The yard lights shone into the dusty rafters. A brush-tailed possum stood on the great iron beam above Mort's desk. Its eyes shone bright yellow through the mortar dust.

Then many things happened at once. Vish lay down on the ground and felt it move beneath him. He put his head under the Audi radiator. There was some fire, flame. He felt the heat in his bare legs and saw the orange light across the gravel. There was a 'Whoomf' noise.

It was then he thought about the petrol tanks beneath the cracked concrete at the front of the front office.

He stood up and started running towards the street.

59

Howie raised himself from the ground beside his wife. The yard was filled with lime dust and petrol fumes. The lights stood on their tall poles, sloping, twisted on their stems like Iceland poppies. Granny Catchprice, dressed in a tattered black, white and red clown's suit, moved into their beam, dust still swirling all round her.

The old chook could walk through hell.

As she turned, she looked as though she came from hell: she had put on a mask, like a witch with long, carved, wooden teeth. She stopped to pick a lump of brick from the bonnet of the Commodore. It was too heavy for her. She pushed it off, scraped it across the duco, down the slope of the bonnet and on to the ground.

Cathy was sitting on the gravel beside him. She said: 'I got no pants.'

Howie helped her to her feet. She tugged down on her T-shirt, more worried about her arse than everything around her. He put his arm round her shoulders and felt she was shaking like a leaf.

'Come on, honey,' he said. 'Come on baby, it's O.K.' He walked her towards the street, towards Granny Catchprice who was now pushing at a clump of bricks which had fallen on the Audi's sleek black hood.

'I need a dress,' Cathy said. 'Where are my shoes?'

'I'll get the truck out,' he said. 'All the gear is in the truck. Once we get the truck out we're O.K.'

It was then he saw the flowers on the gravel, a line of them from the crumpled Spare Parts Department wall to the buckled cyclone gates, splashes the size of carnations. They fell from Granny Catchprice's face – fat drops of bright blood.

There was a noise like a calf bellowing. Howie turned to see a black track-suited figure running over the rubble of what had been their apartment. The noise was Mort. A figure in yellow robes was also stumbling towards them. The noise was Vish. They were both the noise, coming towards Granny Catchprice. She recognized the noise and turned. It was then Howie saw how badly hurt she was – the gelignite had ripped her face back to the bone, up from the gums and teeth to the nose. In the middle of this destruction, her eyes looked out like frightened things buried beneath a muddy field.

'He touched her breasts,' she said.

Howie put his hand around beneath her ribs to steady her. There was nothing to her – rag and bone. As he lay her down upon the gravel, she trembled and whimpered. It seemed too cruel to lay her head upon the gravel. He placed his hand beneath her for a pillow and squatted down beside her.

'It's O.K., Frieda,' he said.

'Rot!' she said.

Howie felt himself pushed aside. It was Cathy, Mort, Vish – the Catchprices. They pushed him out like foreign matter. Cathy took her mother's head and cradled it. Mort held her hand. They made a clump, a mass, they clung to her, like piglets at an old sow.

'Come on, honey,' he pulled at his wife's shoulder. 'Come on.' But they made a heap of bodies which left no room for him.

Howie walked back to the Big Mack truck alone. The engine was new and tight, but it started first off. He threw the long stick back into reverse, and edged the truck back until he felt resistance. Then he squeezed it forward, manoeuvring between the dust silver Statesman with black leather upholstery and the Commodore SS with the alloy wheels. It was a tight fit. He edged slowly past the red Barina Benny nearly sold to Gino Massaro.

But when he came to the Audi, he knew there was no longer room. He felt the resistance as the truck tray caught the Audi's right-hand rear guard, nothing definite, but soft, like a sweater snagged in a barbed wire fence. He increased the pressure on the accelerator just a little. There was a drag, a soft ripping sensation. He knew he was cutting it like a can opener.

'Sweet Jesus,' he said. It felt as good as shitting.

It only made a small noise, a screeee. The diff caught momentarily on a pile of bricks but the old Dodge lifted, lurched and rolled on like a tank, out across the crumpled cyclone fence and arrived, its front tyre hissing, out on to the street.

60

There was this noise in the dark: huh-huh-huh. It came and went. She would do it for a minute. She would stop for a minute. Huh-huh-huh. Benny had Cacka's hurricane lamp. He had that almost from the moment the lights went, but the problem was the matches. He found cigarettes but no matches and he had spent half an hour standing on tip-toe slowly working his way up and down the low rafters of the ceiling looking for the book of porno matches Mort had brought from the bar in Bangkok.

When he came close she struck out at him with the iron bar. It was pitch black. She could have killed him. He never found the porno matches. They were probably in her corner. He found instead an old box of Redheads still above the door frame. He struck the match, raised the sooty glass, and lit the wick. Maria Takis was standing by the work bench, her hands pushed against the wall making a noise like a dog.

'Vishna-fucking-barnu,' he said. 'The fucking turd.'

She stared at him. She made this noise: Huh-huh-huh-huh.

'Don't think you're getting out of this,' he said. 'This alters nothing.'

He came towards her. She held up the iron bar. She had muscled legs like a tennis player. She had them tensed, apart, her back against the wall. Her face was red, veins standing out. She looked so ugly he could not believe it was the same person. Huh-huh-huh, she said. A witch.

Then she stopped making the noise. She stood straighter and tried to lick her lips. 'Get me something clean,' she said.

'There's nothing clean,' he said. 'This is where I live.'

'That.'

First he thought she meant him. She wanted him. She had her hand out towards his cock, his belly. He stepped back. She was pointing at his shirt. He could not believe it. He could not fucking *believe* it.

'Get fucked,' he said.

'Please.'

'It's my shirt.'

'It's clean.'

'You shouldn't get me mad,' he said. 'Not now. You understand?'

he shouted at her. 'You see what has happened? The jealous cunt blew up my *career*. He didn't want it, so he killed it for me.'

She reached out her hand to grab at the shirt. He grabbed at her wrist but she brought the iron bar down with her other hand. The bar crashed down on to the workbench.

He saw then that she was crazy. Her eyes were so hard and dark, he could not look at them.

'Come on,' he said. 'This is my *shirt*.'

'Huh-huh-huh.' Her face was going red again. Tendons stretched down her neck. She started hunching up her shoulder and putting her arm inside her dress, and then she stayed there: Huh-huh-huh.'

He went back to the doorway and looked at the rubble. He pulled out a brick, but it was hopeless. There was concrete and steel reinforcing rod twisted in together. When he turned back he saw she had stepped out of the dress, and lifted it up high as if it might get soiled just touching anything that belonged here. She had an industrial strength bra with white straps. He was shocked by how her stomach stretched, by the ragged brown line down her middle, by the size of everything, the muscles in her legs, the redness of her face. She had buckshot wounds in her arms and thighs. She was trying to spread her dress across his couch with one hand, but the dress was too small and would not stay still. She held it out to him.

'Cut it,' she said.

'Fuck you,' he said.

'Just do it,' she screamed. 'Cut the fucking dress down the side.'

'Fuck you,' he said, 'I'm not your servant.'

'You want this baby to die,' she said. 'You want to kill this baby too.'

She knew he could not stand her saying that. 'Don't you say that,' he said. 'You don't know a thing about me. You think I'm some creep because I live down here.'

'If you're not a creep, what are you?'

'Angel,' he yelled. 'I told you.'

She stared at him, her eyes wide.

'I am a fucking angel.'

They were looking at each other, a metre apart. She had the iron bar in her hand, dressed in pale blue knickers and a white bra.

'Huh-huh-huh.' She hunkered down. She held the bar up. There

273

was a vein on her forehead like a great blue worm.

'This baby needs a hospital, and doctors,' she gasped. 'If we keep it here it'll choke on its cord. It'll be your fault.'

'Why would I kill a baby? I am an angel.'

'Sure,' she said.

'I changed myself,' he said. 'It's possible.'

'See,' she said. She looked him in the eye. 'Now you're going to shoot it.'

'Don't *say* that, I'm warning you. Don't *say* that.'

'Huh-huh-huh-huh-huh-huh.' She held the bar in both hands. She stepped back, leaned against the wall. 'Huh-huh-huh.'

Water and blood gushed out from between her legs, passed through her blue knickers as if they were not even there.

'Shit,' he said.

'Huh-huh-huh.'

He went to the door again, but it was useless. He dirtied his shirt. Behind him, the Tax Inspector was hollering.

'Huh-huh-huh.'

Up in the street he thought he could hear sirens, he was not sure.

'Huh-huh-huh.'

She was backed against the wall, all her pants soaked with blood and water, dripping.

He turned back to the bricks. You could see pale daylight but the stairs were jammed with a mass of masonry and steel.

'I didn't do this,' he said. 'This is not my fault. All it was: I liked you. You never listened to me. I never wanted to do nothing *wrong*.'

Then she started hollering again. He could not bear it. She was shrieking like he was murdering her.

'What do I do?' he said. 'I'll help you. Tell me what to do.'

She did not talk. Her eyes were so wide in her head he thought they were going to pop out. Then she calmed down.

'Cut up my dress. We need a clean surface.' He had razor blades in the old coke stash. He had gaffer tape on the bench. He sliced open her dress and stuck it to the couch with gaffer tape.

'Now – your shirt.'

'No.'

'We don't need to cut it.'

'Forget it.'

'It's coming. It's too soon. It's coming. Help me down.'

He helped her. He put his arm around her. It was the second time he touched her, ever. She was dead heavy, a sack of spuds. He helped her towards the couch.

'Oh Jesus,' she said, 'Oh fuck, oh shit, oh Christ, oh no.'

'Are you O.K.?'

'Oh no,' she screamed. 'Oh noooo . . .'

This time he knew she was dying. It was terrible. It was worse than anything he could imagine.

'Here,' he said. 'It's O.K.' He took off his coat. He put it under her. It was terrible there, in her private parts. He was frightened to look at the hole. It was like an animal. It was opening. Something was pushing.

'I won't hurt you,' he said. 'I never meant to hurt you.'

'Shut up,' she screamed again. 'No.'

He could see the actual head, the actual baby's head. It was black and matted, pushing out from between her legs. He did not know what to do. From the noises that came out of her throat he knew she was going to die. You could see in her face she was going to die. He knelt beside her to stop her rolling off the couch.

She screamed.

He looked. The head was out. Oh Christ. It looked like it would break off, or snap. It turned.

'Cord.'

He did not know what she meant. He was kneeling on rough bricks on his bare knees. It hurt.

She said, 'See the cord.'

He could not see anything.

'The umbilical cord,' she said, her hands scrabbling down in the bloody, slippery mess between her legs. 'Christ, check my baby's neck?'

Then he saw it. There was a white slippery thing, the cord, felt like warm squid. He touched it. It was alive. He pulled it gingerly, frightened he would rip it out or break it. He could feel a life in it, like the life in a fresh caught fish, but warm, hot even, like a piece of rabbit gut. He looped it back over the baby's head. Then, it was as if he had untied a string – just as the cord went back, the child came out, covered in white cheese, splashed with blood. Its face squashed up like a little boxer's. It was ugly and alone. Its legs were

275

up to its stomach and its face was screwed up. Then it cried: something so thin, such a metallic wail it cut right through to Benny's heart.

'Oh Christ,' he said.

He took off his cotton shirt. He threw his bloodied suit jacket on the floor and wrapped up the frightened baby in the shirt.

'Give him to me,' Maria said. 'Give me my baby.'

'Little Benny,' he whispered to it.

'Give me my baby.'

She was shouting now, but there had been so much shouting in his life. He knew how not to hear her. Tears were streaming down Benny's face. He did not know where they were coming from. 'He's mine,' he said.

He closed his heart against the noise. He hunched down over the baby.

'Don't worry,' he said. 'Nothing's going to hurt you.'

61

Maria felt already that she knew every part of her tormentor intimately: his thin wrists, his lumpy-knuckled fingers, his long, straight-sided, pearl-pink nails, his shiny hair with its iridescent, spiky, platinum points, his peculiar opal eyes, his red lips, real red, too red, like a boy-thief caught with plums.

He sat on the edge of the sofa, by her hip. He had one bare leg up, one out on the floor, not easily, or comfortably, but with his foot arched, like a dancer's almost, so that it was just the ball of the foot that made contact with the floor, not the floor exactly, but with a house brick balancing on the floor. He hunched his bare torso around the child and talked to it.

'Give me my baby,' Maria said again.

'Benny,' he said. 'Little Benny.'

He talked to the child, intently, tenderly, with his pretty red lips making wry knowing smiles which might, in almost any other circumstances, have been charming. He cupped and curved himself so much around her baby that she could barely see him – a crumpled blood-stained shirt, an arm, blue and cheesey, and small perfect fingers clenching. She would do anything to hold him.

She asked him once more: 'Please,' she said. 'Give him to me.

He's getting cold now. He needs me.'

But it was she who felt the coldness, the cold hurting emptiness. She stretched her arms out towards him. In the yellow smoke-streaked light of the hurricane lamp, Benny Catchprice's naked skin was the colour of old paper. When her fingers touched him, he flinched, and moved so far down the sofa that the umbilical cord stretched up tight towards him.

'Please. He's cold. Give him to me.'

But he was like a man deaf to women, a sorcerer laying spells. He was murmuring to the baby.

'Give him to me,' she said. 'I'll do what you want.'

He looked up at her and grinned. It was then, as he twisted slightly in his seat, Maria finally saw her baby's face. She thought: *of course*. There were her mother's eyes, bright, dark, curious, undisappointed.

'My baby.' She sobbed, just once, something from the stomach. She held out her empty, cold arms towards the little olive-skinned boy.

Her captor turned away and the baby's bright round face was hidden once again. She could not bear it. She reached out and touched Benny's forearm. 'You want to do it to me, do it to me.'

'Come *on*,' he said incredulously.

He pulled away. It hurt her.

'Please,' she said. The tug on the cord either triggered or coincided with a contraction. She knew the placenta would be delivered and soon, any minute, there would be nothing to join her to the child.

'They lose body heat so fast, Benny, please.' That caught him. He actually looked at her. 'Give him to me.' She held out her arms. 'I'll find you a really nice place to live. Would you like that? I'll get you out of here.'

He began to smile, a bully's smile she thought.

'Just give him to me, I'll pay you,' she said. 'I'll give you money.' She felt close to panic. She must not panic. She must be clear. She tried to think what she might offer him.

'Two thousand dollars,' she said.

'Shush,' he said. 'Don't be stupid.'

'Don't shush me,' she snapped.

He laughed, and kept on laughing until there were tears in his eyes. She had no idea that he was as near as he had ever been to love. She saw only some pretty, blond-haired, Aussie surfer boy. 'Oh, shush.'

On the floor beside his foot, next to his shoes, she could see the shot gun. He had placed it on a garbage bag on top of a plank. It was only as she thought how she might edge towards the ugly thing that she realized she still had the rusty iron bar beside her on the couch, had had it there all the time.

'Shushy shush,' he said to the baby. 'Oh shush-shush-shush.' All her baby's brain was filled with Benny Catchprice's face.

Maria lifted the iron bar like a tennis racket above her head. She saw herself do this from a distance, from somewhere among the cobweb rafters. She saw her ringless hands, the rusty bar.

'Give him to me,' she said. Her voice, scratchy with fear, was almost unrecognizable.

Benny looked up at her and smiled and shook his head.

How could this be me?

She brought down the bar towards his shoulder blade. She brought it down strong enough to break it, but he ducked. He ducked in under and she got him full across the front of the skull. It was a dull soft sound it made. The force jolted him forward. All she felt was *still, be still*, and yet when he turned to look at her, nothing seemed different afterwards from before.

I have to hit him again.

Benny held the baby on his left side, against his hip. He did not have the head held properly. He lifted his right hand up to his own head and when he brought it away it was marked with a small red spot of blood. He actually smiled at her.

'Abortion!' He shook his head. His eyes wandered for a moment, then regained their focus. 'You're such a bullshitter, Maria.'

Maria's legs were trembling uncontrollably. 'I'll kill you,' she said. She picked up the iron bar high again. Her arms were like jelly.

'You're the real thing,' he said. 'I knew that when I saw you.' A dribble of bright blood ran from his hairline down on to his nose. He nodded his head with emphasis. Then slowly, like a boy clowning at a swimming pool, he began to tilt forward. His eyes rolled backwards in his head. He held out the child towards her.

'Take,' he said.

As Benny Catchprice fell, the child was passed between them – Maria slid her arms in under the slippery little body and brought it to her, pressing it against her, shuddering. Benny hit the floor. He made a noise like timber falling in a stack. Maria put her hand behind the damp warm head. She could feel lips sucking at her neck. She brought her arms, her bones, her skin, between her baby and her victim.

It was then, as Benny lay amid the planks and bricks with his bare arm half submerged in puddled seepage, she saw his tattooed back for the first time. At first she thought it was a serpent – red, blue, green, scales, something creepy living in a broken bottle or underneath a rock. Then she saw it was not a serpent but an angel, or half an angel – a single wing tattooed on his smooth, boy's skin – it was long and delicate and it ran from his shoulder to his buttock – an angel wing. It was red, blue, green, luminous, trembling, like a dragon fly, like something smashed against the windscreen of a speeding car.

She took her little boy, warm, squirming, still slippery as a fish, and unfastened her bra, and tucked him in against her skin.

MAJOR NEW PAPERBACKS
From Faber and Faber
'Quality In Your Pocket'

	Available from
Music of Chance *Paul Auster*	7 October 1991
Flynn *Lesley Grant-Adamson*	2 December 1991
Such a Long Journey *Rohinton Mistry*	2 December 1991
In Praise of the Stepmother *Mario Vargas Llosa*	6 January 1992
Immortality *Milan Kundera*	3 February 1992
Mr Wroe's Virgins *Jane Rogers*	3 February 1992
Dirty Tricks *Michael Dibdin*	2 March 1992
An Agent in Place *Robert Littell*	13 April 1992
The Tax Inspector *Peter Carey*	4 May 1992
The Last Shot *Hugo Hamilton*	4 May 1992
The Song Dog *James McClure*	3 August 1992
Radio Romance *Garrison Keillor*	2 September 1992
Kinky Friedman Crime Club *Kinky Friedman*	5 October 1992
A Life of Adventure *Lesley Grant-Adamson*	4 December 1992
Approaching Zero *Bryan Clough & Paul Mungo*	4 January 1993
Sodomies in Elevenpoint *Aldo Busi*	1 February 1993
Cabal *Michael Dibdin*	5 March 1993
They Came From SW19 *Nigel Williams*	2 April 1993
The Lost Father *Mona Simpson*	7 May 1993

PENGUIN BOOKS

Wish You Were Here

Wish You Were Here

CATHERINE ALLIOTT

PENGUIN BOOKS

PENGUIN BOOKS

UK | USA | Canada | Ireland | Australia
India | New Zealand | South Africa

Penguin Books is part of the Penguin Random House group of companies
whose addresses can be found at global.penguinrandomhouse.com.

First published by Michael Joseph 2015
Published in Penguin Books 2015

002

Copyright © Catherine Alliott, 2015

The moral right of the author has been asserted

Set in 12.55/14.86 pt Garamond MT Std
Typeset by Jouve (UK), Milton Keynes
Printed in Great Britain by Clays Ltd, St Ives plc

A CIP catalogue record for this book is available from the British Library

ISBN: 978–1–405–92909–7

www.greenpenguin.co.uk

MIX
Paper from
responsible sources
FSC® C018179

Penguin Random House is committed to a
sustainable future for our business, our readers
and our planet. This book is made from Forest
Stewardship Council® certified paper.

This one's for Jonathan

Chapter One

Somewhere over the English Channel travelling north, closer to the white cliffs than to Cherbourg and whilst cruising at an altitude of thirty thousand feet, a voice came over the tannoy. I'd heard this chap before, when he'd filled us in on our flying speed and the appalling weather in London, and he'd struck me then as being a cut above the usual easyJet Laconic. His clipped, slightly pre-war tones and well-modulated vowels had a reassuring ring to them. A good man to have in a crisis.

'Ladies and gentlemen, I wonder if I could have your attention for a moment, please. Is there by any chance a doctor on board? If so, would they be kind enough to make themselves known to a member of the cabin crew. Many thanks.'

I glanced up from *Country Living*, dragging myself away from the scatter cushions in faded Cabbages and Roses linen I fully intended to make but probably never would, to toss attractively around the Lloyd Loom chairs in the long grass of the orchard I would one day possess, complete with old-fashioned beehive and donkey. I turned to my husband. Raised enquiring eyebrows.

He pretended he'd neither heard the announcement nor sensed my eloquent brows: he certainly didn't look at them. He remained stolidly immobile, staring resolutely down at the Dan Brown he'd bought at Heathrow and had taken back and forth to Paris, but had yet to get beyond page twenty-seven. I pursed my lips, exhaled loudly and meaningfully through my nostrils and returned to my orchard.

Two minutes later, the clipped tones were back. Still calm, still measured, but just a little more insistent.

'Ladies and gentlemen, I'm sorry, but if there is a doctor or a nurse on board, we would be most grateful if they would come forward. We really do need some assistance.'

I nudged my husband. 'James.'

'Hm?'

His shoulders hunched in a telltale manner, chin disappearing right into his neck and his blue-and-white checked shirt.

'You heard.'

'They mean a *doctor* doctor,' he murmured uncomfortably. 'A GP, not a chiropodist.'

'Oh, don't be ridiculous, you're a foot surgeon! Go on.'

'There'll be someone else,' he muttered, pale-grey eyes glancing around nervously above his glasses, a trifle rattled I could tell.

'Well, obviously, there isn't, because they've asked twice. There could be someone dying. Just go.'

'You know I hate this sort of thing, Flora. There's bound to be someone with more general expertise, more –'

'I really think, young man,' said the elderly woman in the window seat beside him, a well-upholstered, imperious-looking matron who'd removed her spectacles to regard him pointedly and reprovingly over her tapestry, 'that if you do have medical experience, you should go.'

She made him sound like a conscientious objector.

'Right. Yes. Yes, of course. *All right*, Flora, you don't need to advertise me, thank you.'

But I was already on my feet in the aisle to let him out, gesticulating wildly to a stewardess. 'Here – over here. Make way, please.' This to the queue of people waiting patiently beside us for the loo. We were quite close to the front as it was. 'He's a doctor.'

'Make way?' James repeated incredulously under his breath, shooting me an appalled look as the entire front section of the plane turned to look at the tall, lean, sandy-haired, middle-aged man who'd unfolded himself with effort from his seat and was now shuffling forwards, past the queue to the bog, mumbling apologies and looking, in his creased chinos and rumpled holiday shirt, more like a harassed librarian than a paramedic in a hurry.

I sat back down again, feeling rather important, though I didn't really sit: instead I perched on the arm of my aisle seat to get a better view. Luckily, a steward had redirected the queue to the loo at the back and I could now see that a little crowd of uniformed cabin crew had gathered around a young girl of about nine who was sitting on the floor, clearly in distress. In even more distress was the very beautiful woman in tight white jeans and a floral shirt standing over her, her hands over her mouth. She was pencil thin with a luxuriant mane of blonde hair, and her heavily accented voice rose in anguish.

'Oh, *mon dieu*, I can't do it again – I can't!'

I saw James approach and address her and she gabbled back gratefully in French, clutching his arm. I'm reasonably fluent, but at that range I couldn't make it out, but then she switched back to English, saying, 'And I have only one left – please – help!'

She thrust something into my husband's hand, at which point I was tapped on the shoulder from behind.

'Excuse me, madam, would you mind taking your seat? We're experiencing a spot of turbulence.'

The glossy, lipsticked smile on the expertly made-up face of the stewardess meant business. The plane was indeed bumping around a bit. Reluctantly, I lowered my bottom, which obviously meant I missed the crucial moment, because when I craned my neck around the stewardess's ample behind as she passed, the crowd at the front were on the floor and James was crouching with his back to me, clearly administering something. They'd tried to move the girl to a more secluded position and shield her with bodies, but a plane doesn't yield much privacy. The blonde, clearly the mother, was the only one standing now, pushing frantic hands through her hair, clutching her mouth, unable to watch, but unable to turn away. My heart lurched for her. I remembered the time when Amelia shut her finger in the door and almost sliced the top off and I'd run away as James held it in place with a pack of frozen peas, and also when Tara coughed up blood in the sitting room and I'd raced upstairs, screaming for her father. You knew you had to help, but you loved them so much you couldn't bear to watch. There was a muffled collective murmuring from the crew and then, without looking indecently ghoulish, I really couldn't see any more, as the mother had dared to crouch down, obscuring James as well.

I went back to my magazine. An interview with a woman

4

from Colefax and Fowler informed me that, on the paint-effects front, Elephant's Breath was all over. Everyone was coming into her Brooke Street showroom asking for chintzes and borders now. Borders. Blimey. I had rolls of the stuff in the attic. Did Laura Ashley circa 1980 count? Probably not. My mind wasn't really on it, though, and I narrowed my eyes over my reading glasses. James had straightened up and was answering a series of quick-fire questions from the mother, whose relief was palpable, even though strain still showed in her eyes. My husband, typically, made light of it, brushing away what were clearly effusive thanks, and came back down the aisle, perhaps less hunched and beleaguered than when he'd gone up it, as quite a few passengers now regarded him with interest. I got up quickly to let him slide in and sit down. The ordeal was over and relief was on his face.

'Well?' I asked. The matron beside him was also agog, needlework abandoned in her lap.

'Nut allergy,' he reported. 'She'd taken a crisp from the girl beside her and it must have been cooked in peanut oil. The mother realized what had happened but had never had to administer the EpiPen before, and she cocked it up the first time. She had a spare one but was too scared to do it in case she got it wrong again. The stewardess was about to have a stab.'

'So you did it?'

He nodded. Picked up Dan Brown.

'Did it go all right?'

'Seemed to. She's not dead.'

'Oh, James, well done you!'

'Flora, I have given the odd injection.'

'Yes, but still.'

'I say, well done, young man,' purred his beady-eyed neighbour approvingly. 'I couldn't help overhearing. I gather you're a surgeon?'

'Consultant surgeon,' I told her proudly.

'Ingrowing toenails, mostly,' said James, shifting uncomfortably in his seat. 'The odd stubborn verruca.'

'Nonsense, he trained as an orthopaedic. He's done hips, knees, everything, but he gets a lot of referrals from chiropodists these days, when it's out of their sphere of expertise.' I turned to James. 'Will she be all right? The little girl?'

'She'll be fine. It just takes a few moments to kick in.'

'Anaphylactic shock,' I explained to my new friend across his lap. Like most doctors' wives I considered myself to be highly qualified, a little knowledge often being a dangerous thing.

'Ah,' she agreed sagely, regarding James with enormous respect now, her pale, rheumy eyes wide. 'Well, that's extremely serious, isn't it? I say, you saved her life.'

James grunted modestly but didn't raise his head from his book. His cheeks were slightly flushed, though, and I was pleased. Morale could not be said to be stratospheric in the Murray-Brown household at the moment, what with NHS cuts and his private practice dwindling. When he'd first decided to specialize, years ago, he'd chosen sports injuries, having been an avid cricketer in his youth, but that had become a very crowded field. He'd seen younger, more ambitious men overtake him, so he'd concentrated on cosmetic foot surgery instead. A mistake in retrospect, for whilst in a recession people would still pay to have a crucial knee operation, they might decide to live with their

6

unsightly bunions and just buy wider shoes. He'd even joked with the children about getting a van, like Amelia's boyfriend, who was a DJ, adding wheels to his trade, morphing into a mobile chiropodist, perhaps with a little butterfly logo on the side. 'A website, too!' Amelia had laughed, 'I'll design it for you.' But I'd sensed a ghastly seriousness beneath his banter. He spent too much time in what we loosely called 'the office' at the top of our house in Clapham, aka the spare room, pretending to write articles for the *Lancet* but in fact doing the *Telegraph* crossword in record time, then rolling up the paper and waging war on the wasp nest outside the window. Not really what he'd spent seven years training at St Thomas's for. This then, whilst not the Nobel Prize for Medicine, was a morale boost.

I peered down the aisle. I could see the young mother standing at the front of the plane now, facing the passengers, her face a picture of relief, casting about, searching for him. I gave her a broad smile and pointed over my head extravagantly.

'He's here!' I mouthed.

She'd swept down the aisle in moments. Leaned right over me into James's lap, blonde hair flowing. 'Oh, I want to thank you so very much,' she breathed gustily in broken English. 'You saved my daughter's life.'

'No no,' muttered James uncomfortably, but going quite pink nevertheless. He tried to get to his feet, his manners, even on an aircraft, impeccable.

'No, don't get up,' she insisted, fluttering her pretty, bejewelled hands. 'I will see you later. I just wanted to say how grateful I am, how grateful we all are. My Agathe – you saved her!'

7

'Well, I administered an EpiPen, but not at all, not at all,' James murmured, gazing and blinking a bit. She really was astonishingly beautiful. I marvelled at the yards of silky hair which hung over me, the tiny frame, the vast bust, the enormous blue eyes. Was she a film star, I wondered? She looked vaguely familiar. A French one, perhaps – well, obviously a French one – in one of those civilizing arty movies I went to with Lizzie occasionally at the Curzon when James was watching *The Bourne Identity* for the umpteenth time. I didn't think this was the moment to ask and watched as her tiny, white-denimed bottom undulated back to its seat.

Once off the plane at Stanstead, on the way to Baggage Reclaim, I saw a father point James out to his son, perhaps as someone to emulate in later life: where all his GCSE biology studies could lead, and the reason he, the father, enforced the homework. The boy stared openly as he passed, as did his younger sister, and I surreptitiously got my lippy out of my handbag and gave a quick slick in case anyone should want his autograph. By the time we got to the carousel, however, most people seemed intent on getting out of the place and had forgotten the heroics. Including the mother and child, who hadn't yet materialized, I realized, glancing around. Perhaps they were hand luggage only? Had swept on through already? Hard to imagine what they were doing on easyJet at all. But then, just as James returned from the fray with our battered old suitcase, I saw them enter the baggage hall. The little girl seemed fine now and was skipping along in front, holding a man's hand. He couldn't be the father, I thought; too thuggish and thickset. Indeed, there seemed to be a couple of similar heavies in tow, whilst the mother strode along in their midst, in sunglasses. Were they staff? Certainly the small, dumpy woman carrying all the Louis Vuitton hand luggage must surely be an employee, and the swarthy man with the cap couldn't be the husband either.

The blonde seemed about to sweep on through, but then, just as she neared the exit she spotted us. She whipped off her sunglasses and came striding across, beaming.

'*Alors*, there you are! *Regard* – look at my *petite* Agathe. As right as what you English bizarrely call rain, and all thanks to you, *monsieur*. My name is Camille de Bouvoir and I am eternally grateful.'

James took her tanned, extended hand. 'James Murray-Brown.'

'Orthopaedic surgeon,' I purred. 'And I'm his wife, Flora.'

She briefly touched the fingers of the hand I'd enthusiastically offered but turned straight back to James.

'I knew you were a surgeon. I could tell by those hands. So sensitive, yet so capable.'

'Aren't they just?' I agreed, although no one seemed to be listening to me.

'And I would like to repay your skill and kindness.'

'Oh, there's really no need,' demurred James, embarrassed.

'May I take your email address? I somehow imagine you would be too modest to get in touch if I gave you mine.'

'He would,' I confirmed, scrabbling around in my bag for a pen and withdrawing a distressed tampon instead, but Madame de Bouvoir had already produced her iPhone. She handed it to me wordlessly and I tapped away dutifully, very much the secretary to the great man. Very much peripheral to proceedings.

'I will be contacting you,' she promised, pocketing it as I handed it back to her. 'And now, Agathe wants to say something.' She gently shepherded her daughter forward. '*Cherie?*' The child was as slim as a reed, with widely spaced almond eyes in a heart-shaped face. Although not yet on the cusp of puberty she was very much in the Lolita mould: destined for great beauty.

She took a deep breath. 'Thank you so very much, *monsieur*, for saving my life. I will be for ever grateful to you and thank you from the bottom of my 'eart.'

She'd clearly practised this small, foreign speech on the plane with a little help from her mother, and it was delivered charmingly. An elderly couple beside us turned to smile. James took the hand she offered, bowing his head slightly and smiling, for who could not be enchanted?

'*Mon plaisir*,' he told her.

Courtesies having been observed, Mme de Bouvoir then kissed James lightly on both cheeks three times. She briefly air-kissed me – only once, I noticed, as I lunged for the second – and then, as a socking great pile of Louis Vuitton suitcases were wheeled towards her by one of her chunky attendants, she sashayed out of the concourse ahead of the trolley, bestowing one last lovely smile and a flutter of her sparkling hand.

James and I gave her a moment to get through customs, where no doubt she'd be met by a man in a uniform, before we waddled out with our bags.

'Great. You know exactly what that will be, don't you?' muttered James.

'What?' I said, knowing already: even now regretting it.

'Some poncy restaurant we've been to a million times

already. We'll have to sit there pretending we never go anywhere smart and endure a lengthy, excruciating meal, which we're force fed anyway on a regular basis.'

'Not necessarily,' I said, with a sinking feeling. I grabbed my old blue bag as it threatened to slide off the trolley.

'We're probably going there tonight!' he yelped.

I avoided looking at him, stopping instead to look in my handbag for my passport. James froze beside me.

'Dear God, I was joking. Please tell me we're not out tonight, Flora. I'm knackered.'

'We have to, James. I've got to get the review in by tomorrow.'

'You're not serious.'

'I am.'

'Jesus.'

'How else d'you think we're going to pay for that bloody holiday? Shit. Where's my passport?' I delved in my bag.

'I've got it.' He produced it from his breast pocket. 'Where are we going?'

'Somewhere in Soho, I think. Oh yes, Fellino's. I have a feeling Gordon Ramsay's trying to take it over and he's resisting.'

'Hasn't he got enough bloody restaurants? Have you texted Amelia?'

'Yes, and she's outside whingeing about us being late. Apparently, we should have let her know the plane was ten minutes delayed. As if I haven't sat for enough hours in that wretched car park waiting for her.'

'Can't you ask Maria to put it in next week's edition? Say you'll go tomorrow?'

'I've tried, but apparently Colin's already let her down.

He was supposed to do the new Marco Pierre but he's got a sore throat, so someone's got to do one.'

'Oh great, so Colin's got his excuse in first, as usual.'

I ignored him. We were both very tired.

'You could google the menu on the web? Write the review from that? Say how delicious the tiddled-up turbot was?'

'Oh, good idea. Like I did at Le Caprice, only, unfortunately, the turbot was off that night, and the scallops, both of which I'd waxed lyrical about. I'd rather keep what remains of my job, if it's all the same to you.'

'But you know Fellino. Can't you ring him and ask what the special is? See what he recommends for tonight?'

'It's fine, I'll go on my own.'

'No, no, I'll come,' he grumbled. 'Blinking heck. Who goes out for dinner the night they get back from holiday?'

'We do, if we're going to go on holiday at all,' I said with a flash of venom. There was the briefest of pauses. James's voice, when it came, was light, but it had the timbre of metal.

'Ah yes, forgive me. For a moment there I thought I was the successful alpha male in this partnership. The high-earning surgeon with a career on a meteoric rise to the stars, providing for his family.'

Heroically, I held my tongue as, tight-lipped, we followed the other weary travellers down the corridor to the escalator. We climbed aboard wordlessly, passed through Passport Control, then trundled out through Nothing to Declare.

Chapter Two

We ran from the terminal building in the pouring rain, not an umbrella between us, the trolley skidding around in front of us on the wet pavement, heading for the drop-off zone, where two pounds secured ten minutes.

'There!' I shouted, pointing as I spotted Amelia in the battered old red Clio she shared with Tara. The trolley span out of control as we tried to escape the hail which lashed our faces and we lunged off at a tangent to retrieve it. The car, when we reached it, was vibrating to ear-splitting music whilst our daughter sat boot-faced within, smoking, engine running, exhaust fumes billowing.

'Where have you been?' she shrieked as I flung open the boot. 'I've been here ages, it's cost me ten quid already. I've had to go round five times!'

'Why didn't you park properly?' I asked breathlessly as James tossed the case in.

'Because I thought that would be even more expensive, and the car park's miles away, and it's raining, in case you hadn't noticed. Why didn't you text me to say it had been delayed?'

'Why didn't you track it, Amelia?' asked James. 'With all that expensive technological equipment at your fingertips that surely would have been the sensible option. "Hello, Mummy and Daddy, did you have a lovely time in Paris?"'

I slammed the boot shut, thinking of the countless times

I'd waited for her in Arrivals, excited as she came back from school trips, skiing holidays, her gap-year travels.

'And some bastard keeps moving me on when I'm literally a second or two over time. Quick, get in.' She was revving up now, glancing fearfully in her rear-view mirror as, sure enough, a uniformed jobsworth bore down. 'Dickhead,' she muttered, giving him the finger, but only once his back was turned.

Soaked to the skin, James and I eased ourselves gingerly into the hideous melee of crisp packets, water bottles, Styrofoam cups, empty beer cans, cigarette cartons, articles of clothing, sleeping bags, fancy-dress paraphernalia, make-up and even a pair of underpants that decorated her car. *Our* car, James would seethe, periodically. As I limbo-danced into the back, my husband in the front dared to turn the music down. Not off, but down.

'It's really cut into my allowance,' she told him grimly as she shifted into first. We pulled away with a lurch. 'And I got stuck in horrendous traffic on the way so, basically, it's cost me a fortune in petrol.'

'Well, it's lucky you got stuck, isn't it, since the plane was delayed,' remarked James. 'Otherwise, it would have cost you even more.'

'It's very kind of you, darling,' I said smoothly from behind, knowing which battles to pick. 'Everything OK at home?'

'Yes, except I had to buy way more food. You didn't leave nearly enough, so that's totally cleaned me out.'

'I left masses! A lasagne in the freezer, two pizzas, and the fridge was bursting with cold meat and salad. We've only been gone three days!'

'Tara had some friends round on Saturday night. They pretty much saw it off.'

'All of it?'

'Well, no, because, as I say, I bought some more. Spent about forty quid, I suppose,' she said wearily, as if exhausted by the responsibility of running a household. She raked a hand through her hair. 'But I'll tot it all up at home and add on the petrol. Let you know the damage. How was it, anyway?'

'Very refreshing, darling,' I said buoyantly, slapping on a smile, determined not to fight quite so soon.

'After all, water is refreshing,' James observed as the windscreen wipers swept away litres of the stuff.

'Oh, shit, you had this? All weekend, like we did?'

'Pretty much. There was a glimmer of hope on Saturday between eleven and twelve and we managed a quick canter through the Tuileries and a twirl round the Place de la Concorde but other than that, it was bars and restaurants.'

'Which you spend your life in,' she said, with a hint of genuine sympathy. 'That sucks.'

'Particularly since yet more sucking ensues tonight, with a visit to one of the West End's premier eateries. Would you like to accompany your mother, Amelia? Endure a slap-up meal?'

'No, thanks,' she said quickly. She was an old hand at these lengthy marathon events. 'Unless Toby and I can go?' she hazarded, for effect only, knowing I was vociferous on the subject of her and Toby the Troglodyte, as James called him, impersonating her father and me. I subjected this to the silence it deserved.

'Still,' she smiled, 'you kids had fun? Hotel not too scabby?'

'Not too scabby, darling.' I returned her grin in the rear-view mirror. Approaching sixty pounds now clinking assuredly into her pocket, she was prepared to be cheerful.

'And did it all come back to you? Paris?'

'Well, I was only eight when I left, but yes, it did. I saw my old school, went to Montmartre, where our apartment was, visited the café we had lunch in, which was still there, that kind of thing. Took a trip down memory lane.'

'Cool. You know what Granny said when I first found out you'd lived there? I said, "Gosh, Granny, you must know Paris really well," and she puffed away on her ciggie and said, "Not really, darling. I only ever saw the ceiling of the Hôtel de Crillon."'

She hooted with laughter as I grimaced. My mother's reminiscences about the wilder side of her youth were, in equal proportion, a source of fascination for her grand-daughters and horror for me.

'Well, that's a fat lie, because Philippe bought us an apartment.'

'She was joking, Mother. Do pipe down.'

I breathed deeply. Counted to ten.

'She came round, by the way,' Amelia went on, swerving suddenly to avoid a cyclist. I clutched my handbag nervously. 'Granny, I mean. To check out Tara's new boyfriend. We agreed, obviously.'

'Obviously,' I said testily. 'But you forget, I've met him, too. And I think he's quite delightful.'

She smirked. 'Because he's going to Durham to do history. Did you spot the ironed creases in his chinos?'

'At least he's got chinos,' commented James, trying to retune the radio into the Test match. 'Unlike the Trog.'

'Ah, but the Trog's got soul, Dad. Try long wave, it's better for Radio 5.' She expertly switched it across for him. 'We were wondering when we were going on holiday, by the way. Is it still the first week in August?'

I stiffened. 'Who was wondering?'

'Well, me and Toby, obviously. I imagine it's OK if I bring him to Scotland? To Grandpa's?'

I tried frantically to catch James's eye in the rear-view mirror, but failed; he was still fiddling with the radio dial – a heroic feat on this white-knuckle ride. The Trog and the Brigadier, James's father? On his Highland estate? Plus James's two sisters?

'Yes, fine, darling,' said her father, who never saw any complication until it reared up and bonked him hard on the nose. 'The more the merrier.'

'Great. I'll tell him. We might bring Will and Jess along, too, they can come in the van. Oh, and they've got a dog, they found it in Streatham, but Grandpa won't mind.'

I shut my eyes and rested my head. This was so like my elder daughter. Spot a small gap and push home the advantage. Within a twinkling there'd be an army of drop-outs dripping around the glen, trailing long skirts, greasy hair, cigarette ash and stray dogs. Exhausting. *Quite* exhausting. And who was going to be cooking for all these people?

'Can we just pause a moment, please, Amelia? Talk about it when I've got over one holiday and got my head round the next? I've only just got off the plane!'

'Yeah, yeah, sure, we can pause,' she said in feigned astonishment, eyes widening in disingenuous wonder at me in the mirror as if I were completely overreacting. Unhinged even. 'I've mentioned it to Jess, obviously, but only, like, briefly. I'll tell them I'll let them know. When you've calmed down a bit.'

I clenched my teeth. What was the point in going away? In having a so-called 'mini-break' when it disappeared so quickly and assuredly down the plughole the moment I returned? I wasn't up to Amelia's strength of purpose, her sheer doggedness, I decided. She should be a shop steward, a trade union official. She campaigned for things and, once she'd got them, beaten her opponent, she popped up again like a mole with something else, waving it like a crusade flag. Had I spoiled her, I wondered? Indulged her? Yes, because all children of this generation were indulged, possibly because we'd had them later and had more money to spend on them. 'They're so lucky!' we mothers would shriek to one another in our designer kitchens over our glasses of Chardonnay. 'Our parents didn't even know which O levels we were taking they took so little interest, and we had to work in shops, Mars bar factories, weren't given bungee allowances!' But our parents had had us in their early twenties – or, in my mother's case, when she was just nineteen – so they were still young and involved in their own lives, not scrutinizing their children's. There was a lot to be said for being a young parent. Except that Tara, who was eighteen months younger than her sister, and therefore had an even older mother, disproved this theory. She was less . . . grasping. Less sharp-eyed. But then, life was easier for her. If you were pretty and clever, life tended to plop into your lap more, didn't it? There was less cause to be opportunistic.

As we neared home, lurching heave-makingly around the corners in our grid of Clapham streets, I wondered nervously if that purple thing I could see poking out of the back of Amelia's T-shirt was another tattoo. Or just a label? I leaned forward to peer, but she braked suddenly at a junction and I nosedived hard into her neck.

'Shit – Mum!' she squealed.

'Sorry, darling – sorry! Just wanted to – to see what speed you were doing.'

'Thirty, obviously, in a built-up area, and that really hurt. I've just had Toby's initials put there in Sanskrit.'

You had to admire her candour. Her carapace. No shame. No guilt. She was eighteen years old and she'd jolly well do as she liked, thank you very much. No doubt always would.

'Your father saved someone's life on the plane,' I said quickly, to change the subject. Needles full of purple dye piercing my darling daughter's neck, the back of which, as a baby, I'd cradled as I'd lowered her into the bathtub, or, later, divided two plaits between as she went off to school, loomed heart-wrenchingly to mind.

'Really? What – mouth to mouth?' She turned to her father.

'No, an EpiPen to the leg. Your mother's exaggerating, as usual. Well, if you're frittering away your allowance on a tattoo, I'm clearly giving you too much. You can foot the grocery bill *and* the petrol. Thank you, Amelia. We can walk to the kerb from here, in the words of Woody Allen.'

Amelia had stopped outside the house and was about to reverse into a space, but her father was already out, slamming the door and walking up the path to our front door, his back rigid.

'What's his problem?'

I sighed. 'He's old-fashioned enough to imagine you at some glittering ball in a few years' time, your hair piled on your head, a silk gown slipping off your shoulders, diamonds in your ears, Toby's initials trailing down your back.'

She gave it some thought. 'Yeah, sounds good. Hasn't hurt Angelina Jolie, has it?'

Angelina Jolie's looks and my daughter's were similar to the extent that they both had long, dark hair.

'No, it hasn't,' I muttered meekly.

'And anyway, Tobes paid, so I didn't use Dad's precious allowance.'

I was too weary to say that her boyfriend paying to have his mark branded on her neck for posterity would probably incur her father's wrath only further, and left the conversation where it was. It was done, and that was the end of it. Apart from a skin graft, of course. Hideously painful and expensive, but always possible and, naturally, where my mind had already fled. Come two in the morning, I'd be creeping downstairs in my dressing gown having not slept a wink, googling it. And ringing Clare in the morning. Clare's twenty-three-year-old son had recently had a dagger removed from inside his wrist before embarking on his new job at Goldman Sachs and, as a neat, cautionary tale Clare had made his fifteen-year-old brother watch from the gallery, to illustrate the lunacy of gap-year indiscretions.

And of course this was Amelia's gap year, she was

bound to spread her wings, make a few mistakes, even. But surely a gap had to be between something? Her A-level results from one of Berkshire's premier boarding schools had precluded university, but photography at art college had seemed a possibility, until Amelia had poured scorn, claiming that all art-school photography looked the same and she'd be better off doing it herself. She'd tossed her dark curls dismissively. 'I'd rather find my own voice, thank you.' I hadn't dared glance at James at this but, to my surprise, he'd jumped at it.

'Right, well, she can jolly well find her voice while she's working,' he'd said hotly as we'd got into bed later that night. 'She can get a job. A proper one. Get off the frigging pay roll.'

Knowing this would go down like a cup of cold sick, I'd suggested the gap year first, as a balm, unaware that Amelia considered it mandatory anyway. Like a polio vaccination.

'Well, of course I'm having a gap year,' she'd said scornfully when I'd offered it up to her magnanimously, beaming delightedly as I did so. 'Everyone does.'

'And then, your father thinks . . . a job?'

'Well, obviously I'll do something short term, everyone does that, too. To pay for my travels. In a shop, maybe. Or a bar.'

No. Long term. For ever, James was thinking. A career. Working from the bottom up, as an apprentice. Whereas I still harboured dreams of further education of some sort, because I didn't care if all her photos turned out like everyone else's, or even if she arranged flowers for three years, I just wanted her to meet someone other than Toby Sullivan, with his ponytail and his van with the mattress inside and his decks – I'd learned not to call them turntables – which she wouldn't do working in a bar and living at home. This, though, I couldn't share with James, whose focus was to stop paying through the bloody nose for his bloody layabout children, not to steer their emotional lives. Well, except Tara, perhaps. Tara had embraced her A levels and was keen to be a vet, and I could see James being very willing to accommodate the expense of her ambition.

I sighed as I got out of the car and retrieved our case from the boot, lugging it up the path to the terraced house in a row of identical Victorian terraced houses. Identical lives, mostly, too. Stockbrokers and their wives, who'd once worked in advertising or publishing, bankers and doctors, hard-working professional people, many of whom I knew and who'd had children growing up with mine, all of whom were battling identical problems. Many far worse than the ones I had with Amelia. Some of their offspring sampled drugs on an epic scale: thank the Lord, Amelia was vociferous in her opposition to them, after a friend had died tragically in horrible circumstances at a festival the previous summer, reshaping my elder daughter's world for ever. I wasn't sure about the Trog, though, and when I'd asked Amelia she'd regarded me sternly and said everyone had to be their own person and what business was it of mine? Only that I cleared up her bedroom and, those funny little papers I found littering her carpet . . . were they really just for his roll-ups? And didn't he smell quite strange? Or was that joss sticks? I'd tried to buy some to remember what they smelled like, but the Indian woman in the gift shop on Lavender Hill had looked at me pityingly, saying there wasn't much call for them these days.

Heaving another great sigh up from the bottom of my recently purchased Parisian boots which, less than an hour ago, I'd been enjoying enormously but were now beginning to pinch, I trudged after Amelia to the front door, secretly admiring her trailing gypsy skirt scattered with tiny mirrors glinting amidst the embroidery, topped by a vintage matador jacket. If nothing else, Amelia had style. She turned to me on the step, twirling the car keys on her finger.

'Oh, just to give you the heads up, Granny's given everything the Swedish look. I said you wouldn't mind.'

I frowned. 'Granny's . . .' I crossed the threshold to the smell of fresh paint and the sound of James spluttering within. My heart lurched as I walked down the hall. I collided with him as he emerged from the sitting room with a face like thunder, pushing past me, hissing, '*Your bloody mother!*' before storming upstairs to his office at the top of the house. The attic door slammed hard.

'Mum . . . ?'

I rounded the corner in gypsy girl's wake to see my mother on her hands and knees, paintbrush in hand, at the far end of the knocked-through sitting room, newspaper thankfully covering the carpet. She was just putting the finishing touches to a heavy sideboard which sat opposite the dining table and which, historically, had been dark oak but was now a streaky shade of pale grey.

She sat back happily on her heels, popped the brush in some turps in a cup and beamed with pleasure. Then she pushed her blonde hair from her eyes, stretched out her slim brown arms and gave me some jazz hands. 'Ta-daa!' My mother is far more beautiful than I will ever be and, when animated, as she was now, could still dazzle.

'Good *God* . . .' I gaped. But not at her beauty.

'Surprise! Don't you love it, darling? You know how you said you hated all that heavy brown furniture? Well, look! The girls and I have transformed it! Given it all a makeover.'

'All . . . ?'

'*Regard!*'

She waved an armful of jangling bracelets to indicate yonder, through the kitchen to the garden, where, sure enough, under cover from the rain on the veranda stood a large chest of drawers, a tallboy, a knee-hole desk, the hall table, all now distressed – in every sense of the word – to a stripy pale grey, which, as far as the naked eye could tell, had been achieved simply by dragging a paintbrush full of white paint across them.

'The girls . . .' I faltered, staring.

'Oh yes, they helped. They were marvellous. Well, Amelia did. It's fab, isn't it?'

My mother still relied heavily on her sixties vocabulary.

'But it's James's stuff, Mum. His family's. Who knows how much it's worth?'

'Oh, very little. I had the local auction house come and look at it first and they said it would fetch barely anything. Said people are chopping it up for firewood these days and they simply can't shift it in the sales. This has transformed it!'

It certainly had. And, in a way, it was quite nice, and I

did hate the heavy brown oak which seemed to loom oppressively and almost consume me sometimes, particularly on gloomy winter afternoons, but . . .

'But you can't just barge in and do it!' I stormed. 'It's got sentimental value, for James at least!'

'I didn't barge in, darling. I told you, I did it as a present. Like a surprise party. I've been planning it for ages. Didn't for one moment think you'd prefer it as it was.'

Her china-blue eyes widened in alarm and she became childlike in her consternation and confusion. She got up from the floor.

'You are *so* mean, Mum.' Amelia rounded on me furiously. 'Granny's spent ages doing this!'

'And did Tara help?'

'Well, she put the paper down and washed the brushes, yes!'

Damage limitation, clearly, on the part of my younger child. I was aware of Tara moving silently around in the kitchen, out of sight, keeping a low profile. I was pretty sure she'd have tried to put the brakes on these two. She appeared in the archway now: petite, pretty and blonde like her grandmother, barefoot in jeans and a white T-shirt. She came across and we hugged silently. Amelia glared at her, daring her to show her true colours.

'It *was* a bit depressing, Mum, all that dark wood,' she said.

'Yes, but it was your father's dark wood!'

'I know.'

It was all in those two little words. *I know . . . but what could I do?* Against the steamroller of momentum that was my mother and elder daughter, what on earth was my level-headed younger child to do except suggest they keep the paint off the carpet and clean up afterwards?

'Well, darling, I can take it off,' said Mum, lighting a cigarette and looking around speculatively, completely undaunted by the magnitude of her actions, at transforming someone's home without a by-your-leave. Oh God, she'd even done the *grandfather* clock! She pursed her lips doubtfully. 'But I honestly think you'll be making a mistake.'

'Mistake? Mistake?' I heard James yelp from halfway up the stairs, clearly thundering his way back down from the office. 'It was a mistake to imagine we could escape this madhouse for one weekend, to have the temerity to claim precisely thirty-six hours to ourselves, to leave the cares and worries of our poxy little lives behind for one single, solitary –'

In one fluid movement I'd stepped across and shut the sitting-room door firmly on his diatribe. I can move when I have to.

'D'you know, I think he's right,' remarked my mother quietly after a moment. 'I'm not sure this break *has* done him much good, Flora. He looked terribly pale and strained when he came in, and he barely said hello to me.'

'Yes, but that's because he was looking forward to coming home to the house he'd left behind!'

'What about taking up sailing again? Getting him out in a boat?' She puffed away on her ciggie and perched on a sofa arm. 'D'you think that might help? He enjoyed that weekend in the Isle of Wight, when you went with the Milligans. And Philippe always loved a sail in Antibes.'

How to explain to this free-spirited, flower-powered

mother of mine that if one took seriously the responsibilities of a house and family, they weighed heavily on one's mind. She came from a different planet to that of my husband: one that had accommodated her getting pregnant when she was nineteen, not even knowing who the father was, and dancing on through life in a glamorous yet highly irresponsible manner, and yet I loved them both equally. How to explain to one that bobbing around in a boat was not going to transform this Englishman's view of his castle, or to the other that she was only trying to be kind? Personally, I didn't care about the grey streaks, just about keeping the peace, and what I wanted more than anything right now was a cup of tea and to take these sodding boots off.

I disappeared, limping, into the kitchen, where Tara was already putting the kettle on.

'What were they thinking!' I seethed, perching on a stool at the island and kicking my expensive footwear off with gusto.

'I couldn't stop them, Mum. You know what they're like when they're in the grip of a good idea.'

I did. And not for the first time it occurred to me how strange it was to have two so different daughters: one who so obviously not only looked like me but behaved like me, too – oh, I knew where Amelia's dark looks and combative streak came from – and another who looked like her granny and behaved more like her father. What would the next one have been like, and the next? I'd often wondered. Right now, though, I wondered if I could gratuitously exploit this one's good nature even further. I kneaded my sore toes with my fingers and sighed.

'I've got to go to this bloody Italian restaurant in Charlotte Street tonight, Tara. Maria wants some copy by the morning. I'm not sure I can sit opposite your father in his condition for three hours. He'll be breathing more fire than the flaming sambucas.'

She paused, but only for a second. Then she nodded. 'Yeah, OK, I'll come. I want to ask you something anyway.'

'Oh?' My ears pricked up. 'Ask away.'

Tara looked a bit furtive. She picked at her blue nail varnish. 'No, it's OK. It'll wait. I'll go and change.'

I was about to say no, tell me now, as I hate having to wait for news of any sort, good or bad, but my phone rang in my bag, and by the time I'd plunged my hand in, rooted around and found it, then assured Fellino that, yes, we were definitely coming, he wasn't to worry – Tara had disappeared.

Chapter Three

It takes experience to canter through a three-course *à la carte* menu complete with *amuse-bouches*, not to mention petit fours, but Tara and I had had years of it. We therefore had certain things down to a fine art. Don't, for example, choose courses that involve lengthy preparation in the kitchen, like slow-roasted, hand-trapped pigeon (you'd be forgiven for thinking they were still trapping it); go instead for the goat's cheese salad or the soup. Never have an aperitif or a coffee, and glance at the menu on the iPad en route. Obviously, I'd ruined my children's haute-cuisine restaurant experiences for life, since they'd been accompanying me on such lightning gourmet missions for as long as I'd been able to pass them off as adults, but needs must. I couldn't sit there on my own, looking so palpably like a restaurant critic, even though, it has to be said, I nearly always warned a chef before I came in, feeling it was unfair to spring it on them.

'It totally defeats the object,' Amelia would say scornfully as we'd sweep into a sea of bowing waiters. 'You're supposed to be the average punter, not have the red-carpet treatment because they know you work for *Haute Cuisine*.'

She was right, of course, but I'd tried it the other way many times and, for some reason, it always seemed to be when the kitchen was having an off day. Too many times

I'd had grudgingly to write a bad review and have my favourite chef ring me in panic:

'Oh, Flora – I can't believe you came in on Thursday! My fish supplier literally let me down at the last minute, which was why the Dover sole was off. I had no idea the muppet in the kitchen would unfreeze a lemon sole instead!'

Once or twice, they'd been tears. 'Oh God, Flora, is there any way you'd come in for a free meal next week? The owner is absolutely going to kill me when he reads I overcooked the rabbit and, if we lose a star, I'll be fired.'

How could I possibly be responsible for the livelihoods of people I liked and admired as chefs? Watch them lose their jobs as I wielded the hatchet? We all had our off days – my copy didn't always bear forensic scrutiny – but my head didn't roll as a result. On the other hand, I couldn't lie, either, say the rabbit had been cooked to perfection, even though, nine times out of ten, I knew it was. This way, I gave them fair warning and, if they got it wrong, they couldn't say I hadn't warned them. They rarely did. I'd write a glowing review and everyone was happy, except my daughter.

'Pathetic. And you're deceiving your readers, you know that, don't you?'

'I do now, Amelia.'

She was derisive, too, of my survival kit. The Rennies she reluctantly accepted, speed-eating being an occupational hazard, but the napkin I brought from home to spit revolting morsels into and spare the kitchens' blushes, she did not. Neither the plastic bag for entire meals 'employed only once, Amelia, when that sweet young guy at Mason's put salt instead of sugar in the meringue.'

'Twice,' she'd retorted. 'Remember when you had those dodgy langoustines you should have reported but instead put them in your bag and forgot about them until people started moving away from you on the Tube?'

I sighed as Tara and I approached the entrance to the Italian restaurant on Charlotte Street.

Fellino, stout and with his waistcoat stretched over his ample stomach, hastened to meet us at the door, hand outstretched.

'Don't have the fillet steak,' he whispered confidentially as he hurried us to a corner table, knowing I liked to get a wiggle on. 'I couldn't get the Aberdeen Angus, so it's a bit tough, but the calf's liver is *magnifico*.' He kissed his thumb and forefinger.

'Thanks, Fellino,' I said, settling down as he flicked pristine white napkins over our laps and in record time had our glasses filled with the wine Tara had ordered by text from the car. Shame. Fillet took two minutes, but never mind; the calf's liver should be equally quick, and Tara sensibly opted for flash-fried prawns.

'And thank you so much for coming. I know you just got back from Paris, I speak to James to check you on your way, we haven't been reviewed for so long, and you know, opposite . . .'

He jerked his grizzled head meaningfully, shrugged and spread his hands despairingly.

'I know, Fellino.'

Rodrigo's new venture had opened across the road last week, to glowing reviews, one of which had been mine.

'He steal our march,' he said sadly, smiling at Tara, who'd taken a bread roll he'd offered her. 'Take a poppy-seed one, *bambino*. Ees better.' She obeyed and replaced the brown.

'Nonsense, you've been here for ever,' I said, 'and your food's just as good. It's only because he's the new boy on the block, that's all. You got our text about starters?'

'I did, and ees coming out right now in two shakes of a lion's tail. I go to see.'

He did, scurrying off, while Tara tucked into bread and wine and I resisted manfully. The temptation, of course, was to eat everything (it was so delicious) and to become the size of a house – oh, and get completely plastered, too – but after a year in my late twenties when I'd been well on the way to looking like the 'Before' photograph in a Weight Watchers ad, I'd imposed my own rules, which I'd pretty much stuck to ever since. No bread, no more than a glass of wine and just taste the carbs, don't eat the lot. This would be sacrilege if I were only doing it once a month, but I wasn't. These days, with the internet and blogging and a bit of freelance on the side, I could be out every other night. Lizzie, my best friend and partner in gourmet crime for ten years, was lyrical on the subject. 'One mouthful of each course is all you need to know about an establishment.'

'But, Lizzie, that's quite rude. And it's supposed to be fun, what we do. Eating for a living.'

'But because you insist on doing it properly, you've come to dread it. You should have widened your net, like I did.'

Lizzie still wrote for *Haute Cuisine*, but not as a restaurant critic: she'd defected to the other side, to editorial, to write their weekly column, and did it with aplomb. In fact, she did it so well she could pretty much write about anything she fancied. She plundered her own life for copy, her friend's, her ex-husband's, mine, she was ruthless in her rummaging and pillaging, but ever since she'd written about 'the crab that twitched', which she swears happened when I took her to Le Gavroche, I'd cut her off my list.

'Please take me. You know I love a good pig-out, and Jackson can't afford it.'

Jackson was her latest beau. Young – very young – black and gorgeous: a jazz singer with nothing to his name besides a second-hand Armani suit.

'No. You lie. You lied about the crab and you lied about the man dying next to us after one mouthful of soup.'

'He did die!'

'Yes, but not because of the soup. Poor Henri Dupont had to instruct lawyers in the end. It cost him a fortune.'

'I won't do it again.'

'I don't believe you. Any woman who tells the world her best friend has piles on her perineum and has to take a cushion along to restaurants is going to invent some fiction about a winking octopus in the seafood salad.'

'The world doesn't read *Haute Cuisine* – according to Maria, we've got a readership of five at the moment – and, to be fair, I didn't invent the piles and there was a cushion. Anyway, no one knew it was you.'

'Everyone who knew me knew it was me, which is everyone who matters.'

She'd sighed. 'Oh, well. Forget the feasting. Can I still come on holiday with you?'

'What d'you mean, *still*? I haven't asked you yet.'

'No, but you did last year.'

'That was last year. Yes, of course you can come. How can I survive it without you?'

'And can Jackson come, too?' she'd asked.

'Of course. He's much nicer than you.'

'But won't James's father mind?'

'Why would he? You brought Neighing Nigel last year.'

'Yes, but he was my age and . . .'

'White? The Brig's got a broader mind than you have, Lizzie.'

'Courtesy of Pentonville.'

'It was Dartmoor, actually, and I'd say Eton and the army did most of the work.'

She'd hugged me then, pleased to get her August plans under her belt, just as I knew my daughter, sitting opposite me now, was about to do.

'*Buon appetito*,' murmured Fellino, having deposited our starters before gliding noiselessly away, as if on skates, back to the kitchen.

'Looks good,' I hazarded, admiring the sheen on my scallops and Tara's pretty beetroot salad.

'Mm,' she agreed, before plunging in. Conversationally, that is. 'Um, Mum, apparently Amelia's bringing Toby on holiday. And of course you've asked Lizzie, which is lovely, so I was thinking . . .' She picked up her fork and toyed with her salad, wondering how to approach this.

'You'd like to bring a girlfriend? Of course, darling. Ask Charlotte. Why not? She loved it last time.'

'Well, no, it isn't that . . .'

I knew it wasn't. Had already worked it out in the

car. What I hadn't quite worked out was what I thought about it.

'I thought I could bring Rory.'

I sighed. Sometimes I wished I'd married the sort of man about whom I could say, *Ask your father*, but he'd just say, *Yes, sure*, so I had to work this out for myself.

'Where's he going to sleep?' Let's cut to the chase.

'In the spare room, obviously.'

Obviously. Except that wouldn't happen. He'd end up in Tara's room, or she in his, and she was only just seventeen, and how did I feel about that? Weary, was how I felt. Weary of having to shoulder the responsibility of making the decisions whilst James took a more liberal view.

'It's going to happen anyway, so why fight it?' I could hear him saying. 'Not if I patrol the corridors after dark with a rolling pin.'

'No, not if you do that. Quite tiring, though.'

I regarded my daughter now.

'Well, I don't know what Grandpa would think.'

'Grandpa won't mind. You know what he's like.'

Unpredictable. As rigid as you like about some things – the way his lawns were manicured, or his ancestral portraits cleaned, for example – but surprisingly unbuttoned about others, as I well knew. I was playing for time.

'I'll think about,' I said, playing for more.

'What's there to think about? We've been going out for ages now –'

'Six weeks.'

'Seven, and you like him, and Daddy likes him, and he gets on with Amelia and Toby. It'll be fun.'

Fun. The annual holiday at James's father's pile in Kincardine: it was never fun. Oh, it might start out that way – in my head, at the planning stage – but it always evolved into a rather tense, tight-lipped affair. It didn't help that I had to bite those lips so hard around James's sisters – well, not Rachel but Sally, who, try as I might to make a new start every year and get off on the right foot, inexplicably found my nerve endings the moment I set foot in the house, the house which they both, as unmarried spinsters, regarded as their domain. And quite right, too, because they lived there, but . . . wasn't it a tiny bit James's, too? The Brig was his father as well. And he the only son. Perhaps we went for too long, I pondered, as I speared a slippery scallop. Perhaps three weeks was too ambitious. But the children had loved it so when they were young: the freedom to roam over all that land after the confines of London, the gloriously scented pine woods to hide in, the picnics by the stream, damming the burn, swimming in the loch. The little boat we'd patched up and rowed about in, catching trout, diving off the side into the freezing, clear water. There'd even been an old pony to ride as it clambered up the steep, rocky path amongst the purple heather behind the house, one girl on its back, the other leading.

These days, of course, they barely strayed from the television in the basement, or the terrace where they sunbathed, should that glorious, pure Scottish sun deign to shine, but still, it was a proper break and, more to the point, it was cheap. Yes, all right, free. And our finances were stretched to the brink these days – disastrous subsidence in our house which had been staggeringly expensive to repair had seen to that – so there was no point looking a gift house in the mouth. Also, if I'm honest, ticking off the whole of James's family in one big flourish, particularly when we saw so much of my own mother in London, gave me a warm glow inside and made me think I'd done my bit on the in-law front for the rest of the year. I chewed briefly on the slippery mollusc in my mouth. How would my daughters' love lives go down with their maiden aunts? Neither had had boyfriends in tow last year. Again, reactions could be unpredictable. Rachel, fine probably – distant, but fine. Sally, sententious and disapproving or keen to be part of the bright-young-thing gang? And then hurt when she felt left out? My heart began to pound.

'I've already rung Sally, just to check,' said Tara, helping herself to some water. She had the grace to blush. 'She's cool about it.'

'You've already . . .' I blinked.

'Just so you'd have one less thing to stress about. I wasn't going round you or anything.'

Well, she was, but at least she'd done it. So I didn't have to. You had to hand it to my daughter, she'd be our girl in Africa one day.

'What did she say?'

'Well, she was thrilled I'd rung, obviously –'

'Obviously!' I could well imagine Sally's delight. She was at her most natural with Amelia and Tara, finding security, I personally thought, in reverting to her youth.

'And then we had a lovely girly chat about which room I could put him in – the blue one, she thought – and how we might be able to drag out the rowing boat, oh, and check out the new Chinese in Kincardine. She thought you'd like it.'

Tara grinned. Sally was a cook by profession, for Scottish house parties mostly, and was frighteningly competitive with me on the culinary front – not just that front either: don't get me on the identical shoes and handbags. She couldn't understand why I wrote chiefly about London restaurants when there were so many good country ones I ignored. 'We do have restaurants around here, you know, Flora,' she'd say, frosty and offended. It didn't matter how many times I told her I simply followed orders and did what Maria, my editor, told me, she felt snubbed, and my current ruse of sampling the eateries and then pretending Maria had vetoed the review was wearing thin.

'Also, she had news, too. She's got a boyfriend.'

'*Sally* has?' I put my fork down.

'Yeah, I know, I nearly dropped the phone. She met him at a house party, apparently. Where she was cooking.' Tara grinned at me. 'The mind boggles.'

'Doesn't it just!'

Sally was mid-forties, pretty – once very pretty – but my heavens she was huge. If you know your P. G. Wodehouse, she looked like that girl who'd been poured into her clothes and had forgotten to say 'when'. To my knowledge, she hadn't been with a man for about twenty years. I gawped, gripped by this information. I picked up my fork. 'Good God. How long? Have Grandpa and Rachel met him?'

'No idea, that was all I got. Except that she's potty about him.'

'Oh, *good*!'

'I know, isn't it?'

It was. It really was. If Sally had a life of her own, it took the heat off me. And my daughters. Who were my life, obviously, since, as Amelia had told me the other day – I believe in all seriousness – mine was pretty much over and I was clearly living vicariously through them.

I sighed, but there was relief in it as well as fatigue.

'Well, it looks like you and Sally have got it all sewn up, Tara. Do I have any choice?'

'Of course you do. I just thought it would help if I did the spadework for you. What's this sauce, by the way?'

'Ginger. Is it not nice?'

'No, it's fine, just a bit . . . no, it's lovely actually.'

Tara was fond of Fellino, too: his family had owned this restaurant for two generations.

'What about yours?'

'Good,' I said, making a quick note on the pad on my lap that the addition of cumin had been masterful, even if I privately thought the infusion could have been done with a slightly lighter touch. The Jerusalem artichokes, however, I noted, had been a lovely and unusual accompaniment to the liver, which had arrived pronto, together with another anxious smile from Fellino. I watched him hasten back to the kitchen. How would he feel about his seventeen-year-old daughter bringing her boyfriend on holiday, I wondered? Well, it wouldn't happen, would it? The lad would be sent packing with a clip round his ear. But then we weren't a patriarchal Sicilian family steeped in Catholic traditions.

'Yes, fine, darling,' I said, taking the path of least resistance. 'But at either ends of the house, OK? The blue room for him and you in your usual.'

'Cool – thanks, Mum.' She whipped out her phone and texted away happily, one hand forking beetroot salad into her mouth, her eyes on the reply.

'Oh, Mum, just one tiny thing.' She coloured slightly. 'Would you mind ringing Rory's mum?'

'Why?'

'Just so she knows the arrangements and everything.'

'Why can't she ring me?'

'She wants to know he's – you know. Been properly invited. And what the arrangements are,' she said again.

'What arrangements?'

'You know, the . . .'

'Sleeping.'

'Yes.'

I crunched hard on my artichoke. So I was to look like the super-keen mother dragging her son to Scotland, and she was to need reassurance that her darling boy wasn't the innocent victim of some sort of honey-trap. No, don't be silly, Flora, I told myself; she just wanted to know the invitation was official, that's all, and that they weren't sharing a bed.

'OK,' I said shortly. 'I'll do it when we get home.'

'You couldn't do it now?'

I gave Tara a level look over our supper. 'No. I couldn't do it now.'

When we got home, Fellino's reputation and Michelin star intact, plus a good review in the bag, or at least in next week's edition, I promised, as he pressed both my hands in his at the door, it was to an uncharacteristic greeting. As I went down the hall to the kitchen to kick off my shoes, put the dishwasher on, swallow a couple of paracetamol and stagger up to bed after what had been a very long day, I heard, 'Hi, Mum!' from the sitting room.

I froze mid-stride. No one ever greeted me without reason. Just ignored me. 'The Thing in the Kitchen', as they'd once jokingly referred to me – I'd stupidly laughed so, naturally, the title had stuck. Without enough irony, to my mind. Suspicious, I retraced my steps, but they were already breaking out, coming to meet me. At least Amelia and Toby were. So the Trog had clearly crawled out of his own bed at home and come across to occupy one of ours, light his strange cigarettes. Oddly, Mum and James were not far behind, their faces animated and excited.

'Have you checked your phone?' demanded Amelia, steering me back in the direction of the basement kitchen, keeping step with me all the way.

'No, I turned it off. It kept buzzing with some strange number. Why?'

'That was easyJet. They rang us on the landline in the end. Kept trying you because you booked the tickets.'

'Tickets?'

'To Paris.'

'Oh. Problem?'

'No, quite the contrary.' Amelia's eyes were shining as I bent down to start the dishwasher. I straightened up. 'You know the girl Dad saved on the plane?'

'Well . . . yes.' I glanced at my husband, who'd slid around the other side of the island to face me. He shrugged modestly but was looking very pleased with himself, blinking behind his glasses. My mother, too, was very bright-eyed, puffing eagerly on a cigarette.

'It was Camille de Bouvoir's daughter. You know, the opera singer? Does glam rock, too?'

'The . . . opera singer?'

41

'Didn't you recognize her on the plane?'

'No!' I scrolled my mind back to the flaxen-haired beauty. Tiny, but big-chested – of course, big lungs and therefore voice. And, now I came to think of it, perhaps with more make-up, and her hair up, making a guest appearance on *Strictly* . . . in a long, pink, sparkly gown, singing whilst the dancers performed their routine in front of her . . .

'Oh! Was that her?'

'The very same. And she's grateful, Mum. *Really* grateful. Oh God!' Amelia clasped her hands with glee and gave a little involuntary jump. 'This is good. This is *such* good news I can't tell you!'

Chapter Four

I looked at the row of shining, animated faces around me: Amelia, Toby and Mum didn't try to hide their excitement and even the famously composed James was having trouble.

'How much?' I breathed, before I could stop myself.

'Oh no,' said Amelia, looking shocked. 'It's not money, Mum.'

'We couldn't possibly accept that,' added James, with a disapproving frown.

'No, no,' I agreed, secretly thinking, Yes, yes. I'd like to see anyone in this room turn it down.

'But what she *has* got, right,' went on Amelia, 'is this amazing place in the south of France. Which she's not using at the moment – not using at all this summer, in fact, because she's touring – and she's asked if we'd like to borrow it!'

'Oh!' I sat down heavily on a kitchen stool.

Tara whooped. 'Where is it?' she shrieked. 'On the coast?'

'No, about an hour inland. Provence. Up in the hills. Sleeps eighteen, stunning infinity pool' – Amelia ticked off the amenities on her fingers, sounding like an estate agent – 'tennis court, party barn, cinema room – all the toys. You name it, we've got it.' She leaped up to embrace her sister, and they danced wildly around the kitchen together, carolling loudly, already lying by a turquoise pool in their bikinis, paperbacks in hand, pina coladas beside them.

I gazed at James, bug-eyed. 'Seriously?'

'Seriously.' He grinned. 'She was so nice.'

'You spoke to her?'

'Yes, you'd written down my email wrong, which was why she had to contact us through the airline. She is so amazingly grateful. The girl is the apple of her eye apparently, an only child. And, to be fair, it's not like she's really *giving* us anything. I felt we could accept the loan of a house, don't you think?'

'Of course you can flaming well accept!' I said with feeling. 'Oh my God – how amazing!' I shot my hands through my hair.

Already, Brechallis House in Kincardine, with its forbidding grey stone walls and black-framed windows flanked on all sides by dark, pine woods and, invariably, cloud and rain, was being replaced – courtesy of a wavy film dissolve – by a white stucco villa complete with vast terrace and pool, surrounded by sun-drenched olive groves and swathes of sage and lavender, not a damp gorse bush or a plague of midges in sight. Oh, the *midges*! I unconsciously scratched my neck just thinking about them.

'When can we have it?' I breathed, snatching up one of Mum's cigarettes from a packet on the island, which I only do in moments of extreme stress or extreme euphoria. I lit it and inhaled greedily. France: my favourite country in the world; the south, this time. Already I was in a sundress – or capri pants perhaps – and a straw hat, off to market under an azure sky to buy *saucisson* and salad to prepare for lunch.

Not to Kincardine under a slate sky in the bone-shaking Land Rover to buy mackerel whose slimy bodies I'd have to gut before cooking.

'Any time we want – it's just sitting there. So we thought – well, same as usual, pretty much the whole of August, just as if we were going to Scotland.'

'And it's got these amazing views, Mum, which you'll *love*,' Amelia told me, eyes alight. 'You can see the sea in the distance, this dear little bay, just like a Cézanne painting, with tiny red rooftops and sweet little fishing boats. Look!'

She was busy on her laptop, flicking up photos.

'Oh! How did you . . .' I moved across to peer over her shoulder.

'She sent us the link,' explained James, looking pretty pleased with himself, I have to say. And why not? For creating such joy in his family, such delight: the girls were flushed with pleasure. *Why not?* I put my arms around him and he squeezed me back as Amelia explained that this was the front, OK, an unbelievable-looking palace, with turrets – towers even. More like a castle than a villa.

'It's like a chateau!' I exclaimed.

'It is,' she said. 'Chateau de la Sauge. Look, it says.' She flipped to a picture of an ornate sign on a wrought-iron gate. 'And this is the terrace . . . and the walled garden with the pool inside . . . and the tennis court . . . and the badminton and boules courts . . . and some of the bedrooms – this is the master one, yours, I imagine. With a four-poster. And the galleried kitchen and the dining room . . . drawing room . . . table-tennis room . . .' And so it went on.

James and I stood, our arms around each other, gazing in disbelief at this slide show, Tara shrieking with delight at every new picture. Toby punctuated proceedings with approving grunts: 'Oh man.' 'Get in.' 'Epic.'

'This would cost a fortune to rent,' I observed.

'Wouldn't it just,' agreed James.

'Megabucks,' confirmed Tara.

'And it comes with a housekeeper, too,' James told us.

'You are *joking*.' I dropped my arms and turned to look at him properly.

'No, she lives in the lodge cottage with her husband, who gardens.' He took a deep breath. 'She does all the cooking.'

James knew he'd delivered the lottery win. The *pièce de résistance*. He'd been saving it. Perhaps even sworn the girls to secrecy. Because, forget the pool. Forget the court and the table-tennis room. Forget the snooker room. We had a cook? Blinking heck. I wouldn't be buying cold meat in the market, I'd be buying floaty dresses and espadrilles!

'Pretty nice to have someone to look after us, don't you think?'

'It's more than nice – it's bloody marvellous. And you, my darling, are a complete star.' I reached up and kissed him squarely on the lips, a rare display of public affection in this house. The girls cheered and clapped.

Bottle it, I thought later, as I went to bed, having said goodbye to Mum as she trotted out to her little red Polo, yet another fag on the go, and thence to her cottage in Fulham: these moments should be preserved, to uncork at a later date when they were most needed. When things were back to normal again, turgid even, to remind us of how we could be, how life should be. That's what I'd like to do. Even Toby had looked almost attractive – what you could see of him amongst the facial hair – brown eyes shining, socks and shoes on for a change, hiding his great hairy toes, as he told us about the time he'd spent in Aix, as a waiter, the previous summer. Picking grapes, too. What a great place Provence was.

As I slapped night cream on my face in the bathroom, my reflection smiled back at me. We'd had some pretty gritty times recently, James and me. I'd had to work that much harder since his private practice had dwindled, forcing us to rely almost exclusively on his NHS salary, and, consequently, I'd been that much grumpier and bad-tempered. The stress of Amelia's exams had taken its toll, plus her disappointing grades, and there'd been a general feeling of battling on amid the strife. To jet off to the sun, to switch off and forget all our petty troubles, to soak up a completely different way of life for a few weeks was surely just what we needed?

We even made love that night, which, let's face it, we were too knackered to do much these days. Well, I was. Despite having just been to Paris for the weekend, that side of things hadn't been an unqualified success, what with both of us being too tired the first night, James too pissed the second, and us having a flaming row about Amelia and what James called 'her spectacularly selfish streak' the third. But tonight, in our own bed, in the house we'd lived in for nineteen years, ever since we got married, tonight it was good.

Afterwards, we lay on our backs, if not still entwined, as we would have been nineteen years ago, at least holding hands. Next door we could hear Amelia and Toby talking.

I hoped no more, but there was nothing I could do about it so I shut my mind to it. Refused to let it spoil things.

'I'll have to explain to Dad, of course,' James murmured.

I turned my head towards him on the pillow. 'I know. I was just thinking that. But he'll understand, surely?'

'Oh, yes. Might be a bit disappointed, though.'

'Mm. We could go up in September?'

'We could.'

We both knew we wouldn't. Couldn't afford the time.

'And the girls . . .' Not ours this time but James's sisters, who, I told him repeatedly, he couldn't be responsible for, not for ever – but I wasn't going to get into that argument tonight.

'Sally will be pleased not to have to help cook for us all?' I hazarded. 'And, you never know, she might even be relieved to conduct her new relationship in private. Not to have to expose her beau to the entire family immediately.'

James grunted non-committally. He'd been as floored as I had about the man's very existence when I'd told him earlier, but he hadn't wanted to sound disloyal.

'I'll probably have to invite Lizzie,' I said cautiously, something I'd already thought about when I was brushing my teeth. 'After all, she was coming to Scotland.'

'But not for the whole time.'

He'd clearly considered it, too, brushing his.

'No, not for the whole time,' I said quickly. 'Just a week or two.'

'A week.'

'Well . . .'

Silence.

'Who's she boring the pants off at the moment?'

'That nice chap, Jackson, the jazz pianist. You liked him.'

'Oh, yes. Well, that's something, I suppose. Although, knowing Lizzie, it'll be all change by August and she'll saddle us with some God-awful toyboy again.'

Lizzie's taste in men got younger as she got older. Jackson was no exception, but it had been dark in the jazz club when James met him. Plus, I'd lied a bit. Told him he was a metrosexual – which I'd then had to explain meant he was pampered and well-preserved, not gay.

'And then there's the age-old question of what to do about your mother,' he said.

'We'll have to ask her, too.'

'I know.'

He did. We'd both seen the light in her blue eyes, although she'd sweetly said nothing. She'd spent her younger, even more beautiful, years jetting around the bays of Juan-les-Pins in speedboats whilst *en vacances* from Paris. She hadn't been back for years. Her lover at the time, my stepfather in all but marriage, had been the wealthy politician Philippe de Saint-Germain, and he'd run my mother blatantly alongside his wife. At his funeral in Paris, both women had been at the graveside, in tears, just as two women had at Mitterrand's. It was the French way. Where had I been, I'd wondered? I don't mean at the funeral – I'd been there beside Mum, just across from his two sons – but in the Juan-les-Pins days? Bouncing around in a Moses basket in the back of the speedboat? I'd asked, one day. Mum had looked vague. Drawn vacantly on her cigarette and her past, and said, 'D'you know, darling, I've absolutely no idea.'

'With a nanny? Back at the hotel?' I'd suggested sarcastically.

'Yes, that'd be it,' she'd agreed, possibly believing it. There was no guile with Mum. Just forgetfulness.

'But that's it on the hangers-on front.' James turned away from me on to his side. He bunched up his pillow and punched it hard. 'We don't want hordes of freeloading friends of Amelia and Tara, or any appendages of your mother. You know what she's like.'

I did. I also thought it probably wasn't the moment to mention Rory, who would no doubt be swapping Scotland for France in the blink of an eye, and, since it was further away, would likely be with us for longer. I'd already decided to veto Will and Jess, but who knew how long Toby would stay? He practically lived with us as it was.

'I'm going to see Camille tomorrow. Tell her our plans.'

I blinked. Sat up. 'Oh?' I gazed down at his immobile form in the darkness. 'Is she coming here?' I went hot at the thought of the frayed stair carpet, the Ikea throws covering the tired sofas, the damp on the sitting-room wall. Wondered, wildly, if I had time to paint it? Who was it who'd said that the smell of fresh paint followed her everywhere? Oh, yes. The Queen.

'No, she's at the Albert Hall this week and rehearsing during the day, so she's invited me to lunch at her hotel.'

'Oh! How lovely!' I was stunned for a moment. Not me, of course. No, of course not me. But why couldn't we both go? 'Are you free?' I demanded. I certainly was. 'Don't you have clinic tomorrow? Private patients?'

He rolled over enough to peer at me over his shoulder in the gloom. 'Free to have lunch with a famous opera singer at the Hyde Park Hotel? Who's lending us a ten grand a week house for the entire summer? I think so, Flora. Peter Hurst is covering my list for a couple of hours; I've emailed him.' He rolled back.

'Oh. Right.' I lay down again. I couldn't help thinking he'd been to enough smart restaurants with me not to get excited about the Hyde Park Hotel, but I forced myself to be the bigger person. 'Do tell her we're completely thrilled, won't you? That we're enormously grateful.'

He grunted. Reached out a backward hand to give me a reassuring pat.

I went to sleep happy, barely needing the eye mask, the socks, the earplugs, the drops of sleep-inducing lavender water on the pillow, the Rennies, or even the swig of Night Nurse – although, naturally, I employed them all anyway, just in case.

The following morning I lay in bed until nine o'clock, luxuriating in my family's absence. Tara had taken a bus to her school across the river; James, after much discussion about which tie to wear, the Tube to St Thomas's Hospital; and Amelia and Toby had walked – or bounced, in Toby's case; he had a funny walk – to their crammer, where they were both doing retakes. About this, James and I had been practically on saucepan-throwing terms earlier in the year. There'd been tears and shrieks from all quarters, mostly from Amelia, who'd baulked at the inconvenience it posed to her gap year, but also from James, who'd baulked at the cost, since he'd already shelled out thousands for private school. Thousands we didn't have. I'd prevailed, though, as I knew I would, but it had been the bloodiest of family battles. At the crammer, she'd met the

Trog, so in some respects I'd scored an own goal, but I was pleased she was having another go, even if it was only at one A-level, sport science. The telephone rang beside me. I lunged in the dark for the receiver, removing an earplug.

'Eau, helleau, it's Penelope Friar-Gordon here.'

I didn't know anyone by that name. I propped myself up on my elbow. Pushed up my eye mask to let the light flood in, and removed the other earplug.

'Sorry, I –'

'Rory's mother.'

'Oh, right.' I struggled to sit up.

'I gather you've kindly invited Rory on holiday with you this summer?'

I came to. The 'kindly' had been crowbarred in somehow. Overall, the voice was distinctly frosty.

'Yes – yes. I was going to ring you, actually, but we've only just got back from Paris, and last night was a bit hectic. To be honest, I only recently learned that Tara's invited him. You know what they're like!'

If I'd been hoping for a spot of mothers-with-teenagers camaraderie, I was disappointed.

'I see. I got the distinct impression from Rory that Tara had invited him a while ago?'

Realizing I was about to drop Tara in it, I became vague. 'Oh, well, I can't quite remember when it was decided. But the thing is, it's France now. Our plans have changed. Provence,' I added happily, thinking that even Mrs Icecold in Gloucestershire would thaw.

'Eau. I thought he'd be doing some stalking?'

For a moment I visualized Rory, in pressed chinos,

perving round Kincardine after the local talent, which was
generously sized and, generally, underdressed. Then it
dawned.

'Oh, no, my father-in-law doesn't ... he no longer
shoots. Just a bit of fishing.'

'Right.' She sounded incredibly disappointed. 'I was distinctly told ...'

What *had* Tara said? That she was from some wealthy
Scottish aristo family whose land marched with Balmoral,
and with whom we shared lavish shooting parties?
Whereas, in fact, the Brig, albeit landed and creaking gen-
try, had acres of scrubby gorse and masses of mangy
sheep?

'Well, as I say, it's immaterial,' I said crisply, disliking
this woman intensely, ' because we're going to Provence
this year.'

She caught my tone. 'Ah, yes, I see. How lovely. And
that's yours, is it?'

'No, it's very kindly being lent to us.'

It occurred to me that it would be simpler to send this
woman my bank statements. Spectacularly overdrawn, no
Scottish pile, no French one either, just a four-bed semi in
Clapham with a mortgage.

'And Rory is very welcome to join us.'

'Obviously, they'll have separate bedrooms?'

'Obviously!' I seethed. Blimey, I was the *girl's* mother;
she was the *boy's*. Was her precious son at the mercy of my
siren?

'Only they are very young. Rory is still only sixteen.'

I shut my eyes. 'They are.' I said quietly. 'Very young.' I
got out of bed and clenched my fist hard. I wanted to say,

D'you know what? He's no longer invited, but knew, for Tara, I couldn't.

'I think I need another word with Henry,' said Mrs Friar-Gordon doubtfully.

Presumably, the husband. 'It's my pleasure,' I said, as if she'd thanked me profusely instead of insulted me, which, happily, wrong-footed her. She remembered her manners.

'Oh, er, yes. Thank you.'

'You're welcome. Goodbye.'

I didn't exactly put the phone down, but neither did I wait for her to reply.

Instead, I peeled off my T-shirt and ran into the shower, emerging a few minutes later, wet and steaming. I was just running naked down the corridor to the airing cupboard at the far end of the empty house for clean pants when the phone rang again.

'Bloody woman!' I shrieked, turning back, just as the door to Amelia's bedroom opened. Toby emerged, his huge, hairy body squeezed into my daughter's Cath Kidston dressing gown.

There was a ghastly freeze-frame moment. Our eyes locked briefly, then my hands flew – one up, one down – but not before his eyes had beaten my hands to it. He disappeared quickly back into Amelia's room.

Shit. Bloody *hell*. I ran on, going as hot as the sun. What was he *doing* here? Well, lying in, clearly, whilst Amelia went to college, which, frankly, *was not on*. Toby staying here at all had slipped under the radar after a supper party six months ago, when we'd had some lovely friends from Wiltshire staying with all four of their children. Naturally, we'd all got roaring drunk, and Toby had been too pissed to drive home. He obviously couldn't go in the spare room, as usual, due to the guests, and Amelia had said, 'Why doesn't he just kip on the floor in my room?' I'd been too tired and drunk to argue. This, then, had set a precedent. Wedged a thin end. And now he'd seen me *naked*. Back in the bedroom, still lacking pants, or any clothes at all, the phone was still ringing. I dived back under the covers.

'Hel*lo!*' I barked, furious.

'What's up?' It was Lizzie.

'Oh. Lizzie.' I groaned. Covered my eyes. 'Toby's just seen me with no clothes on.'

She paused, startled. An excited note crept into her voice. 'Gosh, I didn't know you two . . . does Amelia . . . ?'

'Oh, not like that, Lizzie,' I said, irritated. 'This isn't some torrid Alan Clark mother-and-daughter *ménage à trois*, this isn't an episode out of your life. I ran into him on the landing.'

'Oh.' She was clearly disappointed. 'Oh, well, do him good. See what's in store for him twenty years down the track.'

'Put him off for life, you mean.'

'Nonsense, there's nothing wrong with your figure. If he'd seen mine, he'd be far more devastated. Anyway, France,' she said excitedly.

I narrowed my eyes. Sat up a bit. 'How do you know?'

'Amelia popped round to borrow my tent. She's going to some music festival.'

'Leeds – I know – but not for ages. You have a tent?'

'Remember I went to Glastonbury? With Neighing Nigel? Anyway, isn't it fab? A whole month! For free!'

'Yes, well,' I hedged nervously. 'But we've literally only

just heard ourselves. So, obviously, I'll have to talk to James about exactly who he wants to come and how long –'

'Oh, we *definitely* don't want the Harrisons,' she interrupted. 'Remember they came to Scotland that year and he banged on and on about his bonus and how all his children had got into Cambridge? And she kept passing wet wipes round the Land Rover in case anyone had touched a dead rabbit?'

'No, not the Harrisons,' I said weakly. 'But Lizzie, a month is a long time. I was thinking –'

'Oh, *don't* be so wet, Flora. It'll fly by, you'll love it! You are absolutely not to ring and say we'll have it for less. Think how brown we'll be!'

'Yes, well – oh. Hang on, Lizzie.'

Amelia had put her head around the door. 'Why are you still in bed?'

'Because I am *trying* to get up, but the phone keeps ringing. Why aren't you at college?'

'No classes. It's an Ofsted day. Tobes and I are going to Reading. Is there any petrol?'

'How would I know if there's any petrol in your car?'

'Oh, OK, there isn't. Can I borrow your card? I've got, literally, no money. I'll only put a bit in.'

'No, you cannot borrow my debit card. It is not some magic wand to wave around willy-nill—' Toby had stuck his head above Amelia's in the doorway. He grinned.

'It's in my bag downstairs,' I whispered, mortified.

'Thanks, Mum. Can I give it back to you when we get back? It's just –'

'Yes, just *go*.' Toby was still grinning at me. The door shut on their faces. I waited, horrified.

'I don't think he's told her,' I hissed, aghast, to Lizzie. 'He's just been in. Don't you think that's weird?'

'Who?'

'Toby. I don't think he's told Amelia. And he was *grinning* at me!'

'What, so you think he fancies you?'

'*No.* It's just . . . I mean, surely you'd say – Oh, help, I've just seen your mother with no clothes on? It's just odd!'

'I don't know, Flora. I wouldn't get too hung up on it if I were you. I doubt you're the first older woman he's seen in the buff. That boy's given me the eye before.'

'*Has* he?' I was horrified. 'God, that's *terrible*. You should have *said*. I must tell Amelia.'

'Don't be silly. He's a flirt, that's all. Nothing wrong with that. Anyway, I can't spend all morning on the phone to you, I've got a meeting with Maria at eleven about the summer hols. I want one of the interns to cover for me. And you'd better get up.'

'I've been trying to get up for –' I said, but she'd gone. To see our editor, and no doubt angle for an extra week off in order to come to *my house in France* – in my head, I already owned it, was very definitely the chatelaine – which was what *I* had intended to do, so that I could be free to swan off for longer myself. I shut my eyes and breathed deeply, in . . . out . . . in . . . out. The air exiting my teeth made a strange whistling sound, more like an old woman in the last rattling throes than a much younger, more glamorous one on the brink of her own personal belle époque.

Chapter Five

James returned that evening looking, if possible, even more flushed and thrilled with himself. He was bouncing a bit, too – bounding, almost – and it seemed to me his chest had expanded. He strode masterfully across the kitchen to where I was changing a fuse on the iron, removed the instrument of domestic drudgery from my hands and replaced it with a box of chocolates.

'What are these for? I asked, gazing at the little green box in disbelief.

'Well, you know,' he smirked, hopping about a bit more. 'I just thought I haven't bought you anything for ages.'

'You haven't, and buying After Eights indicates just how long. I think you'll find chocolates have moved on and it's all Green & Black's, these days, but thank you, darling. How sweet.'

He frowned at the box. 'It *is* green and black. What's wrong with you?'

'Not the packet, you fool – oh, never mind. How was lunch?'

'Good, really good.' His eyes shone like a little boy's. He thrust his hands into his pockets and jangled his loose change around, rocking back on his heels. 'God, she's nice, Flora, you'd really like her.'

'I'm sure I would, if I met her properly.' Ridiculously, I was struggling to keep an edge from my voice. When I'd glanced at the clock at lunchtime over my cheese-and-pickle sandwich, I'd felt slightly peeved, but had consoled myself by reaching for my iPad and re-counting the bedrooms at the villa. Ten, including the one in the attic. I'd decided to talk to James about asking the Carmichaels. They'd love it, and I adored Kate and Harry. I was looking forward to ringing and saying, *Kate, we've got this villa in the south of France . . . yes, of course the children, too.* Hear her shriek with pleasure. And, of course, James was busy securing the deal, so I shouldn't be miffed, I'd thought as I'd closed my laptop, put my plate in the dishwasher, flicked the kettle on again, but . . . surely we came as a couple? After all, I was the one who needed to know where the spare linen was kept, where the pool towels were . . .

'She needed to tell me about the keys to the pool house, where the barbecue is. That kind of thing,' James said importantly.

'Right. Yes, well, I can see that might be beyond me.' I picked up the iron again. 'Did you get the keys?'

'No need. They're with the housekeeper, who's her sister, by the way. Her brother-in-law's the gardener.'

'Really?' I made a face. 'Must be a bit galling, surely? Scrubbing floors for your sister?'

'I think it's really nice, actually. A way of looking after a sibling who hasn't done so well. Giving her a job, a free cottage. Her husband, too.'

'I suppose.' I was surprised. James sounded quite strident. And his chin was jutting out in a horribly familiar fashion. Were we taking up positions here? About a family we didn't know? How had that happened?

'And, speaking of siblings who haven't done so well,' he

went on in a rush, 'I rang Dad and Sally. They're really upset.'

'Oh!' Suddenly, I knew what was coming. Why he was a bit punchy and bullish. The chocolates. I put the iron down and sat warily on a stool. 'Oh, James – you *haven't*.'

'I had to, Flora. I couldn't say – Sorry, we can't come this year, we're swanning off to the south of France – without asking them, could I?'

I was speechless. 'But your father! In Provence? He doesn't go out of Kincardine, for God's sake, and Sally!'

'Oh, for heaven's sake, we're not that parochial. Have been beyond the end of the glen.'

'When? When has Rachel ever been beyond the end of the glen? Name me one time.'

He scratched his chin. 'The odd funeral.'

'At the church. In the glen.'

'That's uncalled for, Flora.'

'But we agreed! This morning, before you left! A holiday on our own terms for once, without the extended family.'

'Yes, I know, but it didn't feel right. I felt shabby. Camille completely understood. That's why she helped her sister.'

Camille. He'd discussed it with her before discussing it with me. With a complete stranger. I breathed deeply, teeth clenched.

'I tried to ring, but you were on the phone all morning. In bed, Amelia said.'

'Amelia?'

'I rang her mobile to get her to give you a nudge, but she was driving. On her way to some festival.'

'What festival?'

'Gets back Monday, she said.'

Oh my God, *Reading*. Not the high street, shopping – the *festival*. And I'd thought Leeds, later in the summer. *With my debit card.* I went hot. I simply couldn't tell James. My mind scrolled back to more pressing problems.

'But Sally –'

'Is much calmer now she has a boyfriend, Rachel said.'

'Is *he* coming?'

'Of course. They're a couple.'

'And Rachel?'

'Of course Rachel. I can't have one without the other.'

'Why do we bloody well have to have either!'

James and I had by now squared up to one another across the kitchen island, eyes blazing. I knew he was taking a stand and that I'd have to be very firm if I was going to win this one.

'Why not ask some friends for a change, like normal people do? The Carmichaels – they asked us to Cornwall. I'd love to have them!'

'We still can.'

'Of course we can't! Not with –' I broke off.

Not with Sally and Rachel. They were unusual. Sally, enormous, as we know (absolutely nothing wrong with that), and both unmarried, as we also know (nothing wrong with that either), but both, in their own ways, utterly heartbreaking and awkward.

Rachel, by far the easier of the two, was very religious and extremely quiet. Pious in the true sense of the word. I never quite knew if she approved of me, but I dare say others would say the same. She made a lot of people nervous; Kate Carmichael would be terrified of her. And no doubt get disastrously pissed to hide her nerves. Rachel's standards were hard to live up to and, although she probably didn't mean to, she had a disapproving demeanour. She would, in another era, I think, have become a nun. She was the eldest and had sheltered James and Sally to an extent when their mother had died. Or been shot. Murdered. Except no one ever said that word.

Naturally, that terrible trauma had taken its toll. In that big, draughty house at the head of the glen, when Vicky Murray-Brown had come back that night from Aberdeen – or Dundee, perhaps, I couldn't remember (James had told me very quickly, so many years ago, I'd had to fill in the gaps with my imagination) – and had let herself in quietly at the back door at two in the morning, but of course, not so quietly, being very drunk. And then, after that shot had rung out – and how it must have done so in that huge, echoing house – the dreadful silence that had fallen remained, in a sense, to this day, thirty-odd years later. A ghostly emptiness prevailed at Brechallis. Always had done. Where once a garrulous, headstrong girl, too glamorous for her own good, certainly to be tucked away in an isolated glen with an aging brigadier, had resided as a young wife and mother, now, an old man, a silent daughter and one who talked constantly but whose words were empty, remained. Where once arguing and shouting had filled the air – but at least she'd been a presence, clattering around the kitchen, singing, drinking too much, crying, banging down pans, hollering at her husband and children, desperately unhappy and desperate for love – now, only the wind whistled in her place, through the shabby rooms, the dark corridors. She'd found some comfort in her children, but not enough, and finally, desperately, she'd taken her love to town, with – had it been Fergus? Who did the fencing? Or, no, Darren, a local builder, that had been it. And, actually, now I thought about it, it hadn't been in the faraway clubs of Aberdeen or Dundee but in dour little Kincardine, the small town at the entrance to the glen, with its rows of faceless houses and billowing litter. Teenagers with needles in their arms, and unemployed fathers. Where poverty and despair overwhelmed, but which, from where Vicky sat, staring out at the gorse bushes and the sheep, was the nearest thing to life.

In some stark little pebble-dashed pub Vicky had drunk with Darren and the other regulars one Saturday night. She must have made quite an entrance, flouncing in defiantly in her fur coat, her heart pounding, taking a solitary stool at the bar. After that, she was there every Saturday night. And she made friends. Many were drinking to forget their tough, gritty lives, the monotony of their day-to-day lot, but Vicky was drinking to forget the horrendous mistake she'd made in marrying her much older husband – and in doing so, of course, she made a mockery of him to all his neighbours. In that part of the world, twenty miles made you a neighbour. And geography notwithstanding, he was the laird at the big house. Everyone knew Drummond Murray-Brown.

Home she'd weave in her car in the early hours, along dark, narrow lanes where she wouldn't meet a living soul, let alone a police car, her face sagging with make-up, drink and sorrow, her clothes reeking of cigarettes and her body of Darren's bed. In she'd stagger, feeling her way upstairs in the dark to the spare room, laughing, yes laughing, if the

Brig blundered out of their bedroom to howl in pain and anger, knowing he'd never lay a finger on her.

Not a finger, no. But one night, after she'd gone to town, and come back drunk and sated, he'd lain in wait. Or sat in wait, alone, at the kitchen table, with only a candle and a bottle of whisky. And when she'd returned in the dark, in the middle of the night, there'd been a fearful row. She'd already told him months ago she wanted a divorce. Had informed him one evening, before she'd gone to Kincardine, wearing a silk dress, earrings jangling, slipping into her fur coat, before running down the gravel drive to the car, that she would file for one: take the children to Edinburgh and, more to the point, take half the house and land, as was her right. The house and land that had been in Drummond's family for two hundred and fifty years. Handed down from one generation to another, from father to son. It was to be sold. Divided up, and half the proceeds given to Drummond, half to Vicky. For there was no money to speak of, nothing for Vicky to be paid off with; it was all in the land. Four thousand acres of scrub, peppered with sandstone boulders and bracken and gorse, where nothing of any consequence grew and only sheep scratched a living. Where a large, preposterously ugly, grey stone house presided forbiddingly, its dark windows daring anyone to question its hideousness. He couldn't even afford to let rich bankers come and shoot his pheasant, couldn't afford the infrastructure to facilitate that: the gamekeeper, the beaters. Couldn't get a loan from the bank.

Letters flew from solicitor to solicitor and then back to Drummond. He'd read them at the kitchen table with shaking hands. Half the house and half the land, that was what she wanted. That was fair with three children under thirteen, that was what she needed to release herself. She'd married a man twice her age, it had been a mistake. Hers, she realized. She'd pushed for the marriage, to this confirmed bachelor whom she'd met at a Highland wedding and who had looked rather splendid in his kilt, certainly to a young girl from Godalming, Surrey. Yes, she had pushed him into it. He'd been unsure. But now she needed out. It wasn't going to happen, Drummond said again and again to himself as he read those letters with a horrified, clenched anger. It simply wasn't going to happen. Over his dead body. Or, as it turned out, over hers.

Of course, he hadn't intended to shoot her, or even threaten her, not with a gun – with words, perhaps. But when she'd opened the back door, still giggling, tripping over the step, filling the kitchen with fumes from her painted lips, and when he confronted her and she'd shouted right back in his face, about his sexual prowess, or lack of it, and Darren's overwhelming competence in that department, he'd reached behind the door in a blind rage and, the next thing he knew, she was dead.

Life imprisonment, obviously, for shooting your wife. Nine years, in those days. And some say he'd weighed it up. Some cynical old neighbours on another crag, in another pile, who'd been there for centuries, applied their own warped logic and said, *Yes, reckon Drummond gave it some thought and decided, Well, I'll be out in nine years and the house and land will still be mine. And then my son's.* No one who truly knew Drummond's heart believed that, though, they knew it had been a tragic accident, and anyway, James didn't want the house. And we never, ever talked about it.

When I met him, he told me about it, obviously. I remember it must have been as early as our second date: 'By the way,' he'd said, 'there's something you need to know about me. My father killed my mother.' It was a sort of 'Take me or leave me now' statement. Warts and all. I took him. Loved him for thinking it needed to be out there so soon, wanting no deception, no misunderstandings. No difficult decisions a few months down the track, by which time I might have fallen in love with him. In fact, he pretty much told me, defiantly, 'My father's an ex-con.' Although I was very shocked, I remember liking his defiance, in that wine bar off the Fulham Road. I'd just come out of a long relationship with someone who'd been much more economical with the truth. Truth was what I needed. What I liked.

We were engaged within ten months and, naturally, during that time I went to Scotland and met the Brig and James's two sisters, not spinsters then, just two girls at home with their dad. And Drummond, who'd been out for a good few years by then, seemed just like any boyfriend's father: a little older and crustier, perhaps, because he was, and quite grand and scary in his big Scottish house, but certainly not like anyone who'd spent nine years in Dartmoor.

Just like Eton, Sally told me later Drummond had said, because of course, although James wouldn't talk and I respected that, girls do. And Sally, being the more verbose and vocal of the two sisters, had prattled away in the morning room at Brechallis, on the worn, gold Dralon sofa, hugging a cushion. Up to a point. No one ever discussed that night, when three sleeping children had awoken to a single blasting shot ringing out. A hideous scream. A father in pieces. But Sally told me about the court case. Swift and conclusive due to a guilty plea, but with lots of old friends giving mitigating evidence, supporting and swearing allegiance to an old friend who'd married the wrong girl. Not a wrong-un – different class and generation that these neighbours were, they could see there was nothing bad about Vicky Murray-Brown. It was just that she was not right for Drummond. And Sally told me about Dartmoor, where they visited him and where their father had been so resilient, so cheerful. Saying they weren't to worry. That he had a splendid view of the moor, the smell of heather, just like home. And that the food was better than he'd had in the army, and he was reading loads, making his way through the classics, which was marvellous. He was in charge of the prison garden, too, eating the vegetables from it, and really making the whole experience out to be so much better than it must have been.

And, meanwhile, the three children were sent to boarding school, and stayed with an aunt – Aunt Sarah, Drummond's sister – in the holidays and kind friends at weekends. And whilst nine years didn't exactly fly by, when it became seven – because, of course, he was a model prisoner, Sally said – suddenly, it did. They'd all assumed he would serve the full term, and no one had told them any differently for fear of getting their hopes up. But then, all at once, Daddy was coming home.

'And how did you feel about him?' I'd wanted to ask Sally, but didn't. How did you feel about your father robbing you of your mother with a single shot, which, when I found an old newspaper clipping in a drawer at Brechallis years later, was what had happened. But Sally knew what I wanted to know.

'The same,' she'd told me frankly, looking at me from the other end of the sofa with those wide grey Murray-Brown eyes, bright in her pretty if increasingly moonlike face. 'He was still our father. And, yes, we'd lost our mother, but it had been an accident, a terrible mistake. We could either decide to lose both parents, or keep one. Keep Daddy, which we did.'

They all did. All stood, and have stuck by him, which says a lot for Drummond Murray-Brown, and perhaps not a great deal for Vicky, although they never blackened her name either. Whatever she'd done, she didn't deserve what befell her. An invisible veil of intractable silence regarding their mother descended on the family, and what remained of them was tight, for obvious reasons. Almost twenty years into a marriage with one of the siblings, I sometimes wondered if two out of the three had ever got over it. I suspected they hadn't. James was fine, I knew that. I'm even conceited enough to believe that the girls and I had made him so, but Sally and Rachel were not fine, and I think James felt guilty about that. That he'd survived. Escaped, if you like. And they hadn't. Remained trapped in a house full of ghosts and regrets.

As I faced him now in our Clapham kitchen, I knew. Knew that their lives were entangled more inexorably than those of any other family. Knew, too, that just as we had always, throughout our married life, spent almost a month – a long time in anyone's calendar, my friends were always staggered – with the Brig and Sally and Rachel, so we would now, even in the south of France. It couldn't be avoided. And it had been foolish – selfish of me, even – to imagine it could. To believe that this summer would be any different.

Chapter Six

The ferry crossed the Channel on a rough and churning sea. It felt like a force ten to me, but James assured me it was only a moderate swell, not even a proper gale. You could have fooled me. I'm not one of nature's travellers, though; in fact, on our honeymoon I notched up motion sickness three times in one day: once on the aeroplane to Athens, once on the boat to Zante and, lastly, in the taxi across the island whilst James supplied me with sturdy paper bags and surreptitiously read *The Times*. This time, however, I was not the only one in trouble. Rory was up on deck beside me, clinging to the rail as the others played Perudo in the bar below, no doubt knocking back the rosé, lurching hilariously this way and that as the boat plunged and soared, roaring with laughter as the dice and the cups rolled off the table. Rory and I couldn't look at one another, let alone speak. So intense was our mutual concentration that our knuckles were white with the effort of clinging to the rail, our faces dizzying shades of eau de Nil. It wasn't so much the rise and fall of the great boat in the swell that I had trouble with, it was the uncertain length of the pause in between. The prow would keep rearing up on the crest of a huge wave, hesitating . . . oh God, the *tension* . . . and then swooping down again, like a roller coaster at a so-called funfair. The fact that the pause wasn't always followed by a swoop but sometimes by a dead drop, like a lift plunging from top to bottom, was my undoing. It was this last motion that caused havoc with my stomach and, eventually, despite me gulping desperately into the gale, caused me to vomit over the side. Unfortunately, the wind blew it straight back into Rory's face.

He was terribly good about it. Wiped his face and his pink Ralph Lauren shirt down with a 'Couldn't matter less, Mrs Murray-Brown', even though I'd ceaselessly told him to call me Flora. But it wasn't my finest hour. Naturally, I was horribly embarrassed, but Tara was mortified.

'Mum – how could you!' She flew into the Ladies to find me as I mopped myself down, clutching the basin in an effort not to be thrown across the room, as the boat continued to lurch hideously.

'Well, obviously I didn't intend to throw up in your boyfriend's face, Tara,' I said through my teeth, gritted in case there was more; in case I needed the basin for more than just support.

'Yes, but it's so gross! I am *so* embarrassed.'

Amelia materialized beside us, pale and tight-lipped, but not from the swell.

'Toby's just told me something awful. Apparently, you skipped past him on the landing with no clothes on, is that right?'

'I *ran* to the airing cupboard, Amelia.'

'*Naked?*'

'I didn't know he was in the house!'

'Oh, like you run around the house with no clothes on a lot! You're not doing a Mrs Robinson, are you?' She narrowed her eyes suspiciously at me. 'Trying to seduce him?'

'Don't be ridiculous!'

71

'Well, you're not making a very good impression, Mum. Try harder, OK? I am not impressed.'

Two pairs of appalled eyes bored into mine and then the sisters stalked off, united in their disgust, flashing me horrified backward glances over their shoulders as they went and murmuring mutinously.

Frankly, I was beyond caring, so sick did I feel. I only felt remotely human again when we got to Calais and I was able to change in the loo in a bar and put my dress and Rory's shirt in a plastic bag in the boot of the car. Even then, I have to admit, the smell still wasn't great and, to be honest, whatever they say in the adverts, having six people . in one people carrier is not ideal. We certainly got to know one another pretty well during that ten-hour drive down to the south of France.

Rory's manners were impeccable, really exemplary. But much as I hoped they'd rub off on the rest of us, it was rather exhausting to hear once again how extraordinarily comfortable he was, and did everyone else have enough room? I hoped he'd relax when we got there. Toby and Amelia, at the back, couldn't have been more relaxed, slumped against each other, plugged silently into their music, Toby, whenever I glanced in the rear-view mirror, foraging furiously up his nose with his finger. Tara was engrossed in a book on Virginia Woolf, so it was rather left to Rory to keep the conversational gambits going. He gave us a valiant running commentary on the flat, northern countryside, explaining how the landscape had disadvantaged the Allied troops during the war – did I mention he was reading history? – and how Montgomery had intended to march his men in strict formation over these fields with a view to accessing the beaches below, but the lack of natural topographical camouflage had hindered him. He told us about pincer movements, back-up plans, resources. It really was all extremely interesting, but there was a limit to how many times I could say, 'Really?', or 'That's so fascinating, Rory,' and since it was my turn to drive and James, who'd normally be a willing participant in this sort of conversation, had nodded off, I was rather left flying the flag.

Finally, my mouth dry from chat about the Axis and the Allied powers and eyes glazed from miles and miles of boring French countryside, the vista gave way to more exciting, hilly terrain as we twisted and turned our way across the Alps. James had taken the wheel now and Rory had gone very quiet behind me. I knew why, and truly felt for him – really, I did – but I certainly wasn't relinquishing my front seat. After a while – and quite abruptly – a brightly coloured landscape materialized, as if a roller blind had suddenly been let to fly up. The sky in Normandy had been low and grey – much the same as at home – but now the hefty clouds rolled back to reveal a deep azure blue, uninterrupted by even a wisp of white. As we thankfully opened the windows to greet the warm, still air, heavy with mingled scents of sage and lavender, rows of vineyards and vast fields of sunflowers interspersed with dusty village after dusty village assured us we were indeed in the south of France.

'Nice was once part of Italy, you know,' said Rory, who'd clearly recovered his equilibrium. We passed a rococo-style villa at the side of an olive grove. 'Hence the pastel-coloured stucco you see around here, like in Turin. It was called Piedmont until 1860.'

At least he wasn't reading mechanical engineering, I thought. Or physics.

'I think I knew that,' said James, with genuine interest. 'Although, of course, we're not going as far as Nice.'

'No, but you still see the effects, even this far inland. What are we, about an hour away?'

'From the coast, yes, but by my calculations we're only about five minutes from the villa.'

Even Toby and Amelia unplugged at this. Sat up. Funny how selective their hearing could be.

'Five minutes?' Amelia demanded.

'Just at the top of this hill, according to Camille's directions.' He could have said, 'according to the directions', but he said her name a lot these days. Also, we'd listened to quite a lot of opera in the car, instead of the usual Lighthouse Family. 'We should see the villa any minute,' he went on.

'Chateau,' corrected Amelia as, at that moment, we took a sharp right turn between the endless rows of regimented vines.

At the end of the lane was an elaborate iron gate which gave on to a long, straight drive lined with gently swaying poplar trees. The house rose up before us. Both had been right. It was a villa in the classical Roman sense, flanked by cypress trees and with faded grey shutters, but a chateau in breadth and magnitude. Long, pale and elegant, with a flight of steps leading up to the double front door, which was partly obscured by an extravagant fountain cascading into a round pond in the foreground, it was breathtaking.

'Beautiful,' I breathed, on the edge of my seat now, the horrific journey forgotten.

This was what we Murray-Browns needed, I thought as I gripped the dashboard. This was what we had come for. In the distance, beyond the house, the vale spread out palely below: parched grass shimmered lemon in the bright sunshine and was studded with small farms and the odd charming cluster of tiny houses, their red roofs pierced by slender church spires. Further into the distance, the horizon stretched away to the glittering blue Mediterranean, where little boats bobbed and white sails flapped.

We tumbled out of the car into the intense heat almost before James had stopped, so desperate were we to escape the metal box that had encased, and not necessarily enhanced, our jarring personalities: keen to escape, swim and explore.

'Except we haven't got a key,' I thought out loud, as James and I heaved a couple of cases out of the boot. The children headed off eagerly around the fountain, empty-handed.

'No need, remember? Camille said her sister – ah. Here they are.'

As if on cue, the front door opened and a youngish couple emerged at the top of the flight of steps. The man was very handsome, with dark, flashing eyes in a narrow, tanned face and wearing a pale-blue shirt and tight jeans. His wife, slight and pretty with auburn curls, was in a white broderie anglaise sundress.

'You must be the Murray-Browns.' She smiled broadly, a slight lisp combining charmingly with her heavy French accent as she came down to greet us. The man glided quickly to relieve James of his case, just as servants would in one's dreams. Indeed, it felt like a dream as they introduced themselves as Thérèse and Michel Fragonard, here to look after us during our stay. As he took my bag, Michel looked deep into my eyes. Thérèse, meanwhile, was exclaiming how lovely it was to have us here, shaking our hands as we gushed our enthusiastic responses – both James and I speak French – saying what a fabulous place they lived in and how lucky they were. Introductions to the children were then achieved and the couple led us up the steps and through the front door. In we went, into a huge, double-storeyed hall. It was a tower, in actual fact, or a turret; you could see right up to the ancient wooden rafters. The centuries-old, thick, white walls were plastered all the way to the top with heraldic masonry and crossed swords and there was even a suit of armour in the corner.

'Oh – it's like a castle!' Tara exclaimed, spinning round like a child.

'It was once. Well, a chateau,' smiled Thérèse. 'But a tiny one, *bien sûr.*'

'Looks pretty big to me,' muttered Toby. I could see that Rory was pink with pleasure, and already going across to examine the shields.

Through double doors, we eagerly followed the petite and delicate Thérèse into an inner hall, and then along a corridor into a thoroughly modern and vast kitchen, complete with a highly polished slate island big enough for us all to sleep on and with enough stainless-steel equipment to baffle me for weeks. I circled around, gazing up at the gallery above. I wasn't sure how it would work vis-à-vis smells drifting up, but it was certainly very dramatic. The kitchen in turn led to a comfy sitting room with an enormous television, and then, again via double doors, into the more formal rooms, which were of such size and stature that everything in them seemed lost. They were all furnished in the most terrific French taste, with tapestries hanging from the walls and spindly Louis Quinze furniture dotted about, but very much designed for *petites* French *mesdemoiselles*, not hulking great Englishmen.

'I hope we don't break anything,' I murmured nervously, stroking a tightly upholstered chaise longue and considering Toby's bulk.

'Oh, it would not matter, it is all *brocante* finds,' Thérèse assured me. She seemed to do all the talking, I noticed, while Michel was more watchful. 'Camille, she is so clever, and everything she has found is for really very little in the markets. It is not good.'

She meant in the valuable sense, but the whole effect was very good indeed, and it struck me that Camille was surely a woman of many parts to be able to sing like a nightingale and furnish houses effortlessly, when it took me weeks to decide on a rug for the hall.

'And the bedrooms?' asked Amelia, keen to get to the nub of the matter. We'd been admiring the view over the grand piano in the drawing room down to the olive grove, but Amelia had seen enough olive groves on our drive. Michel, meanwhile, was opening a connecting door to a study, and I saw him glance at James for approval, but my husband was still distracted by the vista.

'*C'est très jolie!*' I assured Michel quickly, moving across to admire the pretty toile-papered room which housed the computer.

Michel nodded and gave me the smallest of smiles back, but his eyes were still on James as he closed the door. He had a dark, brooding intensity that was terribly attractive. Lizzie would be all over him, I thought.

'Yes, yes,' Thérèse was saying smilingly in answer to Amelia. 'Come, I show you.'

We followed as she turned on her elegant, tanned ankles and led us back through the interconnecting rooms to the front hall, then on up the curling stone staircase. The galleried landing which hovered above the drawing room and kitchen had a long corridor peeling off it which revealed one bedroom after another, all beautifully decorated and at our disposal, apart from a locked one – presumably Camille's – at the far end. With so many to choose from, even I couldn't foresee a fight, although I would definitely make sure I was in charge of allocating them, I thought, as my daughters' eyes glinted with intent.

Finally, we reached what was clearly the master bedroom, with a four-poster canopied bed, complete with a little crown at the head of a sweep of heavy red damask. Open French windows issued on to a balcony with a tiny iron table and chairs. Bougainvillea trailed off the balcony rail.

'Oh!' I gasped.

'You like it?' Thérèse smiled.

'I love it!' I assured her, but then realized she was not addressing me. Thérèse was gazing intently at James.

'We do so 'ope you will be 'appy here, Jaimes,' she said earnestly, pronouncing it with a soft 'J', 'and enjoy very much your stay. We are so very grateful.'

'Very grateful,' Michel echoed. It was almost the first time he'd spoken. He had an unusually deep voice. 'My niece, she is so special and precious to us all. The only child in the family, you see. We are indebted. You saved her life. You are a great man.'

In all his years as a doctor, I don't suppose James had ever been paid such a compliment. He went the colour of the damask draped over the bed. The rest of us gawped as Thérèse and Michel stepped forward solemnly and cere-monially to kiss him three times on each cheek.

'Oh, well, no, really, it was nothing. Anyone could have done it,' James blustered, scratching his pink cheek.

'Not anyone. Only a very eminent physician, such as yourself,' Thérèse told him, her amber eyes shining up into his. 'I 'ave looked you up on the internet, and you 'ide your light. You are famous in your field.'

'Good heavens, no. Hardly.'

'Books published.'

'Well, a paper, in the *Lancet*. I wouldn't call it a book. Pamphlet, perhaps. OK, a small book.' James ran his hand delightedly through his hair. Hopped about a bit.

'I should like to read it, Jaimes.'

I bit my lip to stifle a laugh. Knew, if she called him Jaimes again, I was in trouble. I couldn't look at the chil-dren. But Thérèse hadn't finished. She tripped prettily out to the balcony and plucked a sprig of bougainvillea which she then proceeded to tuck into the buttonhole of James's shabby, ancient linen jacket. She stroked the lapel rever-ently. 'There,' she murmured. Was she going to kiss that, too? 'And now' – she glanced around at the rest of us, as if emerging from a reverie – '*à bientôt*. We leave you.'

With a last charming smile, she and her husband departed, the latter, as he shut the door behind them, cast-ing me another of his dark looks, as if confused by the wife of such a great man. Why so scruffy? So smelly? So . . . English?

The moment they'd gone, Thérèse having assured us that supper would be ready in an hour, the children mobbed their father up. 'Oh, so totally heroic, Dad, like, an EpiPen to the leg, so hard,' before disappearing off to argue over bedrooms.

To say that James had a spring in his step would be putting it mildly. He positively bounded around the room, taking off his jacket, but being careful with the buttonhole, emptying his suitcase, humming all the while, pausing occasionally to glance in the mirror and smooth back what remained of his fair hair from his high forehead.

'Lovely girl, that.'

'Very,' I agreed. 'Lovely couple, actually.'

'She had such a charming way about her, didn't she? Very like her sister, in fact.'

'Really?' I said lightly, forcing myself not to say darkly, *I wouldn't know.*

'Yes. They've both got this endearing way of being terrifically sincere and making one feel really . . .' He searched for the word.

'God-like?' I hazarded.

He grinned. 'I'll take that.'

Still humming merrily and refusing to be deflated, he placed his battered old sunhat on a chest of drawers, hung his shirts in the wardrobe, removed the flower from his jacket and popped it in the vase out on the balcony, and then broke out, dear God, into the aria from *The Pearl Fishers.*

Later, when I'd reallocated the children's rooms, telling

them they couldn't possibly take the best ones and must leave the nicest for Sally and her boyfriend – the very idea of Sally sleeping with anyone made my eyes pop – which was next door to ours, and no, not the second best either, that was for Grandpa, and generally shuffling them off to the far end, making sure Tara stayed firmly up here opposite us, I had a shower and changed into something cooler. It was still incredibly hot at seven in the evening and, as I put on a flimsy dress, I was pleased to see that the fake tan appeared to have worked its magic. The wobbly bits seemed marginally less off-putting and, if I walked slowly in my swimming costume to the pool, I decided, so as not to jiggle the cellulite, I might not frighten the natives. I smiled to myself in the mirror as I added a slick of lipstick and a dash of scent, then headed downstairs for a much-needed drink.

Supper was already underway, judging by the delicious smells wafting from the kitchen. As I passed through, out of habit I offered to help, but was told firmly '*Non, merci!*' by a smiling Thérèse as she chopped garlic efficiently, gold bangles jangling. Redundant, I stepped outside on to the vast crenellated terrace. I stopped, momentarily, to let the low sun bathe my face, feeling its warmth, then helped myself to the most sumptuous basket-weave armchair with creamy calico cushions, still in the sun's rays. As I settled back happily, closing my eyes, Michel appeared, as if by magic, to ask huskily what I would like to drink. James had gone for a prowl around the grounds after his shower and I dithered now, held by those mesmerizing dark eyes, wondering what was on offer.

'The champagne is delicious,' he purred.

'Well, that sounds perfect, Michel,' I said, trying not to behave like a sixteen-year-old ingénue and to get a grip. I had actually been on holiday before. Stayed in nice hotels. 'Let's open that, shall we?'

He disappeared with an enigmatic little smile, and I couldn't quite decide if it was a smirk or a smoulder. Was he laughing at me, or flirting? The former, probably, as he no doubt spotted that I was way out of my depth. I determined to be a bit more assertive and, when he came back with a bottle and some glasses on a tray and slowly poured the champagne, handing it to me, I sipped it speculatively as if determining how good it was.

'Lovely,' I declared eventually. I put my head on one side, giving him an appraising look. 'I imagine we've rather ruined your quiet summer, Michel. Just what you need, a crowd of unexpected guests to cater for!'

'Not at all. We depend on people passing through for company.' His eyes didn't leave mine for one moment. 'It can be very quiet, just the two of us, in such a large house. Lonely. Particularly at night.' He meant the evenings, of course, his English not being up to the finer nuances of the language.

'Yes, I can imagine. Although I gather you have your own cottage?'

'The lodge, yes. You passed it at the top of the drive.'

'Ah, yes. Of course.' There was a pause. It went on for longer than was entirely comfortable. 'Won't you sit down?'

He was still standing over me: not hovering uncertainly, more from a position of strength, making me feel uneasy.

'Thank you, but I must help Thérèse in the kitchen.' He inclined his head with a little bow but, again, there was

82

something mocking in the gesture, and the eyes were definitely amused. I wondered if he was goading me on to make amused eyes back, twinkle knowingly, so I deliberately didn't, knowing it was the sort of thing Lizzie would do. Also, I remembered Mum telling me that all Frenchmen were scallywags and I made up my mind not to make a fool of myself.

'Oh, good – is this for us?'

The teenagers were upon me, wrapped in towels, fresh from the pool, hair dripping, faces still damp. I made them take the cushions off the chairs before they sat in wet costumes but enjoyed seeing them lounge delightedly about, then leap up again and line up for champagne as I filled their glasses. Rory sweetly remembered, before he sat down, to ask if I needed a top-up, but was much more relaxed, I thought, in swimming trunks and a T-shirt, laughing with Toby. And since our life had so little jam on it, I was delighted to see them all revelling in the lap of luxury for once, realizing that the exquisite canapés were actually for them too, reaching for them eagerly, telling me excitedly about the amazing pool, which I'd seen from my window.

'Infinity, Mum, so the water literally laps at the edge and seems like it's going to spill out. You feel like you're falling into the valley.'

'It's constantly topped up, automatically,' Toby told us, his huge frame in a large armchair somehow looking better here than it did in London, in our semi. More space for it, perhaps. And, of course, they'd all be brown soon, had caught some colour on their faces already. Suddenly I warmed to these boyfriends of these daughters of mine.

They were just young lads, someone's precious boys, as mine were my precious girls, and I determined not to be judgemental, not to live my daughters' lives for them. Just because I'd made mistakes, it didn't follow that they would, and anyway, it was unlikely either of these boys would break their hearts as mine had been broken at their age, I thought, watching Rory gaze adoringly at Tara. If anything, it would be the other way round. I must stop being so vigilant, so constantly on the lookout for a bastard. These two had far more of James about them in terms of temperament than the man I'd been supposed to marry, the man I'd been engaged to, which was a very good thing.

And much as I'd wanted to invite friends, now that we were here on our own, it was nice to be just us, I thought, as I listened to them chattering away about a bar they'd found, made from logs, down on a terrace below in the olive grove. Yes, to be a family, and to expand into a house and a sun that wasn't usually ours: to eat and swim and tan and laugh together – I wanted that. As James came up the sloping lawn towards us, eyes as alight as his children's at what he'd found while patrolling the boundaries, exploring the gardens, I was so pleased for him, too. If anyone needed a little ego massage it was James, and I resolved to tell him tonight that what Thérèse and Michel had said was true. That he was the cleverest man – after all, hadn't he graduated at the top of his class at St Thomas's when he was twenty-four, then watched, as less able but more obsequious men, adept at oiling the management wheels, had swept past him? I resolved not to make fun.

As he approached the brow of the hill and the terrace, he stopped. Turned around, back to a sound in the distance behind him, and shaded his eyes. I followed his line of sight. Below us, on the valley floor, a dusty white lane snaked its way between the vineyards, the same one that had brought us here. It clearly carried barely any traffic but navigating it now was a small red Polo with a bulging suitcase on its roof. You could almost hear the music blaring from here: almost smell the cigarette smoke from the pair of them, hear the gales of laughter. I smiled. Mum and Lizzie. Who got on like a house on fire and always had done – Lizzie being the daughter my mother should have had – and who had come out a couple of days before us, to stop, sensibly, for a night or two on the way down, but had been told in no uncertain terms not to arrive at the chateau before us. They'd done quite well, I thought: shown unusual restraint, leaving a respectable hour or so for us to meet Michel and Thérèse and settle in. I smiled. Probably been in a bar around the corner all the time.

I guessed Mum was behind the wheel, as the car was shifting and she only had one speed: ninety. That went for her life, too. Throttle out, foot down. Full on. Of course Lizzie admired her, who wouldn't? But she hadn't been brought up by her. We were always moving apartments, moving schools, I was constantly walking into strange classrooms, sitting down at a desk beside yet another slightly guarded child, no brothers or sisters to share the experience with, to moan with later over tea. Mum's boyfriends coming and going. But why hadn't I forgiven her? Why hadn't I grown up about all that? I'd had an awful lot of love, too. Watching Mum and Lizzie make their no doubt hilarious way towards us, I determined I would, this holiday. Make a new start. Try to see her as Lizzie and my girls – and even James, to an extent – did. As a free spirit, someone to be admired and cherished, not as an irresponsible irritant, an extra child.

The car disappeared from view for a bit but then re-appeared as it came round the corner. Down the poplar-lined drive it bounced, before sweeping into the gravel around the fountain. I put my drink down and prepared to go and greet them. As I got to my feet, smoothing down my dress, Lizzie, surprisingly, emerged from the driver's side. My mother, in a bizarre pair of mauve dungaree shorts, got out of the back. Then the passenger door opened and a strange man got out from beside Lizzie. This was not Jackson. He was tall and rangy and very suntanned. He wore a pink shirt and bright-blue linen trousers and was attractive but probably older than he looked, despite the leather bracelets dangling from his wrist. He gazed around appreciatively, as they all did, not yet spotting us at the side of the house on the terrace.

Mum's hand shot up when she saw me. 'Darling!' she called. 'This is just totally and utterly divine!'

As she came tripping across the gravel towards us in pretty gold sandals, Lizzie turned and took a bag out of the boot. The stranger helped her with it and they exchanged smiles.

The children glanced round at me enquiringly. I shrugged, lips tightening. Amelia's mouth twitched.

Slowly, I went to meet them. Lizzie was laughing up at the man now, and pointing at the conical towers in delight. Then she spotted me coming towards her and waved, leaning in to her new companion, obviously telling him who I was. Oh, she was the limit, I seethed to myself. The absolute limit. Jackson couldn't come, so she'd brought someone else – not even told me! Knew I'd say no, probably. Lord knows what James would say. As they came closer, though, I stopped. My mother had paused to let them catch up, and suddenly it was she who was linking arms with the pink-shirted one. She who was gazing adoringly up into the leather-braceleted one's eyes as they came across to the terrace.

Lizzie reached me first. Embraced me warmly. 'Nothing to do with me, Flora,' she said firmly in my ear. 'Absolutely all her own work.'

Chapter Seven

'Darling! How gorgeous! What a pad!' My mother was tripping across the gravel towards me, beaming widely. In another moment, she was embracing me warmly. 'This is Jean-Claude by the way, isn't he heaven? I found him just outside Valence.'

What could I do but shake the hand of the tall, attractive man who was advancing, murmuring, '*Enchanté*,' his smile reaching right up to his sleepy sea-green eyes, which crinkled at the edges.

My smile was a great deal tighter than his and, although I managed to say something in response, it certainly wasn't '*Enchanté*'. Luckily, Lizzie was alive to the situation and appeared like magic to move him swiftly on to meet the others. Mum was oblivious, naturally, cigarette already alight, eyes, too, as they followed Jean-Claude's lean silhouette on its way.

'We stopped off at his antique shop,' she went on in a low, excited voice. 'Such a dear little place, we spotted it because it had the prettiest things for sale outside. Darling little bistro chairs, birdcages, baskets – just the sort of shabby-chic things I like – and inside, we found poor Jean-Claude slumped behind his desk. He'd got a terrible attack of the glums because he needed to get to the *brocante* fair in Aix for more stock – he'd practically run out – but his van had broken down. So I said we'd take him. Wasn't that lucky?'

'Very. So he's off to Aix, is he?' I kept the bright smile going, admittedly slightly encouraged by this news.

'Oh, yes. Eventually.'

'Right. So how long is he staying?'

'Just a few days. You know how it is.'

I did. Just a few days could turn into months with my mother, and in the case of one particular character called Neville, years. 'Is he your stepfather?' the children at school would ask. 'Yes. No. I don't know.' I didn't. What constituted a stepfather? Someone who took you to ballet and swimming (he never did that) or someone who slept with your mother (he certainly did that) before sliding off to some dodgy record company he ran just off the King's Road. Neville, Charles, Tommy, Casper ... all pleasant men, none violent or unkind to me – my mother picked well – but just not what I wanted. Not what I'd read about in Enid Blyton. I wanted a mother who made jam, a father who came home in a suit, a brother called Tim and a dog called Rufus.

'He's the most terrific cook. He's been telling us about how to marinate hams and smoke fish properly. And he does all sorts of fascinating things with pickles.'

'We have a cook. And you know all about pickles, you're forever getting yourself into one.'

'Oh, darling, don't be a bore, he's terribly amusing. And the children will love him.'

'Is he a boyfriend, Mum?'

'Oh, boyfriend, shmoyfriend ...' She waved her

cigarette airily. Saw my face. 'No, of course not,' she said quickly. 'But he is frightfully attractive, don't you think?'

He'd gone to help Lizzie with more luggage from the car and was well out of earshot now.

'Mum, you promised!' I hissed.

'I promised no more unsuitable younger men. But he's older than he looks, darling. At least fifty.'

'But what will the Brig and the others think?'

'Oh, the Brig won't mind, you know what he's like. He's on cracking form, incidentally. Looks divine in his summer gear, very tropical.'

'You've seen him?'

'We bumped into him and Rachel on the boat. They were staying at hotels on the way down, too – in fact, we thought they'd beat us here. Sally and her new man are making their way separately.' Her face puckered a moment and she looked worried. 'Flora, speaking of Sally's new man, Lizzie told me something rather disturbing in the car. She had a chat with Rachel on the boat, and it seems Sally has hooked up with someone . . . well, someone rather surprising. It appears she's lost a bit of weight and she ran into him while she was cooking at a rather grand house party in Fife. Flora –'

'Granny!'

'Darlings!' She broke off suddenly, her face wreathed in smiles as her granddaughters came running across the lawn towards her. Having met Jean-Claude, they were keen to get the lowdown, and looked thrilled to bits. Nothing their grandmother did could ever shock them. They ran into her arms and whatever my mother was about to say about Sally's new beau was lost in a flurry of greetings and exclamations. They immediately went into a huddle to whisper about Jean-Claude.

James had made it up the hill by now and was viewing the scene with dismay. I couldn't meet his eye.

'Lizzie, what were you thinking?' I hissed when she came back with her case.

'I couldn't stop her,' she muttered. 'You know what she's like, batting her eyelids: bat, bat, bat. He was in the seat beside her before I could say, "*Comment s'apelle?*"'

'Oh, I *knew* I should have brought her with us. She's not to be trusted.'

'Well, never mind, he's here now, and it won't be for long. He's actually terribly nice. Come on, show me around. And I need to talk to you.'

I linked her arm in mine and took her off, aware that James was tailing me. He caught up with us upstairs, despite me having taken the stairs at a canter, and cornered us halfway down the corridor. He was breathing rather heavily as he bore down on us.

'Who, pray, is that man?'

'He's an antique dealer on his way to Aix. Lizzie gave him a lift.'

Lizzie glanced at me in alarm.

'He's clearly your mother's latest lover.'

'No, no, of course he's not. He's about fifteen years younger than her.'

'Exactly. Where's he going to sleep?'

'Down the far end.' I waved my hand to indicate a long way away. 'Next to Rory. And Mum can go next door to us.'

'What, and you'll stay up all night patrolling the corridors on account of our daughter *and* your mother? Well, I hope she creeps in his direction rather than ours. I really don't want to lie awake listening to that all night.'

'Well, imagine how I feel!' I said heatedly.

'I can't think what Camille will say.'

'What's it got to do with Camille?' I snapped.

'Well, she's bound to hear about it, isn't she? It's her house. It doesn't look great, does it?' He shot me a venomous look before stalking off pompously.

He was usually quite sympathetic towards my mother: the one telling me to relax about her attraction to increasingly younger men and to go with the flow, that it was no reflection on me. Under the opera singer's roof, however, it was clearly a different matter.

'Unlike James to take the moral high ground,' commented Lizzie as I showed her into her room.

'I think he's got a crush on our hostess and he wants us to all match up. I wouldn't mind, but when the Brig arrives he'll launch into "When I was at Dartmoor . . ." as if it's Sandy Lane, Barbados, but that's all right, apparently. As long as it's *his* family,' I said petulantly, which wasn't like me. I loved the Brig.

'Crikey, I've even got a bell pull!' Lizzie was exploring excitedly.

'It doesn't work. Amelia's already tried it with Tara listening to the row of bells in the kitchen, but they still have to revert to texting me when they want something.' I sat down miserably on the bed. 'I'm so glad you're here, Lizzie. I've a feeling I've bitten off more than I can chew by having both sets of parents here. And now bloody Jean-Claude.'

'Or JC, as your mother calls him – totally without irony, incidentally. It'll be fine, don't worry. Um, listen,

Flora, talking of James's family, we met the Brig and Rachel on the boat coming over.'

'Yes, I know. Mum said. With the Brig looking like something out of a Brian Rix farce and Rachel telling her that Sally has met someone even my *mother* thinks is unsuitable.'

'Exactly. And the thing is . . .' Lizzie scratched her leg awkwardly. 'Well, the thing is, you know how you always say Sally is so competitive with you. So keen to outdo you . . .'

'Oh, *don't* get me started on that. Remember that Christmas when James gave me some pearl earrings, and the next time we saw her she was wearing some which she told me were *much* bigger than mine!'

'I know, and –'

'That Joseph coat I bought, exactly. Which I'd saved up for ages to buy, and then she went straight on the internet and bought the exact same one. Albeit several sizes larger.'

'Well, that's the other thing, Flora. She's lost some weight, apparently.'

'So Mum said.'

'Which means she's much more marketable, if you see what I mean.'

'Well, that's no bad thing, although, knowing Sally, it'll be a couple of pounds at the most and it'll all be back on by the end of the holiday. Oh God.' I glanced at my watch. Got hastily to my feet. 'We must go down to supper, Lizzie. Thérèse said eight o'clock, and I don't want to be late on the first night. James will kill me. He wants us all on parade.'

'Yes, OK, but hang on a moment, going back to this

competitive thing.' Lizzie looked strangely nervous. 'The reason this guy she's with is unsuitable –'

'Is because he's one of Mum's ex-boyfriends. I'm already there, Lizzie.'

'No, not one of hers . . .'

'Shit – one of yours? Please don't tell me it's that chiselled-faced moron you met last time we were in Scotland? The druggy-looking one?'

'No, no, nothing like that. It's –'

'Well, thank the Lord, because, frankly, I sometimes think that despite Amelia being so opposed to it all at the moment it wouldn't take much to skew her in the opposite direction. She is so mercurial, and the last thing I want is some good-looking dude peddling wacky bacc –'

'Oh, *wouldn't* it take much!'

Suddenly, Amelia flew through the open door and was amongst us. I froze, horrified.

'Oh! Darling. I was just saying –'

'Just saying you think I'm so fickle that if some sad boyfriend of Sally's or Granny's turned up with an ounce of grass in his pocket I'd be like – ooh, how exciting, can Tobes and I have a spliff, you experienced old hippies, you? Thanks for that, Mum. No, really. Thanks. I came to tell you supper's ready, by the way.'

She turned on her heel and stalked off towards the staircase, furious. I raced after her, appalled. Flew down the stairs after her.

'No! Amelia, I did *not* mean that! All I meant was that, delighted though I am that you *don't* indulge, I certainly don't want the older generation to think that just because they're with the young, you won't be shocked. Have carte

94

blanche to roll up wherever they want. You know how Mum likes to be part of the cool gang, and –'

Amelia turned on her heel at the bottom of the stairs. I nearly banged into her. 'No, Mum, she *is* cool. Just because she doesn't act as everyone expects an older woman to act, *you* think she's embarrassing. Well, she's not. She's true to herself. And that is so refreshing.'

'Refreshing! To you it might be, because you're a generation removed, but let me tell you, young lady, it wasn't much fun having no example to follow when I was growing up, and I am determined –'

'To revert to the 1950s? Call me young lady?'

'No, I'm just saying –'

'What, Mum? Think about it.' We were glaring at each other in the hall; the colour was high in her cheeks. 'You didn't turn out like Granny, did you? If anything, you're prim and proper, so how does it follow that setting a *good* example is going to create a good child? You should probably go in for a bit of free love and dope-smoking if you really want to take your responsibilities to me and Tara seriously. If you really want us to end up exactly like *you*.'

Her dark eyes blazed right into mine before she turned and marched off. Through the double doors she swept, in her long patchwork skirt, to the inner hall, then out through the open French windows to the terrace, where supper was laid on a pretty Provençal cloth, and where everyone was sitting waiting, ready to eat. Amelia, now on the other side of the table, facing back towards the house, glared at me when I came into view.

Oh, splendid. Splendid. What a terrific start to the holiday, I thought, heart pounding, as Lizzie, who'd clearly

95

been waiting for the coast to clear, slipped past me to the terrace. She shot me a sympathetic look. I walked unsteadily after her and took the only remaining place at the table, which was between Rory and Jean-Claude, and, unfortunately, opposite Amelia.

I shook out my napkin, feeling wretched. I hated rowing with her. Would feel low for days now, worrying as she made me suffer: scowling and sulking and shooting me black looks at every conceivable opportunity, as she was now, across the table. And it couldn't be a more beautiful setting, I thought sadly, as I managed to smile at Thérèse who was setting enormous bowls of daube provençale on the table in front of us. This elevated terrace with its vast urns of pink bougainvillea, its limbs twisting right up to the balcony above, cicadas calling to one another in the soft, balmy air, the heavenly view over the valley and the sea in the distance, surrounded by my nearest and dearest. Let's face it, it was my dream. Why, then, did it suddenly taste so sour? I helped myself to a few pieces of beef and onion and felt it turn to dust and ashes in my mouth.

My phone vibrated in my pocket. Although I always told the children not to look at their phones during meals, I did, surreptitiously. It was a text from Sally: 'On our way. Had a puncture in Rouen but be with you at about midnight. Save us some food.'

Despite my mood, I gave a small smile. Sally never forgot her stomach.

'What?' demanded Amelia opposite me, not about to let me off the hook.

'It's Sally. They're on their way. They had a puncture.' I glanced at my husband to make sure he'd heard.

James nodded, more kindly now that he sensed I was getting it in the neck from our daughter. 'We'll save them some food.'

'That's what she was asking.'

We exchanged a knowing smile, at peace again, as James and I could be in moments. One sulker was enough in a family.

'Not a secret lover, then?'

I turned to Amelia. 'No. I have no life of my own, Amelia. You know that.'

'More fool you.'

The meal continued. Toby looked awkward as Amelia looked mutinous, and I wondered how he dealt with her temper: it must have come his way by now. Mum, rather bucked now the pressure was off her, chattered away gaily. Tara sensed drama and looked nervous for Rory's sake, but she needn't have worried. He smiled gamely and even bravely tried to engage Amelia in conversation. Such was his heroism, it forced me to smile at JC beside me.

'How long have you had your antique shop, Jean-Claude?' I asked.

'Not long. One year, almost. I want for more.'

Don't we all, I thought. 'I'm sure you'll have many more years to expand,' I said encouragingly. 'It's always hard starting a business.'

'Yes, because too many people want to sell crap like me.'

'Oh.' I was startled. 'I'm sure it's not crap.'

'Is that not what you call it?' He frowned, perplexed. 'Your friend Lizzie, she come in and say, "What a load of old crap."'

'She meant bric-a-brac,' I said quickly. 'That's what we call it. Or antiques, of course.'

My mother was sitting beside him and I realized he had his hand on her knee. He saw me look. Smiled. 'You are protective of your mother. But you need not worry. We understand one another.'

'Of course you do, because age is no barrier to anything, is it? We should all just be free spirits and leap into cars with any old passing trade.'

I'd said exactly what had come into my head, employing no filter whatsoever. I was slightly out of control and knocked my wine back boisterously, missing my mouth, so some went down my chin. Amelia was watching me again. Jean-Claude removed his hand from my mother's knee.

'Your mother is a very beautiful woman,' he told me seriously. 'Photographed by Donovan, dressed by Dior, Lizzie told me in the car. A flower of her generation. That sort of appeal never fades.'

'I know,' I said, tears unaccountably springing to my eyes. 'I know, and she's like that inside and out. Which is rare.' I swallowed.

'Your father is dead?' he asked, changing the subject.

'No idea.' I said brightly, blinking hard. 'Mum got a bit confused in the seventies. A bit . . . flowery.'

'Bitch,' muttered Amelia.

'No, darling, Granny would say the same.'

'What would I say?' enquired Mum.

'That you got a bit muddled about my father.'

'Oh, yes, I did. Sometimes I think it might have been Cat Stevens but, in my heart, I know it was probably that

98

frightfully good-looking photographer who keeled over in the nineties.'

'Didn't you think it might be Leonard Cohen?' asked Amelia, brightening to this, her favourite subject. Rory was looking stunned, and I saw Tara make frantic eye contact with me to call a halt to proceedings, but it was too late. Amelia was showing off, enjoying herself. 'After all, Mum's got a similar personality,' she went on.

'Oh, thanks. Depressive? Gloomy?'

'Exactly. And there was that song about Suzanne –'

'Oh, no, that wasn't me,' interjected Mum. 'He'd got the hots for Suzanne Verdal by then, Armand Vaillancourt's wife.'

'But . . . you mean you honestly don't know . . .' Rory asked quietly.

I turned. 'Who my father was? No. And was never tempted to find out. As my mother says, in all likelihood, he's dead and, if not, he'll be married, and who wants that sort of bombshell turning up on their doorstep?'

'I suppose,' said Rory doubtfully. 'But when you were younger . . . ?'

'Oh sure, I wondered,' I said lightly. *Wondered?* I'd been consumed by it. Even stalked a few other possible suspects with my then boyfriend, who was as intrigued as I was. I recalled the two of us gazing down into a Kensington basement kitchen, watching an older man in cords and a jumper eat Sunday lunch with his family. Reading about another in a fashion magazine. But I never did anything about it.

'Mum hasn't got the nerve,' Amelia said. 'You'd think she has, but she hasn't. God, if it was me, I'd have been snipping bits of their hair off, testing for DNA.'

'Yes, you would,' I admitted, knowing she was still furious with me or she wouldn't be so unkind, but also knowing Amelia envied me my exotic parentage. She was at that age when she didn't want middle-class, middle-brow parents, would have loved to have been able to say, 'Mick Jagger might be my father . . .'

'Do you think you ever will? Find him?' Rory clearly didn't like loose ends.

'No. I'll leave it to Amelia to discover on *Who Do You Think You Are?* when she's famous.'

I smiled, meaning it. Wanting her to know I meant it. To my surprise, she smiled back, this sparky, combative, argumentative daughter of mine, whom I loved, along with her sister, more than life itself. And who I truly believed could do something great one day, if she put her mind to it. 'Mum thinks I'm going to be the next David Bailey because I can take a few pictures.'

'Why not?' I told her warmly, sensing an olive branch, knowing we were fine suddenly. Almost fine. Almost agreeing a truce on this balmy, delightful, Provençal evening: almost agreeing it was too beautiful to spoil, no matter how upset or hurt we were. 'Amelia won this terrific *National Geographic* prize –'

'When I was about fifteen.'

'Sixteen.'

'And went on to win another one run by *Countryfile* on TV. A national competition.' It was Toby who'd spoken up this time.

I turned down the table to smile at him, prepared to love anyone who loved my children. I'd often wondered if Mum loved me like that. She didn't seem to. Not in that fiercely protective, perhaps obsessive, way. She just did her own thing and let me get on with mine. I sighed. Knocked back some more rosé. There was no prescription for mothering, of course. Sometimes it was best not to be too analytical, as I was disposed to be. Just let it all wash over you.

The evening wore on in a far more convivial manner than it had begun although, of course, nine bottles of rosé helped enormously. We'd all succumbed to first-night excitement and our relief to be here and, hopefully, the first rows were over and done with. We were settling down now under the soft, navy-blue sky to get seriously pissed.

James had nipped inside to ask Thérèse and Michel to join us after pudding, and Michel had arrived with a tray of tiny glasses, full of something evil-looking, which we all regarded in mock-horror but gulped down heartily. I watched as James, arms extended over the backs of the chairs beside him, expanded happily on his work to Thérèse when she asked him about it, enjoying her interest. Michel sat quietly by, listening, leaning in, picking up tips from the great man. Very occasionally, he'd glance in my direction as I pretended to listen to Mum's prattle and, again, his dark gaze would linger for a few moments longer than was absolutely necessary. Flirting. Definitely flirting, I thought with a sudden rush of excitement and neat alcohol to the head. But why me? I sucked my tummy in and sat up a bit straighter. No one had flirted with me for years, and Lizzie was younger and far more chic, with her snappy little haircut, Agnès B shirt and pedal-pushers. I wondered if she'd noticed? But she was engaged in a heated debate with Tara and Toby at the other end of the table about whether or not feminism was dead, if it had all been sorted out in the sixties. Cigarette stuck to her lower lip, eyes drooping, mouth lurching off to the side; she was clearly spectacularly drunk, unlike the young, who were far more used to shots than us, the white-wine-guzzling generation. Why did we drink the filthy stuff when there were gorgeous liqueurs like this around? I knocked back another thimbleful when Michel slid one across the table to me, together with one of those sizzling stares.

This, along with the laughter, chatter and general state of inebriation, meant that we – or certainly I – completely forgot we were expecting other guests, so when Rachel's car drew up, only James heard it. But then, it was his family, so perhaps he'd been a little more alive to their imminent arrival. At any rate, he set off across the well-sprinkled lawn, and it was only when I heard car doors slamming and voices raised in greeting that I realized they were here.

James materialized from the darkness around the side of the house with his father, who looked older and smaller, as the elderly often do when you haven't seen them for some time. And of course he'd just endured a long car journey; quite shattering for any eighty-one-year-old. Under the twinkling lights hanging in the trees he came across the lawn with his stick, shuffling fast, blinking delightedly. I was already on my way to meet him and when I did I reached for both his hands, which were papery and bony in mine, like birds in rough silk.

'Drummond. You made it.' I kissed him fondly. 'How lovely to see you.'

It was. His delight was childlike, as I knew it would be.

'My dear! What a place! What a *palace*, in fact!' He waved his stick about demonstratively, mouth and eyes gaping.

'I know! Aren't we lucky?'

'*Aren't* we? I say, frightfully good of you to have us, Flora. You didn't have to, you know. Could have had a year on your own for a change, without the blasted outlaws. Or asked friends. But we are *so* thrilled.'

As so often happens, when one does the right thing against one's baser instincts and someone appreciates it, it felt good. I felt warm and happy and so pleased we'd asked them. There would be irritations, of course, but I loved the Brig and revelled in his pleasure.

'And I'm thrilled you're here. I'd show you around, but it's best when it's light. Right now, what I'm sure you'd like most in the world is a drink.'

'Would I!' he roared, squeezing my hands again but releasing them to wave his stick in greeting towards his granddaughters, who were hastening across. 'Darlings! Get the beers in!'

'Got more than beer, Grandpa!' They embraced him fondly. They adored their grandfather, long ago accepting the circumstances of the family tragedy.

Rachel was standing beside me now under the tree lights, her presence quiet and enigmatic as always. She'd probably been there all the time whilst the Brig and I had been talking, without me being aware.

'Really decent of you, Flora,' she said, in her clipped, slightly detached fashion. She was small and squat with a sharp beak of a nose and a no-nonsense haircut streaked with grey. Not a shred of make-up. She rearranged her mauve cardigan around her shoulders. 'I wouldn't have bothered if I'd been you. Would have given us a miss this year.'

'Nonsense, it's lovely to have you.'

It was now. And Rachel was never any trouble. Just a bit socially awkward. She never really initiated a conversation and found it unnecessary to keep one going for the sake of it, so one ended up making all the running, which was a bit exhausting. But then, she'd had a difficult life. Had never moved out of home, and probably never would now. She was the Brig's carer and was happy enough in that role, I think. It was the other one who was trickier. The other one, who, when her car arrived, would bound out of the semi-darkness towards me like some enormous puppy, all breathy and sweaty, ready with some incredibly chippy remark about how this place was lovely, but, my gosh, you should have seen the castle she'd cooked in the previous summer. That really *was* something. I hadn't seen Sally since Christmas, when she'd told me the Christmas pudding I'd brought was too dry and the cashmere shawl I'd given her would be perfect for Barney, her dachshund's, basket.

'Where are the others?'

'About ten minutes away, apparently. They would have been here before us, but they had a puncture. Flora, before they get here, can I just have a word?'

'Of course. In fact, I was going to show you your room first anyway. I had a feeling you'd rather settle in and get your bearings than launch straight into the drinks.'

'I wouldn't mind. I'll just say hello to the girls.'

She went across and greeted her nieces and my mother, and I waited for her by the French windows that led into the kitchen. Her face seemed strained, but then Rachel was hard to read and I knew the best way was to give her time, not to prattle on and fill the silence but wait for her to formulate what she wanted to say. I wondered, as we went silently through the vast house to the front hall and stairs, if this would all be a bit overwhelming for her. Brechallis was a big house, to be sure, but this was on a different scale, and so opulent and richly furnished – over the top, even. She'd need time to adjust. I was glad I'd given her the small, slightly old-fashioned green room with a paisley print on the walls, shelves of paperback books and low lamps. It was somewhat apart from the others and it had its own little bathroom, so she could be private. I showed her inside. She gazed around as I leaned down to turn on the bedside lamp.

'It's lovely, Flora. Thank you.'

I could tell she meant it and was pleased I'd got it right. I crossed the room and opened the French windows on to the tiny balcony.

'I thought you could sit out here and have breakfast if you didn't want to join the throng downstairs. Not everyone does.' Rachel, I knew, liked the morning to herself, usually to sketch in her room or go and paint on the hill behind the house.

She joined me outside, and we gazed down on to the drive below. 'Oh, I'll manage a croissant with the gang. Don't worry about me, Flora.'

'Well, we certainly will be a gang,' I warned. 'When Sally and her boyfriend arrive we'll be thirteen – imagine – for every meal!'

She turned to me and moistened her lips. Looked

worried for a moment. 'Yes, and that's what I want to talk to you about. Sally's boyfriend.'

'Who is he, Rachel? Lizzie and Mum keep hinting darkly that he's entirely unsuitable and that, apparently, we know him. Sally doesn't know anyone that I know, not that I'm aware of.'

'No. She didn't.' She groped for the words. 'But you know how she looks up to you, Flora. Copies you, even.'

I blanched. 'She copies me, but I don't think it's because she looks *up* to me. Quite the opposite, in fact.'

'Oh, she does,' she said quickly. 'She admires absolutely everything you do. Your recipes, your articles, reads everything you write –'

'Yes, but we're both cooks.'

'It's not just that. There's a very obvious hero worship going on.'

I made a face. Not from where I was sitting. More of a gleeful needling. I stared at her, wishing she was slightly more forthcoming. 'What are you saying, Rachel?'

'I'm saying that you mustn't blame her, really.' She looked truly concerned now. 'Of course, it seems extraordinary in the cold light of day but, in the scheme of things, taking everything I've said into account, it also seems quite natural. That if she ran into him, and if the timing was right –'

'Ran into who?' I interrupted, bewildered, wishing Rachel could just spit things out. At that moment, a car swept down the drive, headlights blazing, no doubt illuminating us on the balcony. It swung around the fountain and came to a halt right below us, just proud of the chateau steps.

The automatic outside lights had already sprung into action, so the interior of the sleek convertible clearly showed Sally's blonde head. She was in the passenger seat. Behind the driver's wheel was a dark, male one. For a moment, just a crazy, stupid moment, my heart stopped beating. I gripped the balcony rail. But then it carried on. My heart. *Don't be mad. Don't be idiotic. Not in a million years.*

Sally's door opened and she got out, except – she'd changed. Enormously. She was much, much smaller. Slimmer. In fact . . . she must have lost about five stone. I gawped as she glanced up to us on the balcony. She waved and smiled triumphantly, her usually chubby face chiselled and heart-shaped.

'We're here!' she cried.

I stared down in wonder. Her generally unruly mop of blonde hair, which hitherto had hung down her back in a messy heap, was cut in soft layers, ending around her chin – just the one chin, where there used to be many. My eyes travelled in disbelief down her figure. She was still statuesque, but totally devoid of fat, and not wallowing in a billowing smock but wearing trim white trousers and a smart blue blazer. She looked incredible.

Her companion got out of the car, a lean figure in a creased linen jacket and jeans, but Sally's eyes didn't leave my face for a moment. She would have seen me step back in horror. Would have seen my hand go to my mouth. Because, even before he looked up, I knew who it was. Before that head topped by floppy auburn hair, only faintly flecked with grey, turned, and that intelligent face looked up, blue eyes twinkling, I knew. That the man Sally had met whilst cooking at a house party in Fife and had brought down to the south of France to plunge amongst my family was none other than my ex-boyfriend – my ex-fiancé, in fact. None other than the man I'd spent my formative years with and been very much in love with. His merry eyes met mine in the bright lights, and everything flashed. It was Max.

Chapter Eight

I don't even remember when I met Max. He was just one of the crowd all those years ago, part of the scenery, and although he was incredibly good-looking, there were more interesting boys around. His sort of looks were too obvious, too conspicuous. I liked a bit more subtlety. A touch more light and shade. Six foot four – too tall for me, really; I'm five three – so I remember not considering him at all as we sat around the wine bars and pubs of Clapham and Fulham, me, Lucy, Gus, Fiz, Mimi, Parrot, the rest of the gang. Someone that handsome clearly knew it and he was exuberant and noisy too, with that braying, self-confident laugh. My girlfriends, particularly Mimi, were all over him. It made my lip curl. Everything about him was a cliché, from his floppy nut-brown hair and tawny, ski-tanned complexion to his huge smile, long legs and broad shoulders. The way he drank too much and partied too hard – he was an unusually good dancer, which annoyed me. Who wants a man who can dance? And he drove too fast in his predictable, red MG convertible. Ghastly.

And so I ignored him. And watched as Mimi's skirts got ever shorter, her tops lower as she crossed off the days until she'd see him at the next party, meanwhile, dragging me off to Oxford Street to find the perfect little top to go with her latest mini. We believed, in those days, as my daughters do now, that the perfect top could snare the perfect man, and all day Saturday was spent in the pursuit of it, so that, even if you didn't have a boyfriend, it felt as if you did as you engaged in the ritual of whether he'd like it or not, whilst the boys played cricket, or rugby, never giving us a thought until the evening. We were just one part of their lives, whilst they, I'm ashamed to say, were all of ours. Time not spent shopping was spent discussing them, to a degree they'd have been amazed at. Oh, to an extent, we were involved in our fledgling careers – or degree, in my case – but it was very much secondary to the main event: the snaring, bagging and keeping of a boyfriend. Look, I'm sorry, I'm just being honest.

So I ignored Max, and he, it seemed, ignored me. Until one evening, at a particularly noxious and drunken party in Onslow Gardens, he pounced. As I was emerging from the kitchen, a glass of punch in each hand, one for me and one for Mimi, he put his hand above the door frame, blocking my way into the sitting room. I couldn't go forwards, and couldn't go backwards into the melee I'd just squeezed from. He smiled down from his great height.

'Drinking for two? Not pregnant, are you?'

'Yes, I am, actually. It's due next month.'

'Have you given Charlie the good news?'

Charlie was the boy I was sort of seeing. An interesting, slightly dull but terribly intelligent cove reading bio-chemistry at Imperial.

'I was politely toying with your witty opening gambit, Max. Didn't expect you to run with it. No, I haven't given Charlie the good news because, obviously, I'm not pregnant. We're not that stupid.'

'No, no. Charlie's very clever, isn't he?'

It was true, I did have a weakness for intellectual boys. Perhaps word had got about. I handed him one of the drinks and brushed his shoulder. 'Is that a chip I see before me, Max?'

He grinned. 'Yes, that's it, I'm insanely jealous of Charlie's gigantic Bunsen burner. Is this for me?' He took a swig. 'How kind. Didn't know you were chasing me, Flora?'

'I'm not, it's for Mimi. Deliver it, would you? I'm going to the loo.'

I ducked under his arm and headed for the stairs, and thence the bog. When I came out, having queued for ages, I was pleased to see he had at least given Mimi the drink and that her eyes were shining as he flirted madly with her. We shared a flat, and she was full of him that night in the taxi on the way home, then as we clattered up four flights of stairs in our heels to our pokey top-floor flat in Mendora Gardens.

'Honestly, Flora, he got me a drink without me even asking, and then chatted me up for ages. It's the furthest I've ever got with him.'

'Except he left with Coco Harrington,' I pointed out. I'd seen him lurch into a taxi with her, pinching her bottom as she got in before him.

'Coco's his cousin,' Mimi said quickly. 'There's nothing in that.'

'Second cousin. And posh families don't take any notice of that sort of thing. They're all inbred.'

'You just don't like him because he doesn't flirt with you,' she said petulantly. I thought of his wicked blue eyes twinkling down into mine from under that floppy fringe, then roving up and down the admittedly rather tiny dress I was wearing, which was backless and therefore bra-less, in an attempt to try to rev Charlie up a bit. He was more experimental with the mice in his laboratory than he was with me.

'You're right, he doesn't,' I lied. 'But he does with everyone else, Mimi. He's what another generation would call a rake.'

'I know, but every rake has to gather a few leaves along the way and, one day, when he's mine and we're living in that flat in Chelsea his grandfather left him and I'm pregnant with our second child, gazing adoringly at our first in his cot, I'll be glad he got it all out of his system early and isn't cheating on me. I'm playing the long game, Flora. I've got all the time in the world.'

And off she went, singing drunkenly, to her bedroom, stopping en route for the Nutella and a spoon, then, remembering the long game, putting it back.

The next time he tried it on was at Charlie's birthday party. Charlie lived in now deeply fashionable but then extremely suspect Brixton. His particular dive was a dingy basement flat he shared with two other scruffy scientists. On this particular night it was throbbing with flashing lights and loud boy music – Hawkwind, or something hideous. Max arrived with Coco and some other exotics in his peacock-blue shirt and tight jeans, looking alarmed. He clutched his throat theatrically.

'Where am I? I can't breathe. Have I died and gone somewhere penitentiary? Will the crumpet-catcher survive outside, or will I emerge to find its tyres slashed? So many questions. It's a mark of how much I fancy you,

Flora, that I follow you literally to the end of the earth, if not the Victoria line.'

'Oh, shut up, Max,' I muttered, for more reasons than one. Mimi was in earshot, and a pointed glance told me she'd overheard. 'You fancy everyone, so please don't believe I'm remotely flattered by that.'

'Except that it's you I love!' he roared, grinning delightedly as I stalked off.

Mimi caught up with me. 'You didn't tell me he flirted with you, too.'

'He didn't, until last week. And he only does it to get a reaction.'

'And because you don't fall for him,' she said slowly. She stared at me. 'It's fine,' she added more coldly. 'I won't stand in your way. If you want him, don't hold back for my sake.'

'Oh, don't be ridiculous, Mimi. I don't even fancy him, and neither should you! I'm going out with Charlie, anyway.'

'Only because you feel you should. Because he might invent the cure for cancer one day or something. And because you're too up yourself to go out with fun men.' She stalked off crossly.

'Who are these people, darling?' Max was in my ear. 'Are they all experiments of your boyfriend? Why are they doing that flappy chicken routine with their elbows?' Status Quo were playing to exuberant reaction. 'Some don't seem to wash their hair.' He put his peacock-blue collar up for protection.

'Are you gay?' I asked.

'I am tonight.' He shuddered.

I had to admit, even by Charlie's standards, this lot were

geeky: skinny, lank-haired, hollow-chested, bespectacled. And the boys weren't much better.

'Is that a boy troll or a girl troll?' Max asked in a mock-horrified whisper as a couple took to the dance floor, achingly uncoordinated, glasses clashing. My mouth twitched despite myself. He took my arm. 'Come on. Let's show them how it's done.'

Before I could stop him he'd dragged me on to what passed for the dance floor – a patch of sticky carpet – at which point the music unfortunately changed from Quo to Al Green.

'No!' I gasped as he clasped me delightedly in a tight clinch.

'It's a dance,' he cooed in my ear, 'not a sex act. You don't shout "No!" if a boy asks you to dance, it undermines their confidence. I could be crushed.'

'Nothing short of a runaway truck could do that,' I retorted, wishing he couldn't dance so expertly and move me around the floor in a way Charlie couldn't, wishing I could stop my body moving with his, natural rhythm being about the only thing I'd inherited from my mother.

'You're enjoying your-self . . .' he sang in my ear.

'I'm no-t,' I sang back.

'You're ly-ing. You lo-ve me.'

'I don't even li-ke you.'

He threw his head back and laughed, and I saw Mimi, in a corner of the room, snogging a friend of Charlie's called Derek. You'd have to be really desperate to snog Derek. Before the song ended, I was away, to the garden this time, to join fellow smokers and, hopefully, crowds of people Max didn't know and would hate. I was longing for Mimi to disentangle herself and appear. But she didn't. In fact, Lucy told me she was under a pile of coats with Derek in one of the bedrooms, and since I couldn't leave without at least consulting Mimi – we'd shared a taxi here – and probably should stay because I was at Charlie's, that left me rather stuck. When Max finally left with the cohort of friends he'd brought with him – 'What are we *doing* here, Max?' from the glamorous Coco as they all headed out to the MG – I was at least able to crash in Charlie's bedroom, taking any coats off the bed and depositing them in the hall, knowing, as host, it'd be a lot longer before he came to bed. Knowing I could curl up and go to sleep.

Charlie came in sometime later and I roused myself dozily.

'Hi,' I said sleepily. 'Has everyone gone?'

He grunted something, and I wondered if he was annoyed I hadn't been with him much. He'd either been drinking home brew in the kitchen, which I hated, or having long, intense talks with his lab buddies, and although I liked the intellectual stuff, doing journalism at college was very different to reading chemistry down the road at the real thing. Having bagged my Oxbridge type, I'd begun to wonder if he was for me.

'Get into bed,' I said softly, knowing this wasn't the night to make any decisions or have a drunken row, and hoping he didn't want anything else. Unlikely. Charlie had quite a low sex drive. As he crept in naked beside me, a hand snaked over my tummy. Damn. I held it, hoping a little hand-holding might suffice, but as he moved in for a cuddle I froze. Scuttled to the edge of the bed and switched on the light.

'Shit!'

In bed beside me, naked and grinning hugely, was Max.

'What the fuck are you doing here?'

'You told me to get into bed.'

'I thought you were Charlie!' I could hardly speak. Squeaked instead. 'Where's Charlie?'

'In the bath, asleep. He climbed in, having puked in the loo first; he seemed to think it was the next obvious step. I put him in the recovery position, rather considerately putting a cushion under his head. I did ask if he might be more comfortable elsewhere, but he said he was very happy there and, heavens, it's his house. Who am I to argue?'

I stared in horrified disbelief, clutching the duvet with both hands around my chin. 'Are you naked?' I whispered.

He threw back the duvet to reveal a brown torso and pink boxer shorts. 'Kept my shreddies on. Ever the gentleman.'

'*Never* the gentleman! You must go,' I went on in a low, angry voice. 'Go now! This is outrageous. Get out!'

'But, darling, I can't. Coco took the car. So I have no suitable means of transportation, since the Tubes have long since terminated and I imagine taxis are an endangered species round here. And Mimi and a man who looks like a door are in the other bedroom and, what with your boyfriend in the bath and two pituitary cases coupling on the sofa . . .' He smiled winningly, clasped his hands behind his head and crossed his ankles neatly ' . . . what's a boy to do?'

'I'll sleep on the floor,' I told him. 'Turn your back. I want to put some clothes on.'

He frowned. 'Seems foolish, with an entire double bed

at our disposal. I won't ravish you, you know. Or don't you trust yourself with me?'

I'd already reached down to the floor for my pants and a T-shirt of Charlie's, and wriggled into them under the duvet. I sat up in bed, arms crossed, furious.

'I am *not* sleeping with you, Max.'

'I can see that,' he laughed. 'But what about sharing a bed? Surely there's no harm in that?'

There was a lot of harm, but since it was four in the morning and I was too tired to argue, we did, after I'd tossed him Charlie's dressing gown and ordered him to put it on, which he did, but only after having insisted on modelling it first, in the manner of a mad scientist, finding some test tubes on Charlie's desk, pretending to brew a potion, back hunched, scratching his head naughtily in the way that Charlie had, until even I laughed. It was at that moment that Mimi came in. She looked from one of us to the other and her face said it all.

'I was wondering if we should share a taxi home, but clearly not.'

'Mimi! Wait – no!'

Too late. The door had slammed. I stared, horrified, at the paintwork. Sank back on the pillows and groaned. 'Great. In one evening, you've cost me my best friend – and probably my flat, since her father owns it.'

'Nonsense, you'll patch it up with her, darling. And Lucy's your best friend, not Mimi. I've done my research. And if she does turf you out, you can always come and live with me. I've got a nice little place in Draycott Terrace.'

'Oh, don't be ridiculous.'

'I'm not, I think we'd be good together. But, frankly,

Flora, if you don't put it to the test, we'll never know, will we?' He leaned right over me, an elbow propped either side of my head. I tried to look cross but, God, he was attractive. And when those wicked, glittering blue eyes softened, as they were doing now, he was terribly hard to resist. I'm not proud of myself, but a bit of me felt I had at least resisted for ages and, of course, once I'd let him kiss me I was in too deep, and then, naturally, it was sensational. Sometime later, I lay in his arms, staring at the dawn as it came up behind the thin bedroom curtain.

'Darling,' Max murmured, 'promise me, if you ever run away from me again and I have to chase you round London, don't let it be south of the river.'

I smiled, thinking I hadn't actually thought about running away, and then I fell asleep.

In the morning, of course, there was a bit of a scene. Charlie had staggered in while we were fast asleep. He wasn't best pleased. In fact, he could hardly speak he was so incandescent with rage, and Max and I took advantage of that, wriggling into clothes, finding shoes, keys, money, Max saying in a loud voice what a terrific party it had been and how kind it was of Charlie to have invited him as we hurtled past him standing bug-eyed and spluttering in the doorway. I was puce with shame and stopped to mutter, 'Oh God, I'm so sorry, Charlie, you see –' before Max dragged me down the hall and out of the front door.

'Never complain, never explain,' he told me as we clattered up the uncarpeted basement stairs.

Outside, the crumpet-catcher stood prettily at the kerb, all in one piece. I turned, astonished. 'I thought you said –'

'I lied!' he cried, arms outstretched, smiling broadly.

In an instant he'd concertinaed down the roof and we'd jumped in. We shot out of Branksome Road, around the dustbins and the scruffy-looking cars, the cats returning from a night out, into the crisp air, which clashed violently with our hangovers, and a sunny, bright-blue morn. Off we sped. I'm sorry. But after four months with a very clever chap, having deep conversations in gloomy pubs where everyone drank beer – even the girls – the novelty had worn off. Here I was, flying across Battersea Bridge, wind in my hair, the Thames shimmering beneath me, in a bright-red sports car, beside an incredibly handsome man in a peacock-blue shirt, with nut-brown hair, similarly coloured forearms . . . what could I do?

We had breakfast at the brasserie at Brompton Cross: fresh orange juice and croissants slipped down a treat and there were gleeful grins and more jokes from him whilst I tried not to smile and assumed an ashamed expression, and then I refused to have any more to do with him. I refused to go back to Draycott Terrace and spend the rest of the day in bed, as he suggested, and I refused to walk in Kew Gardens and 'get steamed up in the hothouse'. I also refused to laugh any more than I could absolutely help. It was what I'd missed, though, I realized wistfully. Laughing. Instead, I made him drop me back at my flat – at the end of the road, in case Mimi was at the window glowering – and walked, with fear and trembling, down to number 42.

From the doorstep I gazed up at our top-floor windows, to the eaves where the pigeons roosted, dry-mouthed. Mimi was good fun, but she had a temper. She was also very good-looking and used to getting the boys. Although a bit of me thought that it wasn't as if she was going out with him I knew the sisterhood rules: knew I was in the wrong. I was pleased to see my belongings were not stacked up in the hallway as I opened the front door, and was also pleased to find her in the kitchen, making an apple pie, radio on, window open to the sunshine. Food was our big bond. We'd met on a cookery course in Paris during the summer holiday the previous year, where we'd both agreed, as we sat in pavement cafés drinking espressos and wearing short skirts and feeling very grown up, that in times of crisis and emotional stress there was nothing that couldn't be solved by making a batch of profiteroles. I thought back to that summer – exciting days when you meet a new friend, swap confidences, thumbnail sketch your life up to now and then fill in the details more thoroughly as time went by – and felt sad.

'I'm so sorry, Mimi,' I began humbly, realizing I didn't even know what I was going to say. Was it 'I won't see him again' or 'I'm going to see him again, you'll have to deal with it'? That it depended on her?

She turned. Her face was strained, but she managed a brave smile. She looked me in the eye.

'It's not as if I was going out with him.'

'No, but still. I knew you liked him.'

'And you didn't?'

'I didn't think I did, because everyone else did,' I said truthfully. 'But then, yesterday, I realized that wasn't a good enough reason.'

'So now you do?'

I struggled, wondering how to put it.

'It's fine,' she said quickly, knowing immediately. 'I'm

not going to make a scene over a blatant mutual attraction. Go for it, Flora.'

I felt everything inside me relax. I could have hugged her, but knew from her rigid back as she turned back to roll out the pastry that it would be a step too far, so didn't.

'Thanks, Mimi,' I breathed. I wanted to add – And we won't be obvious. Won't flaunt it in your face in the room next to yours, we'll be at his place, not here; but I knew this wasn't the moment for the geography of the coupling. For the details. Surprisingly, though, she did want to know how it had happened, and I was relieved that I hadn't sought him out: that he'd ambushed me. I wanted to clear that side of our friendship, and she even had the grace to laugh.

'You must have got the shock of your life when you realized it wasn't Charlie. God, the audacity!'

'He's got balls,' I agreed, before realizing that wasn't the most tactful thing I could have said.

I withdrew hastily from the kitchen and scuttled to my bedroom, leaving her to her baking. There, I drew my curtains on the day and went to bed, even though it was barely the afternoon, the sun was still shining, and the pigeons outside my window were still cooing to one another on the crumbling ledge. I needed, though, if I was going to live here with Mimi, for it to be tomorrow. I shut my eyes and snuggled down. For it not to be the day I'd cheated on my flatmate and let a man lead me, uncharacteristically, into temptation.

Chapter Nine

I didn't worry that he wouldn't call the next day, I knew he would, and he did. Luckily, Mimi was out, and I sank happily into the sofa, chatting for a whole indulgent hour, picking stuffing out of the exploding arms, before he went to his parents for lunch, promising he'd meet me tomorrow. The next day, he was waiting outside the London College of Printing, where I was trying to become a journalist in an already shrinking column-inch world, and we went for a drink in Holborn. As we sat on stools at the bar, I thought how easy it was to misjudge someone. He was just a boy. With a very nice face. Who'd driven to see his parents in the country on a Sunday, because he was worried about his sister, who'd fallen off her pony. He was as lovely as someone who was poor with an unfortunate face. It made no difference where people came from, or what they looked like.

There was also the added dimension that I'd gone all the way from hating him to liking him, so that, even then, so early on, the distance between the two made it seem dizzyingly close to love. After a few drinks, we went to the Spaghetti Opera in Fleet Street, which he'd heard about through his contacts in the music world – Max worked for an events company that staged concerts: rock, pop and classical. This particular Italian restaurateur employed impoverished music students to sing whilst the punters ate pasta. Sounds fun, but in reality, having someone draw up a chair and croon – or blast – Puccini in your face on your first date wasn't really ideal, and so we bolted down our spaghetti *al vongole* and beat a hasty retreat to Draycott Terrace.

Those first few weeks swept by in a predictable fashion: drink, eat and retire to horizontal activities, to be repeated again when energy levels recovered. After a bit, though, we emerged and became more inclusive. We spent time with friends, his or mine, at the Surprise, the Phene, the Admiral Cod, the usual haunts. I did tease him initially about his friends, who were the green-sock, tasselled loafers, Barbour-over-a-suit brigade, but apart from Coco, who drank, they turned out to be as normal and insecure about their looks and concerned about their love lives and their jobs as the rest of us. I grew to like them as much as my own crowd. My own friends knew Max anyway, but my college ones didn't, and circled him warily at first. Once they realized he brayed but didn't bite, they embraced him and, after a bit, even Mimi relaxed, and went out with a friend of his called Bertie.

His parents were heaven, and we drove to see them regularly in Hampshire, in their lovely Georgian farmhouse, complete with rambling acres, paddocks and sheep grazing beyond a ha-ha. Although clearly well off, they were steady, sensible people: his father was a local solicitor and his mother a housewife who organized charity events and gardened. She told me quietly one day as I was helping her deadhead roses that she was so pleased Max had met me, because, frankly, some of the girls he'd gone around with before had been a bit racy. Her delicate skin on her beautiful face had puckered thoughtfully, like tissue paper, as she'd paused, trug in hand. Not that any of them had been serious girlfriends, she'd added, resuming her pruning. He'd only had one proper girlfriend before me, an Australian girl called Tiggy who he'd met on his gap year and fallen for, but, geographically, it hadn't been ideal.

And, of course, he in turn met my mother, who adored him, principally because he played backgammon with her for hours on end and laughed at all of her jokes whilst pouring the vodka, all of which encouraged her no end. But he seemed to genuinely enjoy her company.

'Yes, I do,' he agreed, when I put this to him. 'She's good fun.' He nudged me. 'She's where your lighter side comes from.'

I'd grinned, but knew we were both wondering where the darker, more serious one came from. And, like other friends before him, Lucy in particular, he'd asked if I wasn't intrigued.

'Oh, I know the possibilities, I've narrowed it down,' I assured him, and reeled off the names of a captain of industry, a fashion photographer and a musician, and he'd tried to persuade me to discover more. The furthest I'd gone was to take him to a house in the Boltons, where we'd peered down into the well-lit basement kitchen together, where the musician, now a successful producer, was pouring a drink for his wife as she peeled potatoes. Two young children were curled up, watching television on a sofa in the corner.

'I'd be the worst sort of bad news,' I told Max as we stared. 'I don't want to be that. Don't want to be a nasty shock in a letter, or standing on the doorstep. Ruin four people's lives.'

'Change,' he'd said. 'Change their lives and, in time, they'd come to love you. You'd be the cool older sister.'

I made a face. 'Not for a long while, and not to the poor wife. I'd be a horrific jolt, and I don't want that. The other families are all much the same, incidentally. I've checked. Incredibly happy.'

'But what about you? What about your happiness?'

'But I wouldn't be happy, knowing I'd made everyone miserable. I'd be wretched.'

'OK,' he said slowly, 'but what about the truth?'

'It's just a word. Rhetoric. It's not an emotion. A feeling.'

'So not important?'

'Oh, very,' I said vehemently. 'But it doesn't take precedence just because it resonates on moral high ground. It doesn't beat wrecking a family. Anyway, I'm fine, I've got Mum.' I smiled, knowing he couldn't dispute this and that, despite her frivolity, he saw a different side to her: a brave one.

'Brave?' I'd said, astonished, as we'd left her house in Fulham one night after midnight. 'Reckless, you mean.'

'It takes courage to be that happy. Not to let regret overwhelm you. And she's solvent. She's done all that on her own.'

'Done what!' Mum hadn't worked since her early modelling days.

'Made her own money, invested it in property and managed to hold on to it. So far.'

'Well, all she did was stand in front of a camera . . .' I said dubiously.

'Does it matter if it's beauty or brains you're blessed with? Surely it's as much of a crime not to use one as the other? If a first-class brain who could be studying at Oxford was running a sweet shop, you'd say what a waste.'

'I suppose.'

'She's used her assets.' He shrugged. 'Same thing.'

'And had immensely rich boyfriends.' I thought of our fine Parisian years, with Philippe, who was then the French finance minister. I wasn't sure Mum had paid for anything when we'd lived in the beautiful apartment he'd bought for us in Montmartre: I was pretty sure he'd paid for me to go to school, too, in the darling little Madeline ensemble with cape and straw boater.

'Oh, sure, she's taken her chances, but a few years in Paris is just the same as accepting a sabbatical at Harvard. Getting a break for being clever.'

I laughed, loving Max's refreshing view on life, knowing he was good for me, that I could be too critical of Mum sometimes, too judgemental. But then I was allowed to be: she was my mother. And other people, with their cosy, deadheading, trug-wielding, Yorkshire-pudding-making mothers could afford to find her enchanting. They only dipped in.

Max was four years older than me, so I wasn't totally surprised when, after eighteen months, as he was approaching twenty-eight, he asked me to marry him. Girlfriends and I had already discussed this beneficial side effect of dating the slightly older man. Oh, we laughed as we said it, but there was a glaring reality, which obviously couldn't be repeated on the floor of the *Evening Standard*, where I was now working as a fledgling restaurant reviewer under the great Fay Maschler. And I was the happiest girl alive. I'd got my gorgeous Mad Max, who complemented me, just, as everyone said – Parrot, Lucy, Gus – I did him. I'd calmed him down a bit, apparently. I was the brakes, and my friends, who might have initially thought him a bit flamboyant, loved him too now. We happily planned an engagement pary, on my twenty-fourth birthday.

Unfortunately, I was felled by horrific stomach cramps for the two days leading up to it, and on the morning of the party, dizzy with painkillers, I collapsed at work and was taken to hospital. An already erupting appendix was removed from my abdomen and burst as it was placed in the kidney dish. Disappointing, obviously, but it was also a relief that it wasn't more serious. I rang Max drowsily from a phone a nurse wheeled to my bed when I came round from the anaesthetic, and he came rushing in. His face was pale and worried, and he held my hand tight, but gradually, as I talked, he was reassured and relieved, too. I told him to go ahead with the party.

'Don't be silly, it's our engagement party. And your birthday!'

'Yes, but everyone's been invited, and everyone's coming, and it's tonight. In four hours' time. Please, Max. I'll feel wretched if you don't. And it's only our friends in your flat, it's not like it's anything grand.'

Reluctantly, he did go ahead – the alternative, pre-texting and pre-Facebook, being to sit on the phone for the rest of the afternoon. The next day, when I was feeling much better and sitting up, a whole gang of our friends – Max,

Fiz, Lucy, Mimi – came in to see me and said it hadn't been the same. That they'd missed me terribly, but they'd toasted me at midnight and Max had made a short speech about his darling girl. I'd glowed.

The arrangements for the wedding, six months hence, began. I had a gorgeous few days trying wedding dresses on with Mum, who wanted me to go for something elegant and fitted and steered me, quite rightly, away from the shepherdess costumes. We had a heavenly girly time of it, tasting champagne and flicking through folders full of pictures of cakes: Mum, always defiantly feminine, can be quite traditional when she feels like it.

And then, one day, I was in the Coopers Arms in Flood Street, fingering veil material and waiting for Max, when I looked up and saw Coco, on her own, at a table in the corner, dwarfed in a huge camel coat. She looked dreadful and was clearly already plastered. I went across with my drink and sat next to her.

'The blushing bride,' she slurred, the corners of her beautiful mouth lurching with the effort of trying to speak.

'I hope you'll come, Coco? To the wedding?'

She looked at me through dull, dead eyes. 'It's made you bold, hasn't it? This engagement? You used to be scared of me. Now you're trying to be kind. Patronizing. Of course I'll come, he's my cousin.' She seized her drink and knocked back the remains of it. I smelled whisky. 'Who d'you think you are – Diana Spencer? Snaring the prince, so now we all have to cosy up to you? Be your best friend?'

I glanced around, wishing Max would arrive. She got up to go, thank goodness. Wobbled a bit.

'I'll be your best friend, Flora,' she said suddenly, placing both hands on the table for balance. 'I'll tell you something you should know, and that no one else will tell you. On the night of your engagement party, Max fucked Mimi. That's what you should know, and no one else will tell you.'

She staggered from the pub.

I sat, shocked, rocked and immobile at that table in the corner. A few minutes later, the door flew open, and Max arrived on a blast of cold air. He was full of apologies about the bloody Tube and his boss keeping him hanging on and wanted to know how long I had been here. Then he saw my face.

'What is it? What's wrong?'

I told him. And then watched as his face turned grey. And I knew. He sat down and put his head in his hands. Ran his fingers through his hair. Slowly, he looked up, ashen. The party had gone on quite late, he told me. And, eventually, he'd gone to bed, leaving a hard core staying up drinking, playing cards; telling them to let themselves out quietly. Sometime later he awoke to find a naked girl beside him. At first, in his confusion, he thought it was me, then realized it was Mimi. She was already on top of him, working her magic. He told me he had absolutely no excuse. Except that he was quite drunk and very disoriented.

'It was my birthday.'

'I know.'

'My engagement party.'

'Yes.'

'I'd been under the knife, having an operation.'

He didn't answer.

'You came to see me the next day. She came, too. She brought me flowers.'

The horror of the deception threatened to overwhelm me. I felt terribly sick.

I managed to leave the pub. Managed to walk, not home, but to Mum's. She took one look and poured me a very large drink and we sat whilst I cried and told her, and she held my hand. She didn't offer any advice, she didn't tell me what to do, she just looked very sad and very wistful, and once or twice she seemed to be a million miles away, back in her own past. I didn't want to be her in twenty years' time. Didn't want history to repeat itself. I'd never asked Mum why none of the men she'd been with had ever married her, I knew it was too painful.

The only thing she said, aside from consoling me, was, 'He's a very good-looking man.' Not implying anything, just a statement of fact. But I knew. Knew that I was OK-looking – pretty, with an open, friendly face – but that I'd been punching above my weight. I'd be looking over my shoulder for the rest of my life, wondering who was perching on his desk at work, who he was going on business trips with, or, if I was away myself, who was moving in on him at home.

I broke up with him. And, obviously, I broke up with Mimi, and moved back in with Mum, in Fulham. Max was heartbroken. He tried his hardest to win me back. He called me constantly, he loitered around outside my office, my house, but I wasn't having any of it. And the reason I wasn't having any of it, I realized one day on my way into work, was those flowers. Although there'd been other friends around, about five of them, Max and Mimi had approached the end of my hospital bed together, almost as a couple, bearing gifts. The flowers were from Pulbrook & Gould, a very smart shop around the corner from Max in Chelsea, which I used to walk past – nowhere near the wrong end of Fulham, where Mimi and I lived. Somehow, I knew they'd bought them together. Had had breakfast together in his flat, coffee, croissants. And then they'd gone to select them, before coming in to see me. That she hadn't beat a hasty retreat first thing in the morning.

I stayed with Mum for a year – in many ways, she was more like a flatmate than a mother, anyway – and threw myself into having a raucous, non-stop, hectic social life. My friends were brilliant: they partied hard with me, encouraged me to do as much as possible, to accept every invitation. I didn't disappoint them. But towards the end of the year, in November, I overdid it, and broke a tiny bone in my foot, a metatarsal, trying to dance on a table in a nightclub, then jumping off it when the barman, who'd originally thought it a huge joke, turned ugly.

Lucy took me to St Thomas's. James was working in A&E at the time as a young registrar, and something about the way he handled my foot at two in the morning and observed that at least I'd been on the table and not under it, made me warm to him.

'Were you plastered?' He looked up at me with a smile, crouched as he was, tending my ankle.

'Not entirely.'

'Well you're about to be. I'll get a cast on that.' He straightened up.

'Apparently, a surgical boot gives you more mobility? Can't I have one of those?'

'It's a short cut. If you were my girlfriend, I'd want you to be in a cast. It'll mend much better in the long run.'

It made me want to be his girlfriend. To be looked after. To be there in the long run. And he had kind grey eyes, thoughtful ones – not twinkly, naughty ones like Max's.

My visits back to St Thomas's became the highlight of my social calendar. I dressed carefully for them, and when James asked me out for a drink when the original cast was changed for a lighter one, I hobbled off delightedly. His was the first name on my new ankle. With a kiss.

A year later, we were married, and then, not long after that, Max married Mimi. I nearly fell over when I heard. I hadn't even known they'd been seeing each other. Once I'd got over the shock, though, I was triumphant. You see, I thought smugly, pushing through a swing door at St Thomas's, where I had another appointment with James, but this time for a scan, as I was pregnant with Amelia, I'd been right. Of course I'd been right. I'd known all along. Max had never been the man for me.

Chapter Ten

Sally, unused to being the sideshow, was not appreciating the way my eyes and Max's had met in the outside lights of the chateau – me on the balcony, him gazing up – and held on tight. She was alive to the situation in an instant.

'Of course, you two need no introduction, do you? I'd forgotten you know each other.'

Speechless, I dragged my eyes away from Max and back to her, my breath short at the magnitude of her gall. *Forgotten?* Of course she hadn't forgotten. I'd told her the whole story myself, curled up on an ancient sofa in the morning room at Brechallis, when I'd first gone there with James, during one of our girly chats. Starved of company, she loved to drag me off for hours, wanting to know everything. She knew all about Mimi – obviously, she didn't know quite how heartbroken I'd been, because I was going out with her brother – but she knew it had been incredibly traumatic. Thriving on drama, when her life yielded so little, she'd wanted the story again and again.

'I couldn't stop her, Flora,' Rachel, beside me, said in a low voice.

I swung around to her. Her face was drawn in the glare of the outside lights. Sally and Max were getting suitcases out of the boot now, shutting car doors. We stepped back into the relative safety and gloom of the bedroom.

'But this is monstrous, Rachel. You must know that?'

She hesitated, looked wretched. 'I'm not sure Sally's up to that sort of treachery, she's not that deep. I honestly think he flirted with her, she was flattered, and when she realized who he was, she thought, Oh well, so what? It was years ago and he doesn't mean anything to Flora any more. And, I admit, she might have thought – it could be quite amusing.'

'Not to tell me –'

'Yes, that smacks of wanting to give you a surprise, but not a nasty one. Just a bit of a jolt. You know how insecure she is, how everything has to revolve around her.'

'But does she even realize that this has nothing to do with her at all?' I hissed furiously. My hands were shaking as I clutched the necklace around my throat. 'And everything to do with me? That he is here because of me? Is she that stupid?'

Rachel swallowed. 'I think that's taking it a bit far –'

'Oh no, Rachel, it is not!' I knew what he was like, knew his chutzpah.

She licked her lips. 'I know what you mean. It is a bit odd, from his point of view –'

'It's extraordinary!'

'Flora, we must go down,' she said anxiously as we heard noises below. 'It looks even more odd if we hang around up here. We must go and meet them, be normal.' She looked at me imploringly in the dim glow of the bedside light. She was right. Of course she was right. And she was helping me. I needed that. I nodded quickly and, together, we went down the corridor and descended the stone staircase. My heart was pounding. I hoped I wouldn't fall.

When we got to the bottom, they'd already pushed through the front door into the brightly lit hall and were gazing around in wonder.

'Ah, there you are! We wondered where everyone was. Thought you weren't coming to greet us!' Sally's newly bleached teeth glistened as she smiled broadly. She crossed the hall and enveloped me in a mass of lipstick, hair and scent. I managed to hug her back.

'I *do* hope you don't mind, Flora,' she whispered fiercely in my ear, and I actually believe she meant it.

'Sally! How lovely to see you,' I gasped. 'Everyone's still on the terrace, having drinks. You look amazing.'

I turned to Max, as Rachel embraced her sister. His eyes were alight, but it wasn't just amusement: he'd like me to think it was, but there was something else there, too.

'Flora. Lovely to see you.' He stepped forward, and we pecked each other awkwardly.

'You, too, Max. What a surprise.' I kept a bright smile going. I'm good at those. Suddenly, I agreed with Rachel. Sally wasn't deep. Giving me a jolt might be a thrilling by-product, but it wouldn't be her raison d'être for being with Max. She plainly just imagined that this very attractive man, who'd once gone out with her sister-in-law, was now in love with her, because she was so thin and beautiful. But I knew Max. Knew he'd never fall in love with Sally. He wouldn't fall in love with her head.

'Come and see everyone.'

'I thought they'd hear the car, come and meet us! I'm dying to introduce everyone to Max.'

I turned and led the way through the house towards the terrace. I could hear myself breathing.

'What a house!' Max was saying as we crossed the inner hall. 'Is it as amazing throughout?'

'It's pretty special,' I replied. I hadn't heard his voice for so long, it was bizarre.

'It's beautiful,' agreed Sally, stopping to gaze around. We stopped with her. 'Although it's not quite on the scale of the one I was in last year, of course, when I was with the Wards in Angus, which is the neighbouring estate to Balmoral.'

'Yes, I remember you showed me the pictures,' Max said lightly. 'Is that the coast we can see, twinkling away in the distance?' He'd moved to an open window.

'Yes, it is,' I said shortly, removing my tongue from the roof of my mouth, where it had seemingly taken root. I led the way through the kitchen and out to the terrace, where, under the twinkling lights and a velvet sky, my entire family were seated. I was glad it was dark so no one would see my horrified face until I'd had time to compose it. Neither could they hear my heart beating. I introduced Michel and Thérèse, who were clearing away the liqueurs and were the closest, and then as everyone got to their feet, exclaiming, Sally took over.

'Max, this is my gorgeous niece Amelia – and you must be Toby, I've seen your picture on Facebook. And this is my *other* gorgeous niece, Tara – so, by a process of elimination, you must be Rory!'

I stood by in a daze.

'What the hell . . . ?' James was beside me suddenly, staring as Sally went round the table, dragging her beau with her. 'Isn't that Max?'

'The very same.' I swung round to him. 'Did you know?'

136

'No, of course not!' He looked horrified.

'Well, she's your sister!' I hissed.

'Yes, but –' His face acknowledged this responsibility. 'God, Flora. I'm so sorry.'

'Oh my God, look at you!' My daughters were on their feet and shrieking, gawping at their aunt, circling her in wonder. 'How much have you lost?'

'Five stone!' said Sally proudly.

'But how did you *do* it? Was it the five-two thing?' Amelia demanded, clearly wanting to run off and do it instantly. 'Did you starve for two days?'

'No, I met this man.' She smiled and reached for Max's hand. 'It just dropped off.' She half-shielded her mouth with her hand. 'Plenty of sex,' she whispered, in a hideous aside to her nieces.

'When did you two meet?' asked Tara, giggling, but blushing, too, as Amelia, after rolling her eyes at me, made room for them to sit at the young end of the table, where they were handed bread, cheese, Calvados and olives by Thérèse and Michel, who, having been assured the late arrivals didn't want any proper supper, prepared to disappear. Max had paused to greet my mother, who had looked surprised but not incredulous. She introduced him to Jean-Claude. When his back was turned, though, she looked across at me and raised her eyebrows. Everyone settled down to chat, but after a few minutes Lizzie was up from her seat and down to my end of the table.

'Your mother says that's *the* Max.'

'The very same.' I reached for the dregs of someone's wine. Gulped it down.

'Do the girls know?'

'Not yet. They will soon, though. They're already au fait with his sex life. Apparently Sally's going like a train, no doubt with all the zeal of the recently converted.'

'But what's he doing here?'

'Search me, Lizzie.'

Mum was now sitting next to Amelia, and I saw her lean across and whisper in her ear. Amelia froze. She turned to gaze at me. Then, when she could decently pretend to withdraw from the conversation, she scuttled down. Pulled up a chair.

'Is that really your ex-boyfriend, Mum? Granny says it's the one you were engaged to!'

'Yup.' I reached to pour myself some more wine.

'But how do you feel? Isn't that so weird for you? That he's going out with Sally?'

Her face was agog. Max continued to talk to the others, but I knew he was going through the motions, was more intent on us. He couldn't hear us from that distance, though.

'It's more than weird, Amelia.'

'God, I can *imagine*. But he's divorced, apparently, and Sally does look amazing, doesn't she?'

'She does.'

'He's seriously hot, Mum.' She broke off to look at him again. Then back. 'Does Dad mind?'

'I very much doubt it.'

He wouldn't. Once he'd got over the initial shock, he'd assume that these things just happened. That life was full of curious merry-go-rounds and some ended up in your back garden. James didn't have a jealous bone in his body, which had sometimes annoyed me. He was far too relaxed to get worked up about an ex-boyfriend, even if he had been my fiancé. Would I mind if James's ex-girlfriend pitched up? Of course I bloody would. Except, I knew he hadn't had his heart broken by Henrietta. He'd split up with her, so perhaps I wouldn't mind. Perhaps that was different. Yes, it was. But broken hearts mend, and mine had, I thought defiantly, looking at Max chatting and laughing with Toby, Tara and Jean-Claude. Did I honestly feel anything? No. Not in that way. But I was horribly jolted, which wasn't what I'd wanted on my one proper break of the year, particularly such a special one. It dawned on me that, actually, I was furious.

Max deliberately wasn't looking at me, no doubt feeling my eyes on him, but when he excused himself and went inside to go to the loo, I slid away and entered the house via a side entrance, knowing I could intercept him in the corridor. I slipped into the sitting room, which was in darkness, its open double doors giving on to the dimly lit corridor. He tried a few doors before he found the right one and, from my vantage point, I saw he'd put on a bit of weight around the middle. Good. I waited until he'd come out of the bathroom.

'Max, what are you doing here?'

He pretended to look surprised to see me, but I wasn't fooled. Max and I thought alike. He'd left the table deliberately. Had known I'd follow him, I realized with a start. One–nil to him already. His eyes sparkled mischievously in the gloom.

'I'm here with Sally, of course,' he said facetiously. 'I thought you knew.'

'Did you? Did you ask her to let me know?'

'Oh, I didn't do that, but you knew she was bringing someone. You could have asked.'

'I didn't imagine I'd know a man she'd met in Scotland.'

'Does it make a difference, Flora? It's been a very long time.'

'Of course not!' I blustered. 'I just think it's extraordinary of her not to say, that's all.'

He smiled. 'I think she wanted to surprise you.'

'Yes, she would.' So he knew that much about her. 'What are you doing with her, Max?'

'That's a bit churlish, Flora. She's a lovely girl.'

We stared at one another. He knew I couldn't gainsay that. I knew he didn't mean it. Or thought I knew. I couldn't actually read his mind, of course. And he clearly hadn't known her long – was I being paranoid? And horribly unkind?

'She's frightfully glamorous and great fun. Just what I need at the moment.'

I raised my chin. 'I'm sorry it didn't work out with Mimi.' I'd heard through Lucy that they'd parted.

'I'm sorry, too. But I shouldn't have married her. We married in a bit of a rush, for the wrong reasons.'

'What were those?'

'I think you know, Flora.'

'If you're implying for one second that it was my fault, and that you married her on the rebound, it doesn't say much for your character, Max.'

How odd. We'd slipped into talking very earnestly and personally to each other, in furious whispers, as if we'd last seen each other yesterday: this man I hadn't set eyes on for twenty years. As if I'd just picked up the phone when he refused to stop ringing me at Mum's, or bumped into him as he doorstepped me yet again outside her house on my way to work, launching into another row about Mimi. Him telling me she'd wanted her revenge, served cold, that he'd just been a pawn in her game. We both had. That we shouldn't let her win. Trying to persuade me to have a coffee with him round the corner, to listen to him for just two minutes.

'And you didn't?' He gazed at me intently.

'What?'

'Marry on the rebound?'

'Of course not! How dare you!'

'It was bloody quick.'

'A year.'

'Bloody quick. And I gather you were drunk for most of that time, partying hard.'

'Oh what, trying to forget you in a blur of alcohol and then marrying the first man who asked me out?'

He shrugged, his eyes mocking. He definitely had control of this conversation. But then he'd had a while to think about how it might go.

'You've got a nerve, Max. Turning up on my family holiday with a failed marriage behind you, trying to suggest there's anything wrong with mine.' I was shaking.

'You're livid, aren't you, Flora?'

'Yes, I am.'

'Which is interesting. Such a strong emotion. Surely you shouldn't give a damn if I'm here or not? Shouldn't give it a second thought?'

'It's the deceit, the duplicity. You're with a girl we both know is not your –'

'Max?'

Sally appeared at the other end of the corridor. Her feet echoed along it now. 'What are you doing in the dark?'

'Flora was just showing me where the loo was. Come on, darling, let's find our room. I'm bushed, aren't you?'

'Amelia's showing us, she's waiting at the bottom of the stairs. Night, Flora, and thanks so much for having us.'

'Yes, thank you, Flora, we couldn't be more thrilled to be here.' And so saying, he gave me another wicked smile before moving smoothly around to take Sally's arm.

Only when they'd gone did I realize my hands were trembling. I clenched them together hard. I took another moment, then started back unsteadily to the garden.

Most people had drifted on up to bed; it was late. I saw Rachel helping her father make his way slowly inside, his back bowed in his cream linen jacket. Only Mum and Jean-Claude remained seated, deep in conversation at the far end of the table. James was circling it, clearing the last few glasses and napkins in a haphazard fashion.

'Thérèse told us to leave everything, but I think that's a bit off, don't you? I thought I'd at least clear the ashtrays and take the cheese plates in.'

'Yes, I agree.' I gave him a hand, knowing it helped to be married to a man who knew what was OK and what was a bit off. A man of integrity, who would never dream of being manipulative.

'Is the Brig all right?' I formed the words: found a cloth and gathered some crumbs. 'Has someone shown him where he's sleeping?'

'The girls. They're loving being the hostesses with an enormous pile at their disposal.'

'Doesn't happen often.'

'Quite. Make the most of it. Are you OK, Flora?'

He'd paused and was looking at me intently as I frantically swept the table, glad of something to do.

I stopped. 'It is odd, isn't it, James?' I clenched the cloth and looked imploringly at him. 'You must admit?'

'It is a bit peculiar,' he said slowly. 'But I don't think it's some deliberate campaign.'

'I do,' I said vehemently.

'I know, that's why I said it. I knew you would. I just think they coincidentally met and he's divorced and happens to be going out with Sally, that's all.'

'But *Sally*.'

'Steady. She looks terrific.'

'She does, but – Christ, James, she drives *you* up the pole. Let's not pretend she's easy.'

He shrugged. 'I'm her brother. She's bound to be different with him.' He put his head on one side. Gave me a kind smile. 'Come here.' He held out his arms and I walked into them. Held on tight.

'I'm scared,' I whispered.

'Why?' He laughed into my hair. 'He can't hurt us, Flora, don't be silly.'

'I don't know. I just feel incredibly threatened. I want him to go. Now.'

He squeezed me. 'Well, that's not going to happen, darling. Come on, you just have to make the best of it.' He patted my back. 'And you really can't look too thrown, for the girls' sakes.'

'I know.'

I bit my lip as he carried on clearing up. I couldn't be hiding behind my dark glasses all day, skittery and on edge because my ex-boyfriend was amongst us; what would they think? That I was vulnerable, that's what. But he was on my patch. It was outrageous. Imagine if the roles were reversed and James and I were divorced and I'd turned up on his and Mimi's family holiday? It *was* outrageous. Why was I the only one with eyes to see? As James gathered the place mats, I wiped them down. Tried to be sensible. Not so childish.

As we walked inside carrying the debris, we passed behind my mother and Jean-Claude at the far end of the table. Mum didn't turn, but she reached a hand out behind her back. I squeezed it gratefully. She'd looked after me that year before I met James, nursed me at her house. She'd sat on my bed as I'd sobbed. She'd asked me, more than once, if I wasn't cutting off my nose to spite my face. The rest of my life, even. Asked me, if I was so upset, so heart-broken, why I couldn't forgive him? Take him back? Get over my pride?

If anyone had eyes to see what came after pride, she did.

Yes indeed.

Chapter Eleven

'Oh God.' I swung around in alarm 'I've put her next door!' I breathed to James as he closed the bedroom door behind us.

'Well, that's all right, darling. They're hardly going to be at it like teenagers, are they? Especially after a ten-hour drive. And, anyway, so what if they are?'

He was beginning to look a bit cross. I knew I had to keep my paranoia under wraps. Nonetheless, I found myself looking at our double bed, its headboard against the shared wall, as I knew theirs was too. While James was in the bathroom getting ready for bed, I tried to drag it across the floor. It was bloody heavy and I only got it a few inches. It also made a terrible racket.

James shot back into the room, toothbrush in mouth. He stared.

'I thought it might be nice to sleep under the window.'

He removed the brush. 'Flora, you're being absurd! I'm beginning to wonder why it would affect you so much to hear your ex-boyfriend in flagrante with another woman.'

'Shh!' I glanced at the dividing wall in horror. 'And, anyway, do you really want to hear your sister in the same state?' I whispered.

He looked appalled. Hesitated a moment, then put his toothbrush back in the bathroom and hastened to help me.

'Lift, don't drag,' he muttered.

With much puffing and cursing, we shifted the heavy bed to the other side of the room. It left behind an empty, dusty stretch of floor, which, framed by the great sweeping damask canopy, looked most peculiar. I solved that by dragging a chest of drawers across to fill the space. Or started to. James had to help, of course, in the blue T-shirt he wore to bed, his willy poking out beneath it.

'Happy?' he panted.

'Yes, much better.'

He stood up and gazed around. 'Camille will think it's bizarre.'

'Why will Camille know?'

'Thérèse is bound to tell her.'

'I'll just say I'm a fresh-air fiend. Have to sleep under a window.'

'You'll have plenty of it – we can't close the bloody curtains now.' He got on the bed and tried to yank them across.

'Yes, we can, just pull the bed out a bit. It's too close to the wall.'

We went to the other end and were pulling, bottoms up, when Amelia came in.

'Oh, gross, Dad.' She covered her eyes.

'Well, knock, damn you!' James stood up and pulled his T-shirt down.

'Sor-ry. Why have you moved the bed?'

'Your mother wants the air.'

'Oh.' She looked at the dividing wall. Her eyes widened. 'Oh, right. Important not to overreact, Mum. Um, Jean-Claude needs a room, obviously, which means there isn't one for Toby.'

I gazed at her, still panting with exertion, hands on my hips. Infuriating. For her grandfather and Aunt Rachel's sake, I'd insisted Toby nominally had a room. My mother's new boyfriend obviously had to have at least the semblance of separate sleeping quarters, too, since she'd only known him five minutes, which meant my daughter's boyfriend no longer had a smokescreen. I looked at James hopelessly. He shrugged and threw up his hands.

'You sort it out.' He stalked back to the bathroom, muttering darkly about the bloody women in his family.

'Yes, well, obviously, he'll have to go in with you, Amelia, even though it's not what I wanted.'

'It's not my fault.'

'No one's saying it is.'

'I don't see why you have to keep up this bonkers sense of appearances, anyway.'

'Because your grandfather is of a different generation, as is Rachel, in a way, and also, it's the thin end of the wedge. In a twinkling, Tara will be next, and I promised Rory's mother –'

'Oh, grow up,' she interrupted. 'Do you really think Rory and Tara are going to sleep at opposite ends of the corridor?'

And with that she flounced out, having got what she wanted. So why flounce? Why?

I brushed my teeth very hard and drew blood. I stared at it against the white porcelain. No. Over my dead body would my seventeen-year-old daughter disport herself thus. Eighteen was the rule in this family, with at least six months of dating behind them. I spat more blood, pleased with that. I'd just made a rule. A good one. Also, with Tara directly opposite us, Rory would have to be pretty bold to sneak down here. And he was a good boy, I knew that. I got into bed, knowing I wouldn't sleep for ages, that there was too much in my head. After a bit, eyes shut but mind whirring, I heard footsteps padding softly down the corridor. Tara's door opened quietly. I froze. Then I heard her giggle. I leaped out of bed and flew to my door, flinging it wide.

Max was outside, talking to Tara, who was fully dressed at her open door. They stared at me.

'What are you doing?' I asked, wrong-footed.

Max regarded me a moment. 'Borrowing an adapter. I didn't bring one and your daughter said she had two.'

'Right. Where's Rory?'

I threw a wild glance up the corridor, then peered past Tara into her room. She recoiled in mock-horror, squinting in that 'You're so weird' way beloved of her tribe. 'In his *room*?' she suggested incredulously.

'Right. Good. Go to sleep,' I said, as if I'd sorted out something crucial.

I shut my door, but not before Max had managed to look me up and down, taking in my heavily night-creamed face, my very cheap, very short Primark nightie, eyes ironic and amused. His, not mine. I crept back to bed, feeling like a humped beast. Splendid. Oh, splendid.

'Might I suggest, if you're intending to leap up and down all night and patrol the corridors like something out of a French farce, you keep the noise to a minimum?' enquired James sleepily as I curled up beside him. 'God help us if Jean-Claude is down this way, too. Your mother will be here in a minute.'

'He is,' I said miserably. 'Toby's designated room was next to ours, and Mum will definitely do the creeping. So, far from having the quiet end of the house, we've ended up where all the action is.'

'Well, let them get on with it,' he grumbled, turning over on to his side, his back to me, and bunching up his pillow. 'Good luck to them. Everyone will be bonking away like rabbits, but you can rest assured there's one couple who won't be.' He gave a hollow laugh.

I didn't reply. Thought about giving a hollow laugh back, since it wasn't always me that was tired, but decided against it.

Instead, I listened for sounds next door: strained my ears. Nothing. I'd heard murmurings earlier, but only the motion of two people going to bed. And, anyway, why would I care? Max had been married to Mimi for eighteen years, been going to bed with her night after night – why would I care about Sally? I wouldn't. Care was the wrong word. The right word was . . . I thought hard. For ages. When I did locate it, the word which summed up the way I was feeling, it took more than one. Out-manoeuvred. Out of control. Spiralling into the stratosphere. Almost to the point where I couldn't breathe. I knew I'd felt like this once before, when Coco, huddled in a huge coat in the corner of the pub like a fragile bird, had delivered her *coup de grâce*. It was the same flailing experience that I'd do anything to escape from. Next door, I heard Sally giggle. I shut my eyes tight and rammed in my earplugs.

The following morning, Sally came down to breakfast looking flushed and happy. I was already at the table under the trees with some other early risers, it being warm enough to eat outside. I smiled at her brightly over my coffee.

'Morning, Sally.'

'Morning, Flora. I say, James has finally told me who this place belongs to. I couldn't believe it! Camille de Bouvoir, the opera singer!'

'Yes, I know. He was asked not to broadcast it, and you know what he's like. His word is his bond, and all that.'

'Max was flabbergasted when I told him last night, we had no idea. Is she very glam?'

'I've only met her briefly, but yes, she is. Oh, *merci*, Thérèse.' I smiled up at Thérèse, who'd arrived with some fresh coffee. Sally wanted to know if it was Brazilian, Max's favourite, and when Thérèse said she wasn't sure, she asked her in an imperious voice to please check and, if not, to add it to her shopping list? I cringed and pretended to check my phone.

Most people were already up, it being after nine, aside from the teenagers, who wouldn't appear until much later. The Brig was seated facing the view, almost in a trance. The hazy morning light shimmered over the valley floor below us, heralding another hot day, and he looked sweetly delighted in his panama hat, mouth slightly open, as it often was these days, as he rested both liver-spotted, gnarled hands on his stick. Rachel, beside him, poured coffee for both of them. She was wearing an ancient blue shirtwaister which was already dark under the arms. It occurred to me that she really had tumbled into the carer role if Sally had broken free. Rachel had always done the lion's share but, to give her her due, Sally had never stinted. James and I were the slackers, I knew, but then we had a family and lived in the south. I wondered if Rachel minded. She gave so little away. Always a very private person, it was as if, as Tara had once commented, she concealed a lot of things: as if she carried her past around with her at all times. Lizzie, beside her, glamorous in a yellow-and-white striped sundress and gold sandals, provided quite a contrast, reading her emails on her iPad, slim legs crossed. She glanced up as Michel delivered a basket of fresh croissants. I saw him smoulder at her. Ah. Not just me then.

Max appeared, looking impossibly handsome in a pink shirt and khaki shorts, tanned legs beneath them. He smiled down at Sally as he took a seat beside her and she squeezed his leg, leaning in to whisper something. She was wearing a plunging halterneck sundress that revealed acres of bosom. Those hadn't reduced much, I observed as I sipped my coffee. Or dropped. Extraordinary. She really had turned into a very good-looking woman. Perhaps I had got it all wrong. Perhaps they really were in the first flush of love. I pretended to read a guidebook, taken from a pile which the Brig had brought out from the kitchen. Sally leaned diagonally across to me.

'Did I tell you Max and I are going on to St Tropez for a few days after this?' She helped herself to a croissant, then put it back in the basket.

I looked up, as if I had been miles away. Blinked. 'You didn't, no.'

'To stay with the Hamilton-Frasers. Remember I cooked for them when they took that shooting lodge in Perth? I'd love Max to meet them, they've become such good friends.'

'Oh, really?' I was surprised. I'd run into Felicity Hamilton-Fraser coming out of M&S on the King's Road not that long ago. We'd chatted and I'd asked how it had gone, and she'd said, 'Well, your sister-in-law is an excellent cook but we learned not to ask her for a drink. She's feet up in the drawing room making herself very at home, isn't she? And not just one drink, either!'

'Oh, sorry, Felicity.' I'd recommended Sally, who'd been at a very low ebb at the time.

'Oh, it didn't matter, we got quite giggly about it, actually. Put bets on how long she'd stay!'

I'd felt a bit cross then: I didn't want her to be the butt of their jokes.

'Probably just relaxing after all that cooking? It's hard work.'

'This was *before* dinner, Flora. We didn't get fed until well after nine.'

'Heavens! Oh, I am sorry, Felicity.'

'Oh, don't worry, we didn't mind. She was hilarious at the after-dinner games. Any excuse to strip down to her underwear!'

I'd scurried away into M&S. Hadn't told James. He'd have been mortified.

'They've replied, have they, darling?' asked Max.

'No, but they know we're coming. I emailed weeks ago. But you know Felicity, she's so disorganized. It's probably slipped through her net.'

Stupidly, I caught Max's eye.

'We might just see if she makes contact this week, hon.'

'Oh, I'm not fussed either way. We could have a couple of nights at that place you found in the Michelin Guide instead, if you prefer.'

'Yes, we might do that.'

Was she the butt of Max's joke, too, I wondered? That

would be cruel. And would make him a very unpleasant person, surely? Something I'd never known him to be. I thought of the lovely, crazy, funny Max I knew. I voiced this to Lizzie in the kitchen, when we went inside to make some instant coffee, which we preferred.

'It must be for real, Lizzie,' I whispered as we waited for the kettle to boil. 'It makes him the most terrible cad if not, don't you think?'

'Yes,' she said slowly. 'But then again, a marriage break-up does funny things to people, Flora. Makes them desperate. If his life has gone terribly wrong – which it clearly has – there's a temptation to lurch back to the past, when it was peachy. Look at the success of Friends Re-united. He may be here to banish a few ghosts, see you in the flesh and think – what was all the fuss about? She's just a middle-aged housewife carrying a few extra pounds.'

'Yes,' I said slowly. 'That could be it.' I remembered his amused eyes on me in my minuscule nightie last night, taking in my streaky fake-tanned legs. I had thicker ankles since childbirth, too. 'In which case, it'll take a matter of moments.'

'I honestly don't think he's here with the cold, clear aim of breaking up your marriage.'

'No. But . . . maybe to make trouble?'

'It's only trouble if you feel it to be. It's you I'm worried about, Flora, if I'm honest. He's awfully attractive.'

'Oh, you don't need to worry about me.' I hastily grabbed the coffee she'd made me. A bit spilled on my hand and burned me. 'I got over Max years ago.'

I sailed back out to the garden, sucking my sore hand.

*

It occurred to me as I went up later to change that I'd put mascara on for breakfast. And lippy. Something I'd never usually do on holiday. In the privacy of my bathroom, I wiped it off defiantly. Then I put on the shiniest, whitest, total sunblock – I burn very easily – which gave my skin a fishy look. Even the swimming costume I chose was an elderly Boden affair, slightly saggy at the waist and legs. It was very much third reserve for when I ran out of good ones. I added a dreary cheesecloth poncho, chose a trashy novel rather than anything cerebral, and, popping it into my beach bag along with a hat and more sun cream, sallied forth defiantly.

At the top of the stairs I glanced down and saw Sally and Max crossing the flagstone hall below, one step ahead of me, in their swimwear. Sally was in a gorgeous black bikini with a pink sarong tied low around her hips. She was already beautifully brown. Max's hand was resting on the base of her bronzed spine as they crossed the hall. I almost fell over the balcony. Was that *Sally*?

I dashed back to my room. Changed into my expensive new one-piece made from reinforced steel which pulled in all the bits that mattered, including the droopy tummy and the side boobs, as the Australian lady who'd sold it to me had promised. Then I wiped off the thick grease, found a slinky turquoise sarong, applied a touch of lippy and went down.

The pool was a short distance away from the house. To reach it, one had to cross the manicured front lawn, which was constantly watered by spiralling hoses, via a cinder path, duck under a spreading cedar tree, skirt a small lake with a single rowing boat on it, and enter through a charming green wooden gate in a tall, crumbling wall. Inside, there was a beautiful enclosed haven, which had once been an enormous walled kitchen garden. It still boasted large regular flowerbeds to one side, now full of bright dahlias and gladioli, the cutting garden for house flowers, rose-clad walls and a small orchard. Aside from the pool, the rest was laid to lawn, but such was the garden's size, there was even an area with a badminton net. At the far end, an ancient stone barn with a gaping façade had been converted into a pool house, complete with table tennis, drinks fridge and comfortable rattan armchairs with vast, squashy cushions. Behind the barn and over the post and rail fence, a pair of elegant chestnut horses nodded at the flies around them, already hot and bothered, ready to head for the cool of the trees. In the distance, beyond the parched pasture, was the neighbouring vineyard, then the hills of Fayence rose up gloriously in the shimmering heat.

The teenagers were already present and horizontal, having clearly grabbed a croissant and orange juice en route, judging by the glasses and jam-smeared plates dotted about. I'd have to make sure they found their way back inside and put a stop to that tomorrow. Why couldn't they pause for breakfast at the table? They were dozing around the end of the pool nearest the barn, which faced the sun, having bagged the best beds. The boys wore garish long trunks, the girls tiny bikinis, and all were plugged into their iPods, sunglasses on, a paperback apiece. I regarded my girls with pride. Amelia, who'd still like to be thinner, was much more slender than a year or so ago, and Tara had a great figure. Lizzie, in an orange bikini, was face up amongst them, and Max and Sally had not yet appeared. Perhaps they'd got lost.

I found a sunbed in a distant corner, abandoned by the children for being half in the shade, but that suited me. Arranging myself upon it carefully, top half in the shade, legs in the sun, I meticulously removed my sarong, but not until I was sitting down, and even then I let it drape a bit over my thighs, which, despite the fake tan, looked pasty and heavy. I bent my knees to make my legs look thinner and wondered if I could hold this position all morning. I did it for ten minutes and became increasingly uncomfortable and cross.

I hadn't envisaged anything other than total relaxation on this holiday, and having an ex-boyfriend wondering how my figure had changed in the twenty years since I'd last seen him was not in the script. Defiantly, I let my legs flop down on to the sunbed, just as Sally and Max appeared through the garden gate. I snapped them back up again, sharpish. They didn't seem to notice me, though, and took beds, as I knew they would, in full sun, at the more popular, fun end of the pool.

I watched from behind my book, dark glasses and the brim of my hat as they began to shed layers. Sally's legs were long and slim; the only hint of the colossal amount of weight she'd lost was in the slightly mottled texture of her tummy and thighs, but you'd have to be very picky to find fault. I saw Amelia pretending to read but looking with interest, too. Max, in long trunks, was lean and toned, with only a hint of a paunch where, once, he'd had a very flat stomach. He was in pretty good shape, and had a natural tan, which suggested this wasn't his first holiday this year. I realized he looked expensive. His trunks were a good, dusky green. His deck shoes were not tatty and Cornish like James's but sleek and Italian-looking, as were his shorts and shirt, which he folded in a pile beside him, together with a Rolex watch. It occurred to me he'd probably made a lot of money. I knew he was still organizing concerts and events, because Sally had mentioned it last night, but I had no idea how his career had panned out, because, I realized with satisfaction, I hadn't been interested enough to find out. Doubtless, I could have done, we still had one or two mutual friends – Lucy would have known, Parrot, too – but I'd never bothered to ask; had never googled his name, never investigated. You see? I was safe as houses. If he still had problems as far as I was concerned, which – I watched as Sally lay down beside him and they briefly held hands – I was beginning to doubt, that was his lookout. Having seen Sally in her bikini, I was now finding it farcical to imagine Max was here on my account. I smiled. Took my sunglasses off and shut my eyes. How ridiculous of you, Flora. So egocentric. Ridiculously vain. Thank God I could relax.

I have no idea why I fell asleep so easily and so early on in the day, although I suppose I'd had a pretty unsettled night, but I was woken by Tara, her face above mine, concerned.

'You're a bit red, Mum. And also' – she leaned forward confidentially – 'you might want to tuck yourself in a bit.' She glanced down at my bikini line: half my bush was flourishing the wrong side of my swimsuit; my legs were akimbo.

I sat up with a horrified jerk. Rearranged my splayed

limbs – one foot seemed to be on the *floor*, as if I'd been writhing in my sleep – and quickly wiped the dribble from the side of my mouth. I realized the sun had moved. I was now in its full glare, chest and face on fire. Damn. Why had I wiped that sun cream off? And how long had I been like that? I glanced across the pool. No sign of anyone. All beds had been abandoned. Plates, books, glasses and sun cream were littered about.

'What's the time?' I gasped, mouth totally devoid of saliva.

'I dunno, but it must be nearly lunchtime. You were snoring fit to bust, Mum.'

'*Was* I?' I was aghast.

'Come on, they'll be wanting to serve up. Dad doesn't want us to be late. You know what he's like about keeping staff hanging around.'

Tara sloped off, and I quickly found my hat. I wrapped my sarong around my waist and, feeling sticky and drenched in sweat, prepared to follow her. My sarong stuck to my legs. It was no good. I'd have to go in the pool. I was horribly hot.

Thankful no one was around to witness it, I stripped off the sarong and plunged into the pool, obviously not putting my hair under, just wiping my face with my hand. I swum a length of breaststroke in the cool blue water. Bliss. When I reached the other end I saw that, far from being alone, as I'd imagined, one couple was still here. Max and Sally had moved their beds around to the side of the barn, and Sally was naked. She was on her tummy, and around a discreet corner to be sure, but still starkers. I boggled. Max had his back to me and was sitting on his bed beside her, suntan lotion in hand. I watched, mesmerized, as he took a handful and began to cream her back. As he massaged it down her spine, lower, lower, gently into her bare bottom, he turned his head, looked me straight in the eye and smiled.

Chapter Twelve

'But don't you think that's peculiar? That he should be smiling at me while massaging his girlfriend's bottom?'

I was trotting to catch up with Lizzie, who'd spotted a stall she wanted to revisit at the far end of the market.

'Not if he only that moment realized you were there. What did you want him to do, scowl? Look horrified that you were spying? Snatch his hand away? I think, under the circumstances, a smile was quite resourceful of him.'

'It wasn't that sort of smile, Lizzie. Not a friendly one. It was more . . . implicit.'

'Implicit of what? "This is what you're missing"?'

'Yes!'

'Oh, don't be ridiculous. I'm surprised at you, Flora, letting it spoil your holiday like this. You're in a complete tizz about nothing. Rise above. Also, if you could drag your eyes away from your own life for a minute, Jackson emailed me this morning. He can't come, after all. He's too busy rehearsing, which probably means I've been too needy recently and he's relishing some time alone without me.'

'Oh, Lizzie, I'm sorry. I'm sure it's not that, by the way. Jackson's nuts about you.' I bit my thumbnail as she rummaged amongst the shoes on the stall. 'Sorry. I am a bit self-obsessed, aren't I?'

'If truth be told, we all are. Now, what about these? Too bright?'

She was holding up a pair of shocking-pink espadrilles with ribbons. When Madame's eyes were averted, she slipped them on her feet.

'No. I mean, yes. When you get them home, probably.'

Lizzie hadn't known us in the old days, of course. Me and Max. Hadn't known how close we were. She was the wrong person. Lucy would have been better. But, on the other hand, Lizzie was the right person, because Rise Above was just what I should do, and what I'd decided to do only this morning.

I narrowed my eyes and looked into the distance. The market was crowded and packed with stalls under brightly striped awnings which stretched right to the end of the long, gravel square, where, on quieter days, old men played boules and chewed the fat in the sun. Ahead of us, Mum and Jean-Claude were sampling olives from an array of vast wooden barrels on a trestle table. They'd got here much earlier and rung us to say we might like it, this rare afternoon market, very much for the tourists, but quite fun. Lizzie, James and I had driven across to the exquisite hilltop town, perched like a bird of prey hovering over a valley, and made our way in the heat up the little cobbled streets to the top. I'd been pleased to get away, to have a change of scene; James and I were not good at lying by the pool these days, preferring to poke around monasteries and art galleries, as befitted our age, and this was a beautiful place to come. A magnificent church dominated one end of the square, a phalanx of ancient steps running up to its open door, and to either side an avenue of trees with mottled grey trunks provided some welcome shade under a canopy of thick green leaves. Just beyond the right-hand row of trees a low stone wall ran the length of the square – and pretty much the town – in a typically casual French attempt to prevent one toppling down the dizzyingly steep hillside below. No barriers and hideous signs here. The stands were predominantly full of clothes and trinkets, the real commerce having been done yesterday morning, when steely-eyed madames had prodded glistening hams, plump artichokes and florid tomatoes with all the thoroughness of gem merchants. This was a far more flippant affair, and it occurred to me the girls would have liked it, but they'd been intent on their tans when I'd asked, forensically examining first-day white marks and studying factor numbers as if they were revising for exams, determined to go home bronzed.

The world jostled by in strappy tops, shorts and flip-flops under a blazing sun, but my tummy was tight. Up ahead I saw James, who wasn't a great shopper at the best of times, high on the church steps, probably contemplating taking a peek inside. It occurred to me that a moment's quiet reflection within a great dark chasm of peace was just what I needed right now. It might still my soul, bring a sense of proportion to my thoughts, which I knew was sadly lacking. Yes, a wander past the tombs of brave soldiers and Resistance fighters who'd had much tougher lives than me, the opportunity to light a candle for my family, with my husband by my side, could be just the ticket. I left Lizzie to her shoes and made my way through the crowd towards him. As I approached, I realized he was on his mobile. He was laughing and tossing back his head, running a hand through his fine fair hair. His face was alight, eyes bright.

I watched as he laughed out loud, then said, '*Au revoir.*' Au revoir? He pocketed his phone.

'Who was that?'

'What?' He turned. Looked startled. 'Oh, hello, darling. It was Camille.'

'Camille?'

'Yes. Just wanted to know how it was going.'

'Right. She rang yesterday, didn't she?'

'Yes, well, it's the first time she's let the house out. She's obviously keen to know it's all going smoothly.'

'She hasn't let it out, she's lent it to us. Surely Thérèse reports back?'

'I've no idea. Anyway, she'll be here this evening.'

'Here? With us?'

'Yes, she's coming for dinner.'

'But – but, James, I thought she was touring!'

'She is, but her rehearsals are in Cannes. After all, that's where the first concert is. Didn't I say? She said she'd be with us about drinks time.'

'But – do we want her?' I blurted. 'How long is she staying?'

'Well, obviously, the night, and then I've no idea.' He looked affronted. 'It's her house, Flora, be reasonable.'

'Yes, it is, but it's hardly our holiday at all, is it? Everyone assumes they've got carte blanche to invite whoever they please. It's a flipping free for all!'

I made to storm off, but he caught my arm. 'Flora, you're behaving like a spoilt child. Just because Sally has found some happiness and the girls have brought their boyfriends –'

'Oh, I don't mind about that –'

'And your mother has found a friend –'

'Who you objected to, originally!'

'Yes, but I had a good chat with him this morning, he's a nice chap. And now Camille is dropping by – what could be nicer? It's a huge house, and the more the merrier, surely? She's such a lovely, generous, warm-hearted person. I'm surprised at you.'

'Are you? Well, that's because you didn't realize you were married to such an unlovely, ungenerous, cold-hearted person, isn't it?' I stormed off, shaking my arm free.

I shoved through the crowds, boiling with heat and rage, knowing I was behaving very badly. Knowing if this was Amelia – oh, I knew full well where her temperament came from – I'd be livid. Stall after stall of pretty bedlinen, summer dresses, scarves, baskets, Provençal tablecloths in beautiful, colourful prints which, ordinarily, would afford me huge pleasure, passed me by. On I marched. I badly wanted to be alone, but there were so many people and it was so hot, it was impossible. In the tatty jewellery section of the market, where smiling, over-bronzed Mediterraneans sold tin under the guise of silver, Jean-Claude was fingering a faded pink cameo brooch. I made to duck past without him seeing me, but he turned, caught my eyes with a disarming smile.

'You think she like this?'

I stopped. Gazed. It was about the only pretty thing on the stand, and certainly the only thing with any age. I swallowed. 'Yes. Yes, I think she would, Jean-Claude. If you mean my mother.'

'I do. I wanted to thank her. It is so very kind of her to have me. And you, too, of course.'

'Oh, don't thank me, I'm just the tour guide,' I warbled. 'Anyway, I thought you were bound for the market at Aix, not this one? Some urgent mission?'

'I was, but no longer. I got here early when this market opened and all I need is here. Would you like to see? It's being kept for me.'

Oh, why not, I thought, not even bothering to show surprise about Aix: I'd known all along he was staying. He led me across to where another suntanned smiler had a clothing stall, brightly coloured slinky dresses dripping from a railed enclosure. The proprietor greeted Jean-Claude like a brother, her face creasing into a toothless grin, and Jean-Claude, having kissed her three times on both cheeks and indulged in some rapid formalities, moved across to whip away a blanket covering a huge mound in the corner. Beneath it were a cluster of applewood chairs, a pretty wrought-iron bedstead, a fruitwood table, an Aubusson rug, some tapestry cushions, a long length of faded velvet brocade curtain and a box of glasses.

'Oh!' Despite my demeanour, I found myself drawn to the fabric. I crouched down and ran it between my fingers, feeling its luxurious weight. Then I picked up a thick wine goblet, turning it in my hand. 'What lovely things. I haven't seen anything like this. Where did you find them?'

'It was all over very quickly, in the first half-hour. The antiques dealers, they have gone now.'

I picked up an ancient pestle and mortar, enormous and heavy. Gorgeous.

He smiled. Crouched beside me. 'You like your mother. You like these things.'

'It's a family weakness.'

I thought of my Clapham house, stuffed to the gunnels with just this sort of shabby-chic clutter, so that James complained that everything broke within seconds and the girls said they longed for the minimalist cool of their friends' houses, with clean lines and neutral colours and just the occasional flash of orange or lime green. But there was no soul in clean lines. No history. And I didn't like orange or lime green. I liked chipped ivory. Soft rose.

I straightened up. 'Mum had a boyfriend once, in Paris. Philippe. We used to spend whole mornings buying mirrors and pictures in the *puce* at Saint-Ouen. Then we'd have lunch in Montmartre. Philippe wasn't really interested, but he loved Mum. So much.' I remembered him watching with pleasure as she browsed the stands, long blonde hair framing her remarkably beautiful face, always smiling, always happy, other men turning to stare. Women, too. 'We'd spend hours trailing around with her. She'd buy whatever she wanted, and it was never expensive. An old book, a piece of lace. A china doll for me. It gets under your skin after a while.'

'Those sound like happy times.' He was watching me keenly.

I remembered being wrapped in an old fur coat of Mum's, a steaming *chocolat chaud* in front of me, at an outdoor table at Chez Pommette, a mottled mirror propped beside us, the three of us laughing as we played spotting the dog most like its owner, Philippe declaring the winner a poodle and his camp master who minced past as if the most horrendous smell were under their noses. Then we'd go back to our apartment up the steep hill, to our creeper-clad building, where Philippe would cook bouillabaisse, letting me help, showing me how to debeard mussels, clean clams. Make an aioli. I was reasonably convinced that my love of good food and cooking stemmed from these times.

'Yes. They were.' I remembered always feeling safe and secure. Always with Mum, never parked with a nanny, which was surely all one could ask of childhood?

'But yet you still wish it could have been otherwise?'

'How did you know?'

He shrugged. 'Just a hunch. A thatched cottage in the countryside, rows of running beans, the vicar coming to tea.'

I smiled. 'Runner beans. And yes, I probably read too much. And yes, you're right, Jean-Claude, she did her best and I was ungrateful. Have always been ungrateful.'

'That's not what I'm saying. I'm just saying it's not good to be always looking over your shoulder with regret, thinking what might have been. Or what might be, one day. It is better to enjoy the moment.'

I never do that,' I said quickly. 'Look back, I mean.' Was this really what I wanted? An in-depth chat with Mum's latest squeeze on the nature of my shortcomings? But his eyes were kind. I found myself liking this man and marvelling, as always, that, despite the turnover, Mum unerringly went for decent men. She was never one to play a victim to some bastard.

'Let's get a coffee,' he said, sensing a shift in my mood. 'And a cognac, maybe.'

I allowed myself to be led out of the teeming melee to an equally crowded café on the fringes of the market, under the plane trees, beside the old stone wall which dropped away dramatically to the valley below. There was absolutely no chance of a table, except that, in the blink of an eye, and after some quick-fire conversation, Jean-Claude had procured one, out of the blazing sun, under an umbrella, right at the front so we could watch the world go by. He pulled up a third chair for my mother, who'd gone to look at some buttons, he told me.

'I never knew this market yielded such treasures. It's years since I've been to Fayence. And Aix is so overdone, of course.'

I was pleased he'd deliberately reverted to light chit-chat. I looked at him as he ordered for us. He was very attractive and aristocratic-looking. My French was good enough to know his accent was good: Parisian, not provincial.

'How come you've ended up as a *brocanteur* in a little village, Jean-Claude?' I asked when our coffee arrived.

He smiled and lit a Marlboro, offering me one. I took it, knowing I needed it, and the coffee, too. My nerves were shredded. And when I was upset, I lashed out. Which wasn't nice.

'I, too, grew up surrounded by nice things. My father was a diplomat and we lived in many beautiful places. We didn't own them, of course, the grand houses or the antiques, they were ambassadorial, attached to the house, but when my parents' marriage broke up and I lived with my mother, in very reduced circumstances in Brittany, surrounded only by ugly things, I vowed that one day I would surround myself again with attractive *objets*.'

'Attractive women, too.'

'Of course.' He blew smoke above my head and smiled, the smile reaching right up to his sea-green eyes. 'Why not?'

'So that's always been your career? Antiques?'

'No. Not always.' He paused. Seemed about to continue, then changed his mind. 'And you, *cherie*? You like what you do? Eating for a living?'

I laughed. 'Well, put like that . . .' I frowned. 'Actually, no. I don't like it much now. I used to. But I haven't for a long while.' It was odd to hear myself say it. Out loud. Not just to myself. 'I hate putting food in my mouth if it's not for pleasure, which, these days, it isn't, and I hate either hurting a restaurant's reputation and possibly its liveli-hood, or lying to my readers. It's a lose-lose situation.'

'So give it up.'

'Can't. We're broke,' I replied cheerfully. 'Well, not stony broke, but we certainly need the money. There's never enough. I could never afford to be a lady of leisure, like some of my friends. Not that I'd necessarily want to. I have to help James.'

'And James. He too is bored and disillusioned, I think?'

'Yes, you think right.' I smiled. 'But hey. So are most people, probably, if you ask them.'

He shrugged in a Gallic fashion, his neck disappearing right into his shoulders. 'And yet you have free will! You are not beasts of the field. You could change all that in *un instant*.'

'Oh, really?' I gave a mirthless laugh. 'How? And still pay the mortgage? And the bills? Educate the girls?'

'Oh, well, now you put up obstacles. You run scared. And subject yourself to the tyranny of middle-class val-ues. And your girls are young women now, adults. You've done your job there.'

'Right. So what do you suggest we do, Jean-Claude?

Chuck it all in and run a vineyard or something?' I swung my arm over the ancient wall to the serried ranks in the valley below. 'Out here, perhaps?'

He shrugged. 'Yes, of course. Why not? If that's what would make you happy. Life is so simple. If you let it be. Ah, *cherie*! There you are, I was worried!'

My mother appeared, looking radiant, a straw basket over her shoulder full of hats, lace and oddments, bags in the other hand. She kissed us both as Jean-Claude sprang to his feet to help her with them.

'Such finds! Such beautiful stalls! And so lovely to come back and see you both sitting here.' She glowed with pleasure.

Jean-Claude was pulling out her chair eagerly, glancing up at the sun to make sure it was shaded. 'Good. I'm pleased you had success. I feel responsible as a Frenchman – as host *national*.' He placed a hand on his heart with a playful smile. 'It is important you English ladies are happy.'

I smiled and sank into my coffee as they chatted on. English ladies: one very beautiful, one not so, with only relative youth on her side. And how many times had I been in the very same situation? When a boyfriend of Mum's had tried to befriend me. Not in any scheming, Machiavellian way, not to worm his way in, just to help me. But I'd always resisted. Always felt tolerated. It would have helped if I'd been prettier, I'd always thought. To be beautiful was such a prize: to be escorted into a restaurant by a triumphant man – yes, as a trophy, but was there anything wrong with that? Surely only other women said it shouldn't be so? I remembered, after those years in Paris, after Philippe had died – I must have been thirteen – coming back to England and going to boarding school. My choice, not Mum's. I'd read about it: Malory Towers. Philippe had left my mother some money and she bought the pretty house in Fulham and, very reluctantly, let me go. I was deeply unhappy there, a fish out of water in this all-girl, upper-class, alien establishment. One night I overheard a girl in the dorm saying, 'Mummy says her mother's a tart.'

The following day was Sunday, and we were allowed out. Mum arrived with Gerald, her new boyfriend, whom I'd never met before, in his convertible Aston Martin, and they took me to lunch at a local country pub. I didn't speak to either of them. Mum looked flustered and deeply embarrassed as she tried to coax words out of me. I sat there, lumpen in my navy-blue uniform and thick woollen tights, hating her and Gerald, who, a rather nice twinkly banker, said quietly, when he thought I was out of earshot, 'It's too much for her, Susie. Too soon. Don't worry.'

'But she's so sweet, Gerald, darling. I want you to see her sweet.'

'I know. And I will.'

He did, eventually, after about four years, when I finally came round, but only when I'd almost left school. A London day school, which Mum had moved me to soon after that awful lunch, knowing I was miserable. I'd sulked for almost that entire time, which was such a waste, because Gerald was very nice. Unfortunately, his wife, being English, wasn't as accommodating as Yolande, Philippe's wife, had been, and when she found out about Mum, Gerald had had to choose. He badly wanted to leave his wife and marry Mum, whom he loved very much, but then his own

171

daughter, Celia, who was a couple of years younger than me and at a similar London day school, attempted suicide. She slit her wrists in the bath. Obviously, he went home. And the whole family moved to a Jacobean manor house in Devon, as far away from Mum as they could get, and Gerald resigned from his bank and retired to become a high sheriff and shoot pheasant. They didn't need him to work any longer – he'd made plenty of money – and his wife kept a close eye. Which of course is how it should be, keeping families together. Not yielding to a 'home-breaker', which was another expression I'd heard applied to Mum at school.

Mum and Jean-Claude had broken off their conversation to watch me as I stared into space, my coffee cold before me.

'Darling? I said, did you buy anything?'

'Oh. No. I didn't.' Don't sulk. Not again. I could almost feel the scratchy woollen tights. Mum's eyes were anxious. I rallied. 'But I've seen all Jean-Claude's finds – amazing.'

My mother's face broke into a relieved smile, as if I'd actually said, I'm happy with your lifestyle, Mum, and I love your latest man.

'Yes, aren't they?'

Jean-Claude smiled at me over the rim of his cup, patting my back, I knew. Good dog.

And of course it was easier to behave these days; as an adult, not being alone. How I'd wished for a sister or brother when I was young. Yearned. But these days, with James and the girls, who couldn't give a damn, who showed me the light, it was simpler. Although, actually, I'd been shown the light before. Been shown that it was no reflection on me who my mother was and how she behaved. Max had done that. He'd taught me to embrace my exotic mother, to admire her, not to be ashamed. He'd done my small family an invaluable service.

I sipped my cold coffee and swam up from the past to the present. As I broke through the surface, I put my sunglasses on in defence. Glanced around at the bright, bustling market. My eyes snagged on a white dress I'd seen earlier this morning, with a plunging neckline. Sally was engaged in a heated discussion with a stout, wind-battered monsieur. So she was here, too. She held a brightly painted jug in one hand and gesticulated wildly with the other, leaning across his stall of similarly decorated crockery, pursing her lips, showing off, and arguing loudly in terrible French that it was far too expensive. Max was beside her but distracted, staring over the walls of the town across the valley to the luxuriant green hills beyond, hands in his pockets, as far away in his head, it seemed, as those hills. It was inevitable, of course, that I didn't look away quickly enough and that he felt my gaze upon him. There was no mistaking the look he gave me this time as he turned and our eyes met, not over Sally's naked bottom, but over the distance of years: of different lives, marriages, children, the death of his beloved mother, I'd heard, lives spent without each other. It was wistful. Indeed, I'd go so far as to say it was full of regret.

Chapter Thirteen

Camille arrived that evening, fresh from a sexy convertible Alfa Romeo driven by a minder, on a gust of warm Provençal air and Nina Ricci's L'Air du Temps. If she'd also trailed a four-foot Isadora Duncan-style silk scarf, I wouldn't have been a bit surprised. I'd forgotten how beautiful she was and what charisma she exuded. Petite but powerful, she swept across the drive towards the terrace, where we'd all gathered – assembled, perhaps, a little over-excitedly – awaiting her presence. She wore a silk fuchsia shift dress, and two little dogs on leads dangled from a tanned hand. Before she reached us she handed them to the driver, a thick-set individual with no neck and lots of jewellery, who carried her bag. He disappeared around the side of the house.

James had been at fever pitch for the past hour, consulting Thérèse as to which aperitif to serve, which canapés were her favourites, wanting to get everything just perfect. Quite right, I thought, keeping the bitch within firmly in its kennel. She's been so generous – although I couldn't help noticing he'd changed his shirt, twice.

Camille came up the terrace steps, took off her sunglasses and smiled around, taking us all in. 'Look at you, all gathered and looking so heavenly on this perfect evening! Have you found everything you need? All you require?' She went around, kissing everyone twice, whether she knew them or not, which of course she didn't, whilst James, as master of ceremonies, introduced everyone. Our girls and their boys coloured up in excitement, and when she'd turned away, I noticed Toby snap her profile on his phone.

'It's all completely wonderful,' I assured her when it was my turn. 'What a gorgeous place!'

'And you found the town all right? You'll want to go there, it's sensational.' Her voice was a low purr, and she looked deep into my eyes.

'We've been already,' James assured her, handing her a glass of chilled champagne. 'We went this afternoon, it's stunning!'

She made a face. 'But not, I imagine, at that time of day. No, no, *cherie*, you want to go in the morning, before the sun and the crowds. And Seillans is even better. Such hidden treasures, such colours – truly *charmant*. I'll take you tomorrow myself.' She bestowed a huge pussy-cat smile on him, employing her eyes, too. James swooned visibly.

'I say, my dear, you've been inordinately kind to suffer such an invasion.' The Brig beamed broadly at her. 'The last thing you want to do is take us round the ruddy sights. Particularly when you must know them like the back of your hand.'

'*Au contraire*, it's no trouble, and if I show James, then he will know where to take you all, you see?'

James was now hopping around like a Labrador on heat, flushed and delighted in his pink gingham shirt.

'You must be so proud to have such a talented son, Dr–rummond,' she said, pronouncing his name like a drum roll and settling herself down in the centre of the cushioned

175

basket sofa as James topped up her already full glass. 'Thank you, *cherie*,' she murmured up at him.

'Oh, well, yes.' The Brig blinked, surprised. 'I mean, it's always nice to have a medic in the family, isn't it? And he's frightfully good on bunions and wot not. I suffer terribly, you know. But, talking of parental pride – look at you!' His eyes and mouth widened in delight. 'I gather you have a daughter – she must be *so* proud, and all your relatives must be beside themselves.'

Camille made a face. She patted the seat beside her. 'Sit.' The Brig obediently sat. 'My mother was a great opera singer herself, far greater than me, so I think perhaps it is not so extraordinary for them.' She patted the sofa cushion to her left and James also sat obediently; indeed, he almost sat on her hand, so snappy were his reactions. I badly needed a camera. Amelia caught my eye and grinned.

'Your own mother is dead, James? I notice she is not here?'

'Yes. Yes, she is.'

A silence fell. Camille, sensing she'd hit a nerve, turned and clasped the Brig's hand. 'I am sorry, it is still too new? Too recent, yes? I'm afraid I am very sensitive. I pick up on these things so quickly, my emotional antenna is very acute.'

'No, no, not recent. Many years ago, as it happens.' The Brig said matter of factly. 'It's just the circumstances were rather harrowing, so one does rather draw a veil.'

'Of course,' said Camille, pressing on to open the veil. 'Long illnesses can indeed be difficult. I know only too well. My own father died of cancer.'

'Oh, no, it wasn't anything like that. She was killed, you see.'

'*Alors!*' Camille looked stunned. Reared back and clutched her heart.

'Um, Camille, your daughter, she's not with you? Cheese puff?' I interjected, knowing, if pressed, that the Brig was only too keen to confess, and then to give a detailed account of life behind bars at Her Majesty's Prison Dartmoor, regaling anyone who was interested – and most people jolly well were – with an account of all the characters he'd met in there. Donaldson, his cellmate, featured particularly strongly; he was a shaven-headed Glaswegian who'd done time for murder, having knifed someone in a pub brawl. They'd been released at about the same time, and Donaldson had worked for Drummond as an odd-job man on his estate, living, until his recent death, in one of the cottages. They'd been very close. Oh, it was all very uplifting and heart-warming and right on, but I could tell by the look on my husband's face that his father the ex-con was not necessarily the first impression he wanted to give his new crush. I loved him enough to spare him that. Camille was still digesting this information, but I was right in her face with the cheese puffs and my question, so she couldn't ignore me.

'Agathe? Yes, she is here, but she got out of the car at the lodge to see Thérèse and Michel.'

'Of course, you popped in there first.'

She waved her hand dismissively. 'Agathe did, but I was keen to see how you were all getting on. And to see that my room is ready in the tower.'

'Ah, we wondered. Only there's a locked door at the far end of the corridor —'

'My private apartment,' she told me firmly, touching my arm and giving me a level look.

'Of course,' I was flustered. 'I didn't mean . . .'

'Your sister is very attractive, James?' she said, peering around me and waving my plate of canapés away with a bored hand.

'Oh. I suppose. Yes, she is,' said James, surprised, as we all were, not used to Sally being complimented thus.

'She never used to be. Used to be frightfully fat,' the Brig told her in a stage whisper, leaning in. 'But then she ate like a pig. Cooks for a living, you see. Temptation always there.'

'Ah. So your family are all interested in food?' She looked up at me. 'James told me about your job. It sounds so fascinating. And your other sister-in-law? She is in the food industry, too?' She looked at Rachel's ample behind.

Why did I feel she was laughing at us? And the trouble was, Camille had a carrying voice, and poor Rachel blushed. Not one to dissemble, though, she came across.

'No, in fact I don't do much at all, I'm afraid,' Rachel said. 'Daddy's fairly moribund these days, so I'm pretty much around to look after him.'

'Couldn't do without her,' the Brig said warmly. 'Particularly now Donaldson's gone.'

'Melon ball, anyone?' I asked quickly, finding another plate.

'Donaldson?'

'My roommate. Met him at Dartmoor. Splendid chap. Worked for me for years.'

'Oh, but Dartmoor is such a beautiful place! Agathe learned to ride there when she was in England.'

The Brig's face lit up. 'Did she, by Jove! Whereabouts?'

'Actually, her father took her.'

'Ah, splendid. Well, yes, it's a wonderful moor. And, of course, being low-risk and therefore at the top of the pecking order, I had one of the rooms on the top floor, with a panoramic view. Bars, of course, but still. People used to visit and say that, position-wise, it would be the envy of many a country-house hotel. Remember, darling?' He turned to Rachel. 'You never saw my cell, of course.'

'Are you rehearsing or performing, Mme de Bouvoir?' Rachel asked swiftly, seeing Camille look mystified.

'Oh, Camille, please. Rehearsing. The actual tour doesn't start until next week. But you must come. I'm doing one special preview night near here, in Cannes.'

'Oh, well, we'd love to, but I'm sure we wouldn't get tickets . . .' Rachel blushed, realizing she'd looked artful, which she wasn't.

Camille held up the palm of her hand like a traffic policeman. 'I have two. One of which, of course, James shall have; the other, if it is all right with Florence, I will give to you.' She raised questioning eyebrows at me.

'Flora. And, yes, of course it's all right with me. Rachel's very keen on opera.'

'You are?'

'Oh, well, recordings; and box sets,' I heard Rachel muttering as I moved away. 'I don't get to go, of course. Although once, many years ago, with the school, in Edinburgh . . .'

'What did you see?'

'*Madame Butterfly*. But I was only about twelve.'

'But it left an impression?'

It did, and she and Rachel embarked on an animated discussion, Rachel growing pinker with the attention. I wished I didn't dislike Camille. Everyone else seemed to love her. I passed around the nibbles. After a bit, Camille got up and went to talk to the teenagers and Lizzie, who were standing slightly apart, by the balustrade. They chatted for a while and I heard them roar with laughter. Camille stood back and admired Lizzie's dress and I saw Lizzie flush with pleasure at having her Stella McCartney recognized, at being acknowledged as a discerning fashionista. Even Mum and Jean-Claude fell under her spell, as she broke into enthusiastic French to talk to them, although I noticed she addressed Jean-Claude much more frequently than Mum, who, despite her age, was far too beautiful. Mum wouldn't have noticed. She never noticed – or acknowledged – anything unpleasant. Surfed nicely over life's inconvenient hummocks.

Out of frame, Thérèse and Michel were quietly loading the dining table at the far end of the terrace with our supper. Unparallelled delights were appearing from the kitchen. A huge platter of oysters sat on a bed of ice; curling pink langoustines lay between artfully arranged crabs; and there were bowls of tiny pink prawns. From inside, the most wonderful aroma of *lapin à la moutarde* drifted through. My appetite had certainly come back on this holiday, prompted by the joy of eating for pleasure.

'The stops,' Jean-Claude commented to me *sotto voce* as he topped up my glass, his eyes darting towards the laden table, 'are surely being pulled out tonight.'

I smiled. 'Quite.'

Dinner was indeed delicious. A lively, convivial affair, too, with everyone showing off a bit, wanting to be able to say when they got home, Oh yes, I know Camille de Bouvoir. Or even 'my friend Camille', which was how it must always be for the famous, I realized. I was seated well away from her, at the other end of the table, but watched her in action with James beside her. He'd organized the seating plan. She flirted shamelessly with him, but not, I noticed, with Max. Maybe when one was surrounded by attractive people all the time, they rolled off one's back, and someone as interesting and clever as James undoubtedly was – he was regaling her now with some amusing medical story – was perhaps a novelty? And no doubt, having established that Max worked in the music industry, she'd lost interest. She knew all about that. No, it was the operating theatre she wanted to hear about, and James had a good many stories, apocryphal or otherwise, to tell. I saw him reach back into his reserve for more as she threw back her head and roared with laughter, or gasped with horror, depending on which was appropriate.

Her hand went to her heart: '*Non! Mon dieu!* The wrong kidney?'

'It happens,' James assured her. 'And never have an operation at the weekend if you can help it. You get all the part-timers.'

'But surely all surgeons have passed the same tests? Performed the same operations? Surely they are equally good?'

'You'd think so, wouldn't you? But think of the tenors you work with. Some better than others?'

'*Mais oui.*' She pulled a disgusted face. 'Some can barely sing!'

'*Exactement!*' trilled my husband. '*Je n'ai rien à ajouter.*' He turned to Rory, opposite, who was listening. 'I rest my case,' he explained.

'Your French is excellent, James,' Camille said quietly, and, emboldened, he picked up her hand and gallantly kissed the back of it. They smiled at one another.

Oh, please.

Thérèse and Michel served us as usual, providing fresh plates for the rabbit dish after we'd eaten the fish, but I did wonder why they didn't join us. I knew James had asked them. And surely Camille would want to spend time with her own family?

'Apparently, they find it too stressful, cooking and eating. And, actually, I can understand that,' Lizzie, beside me, told me. 'When you've slaved over the bloody thing, the last thing you want to do is flaming well eat it.'

'That's true,' I said, remembering my own dinner parties. 'It's just . . . Camille and Thérèse are sisters. It seems a bit master–servant.'

'That's clearly the way it is,' she murmured. 'They work for her, come what may. Interesting dynamic, isn't it?'

'Very.'

'And where's her man? It can't be that heavy I saw lurking earlier?'

'No, he's in the kitchen having supper. She's divorced.'

'Yes, I know, and, apparently her ex is gorgeous. Thérèse told me. Rich as Croesus, too, comes from some huge landowning family in Grasse. No, I just thought someone like her would inevitably have a guy in tow. The gossip columns link her with Paul Merendes.' A famous film director. 'She certainly seems to have the hots for James.'

Camille appeared to be reading my husband's palm now.

'James saved her daughter's life, Lizzie. She's obviously grateful.'

Lizzie gave me a look. 'I think we all know he stabbed her with an EpiPen, Flora. Even I could have done that.'

In bed that night I snuggled under James's arm, an unusual move for me, since James took any form of bodily contact, even a pat on the hand, as the green light for sex. He gave me a cuddle but didn't seem that interested in pursuing matters.

'Camille's very entertaining, isn't she?' I remarked softly.

'Great fun. And so kind and inclusive, don't you think? She could easily have eaten on her own tonight. I mean, who wants to get involved in someone's else's family? But she seemed to genuinely enjoy us.'

'Well, she enjoys you, darling,' I said lightly into his armpit.

He laughed. 'Oh, hardly.'

I prodded his chest playfully. 'Laughs at all your jokes, hangs on your every word. Picks your medical brains, too.'

'That's because her voice is so important. She wanted to know the internal workings of the larynx and the effect of vibration on the thorax.'

'I'll give you vibration on the thorax,' I murmured suggestively, nudging him.

'It's all to do with the cumulative effect of the muscles, of course. Which I explained.'

'Well, of course. You're the man to do that.' Piqued, I rolled away. 'What with your particular area of expertise being at the opposite end of the human body.' There was a silence.

'As you well know, I trained in every single area of physiology before I specialized. The larynx is something I was particularly drawn to.'

'Depending on who it belongs to.'

He paused. 'Are you peeved, Flora?'

'What, that Camille de Bouvoir finds you fascinating? Not in the least.'

'Only there's an edge to your voice. You're the one usually telling me to stop telling everyone I specialize in athlete's foot and big up my medical credentials. And now that I am, you're squashing me.'

'I am not squashing you, I'm teasing you. Do calm down, James, you're reacting like a schoolboy.'

'I'm reacting because it occurs to me that you don't like not being the centre of attention.'

'Centre of att—?' I sat up. Snapped on the light. 'Centre of attention – me? When? When am I ever the centre of attention? When am I ever anything other than the girls' mother, your wife, Susie's daughter –'

'Oh, you're being ridiculous. And full of rather unattractive self-pity, too. I was right. Jealous.'

'*Jealous?*' I shrieked. 'What, because some heavy-breasted opera singer turns her headlights on you, and reads your palm and –'

'Mum.' The door flew open. Tara appeared, looking horrified. 'Can I just say, these walls are, like, paper thin. We can hear every word.'

'We?' I roared. 'Who's we, Tara?'

She coloured dramatically. Was about to stutter something, but not before I'd flung back the covers, reared out of bed and swept past her. I threw open her door. Inside, Amelia, Rory and Toby, all fully clothed, were huddled on her bed, watching a film on her laptop. I blanched. Pulled down the old Primark number which, as we have already established, was very short.

'Mum, you seriously need to have a word with yourself,' Amelia told me, her eyes cold. 'You're out of control at the moment. And you need to *stop* bullying Dad.'

Speechless, I slammed the door shut, which meant Tara had to open it again to get back in. She shot me a filthy look. At that moment, the door behind me opened and Sally appeared in a pretty pink camisole and boxer shorts. She smiled nervously, clearly wondering what all the rumpus was about, then retreated back inside to report.

I flung myself back into bed, snapping off the light, feeling murderous. I turned away from James, who already had his back to me.

'Caught them all at it?' he asked. 'Got it on video?'

I ignored him, my heart pounding. Then I clamped my eyes and my teeth shut and counted to a hundred. I tried to sleep, but my heart was racing. Also, what had started as light mutterings and muffled laughter next door had fallen mysteriously silent. I tried not to listen and wished I had my earplugs, which had fallen under the bed. After a bit, I heard more muffled laughter, then someone pulled the lavatory chain. A few moments later, the chain went again. I put my pillow over my head and tried to go to sleep.

When I awoke the next morning, James's side of the

bed was empty. A beam of bright light was streaming through a gap in the curtains. It was like being woken by the Gestapo. Indeed, it was so bright it must be quite late, I realized, turning to peer at the clock. Twenty past ten. Why hadn't James woken me? Oh. Yes. There'd been a bit of a row. Deflated, I gazed out of the open window. The sky was clear and blue and the scent of all things warm and Mediterranean wafted through. Voices, too, from the terrace below. Laughter. I was missing out, something I've never been good at. I dragged myself out of bed, reckoning I was averaging about six hours sleep a night, which wasn't ideal on what was supposed to be a holiday, and lumbered off to the shower.

By the time I got downstairs, nearly everyone had gone. As I emerged through the French windows on to the terrace, Drummond and Rachel were just getting up and leaving the table. The Brig greeted me delightedly, with a wave of his stick.

'Flora! How lovely that you slept in. We saved you some brekka.'

'Thanks, Drummond. Did you sleep well?'

'Like a log, my dear. Best sleep I've had for months. Must be the air. James and the others have gone to Seillans, asked me to tell you. Two cars – the whole shooting match went in the end. So kind of Camille. Even the *Kinder* got up early!'

'Oh. Right. Of course. I'd forgotten.'

'They didn't want to wake you. James said you'd had a bad night.'

'Yes. I see.'

'Plenty of time,' Rachel said kindly. 'We're here for ages. I'll come with you tomorrow, if you like? Daddy will be fine without me, won't you?'

'Right as rain! You girls go tomorrow. I'm happy as a sand boy under the trees with the *Telegraph*. Rory gets it for me on his laptop, you know – how about that?'

'Yes. It's . . . amazing.'

'Do you want to go today?' asked Rachel, ever sensitive.

'No, no. I think I'll – just go for a wander, actually. Round here. Around the vineyards, you know. Maybe go to that chapel we passed.'

'Well, don't leave it too late, the sun's getting up,' called Drummond as they carried on their way through the house and on upstairs to attend to their ablutions. I sat down at the breakfast table alone in the sun. It was a still life of broken bread, jam pots and hastily discarded coffee, all abandoned as people pressed on with their day. In my present mood, I realized, the tableau could easily lead to introspection, which was the last thing I wanted. I rose quickly and went to the kitchen to make myself a coffee, drinking it standing up, burning the roof of my mouth, but keen to get on.

Michel appeared from behind a door. 'Good morning.' I'd swear he winked as he said it.

Rude not to wink back, but I resisted and smiled brightly. 'Morning, Michel! A beautiful one.'

'Would you like me to warm a croissant for you?' he murmured, moving closer.

'Er – no, I think I'll skip breakfast. Do me good.' I patted my well-upholstered tummy out of nerves, and his eyes travelled over my body. Instinctively, I sucked everything in. Slowly, his gaze came up. He looked me in the eye.

'As you wish.' He shot me a look from under dark brows, and my eyelashes fairly sizzled with the heat. It occurred to me that if I'd said, 'But if you wouldn't mind popping upstairs . . .' it would be considered perfectly acceptable; all in a day's work for a Frenchman.

Instead, I hastily put my cup in the dishwasher, aware of his eyes still trailing over me, amused, no doubt at this pale Englishwoman's discomfort. I grabbed my phone from the island then escaped upstairs to find my purse, a sunhat and a couple of aspirins for the headache that was already threatening.

A few minutes later I was padding down another set of stairs at the far end of the corridor, stairs which I now realized led up to Camille's tower. I emerged through a side door into a vegetable garden I hadn't even known existed. Neat rows of beans and courgettes stretched out before me, and a gravel path ran through the middle. Presumably, it ran parallel with the drive. I took it and, after a moment, the front gate was in my sights. Who knows where I'll wander, I thought, with a vague sense of mounting excitement. It would be an adventure. A lovely morning alone in a vast, dreamy, Provençal landscape, the sights and smells of which would be enough to suffocate any niggling feelings of jealousy. Oh yes, James had been right, as he so often was. But jealous of whom – Camille? Not for one moment. My daughters, perhaps, with their newly burgeoning love lives? Happily, no, although some friends of mine ticked that box. My mother, then, with yet another beau falling at her feet, yet another exciting start? No.

Who, then? Sally? Was it she who was making my heart beat so fast, my head ache so ominously? I hastened on to the gate.

When I'd made it to the lane, on an impulse I turned left. I walked fast, swinging my arms briskly. Glorious vineyards lined my route, some with single rose bushes at the end denoting, what – the vintage? I didn't know. James would, I thought with a smile. I'd ask him. As I pressed on, the vines gave way to huge swathes of lavender, ready to be harvested, swaying gently in the breeze and humming with bees. The smell was unbelievable. I breathed deeply, taking it right down into my lungs. A tiny part of me was aware that I should take heed of where I was going, remember which turns down these country lanes I was taking, and on no account should I get lost. But I was walking quite fast, for the ridiculous reason that I was a tiny bit apprehensive. As I'd emerged from the vegetable garden I'd seen Michel, behind his green-bean canes. He'd watched me go. For some reason, I wanted to get a move on. Put some distance between us.

As I progressed down the lane, a silly thought occurred, which was that every so often, as I rounded a sharp bend, out of the corner of my eye I'd catch sight of the bright-blue cotton shirt Michel was wearing. I came to a junction and realized with relief that one lane was sign-posted to the village. It surely wasn't far. From there, I could get a taxi back, if I was exhausted. I took the turn gratefully. Now and again, almost testing myself, I'd turn my head quickly. No. It had been my imagination. I ploughed on down the hill. This had been a wonderful idea, I decided, still swinging my arms. Getting away from everyone. Away from the irritants of family life, giving myself time to regroup and come back loving them. I was so glad I hadn't gone to Seillans.

Down into the valley I plunged, the chapel just visible on the horizon, a silhouette in the distance. Too far to walk: the village on the main road was a much better idea. And I'd have a coffee in the shade. I passed a spectacular field of sunflowers, their huge yellow heads bobbing as if in greeting, and then the vines again, mile upon mile of them, as far as the eye could see.

Eventually, I came to another junction, happily still signposted to the main road, but this time, hot and exhausted, I sat for a moment on the small, parched triangle of grass at its base. I leaned my head back on the post. As I did, I turned. There, in the distance, an unmistakable flash of blue caught my eye, before it quickly disappeared behind a tree.

Chapter Fourteen

I got to my feet abruptly. I wasn't seeing things. That had been a blue shirt topped by a tanned face, and it had darted out of sight. I must have walked well over a mile by now, and I was in the middle of vast open countryside, vineyards stretching unceasingly, acres and acres of them, and Michel was following me amongst them. I'd press on. The sign said 'D234', the village couldn't be far, and maybe he was just walking there, too? Maybe that was what he did on a Monday. But something about his eyes in the kitchen and the way he'd looked at me when I'd patted my tummy – did that mean something in French? Take me? Give me a baby? – bothered me.

I hastened on, dry-mouthed, relieved I'd brought a hat. The sun was beating down. Every so often, I glanced around and, for a while, I wouldn't be able to see him. I told myself he'd gone another way. Then – oh God, there he was again, gaining on me: not running, but making up ground steadily, with a long stride. I hurried along the hot tarmac. The countryside was completely deserted, not even the rumble of a 2CV in the distance, not even a Jean-Pierre wobbling on a bicycle, although I had passed a man on one earlier. Suddenly, I remembered I'd walked blatantly through the middle of Michel's vegetable garden. Perhaps he thought *I'd* come looking for *him*? I went hot. Stumbled on.

Actually, it was fine, I decided: because just around the next bend, this road would yield houses, the beginnings of a village; the sign had suggested as much. I was on the right track. It wouldn't be far, and I was being stupid. Patting my tummy meant I was fat in any language, and I'd wager people took that short cut through his garden all the time. It was an obvious route from that side door. And he was undoubtedly going to the village himself, perhaps on an errand for Thérèse. He probably had a shopping basket. I turned. He didn't. His hands were empty. And he was gaining on me. Still not running, but walking very fast, determinedly. I'd never seen Michel move anything but stealthily and quietly; he crept up on one like a cat. Only last night I'd found him behind me in the dark corridor upstairs when I'd slipped up for my lipstick, not bothering to turn on the light. Camille had appeared from her room at the far end, and he'd disappeared, but the more I knew Michel, the more I realized his opening gambit that first day – 'The nights are lonely' – had not been a linguistic solecism. He knew the English for 'evening' and 'night'. I gulped.

Well, if he was going to the village, he certainly wouldn't follow me down this track, would he? My eyes darted left across the vineyard. On an impulse, I plunged through a gap between the vines, still heading in the right direction, but as if taking a short cut. I couldn't see if he'd followed – I was running now, under the relentless rays – because dripping grapes and dense foliage obscured my vision, but the fifth or sixth time I turned around, stumbling over ruts in the sun-baked clay, he was coming through the vines, too, jogging menacingly down the track behind me.

I was incredibly scared. I was running quite fast, and dripping wet. My hat flew off and I didn't stop – neither did he, I noticed, as I glanced over my shoulder, to see that he was gaining on me, his eyes intent and glittering with purpose. I wanted to shout, scream – *Help!* – but no one would hear me and I'd secluded myself totally with this screen of vines. I put my head down and sprinted, hearing him now – oh dear God – behind me. Abruptly, the tunnel of green yielded light, and I was on to a road, which would be empty of traffic, I knew, but was something other than this terrifying tunnel. I could almost hear his breath in my ear, and I raced as I've never done before. As I made it to the road, Michel almost upon me, almost able to grab me by the collar, a car, by the gift of God, rounded the corner towards us. I spread myself like a starfish in the middle of the road, found what little breath I had left and screamed, '*HELP!*'

It all but careered into me. It stopped, just short – only just – and I collapsed on to the bonnet, sobbing, clinging to the silver paintwork. In an instant the driver's door flew open.

'What the –?' Max got out. Max, in khaki chinos, a white linen shirt and sunglasses, which he whipped from his face. He looked horrified, pale under his tan. 'Flora! Dear God.'

He hurried around and I threw myself at him: clung to his chest, sopping wet, sobbing with fear and relief, unable to say anything except 'Michel' in a strangled gasp.

And Michel was indeed amongst us; bent double, clutching his knees, panting. Sally, too, as she emerged from the passenger seat of the car, elegant in a pale-blue dress. Her hand went to her mouth.

'Flora – what's happened?'

'Michel,' I managed. 'Followed me, from the house. Chased me. Through fields. Oh, thank God you've come.' I was still clamped like a limpet to Max. I had no idea I could feel so frightened.

'She took the wrong phone,' panted Michel, holding his side, his face wracked with exhaustion. 'Took Thérèse's, by mistake, from the island in the kitchen. I came after her. Thérèse worried she get lost; the Brigadier, he say she gone to the chapel. So far. Madness. Then she begun to run. I was worried, thought she'd gone mad. The sun maybe. Crazy lady ran through middle of vineyard' – he turned to point back to where we'd come from – 'she never find a way out. Like a labyrinth! I run after her, but she fled. I so worried, think she ill.'

He did indeed look incredibly concerned. All three of them did: Sally, in her pretty blue dress, sunglasses off now, peering; Max, whose chest I managed to prise myself from, gazing down at me with anxious, lovely eyes; Michel, still heaving, holding out my phone, bewildered.

I stared at it, trembling, stupefied. Put my hand into my skirt pocket. Brought out an identical iPhone, but not mine. Thérèse's. We swapped silently.

'You scared me,' I whispered.

Michel looked more than concerned now. He looked taken aback.

'I so sorry. You think . . . ?'

It took another moment for the penny to drop. I watched it clatter down. Watched him comprehend completely and look aghast. I felt so ashamed. Mortified.

'Camille, she will –' he stuttered.

'This doesn't have to get to Camille,' Max said firmly. 'Nothing's happened here. Flora had a fright, that's all.' He had an arm around my shoulders in a comforting, brotherly way. I could feel my trembling desist. 'But no harm has been done. She simply got the wrong end of the stick, as so often happens.'

Did it? Max and Sally shepherded me gently into the back of the car, as if I were a day-release patient. Then Michel got in. He'd resisted initially, saying he'd rather walk, but they weren't having it. He practically sat on the door, so anxious was he not to be near me. Do these things often happen, I wondered? Or was I losing my mind? Kind, thoughtful gardener, brother-in-law of generous hostess, hurries to give guest correct phone lest she finds herself hopelessly lost in unfamiliar landscape, whereupon she breaks into a gallop and fears she's going to be attacked. How common was that?

We drove back in silence. I felt numb, if I'm honest. So relieved it was all over, but knowing, somehow, it wasn't. That it was only the beginning.

On the gravel sweep in front of the house, the car stopped. Sally, annoyingly, nipped round and helped me out of the back. I tried to shake her off, but she insisted, and I'd swear she put her hand over my head, like they do in police dramas. Fear and shame were rapidly turning to a feeling that I'd been extremely foolish. And Sally was evidently enjoying herself. A shaken Michel got out, too, and Max had some quiet man talk to him, about how he wasn't to worry – no doubt, hysterical females featured; no doubt, he was apologizing on my behalf – I couldn't really hear. I was too busy trying to get rid of Sally, who was escorting me through the hall and up the main staircase, one arm round my shoulders, the other hand holding my elbow.

'I'm fine, Sally, thank you.'

'Have a shower and a lie down.'

'I will.'

'And drink a lot. You'll have lost fluid with all that sweating.'

'I know.'

'And a couple of aspirins.'

'Yes.'

'I'll get them for you.'

'I have some.'

'Mine are very strong. You'll need them.'

'I have strong ones.'

'Mine are prescription.'

'I'm married to a doctor. I've got fucking knock-out drops.'

'There's no need to swear. I know you're distressed, but you must stay calm. Try.'

Eventually, at my bedroom door, I shook her off. I showered long and hard, warm then cool. Then I wrapped myself in a huge towel and lay on the bed, staring up at the ceiling.

At length, James and the others returned. I heard the cars beneath my window and the doors slamming. Voices were high and exuberant, but then I heard Max's voice, quite low, and their voices lowered, too, to hushed tones. After a bit, there were footsteps on the stairs, and James came into the room, white-faced.

'Good God, darling, are you all right?'

I silently thanked him for that.

'Yes. I am now. Just got a fright.'

I propped myself up a bit as he sat on the bed beside me. 'Poor, poor you.' He took my hand. 'But why did you think . . . ?'

'I don't know. I just panicked, I suppose. He sort of . . . twinkled at me, in the kitchen. And before.'

'Twinkled?' He looked horrified.

'Oh, no, not that. With his eyes.'

'Oh.' His face cleared with relief. Then he frowned. 'And you thought . . .'

'Well, I didn't know what to think, James. This man, racing after me through the countryside.'

'But why were you rushing off alone anyway?'

'I wasn't rushing, I went for a walk. You'd all gone, and I didn't want a solitary morning by the pool.'

'Dad and Rachel were here.'

'Yes, under a tree, reading. Which didn't really appeal.'

'So you thought you'd stomp off in a show of defiance?'

'No! Not at all. I just fancied a walk.'

'It's three miles to the village from here, Flora. In the midday sun –'

'I had a hat, and sunscreen, and money and a phone. Or so I thought.'

He got up off the bed and crossed to the window. Gazed out. After a moment, he came back, lips pursed. He looked down at me. 'It's incredibly serious for a man to be accused of sexual harassment . . . you know that, don't you?'

'I didn't accuse him!'

'I know, but –'

'Whose side are you on?'

'I'm just saying that Michel is very distressed.'

197

'*I'm* distressed!'

The door flew open. Amelia came in. Nodded above the bed. 'Window's open, Mum. Calm down. We're all on the terrace.' She leaned across and shut it. Sat down on the bed beside me. 'Are you OK?'

'No, I am not. Your father thinks I've deliberately tried to incriminate an innocent man.'

'Oh, don't be ridiculous,' retorted James.

'Max said you were very scared,' said Amelia.

'I was. But I thought it was going to be kept quiet. Camille . . .'

'Michel broke down, upset. Camille heard. Max had to explain. And Sally helped, obviously.'

'Obviously.'

James turned to Amelia. 'Apparently, he twinkled at your mother.'

Amelia frowned. 'Twinkled?'

'Gave me the eye,' I muttered, feeling incredibly foolish.

'Oh God, he flirts with all of us. Frenchmen do that. Did he say anything?'

I cast my mind back to the conversation in the kitchen. 'Well, he – he asked me if I'd like a croissant warmed.'

James got off the bed. I saw him exchange a look with his daughter. 'I think we'll just draw a line under this, don't you? Forget about it. Come on, darling, come down. We're all going to have a late lunch. But I think you should apologize to Michel.'

'God, yes,' spluttered Amelia, in a voice that suggested her father had been far too restrained. 'This is beyond embarrassing, Mum. You need to get out more.' James shot her a warning look as, with a flounce, she left the room. He hesitated, then followed her.

The door, as he closed it, blew the window above my head open again; it had been shut, but not clasped. From the terrace, hushed voices drifted up: Amelia had clearly rejoined the young and was recounting the drama from my viewpoint. There was a pause when she'd finished.

'She's at that difficult age, of course.' My daughter Tara – the good one – observed.

'Does that send women bonkers?' Rory asked.

'Can do,' Toby replied soberly. 'My mum went totally mental.'

'Maybe she's fantasizing?' Tara said. I imagined a huge and general sucking in of cigarettes as they all gave this some thought. 'How did she look?'

'Awful. Crazy. And naked, but for a towel.'

I leaped up on the bed. Flung wide the window. '*I have had a shower!*'

Unfortunately, my towel dropped as I held the window. I snatched it up. Slammed the window shut and fastened the clasp. Silence from below.

I fumbled around the room, finding some clean clothes, my hands fluttery and trembly. As soon as I was dressed, I went downstairs and out on to the terrace. Everyone avoided my eye, even Tara, who could always be relied upon. The Brig and Rachel approached from the trees where they'd been doing the *Telegraph* crossword, and a general look flew around that they didn't need to know, and shouldn't be told. Camille and Lizzie were absent. At length, they emerged from the house together; they'd clearly been talking. Camille, with perfect manners, sat next to me and patted my hand.

'Poor you. What a fright.'

I glanced at her gratefully, but her eyes told me she didn't mean it. She was livid.

'I'm so sorry,' I stuttered. 'Feel such a fool.'

This helped a bit. But not much. She nodded. Didn't speak.

'I'll go and apologize.'

She held my wrist in a vice-like grip under the table. 'Not yet. He is very upset.'

Lizzie slid in on the other side of me. 'It's fine,' she muttered, flicking her napkin out on her lap. 'They're making a meal of it.'

I thanked her with my eyes. Mum and Jean-Claude drifted back late from Seillans, and as they sat down, chatting away about what a lovely time they'd had, we all tucked into huge platters of charcuterie and melon and tomato salad as if nothing had happened. Thérèse, though, when she came to remove the plates and replace them with fresh ones for a plum tart, banged mine down so hard it nearly broke. Everyone round the table jumped. Her eyes, when I glanced up at them, were glittering with fury, as I'm sure mine would be if someone had accused James of something similar.

Years ago, James had asked a nurse, in the operating theatre – in a pass-the-scalpel moment – if she'd had a good weekend. She'd replied that she'd had a lovely time punting with her boyfriend, and James had jokingly said he didn't need the details. She'd reported him to the disciplinary committee for inappropriate behaviour. James had come home ashen-faced. He'd gone straight to the sideboard and had a large whisky, which he never did. He'd actually had to restrain me from driving to the hospital and beating the door down. The disciplinary committee! My kind, gentle James! I knew how Thérèse felt and shrivelled under her angry gaze. I didn't touch my tart either, in case she'd spat in it.

After lunch I had a long discussion with Lizzie, not in my room, where the world clearly overheard, but at the bottom of the garden in the olive grove, where only a donkey grazed. In the shade of an ancient, crooked tree, perched on a heap of stones, amidst prickly dry grass and chattering cicadas, I cried, and she hugged me. I explained, and she got it, but no one else would. We were the only two middle-aged women here. Sally and Rachel didn't count somehow. But Lizzie understood.

'But you'll have to apologize, I'm afraid. Just so it doesn't look like you still believe it.'

'I don't.' I wiped my eyes.

'I know, which is why you have to.'

'I know.' I clutched my tissue. 'Will Thérèse be there, d'you think?'

'I don't know. But I'll come with you. Come on. Let's get it over with.'

We got up and went around the side of the chateau to the front drive. As we walked up to the lodge house, my heart pounded.

Thérèse came out. Perhaps she'd been waiting for us, watching from the window. Either way, she stood on the front step, tiny, inscrutable and, on closer inspection, quite lined, unlike her tanned, smooth-skinned husband.

She was wearing a printed dress with an apron tied firmly over the top, which I'd never seen her wear before. It seemed symbolic somehow: as if it were to remind me that they were subservient and defenceless. It occurred to me this could have been turned into a joke: 'You thought what? Oh, Flora, you are *priceless*! Listen, everyone, Flora thought he was chasing her for her body!' Why hadn't it been? It also occurred to me that at no point had Michel shouted, '*Votre portable!*' Waved it in the air. I spoke French. I'd have understood.

Thérèse listened as, falteringly, I explained, then she went to get Michel. I clearly wasn't to be allowed in. He came out and stood, head bowed, in servile attitude, as I apologized profusely, Lizzie beside me.

When I'd finished, he nodded, looked a bit sad, but said he accepted my apology and was sorry for having frightened me. Which was nice of him.

We turned to go but, as we did, Agathe appeared. She slid into the doorway to take her uncle's hand. As she looked up at me, I caught my breath. Side by side, I could see that her eyes were identical to Michel's. Her mouth, too: sullen, yet full and sensual. There was a striking resemblance.

'Lizzie, did you see that?' I breathed, once we were safely out of earshot, hurrying away down the drive.

'What?'

'The child, Agathe. So like Michel!'

She shrugged. 'A bit. But a lot of French children have that surly, Mediterranean look.'

'Lizzie – she's the *image* of him!' I was fired up.

Lizzie swallowed. She hesitated, then gave me a funny look as we approached the house. Paused a moment. 'Maybe don't lie by the pool this afternoon, Flora. I'd keep out of the sun for a while. You've had a nasty shock.'

She gave me a quick hug, but then went on her way to the pool, looking thoughtful.

Chapter Fifteen

Of course, it hadn't escaped my notice that I'd clung to Max like a barnacle. Drenched his shirt, no doubt, with my sweat, but he hadn't cared: he'd held on tight with strong, protective arms like men do in the movies. He hadn't peeled himself off. Not even when Sally got out of the car. Well, you wouldn't, would you? If someone was that distressed?

I thought about this, and about other things, as I sat under the walnut trees with Rachel, in her quiet spot. She was fair-skinned and only troubled the pool to swim once a day, when no one else was about; otherwise, she sat here with Drummond and read or sewed. He'd gone for a siesta now. Others had, too. Lizzie, Mum, JC, Max and Sally – the latter for a siesta *complet* perhaps, as James and I used laughingly to call it. And the young were catching rays by the pool. Rachel and I sat in companionable silence, her embroidering and me pretending to read, remembering occasionally to turn the page. Thank God for a quiet sister-in-law. What I wanted, more than anything, was to be alone, with my crackpot theories and ideas, to mull over my derangements in peace, but I knew I couldn't do that on a family holiday. Knew it would look odd. Look where it had got me this morning? I knew I couldn't self-indulgently draw attention to myself by going on another long walk, or by driving to a deserted monastery or finding a church to poke around; everyone would raise their eyebrows. I had to stay put, at least for a bit, and being with Rachel was the nearest thing to solitude, just as being with Sally was the nearest thing to being in a crowd. It was a wonder James was so normal with such siblings. Except, at the moment, I hated him, of course, so he wasn't. He was odd, too.

I watched surreptitiously over my paperback as Rachel stitched her tapestry. What passions boiled beneath that smooth, pale brow, I wondered, the one she presented coolly to the world? This wasn't the eighteenth century: surely it wasn't enough for her to be the unmarried sister, alone in a Scottish pile caring for her aging father, going to church, visiting the elderly in the village, dabbling with her watercolours? James and I had discussed it at length, and he'd always assured me it was, before changing the subject. His family was off limits. A closed book. We couldn't know everything about the person we were married to – I respected that – and I knew they'd suffered a terrible trauma, but I'd had an unusual upbringing too, and I was completely transparent. Too much so, probably. And although it all tumbled out of Sally, it was generally rubbish, as if she covered herself with garbage and hid beneath it, so one never knew what made her tick either. Both sisters were opaque in different ways.

I was rarely alone with Rachel, and if I'd been my normal self I'd have relished the opportunity to ask questions, enquire gently if she was happy with her lot, but I wasn't, so I didn't. I was the one with the problems, not her.

'I don't suppose you'd like to drive into Callian, would you, Rachel? There's a chateau that's supposed to be quite interesting. We could have a drink and be back in time for supper.'

'Flora, I'd love to, but I promised Daddy I'd go tomorrow, it's on the way to Seillans. He's really looking forward to it. Apparently, it's got a moat. We're going to set off early, before the sun gets too much. It might take the gloss off it if I'd already been with you. Come with us in the morning?'

'Yes. Yes, I might.'

We left it at that.

A little while later, probably twenty minutes or so, a shadow fell over my book. I looked up. Max was there in a dark-blue shirt. He smiled.

'Would either of you ladies like to come into Callian? There's a church worth seeing, twelfth century. We could have a drink.'

'And a chateau,' smiled Rachel, putting down her work. 'Flora and I were just saying; it's all in the guidebooks in the kitchen. Do go, Flora,' she urged. 'You'd love it. Don't wait for us.'

'Is Sally coming?' I shaded my eyes up at him. I absolutely knew I didn't want to go with him and Sally and frantically searched my head for an excuse.

'Sally's asleep. I think I'm going to leave her. Do her good to rest.'

Why, was she pregnant, I wondered wildly?

I nodded. 'Sure. I'll come.'

Why not. My heart was pounding, though, as I closed my book. I'd clung on to that shirt quite tightly. Not the clean one he was wearing now, the one in the bottom of his wardrobe, in a heap, or in a linen bag, if Sally was that organized.

'I'll get my bag.'

'OK. See you at the car. Let's take mine.'

'Fine.' As if it were a perfectly normal thing to do.

We walked back towards the house together, peeling apart as I went upstairs.

In our room, James was flat on his back on the bed, snoring for England, catching flies. I crept around, finding my straw bag, a hat, changing my shoes, looking in the mirror in the bathroom. My face was a little flushed, so I dabbed some translucent powder on. I brushed my hair, still long – too long probably, for my age, but heavily highlighted now to hide the grey. I studied my reflection, wondering why. Knowing why. I added some lipstick. Rubbed it off hastily. And no scent. But it was hot, so I did blast more deodorant under my arms.

I crept out, shutting the door softly. On the landing, I met Drummond.

'Going out?' he asked, looking at the straw bag over my shoulder.

'Yes, to Callian. Have a poke around.'

'Ah – with Max. Yes, he asked me earlier, but Rachel and I are going tomorrow. Nice chap. Have fun, my dear.'

And on he went. Right. So when Max had asked both me and Rachel, it was in the certain knowledge that Rachel would decline. I paused for a moment, uncertain, my hand on the polished banister rail. I wasn't far from my room, and the girls were right about the acoustics. I could hear James's snores as if I were right next to him. It wasn't the most seductive of noises. In a twinkling I was tripping downstairs – like Cinderella off to the ball, except in wedged espadrilles, not satin slippers, oh, and my new sundress, which I'd quickly changed into in the bathroom but neglected to mention just now – down the majestic stone staircase, across the flagstone hall. Ancestors glared down in a censorial manner from gloomy oils as I went, and I wondered how many far more glamorous mesdemoiselles had escaped thus, under their disapproving gaze amid the crossed swords and suits of armour, on secret assignations?

Max had put the roof down on his car, and I slid in beside him. We exchanged a quick, hopefully not too complicit, smile. As we sailed down the long gravel drive, through the iron gates at the end, and purred along the lane between the vineyards, I felt exhilarated. Safe, too, which was strange, given who I was with, but Max and I knew each other extremely well: knew we could sit in silence for a bit and not make small talk, just let the warm wind whip through our hair, the heady scent of sunflowers and lavender wash over us. It helped that we'd been in each other's company for a few days already, softening the shock of being together again after all these years. As we slowed down to go through a tiny hamlet, an old woman dressed in black hobbled out to cross the road, her equally elderly chihuahua on a lead beside her. Midway, the dog decided to relieve itself. We waited. And waited. Madame glared at us.

'D'you get the impression she's indignant we're even watching?' murmured Max.

'Possibly the crossest Frenchwoman I've seen to date.'

'Steady. The competition for that title is stiff.'

'Oh, really? Are they notoriously bad-tempered?'

'Suspicious is more the word I'd use. But they have good cause to be. Their husbands are rascals.'

'That's what Mum says.'

'Sensible woman, your mum.'

I smiled. Looked at his profile a moment. I took a strand of hair from my mouth. 'Max, I was really sorry to hear about your mother.'

He nodded. Didn't look at me, though. 'Lucy?'

'Yes.'

Finally, he turned his head. Gave me a sad little smile. 'Thanks, Flossie.'

His old nickname for me. It took my breath away for a moment, but he'd said it without thinking.

'Cancer?'

'Yes.' He looked straight ahead again. 'I gather you wrote to my dad.'

'Yes. I was so fond of her.'

'I know. Thanks for that. He appreciated it.' Madame finally achieved the other side of the road, and we drove on. After a while, Max's mouth twitched. 'Notice you didn't write to me, though.'

'Well, I –'

'Didn't want to give me ideas?' He turned and gave me his wolfish grin.

'Oh, don't be ridiculous!'

He roared with laughter. 'Still so easy to tweak!'

I shook my head wearily, but found it hard not to smile, and the mood in the car was light as we drove into the beautiful town of Callian. We climbed up and up, snaking around the steep hill to the medieval town perched on top. Both sides of the road were already chock-a-block with parked cars, some at crazy angles.

'*Centre ville*, d'you think?' suggested Max.

'You mean in the total absence of spaces?'

He shrugged. 'Fortune favours the brave.'

Miraculously, it did. As we approached the city wall, which was draped with pretty bunting to announce that the town was *en fête*, a car drew out of a space just next to the old gates. Max reversed in expertly, but it was tight. I swivelled round to help him.

'About two foot.'

'Thanks.'

'Stop – *cripes*!' He'd nearly hit the car behind. When he'd finished the manoeuvre he turned.

'Did you just say cripes?' he asked incredulously.

'I was going for Christ and changed my mind,' I admitted, busted.

'Thank you for not blaspheming, Flossie. I'm a sensitive chap and I'd have been truly shocked.'

I narrowed my eyes at him as we got out of the car. 'Don't push it, Max.'

'What d'you mean?' He looked at me with mock-bafflement.

'The Flossie business.'

'I called you that earlier!'

'That was different. Don't take advantage.'

'Why ever not?' He roared delightedly as he locked the car. 'Haven't you seen the flags?' He nodded up at the bunting. 'It's open season!'

More head-shaking and lip-biting from me as, together, we sailed on through the ancient archway into town.

Strange how the years rolled back. We could have been walking down Marville Road to Mum's for a drink in our old trainers, or coming back from walking the dogs at his parents' house, strolling down the lane, our hands brushing cow parsley heads, in time for lunch. No nerves, no need to explain anything, just a lot to find out. I think we both knew we weren't going to the chateau, which was on the other side of the hill, or the medieval church in the Latin quarter. Instead, Max headed for one of the narrow side streets off the main square, as yet not particularly crowded, its restaurants still laid with paper cloths for drinks, not white linen for supper.

We found a pretty place with a raised terrace and a pagoda dripping with grapevines. There were a few empty tables outside. The waiter arrived almost immediately, pleased to have some custom, and Max ordered a beer for him and a glass of rosé for me. When he'd gone, he took off his sunglasses, folded his arms on the zinc table and leaned across. He smiled. Right into my eyes.

'So.'

'So.'

'How have you been?'

'For the last twenty-odd years? Fine. Apart from today.'

'Oh, today.' He made a dismissive gesture. 'Crossed wires. A mountain out of a molehill. Too much fuss made about nothing. I'm not interested in that, I want to know about the rest of your life. Quite a lot to catch up on, one way and another.' Our drinks arrived and he took a sip of beer.

'Not really. Only if it's complicated,' I told him. 'Mine's pretty straightforward. I could probably do it in about five sentences.'

He smiled. 'OK. Go.'

'No, you.'

'What, from the beginning? In my case, we'll be here all night.'

'Edited highlights, then.'

He paused. And, as he did, I studied his face. A few lines, obviously, and he was going grey at the temples. His hair was swept back instead of flopping forward in a fringe which he used to push back impatiently. His cheeks were slightly more sunken, but that only highlighted the good bones. It suited him. He gazed beyond me in thought. Came back and flashed me that grin.

'Well, you dumped me, obviously.'

'Obviously. You cheated on me.'

'I made a tiny mistake.' He held his thumb and forefinger a centimetre apart. 'A small slip.'

I winced. 'Unfortunate analogy.'

He inclined his head, accepting this. 'Anyway, there was no forgiveness from you. No Christian mercy.'

'This is old news, Max. Shall we fast-forward? Reader, you married her?'

'Oh, you mean Mimi?'

'I imagine I do.'

He shrugged. 'What was a boy to do? You'd snared your medic by then.'

'Ah, yes, of course. The stereotypical bourgeois girl on the hunt for a nice professional man. Thank God I found one.'

'You always did like clever coves.'

'Didn't I just?'

'Did you love him?'

'Yes, of course I did. Do!'

'As much as me?'

Merest pause. 'Of course. More than you,' I retorted, to make up for that pause.

'*More* than me,' he repeated incredulously, eyes widening in mock-surprise. 'And yet we were engaged to be married.'

'This is childish, Max. I wouldn't be so rude as to ask if you loved Mimi.'

'But you'd still like to know. I did, actually. Mimi was a slow burn. She crept up on me. And was very sweet. She helped me get over you.'

'Which is weird, really, when you think that she instigated our split.'

Max waved a disdainful hand. 'That wasn't her fault. She was pissed. You overreacted.' His eyes twinkled. 'Because of your mo-th-er . . .' he sang, grinning.

'Ah. Mr Amateur Psychologist speaks.'

'Nothing amateur about it, I studied at the master's knee. Lesson one: do not repeat parental mistakes.' He wagged a stern finger. 'Do not replicate a behavioural pattern.'

'Shall we move on? Tell me more about Mimi.'

He shrugged. 'What's to tell? Mimi and I got married and we were very happy. For a bit.'

'Children?'

'A boy, Mungo. He's with his mum at the moment.'

I wondered at an only child, but didn't ask. 'And you're in the music business?' As soon as I'd said it, I wished I hadn't.

He blinked in delight. 'You know I am. You overheard me telling JC about it the other night. Your mind was not remotely on Lizzie's new shoes.'

I flushed, and when he saw, he became kinder, which he was.

'Yes, you're right. I put on shows, organize concerts. That type of thing.'

'Celebs?'

'Some.'

'Like who?'

'Robbie Williams?'

'Close personal?'

''Fraid not. Purely a business relationship.'

'So what went wrong?'

'With Robbie?'

'Obviously not with Robbie.'

He shrugged. 'Nothing cataclysmic. We argued a lot. Mimi's quite . . . controlling. And I went quiet on her when she nagged, which only made it worse.'

'About what?'

'What did she nag about? Promotion, mostly. How I should move on and up in the world. She's pretty ambitious. I don't know, what d'you want me to say? I should never have married her? Or – I married her because she worked on me night and day and she's a good-looking bird and she can be very entertaining and you'd married some-one else?'

'Please don't tell me you married her to spite me.'

'Don't flatter yourself. Why would I wreck my life for you?'

I stared at him. After a moment he gave me that grin again. More indolent than wolfish this time. He sank into his beer. It struck me he was quite lazy. Capable of taking the line of least resistance. Part of his charm, in a way.

'What are you doing here, Max?'

He wiped some froth from his mouth. 'Courting Sally. What does it look like?'

'Old-fashioned word.'

'Old-fashioned girl. OK, shagging Sally.'

'Why?'

'Oh, hello, back to you. You mean, am I here on your account?'

I held his eyes. Raised my eyebrows, undeterred. Suddenly, a blowtorch smile lit up his whole face.

'Of course I am!'

I took a moment. Wrong-footed. 'You are?'

'Well, I didn't engineer it, if that's what you mean. But when Sally mentioned her brother was being lent a house in France courtesy of a grateful patient, and did I want to come, I didn't think, I couldn't possibly bump into Flora after all these years; I thought, great, why not? After all, my marriage had collapsed, I'd never really got over you, and I figured you might a) have the happiest marriage under the sun, in which case I'd go quietly, or b) be trapped in a monotonous, boring relationship and be going through the motions on account of the children, who are actually young women now, so pretty soon it'd just be you and the medic.'

He was laughing at me with his eyes. My mouth was dry, despite the rosé. 'And what have you decided?'

He lifted his beer to his lips, still holding my gaze. 'Jury's out, Flossie. Somewhere between the two, I'd have said when I arrived, but this last twenty-four hours . . .' He shook his head. 'I'm not so sure.'

Chapter Sixteen

'Well, you're wrong,' I said shortly. 'There's absolutely nothing wrong with my marriage. We're extremely happy.'

'Congratulations. No nineteen-year itch?'

'Not even a tickle.'

'I'm glad.'

I think we both knew we were stretching the truth: he certainly wasn't glad, but it was nice of him to say it without sarcasm, and I was exaggerating, but in only one respect. I had no itch with James, just with my life. With the relentless monotony of it – his word. The work which I increasingly disliked, the endless worry and bickering with the girls, the mortgage, the daily grind, the general keep-buggering-on-ness. That was the irritation. And sitting here, opposite an extremely attractive man, with whom I used to be in love and who was clearly still interested enough in me to want to join my family holiday, gazing deeply into my eyes on a balmy, Provençal evening under a vine groaning with swollen grapes, was really not going to help. Or else it really was, depending on how you looked at it. Temporarily, a little voice in my head said. Temporarily, surely, it's OK to relieve the irritation? Apply a little soothing balm? Forget everything for five minutes? Where's the harm?

'You're still easy on the eye, Flossie.' He looked at me narrowly.

Max didn't do conscious charm. I knew he meant it. But no middle-aged woman with cellulite and thread veins and the odd hair cropping up in unlikely places needs to be told that she's still attractive and hang on to her sanity. I felt mine slipping.

'Rubbish,' I muttered, meaning, *Tell me more*.

'You are. You've still got your own hair, your teeth.'

'Actually, these come out at night.' I tapped a front one.

'Ah. I thought I heard the rattle of porcelain in a glass next door.'

I thought of him lying awake in the adjoining bedroom, listening: not to that, but for anything else. I thought of me lying awake, listening, too.

'You're not being very kind.'

'To whom?'

'To Sally.'

'Sally knows the score. She knows I'm playing it for laughs. That I've come out of a long marriage. And I'm not serious. I was upfront about that.'

I believed him. 'Still. She doesn't know the whole story.'

'Oh, you're not the whole story, Floss, don't get ahead of yourself. I'm also here for the sybaritic free holiday. The wine, the *grande maison*, the Mediterranean sun – who'd turn that down?' He grinned.

'Not me,' I agreed.

'Think of yourself as an added bonus. The bonus ball. D'you want to do the chateau?'

'Not really. Do you?'

'No. D'you want another drink?'

'Yes, please.'

*

217

Back at the ranch, when we rocked up an hour or so later, drinks were in full swing on the terrace, and supper was being laid out. I slipped upstairs whilst Max strolled off to field any questions and wax lyrical about the chateau. Our first lie, I thought with horror, but also with a frisson of excitement as I looked at my flushed cheeks in the bathroom mirror, my bright eyes. I crept across to the window and listened to the chat and laughter below. Max was handling it beautifully; nobody was in the least curious or suspicious, it seemed. I had a quick shower, recovered my maxi dress from the floor of Tara's bedroom opposite, where, having tried it on, she'd discarded it, and went down. If I'd felt in control, though, I'd reckoned without my elder daughter's antennae. She saw me approach through the French windows and beetled across the terrace like a heat-seeking missile to intercept me.

'What was *that* like?' she whispered, as I helped myself to a drink from the tray held by Thérèse, who, incidentally, still wasn't smiling.

'What was what like, darling?'

'Don't be coy. A date with your ex.'

'Don't be silly. We went to look around a chateau. No one else wanted to.'

'Did you ask Dad?'

'Couldn't find him,' I lied. Second one.

'Well, come on. Give.'

'Fine.' Exhilarating. Unbelievably exciting. 'Nice to touch base again.'

'Is he still hot for you?'

'Don't be ridiculous, Amelia.'

'Did you talk about old times?'

'A bit.'

'What, like, how he broke your heart?'

'He didn't. I broke his. Where's Daddy?'

'Gone to the chateau with Camille and Sally.'

'Oh, right.' I felt myself flush. It broke out all over me. I gripped the stem of my glass. Met Max's eye across the terrace, which told me he, too, knew. Also that he'd deal with it.

'Didn't you see them there?'

'No, but it's a big place. Must have missed them.'

At that moment, tyres crunched on the gravel at the front of the house: car doors slammed and voices carried. Not long to think about how to handle this. In an instant, they were upon us, Sally most of all.

'Max, darling! We looked for you and couldn't see you. Rachel said you'd gone to Callian.'

'Yes, we did, but we couldn't park so we abandoned it. Just drove round it.'

'I thought you said it was a big place?' Amelia asked me.

'Callian? It is. Well, intricate, anyway. Lots of winding streets.'

'Oh. Right.'

She looked confused and I wondered why I couldn't just say, Look, we hadn't seen each other for almost twenty years, we needed a drink to catch up. What was wrong with that? Nothing. Unless there was something wrong with me. Which there wasn't. And I'd say it to James, later, in bed, I determined. No secrets.

James, though, didn't seem to have his mind on where his wife had been, or the spirit of full marital disclosure at all: he was too busy making sure Camille had a drink, that she wasn't short of olives or tapenade and didn't need her wrap. His own colour was pretty high, too, I thought: his eyes shining. Perhaps this was what our marriage needed – what any lengthy marriage needed – a little light flirtation? To oil the wheels, make us feel young and invigorated and sprightly again, so that when we came together, sparks flew? It was surely how the French operated, I thought, seeing Michel back to his old ways as he sidled up to Tara and asked if she was sure she wouldn't like *un petit feuilleté aux anchois*? Rory bridled when she giggled. Perhaps it was the climate? I knew, though, that there was no danger in James's flirtation: knew instinctively Camille wasn't serious, even if he was. In fact, I wondered what her game was. And when would the main event, her current beau – oh yes, Lizzie had done some digging and discovered she definitely had a love interest – appear? Would she then depart with him, I wondered, watching her circulate around the terrace, looking stunning in a long pink skirt and silky white camisole: finally exit stage left and leave us in peace?

She floated across the terrace towards me with a wide, welcoming smile. Why was I such a cow?

'Did you have a lovely time? Did you like my Callian?'

'Loved it,' I enthused, trying to make up for my treacherous personality. 'It's beautiful, Camille, you're so lucky to have a gem like that on your doorstep.'

'But you didn't make the chateau, I hear. Too busy?' She waggled her eyebrows knowingly at me.

I laughed. Fell right into the Girls Together conspiratorial trap. 'Oh, you know. It was nice to have a chat. Max and I haven't seen each other for years.' Why was everyone so interested?

'Ah, *oui*? I didn't know you were old friends? Ah, *cherie* – have you met Flora?' This to the quiet child who'd crept up on us stealthily, like a shadow.

'Only very briefly.' I smiled and held out my hand. '*Bon-soir*, Agathe.'

She took it and smiled shyly. Then turned to her mother. '*Maman* – couldn't you just for once come back and eat with us tonight? Not these complete randomers?' She wasn't to know, of course, that I spoke fluent French. Camille did, though.

'Agathe! *Ne soyez pas impoli!*' she chided. 'But yes, tonight, I will.'

And so she did, turning away, which was a relief. And what with her absence, and the time I'd had earlier with Max, I found myself feeling quite buoyant and being altogether delightful at supper: really rather funny and light-hearted for me. A person I remembered. I saw James smiling at me as I recounted some tale the girls loved to hear and prompted me to tell, about how I'd once lost a shoe outside Harrods, found it again in the crowd with my foot, only to discover, when I got on the bus, that I'd got odd shoes on, one of which didn't belong to me. 'It *has* to be one of Mum's fibs,' insisted Amelia, as she always did. 'No, no, quite true,' I declared, as everyone roared.

Oh yes, I thought, lifting my glass to my lips: she's still there, that person, the one you all remember. Just very hard to find.

I found myself saying yes to everything that night. Could Tara have a few euros to buy a dress she'd seen in the market? Yes. Could Lizzie borrow my new sarong tomorrow; she'd spilled wine on hers? Yes. Could my mother take our car to the lake for a boat trip with Jean-Claude? Yes. I even said yes to James that night. Quietly, though. Indeed, we made almost no sound at all.

The following morning, as usual, dawned bright and clear. Aside from Drummond and Rachel, who'd gone sightseeing, most people decided on a lazy day by the pool, and that suited me fine. I wanted to lie still, get a tan, pretend to be asleep and reflect on yesterday's conversation. Hug it to myself. Tell myself it was lovely to be admired again after all these years and that was that. It was a bit of a strain keeping my knees bent at all times in case Max should appear, but he didn't, taking the Reading Under the Walnut Tree option, along with James, who was not a sun worshipper. It occurred to me that not many men would be happy to sit with their wife's ex-boyfriend and discuss the new biography of Napoleon they both happened to be reading, but James was not many men. He was rather exceptional. Rather lovely, I told myself sternly, lest I should compare him in terms of physical attributes, in which department he might be found wanting, but which were not important.

Sally, however, had other ideas regarding my solitude and, unable to amuse herself for five minutes on her own, or concentrate on a book, lay down on the empty sunbed beside me. I groaned inwardly but smiled, tipping up my hat, which covered my face, for a brief second, before replacing it, hoping she'd get the hint.

'Flora, can I talk to you for a moment?'

'Of course.'

'I mean, girl to girl?'

Oh God. What had he said? I removed my hat and

looked at her. Her face was a bit drawn: worried. I felt my mouth dry.

'What's wrong?'

'Did you know that Max and Camille had had a thing?'

I stared at her. Sat up and turned to face her properly.

'*What?* They don't even know each other.'

'Yes, they do. Max told me last night. I think that's why we're all here.'

I stared at her for a long moment. 'Sally, I have no idea what you're talking about. Max and *I* had a thing –'

'Oh, yes, years ago, old history.' She waved a dismissive hand. 'I know about that, but this was six months or so ago, after his marriage had finished. She was the girl before me.'

'I don't believe it.'

'Why would he lie?'

'But – but they don't even look like they know each other, let alone had an affair.' My mind span.

'Because it was kept so quiet. She didn't want yet another relationship to get in the papers. Her ex-husband is threatening to fight for custody of the child. She didn't want to jeopardize anything.'

I put my fingers to my temples, trying to make sense of this. From the other side of the pool, Tara and Rory looked up, eyes trained on the intense whispers. I lowered my voice.

'How did they meet?'

'Through the opera. Max produced one of the shows she was in. It was in Rome, in St Mark's Square. Lots of famous classical names, plus some modern ones – Katherine Jenkins, Paul McCartney, the Opera Babes – it was huge. Televised on enormous screens in the parks. You know the sort of thing.'

'Yes.' I might even have watched it.

'She fell for him, and they had a fling.'

'Who broke it off?'

'He did.'

'Why?'

He said she was too intense and too spoilt. Wanted everything to revolve around her. And, of course, by that time, towards the end, he'd met me.'

'Right.'

'We weren't actually going out, but we were seeing each other. Also . . .' she hesitated. 'He's never quite got over an old girlfriend. He told me that at the time.'

I stared at her. Sat very still.

'Well, not you, obviously, Flora.' She laughed.

'Obviously!' I laughed back, but my head said, *fucking hell*. I was *engaged* to him, Sally.

'Max has had loads of girlfriends,' she said kindly. She patted my hand. 'He's a very attractive man.'

'Yes.'

I wasn't so sure. I knew Max much better than Sally did. He wasn't a roué. Had never been a player. I sniffed a man covering his tracks, littering it with phantom girlfriends.

'So . . .' I felt my way. 'After he and Camille split up . . .'

'There was nothing to split, Max said. It was just a casual thing on location as far as he was concerned. And when I got James's email saying he'd administered an EpiPen to a child on a plane and the mother had lent him a villa in France and would we like to come, I didn't think to ask who it belonged to, just squealed and emailed back, "Yes, please!" So that was all I knew to tell Max.'

Camille had also asked James to keep her name quiet. Claimed she didn't like people knowing where she lived.

'So Max didn't know who it belonged to?'

'Any more than I did.'

'But *she* knew.' I was thinking aloud. 'About you. She knew he'd probably come with you.'

'Exactly.'

I stared, horrified, as the full implication dawned. 'You think she engineered this whole thing? To see Max?'

'I do. Think about it, Flora. She asks for your email at the airport to send you a bread-and-butter thank you, and when she sees the name she thinks – hello: Murray-Brown. That's an unusual surname. She knows Max is seeing a Sally Murray-Brown. So she investigates. Asks James to lunch. Discovers he does indeed have a sister called Sally. So she suggests his entire family come out. But asks that he keeps her name quiet.'

'Odd.'

I recalled her at the airport: very much in a hurry at the baggage carousel, to which she'd arrived late, making for the exit and leaving her minions to collect the luggage. At the last moment spotting James and having no choice but to come across, but hardly on a mission. Then, suddenly, lunch at the Hyde Park Hotel, and then, lo and behold, the surprise holiday, hurtling down the tracks. I felt a nasty taste in my mouth. For us, as a family. For having been duped. And for my James. Who, even now, was probably mixing her favourite lunchtime Bellini in her favourite tall glass, with sugar on the rim, running around after her like a puppy dog, making, if I'm honest, a bit of a fool of himself. Which Camille encouraged in order to . . . what, make Max jealous?

'Does she strike you as the type to make a huge, magnanimous gesture?' persisted Sally. 'Or the type to casually write an email of thanks, not even a letter?'

'The latter,' I agreed.

'I reckon we're all here because she wants to try to get Max back.'

I shook my head, staggered. My heavens, she was cool. A very smooth operator. Although, of course, what Camille didn't know, I thought, my head spinning, was the subtext. That Max and I had once been together, had been very much an item and were quietly getting to know each other again. And that once he'd got over the shock of whose house he was in – I remembered Sally saying he was flabbergasted – he wasn't averse to spending his holiday here, because he, too, had an agenda. Had known all along I was coming.

'So . . . what is it that worries you, Sally?' I said carefully. 'I thought you and Max had a very casual relationship?'

'We do,' she said quickly. 'He was straight with me from the beginning, as I was with him. Absolutely no strings attached. We're playing this one for laughs. Otherwise, I wouldn't have got into it,' she said firmly.

'Right.' I was surprised at her vehemence. Rather admired it.

'I was just a bit shaken, I suppose. To discover the lengths she's gone to, to engineer this. And I feel a bit bad for James.'

'Me, too,' I agreed, as, at that moment, Max came through the gateway to the walled pool in swimming trunks and a pink shirt, a book and towel under his arm. As he peeled off for a swim, Sally got up and sashayed around to greet him. She rose up on her tiptoes to give him a kiss, then took up position on the bed beside the one on which he'd placed his book and towel. Max reached down and gave her hand an affectionate squeeze before walking around to the deep end to dive in. Just then, Camille appeared through the gate at the other end of the walled garden. I'd never seen her by the pool before. She wore a green silk sarong around her hips and a white bikini top, which just about encased her considerable bosoms. Her figure was to die for; slim and brown but curvaceous, she was a veritable pocket Venus, and in keeping with the mythological analogy, her blonde hair flowed in ripples down her back. If Max saw this vision of female pulchritude, he didn't acknowledge it. His eyes didn't flicker towards her. Instead, feet poised on the edge, he raised his arms and executed a neat swallow dive into the shimmering blue water, hardly rippling the surface.

Three pairs of female eyes watched intently as he travelled the length of the pool underwater. Before he made it to the other end, I quickly pulled mine away. Drew the brim of my hat defiantly over them. Oh, no. Count *me* out, I thought in horror. Count me *right* out of the equation.

Chapter Seventeen

That evening, as we dressed for dinner, I told James what Sally had told me. He listened, but I could tell he didn't want to believe me.

'Oh, no, I think that's just a coincidence, darling.'

'Do you?'

'Yes. You girls with your conspiracy theories. I'm sure Camille was as surprised as anyone when Max turned up.'

'But did you even know they knew each other? Let alone had an affair? I mean, they kept that very quiet, didn't they?'

'Well, for obvious reasons. He's with Sally now, and if Camille's going through a custody battle – I knew about that, by the way, she's having a terrible time with her ex. He's called Étienne de la Peyrière, and his family rule the roost round here. Own half of Grasse. I'm going to see if I can get her some help. Chap I was at Cambridge with is a brilliant family lawyer.'

'I'm sure she's got the best that money can buy already, darling.'

'Well, she seemed pretty interested.'

'Right.' I tied the strings of my espadrilles in a bow. 'Thérèse told the girls he's nice.'

'Who?'

'Étienne de thingy.'

He laughed hollowly. 'Not according to Camille, and she

should know. I gather he's a complete shit. Have you seen my blue linen shirt?'

'You didn't put it in, it was dirty.'

'Damn. And I've run out of contact lenses, which is annoying.'

'Why?'

'Well, I'll have to wear my glasses.'

'James, don't . . .'

'What?'

'Nothing. Come here.' I was sitting on the bed. I stretched out my hand and he came across. Sat down beside me.

'We're all right, aren't we?' I asked him.

He laughed. 'Isn't that the sort of thing they say in *Friends*?'

'But aren't we?' I persisted.

'Of course we are. And last night was lovely.' He kissed me perfunctorily. 'And you're enjoying catching up with Max?'

'Oh, yes. We went for a drink last night, which is why we didn't make the chateau.'

'Yes, that's what I assumed. And the thing is, Flora' – he hesitated – 'it's making us much better together. Getting out more, I believe it's called. Mixing with different people. Sparks us up a bit.'

'Yes, that's what I thought, too. A couple of days ago. Yesterday, even. It's just . . .' I still had his hand.

'What?' He brushed my fringe from my eyes. An affectionate gesture.

'I just think we should be careful.'

He laughed. 'Oh, don't be silly, darling, we're not seventeen.'

'No.'

'I'm really not worried I'm going to find you snogging in the undergrowth with Max, if that's what you mean.'

'I don't mean that.'

'Nice man. I like him.'

I nodded. Odd man, my husband. Plain *odd*.

'Camille has got tickets to an Andrea Bocelli concert in Cannes on Friday,' he said. I now had no illusions about Camille leaving us. She was here for the duration.

'Has she?' I got up and found my earrings on the dressing table. Popped them in and turned. 'You go. You know I hate opera. How many tickets?'

He hesitated. 'Two.'

I smiled down at him. 'Honestly, go. You know I don't mind.'

I didn't. Did that make me odd, too? No, because I knew why she was here, even if James didn't believe it. Would I have minded if I'd thought she really was after my husband? Yes, of course. I quickly added some blusher. Caught my own eye in the mirror. But she wasn't.

Supper that night – a barbecue, which made a pleasant change – found me placed next to Max. I won't pretend I didn't engineer it. Once a noisy conversation was under way at the other end of the table, Amelia and Toby on either side of a debate about legalizing cannabis, both waving spare-rib bones at each other, everyone else lining up to take sides, I came straight to the point.

'I gather you and Camille are not exactly strangers.'

He grinned. 'Sally didn't waste much time.'

'But why did you pretend you didn't know her? I can

understand not wanting to appear over-friendly, but we didn't even know you'd met.'

'To tell you the truth, I was so bloody shocked when Sally told me whose house it was, and then, when she appeared on the terrace that first night, I didn't quite know how to handle it. She pretended she didn't know me, so I took my cue from her. Let myself be introduced. After all, it's her custody battle.'

'So you know about that.'

'She told me in Rome.' He shrugged. 'I assumed that was the reason for blanking me here in front of her family, her sister.'

I speared a tiny caramelized onion thoughtfully with my fork. 'You realize we're all here on your account? Every single one of us?'

'Bollocks.'

'It's true. For once, I agree with Sally. Camille has master-minded this whole shebang. You have no idea how manipulative women are, Max.'

'Oh, I think I do.'

I'd forgotten he'd been married to Mimi. I wondered, for a moment, what it must be like to be Max. To be so attractive that women fought to get close to him. Arranged their lives around him. Not this one, I thought, ignoring the fact that his blue eyes looked even brighter now his face was tanned, his hair slightly flecked with gold. And, anyway, part of me thought that he was really only inter-ested in someone as ordinary as me because I'd resisted him.

I was conscious of Amelia's eyes on me towards the end of supper and, after pudding, she followed me into the

231

kitchen, as I helped take some dishes in. She stood over me as I stacked the dishwasher under the island by the sink. Could have helped, of course, but she had other things on her mind.

'Tara and I really aren't happy about it, Mum,' she said pompously.

'About what?'

'You flirting outrageously with Max, and Dad being knocked sideways by Camille.'

Tara appeared, hastening to her sister's side from the table. This was clearly a pre-arranged pincer movement. She nodded solemnly and they both looked po-faced. Any minute now some arm folding would go on. They folded their arms.

'I'm not flirting, Amelia, and anyway, you were really rather interested yesterday.'

'Yes, but it's too much now,' said Tara. 'It's all a bit – you know – weird. And Dad's even worse.'

We turned to look through the open French windows. James was rocking with laughter at some comment of Camille's – one supper with her own family in the lodge had clearly been enough, and she was back with a vengeance. He was looking, I have to say, quite attractive as he embarked on yet another orthopaedic anecdote.

'Dad's just having a nice time. Enjoying the attention.'

'He looks like he's going to stick his tongue down her throat. It's gross. Anyway,' went on Amelia, 'I think she's secretly after Max.'

'What on earth makes you say that?'

'She keeps sneaking him furtive glances, and he is really good-looking. How come you snared him, Mum?'

'Thank you, Amelia. I had my moments.'

'What, in the Wimpy Bar? With your flared jeans?'

Lizzie had joined us now, sensing girl chat. She took out her Marlboro Lights and leaned against the draining board, but misjudged it and staggered slightly.

'Frankly, I'm just jealous no one fancies me,' she pouted. 'I'm the bloody single woman here. You might have invited some sex-crazed Lothario on my account, everyone's shagging except me.' Her mouth lurched at the corner as it did when she was pissed, and she fumbled to light her cigarette.

'No one is shagging, Lizzie. And anyway, yesterday you said there was a glimmer of hope on the Jackson front.'

'False alarm. He's still up to his eyes with work. Speaking of which, did you get Maria's email?' She blew out a thin line of smoke and attempted to fix me with swimmy eyes.

'Yes. I did,' I said shortly.

'And you're not going back?'

'No, I'm bloody not.' Ever, I thought to myself, wondering if I meant it, or if it was just holiday bravado. I took a slurp of the Cointreau she'd brought in with her.

'Going back where?' demanded Tara, ears pricked.

'Maria's calling a meeting. The magazine's been taken over, so . . .'

'You knew that. That happened months ago,' objected Amelia. 'You said it didn't matter.'

'Yes, but the knock-on effects are now rippling out. The implication is that anyone who wants to keep their job had better show up for this meeting.'

'But you're on holiday.'

'I know.'

They looked thoughtful. 'You could just go for the day?' suggested Amelia. 'Get a plane from Nice?'

'Yes, that's what I thought I might do,' agreed Lizzie.

'Oi, are you lot coming or what?' Toby's voice floated across from where he and Rory were shuffling cards at one end of the table, ciggies and candles lit. The girls drifted off to play Vingt-et-un, bored now that we were talking shop and not men.

'Watch yourself, Mum, OK?' was Amelia's parting shot to me. I rolled my eyes theatrically.

'But not you?' asked Lizzie, her mind still on flights home. 'You're really not going?'

'I'm really not going. If they want to sack me, they can jolly well get on with it. Give me a nice fat redundancy package. I'm not going back to grovel.'

My eyes were on Max, at the table, helping Drummond, who could be jolly stiff, to his feet. He steadied him, found his stick and then stayed with him a moment as Rachel came round from the other side of the table to take him inside and up to bed.

'Night, all.'

'Night, Drummond.'

'Night, Grandpa!'

He gave a cheery wave to the young with his stick, still brimming with delight at being here, amongst his family, in the warmth, which he can't have felt on his skin for years: since his days in Africa probably, in the army. Thanking his lucky stars for being alive when so many of his contemporaries weren't, before shuffling in.

'Right. Well, I don't have the luxury of choice, so I might. Go back.'

'It's not a luxury, Lizzie, I don't have that either. We need the money as much as you do. It's just . . . I've come to the end of something with that magazine.'

I had. Had known it for some time now but had been in denial. Because I used to love it so. And I'd made myself believe I still did, but I didn't. I still loved the food: was still excited when something new hit my taste buds, some innovative combination of flavours. That moment when I realized there was someone highly creative in the kitchen was still a thrill. I remembered discovering Antoine Edelle in a tiny restaurant in Tooting, being struck by his prodigious talent, praising the young chef to the skies and being delighted when, a few months later, he opened in Greek Street to rave reviews. The delight in all that was still there. And it more than made up for the mistakes I couldn't help noticing, like Thérèse putting too much wine in the marinade tonight or balsamic in the vinaigrette. And the food was good here. Or last night, how the creamy morel sauce was just slightly too rich, badly needing a dash of lemon to cut through it – I'd seen Jean-Claude's face after his first mouthful, knew he knew, too: he approached food with a great solemnity, I'd noticed. Yes, most evenings I noticed something, but it didn't taint my pleasure. Noticing flaws was an occupational hazard, and I was proud of my training, my finely tuned palate. It defined me. But I wanted to turn it in another direction now. Do things differently. I knew how, too. Just couldn't quite admit it. Even to myself.

I swam up from the depths of my reverie. Helped

myself to another slurp of Lizzie's Cointreau. 'To be honest, Lizzie, I think it's all just a storm in a teacup. Maria's holiday in Tuscany got cancelled at the last minute because her husband had to go to New York. She's probably a bit jealous of us all lying here in the sun.'

'I know, I wondered that. She's really pissed off, apparently. I spoke to Colin. Serve her right for marrying an über-rich banker.' She sighed. Stubbed her cigarette out in a cheese plate. 'Perhaps I'll play it by ear. See if we get any more missives tomorrow.'

'Exactly. I would.'

Lizzie had been standing with her back to the draining board, facing the garden. She focused her gaze on the candlelit table. 'I say, James is having fun, isn't he?'

I turned. Dried my hands. My husband was on his feet now, mimicking someone with an exaggerated limp. A hunched back, too, apparently. Was he Richard III? Camille was laughing prettily, clapping her hands with delight.

'Is he making a fool of himself, Lizzie? The girls think he is.'

'Of course not, he's on holiday. I haven't seen him like that for years, it's really lovely. He's such good company.'

I glowed. Lizzie had sat next to him at supper.

'It's good for us, isn't it, Lizzie? All of this?' I looked out at the lively table, a game of cards at one end, explosive laughter at the other, the lights strung so prettily through the trees on the lawn.

''Course it bloody is. Christ, we're not dead yet. Let the young shake their heads and suck their teeth, I'm not reining in. Not for one moment. In fact, I'm going skinny-dipping with Sally.'

'Is that where she is?'

'Yes, starkers in the pool. Come on. While the kids are playing cards.'

She grabbed my arm and, full of Cointreau, we hastened off. Giggling like schoolgirls, we ran out through the side door and then around the other side of the house. We picked our way across the sloping lawn, through the spinney in the dark, and under the cedar tree to the gate in the old walled garden. A few minutes later I was beetling back alone, eyes wide, fully clothed. Mum was in the pool, too.

In the pitch black, my mind not on the route I seemed to have veered from, I cannoned straight into someone in the dark. I shrieked.

'Oof – steady!' Arms came out. It was Max.

'Oh – God, it's you!' I clasped my heart with relief.

He laughed, steadying me. 'Who did you think it was, the bogeyman? Word is the girls have got their kit off down at the pool. Couldn't get down there quickly enough.'

'Yes, but, actually, maybe not, Max. Mum's in there.'

'Oh. Right.' He turned about abruptly.

'Exactly.'

We went back up the cinder path together. I grinned up at him in the dark, lurching only very slightly. 'Odd, isn't it? Amelia and Tara would be horrified if I went in, but I think I'm still young. So why am I aghast at my own mother?'

'I think it depends,' he said carefully.

'On what?'

'On whether the pool has underwater lights or not.'

I giggled.

'Do you still smoke?' he asked.

'Occasionally. But, like skinny-dipping, not in front of the children. I operate a strict regime of hypocrisy.'

'Let's have one over here, then.'

He drew out a pack and we wandered off the beaten track a bit, towards the horses' field beyond the spinney. It was a moonless night, with just a sprinkling of stars above, like diamonds tossed carelessly on to black velvet. The horses came ambling across the field to greet us, and we stroked their velvety noses. Let them blow into our hands. Max lit two cigarettes the way he always used to and passed me one. We leaned back against the fence.

'You haven't lost that habit, then,' I observed.

'I have, actually. Haven't done that for years.'

Instantly, I was transported back to the many times he'd done it for me: on the top of the number 19 bus as we rumbled back from the West End after the cinema. Inside the cinema, in the days of little ashtrays between the seats. In the Italian bistro afterwards, him lighting both from a candle dripping with wax as we argued about the film, never agreeing on anything we'd seen. And then, of course, in bed, at his flat. Flicking ash off the navy-blue sheets into a small pewter ashtray on the floor beside us that had belonged to his grandfather. Burning a hole once. I could tell Max had gone to these places in his head, too. We didn't speak, just smoked in silence. At length, Max cleared his throat.

'I miss you,' he said simply. 'Miss those days.'

I swallowed. Kept my face free of expression. 'You're idealizing them, Max. Because it was our youth. That's what people do. Because we were young and carefree, we look back fondly. But we can't recapture it.'

'You do, too?'

'Look back? As a rule, no. But I did just then.'

'We were good together, Flora. We never stopped laughing.'

He'd deliberately conjured up a very seductive image: one that was hard to resist and one which, when I was young, when he'd betrayed me, had been the hardest. Max and I would laugh until the tears rolled down our faces. Until our sides hurt and we had to sit down. About anything. Nothing. Someone in the street going so fast they were bent at right angles. Max would suddenly mimic them, going right up beside them as he did it. A shop assistant or waitress with a funny turn of phrase, which we'd employ for the rest of the day, in a Sybil Fawlty voice – 'Ta ever so.' 'Will you be wanting sauce with that?' 'If Madam would kindly desist from smoking.' So many things collectively tickled us, and life was so serious now. It seemed to consist of a series of problems to be solved in rapid succession, popping up like moles the moment the last one had been bashed on the head.

'Nothing's that funny now,' I observed.

'It can be.'

He reached up and brushed the hair from my eyes, something James had done earlier, but this time an electric current shot through me. I steadied myself on the fence, knowing I was full of Cointreau and giddy on warm Provençal air under a starry sky. That this wasn't real life. We stubbed our cigarettes out simultaneously and glanced at each other. Or I did. I was aware Max had been watching me for some time. I was shocked by the intensity of his gaze: by the depth of feeling. Suddenly, all the years rolled back in a snap, as if I'd let go of a roller blind I'd been hanging on to, to keep the darkness in place. The light flooded in and, with it, a myriad of other memories I'd shut out. Bright, sunlit ones, like playing football with his small cousins in Hyde Park, Max in goal, deliberately letting them shoot past him, their shrieks of delight. Driving to the coast in his convertible MG, me hanging on to the surfboard we'd tied above our heads which threatened to disappear at any minute. Running down dunes in our swimming costumes into a freezing North Sea. Lying on our backs in the sand, windmilling our arms to warm up. Sleeping on his roof terrace in South Kensington during a heatwave, being woken by thin clear light and the rattle of milk bottles below. It might have been twenty years ago but, right at this moment, it felt like yesterday. So when he took me in his arms and kissed me, it felt entirely natural. In fact, it felt like the most natural thing in the world.

Chapter Eighteen

At length, we pulled apart, our hearts racing. I say at length, because the kiss was a long one: I'd like to tell you it was brief and hurried, but it wasn't. It was also highly charged and emotional; full of longing on his part and high excitement on mine. Afterwards, we held each other tightly and I could hear his breath roaring in my ear. Then, as one, we stepped back in shock. Gazed at each another. 'Blimey' sprang to mind, but happily not to my lips.

'I've got to go,' I muttered, and he nodded quickly in agreement.

It occurred to me, as I saw the shock in his eyes, that he was as taken aback as I was. This hadn't been premeditated. He hadn't planned this in any way. He'd just meandered down to the pool full of food and booze, as I had, with a cheeky desire to surprise some naked women. He hadn't followed me or engineered it, any more than he'd engineered us dipping out of sight of the teenagers to have a cigarette. It had just happened. But . . . had it been lying in wait all these years? Ready to ambush us? Had it been tucked away in our minds as something to do one day? To finish what was started – and ended so brutally – all those years ago? It seemed to me I'd just melted into his arms and turned my lips up to his without a second thought.

No time to speculate further, though, because as we emerged from the spinney, the house was in sight, lit up in all its glory. My adrenalin was pumping fast as we walked up the sloping lawn and I felt the words 'Adulterous Witch' writ large on my face as we rounded the corner and approached the post-dinner table to sit – rather conspicuously, in retrospect – as far apart as possible. Neither of us got a second glance from the others. They carried on drinking and laughing and playing cards, as if we hadn't been missed at all. Max went to the far end to watch the game and I pulled up a chair beside Jean-Claude, who was talking to Thérèse. It was all too easy, wasn't it? I thought, picking up a stray drink, my hand trembling ever so slightly. An extramarital affair? So simple. No wonder it happened so often. Not that it was ever, *ever* going to happen to me.

James was opposite me, beside Camille, who was talking to Jean-Claude and Thérèse now.

I smiled. 'I'm off to bed,' I told him. There. Quite normal, that two-timing voice of mine.

He smiled back, and something in his eyes told me he remembered our conversation in the bedroom earlier. About us being all right.

'Me, too,' he agreed.

We got up as one, as a happily married couple, and said goodnight rather generally. I didn't look at Max or my daughters. Together we walked through the house to the hall. Up the curling staircase we went, James pausing to collect a paperback he'd left on the landing windowsill. I waited for him as he riffled through the pile. My heart was still pounding and I was terrified he'd hear it. Once in our room, I brushed my teeth, slipped quickly into bed, then turned away and shut my eyes. James was only just behind me. He turned out the bedside light.

'Night, darling,' he said sleepily.

'Night.'

He, too, turned over and was asleep and snoring in moments. I lay there for what seemed like hours, waiting for my heart rate to come down, waiting for my breathing to return to normal. Wondering if I'd ever be the same again. Well, I wouldn't, would I? I'd kissed another man. I'd irrevocably changed, in the space of ten seconds, the nature of our marriage. It would never be the same, I'd seen to that. It's very fabric, intricately woven over many years, had been yanked, and when a loose thread revealed itself, pulled apart. What would happen now? How would this change manifest itself? I was so transparent – everyone said so – would he guess? Would I have to tell him? We told each other everything. Always had done.

The following morning I awoke with a start. Abruptly, as often happens, when something extraordinary has happened. But, strangely, in the soft warm light that streamed through a gap in the shutters, what had felt so momentous and painful and totally wonderful all at the same time a few hours ago suddenly seemed faintly ridiculous. What a fool I'd been. To get pissed like that. And how stupidly I'd behaved. It had been late and dark and all my senses had been skewed with drink, but really. In the excitement of the moment, and in the middle of the night, it had felt far more portentous than of course it was. Just a stolen kiss with an ex-boyfriend in a dark wood. Stupid, Flora. But not the end of the world. Move on. Don't, whatever you do, breathe a word to James – I can't believe you considered that last night – and never, ever, let it happen again. There. Job done.

James stirred beside me. He turned over and hugged me from behind so that we slotted together like spoons. Sleepily, he kissed my shoulder. My eyes bulged slightly at the opposite wall as he kissed me again. I wasn't entirely sure this was what I wanted, but on the other hand . . . maybe it was. To prove that last night had indeed been an aberration. A silly deviation from real life. James pulled me in closer and I acquiesced. Yes, last night had just been a ridiculous episode not to be repeated: to be put down to drink, holiday madness and happenchance.

Ten minutes later James was bounding around the bedroom like a teenager, humming loudly and running me a bath. He was fresh from the shower, stark naked, towelling his shoulders vigorously, his love life a positive riot at the moment.

'This holiday has done us the world of good, darling,' he declared heartily, bending over the bed and planting a kiss squarely on my lips. 'It was clearly just what we needed!'

Clearly, I thought guiltily as I watched his bare bottom retreat back into the bathroom. I wasn't convinced it would necessarily feature in any agony aunt's advice on how to reignite a tired, marital sex life, though. I wasn't sure kissing an ex-boyfriend and letting your husband have his ego massaged by a sexy soprano would necessarily be amongst Graham Norton's Top Tips in the *Sunday Times*.

Speaking of that very same sexy soprano, the sound of her dulcet tones began to filter up through the floorboards. Except they weren't dulcet and the floor wasn't providing much of a filter. They certainly weren't pleasant. She was belting out scales, at full volume and at an increasingly high pitch, whilst accompanying herself on the piano. As they got higher and higher, they became shriller and shriller. Then came the arpeggios. *Screeching* arpeggios. She was certainly very good, but very, *very* loud. I had no idea one person could sing to that volume; it sounded more like a fully blown choir. Would the windows shatter, I wondered? Instead, our door flew open. Tara, tousled and astonished, put her head around.

'What is that *terrible* noise?' she whispered.

'It's Camille practising.'

'Make it stop,' she begged.

'You're lucky to be hearing it at all,' retorted James, appearing from the bathroom with a towel around his waist. 'People pay good money to hear that.' He cocked his head appreciatively as the floorboards rattled.

'*La – la – la – la – LAAAAAA!!!!*'

The whole house shook. And must be awake, too.

'Sounds like she's being stabbed,' Tara said. She shuffled back to bed and I pretended not to hear Rory muttering to her as she closed the door.

On and on it went.

'Bloody *hell*!' I heard Sally shriek from next door, then she dissolved into giggles. I wondered if her sex life had been pepped up, too? As a result of last night? I shut my eyes tight. No, I did *not* want to think about that. Instead, I leaped into the bath James had run me and agreed that no, I didn't think Camille would mind if he went down and slid quietly into the room to listen, keeping to myself the view that he would be in a minority of one. I visualized him, creeping into the drawing room with the grand piano in the window, polishing his glasses and perching on a sofa to listen adoringly. Indeed, when I went down later – the noise too deafening to do anything else – this was the scene I encountered. Except it wasn't Camille playing the piano, as I'd imagined, but Michel.

He scowled slightly at being interrupted, even though Camille hadn't seemed to notice. James frowned and motioned me away, as if he was acceptable at an operatic masterclass, but I wasn't.

So Michel was rather talented, I thought, closing the door quietly, as Camille broke into the aria from *Madame Butterfly*. It was one thing to thump out scales but another to play this. Not just a gardener. At the end, James applauded loudly.

'Bravo! Oh, bravo!'

I cringed for him and, unfortunately, he burst into the kitchen glowing when I still had two fingers down my throat in mock-disgust.

'What are you doing?'

'Got something stuck.'

'Oh. Isn't she marvellous?'

'Marvellous.'

'And guess what, she's been asked to perform that aria on stage tonight, with Bocelli, practising as a preview for her tour. So I'll actually see her in action!'

'Oh that's great, James.' I really was pleased for him. He was having the time of his life. 'So' – I suppressed a smile – 'she'll step up on to that stage, vacating the seat beside you – and everyone will think . . . she's with you!'

'Yes!' He squealed. Then realized. 'I mean – no.' He looked worried.

I laughed. 'Don't worry, darling. It's only one night. Why shouldn't you look as if you're escorting a celebrity? I'd be chuffed to bits if I was, and it was – I don't know, Michael Bublé, or someone.'

He shot me a grateful look, and I knew in his head he was already wondering if she'd kiss his cheek before she got up from the seat beside him, like they did at the Oscars, enjoying his fantasy to the hilt.

The next visitor to the kitchen was not so euphoric. Lizzie swept in, smartly dressed in a navy-blue jacket and skirt, clutching an overnight bag.

'Just as well that dreadful caterwauling woke me up. I'm going to catch the 11.50 from Nice, if I can.'

She dumped her bag and clip-clopped in her heels to the cappuccino machine in the corner.

'Oh really, why?' James looked surprised.

'Hasn't Flora told you?' She glanced around. 'It's the day of reckoning. Maria is summoning the troops.'

James raised his eyebrows at me.

'Lizzie's exaggerating,' I said smoothly. 'Maria's pissed off because she's stuck in the office, so she's trying to wreck everyone else's holiday. You frighten too easily, Lizzie.'

Lizzie arched her eyebrows at this: it was patently untrue. She really didn't, as a rule, and I really did, but right now, our roles seemed to have been reversed. Generally, it would be me getting the first plane back and Lizzie who'd be dragging her feet and telling me not to panic. But not today. Today, as she bustled about behind me, finding her iPad, checking timetables, I sat at the kitchen table sipping my coffee, watching the morning sun cast a shimmering haze over the lawn, heralding a beautiful day and the promise of more heat to come. Today, I was happy to let the real and stressful world wash over me in a liberating manner, as I gave myself up to the delights – which, let's face it, were coming in many unexpected guises – of my much-needed Provencal holiday.

Sally and Max were next down, and we all greeted each other cheerfully, as if a starlit snog had never happened.

'Morning!'

'Morning, all! A lovely one, as ever.'

Max's eyes snagged on mine and then darted away, but you'd have to be very acute to notice, and no one did. Jean-Claude and my mother were next, looking stricken.

'Terrible, *terrible* noise!' Mum whispered, coming in, clutching feebly at the furniture in mock-horror and looking appalled.

I frowned as Camille came in through another door on a cloud of Diorissimo, in tiny white shorts and a strappy top. For an opera singer, she was minutely built and I wondered where the strength and power of that voice came from? All in the spectacular lungs, I imagined.

'My darlings, I hope you don't mind fending for yourselves tonight, I've secured a few more tickets for tonight's performance. Michel and Thérèse are coming with me.'

'Oh, no, not at all!' we all chorused instantly.

'Of course not, you've been so kind,' I said, as she ignored us anyway and swept on out to the terrace, taking the coffee Lizzie had just made for herself, leaving her looking startled.

A cosy camaraderie prevailed in the kitchen: a palpable relief at the thought of being on our own tonight, without any member of the de Bouvoir family.

'We could go out?' suggested Sally quietly over her coffee as she sat down opposite me.

'Or I could cook?' said Jean-Claude, joining us at the table. 'I'd like to.'

'Really? Would you?' I turned to him in delight, always keen to reject the Eating Out option these days. And we were so happy here, weren't we? In our womb-like existence. Our own little world. I wanted no intrusion from the outside world, no reminder of reality, no piercing of my bubble. Indeed, I'd almost forgotten the chateau belonged to Camille at all.

'Of course, I would enjoy to do it.'

'Splendid!' declared the Brig, who'd just appeared. He settled himself down at the table, too. 'I do find restaurants so damned uncomfortable these days. And they nearly always have a battery of steps for me to fall down.'

'I'll shop for you, if you like?' I offered. 'I'd like to do that.'

Jean-Claude smiled. 'Ah, but you are forgetting I won't know what I am cooking until I have gone to the market. Until I have seen the meat and smelled the fish. *Alors*. You make the lunch, *cherie*. Let us do all of the cooking today, so that Michel and Thérèse have the whole day off.'

'Perfect!' I said happily. I liked cooking, too. So did James. Adored it. Maybe we'd do it together? His eyes told me we would.

'That would be really nice, darling,' he said.

So, with Michel kindly taking Lizzie to the airport – she left with regret and promises to be back soon, muttering darkly about there being no way she was spending more than a day placating Maria – James and I, having looked at the map, and James having been assured by Thérèse it was the best place to go today, prepared to set off for yet another exquisite hilltop village, this time that of Mons.

Amelia appeared through the front door just as we were loading up the car. Her eyes were bleary from sleep and she picked her way gingerly in bare feet down the steps and across the gravel drive, but she looked pleased.

'Where are you two off to?'

'Sightseeing and food shopping in Mons.'

'You crazy kids.'

'Want to come?'

'Nah. Have fun, though.'

I smiled, knowing she was pleased to see her parents together and looking happy. As I threw in a couple of straw baskets I'd found in the pantry, I caught a glimpse of Max, who'd moved further down the garden to sit under the walnut tree with a book. He was watching us go from under the brim of his hat. That must never happen again, I thought, as I slammed the boot shut. Never. Nevertheless, a glance in the rear-view mirror as I drove to the end of the drive told me he'd watched the car all the way down, and I felt an unmistakable tingle of excitement. It was a long time since I'd been watched by a man. Aside from traffic wardens, of course.

'We'll probably leave at about four, Camille says,' James was telling me as I turned down the lane, excited at his own plans, oblivious to my world. 'Otherwise, the traffic builds up. We'll have drinks by the sea first, and then supper, which she's booked.'

'Lovely, darling.' I turned from behind the wheel and smiled at his evident pleasure. I always drove on holiday, and James map-read. The other way round, and I felt sick in minutes and we ended up lost and having a flaming row.

'Turn right here,' he told me. 'And I imagine we'll be back quite late, so don't wait up,' he said, casting me a furtive look.

'No. I won't,' I assured him with a smile. 'You know Max is going, too, don't you?' I said, hoping he did. Hoping it wouldn't burst his bubble.

'Yes, in an official capacity,' said James pompously. 'His company is organizing the concert and, since he's here, he thinks he ought to put in an appearance.'

'I can see that.'

'Oh, yes. Me too.'

I was glad he could see it. I, on the other hand, could also see Camille, surrounded by adoring men. I was convinced Michel was not immune to her charms – my own thoughts on that, I heroically kept to myself – and, of course, James was beyond hope and she wanted Max to witness this. As we'd cleared the breakfast table, Sally had told me that Max had felt the pressure to go, but that she hadn't been invited.

'Perhaps there are only a certain number of tickets?' I'd suggested. Rachel, I'd noticed, originally the first to be invited, seemed to have been forgotten. Naturally, she hadn't said a word. 'James says it's sold out.'

'Except you'd think the star of the show would be able to wangle one more, wouldn't you?' she'd said crossly.

Or even the organizer, I'd thought privately, but I didn't say. I couldn't meet Sally's eye as it was.

James and I parked easily halfway up the hill to the village, remarking as we got out how in England we'd have to search high and low for a space. We walked arm in arm up the steep little cobbled street, dodging pots of geraniums and bougainvillea littering front steps, cats sunning themselves and neighbours strapped into pinnies discussing the business of the day. The sun was high in the sky now and, as we climbed, it cast a rich, warm glow on the scattering of red roofs which began to reveal themselves in the depths of the dizzying valley below, in the vast dramatic expanse of the dusty plane peppered with olive groves. As we strolled ever upwards in the sunshine, passing a clutch of old men playing pétanque in the mottled shade of trees, sipping their pastis, it occurred to me that I hadn't been happier in a long while. Before we embarked on the market, we stood for a moment, still arm in arm, on the terrace at the top of the promontory, by a cooling fountain, gazing down at the panoramic view, the abyss freckled with tiny farms nestled amongst groves and vineyards, banking right up at the sides to oak- and pine-forested slopes, then through the valley floor to the sparkling sea beyond.

'I could stay here for ever,' I told James, as we stared, surprising even myself. 'Never go home. I love it.'

He laughed. 'People always say that when they're on holiday.'

'We don't.' I reminded him.

'That's because we always go to Scotland.'

'True. We should do this more often.'

'I know.'

But we both knew we wouldn't. That this was a one-off. A treat to be savoured. Knew, that with crippling bills — shoring up the house before it slid down the hill had hit us badly — and a mortgage, we'd be in Clapham, and periodically Scotland, for the rest of our lives: watching anxiously as James's private practice dwindled and younger men leaped ahead, hoping we could limp on until he retired and drew his ever-decreasing National Health pension, which was, oh, only another fifteen years or so. As if the sobering thought had struck us simultaneously, we turned, as one, away from the seductive view, the other world it presented, and with a certain forced jollity now, strode away to the market to squeeze the melons.

Salad Niçoise, James had decided, with fresh tuna, which he was sure we'd find easily. Also, some delicious plump black olives from a barrel, freshly laid eggs, green beans, tiny new potatoes and tomatoes you could smell at twenty paces – oh, and some asparagus tips, too. This was to be a salad unlike any you could make at home.

The market was well under way and bustling with critical intent, for, unlike the one for tourists the other day that was full of handbags and dresses, this was for serious gastronomes only. Every local French housewife worth her salt was here; the place positively bristled with them. They sniffed and prodded the abundant displays of brightly coloured peppers, vibrant green courgettes and creamy chicory heads which looked, to our eyes, spectacular, often dismissing them and certainly bartering energetically, before they deigned to make a purchase. James and I got into the swing immediately, food shopping and cooking being one of our great shared pleasures. Cheeses being his speciality, he beetled off, nose twitching, to some creamy, blue-veined Roquefort he'd spotted. *Saucisson* and other charcuterie were also on his agenda, whilst the fruit, veg and fish were mine. As I went slowly past a string of stalls, squeezing and smelling, not ignoring misshapen, lumpy tomatoes, knowing looks were not a guarantee of ripeness or flavour, buying a fat bundle of white-and-mauve asparagus here, an irresistible orb of purple aubergine there, I wondered if I'd ever tire of a market like this. Ever stop marvelling, as I entered the fish stalls, at the baskets of scallops heaped on the floor beside the tables, the tiny pale shrimps in buckets, the vast, pale-pink langoustines, bright-red mullet, clams, plump soles, oysters like silver medals in their creamy, corrugated shell beds, soft crabs, boxes of winkles, everything ripe for bouillabaisse, which, personally, I'd have made but I had wanted James to choose the menu. Would I tire? I thought not. This was what I loved about food, what I missed: the instinctive sensory pleasure, not having to rate it out of ten. Eventually, I found what I looking for and seized upon the perfect tuna. Having examined the pink gills and bright eyes, I deemed it unmistakably this morning's catch and ordered a large slice.

Before we left, with our bulging baskets, happy with our purchases, we stopped for a drink, in the square, under the trees. I had a coffee, dark and bitter, and James had a beer. Together, we sipped and watched the world go by: two people content not to speak, just to be. The previous night flashed briefly through my mind but, already, it seemed like a dream. Something that might never have happened. Perhaps it hadn't? Perhaps I'd imagined it all. I manoeuvred my legs into the sun, making sure my face was shaded by the umbrella.

'Have you noticed how much slimmer the people here are?' I said after a while as the crowd flowed by.

'It's the diet. Less McDonald's.'

'And the way of life. The fact that they shop for fresh food every day. That's exercise in itself. No Ocado deliveries here.' I smiled. 'Are we turning into Francophiles, d'you think?'

'You always have been. All those formative years. It's in your blood.'

I sighed contentedly. 'It speaks to me, James, this country. I don't know why. I feel at home here.'

There was the smallest of pauses. 'Then we must come back more,' he said lightly.

I didn't answer. As I drained my *café noir* I narrowed my eyes at the church at the far end of the square, huge and looming, dominating proceedings and refusing to be ignored, as French churches do. I nodded towards it.

'Shall we pop in? Take a look?'

'Why not? Or – tell you what, darling, you go. I'll watch the bags. Don't be long, though, we need to get back and get this fish out of the sun.'

'Oh. OK.' He was right, I supposed. It was a lot to cart around, but it would have been nice to go together.

'I'll get the bill,' he told me as he waved to the *garçon*.

I put my sunglasses on and wandered off, pushing back through the market and pausing only to make an irresistible purchase of tapenade, the gleaming Provençal olive spread, to ladle on to crusty fresh bread and pass around before the salad. After I'd climbed the steep phalanx of steps, worn smooth by generations of pilgrims, and crossed the ancient threshold into the vast, brown chasm, candles flickering at the far end by the altar, the cool, the gloom, the peace and the emptiness enveloped me. I felt, not sadness, as Lizzie always said she did with a shiver, if I was with her, already making for the exit, but tranquillity and calm wash over me. I sat in the nearest pew and said a little prayer. Then I went to the tray of tiny candles. Popping my two euros in the box, I took a taper. As I lit a candle, I shut my eyes. Prayed hard. But not a small duty prayer this time, not a thank you for getting us here safely, a proper Please God one. I prayed for longer than I expected, because I had quite a lot to say. There was a bit about forgiveness, obviously, but then other things. Things I didn't even know were on my mind. Things no one had asked me about in a long time but which I felt a sudden compulsion to share. To divulge.

After a while, I sensed a presence beside me. I opened my eyes and raised my head. It was James, with the bags.

'Thought you weren't coming in?' I said.

'Changed my mind. What did I interrupt?' His eyes were kind. Soft, grey eyes I loved. 'What were you praying so hard for?'

I smiled. Linked my arm through his. We made for the door. 'For us. For the rest of our lives. For some sort of guidance through this crazy, uncertain world in whatever way,' I glanced up and gesticulated, open-palmed, to the heavens, 'that He sees fit.'

Chapter Nineteen

Jean-Claude cooked for France that night. James and I thought we'd acquitted ourselves pretty reasonably at lunchtime, the tuna having been seared to pink perfection and served on a bed of pale-green endive so springy it fairly exploded in the mouth, with soft-boiled eggs, plump anchovies and olives accompanying, but it was nothing to the meal Jean-Claude produced and I wished my husband had been there to witness it.

Escargots were first flamed in cognac then added to sautéed ceps and shallots and served with a cream, mustard and tarragon sauce. Then came a perfectly pink rack of lamb with a fragrant herb crust. It was accompanied by a truffle and Madeira sauce, dauphinoise potatoes, tiny shelled peas and blanched artichokes. All this was followed by a sublime chocolate fondant, surely the ultimate test for any chef. Mum acted as sous-chef, chopping and washing ingredients as he quietly got on with the main event. He issued a few low instructions to her, but he also thanked her every time she put a row of prepared vegetables in front of him, I noticed. I'd been perched at a stool in the kitchen, having my nails painted by Tara. She liked this man, and he liked her, I could tell. Watching them took me back to the days of Philippe: not just the cooking, which they loved to do together, but the way Philippe would look at her when she stopped to stroke a dog in the street or gave money to the beggars who gathered at the foot of the steps to Montmartre. It was the same tenderness Jean-Claude had on his face now as she dithered, on the point of putting the snails in front of him, then dashing back to the sink to give them a second wash. She was happier than I'd seen her in a long while. Not that Mum ever presented anything other than a cheerful façade to the world, that wasn't her style. But as she shimmied around the kitchen in the pretty dress she'd found in Fayence, popping out proudly to announce each course to the assembled family on the terrace, who cheered and clapped each announcement – Mum dropping a low curtsey as if she'd cooked it all herself, then executing a pirouette, arms above her head, to make her granddaughters laugh – I saw a light in her eyes I hadn't seen for years.

There was certainly a less formal atmosphere that night, without Camille, and without being waited on by Michel and Thérèse. Spirits were lighter and more frivolous. I liked it. In fact, I wished we didn't have the de Bouvoir family watching over us all the time. Wished we could have more nights like these – but then, I reasoned guiltily, we wouldn't be here at all if it wasn't for them. It was also something of a relief, I realized, not to have Max here. It gave me a respite from my feelings, anyway. I wondered if he'd disappeared on purpose. Sally had said it was a spur-of-the-moment decision to go to the concert: had he deliberately given us both some space? It would be a kind gesture, and very like him. I sank hastily into my wine.

At the end of the meal we all clapped like mad and raised our glasses to Jean-Claude who, flushed and smiling, appeared from the kitchen, framed in the French windows. He'd barely eaten a thing, so intent had he been on getting each course to the table, hot and perfect. After a self-conscious little bow he finally sat down beside me and gratefully accepted a cognac.

'That was unbelievable, Jean-Claude,' I told him. 'And I mean that from a professional point of view, not just as a grateful and greedy holidaymaker.'

'I told you.' He smiled. 'All Frenchmen can cook.'

'Don't give me that. You're professionally trained.'

He smiled and swirled his cognac around in its glass, avoiding my eye. 'Perhaps,' he admitted at length.

'Where?' I demanded, turning in my chair to face him properly. 'And what's with the bric-a-brac – lovely though it is,' I added quickly.

He laughed. 'Only so very recently you applaud my artistic tastes. Admire my finds in *brocantes*. Now you prefer my culinary skills?'

'You've clearly got taste in spades,' I told him, 'be it antiques or haute cuisine, but even I could source a few bedsteads and lamps. I certainly couldn't cook like that. Come on. Give.'

He sighed. Shrugged. 'I trained with Thierry Dupuis in Paris. I work for ten years under Hugo Monfleur in L'Escale before finally opening my own restaurant just off the Rue Saint-Honoré seven years ago. I gain two Michelin stars in three years.'

My mouth dropped open. 'You're kidding.'

'I'm not.'

'What happened?'

He spread his hands, palms up, in a hopeless gesture. 'I got divorced. The recession bit. I owed people money. I had to sell the restaurant to pay my wife. I opened another, in a less elegant part of the city, in Jardin des Plantes, and it didn't work.' He shrugged expressively. 'These things happen. It's happening all the time, all over Paris. London, too. You open, you close. Oh, and did I mention that the maître d' had his fingers in the till? And, because I was so busy in the kitchen, I didn't notice until it was too late? Until we closed, in a blaze of bad publicity, orchestrated by my ex-wife, who works for *Paris Match*, and who saw to it that the magazine covered my fall from grace?'

I stared as he gazed, narrow-eyed, into the distance. Hurt eyes. Right. A glimpse of this man had been apparent these past few days, but I'd had no idea. I'd noticed him tasting dishes with critical relish, thoughtful as he savoured a mouthful of soup; it was something I recognized. And I'd seen him assiduously picking over *moules* in the kitchen, considering himself unobserved, but now I got the complete picture. And to have had a restaurant in such a prestigious part of Paris. I wondered if I'd heard of it.

'La Terrasse,' he told me when I asked.

I had. One of the premier establishments on the Right Bank, very much in the vanguard of a new wave of French cooking: I had no idea it had closed.

'But it is a mistake to cook and also to own and manage. I couldn't do it. Couldn't trust anyone, but couldn't do it all on my own.'

'You do need a good manager,' I agreed.

'*Exactement.* But everyone is in it for themselves these days, siphoning off what they can. You have no idea.'

I looked at his tired, much-travelled, handsome face as he massaged his brow with his fingertips. I visualized him years ago, as a young man, in the heart of Paris. A chic, cultured, good-looking man. Walking in the Tuileries Gardens perhaps, with a glamorous wife in a Chanel coat, two small children in private-school uniforms. I knew he had two boys, grown up now. A little dog maybe: the ultimate Parisian family. Living the dream. Then the fall from grace.

'Oh, I know shit happens, Jean-Claude. I'm in the same business, remember? I see restaurants open and close all the time, sometimes by dint of my pen. So then what? After the divorce. Your wife kept the house?'

'She did. In the Marais. Her father was a divorce lawyer, which helped, and anyway, I just wanted to get away. I left her nearly everything. I'd had an affair, after all, so of course I felt guilty. And when the second restaurant closed, I felt such a failure. Very . . . how you say – humi—?'

'Humiliated.'

'Exactly. So I came down to the south. Decided to move right away from Paris. I wanted to get away from food. Find a different life.'

'But you miss it?'

'I didn't, for two whole years. It was a relief. But, you know, when you create for a living, and then you stop, at first you relish the peace, but then, you itch. Your fingers, you know?' He waggled them ruefully. 'Because it's not a job. It's not an occupation. It's in the blood. Like breathing. For me, cooking is like breathing. So you see, the oxygen, it is gone. And cooking for you tonight . . . ah, *mon dieu*!'

I saw something in his eyes which only came from talking about something – or someone – you adored.

'Would you ever go back to being a chef? Now?'

'In Paris, *non*. I'm done with that city. For ever. But down here, in the south . . .' He shrugged expressively, his head disappearing into his shoulders. 'Who knows? I think it is unlikely, because I don't want to work for anyone else, and to open again on my own – with what?' He spread his hands in an eloquent, empty gesture. 'Buttons, as you say in England? Everything boils down to money, *ma cherie*.'

'I know.' I did. I sighed. 'And what happens when Mum goes back? To England.'

My mother came to sit beside us, glowing with pride for her man. He took her hand.

'I hope she won't go too quickly. I've asked her to stay on for a bit with me, in Valence. Have a bit of a holiday. Maybe help with the shop.'

'Oh. Right.' Controlling as I could be about my children, I could hardly tell my sixty-something mother it was out of the question. And how happy she looked.

'You didn't come through Digne, did you, darling?' Mum lit a cigarette, beaming. 'James said you took the autoroute, but it is complete heaven. A charming, bustling little town with a terrific café society – a bit like Aix, but much smaller. Not nearly so crowded. I thought I could go off to the markets while JC is manning the shop and look at things he doesn't do yet, maybe branch out into linens, antique tablecloths. A bit of lace, that sort of thing.'

Jean-Claude squeezed her hand fondly, but he made a face. 'Except the rest of the south of France has already branched out that way. But we will see.'

'Or maybe dried herbs? In bags? No reason why it has to be exclusively antiques?' she suggested.

Jean-Claude and I roared. 'Herbes de Provence, Mum?

Yes, that's novel. What, in little sacks? I'm sure no one else has thought of that.'

She pouted good-naturedly. 'You tease me, but you wait. I'll think of something. Something to give him an edge.'

I envied them for a moment: their adventure, their happiness. Knew it could end in tears, this holiday romance of Mum's, as all her affairs did, but there was something different about this man. For a start, he was no longer married. A first, for my mother.

The evening slipped on. The children, entirely of their own accord, washed up, and then sauntered off for a swim. Mum and Jean-Claude had an early night and I sat with my in-laws, playing bridge, something I hadn't done for years. It took me back to the days when I first went to Scotland, when James took me home. We'd been going out for some time – might even have been engaged – and I'd been dying to meet his family. He'd cautiously described his sisters on the long drive up, explaining why they hadn't made the move to London, or Edinburgh, or indeed any town at all, as most young people did, why they were so resolutely at home with their father, trying not to make them sound odd. I'd been intrigued. We'd played bridge after supper that first night, and I'd weighed them up. Rachel, I could just about understand: quiet, but with an inner strength, which James told me stemmed from her religious beliefs. But she also seemed to have a strange and misplaced sense of duty, which certainly Drummond didn't expect or encourage. It was as if she, as the elder, less attractive sister, was happy to have an excuse in her widowed father to stay where she was, for ever. Sally, I could never fathom. Already a size sixteen, in dresses that looked like tents, she seemed to grow daily, with every huge meal she cooked and ate furiously. I'd never seen anyone shovel food in so fast; it was as if it were a daily challenge. There was a terrible moment on the last day of our visit when she couldn't get out of a dining-room chair, a carver with arms. We'd had to help her. But I'd always known there was a very attractive woman in there. It was as if Sally were determined she would never emerge. And yes, she was silly and unpredictable – hysterical, sometimes – but she could be bubbly and charismatic, too. Why would she stray no further than the surrounding glens? Never work further than Perth? I'd asked James on the way home. Surely she could come and stay with us? Perfect her culinary skills at one of the London colleges? She was still young; it was never too late.

He'd laughed hollowly. No, no, Sally was better off where she was. And anyway, that would leave Rachel on her own. Sally was fine. And she'd certainly seemed it as she'd clucked excitedly around me on that first visit, thrilled to have a visitor, a potential sister-in-law, showing me every inch of the huge, dreary house, the sterile, windswept garden, where nothing grew except a few hardy shrubs; she was proud of everything. But I'd sensed an underlying nervousness, too. And she'd seemed almost to have to steel herself to go into Kincardine, the tiny town twenty minutes away – twenty minutes to the nearest pint of milk. Now, though, as she laid down the dummy hand opposite me on the bridge table, pretty stacking rings glittering on her tanned fingers, the metamorphosis wasn't just amazing, it was extraordinary. Yes, she was still excitable and watched over carefully, I realized, by Rachel, who had always kept an eye on her, interrupting her sometimes when she was getting out of control, when her voice rose too shrilly, smoothing over conversational faux pas – but there hadn't been many of those this holiday. She'd been much calmer. Better company. What had happened to spark the transition? To make her slim down, leave Scotland, have her first proper boyfriend? Something must have, I was convinced. I watched the sisters as I played cards with them, both so impenetrable and guarded in their own ways.

After another hand, Drummond yawned, and I used it as my cue.

'Yes, I'm tired, too. In fact, I'm ready for bed,' I said, stretching. 'Sorry, everyone, to break up the game.'

'Don't be silly, my dear, I'm ready, too. I'm thrilled you played a couple of hands. Just like old times, eh?' He patted my shoulder. 'I'm off. *Bonne nuit*, everyone.'

Drummond got unsteadily to his feet and both his daughters went to help him, holding his elbows. Rachel reached for his stick, which was propped against the table. She was making to move off with him and take him upstairs, when I said, 'Um, Rachel, you wouldn't give me a hand laying the breakfast table, would you? Only Thérèse and Michel usually do it, and I thought maybe we should . . .'

'Of course!' Rachel, ever solicitous, was shocked she hadn't thought of it herself. She flushed a bit as Sally took over Drummond. I wished I'd had the presence of mind to think of something else, something that wouldn't have made her uncomfortable.

'I'll take Daddy,' Sally assured her, already making steady headway towards the house with her father. 'I've been looking forward to an early night, since Max is out. Toodle-oo!'

'Night!' we both called, as Rachel began busying herself, clearing the debris of ashtrays and glasses from the table. I stayed her hand.

'Rachel, that's not why I asked you to stay. It was all I could think of.'

'Oh?' She paused. Looked down at me enquiringly.

'Sit down a second.'

She sat. Blinked. Looked nervous. 'What is it?'

'I'm just so intrigued. By Sally. Last time I saw her, at Christmas, she was enormous. Played clock patience constantly by the fire, ate tin after tin of Quality Street, barely left the house except to collect the groceries, got terribly upset when she thought someone had taken her favourite cushion from her bed – cried, even, remember?'

'Yes,' Rachel admitted, as we both recalled her running into the drawing room, shaking with sobs, accusing everyone until it was finally found, not on the bed, but under it. She was like a child.

'And now here she is,' I went on, 'slim as a blade, looking gorgeous, a handsome man in tow, off to visit friends in St Tropez – what's happened?'

She laughed. 'Yes, it's amazing, isn't it? Such a turn-around.'

'But what precipitated it, Rachel? Something must have done.'

She shrugged. 'The weight loss, I suppose. If you lose five stone, it's bound to make a big difference.'

'But what galvanized her to do it? To lose it in the first place?'

'No idea. She just did.'

I felt she was being evasive but couldn't be sure.

'What, she just woke up one morning and thought, I know, I won't have four Weetabix for breakfast, I'll go for a run?'

'I suppose . . .'

'It was January, wasn't it?'

Rachel blinked rapidly. Looked beyond me. 'Yes. January. The fifteenth. Just after Donaldson's funeral.'

'Donaldson?'

Her eyes came back. She gave me a peculiar look. 'You remember, Flora.'

'Yes, of course I remember Donaldson.'

He'd been Drummond's right-hand man. His batman, almost. Orderly, I believe it's called in the army. The man he'd brought out of prison with him. The man he'd been close to and had given a cottage on the estate in return for manual labour. Drummond had adored him. They'd shared a cell, and Donaldson, a seasoned convict, a reoffending prisoner, had helped him through some very dark times. They'd been released within six months of one another, and Donaldson had arrived at Brechallis almost immediately. He was a reformed character who spent all his time mending fences, tending the sheep, which he'd learned to do, turning them upside down and clipping toenails, dagging and shearing them, clearing streams. But I'd always been a little scared of this tough, heavily tattooed, inscrutable man. He'd keeled over in a ditch, just after Christmas, trying to release a ewe from some brambles. Heart attack, apparently. Drummond had been terribly upset. He wasn't that old, either; must only have been in his late fifties. James went to the funeral, I remember, but I didn't. But why should his death be the catalyst for Sally to lose weight? I opened my mouth to voice this.

'Coincidence, I'm sure,' Rachel said quickly. She got to her feet. 'I've no idea why I even mentioned it.' She brushed some imaginary crumbs from her lap, not looking at me. 'Sally just got to a stage when she couldn't look at herself in the mirror any longer, that was all.'

'She hadn't been able to do that for a long time,' I said slowly.

It was one of the things I knew about Sally. She avoided mirrors. There were none at Brechallis, except in Drummond's and Rachel's bedrooms. I'd had to put one in the guest bathroom. We all knew Sally didn't like seeing what she'd become; it was common knowledge, even if no one ever mentioned it.

Rachel swallowed. 'Yes. Well. I think it just all came to a head. Anyway, I'll go and get the place mats for breakfast and then I think I'll turn in, Flora. Goodnight.'

She turned and went quickly inside, the conversation over, a curtain firmly drawn. And there was absolutely no chance of reopening it, of that I was sure.

Chapter Twenty

The following morning I awoke late, as seemed to be my wont these days. I'd heard James returning in the early hours, full of the joys, slightly pissed and making just a bit too much jolly noise as he said goodnight in loud stage whispers to his opera comrades on the landing. Faux tip-toeing around the bedroom, he'd banged into furniture and shed his clothes before falling into a noisy, snoring slumber beside me, no doubt dreaming of being on stage in tights and a codpiece, singing his heart out to his leading lady. I, meanwhile, despite the earplugs, couldn't go back to sleep. I tossed and turned, finally waking – I peered at the clock – at a quarter to ten. Annoying. A waste of another day. On the other hand, what was the rush? What, apart from the sun, which even now was streaming in through the shutters James had left ajar, did I have to get up for?

I sat up, stretched languidly and reached for my iPad. I tried not to read emails on holiday, but a glance at the recent additions told me there was one I really should open. I grudgingly complied.

Dear Flora,

Since you didn't feel inclined to attend the crisis meeting I called, and since, as you know, I have to lose at least three members of the

*team in order to ensure the magazine remains viable, I am afraid
I have no alternative but to make you redundant. It goes without
saying that your hard work and loyalty to* Haute Cuisine *over the
years has been exemplary, as has your commitment. I had hoped
not to end our working relationship by email, but I'm afraid you
left me no choice.*

    *I do hope we can remain friends and wish you all luck for the
future.*

Best wishes,
Maria

I stared, shocked. In fact, I had a bit of an out-of-body
experience. Almost felt as if I were floating up on the ceiling, looking down at myself. I wasn't sure I'd had such a
jolt before. Oh yes, of course. In the pub. In Chelsea. With
Coco. Now, though, despite the world wobbling briefly
and me observing it from on high, it righted itself soon
enough. I floated back down. Because part of me had
known. A small part of me had thought, Don't go back
with Lizzie. Then Maria will have to make you redundant.
Just a small part. One I hadn't even properly admitted to
myself, let alone to James. And a mighty big part of me
realized now that I was relieved. It was sad to hate a job I'd
loved so much, but I did, and I'd wanted someone else to
make the decision for me. To push me. My lip curled,
though, when I reread the email. Crisis meeting? What crisis meeting? She hadn't originally couched it in those terms.
And when had she previously mentioned making anyone
redundant? Never. And if she'd hoped to have the conversation in person, well, then, she'd already decided my fate,

hadn't she? I'd have returned to be informed by Maria, in that little-girl voice of hers, as she peered over the spectacles she wore for effect – we'd all sneakily tried them on – from the other side of her vast, glass-topped desk, and looking down her nose, so tiny after so much surgery it was a wonder she could still breathe through it, that there was no way she was responsible for this decision. That the powers that be – Didier in particular, from the parent magazine in Paris – was forcing her hand and she wished it could be otherwise. Then she'd flick back a sheet of expensively highlighted blonde hair, cross her minuscule knees in her tan leather Christian Lacroix skirt and wait for my reaction.

I thought for a moment, heart pounding, bolt upright in my Primark nightie. Then I reached over the empty expanse of bed for James's phone, which was on his bedside table. Reading the number from mine, I rang Maria's mobile. She answered immediately in her breathy whisper.

'Hello?'

'Maria, it's Flora.'

Shocked silence. Had she known it was me, she wouldn't have picked up, but I knew she wouldn't recognize James's number.

'Oh, um, Flora,' she faltered. 'I'm so sorry.'

'Don't worry, it's not your fault. As you say, it's out of your hands. Can you tell me what the redundancy settlement is?'

'Of *course* I can, darling. Hang on.' I heard her mobile clatter down on the glass desk as she riffled nervously through some papers. She returned a few moments later and mentioned a sum of money so large it made me blink.

'Right. A year's salary, then.'

'I'd have liked it to have been more – you've worked for us for nearly eighteen years – but it was the best I could do, Flora.'

'It's fine, Maria. More than I expected. Thank you.'

I doubt if anyone had ever thanked her for firing them. She became expansive in her relief.

'Well, I told them there was no fucking way I was letting you go without a fight, and without a decent package. In fact, I was in the boardroom for two hours on your behalf, giving them what for.'

'And you'll give me good references? Explain the economic imperative for letting me go?' I asked briskly, cutting through the crap.

'Of *course*, darling, glowing references. I suspect you'll get a job on a rival magazine in moments, *and* pocket a year's salary.'

'We'll see,' I said shortly. 'Anyway, I must go.'

'And we'll meet up?' she said urgently. 'We've been friends for years, Flora. No hard feelings?'

'None at all,' I told her, before saying goodbye.

We'd been colleagues for years, not friends. Maria was far too brittle and self-absorbed for me: I doubted I'd ever see her again. But my own phone was ringing now and I lunged to answer it, recognizing the number.

'Lizzie.'

'Oh, Flora, I'm so sorry!' she wailed. 'I feel such a heel!'

'You kept yours?'

'Yes, but only just. I had to creep and crawl around her office for hours, until I thought I was going to be sick all

272

over her carpet, all over her Manolo Blahniks. I just feel so bad for you.'

'Don't,' I told her. 'I half expected it. Half . . .' I paused. 'Wanted it?'

'If I'm honest,' I admitted. I swallowed. 'I'm tired, Lizzie. Tired of doing the same old thing, hammering out copy about another bloody artichoke or another steak tartare and pleasing everyone except myself. I want to go. It's time.'

She was silent on the other end. 'Have you told James?'

'Not yet. Only just heard. Might go and do that now. Are you coming back?'

'You're joking! I'm doing all your bloody restaurants now. Forget the editorial column, I've got breakfast at The Connaught, followed by lunch at Le Caprice and dinner at La Rochelle – they've sacked Henry, too. I'm eating for three!'

I smiled. 'You'll be the size of a house.'

'Don't. I've already googled bulimia. We're all going to miss you so much, Flora. Everyone's devastated.'

This did threaten to choke me. The band of brothers in the little office on Charlotte Street, up those rickety stairs, crammed into our cave, whispering about Maria as she sat in splendid isolation in the room above, united in our common dislike of her. Years ago, we'd all bashed away at word processors, the air full of cigarette smoke and expletives as we mistyped, ashtrays overflowing. No cigarettes now, of course, and only laptops and iPads, so much quieter, but always laughter: me, Henry, Lizzie, Colin, Fatima, Sue, Blodders, Pat, Toenail – I'd miss them all. Miss the banter. The camaraderie. But let's not get too carried away. Let's not oversentimentalize. These days, a lot of copy was written at home; journalism had become a lonely business. Still, I put the phone down feeling sad and nostalgic, and promising I'd ring Lizzie for a proper chat later and, yes, come in and have lunch with them all. At Bellingdon's, our favourite haunt on Charlotte Street, which she'd organize. For Henry, too. Poor Henry. His partner, Graham, had recently been made redundant as well. Then I got out of bed to have a pummelling, invigorating shower and threw on some clothes.

I found James in the drawing room with Camille. I'd followed the music. The hills were alive. There he was, like a dutiful gnome, but taller, on the edge of his chair. This time, she was at the piano, swaying slightly and singing softly as she played.

'Oh – darling.' He got up as I came in, just a bit too quickly. Gave me a hug. Unusual.

'Did you have a good evening?' I asked.

'The best,' he told me warmly as Camille continued to play, not deigning to stop and greet me, I noticed, or even turn and smile.

James put a finger theatrically to his lips, and we crept out. He led me through the open French windows to the garden, where a few people were still having breakfast. He shut the glazed doors quietly behind us.

'It was an amazing evening,' he told me, glowing. 'Gosh, she's got an incredible voice, Flora. It's not until you actually hear her sing, in the flesh, that you realize how extraordinarily gifted she is. Ask Max.'

He and Sally were at the breakfast table in the garden in the sun. I turned.

'Oh, she's quite something,' Max agreed, glancing up from his iPad. 'It's a phenomenal feat to project a voice across three or four thousand people, plus an orchestra of about seventy-odd instruments, with absolutely no amplification at all. One forgets.' There was genuine respect in his voice, and I wondered if Camille had wanted this: for Max to see her at her very best. We didn't meet each other's eyes.

'The whole place erupted when it was announced she was going to make a guest appearance,' went on my husband, eyes gleaming, extraordinarily star-struck. 'No one knew, you see, and you should have heard the roar when she got up to take to the stage – they went berserk! I've never heard such applause! First, she did the duet from *The Magic Flute* with José Carreras – he was also making a guest appearance – and then she sang an aria from *Carmen*. And my God, when she'd finished, you could have cut the air with a knife. Could literally have heard a feather drop. We sat in complete silence. I'm not ashamed to say I cried I was so moved, and even Max here looked a bit moist as we clapped away. We all got to our feet – the whole place was on its feet, wasn't it, Max? – cheering and stamping for ages. Extraordinary!'

'It must have been.'

'And they *implored* her to do another one, wouldn't let her go back to her seat. So she sang "*Un bel dì*" from *Madame Butterfly* – you know?'

'No.'

James and I never went to the opera. I didn't think he liked it. Plus, we couldn't afford it.

'Yes, you *do*.'

'I don't, James. Why would I?'

'It's always on the radio.' He put his hand to his heart. Stood up straight. *'Un bel dì, vedremo, levarsi un fil di fumo, sull'estremo confin del mare,'* he warbled loudly, and only half ironically. James can't sing. At all. He's tone deaf. I felt my eyes widen. Max looked away. *'E poi la nave appare –'*

'Da-ad!' Amelia, at the far end of the table, let her mouth drop theatrically. 'God, stop him, Mum. It's embarrassing!'

Tara was pink, too, but their father was in the grip of an infatuation. He simply laughed at his daughters' distress.

'You girls should get out more,' he joked, gaily plucking a croissant from the basket. He tossed it in the air, bouncing it on his arm like a cricket ball before catching it and munching away heartily. His eyes shone. 'Get some culture.'

The girls made weary eyes at him, and I sneaked a look at Max. James was not normally so foolish and susceptible, and Camille was a very beautiful and talented woman. Max surely couldn't be totally immune to her charms if my husband was so bowled over. As if on cue, Camille appeared through the French windows in a crumpled little white dress. If anything, she looked slightly tired and vulnerable, always a winning combination with men. James gazed at her as if he could eat her up and even Max gave her a longer look than he would normally. He glanced quickly away, but I wondered if her magic was finally working.

'Pool, d'you think, darling?' asked Sally, perhaps wondering, too. 'Another hideous day in paradise?'

'Why not?' Max agreed, getting to his feet and gathering his iPad and book. It was Camille's turn to watch him go. Plan her next move.

Agathe, the ghost child, appeared out of nowhere beside her. She tugged her mother's arm. As Camille bent down, she whispered in her ear, cupping her hands around her mouth, something I'd always told my children was incredibly rude.

Camille nodded grudgingly and allowed herself to be led away. Agathe cast us a glittering, menacing look from her dark eyes as she tugged her mother towards her sister's cottage.

'Pool for you, too, darling?' asked James, gathering up his own book. *A History of the Royal Opera House.* Dear God.

'In a mo. Or I might drive into town. Actually, James, have you got a sec?'

'Sure.' He looked surprised, catching something in my voice.

He made to go back into the house with me, but, knowing the acoustics of our bedroom, I turned and walked the other way, off down the sloping lawn towards the olive grove, chewing my thumb. James caught up with me, and I was aware of Amelia's eyes following us. When we'd gone through the little gate at the bottom, into the longer grass of the orchard, I turned.

'I've lost my job, darling. Maria's made me redundant.'

'Shit.' He stopped. Looked aghast. We stared at one another under the dappled shade of an olive tree.

'But I've got a year's money.'

His face cleared a bit. 'Well, that's something, I suppose. You'll find another job within a year. But what a shaker, Flora. Right out of the blue. Are you OK?'

'I'm fine, actually. And it wasn't so out of the blue. I half expected it.'

'Oh? You didn't say?' He frowned; looked searchingly at me.

'Well, only half,' I said quickly. 'And I didn't want to worry you.' If pressed, I could feel rather guilty about wilfully reducing the family fortunes, not going back to fight my corner. 'And the thing is, James' – I felt my way carefully – 'I may not get a job in the same field.'

'We can't afford for you not to work, Flora.'

'I know. It's just, I don't know if I want to do the same thing.'

He raked a hand nervously through what remained of his hair. 'Well, I'm not sure *I* want to do the same thing, removing bloody bunions day after day, hoiking out ingrowing toenails. But there is something of an economic necessity. A bit of a bloody mortgage to pay, and –'

'Not much.'

'What?'

'Not much of a mortgage left.'

'No, but still. We can't afford for you to do frigging Pilates classes or wine-tasting courses. Flog cashmere gloves at Christmas fairs like some of your friends.'

The wives of rich bankers, he meant. I knew that. And I didn't want to either. Knew I'd tire of that sort of life in seconds.

'No, but the thing is, James, there are other ways. Other . . . hang on.'

Tara and Amelia had made their way down the lawn and were even now picking their way through the field of sharp grass in their bare feet, towards us. We waited.

'What's happened?' asked Tara, before they'd even reached

us. They looked alarmed. Clearly, they'd been watching us from the breakfast table.

I swallowed. 'I've lost my job, darlings.'

'Shit.'

Why did all my family say that?

'Told you,' muttered Amelia.

Tara put her arms around me, hugging me tight. 'Oh, Mum, you must be devastated!'

'Not too devastated, if I'm honest. And don't worry, they've given me lots of money.'

'Oh, well, that's a relief.' She let go. It obviously was.

'How much?' asked Amelia.

'Never you mind,' said James. 'Your mother's being very brave about it, but it's clearly been a terrible shock.'

'Did Lizzie keep hers?'

'She did.'

'But you'd been there longer?'

'Not much. And, anyway, I'm pleased for Lizzie. She needs it more than me. She's on her own.'

'And your mother will get another job in no time.'

'Of course you will,' agreed Amelia. 'Didn't that chap at *Gourmet* headhunt you only last year?'

'Of course!' James struck his forehead with the palm of his hand. 'Well remembered, Amelia. Give him a ring, darling.'

'Well –'

'Or Malcolm Harding? At the *Sunday Times*? He was always bothering you, always wanting you.'

'I just might give it a bit, James.'

'Oh yes, a couple of days.'

'She's in shock,' Amelia told him sternly. 'You're rushing her, Dad. This is huge.'

I felt bad that it wasn't that huge. But then I'd always told my girls a career was so important. The cornerstone of their life. Marriage and babies slotted in. Why? When I'd never really believed it? Marriage and babies were far more important.

'Come on.' My elder-statesman daughter took my arm. 'I'm going to make you some tea. With lots of sugar in it.'

I allowed myself to be led away to be fussed over, feeling a bit of a fraud, if I'm honest. But it was a rare experience in my household, and one I was unwilling to pass up.

Word spread fast. One by one, people came up to commiserate and squeeze my shoulder as if I'd suffered a bereavement. I wondered if this was how people felt when someone they loathed had died and, inside, they were quietly rejoicing. Guilty. But, on the other hand, why should I dissemble?

'I hated it,' I told Max defiantly, when he came to find me. 'I was longing to go. This is a blessed relief.'

Mum was with him. She understood immediately. 'You'd done it too bloody long,' she told me, lighting a cigarette and handing it to me. I dragged hard. 'Everything has a shelf life.'

'Exactly,' I said gratefully. My mother had skipped from one passion to the next all her life and was the happiest person I knew.

'And work is so overrated,' she told me firmly, rather undoing the wisdom.

Camille, after all of half an hour with her own family,

was back amongst us on the terrace. She approached my chair as if I were in A&E, took my hand and pressed it between her two, bird-like ones. 'Your heart is breaking quietly, I know,' she said softly, crouching down. 'It is your life. Your career. You've given your best years. And for women, because we battle so hard, because we smash through the glass ceiling, it is so much harder to bear. Rejection. It cuts us, here.' She pressed my hand to her heart, which was beyond embarrassing. Her breasts were enormous.

I cleared my throat. Extricated my hand with an awkward wiggle. 'No, actually, Camille, you're wrong. It was time for a change.'

'Quite right. The show must go on.' She gave a brave smile and leaned forward to kiss my cheek. 'Such courage,' she whispered, before fluttering away, all male eyes upon her.

That evening, however, I'll admit, I hit the bottle. Despite my relief that the decision had been taken out of my hands and that I'd been generously compensated, there was a need to drink and reflect on how I'd spent most of my adult life: in restaurants, getting to know lovely patrons like Fellino, forging relationships that spanned years. With friends like Lizzie and Colin, meeting deadlines – just – scribbling copy, in editorial meetings. It was goodbye to all that and hello to a different way of life.

Unbeknownst to the rest of my family, I knew this for sure. Felt something click firmly into position within me. I knew I had to be strong, though, to follow through. To really mean it, and deliver. I'd talk to Jean-Claude later. Not tonight. Tonight I just wanted to reminisce and tell my stories. About the time I'd found a wedding ring in my soup, or the waiter who'd flambéed not only the crêpe Suzette but his wig, too. We'd had to stamp it out. The time Lizzie and I had got so disastrously pissed she'd thrown a bread roll at the disapproving couple on the next table and we'd been evicted. Less amusing stories, too, like the time the IRA had planted a bomb in Hyde Park when I'd been at the Berkeley. The horrific scene that had met my eyes as I ran out at the blast. Those enormous brave horses on their sides, the terrible carnage, the young soldiers. Or the time a man had sighed deeply at the table beside me, clutched his heart, fallen from his chair and promptly died. Or when a young man had run into Boulestin, interrupted a couple at the next table and presented a ring to the girl. She'd got to her feet and run off with him. My job, played out as it was in public places, had a certain theatrical element to it; a certain – curtain up – which made it unpredictable. It was live. It was a performance. As was the food. And sometimes it was unbelievably amazing, and sometimes – rarely, thankfully – memorably bad, to the point where I'd have to spit it out. Always, though, I was the revered guest, the star attraction. The red carpet would be rolled out as I was ushered to my table by the maître d', his poker face giving nothing away. Time for someone else to have that thrill, I thought, raising my glass of Sancerre to my lips. Time for some younger – cheaper – reviewer, to be giggly and incredulous, as James and I had been in the beginning at this free lunch for life. Time to move on.

In the moonlight, sitting as I was at the head of the table, I watched as an owl soared up into the dark velvet sky, hooting softly, circling the trees. As it landed on the branch of an oak, it seemed to be in pursuit of something. A mouse? A mate? I was more than a little pissed, but as the owl took off again it suddenly seemed imperative to see if he'd achieved his quarry. Toby and Rory were talking across me now, not rudely, just animatedly, about cycling in London, which Rory did and Toby didn't; a conversation in which I'd previously been participating, adding my two pennyworth. They could manage without me. I stood up – slightly unsteadily, it has to be said. Without disturbing them, I moved quietly down the garden towards the olive grove for a ciggie with the wise old owl: a lean against an ancient, gnarled tree, which had seen a few of life's sea changes. For some time alone, to think.

As I tiptoed down the slope, not wanting to disturb the table, I stopped, abruptly. Snagged on a sound. Muffled voices were coming from my right. I turned, and in the faint half-light of the moon saw two figures, locked in an embrace, in the little gazebo where the barbecue was. At first I thought it was Thérèse and Michel. Then I realized, with a sickening thud of my heart, that it wasn't them at all. It was James and Camille. My husband was kissing Camille with all his might. His eyes were shut, his arms wrapped tightly around her as he towered over her, clasping her to him, giving the embrace every ounce, every fibre of his being.

Chapter Twenty-One

Perhaps if I hadn't been so inebriated I might not have charged in quite so precipitously. Might have given it some calm and measured thought; taken a moment to consider and reflect. Instead, I resorted to immediate intervention and robust rhetoric.

'*What the fuck are you doing!*' I roared. Very loudly.

The whole world stopped. My world, my daughters' world – if I'd thought about it – my mother's, James's. I couldn't have been more destructive if I'd tried.

James and Camille sprang apart like repelling magnets. Camille disappeared out and around the side of the gazebo, melting into the darkness – with a degree of practice, I felt – like a spirit of the night. James stood there, rooted, dumb and horrified, caught in the headlamps that were my eyes and in the elaborate wooden structure – more Gothic temple than garden shed – like a fly in a web. I marched towards him, incensed. He backed away, into the barbecue: tripped over a gigantic set of tongs lying on the floor and fell over backwards with a terrific clatter. As I stood over him, fists clenched, speechless, both daughters rushed up.

'What's happened!' cried Amelia breathlessly. 'Why were you yelling? Oh God – Daddy! Are you OK?' She and Tara lunged to help him. With great presence of mind, I swam to the surface.

'Your father's drunk,' I managed. 'I found him flailing around in here.'

'Well, help him!' retorted Amelia, gently helping her shaken father to his feet. Tara found his glasses. 'Bloody hell, we've all been in that state, including you! You're not such a model of sobriety yourself tonight, Mum. I thought something terrible had happened!'

It had.

'You frightened us,' Tara told me angrily, rounding on me. 'Dad blundering around plastered hardly warrants you yelling like that.'

'Poor Daddy, did you hit your head?' asked Amelia gently.

'Yes,' he bleated.

'Bastard!' I couldn't resist roaring.

Amelia swung around. 'Mum, you have seriously got to stop thinking that the world revolves around you. If Dad decides to get drunk on his holiday, so bloody what. Get a grip, live your own life and *leave him alone*! Come on, Daddy, let's go and find you a chair. Black coffee for you.'

James, blinking in terror in the moonlight and sheltering cravenly behind his daughters' misapprehension, willingly allowed himself to be led away up the garden path to the top of the sloping lawn. As they reached the table under the trees, Amelia turned and cast me a last black look. A space was made for her father to sit down, the boyfriends muttering incredulously at my over-the-top reaction. Sensible James. Safety in numbers, of course. Even at this remove, though, I could feel Max's eyes upon me from the opposite side of the table. I wondered if he knew what had happened. But how could he? From that angle, it would be impossible to see around the corner into the dark gazebo. I just felt that Max had extrasensory perception, somehow: that he was extraordinarily tuned into me and knew I wouldn't scream if my husband were merely drunk. Mum, too, gave me a searching look as I approached. Bidding everyone a shaky goodnight, I went up to my room, trembling, I noticed, to wait for James.

The length of time he took to reach our room was important, I knew. If he was ages, hoping to sneak in when I was asleep, or had calmed down, it was bad news. If he practically followed me up, it was better. Almost as I'd shut the bedroom door and went to sit on the bed, clenching my hands tight, the door flew open. James appeared, white-faced.

'Oh God, Flora, I'm so sorry,' he breathed, shutting the door and crossing the room quickly. 'I don't know what came over me.'

'You fucking bastard!' I spat between clenched teeth. Real spittle, I noticed, shot out.

'Yes.' He looked shattered. Really devastated. 'Yes, I am. I know that. And you have every right to say it. I am so, so sorry, Flora. I regret it with all my heart. I wish to God it hadn't happened.' Bravely, he crept to sit beside me on the bed.

'And what else has happened, eh? What else, James? How many stolen kisses in the moonlight? Or worse!'

'None!' he yelped, leaping off the bed beside me. 'None, ever! That was the first – and last – and absolutely nothing more than that. Nothing worse, I promise!'

I could read James like a book. Knew he was telling the truth. He was incapable of lying. If we didn't want to go to

286

a dinner party, I'd tie myself in knots, thinking of an elaborate excuse, as he'd say, 'Can't we just tell them we don't want to come? That it's too far and we're out the night before, which we are?'

'No, of *course* not,' I'd tell him. 'We'll say you're on call.'

So I could lie and he couldn't. And looking at his frightened, wide eyes behind his glasses as he perched tentatively beside me, I knew the whole story. That his infatuation had led to one stolen kiss in the moonlight, on a balmy Provençal evening, with a very beautiful, very famous woman. But no more than that. Why, then, did I continue to vent my spleen?

'Oh, so you say!' I roared. 'But how can I tell? How do I know what you were really up to last night in Cannes?' I couldn't resist it. I held all the cards, you see. It was so rare. Such a novelty. Such a pity to waste them.

'Nothing!' he whimpered, terrified. 'Honestly, nothing happened – and, and Max was with us the whole time! Ask him!'

Max. That did give me pause for thought. Or slowed me down, at any rate. But not to a grinding halt. Still I swept on, with a valid point, this time.

'And what if I hadn't spotted you, James? What if I hadn't pottered down to have a quiet ciggie in the olive grove? Would you have allowed yourself to be led off to her private quarters? You certainly seemed to be enjoying yourself!'

A mental image of her wrapped in his arms, his eyes shut, face suffused with rapture, came careering back to both of us. He took a moment.

'I don't know,' he said honestly. See? Can't lie. I held my

breath as he thought earnestly. 'I hope not. Believe not.' He looked beyond me as he considered it truthfully. His eyes came back to me. 'No. I agree I was loving that terrible, stolen moment, but the instant it changed to something much more duplicitous, to being led by the hand, creeping round the house to the back stairs, for instance – something would have kicked in. I know it would. In fact, I'm sure of it. I honestly believe that, Flora.'

I did, too. No way would James sneak off to Camille's bedroom up in the tower on a family holiday; locking the door behind him, shedding clothes, hopping round the room trying to get out of his trousers, glasses off, blind without them as Camille waited patiently in bed – no. Banish that image. We both knew it wouldn't have happened. Any more than I would have succumbed to – well. You know. I swallowed, alive to the parallels. To the fearful symmetry. But that was different. Was it? Yes. Definitely. Max was an old boyfriend. I'd kissed him before. It hardly counted. Or did it count more? Surely there was more latent emotion, more feeling between the two of us than there could be between Camille and James? James was ridiculously flattered to be courted by her, and Camille . . . what *was* she up to, I wondered?

'You've been an idiot,' I told him coldly. 'You've been taken in and used. She's in love with Max, James. She's trying to make him jealous. You've been a pawn in her game.'

This hurt, I could tell, and I wished I hadn't said it. I'd never deliberately hurt James, but I was a bit out of control. And a bit out of my depth, situation-wise, too. What did one say or do when one's husband was caught with his trousers down? Surely one got out the big guns? Surely the little ones wouldn't do? I had to make a *bit* of a scene, surely? Couldn't just climb into bed and read as usual? James gazed at the carpet, ashamed. But I wasn't finished.

'I'm disgusted with you, James. Absolutely appalled. That you could betray me like this, and our children, on a family holiday.' Yes. This was the stuff. This was more like it.

'I know, Flora. I'm so sorry.' He gulped. His hand crept along the bedcover and found mine, gripped it hard. He turned huge, pleading, pale-grey eyes upon me, blinking rapidly behind his spectacles. 'Please don't say anything terrible, please. Something that can't be unsaid. It will never happen again. I'll do anything. I'll go home, if you like. We can say the hospital rang, that Peter Hurst's been taken ill and I need to go back. I'll do anything to save us, to recover this. I love you more than anything in the world – you know I do. It was just a silly infatuation, an idiotic mistake, but it will never, ever, happen again. I've been a vain, gullible fool, but please God don't say any-thing terrible. Words we've never said before.' He was near to tears, and I realized I was, too. I thought of his look of rapture as he kissed her. Something I hadn't seen for a long time – because marriage wasn't like that, was it? Particu-larly a nineteen-year-old one. You didn't go around in a state of unadulterated bliss, gazing into each other's eyes, holding hands.

I sighed.

If we'd been in London, I realized, if this had happened at home, we'd have slept in separate bedrooms. But we couldn't do that here. I could, I supposed, go to Lizzie's room, which was empty, but that would involve making a scene, and I didn't want that. Instead, we both went separately to the bathroom – not together, as usual, one having a pee whilst the other brushed their teeth – then, nightclothes on, we stole into bed and turned away from each other. I tried not to think about what might have happened if I hadn't intervened. The next kiss. I was sure there would have been one of those. The panting and the mutterings before he resisted the bedroom in the tower. Tried not to imagine James's lovely heart beating rapidly, so smitten, his passions so aroused, but it was hard. His heart and mind and soul and sex drive – sex was very important to James, he took it seriously – had been mine for so long. I couldn't help but feel hurt, even though my head told me this episode was a nonsense. Couldn't help but feel wounded in the moment, not yet an hour after the event.

Eventually – and I knew James wasn't asleep, heard none of the rhythmic snoring I usually did the moment his head hit the pillow – I got up, took a sleeping pill in the bathroom, came back and fell into a dreamless coma.

When I awoke, a cup of tea was beside the bed. A few sprigs of lavender, too, in a tiny vase. The tea was a bit cold, but I drank it. He obviously hadn't wanted to wake me. When I went down, quite late, he and his father were at the breakfast table.

'Hello, darling.' James's eyes were anxious.

'Hello.'

'Thérèse has made some pancakes. I kept a couple warm for you. Would you like them?'

'No, thank you.'

I helped myself to coffee and a croissant.

'Would you like a little trip today, darling? Shall we go into Grasse, perhaps? It's the centre of the perfume industry, apparently. You could try a few out?'

'It'll be terribly crowded, James.' I was trying to be nice, but it was hard.

'Camille's ex owns one of the scent factories there, apparently,' Rachel said, joining us, sitting down.

Silence at the mention of her name.

'Or Tourrettes, perhaps? There's a glorious view from the top of the hill?'

'Yes, perhaps.'

Or perhaps some time alone, to think, I wanted to say. Not about anything drastic, just some time apart. Surely that would do us good. But James was a bit frantic. A bit scared. I could be a bit chilly, you see. A bit scary. But sometimes, when I was in a corner, I didn't know how to be anything else. And him being scared made me worse.

'Or there's an art exhibition in Seillans, I keep seeing the posters advertising it. You'd like that, wouldn't you, darling?'

Rachel wasn't stupid. She looked from one to the other of us. Didn't say anything.

'Lovely,' I said faintly. 'Let's do that, then.'

'Leave in about twenty minutes?'

'Perfect.'

It was as if we had a date. Drummond glanced up from the iPad he'd been engrossed in. Getting the *Daily Telegraph* every day courtesy of Rory had made his holiday. 'To a gallery, you say?' Drummond was fond of art.

'Yes, but let's let James and Flora see if it's any good first,' said Rachel quickly. 'You know what these Provençal shows can be like. All vibrant colours and cubist disasters. Cézanne gone wrong.'

'Oh. Yes. Ghastly.' Drummond shuddered. 'Quite right. Can't be doing with all that.'

He went back to his newspaper, and Rachel and her brother communed silently, James thanking her with his eyes. They were very close, these two. Sometimes, over the years, it had surprised me how close, because neither was demonstrative about it. There was no big hug, or 'Lovely to *see* you!' when we went to Scotland. But James would go out on the hill with her a lot. Long walks. She wasn't a night bird like Sally, who would stay up until three drinking and talking, but she liked walking and James liked her company. She hardly ever came to London – in fact, I could count on one hand the times in our married life she had – but if I lost my phone and borrowed his, or vice versa (oh yes, that happened regularly) Rachel's was possibly the most recent number I'd see. They talked. It occurred to me he might conceivably tell her about last night. Which would be fine. She'd be good. Was quietly good at most things in life, even though she didn't lead a busy one, or a married, complicated one. But perhaps that gave her special insight? No, I wouldn't mind if he talked to Rachel.

The children appeared. James endured a certain amount of teasing about his condition last night and the state of his head this morning. Drummond roared with laughter. Happily, he'd been in bed and was none the wiser. And he loved their jokes.

'Was your father a bit squiffy last night, then?'

'He was off his head, Grandpa. Fancy a nice glass of

beer, Dad? Or perhaps a few press-ups and a jog around the block?'

'Bugger off, you lot,' James said good-naturedly, pleased to have their presence, which diluted their mother's. 'When *haven't* you woken up with a hangover?'

'Not often,' agreed Toby seriously. He straddled a chair backwards and got out his tin of tobacco, reading the situation wrongly, as usual. 'And, actually, I sometimes wonder if I ever draw a sober breath. One day just merges into the next, you know? It's like a total blur, man.' There was a silence. 'I mean – out here,' he added quickly, glancing up from his tobacco and seeing James and I join forces in the stony-look department.

'How's that management-consultancy application coming on, Toby?' asked James, uncharacteristically. It was the sort of thing I might have said, or badgered him to ask, but he wouldn't. Would regard it as interfering, or controlling. I realized he was doing it to please me.

'Yeah, I've almost filled it in,' replied Toby, surprised. He put the lid back on his Golden Virginia. Swung his legs round and sat properly on his chair. 'Sending it off when I get back.'

'Good.'

'Great,' said Amelia, under her breath. 'Two of them now. Happy days.'

'Life is not all beer and skittles, Amelia,' I told her, wondering why. This was surely entering a battleground I neither needed nor wanted on holiday. Perhaps I was supporting James. Showing I appreciated his solidarity. To my surprise, she didn't flare up or stalk off.

'I know, but do you know why we all think it is? Why we all regard it as one huge bowl of cherries?'

'No, do tell?' asked Drummond delightedly. He adored Amelia. Admired her spunk, he said, which always made her giggle.

'It's because you've kept us as children for too long. Poring over us, controlling us, always so interested in our lives, wanting to look at our Facebook pages – we're incapable of functioning on our own. If fifty is the new forty, eighteen is the new fourteen. I'm just a baby.' She widened her dark-brown eyes. 'It's not my fault I'm so reliant on you, Mummy, so helpless. You've made me that way.'

'Your generation grew up much quicker,' Tara agreed. 'You were left to sink or swim, so you swam.'

'That's true,' agreed Drummond quietly.

'You've coddled us,' said Amelia, warming to her theme. 'So now we can't grow up. You'll have to look after us for ever.' She gave a bolshie grin.

'I might have known it was my fault,' I said.

'Actually, it's the fault of technology,' said Rory. 'The only reason my mother can get hold of me every day is because of my iPhone.'

'Does she?' I asked, surprised.

'No, because I've turned if off. Told her there's no signal. But she would. Not every day, but a lot. She can't stop herself. And it's not healthy.'

'No,' I agreed, thinking of my own upbringing. James's. Were either of those any healthier?

'I think there's some middle ground,' said Rachel sensibly, 'which perhaps the next generation will find.'

'You mean when we have children?' Tara asked her.

'Exactly.'

This sobered them up a bit, as they contemplated how they'd do it.

'I'll let them do exactly what they want,' said Amelia predictably. 'Make their own mistakes. Learn by them.'

I smiled. No point even being drawn into this one. It struck me that James and I could never part. Never go our separate ways. This was such a two-pronged effort. Such a struggle.

'Yes, well good luck with that,' James said shortly. 'I hope you enjoy clearing up the mess.'

'So many children are still living at home at thirty,' Rory said. 'Did you know, in Spain, the average child leaves home at twenty-eight?'

'Exactly, because our development has been stunted,' Amelia told him. Nothing was ever her fault.

'No, because of economics. Your generation could buy your own houses. We'll never be able to do that,' Toby told us.

James's eyes sought mine in mock-horror. I didn't respond, though. The thought of thirty-year-old Toby and Amelia living with us was indeed appalling, but I wasn't ready to join James on any jovial level yet. I drained my coffee and made my way back upstairs, leaving them to their discussion, which would go on for ages, round and round in pointless, rather boring circles, with Amelia feeling more abused and aggrieved at every turn.

No sign of Camille, of course, I noticed, pausing a moment at the tall window halfway up the stairs, where all the discarded books seemed to gather on the sill. I gazed out down the front drive to the lodge. She'd made herself very scarce. Had gone into Cannes with Max, Sally told me, when I'd run into her just now at the foot of the stairs. Sally had been on her way to the pool. I'd been startled, but she hadn't looked remotely concerned.

'They had to tie up a few loose ends, business-wise, after Wednesday night's performance. The sponsors wanted to have lunch with her, take some photos for PR, that kind of thing. It was part of the deal, apparently. And she didn't want to go alone. Obviously, Max had to go because he's the promoter.'

Obviously. Or was Camille's plan working? I knew Max had been alive to the fact that something had happened last night in the gazebo. Were these men, one by one, falling like flies, slotting perfectly into her grand plan?

'And, actually, it's lovely to have a quiet day without the boyfriend around,' Sally giggled. 'I've put a treatment on my hair – it feels like straw with all this sun.' She patted her oiled locks. 'And I'm going to bake all day and read a crappy book. No need to impress Max with a Booker Prize winner today!' She flourished a fluorescent paperback gaily before sorting through the basket on the hall table where all the sun creams were tossed, ready for a peaceful day by the pool.

I watched as, suntan lotion retrieved, she appeared beneath me now, and went through the front door and down the steps. She padded across the gravel drive in her espadrilles, a basket swinging from her shoulder, hat in hand, long legs already brown and unbelievably slim. As she went, she passed Michel coming in the opposite direction, down the box-lined drive from the lodge, towards the house. He carried some vegetables in a trug. They smiled and exchanged a few pleasantries before moving on. Sally tracked right across the sloping lawn towards the walled garden and the pool. As he came closer to the house, Michel stopped. He looked up at the tall window where I was standing, and gave me a very direct look. A very cold look. Flustered, I moved away. But it had chilled me. Why, I didn't know. Clearly, he had just glanced up, sensing someone's eyes upon him, that was all. I hurried on up to my room. Quickly, I changed my shoes, found my basket, slicked on some lipstick and made to go back downstairs. Before I did, I closed the shutters against the sun to keep the room cool. In the front drive I saw James already waiting, leaning against the bonnet of the car.

I put my dark glasses on as I went down the front steps into the gravel and the glare of the sun. I might not be looking forward to this little trip, but I was glad we were doing it. Could see the sense, actually. It would clear the air. Draw something of a line. James had parked on the far side of the fountain under the trees in the shade, and I didn't hurry as I crossed the drive. Trailed my fingers a moment in the cool water. It was hot and, anyway, he'd kissed another woman last night. Let's not forget that. He could wait. As I reached the car and put my hand on the door handle I caught sight of his face across the roof. It wasn't the Flora-pleasing one of last night: the abjectly apologetic, craven one. It wasn't even the nervous one of this morning at breakfast, let alone the scared one. It was a furious one. Indeed, it was pale with anger. I blanched with shock as his eyes hit mine, glittering behind his spectacles.

'Get in,' he said tersely. 'We have a lot to talk about.'

Chapter Twenty-Two

We shot off up the drive at speed. Shocked, I put my hand out on the door to steady myself. Gravel sprayed beneath the tyres. My husband did not drive like this; like something out of an American cop drama. And why was he driving at all?

'So,' he said curtly. 'You and Max.'

I inhaled sharply. Felt the blood drain from my head. Had he really said that?

'What d'you mean, me and Max.' See? I can lie. Instinctively. Reflexively.

'Don't try to fib your way out of it, Flora. You were seen. Grappling and panting in his arms the other night. Michel saw you.'

'Michel?' I repeated faintly, my head spinning.

'Yes, he was going back to his cottage. You weren't quite careful enough, you see. Away from the house, sure, but not from the staff.' James's face was dangerously pale as he whipped a glance across at me. 'You disgust me. In so many ways.'

'How did you? I mean –' I was horrified, and hot with shame at being caught. I was scared, too. More so than James would have been.

'How did I find out? He told Camille, who's just rung me. Don't try and deny it, Flora, you know full well what happened. And who knows what else, too.'

I recalled Michel's face just now. Vengeful. That was the look I'd been unable to place. And, of course, I'd accused him of something terrible earlier on in the week. Revenge was surely a dish best served cold.

'Nothing else,' I whispered as we sped along the lanes much too fast, vineyards flashing by. The sun was beating down, hotter than ever, a furious heat, it seemed. Sunflowers glared and nodded accusingly at me, their enormous, round faces scarily nightmarish: not so pretty today. I somehow found my voice. 'Honestly, James, just one kiss. I swear to God. Swear on the girls.'

He glanced at me at this.

'I – don't know why it happened. A warm night, too much to drink – who knows. It was a nonsense. Just like . . . well.'

'No, nothing like me and Camille. And no, we are not all square, not remotely, if that's what you were going to dare to suggest. In the first place, you haven't even had the grace to apologize and you made me crawl.'

'I'm sorry, James.' I looked down at my hands.

'Really crawl.' His lip curled.

'I'm truly sorry. It meant nothing. I promise.'

'And, in the second place, which is far more pertinent, I don't believe it meant nothing. There is a world of difference between a stolen kiss with a famous opera star with whom I am childishly infatuated, and falling into the arms of a man with whom you were once head over heels in love and engaged to.'

'I disagree.'

'Oh really? Don't be fatuous, Flora. Even I, who don't fit into the jealous-husband mould, can see that he still adores you, which, up until now, has given me something of a perverse pleasure this holiday, I'll admit. Something of a gratuitous kick. Knowing you're mine and not his. But now I know the pleasure is all his.'

'Of course it's not! I told you, it was a drunken one-off.'

'And you felt absolutely nothing?'

'I —' I tried to answer honestly, as he had last night: knowing James would demand nothing less. Would see through anything else.

'I — yes. I felt something.'

A muscle went in his cheek. I lunged for the lie instead.

'I felt transported back in time, that was all. A trip down memory lane.'

'You wanted him.'

Why was it all about sex, for men?

I sighed. 'No. That I can answer truthfully. If you mean — did I want to charge upstairs and take all my clothes off — no. It was more . . .'

James thumped his chest with his fist. 'More in here?'

I felt panicky. He wanted me to be honest, and what was the result?

'I was moved, OK? Touched. God, James, who wouldn't be?'

He nodded. 'You got a glimpse of the life you could have had if you hadn't settled for second best.'

'Oh, don't be absurd!' I turned to him in horror. This was very unlike him. James was famously self-assured. Not arrogant, but happy in his skin. 'You're saying that out of anger — you've never felt that, I'd know it. You're saying it because you can, because it conveniently fits the argument.'

'I don't think you're in any position, Flora, to determine what I can or can't say.'

'No. I realize that.'

'You didn't even have the decency to let me off the hook last night, knowing you were in the same boat. That's disgraceful.'

'I know.'

'It makes me dislike you as a person.'

'Don't say that, James,' I said quietly.

'It's true.'

We drove on in silence. I sensed a clenched calmness sweep over him. Knew he was livid, which rarely happened.

'I think we need some time apart.'

I swallowed hard. 'You said last night we shouldn't say anything terrible. Words we'd regret. That's something terrible.'

'I know, but it's what I feel. I don't know you at the moment, Flora. Can't bear to look at you.'

'You mean a day or two? A week? I could go to Mum's when we go back.'

'No, I mean one of us goes home now. I can't bear this situation. Won't be able to cope. I'll take you to Nice this afternoon. When we get back. There's a flight at six. We can tell the girls you've decided to fight for your job. Gone to see Maria.' He pulled sharply into a layby beside a field of lavender, jerking to a halt. 'Something you should have done anyway, like Lizzie.' He turned in his seat behind the wheel to face me properly, his eyes furious. We were clearly not going to an art exhibition in Seillans. 'You need to think about what you want, Flora. Do you want to continue to support this family, to make it a joint effort, or d'you want to play the frivolous frustrated housewife instead? Chuck in your career and have an affair with an old boyfriend? Or even make a life with an old boyfriend? After all, he's single, and it's clearly why he's here, which is pretty elaborate when you think about it. He obviously has no feelings at all for my poor sister.'

It was my turn to flare up. 'Well, that's not my fault! And I'm insulted you'd suggest for one moment that I'd disappear with him. You're being totally disingenuous. You know that's not true. I told you, it was a stupid indiscretion, and yes, I should have gone easy on you last night, under the circumstances, but human nature isn't always like that. I *was* incensed, still *am* incensed at the thought of you kissing another woman, because I love you, James.'

We were silent a moment, both inwardly fuming; both very hurt. Both having hurt each other and knowing it had changed our marriage in some way which felt irreparable at the moment, and terribly sad, but reason also telling us it was only the here and now, sitting in this car fighting, not the reality long term. So why did I have to go home? The thought appalled me. A kiss each. Stupid, but not a tragedy, surely? But I couldn't see into James's mind completely. He'd always kept a tiny bit back. Not his love, just a part of him, which made him special, I thought. Interesting. He was less heart on sleeve, warts and all, than I was. But what if that something was a slight meanness of spirit? He turned away from me now, to look out of the window across the fragrant mauve valley, his face a mask. There'd been a handful of times when I couldn't see into his soul and this was one of them.

'Come on, James.' I reached for his hand. 'Let's sleep on it. You've just found me out, and you're incensed, as I was incensed last night, but I'm calmer now, after a night's sleep. Can see it for what it is. A silly mistake. Ruining everyone's holiday is not going to help.'

'We wouldn't be ruining everyone's holiday, just yours.' He said this coldly. He really did despise me right now. 'I can't help it, Flora. I can't stop seeing you in his arms. I want to kill him.'

And James was such a mild man.

'And we can't ask Sally to leave, to take him away. Can't tell her what you've done. Which is pretty atrocious behaviour towards your sister-in-law, incidentally.' He started the engine again. 'No. You'll have to go home.'

We drove on in silence.

In point of fact, we did go to Seillans, or at least we parked outside the gallery, up on a pavement in a tiny side street. James went inside to get a brochure to prove we'd been. I sat still, staring ahead. He was right, I wasn't a nice person. I'd betrayed him, and also betrayed Sally, and then been a total hypocrite last night. Home in disgrace was the best I could hope for. But I was still shocked by his decision.

I thought of the house in Clapham – musty and dark, north-facing, but I'd never really minded; had resolutely painted it creamy, light colours to compensate, but it seemed gloomier than ever somehow, these days, and always much darker, of course, after a sybaritic holiday in the sun. But Clapham was the truth, the reality. This was just a dream. I gazed around at the ebb and flow of beautiful, tanned people in holiday mode on the cobbled street which led down to the main square, where pretty bunting stretched between the mottled plane trees beneath an azure sky, and where waiters were setting tables for lunch around the fountain. This wasn't real. Except, for some people, it was, I thought, singling out those who clearly weren't tourists: those with their basketfuls of groceries, with more purposeful looks on their faces as they dodged the ambling crowd, tiny dogs trotting beside them on leads. Of course, they had their dramas, their disappointments, their tragedies even, but didn't this glorious setting, this heavenly climate, make everything more bearable? Being tired and cross here wasn't the same as being tired and cross in the Southside Shopping Centre, or trudging up Lavender Hill in the rain with shopping, or sitting on the South Circular in a traffic jam. And I had to leave. James knew it was a punishment. Knew I'd feel it keenly. He was being deliberately harsh.

I watched as he came out of the gallery a few minutes later, shutting the door on the predictable blaze of sunny landscapes in the gallery window, his face set and angry. Of course, he was still in shock. He'd only just found out. He was bound to be upset. I felt nervous, though. James didn't make empty gestures. He didn't order his wife home from holiday without meaning it. And, however it might look to outsiders, he wore the trousers in this marriage. I might make all the noise as I flapped about with the smaller sails, rushing from side to side shrieking, as one boom after another swept over, threatening to decapitate us, narrowly missing us, but James's was the hand on the tiller.

We drove home in silence, my mouth inexplicably dry. James took a detour through a couple of unfamiliar villages to give us time: to enable us to tell the folks back home we'd had a lovely time at the gallery. I knew it was giving us time, too, as we purred slowly past the old men playing boules in the main square, or sitting outside a bar with a café cognac, their wives gossiping on doorsteps or outside shops: I also knew from his taut, clenched face that, instead of calming down, if anything, James's quiet fury was gaining momentum.

'You tell them I'm going,' I told him when we reached the chateau, pulling up at the open front door. 'I might burst into tears and give the game away. You tell them I'm going back to see Maria.'

'Sure,' he said, as if I'd asked him to tell them they were having pizza for lunch.

I knew he'd be fine, too. Knew he'd make it so casual and low key they wouldn't bat an eyelid: *Oh poor Mummy, what a bore, but she'll be back in a couple of days*, I could hear Amelia saying, before going back to her iPad, or her book, in the sun. And then, when I didn't come back, he'd say I was working things out with Maria, and they'd nod, knowing Mummy was being responsible, as adults had to be sometimes – not them, of course, not yet. They were the new fourteen. And James would wander off to read his book under the trees, mission accomplished: which made him quite a consummate liar, too, really, didn't it? Quite the deceiver. And why was my crime so much more atrocious than his, I thought defiantly as I climbed the stairs to my room. So much more heinous? Because we both knew it meant more, I reflected, packing a bag, wondering if I should take the lot: if I'd be back. Would James summon me, after a decent length of time? Probably not, I thought, with rising terror, but still, I only took hand luggage. Let him sort the rest out. Odd that I wasn't fighting this, I pondered as I packed my sponge bag in the bathroom. Not putting my foot down, saying, Don't be ridiculous, I'm not a child, of *course* I'm not going home. Just going quietly.

As I was rooting around for my passport in the bedside drawer, zipping it into my bag on the bed, the door opened. Tara came in, pale-blue eyes wide.

'Daddy says you're going home.'

'I think I should, darling,' I said, forcing a smile. I might have known this one wouldn't go straight back to her iPod. 'I've had that job for eighteen years. Can't just throw in the towel. If I was in London, I'd march round and have it out with her, so I think I'd better march home and do the same now.'

'I suppose.' She bit her thumbnail and sat on the bed in her bikini, slim and brown. I threw a few more bits in my bag. 'Except yesterday, you said you didn't mind.'

'Shock, I suppose.' I kept the bright smile going, making myself look at her and trying to appear as cheery as possible. Her blue eyes in her tanned face looked worried. 'Is everything OK? Daddy seemed a bit ... you know. Clenched.'

'I think he's a bit cross I didn't think of it sooner. I mean, going home,' I said, trying to stick as close to the truth as possible: the best way to lie. 'I should have been the one to see our finances wouldn't survive this, but I was a bit swept away with the glamour of being here. All of this!' I swept my hand to indicate the high-ceilinged room, its elaborate cornice, the canopied bed, the chandelier, the view out of the open window to the hills and the sea beyond.

She nodded. 'And you'll be back?'

'Of course I'll be back, darling!' I gave her a hug. Squeezed her tight. 'Now, I'm going to put you in charge of making sure people don't treat the place too much like home: empty the odd ashtray, chivvy the others to stack the dishwasher occasionally to help Thérèse . . . d'you think you can do that?'

'Of course.' Tara did that sort of thing anyway. She walked to the door with me as I picked up my bag. 'Rachel says she'll take you to the airport.'

'Oh, really?' I stopped short of the door. 'Not Daddy?'

'No, he's gone to the vineyard to get some more wine with Sally and Grandpa. He said he'd told you? Said goodbye already?' Her brow puckered and her worried eyes searched mine.

'Oh, yes. Yes, of course he did. I forgot. I thought he meant he was going later, after supper.'

'But he said goodbye?'

'Of course he did, darling, stop worrying!' I laughed, squeezing her shoulders as I went on, but only my mouth was smiling; my head was spinning. Crikey. Where was James? In his head? Shot of me already?

I prattled on about it being good to be able to give the plants back home a watering, that I was pretty sure Maddy, our neighbour, didn't get round to it as often as she might. About how I'd have lunch with Lizzie, maybe launch a sustained attack on Maria, a show of force – 'girl power!' I joked, raising a clenched fist. Tara raised a thin smile.

At the foot of the curved staircase, in the cool of the limestone hall, Rachel was waiting with her handbag and her car keys. I got a shock when I saw her eyes. Scared.

Knowing. Had he told her? My heart jumped. What had he told her?

'Bye, darling!' I said brightly to Tara, giving her another quick hug. 'Say goodbye to the others for me!'

'Aren't you going to? They're only out there.' She pointed to the terrace, which could just be seen through the French windows of the inner hall, where some of the party were gathering for lunch. It would be odd not to say goodbye to my other daughter, who was ambling across in a sarong, book in hand. She saw me through the open door and came across.

'Ma. Gather you're deserting us.' She took off her sunglasses. Looked surprised. So I'd got that a bit wrong, too.

'Yes, off to grovel,' I chortled, giving her a hug.

'Unlike you?'

'Oh, I have my obsequious moments.'

'Well, if she says no, spit in her coffee.'

'Will do. Bye, everyone!' I tripped across the hall and stuck my head around the door, but didn't set foot outside. The boys went to get up, but I was too quick for them, gave them a cheery wave and darted back.

'Say goodbye to Mum and JC for me, will you?' I asked Amelia as I returned to the front hall.

'They're only by the pool.'

'I know, but we've got to hustle if I'm going to catch this plane. Toodle-oo!'

And, with that, we were off, Rachel and I, leaving my daughters standing together on the front steps watching us go, their boyfriends, unperturbed, already back to their game of cards. But blood was quite thick, I thought, as they shaded their eyes with their hands, waving uncertainly as Rachel and I drove off. And their faces said it all as I studied them in the wing mirror: how unlike Mum. Totally unlike Mum. But I could put it down to age, or hormones, or, of course, their father.

As we swept up the drive it occurred to me that Rachel's fingers on the steering wheel were tight. She'd barely said anything. Her mouth was pursed, too, as she stared straight ahead at the road. I felt cross suddenly, at this melodrama. OK, nothing much happened in Rachel's life, but could she please get a sense of proportion? Could everyone get a sense of proportion? Including James?

'Rachel, what's he said to you? James? You look like I've fallen so far from grace there's no hope of redemption for me in this world, let alone the next. As if I'm a scarlet woman!'

'You're not, are you?' She glanced at me.

'No, of course I'm bloody not! I kissed him, for God's sake, after a drunken evening. Just as James . . . anyway. And now I'm being sent home in disgrace like a fourteen-year-old.'

'He can't help it, Flora. I know it seems like a huge over-reaction, but it's not his fault.'

This annoyed me. The sister knowing more than I, the wife, did.

'Well, he *can* help it, if only he'd give it a bit of rational thought. He's jolly lucky I'm complying and not staying for a stand-up, knock-down fight.'

'He was so sure of you, you see. Knew you'd never stray. This is shattering for him.'

'A kiss,' I said weakly, knowing she was right. That James was shattered. That I couldn't have stayed.

'It's what it symbolizes. And who it was with. I think

he was almost enjoying having Max here, knowing he was desperately in love with you and that you wouldn't give him a second look.'

I was silent. It was indeed so terribly different to him and Camille. I licked my lips. Swallowed. We drove on in silence. I knew they went deep, these siblings, but I wondered how deep. Deeper than with me? I felt jealous. Knew it would take so long to undo this. I also felt utterly exhausted.

The magical scenery swept by. At length, though, the vines, the sunflowers and the lavender gave way to villages, then ribbon development, then solid urbanization. As we reached the outskirts of Nice, where washing hung from tenement windows and stray dogs trotted purposefully along pavements, a couple of women, tottering in mini-skirts and heels, shoulder bags on chains, stepped out in front of us at a pelican crossing. Rachel stopped sharply. We watched as they made their way across, cackling with laughter, leg muscles bulging from the strain of the heels, faces over made up, on their way to town. As she shifted into first gear, Rachel said softly, 'It's to do with Mum.'

I gazed straight ahead. Nodded. 'I know,' I said, equally quietly. We drove on.

I did know. About James, Rachel and Sally's mother. Drummond's wife. Of course I did. I watched as the two women disappeared from view in my wing mirror. About how she'd tottered – or driven – into town with a faceful of slap. Until Drummond had had enough. They'd all had enough. I blinked rapidly as Rachel took the slip road up to the airport. And of course I'd been conscious of the nature of our bond in the early days: how we'd clicked so quickly. Why, perhaps. Why I wasn't shocked by his childhood. Because I'd endured something equally uncon-ventional, with my own mother. Why he totally understood about me being unable to forgive Max's infidelity. As he was unable to forgive me now. He'd always said he'd be incapable. Made that clear. I used to joke and ask what he'd do if I ran off with the milkman?

'Oh, tuck a child under each arm and head for the wide-open spaces,' he'd say. Meaning it.

'My children, too!' I'd retort, knowing it would never happen: that I never would.

'You'd have to fight me for them.'

A grim courtroom drama had flashed through the ban-ter like a sharp knife. He'd already contemplated it. Thought it through. And now, here he was, making me head away from my children; my girls, standing uncertainly together in their bikinis and sarongs in the drive, shading their eyes to watch me go. What was he putting in motion? When all the time . . . the ecstasy on his face as he kissed Camille swept back to me in a rush, like the tide surging up the beach: the complete and utter abandonment.

'I'm sorry!' I said to myself as we approached the ter-minal building, but actually aloud, too. 'No, I'm sorry, it's just not on!'

Rachel came to a halt behind a row of cars outside Departures. She didn't speak.

'It's not fair, Rachel. And I won't tell you why, but it's not.'

She looked neither surprised nor startled by my out-burst. In fact, she didn't look at me at all. We both got out of the car and she waited while I went around to the boot and got my bag. I came back and kissed her. Thanked her for the lift.

'I'm sorry. None of this is your fault.'

'And none of it is yours, either, really,' she said ruefully, so ruefully that I caught on her tone. But she was already getting back in the car, putting on her seat belt, glancing in her rear-view mirror to pull away. And then she was off.

I stood for a moment, mid-pavement, the warm breeze snaking around my bare legs, watching her go. I turned and walked towards Departures. As the glazed doors slid open automatically I felt the chill of the air conditioning. A blast of reality. I was still musing on Rachel's words as I glanced up at the screen to check my flight. Delayed. Oh, splendid. By how long? It didn't say. And it wasn't the only one, either: many were, I noticed. Resignedly, I joined the queue behind the familiar orange easyJet desk.

The commuters were the usual suspects: middle-class, middle-income families disgruntled at being herded like cattle, with only a distant memory of the glamour of a bygone era of air travel, too poor to upgrade to a better, classier airline. As I queued, I became increasingly incensed by Rachel's words. *Not your fault*. Too right, it wasn't my fault. We'd both had a difficult time, a difficult upbringing. Both been true and loyal throughout our married life and both had a minor indiscretion, astonishingly, within days of one another. Wherein, then, lay the difference? All of a sudden, I caught my breath. Not in the same queue but leaning languidly against a desk at the next counter was a more urbane, sophisticated sort of traveller. One in a crisp chambray shirt, stone-coloured chinos, with a deep tan and very deep-blue eyes. It was Max. Watching me. Waiting for me, even. I swallowed. Left the line of passengers and walked towards him. Herein, of course, lay the difference.

Chapter Twenty-Three

'You are absolutely the last person I need to see,' I told him, dropping my bag, practically on his foot. 'You are the reason I've been sent home in disgrace.'

'I know.' He tried not to grin. Failed. His eyes sparkled naughtily.

'What are you doing here?'

'Waiting for you.'

'You knew I'd be here?'

'Sally told me.'

'Well, I'm on my way home, Max.'

He affected a long face. 'Shame.'

I narrowed my eyes. 'And my marriage may well be over.'

'I doubt it. Come on. Let's go and have lunch.'

'Use your eyes, please. I'm getting a plane.'

'I know, but it's delayed, they all are. Baggage handlers' strike, didn't you know?'

'No. I didn't. Shit. *Bugger.* I'll ask,' I cast about wildly.

'I already have. At least five hours, they say. Most are leaving tonight, though. You'll be OK.'

'Will I?' I said grimly.

'Come on, I'm starving. Let's go into Nice.'

'No, thanks. I'll get a sandwich here and wait.' I sat down on my case. A bit like Paddington Bear. But it was small and squashy – hand luggage, remember – so I wobbled precariously.

'Oh, don't be absurd, you've got hours! The only reason this lot aren't going anywhere is because they haven't got some knight in shining armour waiting to whisk them away for a slap-up meal. Where's the harm, Flossie? I'm not going to jump on you. Don't get ahead of yourself.'

The harm, as we well knew, was in the chat, the drink, the banter, and how it would look to James. But, actually, I was becoming increasingly furious with that man. It occurred to me that I had broken away from Max of my own volition: would he have broken away from Camille if he hadn't been interrupted? Forget running up to her bedroom in the tower – we all knew he wouldn't do that – but what about a lengthy grapple in the gazebo? Not one kiss but several? A spot of first base? He'd have been up for that, I bet. How dare he send me home?

'Wait here,' I muttered. I strode off to find an orange-clad easyJet official, no mean feat at the best of times, but particularly impossible in an airport packed with furious commuters. Eventually, I tracked one down. He indeed confirmed that nothing was leaving the tarmac for at least five hours, but most would go before midnight. Hopefully. Maybe. Fingers crossed. I came back.

'OK, you're on. But I warn you, I'm in a filthy mood, Max. And if I had to choose anyone to have lunch with right now, you wouldn't be top of my list. In fact, you'd be right at the bottom.'

'You've completely charmed me, Flossie. I'm putty in your hands.'

'Oh, sod off.'

'Where did you learn to flirt like that?'

'Funny.'

Outside, in the short-term car park, we found his silver Mercedes, which, through the miracles of modern technology, converted to the roofless variety in seconds flat. I slid nervously into the passenger seat, aware he was still laughing at me.

'I might have known you'd end up with a car like this.'

'I haven't the faintest notion what you mean.'

'An incredibly obvious crumpet-catcher. A topless model.' I dragged a scarf out of my bag and wrapped it around my head, then put on some dark glasses.

'You're travelling incognito?'

'You're public enemy number one, Max.'

'And you know so many people in Nice.'

'I'm not taking any chances.'

'You look a bit like my cleaning lady.'

'It's a look I rock regularly.'

We set off.

In the event, we didn't go into Nice. The centre would be impossible, he told me, far too crowded, and there wasn't anywhere remotely acceptable on the outskirts, so we'd drive along the coast for a bit, to a little place he knew. Of course he did, I thought, watching him out of the corner of my eye as we swept along the coast road. His older, now familiar face was tanned and handsome, blue eyes narrowed behind sunglasses, a cornflower-blue shirt conveniently matching those eyes and the sea beyond – his underpants, too, no doubt – brown arms and hands muscular on the wheel. The wind was in our hair – I'd ditched the scarf by now, as it threatened to throttle me – and the sun on our faces as we flew along at speed. A vast stretch of Mediterranean swept away to the horizon on our left: tiny sailboats bobbed, speedboats trailed snakes of white foam and girls waterskied in bikinis. It was a long way from Clapham. Riviera Radio played the while, and some French crooner sang, not quite 'The Girl from Ipanema', but something impossibly similar. Then came the adverts, asking if we were all right for drinks cupboards aboard our yachts? If our Ferraris could do with a service in Cannes? Everyone here, it seemed, was rich: basking in the sunshine and their wealth. Including Max, of course, I thought, glancing at the rest of his sartorial ensemble – chic chinos, Italian shoes – comparing it again to James's ancient Crew Clothing which he dragged from the bottom drawer year after year. I sighed. But then, in a highly uncharacteristic move, I decided to surrender to the moment, reasoning it was highly unlikely I'd ever be in such a car again, with a man as handsome as Max, in such an utterly sublime setting. Defiantly, I leaned my head back on the expensive blond leather headrest. Occasionally, I caught Max glancing at me, amused. The next time he did, we both smiled. But not in a clandestine way, more in a 'This is OK' sort of way.

The restaurant was well off the beaten track, which pleased me. We drove up a narrow lane into the hills, navigated a series of hairpin bends, then climbed, almost up a dirt track, through pine woods. A few goats turned to stare amongst the sweet-smelling needles. Cicadas sang their deafening music. Right at the top, we parked on a promontory. I stepped out of the car and turned. Gasped. The most beautiful sea view met my eyes. The restaurant and its terrace were perched perfectly to make the most of the sun-drenched bay below. I felt sure someone out at sea aboard their gin palace must even now be sipping a Martini, shading their eyes up at us and murmuring, 'Darling, that must be a terrific place to eat. What a position. Let's go.'

And here I was. Of course, I shouldn't be, I thought, as I followed Max inside, but no one would ever know.

'This is gorgeous, Max,' I conceded.

'It is rather special, isn't it? The patron is a huge fan of Camille, which is the only reason I've secured a table.'

'He thinks you're coming with her?'

'Yes, you're going to be a colossal disappointment.'

'Story of my life.'

I whipped out my lippy and hid behind Max as he explained, to a swarthy maître d', in perfect French, that I was Camille's personal assistant, and we were hoping she might show up for coffee, but that she had a terribly tight schedule. It was something James would never have done and, as we were shown to our table, although I was cross with my husband, I was pleased about that: I mentally notched up points in his favour.

'You haven't lost your devious ways,' I told Max as chairs were pulled out with a flourish at what my practised eye told me was the best table on the terrace. The only free one, too; all the others occupied by beautiful people sipping champagne and eating oysters under a burgeoning pagoda of trailing vines and pale-blue lobelia.

'Needs must,' he told me airily.

We sat and admired the view, although, once he'd glanced at it, he removed his glasses and smouldered naughtily in my general direction. I remained resolutely glued to the seascape but caught his expression out of the corner of my eye. Too obvious, I told myself. Who wants a man who smoulders?

The trouble was, after a couple of glasses of rosé, which was chilled and delicious and slipped down an absolute treat as we waited for our escargots, smouldering didn't seem so terrible. In fact, it seemed really rather welcome. And, apart from anything else, I reasoned, as I listened to his entertaining music-world chatter, about which I'd asked in order to steer him away from more personal matters, when would I next be sitting at a table like this, obsequious waiter filling up my glass and hovering solicitously, in light of my recent dismissal? Max must be quite a big deal in his own right, I realized, for them to be sanguine about him appearing without the star herself. What exactly was his relationship with Camille, I wondered? I asked him.

'Oh, you mean you're no longer interested in the logistics of a two-month tour of the States complete with sound crew and diva? You're cutting to the chase?'

'I needed to ease myself in. Ten minutes on how you decide which venues to play and which to resist has helped enormously. That and two glasses of wine.'

'Excellent news. Well, as you already know, Camille and I had an affair.'

'Had?'

'Definitely past tense. But I was certainly bewitched by her, I admit that. Entranced. As James is now.' He grinned at me. 'She has a tremendous ability to ensnare men.'

'In an incredibly obvious way.'

'And when you hear her sing, you're lost. I was, for quite a while. And then, of course, there's the vulnerability; the

318

little girl lost in a world that's only after her talent. You want to protect her, look after her.'

'And you left Mimi for her.'

He frowned. 'How did you know?'

'I worked it out. Never quite believed the fling-on-tour bit. Men always leave their wives for another woman. They rarely step into a vacuum.'

'Aren't you the wise old sage. Yes, all right, I left Mimi for her. I was besotted, at the time. Flattered, too, I suspect. But then, little by little, you see the other side of Camille. The ego, the arrogance, the self-absorption.'

'Little by little?'

'I know. Women see it sooner.'

'But then we're not trying to get into her capri pants.'

'True.'

I paused. 'So . . . were you in love with her?'

'I think I was, for a bit. But it's funny how, once that goes, it disappears remarkably quickly.'

'And it has gone.'

'Yes.'

It wasn't at all what he'd said before. Before, he'd said he'd felt very little for Camille. I was pleased, in a way. Max wasn't a shallow man. I'd been perplexed by that.

'So now?'

He shifted in his seat: a regrouping gesture. 'Now I'm thinking of working with Jonas Kaufmann, in Italy. He's asked me.'

'That would be good, surely? He's equally famous?'

'He is, and it would get me away. I could delegate Camille.'

'And Mimi?'

'Yes, well. That's another story.' He looked beyond me, into the distance. Leaned his elbows on the table and massaged the bridge of his nose wearily.

'Would she have you back?'

'She would. Just. We'd have to work hard, obviously.' He leaned forward and played with his fork. His face had dropped. 'It wouldn't be easy. I'm realistic about that.'

'But at least she'd forgive you. At least – your family, your son . . .'

'I know,' he said quickly.

'A second chance, surely?'

'Yes, but you can never snap right back to where you were, Floss. This isn't a fairy story. There'd be days when she'd still hate me, find it hard to forgive. Gloomy Monday nights in January when she'd rehash what I'd done. There'd be sulks, rows, bitter recriminations.'

'You could have counselling?'

'*More* counselling.' He groaned. Rubbed his eyes again. Then he sighed. 'Yes, we could. And it might work. But it's never going to be exactly the same.'

I remembered thinking that the other night: that James and I would never be the same, that we'd sullied our marriage. But one kiss each. Come on. It was nothing to what Max had done.

'But I got it wrong in the first place, you see,' he said into his plate of snails as they arrived. '*Merci.* If I'd got it right with you, none of this would have happened.' Blue eyes flashed across the table to meet mine.

'That suggests other people are at fault. It shifts the blame. I'm not so sure it wouldn't have happened anyway.' I refused to be seduced.

'You mean I'd be a shit whoever I married?'

'No, because you're not. But I'm not convinced you can abdicate responsibility like that. Say, Oh, if I'd been with her, I'd never have strayed.'

We ate in silence for a moment, attending to the tricky business of eating escargots but also alone with our thoughts.

'You know this is my last throw of the dice, don't you, Flossie?'

'I know.'

'That, despite all the banter, if you said yes, I'd forget Italy, forget Kaufmann, forget going home. Follow you wherever. Do whatever you wanted.'

I concentrated on extracting a snail from its shell but, actually, I didn't need to. Knew I could look up into those deep-blue eyes, heavy with meaning, and love, actually, and have no problem saying what was in my heart. I put down my fork.

'The thing is, Max, you felt I got away from you. And I'm not saying I felt I'd had a lucky escape – I loved you very much at the time – but I married the right man. And I knew that the moment I walked down the aisle with him. I haven't spent the last nineteen years with you burning a hole in my heart, full of what ifs.'

He met my gaze. I held it steady. Max nodded slowly. 'Whereas I have. James is a lucky man.'

I swallowed. 'Not really. I'm a shrew. And a nag. And I'm preachy and full of ridiculous neuroses. I drive my family mad. And I haven't aged particularly well. I've put on too much weight and my chin is a bit droopy. That surely helps, Max?'

He laughed. 'No question.'

'But it's true, isn't it?' I insisted.

'You mean, have I enshrined something – someone – in my heart who doesn't exist? Is it a relief to see her for what she really is, all these years later?'

'Yes. I mean, come on.' I rolled my eyes expressively. Almost held up my bingo wings. Not quite.

'You never were an oil painting, Flossie.'

I threw my head back and laughed. 'Thanks!'

'But not every man goes for arm candy.'

'No, but many men are distracted by it. And I think I'd have spent my life looking over my shoulder if I'd married you, Max, something I've never done with James. Women . . .' I didn't say – like Mimi – didn't want to dredge that up 'will always home in on you.'

He played with his spoon. 'I'm not asking for violins to be played, but it can be a curse, sometimes. For a man. Not to be taken seriously.'

Good looks, he meant. I thought about it. About people like Robert Redford and George Clooney, wanting to be famous for directing rather than acting.

'Nah.' I shook my head. 'Sorry. Given the choice, you'd never give it back. Never look any other way.'

He smiled. Very attractively. Eyes creasing with laughter lines – he, of course, had aged terrifically. 'Maybe not.'

The waiter came to take our empty plates and shells. Provided finger bowls, which we used. Asked if we'd like more wine. I declined. He left us alone. Max's eyes met mine. Held them.

'So that's a no, then, Flora?'

I smiled sadly. 'It's a no, Max.'

'Not even a moment's hesitation.'

'Not even a heartbeat. But I'm very flattered. On the other hand, you didn't leave Mimi for me. You didn't break out of a long, comfortable marriage out of passion for Flora Murray-Brown. You broke out for Camille. Then, when you realized she was shallow, you thought – shit, now I'm single. Hm, I wonder how old Flora's doing? Always liked her. Got a bit of depth. Ooh, look, here's her sister-in-law. Might ease in there, tag along on their family holiday, see if there's still a spark. Oh hello, yes, still fancy her. Even if she hasn't aged brilliantly. And although Mimi says she'd have me back, she's going to be bloody furious. I could have a fresh start with Flora. She's a laugh. We've always got on. Let's face it, we were engaged, should have been married. And she knows me very well. There'd be so much I wouldn't have to explain. We could have fun for the next few years together; maybe not get married, just see how it goes. And I feel like a change.'

I looked at him steadily. He held my eyes and, this time, didn't try a grin.

'We're all fallible, Flossie,' he said softly at last. 'All human. And maybe you're right. Maybe that encapsulates it. But is it so terrible?'

'No,' I said slowly, 'it's not terrible. It's reasonable, at our age. And realistic. But don't dress it up as something else. As a grand passion. You know very well that if we ran away together – which there isn't the slightest chance of our doing – we'd still end up getting on each other's nerves. Cracks would appear, as they have with you and Mimi – me and James, for Christ's sake. Nobody's perfect. There are no fairy-tale endings. You just have to keep buggering on.'

He nodded. 'You're right. You are preachy.'

'Which you'd forgotten. See? And, after a bit, it would irritate you. Drive you mad. Ask James. My daughters. They'll tell you. Go back to Mimi, Max. And give her my love.'

His eyes widened at this. 'She feels that she shat on you from a very great height.'

'Did it bother her?'

'Of course. She's not a bitch. She was just . . .' He shrugged.

'Overtaken by something more important than our friendship. I know.'

I did know. Mimi and I had been friends. Shared a flat. And I'd forgiven her years ago because, in a way, she'd delivered me to James.

'I'm going to preach again.'

'Jesus wept.' Max put his head in his hands.

'Sometimes the hardest route is the most worthwhile.'

'Wait. Hang on.' He folded his napkin lengthwise. Leaned across and put it round my neck, like a dog collar. 'Go on.'

I pulled it off. 'I mean it, Max. You're scared of going back to Mimi because she's a strong woman and you know she's not going to be pathetically grateful to have her man back and give you a hero's welcome.'

'I'm not saying she'd make me pay . . .'

'No, because, as you say, she's not a bitch. But you're going to have to put your back into it, not just swan in being suave and charming, and that makes you nervous. But it'll be worth it.'

The waiter brought the bill. Max paid in silence and I

324

watched him: loving him, in a way. Not like James, but just in an incredibly fond, 'What a shame I don't see you any more, I was extremely close to you' sort of way. And if he really searched his heart, I think that was actually the way he felt about me. He'd deny it, but I'd say it was so.

We walked to the car in silence. He had his arm draped around my shoulders, and that felt entirely right. We got in and he started the engine. The car bumped slowly back down the goat track, then navigated the zigzag lane through the pines, before we sped back along the coast road. The forested hills were to our left this time, the glittering expanse of water to our right, the sun beating down. When we stopped at some lights I could see he was deep in thought: it was almost as if I weren't in the car any more. I took a strand of hair from my mouth.

'What are you going to do about Sally?'

He turned. 'Hm? Oh, you don't need to worry about Sally. You'll be surprised to hear she wanted even less from this relationship than I did. No strings. I should think she'll be glad to see the back of me.'

I recalled her skipping gaily off to the pool with her book and her oily hair. For a day, I'd thought; but perhaps Max was right. Perhaps she didn't want anything. We'd all just assumed she did. But Sally didn't subscribe to that Darwinian instinct to settle eventually on one person. Like Rachel, she preferred her own company, but she was less straightforward about it: dressed it up differently. Assumed a more elaborate disguise, a camouflage of constant chirruping, in order to appear – well, like everyone else.

'I'll ring her this evening. Tell her I've got held up with work in Cannes and won't be returning. Then I'll have dinner with her when she gets back. She won't mind a bit.'

No. She probably wouldn't. Might even be relieved. She was a strange one, Sally. The only person she'd possibly ever been close to, outside of the family, had been Donaldson, but although my girls had wondered about that, Rachel and I had always thought no. No, this wouldn't shatter Sally.

We drew up at the airport right outside the Departure doors, Max ignoring the drop-off zone. He got out and went round to take my bag out of the boot. When he came back we stood facing each other: no embarrassment, just smiling. He opened his arms and I walked into them. He hugged me and I laid my cheek on his shirt, still smiling. When we drew back, he looked quizzical.

'By the way, did you ever contact your father again?'

My mouth dried. I retreated quickly into myself, behind my eyes. Closed the shutters. An angry horn blared loudly, a taxi driver behind us, outraged at Max's audacious parking. He was shaking a Gallic fist and shouting, leaning almost out of his window in rage. Max threw up his hands in response and a furious exchange broke out between the two men, with absolutely no serious intent on either side. Max came back to me. Grinned.

'Better go.'

'Yes.'

He held me again. 'Take care of yourself,' he whispered.

'And you.' I whispered back. 'Great care.'

Then he turned and went.

Chapter Twenty-Four

I joined the easyJet check-in queue for the second time that day. It snaked for miles and, on another day, at another time, I'd have found an official, asked questions, demanded answers – been embarrassing, my daughters would say: 'doing a Mum'. Right now, though, I just took it on the chin. I was feeling numb, so standing in a daze in a queue of complete strangers, thoughts chasing around my head, suited me. I welcomed the complete inertia in my body to counteract my very fast brain.

The man in front of me turned and gave a wry smile. 'Not much we can do about it, is there?'

I gazed at him. Middle-aged, nice, open face, balding. Actually, there was.

'Excuse me,' I muttered, sort of to him but also to the young chap behind me, who was weighed down with an assortment of backpacks and was blocking the way. I muscled past and through the throng, in the direction of the main concourse. Then I span around, looking for signs. Ah. That way. Down the escalator I went, following directions to the station. In the end, I had to get a taxi across town, as the station was not situated within the airport, it transpired, and then, when I reached it, I spent ages trying to work out a French timetable. In the end, I gave up. I explained my destination to the girl at the window, through the grille, and was told that '*Bien sûr*', it was indeed possible to get a train, or at least in that direction. There was one to Grasse in half an hour, but from there I would have to get a taxi, or a bus. No trains. 'C'est difficile.' Lots of shrugging. It was not an accessible place. I'd manage, though, I decided, bag clutched on my knees half an hour later, as the train, with surprising punctuality, departed.

The journey was beautiful. If I'd had a mind to appreciate it, I'd have experienced the route swooping up over mountains dense with pine and then dropping down dramatically through tunnels to emerge into fabulous countryside. Even in my dry-mouthed, shallow-breathed state, I sensed the drama of my surroundings. After the Massif Central came hilltop villages, old men staring at the train as if they'd never seen one before as they herded sheep or goats. After an hour or so, we trundled into Grasse and I realized I hadn't released my grip on the handle of my bag the entire journey. My hands were white. I flexed them gingerly. As I got off the train I tested my knees, too, stiff from holding the exact same position, a heavy bag resting on them.

The taxi was sick-making. The car was old and very proximate to the ground. None too clean either, and the driver smoked continuously. I opened the back window and gulped down air, hoping I wasn't going to throw up, but relieved, in a way, to have something else to concentrate on. We lurched on for miles, swinging around bends without slowing down, me being thrown around in the back. As we drew closer, finding the chateau seemed to be entirely my responsibility, despite my giving the driver the address. Lots of raised hands – both of them off the wheel at the same time – as I directed him into another wrong turn, and another. Plenty of *'Merde!'* and murderous glances at the meter, which I'm sure he was not disappointed to see rocketing but wanted me to be aware of, aware that this was all my fault, in case I quibbled, no doubt. Finally, he flung me around yet another hairpin bend, but this time on to a dusty lane I recognized.

'Alors – ici!' I told him, leaning forwards. *'Au bout de cette voie – là-bas!'*

'Ah, oui,' he muttered, as if he'd known all along. I got the distinct impression we'd been carefully circumnavigating the house for some time.

'Ici – ce côté de la porte,' I told him firmly and, obediently, he stopped short of the gates.

I paid him, practically all the money I had, then waited a moment for him to go. I inhaled great mouthfuls of fresh air. Before turning around, I composed myself a moment, in the dust the taxi had left in its speeding wake, which hung, suspended, then I turned and walked through the tall iron gates to the chateau with my old blue bag. I felt a bit like Maria returning to the abbey. Or had she been fleeing from it? I could never remember. Was always in too much of a drunken haze on Christmas Day, just about coming round for 'Edelweiss'.

As I passed the lodge cottage perched at the end of the drive, I saw Michel and Thérèse bent double in their vegetable garden. They straightened up when they saw me, yellow corncobs in their hands, staring as I went by in that blatant, French way. I didn't greet them, and they didn't acknowledge me either. Agathe was with them, a basket full of tomatoes over her arm as she shaded her eyes to watch. On I strode, feeling, not like Maria now, more like

Clint. Yes, in some spaghetti western: a gun on each hip, ready to shoot from both. I hesitated, though, when I got to the front door, flung wide, as usual, to reveal the ubiquitous tangle of flip-flops, paperbacks, sun cream and hats strewn on the hall table and the floor. Should I go inside and upstairs to my room to ponder what to do next? Let people find me? Spread the word themselves? Or should I go round the back, brazen as you like, to encounter them all on the terrace or under the trees, announcing, quite simply, that I'd had a change of heart and wasn't going home at all, and did anyone know what was for supper?

Upstairs to my room.

I crept up the stone staircase, feeling a bit foolish now. It had seemed so right at the airport. Also on the train. Less so in the car. And now . . . I wasn't sure I could pull it off. I left the bedroom door ajar so that I might be seen or heard. Sat down on the bed. But nothing happened for a long time. I could hear voices below on the terrace. I coughed. Coughed again. Still nothing. Finally, I opened the shutters, which had been shut against the heat of the day, with a bit of a bang. Silence below. Then murmurings. At last, footsteps on the stairs, and Tara came in, eyes as wide as when I'd left her, still in her pink bikini.

'Mum! What are you doing back?'

'I had a change of heart, darling.' I bustled around the room being busy, unpacking my bag, which I'd deliberately left full to give me something to do, popping creams back in the bathroom, nightie under my pillow. 'Decided I could say everything I wanted to say to Maria on the phone and that it was pointless going all the way back just to have a conversation.'

'Right.' She looked stunned. 'But what about doing it in person, all that "much better face to face" stuff?'

I felt weary already. Had I said that? I could never remember my own web of lies.

'Well, yes, of course. Ordinarily, that would be the way forward but, you see, there was a baggage handlers' strike and I wouldn't have got a flight until the early hours. I didn't fancy a night on the airport floor.'

'Oh God, no.' Tara and Amelia had passed swiftly through the age of finding it fun to sleep on the floor of a soggy marquee after a party; indeed, my elder daughter had been known to book herself into a B&B after an eighteenth in deepest Wiltshire. Why hadn't I thought of that earlier? The truth?

'So will you go back tomorrow?'

'No, I think not. I shall ring Maria now. Tell her my position.'

'Which is?'

'Well, I'll . . . give it some thought.'

'Presumably you've been thinking of nothing else!'

'Yes, but –'

'Blimey – what are you doing back?' Rarely have I been so pleased to see Amelia.

'Baggage handlers' strike,' I told her.

'And she's changed her mind about the face-to-face bit,' put in Tara.

'Well, as I say, I can do it on the phone.'

'Oh, right. What about the sustained attack with Lizzie? "Girl power"?' Amelia raised her eyebrows.

'She'd have to have spent the night at the airport,' Tara said helpfully.

'Oh, gross.'

They watched me bustling around for a bit then turned to go, satisfied – or bored, perhaps – just as the boys appeared in the corridor. Their eyes were large as they peered over their girlfriends' heads at this strange woman, totally unlike their own mothers – I'd met neither, but the spectre of Rory's plagued me constantly – who boomeranged back and forth on a family holiday. The girls tactfully turned them around, and I sat down wearily on the bed, rubbing my aching brow with my fingertips. I listened to them amble downstairs. Knew they'd eventually spread the word, but knew it could also be a while, so dull and inconsequential was I, only really useful as a provider of food or fresh laundry, and since that wasn't necessary with Thérèse to do it, of no real consequence at all. They wouldn't rush to find their father.

I lay down on the bed to wait. Sat up, almost immediately. Swung my legs round and braced myself as his familiar footsteps sounded up the stairs. For the first time in my life, I felt scared. I remembered his fury on the way to Seillans. His taut, white face. But as he came into the room and shut the door behind him, I knew. Five hours alone had cooled his temper, just as it had mine the day before. He was no longer ablaze. On fire. That sort of combustion and momentum cannot be maintained unless you're a certain type of person, and James wasn't.

'What happened?'

'There was a baggage handlers' strike. I could have gone much later tonight, but I changed my mind.'

'Oh?'

'Yes, I've had a long time to think about it. Also, Max

was at the airport, James. Waiting for me, I think. Well, yes, he was. I was so furious with you for sending me home, I had lunch with him. After all, I had five hours to kill.'

James didn't say anything. A muscle went in his cheek, though, as he stared down at me.

'And I knew I no longer had any feelings for him, which was why it was all right to go, and I don't know if you'll understand that, but I'm telling you anyway. It's the truth. We had lunch in a very beautiful place overlooking the bay, with delicious wine and seafood, and he's terribly attractive, and I felt absolutely nothing, except an old bond of friendship and familiarity and a wish that we'd remained friends.'

'Bully for you. How nice of you to come all the way back to share that with me.'

'The point is, James, I never did feel anything. It was just a silly, drunken, summer-holiday indiscretion. I haven't been hankering away all these years for Max.'

'Again, my thanks to you for clarifying that.'

'But that's not what I came back to tell you.'

He stared at me. Didn't speak.

'I came back to tell you that – that –' Unaccountably, my knees began to shake. Physically tremble as I sat there. I put my hands on them. Began to feel tears sting behind my eyes, streaming down my face. A lack of air.

'I came back to tell you about my father.' I felt the air rush out of my lungs as if from a vortex. 'I've known all these years, but I've blocked it. I've blanked it.'

And then I broke down. Dissolved. I felt James sit beside me. He didn't say anything. Didn't put his arm around me, not that I was expecting it. I wasn't going for the sympathy vote here, that hadn't even occurred to me. I knew it wouldn't occur to James either. I just knew I couldn't keep it in any longer and that there was only one person I could share it with. I sobbed quite loudly and violently, and he got up and shut the windows. The shutters, too, plunging the room into deep gloom. Then he sat down again.

'Years ago,' I blurted out, quite loudly, 'Max and I went looking for him.'

'I know. You told me.'

'But I didn't tell you we found him.'

'No.'

'Because – well, you see –'

'You don't have to tell me.'

'I do,' I said fiercely.

'Right.'

I gulped. 'We tracked him down through his sister, in Brighton. Max and I went through Mum's things one day, in her bedroom, when she was out with Neville at the races, like a couple of budding detectives. We thought we were so clever. We found letters. Not from him, but from this sister, referring to someone called Tom, who was so sorry. And this sister – Sonia, she was called – was wondering if there was anything she could do. Max and I knew it was my father; we were convinced. Mum had clearly been left in the lurch with a baby and, for some reason, had never breathed a word. We got the train down to Brighton, to Sonia. She was still living with her parents, a mean-looking, closed-up couple. Sonia was better. The house was horrible, though, James, almost a slum. Max and I were horrified.' I took a deep breath. 'It turned out

Tom was in prison. For drugs. Not just possession, for supplying. Young people. But also for conning old ladies out of their savings to buy the drugs. He'd become notorious in Brighton. When her parents finally left the room, Sonia showed us the newspaper clippings. The trial. My mother beside him, looking shocked. So young. A baby – me – in her arms. He was very good-looking. Chiselled features, wavy, dark hair. He'd hit one of these old ladies, one of the ones he preyed on, and she hadn't died but was very shaken up. This was all reported as the trial went on. After that, Mum wasn't by his side any more with me in her arms. There was a picture of the old lady in her hospital bed, with black eyes, bruises.'

I was shaking, my voice rising hysterically. James's arms were around me now, holding me close as he sat beside me. It was only now I'd even noticed.

'He was charming, apparently. He'd worked his way into the old ladies' lives, their homes, by valuing their antiques. He was a dealer. In so many ways. It was mostly widows with death duties to pay. He'd sell their paintings and then keep most of the profits, giving them only a fraction. Then he'd sell more and more of their possessions, until this old lady – Cynthia Chambers, she was called – refused to part with her silver. So he beat her up. That's my father. That's my father, James.' I shook and sobbed as he held me.

'Max asked me about it as I left, said, "Did you ever contact your father again?" I couldn't speak. Hadn't let myself think about it for twenty years. Just ignored him. But I did follow it up.'

'And?'

I struggled.

'Don't say. Not if you don't want to.'

'I *do*!' Vehemently. I licked my lips. 'Max and I left the house in Brighton shocked and horrified. He asked if I wanted him to come to the prison with me. Meet him? I said no. But later, I went on my own and didn't tell him. I was so ashamed. So embarrassed. Max's parents were lovely. And, obviously, I didn't tell Mum.'

'Not even that you knew?'

'No. I decided she was so appalled and horrified she'd tried to protect me. Her one bad apple. All the others were so lovely, James. Philippe, Neville . . .'

'I know.'

'I didn't want to hurt her.'

'No. But you went to see him?'

'Yes.' I shuddered. 'Horrible. Unbelievably horrible. Again – I blanked it. A queue of women outside, a sort I was so unfamiliar with. Scary-looking. Bleached blondes chewing gum, chain-smoking, although most of them looked scared, too. We were shown to a big room with small tables and a chair either side. A complete stranger came in and sat down opposite me. Tried to take my hand.' I shook my head. 'I'm not sure I can even tell you about it, James.'

'Then don't.'

'But it hurt that Max knew and you didn't.'

'Yes. But that was timing. Circumstances.'

'Yes.'

'And he doesn't know this. Don't rehash it. Don't pick that scab. It's not healthy. You've told me, and I know. That's all that matters.'

'Don't you want to know where he is now?'

'Only if you want to tell me. You don't have to.'

'He lives in Singapore. With his third wife. She's Thai. I have half-brothers and sisters. I have no idea how many.'

'No.'

'I don't have to, do I, James?'

'No, you don't have to.'

'I was so scared that if I told someone – you even – I'd have to find out. That those were the rules. Wasn't allowed to just – let it lie.'

'Although your mother did. Sensibly.'

'Yes.'

'There are no rules, Flora.'

'Amelia would disagree. Tara even, they'd –'

'Be forensic, I know. Pore over it. And be aghast you hadn't looked into your new family, dug it all up. It's fine, Flora, leave it.'

'He may even be dead now, for all I know.'

I felt calmer, suddenly. Shattered, but calmer. It was out. And it had been in there for so long: buried very deep. With a heavy boulder on top. Max had been sworn to secrecy years ago and I knew he'd never share it with anyone. Max was genuine. And I didn't blame him for bringing it up just now. I might easily have done the same. But he had no idea what reaction those few words would provoke: 'Did you ever contact your father again?'

He'd unwittingly lit the blue touchpaper. And I'd quietly gone up in smoke. Imploded inside, in that easyJet queue, perhaps the combustion more tremendous for being buried for so long. And then I'd run to the one person in the world I knew I needed, come what may. James.

We sat on the bed together, side by side, and I knew exactly where we both were, in our heads. In Bistro Vino,

South Kensington, many years ago. Nineteen, to be precise, after I'd happily agreed to marry him. After he'd told me about his father and his mother, and after we'd agreed, holding hands in the candlelight, the wax dripping down the bottle, to so many things: mostly that we hated duplicity more than anything in the world; that we would never deceive one another. That his mother had hurt his father too badly for James ever to marry anyone who might eventually be capable of such a thing. That I had been a child of a one-parent family for too long not to want a forever marriage. And Max had deceived me and I never wanted to feel like that again. We didn't go into it deeply, we weren't heavy about it, but it could have been written in blood.

But there'd been another pact, too – an implicit, tacit one – that night. I'd been the one gingerly to broach it, wondering if two people, however much in love they were, needed to know absolutely everything about each other? Wondering if a person could still possibly have, not a secret, but something they felt they never wanted to share with anyone in the world? Meaning my father. Because, once shared, I'd gone on hesitantly, it was out there for real. Enormous. Uncontrollable. And before I'd even got to the end of the sentence, James had agreed. I remember the light in his eyes in the flickering candle flame: those eyes as they seized on something they recognized completely.

'I agree,' he'd said quickly. 'As long as it's not something that affects the other, why should anyone own the other completely?'

'Yes,' I'd said, surprised at his alacrity, and the way he'd put it. But so, so relieved. Knowing I wasn't ever going to be probed but had at least admitted to owning something he'd never know. And he'd never asked. As I had obviously never asked him.

But it was different now. I'd told him my secret. And, childishly, I wondered if he'd tell me his. I felt so much better having divulged, I realized. Exhausted. Shattered. Spent. As if I'd been sick, actually, which in a way I had, I'd spewed it out, but – it was all so long ago. It had felt huge then, in Bistro Vino – enormous. Had become more so because I'd hidden it, I realized. But now that it was out – why, it wasn't that momentous at all. My father. Just a sad old loser – a violent old loser – who'd procreated carelessly and produced quite a few children along the way, one of them being me. But I'd been lucky enough to have my mother. I breathed in deeply. Let it out slowly. I realized I felt almost evangelical about how much better I felt. I reached for James's hand. And maybe . . . just maybe.

But he was getting to his feet. Walking around to the window. Leaning over the bed to open the shutters. Then the window. Light poured in. He stood, staring out. Letting the air, the voices, the world, flood back in. No longer cocooned here in the dark, in our closed-off, womb-like world, everything changed. I licked my lips, knowing another opportunity might not come my way for years.

'James . . .'

'Come on, Flora. Have a shower, freshen up, or whatever, and then come down.'

He turned from the window to look at me, his eyes so guarded, so blank. I felt afraid.

'Yes,' I whispered. 'Yes, I will. And . . . thank you, James.'

He gave me the ghost of a smile, but didn't hesitate for a second. In another moment, he was gone.

Chapter Twenty-Five

I did as instructed and showered, changed and then went down. It was almost drinks time, almost six o'clock, and I needed one very badly. I felt exhausted and utterly drained, but so, so glad not to be back home in Clapham. I avoided the kitchen, where I could hear people talking, and instead walked down the corridor to access the terrace via the drawing room, deep in thought. Unfortunately, as I pushed through the door, I realized I'd chosen the same room my mother and Jean-Claude had elected for a quiet tête-à-tête. They were sitting on one of the long, creamy sofas, holding hands.

'Darling, how lovely!' Mum jumped up and clasped her hands together prettily, eyes alight. Jean-Claude got to his feet, too. He clapped me on the back as Mum hugged me.

'First of all, I couldn't believe you'd gone, and now, like a miracle, you're back!'

Particularly without saying goodbye, she meant, but was too nice to say it. Mum never emotionally blackmailed, or applied pressure, she was too generous for that: just focused on the good things, like me returning. Not for the first time, I hoped I'd mostly inherited my mother's genes and not Tom's. Obviously, this had preoccupied me at times. Was it why I was impatient? So volatile? The girls had often said, 'You're so different to Granny!' And I'd cringe. Amelia would go on to say sagely, 'You're probably like your father.' It hadn't frightened them, this mythical grandfather, because, naturally, they'd glamorized him. A French count whose aristocratic family Mum had protected. A diplomat with a high-profile career. A film star, already married with a family. After all, Granny had been so beautiful, her men so exotic. They'd never thought of a low-down crook. How disappointed they'd be. And, naturally, I worried for their genes, too. Why did Amelia have a temper? Tara, so indecisive? Or was it all nonsense anyway and far more to do with nurture than nature? I hoped so. And, of course, there'd been Sonia, who'd done the right thing, reached out to Mum. Tried to help. Maybe they weren't all bad apples in that family. And maybe Tom – I could never, even in my head, call him my father – had just taken a wrong turn? Some of the children's friends took drugs, I knew that – Toby, probably – it was not unusual. And if Tom had become addicted, well, then the natural extension of that was . . . no. No, it was inexcusable. This was where Tom and I always parted company. When he hit the old lady.

I gasped as Mum held me now, not from the pressure, but at the thought of how she must have suffered, on her own. She held me at arm's length, eyes dancing. 'I am *so* pleased,' she said.

'And I'm glad to be back, Mum,' I said, with unusual warmth. She blinked, surprised.

I wasn't always very nice to her, I knew that. Was impatient; scornful. But what a brave decision she'd made not to share Tom with me. Not to burden me with that baggage. If only I hadn't gone looking. I could have luxuriated in the same blissful ignorance as Amelia and Tara.

Something in my make-up, though, meant I'd always have searched. Without Mum's bedside box, I'd have found him anyway. Tracked him down through Interpol or DNA. I have that relentless, probing nature.

'And you're staying? Not dashing off again? Amelia said there was a baggage handlers' strike or something . . .'

'Oh yes, I'm staying. This place is too gorgeous to leave, Mum.'

'I know. Which is why . . .' she glanced at Jean-Claude, who nodded. 'Why I need to tell you my news, too.'

All at once, I realized her eyes were shining for other reasons.

'Oh?' I felt myself harden. Hated myself for it. But I knew what was coming.

She still had my arms. Made to sit down, but I remained standing. She hesitated.

'Darling, I'm going to stay in France, with JC. Move back over here.'

'We want to give it a try,' said JC, who'd seen my face.

'What, for ever?' I said, not liking my voice. 'I thought you said a few weeks?' What was wrong with me? Why was I like this? But I was upset. And this was always my knee-jerk reaction: to lash out.

'I miss France,' she said sadly. She perched on the cream sofa. Instead of standing stonily above her, I made myself perch beside her. Jean-Claude went to sit opposite. 'I realize that now. I had so many happy years in Paris, and down here I feel . . . well, I'm much more myself. I'm much more Mediterranean than English, Flora, this place speaks to me.'

'It speaks to me, too,' I said, before I could stop myself.

'Everything about it. The way of life, the people, the accent on prettiness and charm – I love prettiness and charm. I'm possibly even twee – is that so terrible? In England, I feel I'm constantly saying sorry for the way I am, for being feminine, rather than feminist. I don't like feminists, they scare me.' She hesitated. 'And I like men. I love the difference between men and women – *vive la différence!* – why not! I'm freer to think that sort of thing here. You'll scoff, Flora, but I know I'll be perfectly happy bagging up lavender bags and tying pretty ribbons on them on a sunny doorstep, cooking for Jean-Claude in the evening. It's my idea of paradise. And I wouldn't have to apologize all the time.'

To me, she meant. The apologizing bit. She'd phrased it as if she needed to apologize to the whole world, or at least the whole of England, but she meant me. Sorry for being scatty, for not having a tidy house, for feeding the birds in the park every day. For tie-dyeing all her T-shirts, chain-smoking, taking in stray cats, wearing ribbons in her hair, baseball caps, for always being in the pub with a man, playing canasta, roaring with laughter, at her age. I was a drudge. Always her brakes. And she wanted to get away. Or was I being paranoid? Was it absolutely nothing to do with me? I'd miss her so much, though. A huge lump filled my throat. So much, it hurt. She'd always been round the corner, always. Just there, for me. *Me*. So much, I'd taken for granted. I felt panicky. Thought I'd grown out of that feeling. The terror of Mum dying. When I was young, I'd awake bolt upright in bed, covered in sweat. I knew I had to be grown up now. Let her go. But if only it were Paris. Not so far. Deep in the south of France.

343

'It's a plane ride away,' she said gently, knowing.

'Yes.'

Up to now, though, I'd see her three times a week. Four, sometimes, if I popped in on a Sunday. Didn't I mention that? And yes, I usually went there. Oh, she came to Clapham, but mostly it was me making the journey. Well, you know, a lot of my restaurants were in her neck of the woods: Chelsea, Belgravia; I'd pop in after lunch. No reason to shop in M&S in the King's Road, though: there was one much closer to home. I looked at Jean-Claude, who was watching me.

'I'll look after her,' he said gently. And I knew he would. Knew she'd chosen another good egg, and that, even though they'd only known one another a short while, there'd been an instant rapport. They'd recognized each other. But Mum knew I wasn't worried about that.

'If it doesn't work out, I'll be back,' she said, to keep my panic at bay.

'It will work out,' said Jean-Claude, more realistically. The truth, which I needed. I looked across at him gratefully.

'And will you carry on with the shop?'

'Of course!' said Mum in surprise. 'But I'm going to make the outside so much prettier. Paint all the window frames a dusty pink and have a little reopening party. Invite the locals, get to know them all. It'll be so much fun!'

'Despite the crowded market?' I wasn't talking to her now. She sounded too much like a character in *Miranda*, or *Ab Fab*. 'The other night, you said it was so seasonal?'

'You're right, it is.' More truth from JC. 'And sometimes, I think . . .'

'What?' I said quickly.

'Nothing. Because that's a crowded market, too. And I don't want your mother to put money in. She can buy the pink paint,' his mouth twitched, 'but that's it.'

'Oh, but JC, that's how we're going to expand!' Mum exclaimed, lighting a cigarette, crossing her tiny knees and blowing smoke out excitedly. 'Buy another shop, in the next village perhaps, or –'

'If you touch your savings, it's off. *Fini*,' he said firmly. 'I'm not interested.'

She pouted. He turned back to me.

'And I don't think she should sell her house, either.'

'But I'll go to Flora's when I'm in London, I won't need it. Why would I –'

'Rent it out,' he told her, interrupting. 'Rent the London house, don't sell. That way you'll have an income.' He turned to me. 'You tell her, Flora. Never get rid of property, especially in a capital city. Lease it.'

I sighed, at a loss against his rational argument. How could I tell her she was being foolish, when she had someone more sensible than me at the helm? All I could do was nod, agree with JC, give them my blessing and hope my highly emotional state – I was now on the verge of tears – had more to do with the past twelve hours than with me, a happily married woman with two children, being unable to live within a ten-minute drive of her ditsy, impossible, highly irritating mother.

I should be delighted she's having another chance, I thought as I went out to the terrace. Too many people were gathered there, so I slipped through the French windows to the kitchen. A life in the sun with a gorgeous man

345

who loves her. I shouldn't be helping Thérèse lay the table for supper – I delved into the cutlery drawer – with stupid, shaking hands. I doggedly put the knives, forks and spoons around the table on the terrace, ignoring Thérèse, who sighed and clucked, following me out and replacing them with the spoons she wanted – pudding, not soup – and sharper knives for steak.

But, actually, I'd known this was coming. Had known the other day, when, although they'd talked in terms of a holiday, a few weeks, they'd meant a lot longer. I'd had a while to get used to it. Mum had carefully seen to that. I knew I couldn't trust myself to talk about it yet, though, and since I couldn't sit quietly in a corner on my own without drawing attention, activity was best. I began to clear up the terrace, plumping cushions, collecting stray glasses, retrieving clothes from the floor, books from under chairs. The girls caught my mood and, assuming it was a bad one rather than an upset one, quietly got up from their comfy chairs to help. They were slightly in the dog house anyway, since I'd caught them coming out of Camille's room in the tower earlier, having a snoop. They went to the kitchen to fill water jugs, find glasses for the table, giving each other 'What's up with her?' looks.

James had bought a bottle of port from the vineyard he'd got the wine from and was showing the boys how to decant it properly, straining it through a piece of muslin he'd found in a drawer. Mum, pleased to have told me, to have got that over with, skipped off down the garden to pick some flowers for the table. JC sat on the terrace and watched her go with a fond smile. She was younger than me, in spirit, I thought as I paused in my clearing up to watch her bend down and gently pluck nasturtiums from their base, gathering them in a bunch. Always had been. Lighter. Kinder. Nicer. I got Tom. Aware I was in trouble now, I hummed away to the music Rory had put on the iPod in the kitchen: Jack Johnson, or Mumford & Sons, chosen, diplomatically, to appeal to all ages.

Sally appeared in a wafting blue kaftan-style dress, more the sort of thing she used to wear in Scotland. I realized I hadn't given her a thought. She looked happy and relaxed, though, helping her father down the step to the terrace. Drummond, bathed, florid and fragrant with Trumper's aftershave, looked even more delighted than usual.

'My dear!' He raised his stick exuberantly. 'So glad you're back. Excellent decision. Wretched magazine. Their loss, not yours.'

'I'm glad, too,' Sally said warmly. 'And I gather you had lunch with Max,' she went on, and boy, was I pleased I'd told James. Imagine how that little revelation could have ricocheted around the terrace.

'Yes,' I said breathlessly, as James continued instructing the boys, not turning a hair.

'He rang earlier,' she went on. 'He's got so much on at the moment, I don't honestly think he'll be back.'

'No, he – sort of said.' I was nervous of knowing more than she did. Of being better informed. But she was so nonchalant. Happy, almost. I believed Max now – not that I hadn't at the time – but I was glad of this clarification. Their liaison had meant possibly less to Sally than it had to him. Just because I, Flora Murray-Brown, took every relationship seriously, whether it be a blood tie, a best friend, an ex-lover, my neighbour, my cleaning lady even, it didn't mean everyone did. Some were happy alone. Better alone. Stronger, perhaps.

Rachel appeared. It occurred to me that, for once, she didn't look so composed, so serene, but she wouldn't meet my eye, so I distracted myself by listening to the general chatter as we sat down to fillet steak, hollandaise sauce and salad. Camille had gone for good, it seemed, back to Paris, according to Thérèse, so when Mum shared her news, it was with family and friends. With people who knew and loved her. The girls were surprised and delighted.

'But Granny, that's fantastic! You and JC are just made for each other. Tara and I have said so all along, haven't we?'

'You're one of those soul-mate couples, you know?' Tara said earnestly. 'That you read about? Who sometimes take years to find each other, but when they do, you just know it's right.'

The older members of the party smiled at their plates.

'It's brilliant, Mum, isn't it,' she went on, turning to me. 'Don't you agree?'

'I do,' I said carefully. 'But Granny's going to live in France, don't forget.'

'Oh, Granny, we'll miss you!' Despair now, and real shock, as the implications dawned. But youthful idealism and enthusiasm returned as Mum quickly outlined her plans.

'No, because, look, on easyJet it costs practically nothing and they fly straight to Nice, two flights a day. And you can come out every holiday, not just in the summer. Imagine having a granny in the south of France! How glam is that? You'll be in St Tropez in a jiffy. And, anyway, I'll be back and forth.'

'Will you?'

'Of course I will! And think how brown you'll be – a year-round tan!'

'And we could come out and revise with you?'

'Exactly! Bring your books and laze in the sun.'

They were loving this already. In their mind's eye, they'd recreated a luxurious setting just like this one: a huge garden full of tropical palms, an infinity pool, a view of the sea, whereas the reality would be a tiny back yard, or even just the front step of the shop, in a provincial, dusty town, above which, Mum and JC would live. Not that it would bother Mum. She'd make it pretty. Fix windowboxes, fill them with trailing plants, add a balcony, perhaps. Arrange pots of herbs around the front door, bring the antiques outside and sit amongst them in the summer, sewing and chatting to new friends, playing backgammon, basil and thyme wafting. She'd persuade the girls when they came out that it was charm, not glitz and glamour, that was important: get them sewing, too. For now, though, as they adjusted to Granny not being round the corner, where they often went straight from school or college, or later on in the evening for a glass of wine and no doubt a cigarette, baring their souls in a way they never would to me, she let them think they'd be jetting out every other week to join the smart set. In reality, of course, flights to Nice not being cheap, once a year they'd drive to Portsmouth, put their old Clio on the ferry and drive mile upon mile to see her. They'd miss her so much. More than they knew. We'd all miss her so much. She was, quite simply, the lynchpin of this family. Just as she'd been in my small one, years ago. James caught my eye in sympathy, and I was grateful.

Supper rattled along and I held my own with Mum and the girls, exclaiming, delighting in their every plan and idea for her new life, but I was glad when it was over. There was a limit to the extent that I could say, 'Yes – terrific idea!' or 'Why not sell greeting cards, too?' and sound like I meant it. Now, with pudding over, I could leave them to their cheese and port and legitimately help Thérèse in the kitchen, even though I could tell she didn't want me. All the while, whilst I was pottering about and getting in her way, putting the dishwasher on when it wasn't quite full, causing her to tut and open it again, I kept an eye on the table. If someone had a plan, I had one, too. One that would help, I knew. I was waiting for the one who I was sure would go early to bed, with her book. Who'd rise quietly from the far end of the table and slip off. Ah. There. As she duly bid goodnight to everyone and came through the kitchen, I intercepted her.

'Rachel – could I have a word? Before you go up?' My voice was a bit breathless.

She looked surprised. But then – not so surprised. Instantly, the shutters came down. 'Well, I was just going to help Daddy . . .' She turned. Drummond was a few steps behind her.

'Oh, nonsense,' he roared. 'You fuss too much. I'll be absolutely fine! Anyone would think I was an old crone. Go on, Rachel, you girls go and have a natter and a glass of something. You never have a night with the younger crew.'

'Because I'm happy with my book.'

'It won't take a mo,' I pleaded, and anyway, Drummond was already on his way past us. Waving his stick in a

350

backward salute, he successfully negotiated the step up from the kitchen to the hall, and was shuffling eagerly – showing off, almost – across the limestone floor to bed. Rachel looked scared.

'Let's go through here.' I knew I had to be firm. Seize the initiative and the moment. Not let her dither. I led her down the corridor and through the door to the drawing room, but it was a huge, formal room, the only light, when I flicked it on, being the bright, overhead chandelier. I hesitated in its glare. Rachel, to my surprise, wisely crossed through and opened the French doors to the terrace on the west side.

'I'd rather be outside,' she told me, as we slipped out into the night.

In the dark, I decided she meant, and my heart began to pound. I'd thought, given half a chance, she'd run, but there was something decidedly collaborative about her now.

We walked down the sloping lawn, away from the house, in silence. On we padded, distancing ourselves from the chattering family around the table, from the twinkling lights strung between the trees. The buzz of voices became more muffled in the still night air. I realized we were heading for a tiny terrace the children smoked on, a round, stone one, which came equipped with a small iron bench. It was in a natural hollow just short of the orchard; a sunken space that someone – Camille's landscape gardener, no doubt – had realized would make a delightful sanctuary to catch the setting sun. The evening air was heavy now with the powerful scent of the rosemary bushes he'd planted strategically in a circle around it. There was a tiny candle on the little mosaic table and a lighter the children had left. I went to light it, but Rachel stayed my hand. The faint glow from the house made our faces just visible, and that was enough for her tonight. Also, I realized, it would threaten our privacy.

We sat down on the bench side by side, and I wondered how to embark on this. How to phrase it. Rachel, I knew, was not going to assist me. It helped that we weren't facing each other. I could study my hands. I licked my lips and dived in.

'Rachel, I know – have known, for years – that James has been keeping something back from me. But, out of respect for his privacy, I've never asked him what it is. I asked him tonight for the first time, but he wouldn't tell me.'

There was a silence.

'And now you're asking me.'

'Because I feel I need to know.'

'Why, so suddenly?'

'Well . . .'

'Because you divulged something yourself?'

I turned. Blinked at her. 'How did you know?'

'I don't. I'm guessing. But, often, people don't question a secret if they have one themselves. But now that you've shared yours, you feel you have a perfect right to know his, is that it?' Her voice was uncharacteristically hard. I was startled.

'No. No, of course not. I just –'

'And now that your mother's deserting you, you want to clutch at another security blanket. You need to be sure of

James. You don't want this loose end. You want to claw something back, for you. Have all of him.'

I stared, shocked. Her expression was not one I recognized. It was tough. Unfriendly. All of a sudden, though, it collapsed back into the Rachel I knew.

'Sorry. I didn't mean that, Flora. Well . . . I did, and I didn't. I didn't mean it to sound so harsh.'

I gulped. Nodded. 'No. But . . . God. You're right, I suppose. I do feel a bit like that. A bit quid pro quo. A bit – now it's your turn. And I am upset about Mum. I hadn't analysed it to that extent. I suppose I am being a bit desperate.' My breath was becoming shallower. 'And I shouldn't be asking you, Rachel. It's James's secret and, if he doesn't want to tell me, I've no business going around his back. No business –'

'Except, it's my secret, too,' she interrupted.

I held my tongue. Held my breath, too. In the still night air, the cicadas paused in their chattering, and it seemed to me that, should a feather drop from a passing night owl, should a field mouse scuttle by, I'd hear it.

'And the thing is, Flora, I've always thought that one day you would know. That it was really just a question of time. A question of when. And I imagine that moment's arrived.'

Chapter Twenty-Six

We sat in silence for a moment before Rachel spoke again. At length, she cleared her throat. Her tone, as she went on, was contemplative, reflective.

'D'you find, as you get older, Flora, that you're more accepting of others? Their foibles and habits? Faults, even?'

I blinked, wrong-footed. 'Up to a point, yes. I try to be less judgemental, if that's what you mean.'

'I think it is. When you're young, everything is so black and white. So categorical. People are honest or dishonest. Trustworthy or unreliable. Good or bad. And, once that label is there, it sticks. We press it down hard with the heel of our hand. But I'd like to think I've become more accepting – more realistic, anyway – as I've got older.'

It occurred to me to think Rachel had never been anything other. At least, that was how she presented to the world. It was me who was quick to judge, to proclaim on someone.

'You've always been generous-spirited, Rachel.'

'No, I haven't. I was very hard on Mummy.'

I glanced at her. I'd never heard her say that. Only refer to her as 'our mother'.

'She was not so terribly different to your mother, Flora.'

I must have looked shocked: felt it, too.

'Who is completely delightful and enchanting,' she went

on quickly. 'Which Mummy wasn't, always. I'm just saying, there were some similarities. Both high-spirited women, young at heart – young, full stop, in my mother's case. Light-hearted. Fun. I was serious-minded and bookish. And I minded very much about her frivolity, as I saw it then. I was hard on her.'

'You were very young,' I reminded her.

'Yes. But I was . . . priggish. I hope I'm less so, now.'

It occurred to me that a young, bespectacled Rachel in dreary clothes and constantly with her nose in a book could have been described so.

'Sally was more like Mummy. But I was so disapproving, I even turned Sally against her. A bit. And Sally always looked up to me. Sally would say – Oh, but it's so dull here, Rachel, we know that. Mummy dresses up to go into town occasionally, to have some fun, buy clothes and have her hair done, just because she's bored: what's wrong with that? But I told her it was more than that. That she was staying out late, drinking with local men. Coming back very drunk in the small hours. Driving whilst drunk.'

'Which she was,' I reminded her.

'Yes, but I could have protected Mummy more. I told James, too. Went on about it. In a way, I think I poisoned them against her.'

'But she was out of control, Rachel. You had good reason. And why should you shoulder all that knowledge yourself?'

'Some older sisters might have done. But we were alone a lot in that cold, echoing place and, sometimes, stories were our only company. And, don't forget, I read a lot. Lived through stories, really. So I'd embellish. Say she was a disgrace, even though, on that particular day, she might only have been seeing a girlfriend for supper. My imagination ran riot. And Mummy and I didn't get on. I adored my father and hated his sadness. But . . . there were only two people in that marriage. I shouldn't have got involved. Shouldn't have taken sides. It was for them to work out.'

I shrugged. 'OK, but I think it's inevitable. Eldest child, you love them both, but side more with one –'

'Yes, but I didn't really,' she interrupted. She twisted round on the bench to face me. 'Love them both. I came to hate Mummy, and I idolized my father.'

I waited. Wondered what was coming.

'The night that . . . Mummy went into town, I told them about Darren, the builder she was seeing.'

'Told who?'

'James and Sally. Upstairs in my bedroom. Aunt Sarah's old room. We were all under the bedclothes, hugging our knees in the dark in that huge, spooky room, which hadn't been decorated since Daddy's childhood, with the big brass bed. I told them she was sleeping with another man.'

'Which she was.'

'I . . . don't know.'

She looked scared for a minute.

'Well, Rachel, everyone in the village said she was, it all came out in court. Darren's wife said so. It was in the paper I found.'

'Yes. It's just, I didn't know for sure. I was guessing. And came down against her. In a child's mind, that is obviously the ultimate treachery. One parent cheating on the other. Your mother sleeping with someone other than your father. They were incredibly shocked. Sally sobbed. She was only eleven. James shook, I remember. Physically shook with rage. Sally and I had to hold him. He went so white. I hurt him very badly. Couldn't have hurt him more if I'd stabbed him.'

I gazed at her, imagining it. Three children in their nightclothes, huddled together in bed.

'Anyway, that was the night Daddy got so drunk. I went down to the kitchen and tried to take the bottle away from him, but he wouldn't have it. Just sat there at the table with his whisky, staring at the door, waiting for her to come in. I went back upstairs and told James and Sally how upset he was, and nobody went to bed that night. We sat on my bed, frightened, in the dark. Squished together, still holding James, who was trembling.

'But you went to sleep eventually? I thought –'

'No.'

Thought the shot had wakened them, I was about to say. That's what I'd been told. I stared at her.

'Eventually, we heard the car, coming up the drive. I got out of bed and ran to the window. I remember seeing her get out of the car, staggering about. James was beside me. We saw her swaying in her high heels, which she took off. She was barefoot as she approached, clothes all askew. Sally was still crying quietly in the bed. We watched as she came stumbling, giggling even, towards the house. James was completely rigid beside me. Then we heard her come in. Obviously, she tried to creep in the back door to the kitchen, but she was met by a terrible roar from my father. We clutched each other as we waited for what would happen next. Daddy called her all the names under the sun – a whore, a tart, an adulterer, a cheap and trashy tramp. Mummy was shrill, defensive at first, but then derisive – abusive even. Very drunk. She was caustic and cutting. I remember hearing, 'Compared to you, *old man.*'

Then we heard a scuffle. We ran to the landing. James and I fled along the passageway and down the back stairs to the kitchen. They were fighting in there, really fighting. Wrestling. I remember racing to separate them and, as I did, I passed Daddy's gun, at the foot of the stairs, which was unusual. It was always in the gun safe, always – he was meticulous about that. But the fox had been prowling round the chickens the last few nights. He, or James, had put it there for easy access.'

'James doesn't shoot.'

'He did. Loved it. Rabbits, pheasants. Grouse, even. I saw James glance at it, too, but for longer than I did. Really stare.'

Oh dear God. I went cold.

'I don't remember much of what happened next, because I was so intent on separating them. Daddy had a hand round Mummy's throat and her knee was up in his groin. Daddy gasped in pain and I remember pushing him back hard, in the chest. He let go of Mummy, but she still had his hair. Chunks came out in her hands, but I managed to push them apart and give Daddy a superhuman shove, back against the wall. And then a shot rang out.'

Both hands flew to my mouth in horror.

'But how – it was Drummond!'

'No.'

I gazed at her. 'James shot his mother?' I breathed. 'Jesus Christ, Rachel – it was James?'

She stared back at me, her face like porcelain in the

darkness. 'Mummy was face up on the floor, arms and legs splayed out, blood gushing out of her mouth. Pumping. Her chest was covered in blood, too – soaked. At the foot of the stairs was Sally, in her pink nightie. The gun was in her hands.'

I went silent in horror. When I came to, both my hands were clamped over my mouth. At length, I extracted them. '*Sally* shot her?'

'Yes. James was frozen, still halfway down the stairs. I'd thought he was behind me. Had felt someone on my heels. But it was Sally. It was her glance I'd felt rest on the gun and, in the confusion, I thought it was James.' She swallowed. 'There was a moment when we were all suspended in time like that. The entire family, in the kitchen, in total shock and disbelief. And then the whole scene came to life. Jerked horribly back into action. Although, bits of it, I've blanked. I remember Daddy rushing to Mummy, bending over her, but there was so much blood. He was slipping in it. An unbelievable amount of blood. I remember lots and lots of screaming. Me, I think, mostly. Hysterical. James was still frozen. Then I remember Daddy taking the gun from Sally, who'd lowered it but still had it in her hands. He wiped it with a tea towel. Then he clutched it hard, before tossing it aside. I remember him dashing for the telephone. Ringing the police, the ambulance. Saying there'd been a terrible accident, to come quick. Then I remember him breathing very hoarsely, like a death rattle, herding us back up the stairs, to my bedroom.

'Up, *up!* Go! Quick!'

We ran to my room. Away from Mummy. Terrified. And, once he'd shut the door on us, he raced back down.

The police came very quickly, considering we were so remote. It all happened very fast. But they came by helicopter, you see, from Dundee. I remember it hovering outside the window, the trees all whipped up and important-looking, like something in an American movie, the long grass rustling as it landed. Daddy's footsteps were pounding up the stairs again. He flew in.

'Is she dead? Is she dead?' I shrieked, knowing she was. I was hysterical. The other two were silent.

'Yes, she's dead. The gun went off by mistake in my hands. I only meant to frighten her.'

I remember the three of us staring at him in the darkness, bewildered.

'But . . .'

'Yes, that's right, went off in my hands.'

'But – you didn't have the gun, Daddy.'

'I did, I had the gun. Remember that. If you do anything for me this night, you'll remember that. Rachel?'

'Yes, Daddy.'

'James?'

'Yes, Daddy.'

'Sally?'

'Yes, Daddy.'

She shuddered. 'None of us will ever forget that. As the police banged on the front door, down he went. And there we stayed, huddled and terrified, as I, Daddy's natural supporter, rammed it home. Sally, in prison? Unthinkable. Of course, I didn't know that might not have happened.'

'Daddy shot her by accident, yes, James?'

'Yes.'

'Sally?'

360

'Yes.'

We were so scared.

A kind policewoman came up, and we were wrapped in blankets and helped downstairs. Sally was carried. We were taken down the front stairs, not the back ones to the kitchen, but outside to the front drive. We passed Mummy, on a stretcher. She was covered in a blanket, about to be taken to the helicopter. I remember her face. There was no blood on it now, it was pure white above the red blanket. Daddy was talking to a policeman. We were driven away in a car. After that, it's all a bit of a blur. At the police station, we all told the same story. We were in shock, deep shock, and doing exactly as we'd been told, which was something we'd always done. We always obeyed my father. Never questioned him.'

She breathed deeply: gave herself a moment. 'And then we went to Aunt Sarah's, in Kent. She came and got us. And it all became sort of . . . surreal. Otherworldly. As if we'd simply come to stay, which, of course, we never did. In this nice, creamy, Edwardian house in a row of other houses outside Tunbridge Wells, with a big back garden and a cedar tree. It was as if . . . nothing had ever happened. I remember one day, at teatime, our cousin Paul said something about Scotland, and Aunt Sarah shot him such a look. It was never, ever mentioned again. It was as if our parents had been airbrushed from our lives. We even went to school with Paul and Anne for a couple of months. No mobiles, of course, in those days, and I don't even remember us talking to Daddy on the phone. Perhaps we did. I don't know. As I say, I've blanked a lot.'

I stayed very still.

'After that, of course, there was the court case. They decided not to put us in the dock, not to question us further, since my father had made a full confession. The gun had been there for the fox – of course, it shouldn't have been loaded, or out of the safe, he was genuinely culpable in that respect – and in the heat of the moment he'd grabbed it and it had gone off in his hands by accident. We thought he was going to be charged with manslaughter, and it was a terrible shock when they changed it to murder, which carries a mandatory life sentence. But life sentences vary – the shortest, at the time, being nine years, which Daddy got. I remember Aunt Sarah taking the phone call in the hall by the front door. We hadn't been allowed near the court in London, and no newspapers had been allowed in the house. I remember her coming back through and collapsing at the kitchen table.

'Nine years!' She covered her face with her hands. 'Nine years!' she sobbed. I rushed to comfort her, horrified. Then I looked up and saw Sally, white-faced, in the doorway.'

Rachel swallowed. Blinked rapidly into the dark night. 'After that, we went back to Brechallis, and Daddy's other sister, Belinda, came over from Ireland.'

'The spinster.'

'That's right. The teacher. She took over. Became our carer, I suppose. And we all went to boarding school. Just came home in the holidays, when Belinda would appear from Ireland. And, again, it was never mentioned.'

'Not even between the three of you? In the holidays?'

'Never. Because that would have given credence to the truth. It would have made it real, and Daddy didn't want that. The weird thing is . . . we almost came to believe it, I think. In our minds. Again, we didn't discuss it, but I think we all believed Daddy had killed Mummy by accident. That was definitely what had happened. Once, at school, someone in my dorm said, "Golly, poor you. And your poor father. What a dreadful thing to have to live with." I remember having to go to the san. Spending the night in there.' Rachel shut her eyes. I sat by quietly, shocked.

'Anyway' – she composed herself – 'we would go and visit Daddy at Dartmoor and, as you can imagine, he was always on good form. Always made light of it. Showed us his tapestry, or whatever he'd been doing, said the food was tremendous, that sort of thing. He was in charge of the vegetable garden eventually, had a team working for him. Said it was just like the army – well, you've heard him.' I had. Often. 'And time – years – just sort of drifted by. We got on with our lives. What else could we do? As we got older, I'm sure we all realized that Sally wouldn't have gone to prison, but . . . would she have been taken into care? Would we all have been taken into care? What would have happened? She would surely have been all over the papers, revealed as the girl who shot her mother, how would that have affected her? As it was, she was growing up OK. Or so it seemed. She never . . . formed any real attachment to anybody, though. No schoolfriends, nothing. But then I didn't really, either. James was better. Brought friends home, went to stay with them – but you were the only girl he brought back.'

'But not the only girlfriend.' I knew that.

'No, but the only one we met.'

My breathing became quite rapid. I tried not to think

about my poor darling James. To concentrate on what she was saying.

'Anyway. Daddy did form a close friendship. Inside.'

'With Donaldson.'

'Yes. Who'd also been in the army. As a private. And they formed this sort of officer–orderly bond, which suited them. And when they were released at much the same time – Donaldson was a lifer, too – as you know, he came to live on the farm.'

'Yes.' He was a surly, rather scarily brooding man, but quite good-looking in a dark, rough sort of way.

'What we didn't know, until much later, was that Daddy had broken the pact. The sacred, unshakable rule that the rest of us had kept.'

I stared at her, mute. Found my voice. 'He'd told him.'

She nodded. 'And what James and I also didn't know – in fact, I'm not sure James even knows now; I only found out by accident – was that Donaldson used it. With Sally. Let her know he knew. Turned the screw. Taunted her with it. Sally had always been the most panicky and nervous of the three of us, but I'd thought that was only natural. Had thought she'd be better when Daddy got out. So I'd stayed at the farm, thinking – all will be well when he's back. I can go. Have a life. But, if anything, it got worse, and I didn't know why. Couldn't work it out. She was even more teary, more fluttery – hysterical, at times. He bullied her, you see, and I think . . . blackmailed her. Certainly, she has no jewellery left. I think Sally realized she could never escape her past. And she got fatter and fatter, as if in defence. Ballooned to – well, you know.'

'Yes.' I inhaled sharply, remembering her cramming the

food in: standing right inside the pantry, taking it straight from the shelves to her mouth – pork pies, cold potatoes – so scared and unhappy. 'Oh God, Rachel, you couldn't leave her.'

'No. And she couldn't tell our father. He adored Donaldson. It would destroy him. Break his heart. Daddy had done so much for Sally, anyway.'

'And then, finally, Donaldson died.'

'Yes. Six months ago. And Sally escaped. Up to a point. In a manner of speaking. She lost all the weight, anyway – that was miraculous – and she worked further away from the glen. She made a few friends, too, proper ones, not just boasting about people she worked for. And then she met Max. But I knew she'd never form a proper relationship. She was too damaged for that, a psychologist would no doubt say. Which I think suited Max, too.'

'Yes,' I agreed. 'Although not in such a complicated way.' God, Max was a simple creature compared to this.

'No. No, of course not.'

'And James?' I asked, with a lump in my throat. 'D'you think . . . I mean . . . is he damaged, too?'

'You mean, enough to ever properly connect?'

'Yes!' I whispered, scared.

She covered my hand with hers. 'Oh, come on, Flora. Do you even have to ask? Of *course* not. Why are you even saying that? You know that's not true.'

I felt relief flood through me. 'Yes. I know that's not true. It was – well, it was that nightmarish tale you've just told me still speaking, I suppose. I was still in it.'

Still with that little twelve-year-old boy, frigid and terrified on the stairs. Keeping the real story of what had happened that night to himself, all his life. What *must* that be like? Terrible, but not as terrible as it had been for Sally. Of course not. But still. A ghastly secret. And secrets have to be kept. It's imperative. Because, look what happened when Drummond told only one person? Donaldson? It spiralled out of control. They *have* to be kept. So that if a bit of me was even remotely hurt that he hadn't told me – which it wasn't – I knew why.

Rachel and I sat together in the heavy, warm air, the fireflies playing in the tree lights which twinkled in the distance. I thought about what true love really meant. It meant sacrifice. As Drummond had done for Sally. And as Rachel had for Sally, too, never leaving her. It was something visceral, unspoken and profound that could never be put in Valentine cards or whispered in ears, because it was so completely silent and unutterable.

After a while I turned to her. 'Are you going to tell James you've told me?'

She barely missed a beat. 'Yes.'

I was so grateful. I told her so. 'I – don't think I'd be able to hide it, you see. The fact that I know. We're so in tune with each other. So tight. I'd find it impossible not to say. It's so huge, and I am so transparent. It would be all over my face.'

'I know. And the thing is, I always thought it would come out one day. That you'd know the truth. Even though James and I never discussed it. Because you two are so strong. I didn't think he'd be able to keep it inside for ever.'

'Except he did. You told me, Rachel.'

She turned to me properly in the darkness. 'But the

thing is, Flora' – she gave a small smile – 'he asked me to tell you.'

I felt my eyes widen. 'James did?'

'Yes. Said he wasn't sure he'd be capable of doing it. Without breaking down. And don't see that as a sign of weakness, Flora, that he asked me.'

'I don't.' I was so relieved. James had wanted me to know. Just hadn't been able to tell me himself. My eyes filled with tears.

'When did he ask you?' I whispered.

'Tonight. Before supper. He came and found me in my room. He said he owed it to you.' I inhaled sharply. She went on. 'I wanted to give myself some time to compose myself, think how to put it. He'd said at some point would I talk to you; he didn't mean tonight. In the next few months I think he meant, maybe when you came to Scotland. But you stopped me in the kitchen and there was no escape. I could see it in your eyes. I knew you wanted it now. And perhaps it's better this way. That it's over. Done.'

We sat very still. There was no sound, apart from the odd cicada chattering in the long grass, but I sensed something, or someone, close by. Slowly, I turned my head towards the sea. There, in the darkness, just below us in the olive grove, a small candle in a jar in his hand, was James. Waiting. He'd known I couldn't wait, too.

Rachel got to her feet. She reached out for both my hands in a swift movement and took them in hers. We held on to each other for a moment. Held each other's eyes, too. Then she turned and slipped away, into the night.

Chapter Twenty-Seven

I made my way towards him, through the rough, spiky grass in the orchard, which prickled my bare ankles, picking my way in the dark around the hassocks which would suddenly rear up in clumps. As I approached, he put the candle on the ground and held out his arms. I walked into them, and we held on tight. For a moment I was transported back twenty years: to when our love was new and he was a junior doctor at St Thomas's and I was a budding young journalist on the *Evening Standard*. It was that same intense, enveloping embrace of those early days. We held each other fiercely. After a while, our grip loosened and I lay my head on his chest. I could hear his heart beating. His voice, when it came, was a bit thick. Muffled.

'I'm not sure I'll be able to talk about it, Flora.'

'There's nothing to talk about. I know everything. There's nothing that needs to be discussed.'

I knew he wouldn't want me to say, God, James, how *awful*! Poor you. Poor Sally! How have you kept it hidden all these years? So I didn't. Waited for his cue, if there was to be one.

'There is one thing I do have to say, though,' he went on, more calmly, having cleared his throat. 'And that's that you must never tell a soul. Not the girls, not anyone.'

'James, that goes without saying.'

'Yes, but it needs saying. Because I believe by law – I

368

don't know, but I have a fair idea – the three of us, me Sally and Rachel, and you too, now, might be complicit.'

I raised my head.

'What d'you mean?'

'There's something called an accessory after the fact, which, as I understand it, makes it a positive duty to report a crime.'

'Oh, James, that's absurd! Your father's already served a life sentence. And Sally was eleven!'

'Yes, you may be right. I don't know. I've never asked and have never even trawled the internet for information. Because I don't want to know.'

'No.' I was scared suddenly.

'But, as you say, she was eleven, so perhaps not.'

'I agree, though,' I said quickly. 'About never telling a soul. Especially not the girls,' I added fiercely, protectively. I lay my head on his chest again.

A silence flooded between us.

'That's the thing about secrets,' I said, breaking it eventually. 'I was thinking it earlier. They're better kept.'

'Yes, but once you'd asked me, I knew you'd be hurt if I didn't tell you. I didn't want it smouldering away in the background of our marriage.'

'And it would have done.' I lifted my head: we'd given ourselves enough time now. Could look at each other properly in the faint moonlight. I took a step back and searched his eyes. They were hurt and pensive. Like a small boy's. As I gazed, I realized that, actually, there were some things I would like to ask him. Like whether he thought that not being involved that night was what had saved him? Emotionally? The rest of his family – Rachel, delivering the shocking news to her siblings about their mother's infidelity; Drummond, leaving the gun out and loaded at the foot of the stairs; Sally using it – had made huge mistakes, were all, in different respects, responsible, something they'd never recover from. They'd carry it to their graves. But James had been an innocent bystander. A spectator. Was that how he'd escaped? Been the only one able to lead a normal life? I didn't ask. And never would.

What I did know, though, was that the two of us had changed. That in the wake of these revelations we'd be subtly different for ever. Perhaps more gentle with one another. More understanding. Perhaps not, in time. Perhaps things would just return to normal and it would all disappear into the ether again.

'D'you want to walk down to the headland?' he asked.

'What headland?'

'The one further down the hill, with the best view of the sea. Haven't you been?'

I knew he was teasing me. Was pleased. I became jocular, too. 'No! Who have you been with? Something else you're not telling me?'

I might have chosen better banter. Nerves, I suppose, but James smiled, knowing I meant well, that I was rallying. Joining him in lightening the mood. Being stoic about it.

'Amelia, actually. She was taking pictures down there. With her proper camera, not that stupid one on her phone.'

'Oh, good.'

'She showed me some. They're not bad.'

I smiled. 'Try telling her that.'

'Well, at least she's finally decided to go to art college.'

'I know, she told me. Northumbria, apparently.'

'Which will no doubt change.'

Normal humdrum conversation, which helped. We walked on together, using the candle to light our way to the other side of the orchard. Through the gate we went, shutting it on the donkey, who'd followed, and then down a little lane in the dark, a couple of pilgrims with their juddering candle. We needed some time, you see. Couldn't go straight back to the others, not just yet. The change of scene, the walk, clinging to motion, helped us to get our breath back. Helped distance us from any nightmarish scenes, to return from the past to the present. When we'd found the headland he meant, just a flat rock really, which we climbed up on to, it did indeed have a bird's-eye view of the sea, lights twinkling from boats. In fact, it was so beautiful, it was almost impossible to be anywhere else except the here and now. It would do the trick. We sat with our arms around each other, facing the view, soft breeze on our faces.

'It's funny,' I mused at length. 'In no time at all we'll be back home. Getting on with life. And these things, which neither of us knew anything about before we left, will be there with us, in the house. Around us in our daily lives.'

'Yes, except in a way, they'll be smaller for each of us. Certainly not bigger. Because they'll be shared.'

'Yes.' I turned to him, pleased. 'You're right. I hadn't thought about it like that. We've diminished them.'

'Waved our swords at them.' He smiled.

'Chopped their heads off!'

'Exactly.'

We squeezed each other. Turned back to the view.

'It's funny to think of being back in Clapham at all,' he said, after a while, with unusual despondency.

'Yes, isn't it?' I turned back to look at him. Couldn't gauge his expression. But then it was dark. 'James . . . you're not thinking . . .'

'What?'

'Well – I'd stay here in a heartbeat!'

'Oh, Flora.' He laughed. 'How could we? I've told you, that's just holiday talk.'

'No, but think about it, James. We could. I have no reason to go back now –'

'Yes, but I do!'

'But you hate it.'

'Well, of course I hate it. It's work. Lots of people hate work. But that's life, my darling. That's the deal. You work hard, you keep your head down, and if you're lucky – you make it through to the other side. To your retirement package.'

'Which is tiny. And also, a good fifteen years away.'

'Fourteen.'

'And it won't be much, James. We know that. They've whittled away at your job – taken away all the good stuff, the stuff you like, the interesting operations – and now they're hacking away at your pension. And they'll probably change the rules again before we get our hands on it. You'll probably have to work another five years, till you're sixty-five or something, before you even get a sniff of it. Do millions more toenails and corns, bugger on till then.'

'Yes. Thank you for reminding me. I know what my job description is. But what's the alternative?'

'Well, there *is* an alternative, don't you see?' I turned to him eagerly on the rock. Took a deep breath. 'There is always an alternative.'

He gave a hollow laugh. Dropped his arm from around my shoulders and drew up his knees. Hugged them. 'You're just intoxicated by this holiday, Flora, that's all. It's been too much for you. Too much for all of us. Too spoiling. We should have had a week in Bognor,' he said gloomily.

'But so many things have happened out here.'

'Yes, quite enough, if you ask me. Just drop it.'

He meant that. Had said it quite tersely. Changed the tone. And we'd been so close a moment ago. I knew I was ruining the moment. Nevertheless, I wouldn't drop it, because something told me that this *was* the moment. Something told me this was the night. When souls, already laid bare, emotions, already running high, were open and receptive. I had to seize my chance.

'So many life-changing, perspective-altering things have happened,' I went on in a low voice, trying to keep it steady. 'Don't you see? It's made *us* different. Made *me* feel differently about –'

'Life?' he offered sarcastically.

'Yes, OK, if you like,' I said defiantly. 'Life. About needing to grab it.'

'With two hands?' he offered, eyebrows raised.

'James, listen, please!'

He sighed. Removed his glasses and rubbed the bridge of his nose wearily. Replaced them again. 'OK. So what do you suggest? Buy a vineyard? Make our own wine and try to sell it? Flog it to derisive Jean-Pierres, like every other idiotic, idealistic English couple who've ever read *A Year in Provence*?'

'No, not a vineyard. A restaurant.'

'Ha!' He threw his head back and barked out a laugh to the stars. 'A restaurant!' His face, when it came back, was delighted. 'In France! *Les ros-bifs anglais?* Les Feesh and Cheeps? You must be mad!'

'Except we're not *les ros-bifs anglais*, are we, James? Cuisine-wise, we're as sophisticated as they are. Both of us. And, anyway, we'd have a French chef.'

'Who?'

I paused. 'Jean-Claude. He's brilliant. And I should know, it's my job to know. Trust me, he's out of this world. First class. He cooked for us the other night. It blew me away. It's what he did before the antiques.'

'Yes, I know, but –'

'In Paris, James. Rue Saint-Honoré. La Terrasse.'

'Off the Tuileries?'

'Right there. And then in the Jardin des Plantes.'

'He didn't say.'

'He wouldn't, to you. He's modest. And broken, too, by the experience. I had to prise it out of him. But you know me.'

'I do.'

'He was screwed over by the staff, who had their fingers in the till, and then by his ex-wife. He lost all his money. Took his eye off the ball. He's never got back in. He had two Michelin stars.'

James gazed at me. I licked my lips, knowing I had his attention.

'He has no business acumen whatsoever. None at all. You have loads.'

'Well, I –'

'Yes, you have. You know you have. You run your private practice yourself –'

'Such as it is.'

'Exactly, such as it is. Vanishing daily. But no other surgeon does that. They all have help. You could run that entire hospital if you felt like it – you've often said it's the side you should have gone into. A restaurant would be a piece of cake. And I know people in Paris, James. Influential people on the best magazines, newspapers, who'd write it up for us.'

'You want to do it in Paris!' he cried.

'No, down here, in Provence. But Paris is where the reviews will come from. I can get it on the map.'

'And where will the money come from, eh? To run this exclusive, Michelin-starred eatery? I presume that's what you're going for? Fine dining? Top end? How are you going to pay the staff, the waiters?'

'We'd have to sell Clapham, obviously.'

'Right!' he yelped, rocking back on his haunches.

'Probably for about two million pounds.'

He barked out another laugh. 'Oh, don't be absurd!'

'I promise you, James, you have no idea. That is what four-bedroomed houses south of the river like ours go for, even though we bought it for diddly squat twenty years ago. But we wouldn't spend it all on the restaurant, we'd buy a house, too, with some of the money. There'd be enough – it's cheaper out here. Mum would help with the restaurant.' My mother could do that. She'd been left a healthy inheritance by Philippe. Not as much as his wife, but a substantial amount. Some of which she'd used to buy Fulham, some of which she still had.

'How d'you know she'd want to?' he asked defiantly, but there was less conviction in his voice. Mum had to be constantly restrained from spending her money, from giving it all to us, which James found emasculating. She'd wanted to pay the school fees, but he hadn't let her. She'd clasp her hands with glee at this, sink in all of it, not that we'd let her. We'd have to rein her in. Somewhere small, I was thinking, in a bustling market town. Not remote. Passing trade was crucial. I'd even wondered about Jean-Claude's current premises, in the middle of a busy town, Mum had said. We'd walk to the market for the produce. I would. With Mum. Baskets over our arms. Meat and game, we'd source from local farmers. Just twenty covers, perhaps. And a few outside on a terrace. A small menu. Three choices for lunch, four for supper. But with the menu changing daily, according to what was bought. And I'd buy the best. Had spent twenty years training for it. Tasting for it. Moving, unknowingly, towards this day.

Word would spread, derisively at first – 'Les Anglais, they've opened a restaurant!' But when they came to mock, they'd eat their words. And how many French restaurateurs did I know in London who said they only employed English staff these days, not French, because they worked harder? And boy, we'd work hard. James would work his socks off, I knew, although, in time, I hoped he wouldn't have to. As I say, we'd keep it small. To begin with. After that – who knows? A larger premises? More covers. But no. For the minute – petite. Manageable.

James jumped off the rock. He was pacing about, hands in his pockets jingling his change, keeping his face averted in an effort to show he was not infected. Like so many foodies, we'd sat in countless restaurants over the years discussing the winning formula, how to do it properly, what would make a place really stand out. But we'd only ever dreamed. Had never really meant it.

'And the girls?' he said, forcing some sarcasm into his voice. 'They'd commute from London?'

'The girls are only with us for the holidays, James. Tara's in her final year, and now that Amelia's finally decided to go to college – yes, they'd commute, if you like, in the holidays.'

'Which they'll tire of. The novelty will wear off. All their friends are in London.'

'Except Mum's going to keep her house. Jean-Claude has persuaded her to do that. They'll always have a base there.'

'Oh, great, two teenagers living it up in Granny's Fulham pad. It'll be a drug den in no time!'

'No, because, if they are there, I'll go back. They'll come to France for the first couple of holidays, but when, as you say, they want to be in London, I'll be there, too. The restaurant will be up and running by then. You won't need me all the time. And I can do some good PR in London, go and see reviewers, travel writers. Spread the word.'

I'd thought this bit through very carefully. The girls were my top priority: always had been. But I could still make use of my time back home with them.

'And, anyway, they're not children, James. Amelia's nearly nineteen. They're young women. Plenty of their friends have parents who live abroad.'

'Plenty?'

'Emma's in Cyprus, Polly's in Dubai –'

'Well, yes, army. Or work.'

'*We'll* be work,' I said fiercely, clenching my fists. 'Working abroad. And crikey, they've had all their young life with us. It's not as if we shunted them off to boarding school at ten.'

He massaged his forehead hard with his fingers. Kneaded it. 'I don't know, Flora. It's such a risk. To give up everything, my work, my whole career. All my medical training.'

'You hate it. Hate what you do. What you once loved has turned around and bitten you hard on the bottom. You are so disillusioned. And this is not a risk.'

'Of course it's a bloody risk! It could so easily go wrong. Go tits up and leave us penniless! God, I don't even know why we're talking about it. This is silly talk. Forget it. Forget I even discussed it with you – indulged you. I was caught up in the emotion of another moment, one that happened thirty-odd years ago. Vulnerable to – to emotive chatter.'

'It is not emotive chatter.'

'Oh, trust me, it is. It's holiday-itus. Crap. Pipe dreams. Forget it, Flora. We go back as planned, to our boring but salaried jobs, next week. Or, at least, I do.' He shot me a flinty look. 'You'll look for another. I'm cross you even made me talk about it. Took advantage of the situation.'

He turned angrily on his heel and stomped off along the lane towards the olive grove, leaving me on the rock, looking out to sea, a flickering candle at my feet. I watched him go. Saw his tall, familiar figure wend its way up the hill, along the zigzag path, through the gate to the orchard. I lost sight of him then. But knew he'd march crossly. Go back up the sloping lawn to the house, shoulders hunched, up the terrace steps and straight to bed. I turned and looked out at the vista before me. The soft lights of the few farms freckled in the valley beneath me glowed whilst the twinkling lights in the bay beckoned. The heavy night air was soft on my face. I stayed there, on my rock, hugging my knees, breathing in the scents of Provence, gazing a while. At length, I climbed down, picked up the candle in the jar and, having given him some time and some distance, followed my husband thoughtfully back to the house.

Chapter Twenty-Eight

We were awoken the following morning by a terrible rumpus. I'd been fast asleep, having finally dropped off in the small hours, my head too full of the night's events to fall precipitously into the arms of Morpheus, so it was an almighty jolt to hear shouting – swearing, even – all in French. It took me a moment to wonder where I was. It didn't help that the voices were unfamiliar or, at least, the protagonist's was. An angry, voluble man. Livid, even. I sat up in bed, realizing I was covered in sweat. Throwing off the sheet for some air, I tuned my ear into the incredible row beneath me. Who could it be?

'What the hell's going on?' growled James, still half asleep beside me.

Amelia burst into our room, wide-eyed in her pyjamas. I pulled the sheet up quickly.

'There's this really fit guy in the kitchen, right, looks like Johnny Depp, who's clearly Camille's husband. He's kicking up shit with Michel and Thérèse.'

'How d'you know he's Camille's husband? Pass me that T-shirt, please.'

She tossed me one from a chair. I wriggled into it. 'Because Tara and I crept into her room in the tower when she wasn't there, remember? Had a poke around, found a few photos – we showed you, so don't pretend you don't know.'

'Oh. Right,' I said guiltily. I'd been cross, but interested, too. 'Is Camille down there?'

'No, she left. You know that.'

'I just wondered if she'd come back with him.'

'Why would she do that? They're estranged, remember? Duh. No, they're down there fighting over the girl, Agathe.'

'How d'you know?'

'My French is not that limited, Mother. I did get an A at GCSE. You'd be better, though. Go on, Mum, go suss it out.'

'Don't get involved,' mumbled James sleepily as, with as much of a nose for gossip as my daughter, I tumbled out of bed. I slipped into my dressing gown – pausing only for a quick pee and a ruffle of my curls, should Johnny Depp be interested in the over-forties bedroom look – and crept down the passage towards the gallery. The landing ran right around the kitchen and drawing room on the first floor, affording a perfect view. Obviously, I kept well back from the action and slid against the wall, crouching down low, as the shouting, if anything, got more furious.

Tempers were indeed frayed: someone was incensed and, actually, I think I could have crept right to the edge and dangled my legs through the spindles and no one would have noticed. From a distance, I could just see, as Amelia had so rightly said, the top half of a very attractive dark-haired man with fine Latin features. He had slightly hooded light eyes in a narrow face, and a very straight nose. More of a young Alain Delon than a Johnny Depp, actually. He was sitting at the kitchen table by the open French windows in jeans and a blue linen shirt, sleeves rolled up to the elbows. His profile was towards me and he was firing off a stream of invective, his face, under his tan, pale with anger.

'She's an animal!' he was saying, in a cultivated Right Bank accent, spitting out the words. 'She let's me discover, through a DNA test, when she already knows the result. Let's me take it, because she hasn't the guts to tell me herself. What sort of a woman – what sort of a *mother*, is she?'

Michel and Thérèse sat opposite him, dark heads bowed in silence. Thérèse had her apron on over her dress and Michel was in his *bleu de travail* overalls. They didn't look at him. Gazed down into their laps.

'And you two – you go along with it. Duping me, selfishly, just to get what you want, neither of you having the courage to tell me, when I've been so kind to you. Letting you see Agathe as much as you want, because I know you adore her – and now I know why! The reason! You're filth. You . . . *you*!' – he swung round to Michel – 'disgust me.' His lip curled, but it was quivering, too. He turned to Thérèse. 'And you – you let him. Let him sleep with my wife. Your own sister!' At this his voice cracked with pain. Horror, too. He threw back his head and gave a primeval cry.

'You have no idea, Étienne' – Thérèse's voice, when it came, was low, trembling with emotion – 'how much that cost me. How much. But you also have no idea – *tu ne comprends pas*' – she clenched both fists on the table and leaned forward, her face contorted – 'the lengths a woman will go to to have a child.'

'There are other ways,' he whispered angrily, leaning forward also, right into her face. His fists were balled, too. '*Were* other ways, available to you.'

'Expensive ways.'

'Which Camille paid for. Don't give me that crap!' He flung himself back in his chair.

'Yes, she did, four times. But the last time, when it didn't work, the doctors said they wouldn't do it again. That was my last chance. No more IVF.'

'There was another hospital. Where they said they'd do it again. You told me.'

'Sharks, at a private clinic, with their eyes only on Camille's money – the hospital told us that, too. Told us private clinics would let us go on for ever, compounding our grief, our disappointment. But it wouldn't work. Not for us. This was the best way. The only way.'

'Why didn't she do it properly, then?' Étienne lurched forward across the table again, right into her. 'Be a surrogate mother, have all the tests, go through the motions, all the procedures?'

All three faces at the table knew why. Said it all. 'Camille wouldn't do that,' Thérèse said eventually. 'I knew. And I wouldn't ask. She'd paid for all the IVF . . . done so much already.'

'She'd throw money at something, but she wouldn't consider putting herself out,' spat Étienne. 'Wouldn't put herself through it, all those hospital visits, hoops to jump through, tests to take – but a quick fuck with her brother-in-law, who she's always fancied – *pas de problème*. It would amuse her. Appeal to her warped sense of humour. And to be granted permission?' He gave a hollow laugh. 'What could be better? She's sick, I tell you.'

'I didn't care. Still don't care, now,' Thérèse said defiantly. 'I told you, I'd do anything.'

'I bet she didn't even think she'd get pregnant. Thought

it was just a quick shag. I bet that was a nasty surprise. After all, she never did with me.' His voice lurched at this. He couldn't look at Michel. Turned away.

'Maybe. And, yes, I think you're right. She told me she thought she couldn't,' said Thérèse. 'But she did. And she selflessly had the baby for us – she didn't have to do that.'

'Selflessly!' Étienne lunged right across the table, his face twisted and I saw spittle fly from his mouth. 'Camille never did anything selfless in her entire life. She never wanted children, I knew that when I married her, but I thought I'd talk her round, I was so in love with her. I couldn't believe it when I did, when my campaign prevailed, when, so suddenly, almost overnight, when she'd been adamant about not having any – only the week before – she agreed. But she was already pregnant by then, and she knew it. Of course, I didn't question that it was mine. And, in a way, once she'd got used to the shock, it must have suited her. She'd have the child, which would satisfy me – my irritating, persistent pleadings – and round off her public persona in one fell swoop. Make her profile warmer, more accessible, more *human*. A constant complaint of her PR people. Too much the ice maiden, they said. But she'd never really have to look after Agathe. She would always be with you when it was her turn for custody. An equal share, the judge said, but I didn't understand that. Why shouldn't Agathe be with me the *whole* time, when, in Camille's care, she was always with you? So when I fought it, eventually, in the courts, stupidly – oh, *so* stupid.' He screwed his eyes up and thrust the palms of his hands into them. 'You all watched. Stood by and watched.'

He removed his hands. 'And, at first, it goes well for me. The judge is sympathetic, I can tell, until Camille, knowing she's about to lose, knowing the judge will side with me and knowing, too, what that will do to her image: Camille de Bouvoir loses custody of her child – imagine! She insists I have a DNA test. *Merde!*' He hit his forehead with the heel of his hand, his face tortured.

Two figures crept to join me: Amelia and Tara, in their pyjamas.

'Is it good?' whispered Tara, crouching down beside me.

I made an anguished face. 'So sad.'

They hugged their knees.

'Thank God they had the humanity to let me know out of court, privately, when the results were in. But *you* knew. You could have told me the truth. Instead, it comes like a grenade, landing in the middle of my life. And, immediately – I know the rest. Know the father. It comes to me like another bomb, an unexploded one this time, one I've been sitting on for years. I wouldn't let myself believe it at first, would not let myself consider it. The horrible truth.' He gave a strangled sob and his head dropped into his hands. Tara gripped my arm. 'So now, I lose Agathe completely,' we heard him say in a muffled voice. 'I am worse off than when I started.'

There was a terrible, chilling silence.

'Never, Papa.' A small voice made the three of us jump. Our heads swung to the left. Through the French windows at the opposite end of the room, from the garden side, a small figure in short, floral pyjamas had crept in.

'Agathe?' whispered Tara, who couldn't see. She craned her neck. I nodded. Put my finger to my lips.

'You will always be my Papa – always. Now and for ever. I don't care what a court says. If you don't.'

Étienne clearly couldn't speak, so overcome with emotion was he. But in an eloquent gesture, as she approached, he drew her to him with an outstretched arm. With the other, he wiped his face, which was wet with tears. She stood beside him, her arm around his shoulders, his around her waist.

'And Thérèse and Michel will be my uncle and aunt, even though Thérèse has been like a mother to me, always, and Michel, a second father. That is how I'd like it to remain. As it's always been. The three of us. Just as it is now. During the week with Papa in Grasse, the weekends here, with Thérèse and Michel. Just as always. But I don't want to see *Maman*. Don't want to go to her in Paris, in the holidays.'

Tara squeezed my arm. 'Quite brave,' she whispered.

Étienne swallowed. He composed himself. 'At all, *chérie*?'

'She scares me,' Agathe said in a small voice. 'When I know I'm going there, when you drop me off, I sweat. And when I go up to her apartment, she never comes to greet me – her maid lets me in – and when I do see her, she says, "How long are you staying?" I know she doesn't want me. She's happy when I'm in my room, or watching TV. If we go out, we go shopping, for her. Chanel. Saint Laurent. I sit on a chair. And I never say the right thing. And always she tells me to speak up. And, sometimes, when I'm there, I wet the bed. That makes her very angry. And she's right, I'm too old, I shouldn't. But she doesn't like me,' she finished sadly.

'She never liked anyone very much, *chérie*,' said Thérèse

softly. Her own sister. 'It's just how she is. She can't . . . trust. And if I told you, as a child, she, too, wet the bed . . . Our mother, you see. Your grandmother. Camille was so pretty. Too pretty for her. With this brilliant voice. Like our mother. It was not the same for me. But that's another story.'

So many stories. Tragic ones. Stretching back and back in time. Affecting so many children. How many more, I wondered? Sally. Rachel. Camille, too, it seemed. James and Thérèse were survivors. Me, too. By the grace of God and the skin of our teeth. The ones who got away. I squeezed my own children's hands tight.

'But if that's what you want, *ma chérie*, I'm afraid I am not the person to implement it,' said Étienne sadly. His voice was broken. 'Not in a position. I am weaker now than I ever was. I have no claim on you.'

'No, but I am in a position,' said Michel, speaking for the first time.

The girls and I shuffled along the wall a bit on our bottoms, in a bid to see his face properly through the banisters. It was pale and tense. Determined. 'From now on, what you want, Agathe, is exactly how it will be, with no one telling you what to do, or where to go. In our hearts, we have always acknowledged and regretted the terrible wrong done to Étienne. And I know you will love her now, Étienne, as you always have done, because you are a good man. We are her aunt and uncle, you are her father. Her mother will not care one fig; she will be relieved. She is not maternal. The situation will remain unchanged, but Agathe, you will never have to go to Paris again. If she objects, wants you as an adornment, to be photographed with her, like she did in London, taking you out of school for two days, I will tell her that I will go to the press. Tell them the real story. I do not care. But she will. Very much she will care. You will be with your father and your aunt and uncle here, in Provence. Not go to Paris.'

'I'm ten, anyway, next month.'

'Exactly. Next month you are ten. In a few years, a teenager. A young woman.'

'And can I still come on holiday to Antibes, in September, before school, like I was going to, with you?' She turned to Étienne.

He shrugged, unable to hide his sadness. 'If Michel —'

'No, not if Michel,' Michel broke in. 'I told you. Everything will remain the same, with this' – he flicked a dismissive hand at the piece of paper in Étienne's hand – 'as if it had never happened.'

Thérèse got up. She whipped the sheet from Étienne's hand. Walked to the island and lit the gas on the stove. As the flame leaped into life, she held it within. Burned it, before the three of them.

'DNA,' she said scathingly. 'What is DNA to ten years of love and devotion. Ten years of unconditional love.'

A silence enveloped the four people below us; they were suspended there like characters in a play. Up in the gallery, we, too, turned to stone, hardly daring to breathe. The silence was finally broken by Agathe. Her voice, when it came, was shrill and unnatural. It had a crack in it.

'And you will love me just the same, Papa? Even though . . .' She didn't make it to the end of the sentence.

'Don't say it,' Étienne whispered fiercely, and equally brokenly, holding her close. 'No one knows it. Except the people in this room. And your mother. Who won't want anyone to know. So don't say it.'

She nodded, and they clung on to each other tightly. Agathe had both arms around his neck, hiding her head in his shoulder.

Upstairs, I glanced at the girls and saw them both blink away tears. My own eyes were full, too. We silently got to our feet in the shadows, feeling horribly like interlopers now. Quickly, we slid back along the wall, swallowing a bit, and, like spirits, disappeared out of sight, back down the corridor, fleet of foot, to our rooms.

The girls crept into mine and sat on the bed, which was empty. We could hear their father showering in the bathroom.

'Wow,' said Amelia.

'What a bombshell,' agreed Tara. 'So Agathe is Michel's, is that it? Did I get that right, Mum? They were speaking so fast.'

'You did. And she is. But we keep it to ourselves, OK?'

'Definitely. We shouldn't have heard it at all. Bloody hell, though. Who would have thought?'

Well, I had thought. In what I imagined was a mad moment. And I wondered how many more people might have done, or would continue to do so, over the years.

'So Camille shagged her brother-in-law,' said Amelia. 'How weird is that?'

'Or magnanimous,' I told her. 'Depending on how you look at it.'

Amelia gave me an arch look. 'Crap. I bet she loved it. She's like that, I can tell. And Michel is very good-looking.'

'They're both amoral,' Tara said. 'Similar types. Thérèse is the only decent one in that family.'

'Except Michel was generous to the husband, just now,' I reminded her. 'About seeing Agathe.'

'Oh, yeah. I meant sex-wise, that's all. I agree, he was good about Agathe.'

'I want one of those,' said Amelia wistfully, hugging her knees to her chest and gazing into space.

'What, a child?' I said, alarmed.

'No, a Johnny Depp lookalike with a six-pack and a heart of gold.' She shivered, her eyes on fire. 'Wasn't he amazing? All heart and soul and stunning good looks.'

At that moment, Toby blundered through the door, which was ajar. He was in his boxer shorts with a minuscule T-shirt which bore the legend 'Keep Calm and Marry Harry' stretched taut across his chest. Unshaven, as he had been for days, he reeked of stale bed. He scratched his balls.

'Oh, man, what time is it? Why are we all, like, awake?'

Amelia looked him up and down. Her lips pursed. She looked older, suddenly. 'Toby. Why the fuck have you got my T-shirt on?'

Toby glanced down in surprise. 'Needed a slash. Down the corridor. It was all I could find.'

'Well, take it off!' Amelia leaped off the bed.

Toby saw something in her eyes and, in panic, started to wrestle his huge, hairy torso out of the tiny T-shirt. Quite a lot of tummy protruded over his shorts.

'Not here, you fool!'

She turned him around and hustled him back to their room, but the T-shirt was stuck over his head so he couldn't see. He walked straight into our door.

'Ooof! *Ow!*' he roared plaintively, doubling up in pain.

Totally without sympathy, Amelia continued to steer him on. Before her own door shut, we heard her mutter darkly, 'Shut up, Toby. You'll live.'

I sat there a moment with Tara. We pulled the sheet up over our knees.

'Do you really think Michel's amoral?' I asked her.

'God, yes. He's the biggest flirt ever. A pest, actually. You certainly wouldn't want to be on your own with him. Apparently, he made a move on one of Camille's opera buddies when she came to stay, followed her down to the pool on her own.'

'How d'you know?'

She flushed. 'We found a letter on Camille's bed, complaining about him. It was recent. This summer.'

'Right.'

'Why?'

'Oh, nothing. Just wondered.'

She laughed and got off the bed. 'Still wondering if he was after you in the vineyard, Mum?' She regarded me kindly. 'It was from Atalanta Guggenheim, the American soprano? Legs up to her armpits? Face of an angel?'

'Oh. Right.'

She seized a dress from a chair in the corner. 'Is this mine?' she asked incredulously.

'Might be. I was trying it on.'

'It's way too small for you.'

'It's Lycra, Tara.'

'Yes, but that doesn't mean it's elastic! I hope you haven't stretched it.' She gave me an outraged look and flounced out.

James came in from the bathroom, toothbrush in his mouth. 'What was that all about?'

'I borrowed a dress of Tara's.'

'No, the rumpus downstairs.'

'Oh. That.'

I hesitated. He had been so smitten so very recently. I wasn't sure he was ready for the object of his desire to be quite so tarnished.

'Camille's husband's here. Raising merry hell about how little he sees of Agathe.'

'Ah.' He nodded. 'Well, she's a very devoted mother, of course. Likes her daughter with her as much as possible.'

I nodded. 'Right.'

James turned and wandered back to the bathroom, still brushing his teeth.

I smiled to myself in the empty room.

Chapter Twenty-Nine

The Murray-Brown family sailed for Portsmouth five days later. Our bodies were rested and tanned – and possibly a little plumper, having supped copiously at the land of milk and honey and done little more than flop by the pool – and our hair was a shade or two lighter but, most of all, our minds were made up. In particular, James's. There'd been a bit of a sea change. A bit of a Damascene moment, two days after Étienne had appeared. He'd stayed, Étienne – after all, it was his house, too: the divorce had yet to be finalized and Camille wasn't there – only for a few nights, and in the lodge with Agathe, not in the chateau, but he'd stayed. And God he was nice. He did little more than introduce himself that first evening, strolling slightly self-consciously on to the terrace, ruffling his hair and saying he couldn't really be next door and not say hello, and also did we mind if he used the pool? We'd all got to our feet in a flurry, lolling as we had been in chairs, saying, 'Of *course* we don't mind,' and golly, it was far more his pool than ours. Then we'd persuaded him to stay for a drink. We'd all liked him immensely, then, and the odd times we'd bumped into him in the grounds over the next few days. He was so courteous, so friendly, so *charming*. Or, at least, the female members of the party thought so, possibly because he was the best-looking man we'd ever seen. I'd had to kick Tara to stop her staring with her mouth open when he'd passed us on his way to his car, and Amelia seemed to have urgent business tidying up the pool house when he took his evening swim.

The men couldn't really see the attraction. Toby sulked, but James liked him very much, principally because he got the internet working again. It was temperamental, Michel had explained, with his lugubrious shrug one morning when Drummond had been unable to get his *Telegraph*; and he was not technical, he'd said apologetically. Neither were we. But Étienne knew precisely which provider to ring and harangue in his native tongue, and then which buttons to press. And James, who was the least web-oriented of us all, who didn't even own an iPhone, just a cheap supermarket model, seemed, strangely, the most grateful.

I crept down in the early hours one night, having woken and found the bed empty beside me, to discover him in the study, where the main computer was, staring at the screen. He cleared it quickly when he heard me come in. Stood up, shielding it.

'What are you doing?' I peered around him.

'Nothing.'

'Well, of course it's not nothing. What were you looking at?'

'I was bored. Couldn't sleep. Came down to read my emails.'

'I don't believe you. You hate doing that on holiday.'

'OK, I was looking at . . . porn.'

'Porn? You? Don't make me laugh.'

I pushed past him and sat down.

'What's so funny about that?' he yelped. 'I do have a sex drive, you know.'

'Yes, but you hate porn. What were you looking at, James?'

I tried to see if he'd minimized anything. He had. I pulled it up.

Restaurants à vendre en Provence.

I caught my breath. Stared.

'I was just – just looking out of curiosity,' he faltered. 'Just window shopping. No real intent, no –'

'And last night, too,' I breathed, ignoring him. 'I heard you get back into bed. What have you found? Oh, what have you found, James?' I swung around to him on the chair, my eyes shining.

'Well, no, Flora, nothing. You are not to get excited. It's just that – well, OK, this one . . .' He shoved me across on the chair and scrolled down with the mouse. 'Near Seillans, right, has a view . . . and also a terrace . . .'

And there we sat, bottom to bottom, a middle-aged couple in our jim-jams, poring over a heavenly-looking stone building in an olive grove beside a river, with covers for thirty. Too remote, though, we decided, scrolling back to another he'd found, this time in the centre of a very pretty village, opposite the *hôtel de ville*, which came with a separate house. And then another, so big it was a restaurant within a house, really: beautiful, shuttered and chateau-like, again, *centre ville*; the owners had simply converted their huge hall to accommodate tables, just twenty covers. This one, we loved. It had two kitchens, one for the private family side, one for business. We sat salivating over it until four in the morning, before dragging ourselves up to bed. We slept until noon.

'What have you two been doing?' asked Amelia, when we finally joined them by the pool, having grabbed a coffee en route. She peered at us over her book and sunglasses as we skirted past them.

'Just having a lie-in,' I told her.

'Oh, gross. Too much information.' She went back to her book.

'Better than sex, actually,' muttered James, as we lay down together on adjoining sunbeds on the opposite side of the pool. I giggled.

'They're *giggling*,' Tara told her sister in horror.

Amelia sat up. Regarded me from across the water. 'Don't get pregnant, will you, Mum? You told me the other day your Mirena was running out. I'm not going to have to talk to you about contraceptives, am I?'

She was showing off for the boys' benefit, to demonstrate that, unlike some families, we did pretty much talk about anything. The boys giggled, suitably bug-eyed with awe at Amelia's neck. I told her to wind it in, in no uncertain terms, but it did occur to me there were some things that would have to be talked about and, in a way, surely better done out here than at home?

The following evening, our penultimate one as it happened, we managed to corner them whilst the boys went to help Michel at the bottle bank.

'Won't take you a mo, boys,' I'd said cheerily, engineering the whole thing. 'And Michel will be glad of the help.'

Michel looked like he couldn't think of anything more irritating than having two grunting teenage boys along for the ride in his pick-up, but they settled in the front seat beside him and set off in a crunch of gravel, several weeks of louche living rattling in bin liners in the back.

I grabbed a bottle of rosé from the fridge as James shepherded the girls to a quiet spot at the bottom of the garden: the round stone terrace where Rachel and I had talked. As I approached with the wine and the glasses, the girls were sitting side by side on the bench, opposite their father.

'What's going on?' asked Amelia with wide eyes, not fooled for one minute.

I poured the wine and then we explained, between us, James doing most of the talking, for a change. About our careers. About how mine had obviously hit a sudden buffer and how Daddy's was – well, not entirely what he'd imagined it to be as an idealistic young medical student. And how, now that we'd educated them, got through the worst bit – school fees, etcetera – seen them through all of that, and now that they were young women, almost –

'Shit. You're not splitting up, are you?' said Tara.

'No, of *course* not. Of course not, darling.'

'Bloody hell. Yesterday's lie-in really would have been a last hurrah if they were,' observed Amelia.

James ignored her and carried on. Said how, of course, careers didn't always live up to expectations – one had to be realistic – but how it was also important to recognize it was possible to do something about it. Take a view. Maybe make some changes, before it was too late.

'Don't tell me. You're running away to the circus. You'll throw knives at Mum, who'll be spreadeagled in a bikini. Paul and Debbie.'

'Shut up,' muttered Tara, who was more intent.

'No, we're going to be restaurateurs,' James told her.

She gaped. 'Restaurateurs?' She had to think about it. 'What, run a restaurant?'

'Run and own a restaurant. Out here. In France.'

'How?' They both blanched.

So we told them. About how we – I – had all the experience under the sun to ensure it had the right ingredients to make it a successful enterprise. About Jean-Claude, who we'd talked to last night, and who had once been one of the most celebrated chefs in Paris, and about Mum. About how we all spoke French. How it could work. Would work. How brilliant it could be.

'What did Jean-Claude say?' asked Amelia.

'He leaped at it.'

He had. I recalled how James and I had broached it with him, gingerly at first, but he'd caught on like a forest fire, halfway through James's semi-prepared speech: had jumped to his feet, eyes shining: 'You mean you'd finance it? Run it? I'd just cook, be in charge of the kitchen?'

'In total control of the kitchen, yes. We'd do the rest.'

'Everything I hate, can't do. Loathe. The business side, the politics, the hiring –'

'I'm good at that,' said James firmly.

'And I know people in France. Magazine critics, contacts –' I'd told him.

'So do I,' he'd said vehemently, turning to me. '*Moi aussi.* Friends, who regret now what happened. Have some shame.'

'Exactly. Of course.'

'But not in Paris. I can't go back yet.'

'No, not in Paris.'

'But . . . maybe one day.' His eyes gleamed, remembering what he'd lost. What had been taken. Some unfinished business.

'That's a long way down the track, JC,' James had told him firmly, but his eyes had gleamed a little, too, perhaps at some unfinished business of his own. His own, unfulfilled career. 'Let's start small. Build a reputation. Here, in the south.'

'The best reputation. I would never let you down, never. You'll see. People will come from miles.'

'From Paris?' James had joked.

He'd turned a serious face on him. 'Of course. *Bien sûr, mon ami.* When they know I am cooking again.' His back straightened.

I'd breathed in sharply. Golly. I looked at my mother, who'd been silent the whole time.

'Mum? What do you think?'

I wondered if she'd seen herself more quietly: on the steps of the shabby-chic antique shop, painting chairs, mending old lace, her legs in the sun. But I was wrong: her face suddenly wreathed into smiles.

'Of *course*, yes, darling, of course! I'm in shock, that's all. My one, my only reservation about coming here with JC was leaving you behind. We've always been within minutes of each other, but to be here with you *both*.' Her eyes sparkled, and I realized they were full of tears. 'It's too much to hope for, at my age. All my life,' she admitted, 'I've never dared hope too much. Then you get through, you know? If you don't expect too much. Don't think too much. Don't go deep. Have only happy thoughts. See only nice things.'

It had always been her defence mechanism, I knew. And who was I to knock it? My mother had never been down, subject to depression or moods; she just didn't allow herself. She skated across the surface of life.

'But what about the girls?'

'They'll come, too,' I told her quickly. 'That's the only condition. In the holidays. Or, if they hate it, we'll go back to England then, and you and Jean-Claude will hold the fort. But, having said that, if they're not up for it at all' – I looked around at everyone – 'it's a deal breaker. The whole thing's off.'

Jean-Claude looked shocked, but Mum didn't. She looked very knowing.

I wished I felt half as knowing as James and I sat with our daughters now at the round mosaic table in the sunken terrace, the girls' faces not so jokey now, not so flippant. Digesting. Absorbing. Watching us closely.

'So, basically, we'd move to France,' said Amelia flatly.

'Yes. We'd sell Clapham, buy a place out here – you get more for your money, so it would be nice – and this would be our base. Provence.'

'But . . . what about all our friends? Tara and I don't really speak French.'

'We'd keep Granny's house. In Fulham.'

'Oh!' Having both looked tense and worried, they brightened considerably.

'You mean Tara and I can go there in the holidays? It'll be empty?' Already she was filling it with friends, loud music, everyone spilling out on to the pavement, smoking, drinking, neighbours banging on walls, the whole street vibrating, throwing the best parties in London, the coolest place to be: *Are you going to Amelia's? Her parents have, like, given her this house . . .*

'No, not empty, because, if you're there, Daddy and I will be, too.'

'Oh.'

Tara looked slightly relieved, though. 'So we can choose where we want to be?'

'Up to a point,' said James, more sensibly. 'The family won't be totally dictated to by you. We'd like to think a couple of weeks at Easter here in the sun, perhaps bringing friends; likewise, six weeks in the summer might be very pleasant, at the restaurant's busiest time. Grandpa might be persuaded to come, too. Whereas Christmas, we might spend in Fulham, whilst Granny and JC hold the fort.'

'Yes, and we could pop out for the odd weekend in term time. Pippa Foster does that, to her parents' in Guernsey. It's the same, really, isn't it?' said Tara.

'Exactly. As much as you want,' I agreed.

'And you'll pay?' said Amelia, naturally.

'Within reason,' said James firmly, knowing how inclined I was to promise the earth.

'Say a couple of times a term?' suggested Amelia, keen to firm things up.

'Yes, perhaps about that.' James couldn't help smiling at his elder daughter, whose negotiating skills were akin to his own.

'So, two weekends a term – perhaps with friends –'

'Or perhaps without,' said James crisply.

'Easter and the summer in the sun – and home for Christmas.'

'So we don't miss the parties,' agreed her sister.

They shrugged.

'Cool.'

Their eyes were alight, though. Not so cool. I could see we'd sold it to them. But they had to be realistic.

'Clapham will go, our home for twenty years, and that will be sad. But you'll have a bedroom each at Mum's.'

'We could sell Granny's and keep Clapham?' suggested Tara, but Amelia frowned. Fulham appealed to her. I'd always suspected my daughter of being a closet Sloane.

'We could,' I said, 'but I want Mum to have her independence. In case . . .'

'. . . it all goes wrong with JC?'

'Yes. But I don't think it will,' I said quickly. 'Even though they've just met.'

'It won't,' Amelia agreed. 'They've, like, found each other. After so long. I can sense it. It's amazing, isn't it? That it can actually take so long, a lifetime perhaps, to find the right person? Who you truly click with?'

'Yes, Amelia.' Her eyes were on the pick-up truck appearing in the distance, a cloud of dust behind it. A slight cloud appeared in her own eyes, too. 'It can take a very long time, my love.'

Important to get it right, though, I thought.

And so we were going home. Drummond, Sally and Rachel were leaving the same day, but Rachel was driving to Relais Saint Jacques, she thought, to break the journey, attempting it in one go being too much for her father. I'd sat looking at the map with her very early that morning in the kitchen, a pot of strong coffee between us. She'd looked around wistfully.

'It's so sad to leave. This has been such a – well, a cathartic place to be. Like a retreat, or something. It's as if we all needed it.'

She and I were alone, cases packed beside us.

'I think we did need it. And, sometimes, you have to step right away from your life before you can see it properly. I think we all did that here.'

'Toby! Will you stop arsing around and get out of bed!' floated down from the gallery upstairs. We smiled. A door slammed.

'I know. I definitely needed to get out of the glen.'

'For good?' I asked tentatively.

'No, of course not. Daddy would never sell. But . . . well, I've persuaded him to sell a few of the cottages and buy a flat. In Edinburgh. In New Town. He's so enjoyed getting away, and he can see how remote we are now.'

'Oh – so you and Sally can have a bit of city life?'

'With him, too, yes. Or without. I'm going to employ a housekeeper. A sort of – carer,' she said bravely.

I leaned forward and hugged her. 'Well done.'

'I interviewed one before we left, actually. Didn't have that particular epiphany here. I've been thinking about it for a while. She's called Heather, and she's a tall, handsome Geordie of about fifty. Divorced. Daddy thought she was a friend of mine who'd come for tea. He liked her enormously. Flirted, even. But she can handle that. He asked me, casually, the other day, if my friend Heather would be back?'

'Yes, for ever!' I gave a snort of laughter.

'Well, for three weeks at a time. And then a week to her mother in Durham. For a break. Which she'll need. Then either Sally or I will take over.'

'Or he could come to Edinburgh?'

'Yes, if we're working. Or studying.'

I paused. 'Studying?'

Her cheekbones coloured slightly. 'I've . . . applied to an art school there. Leith's.'

'Oh, Rachel, that's brilliant!' Rachel spent so much of her time painting on the hill, and not just watercolours. Oils, these days. She was good.

She shrugged. 'I haven't heard yet so, who knows, I may not get in.'

'You will.'

'But I thought – you know. Meeting people. And . . . I don't know. Something about your mother, Flora, has inspired me. Something about it never being too late.'

Through the window, we could see Mum and JC, packing their car.

'It isn't. Ever.'

'She is rather tremendous, isn't she? You're so lucky.'

'She is. And I am.'

'Always – in the words of Monty Python – looking on the bright side of life.'

I smiled. 'Quite. And Sally?'

'I'm persuading her to apply to the Jamie Oliver Italian in Edinburgh. Her agency work is a bit unpredictable – she'd be better with a stable job, where she gets to meet people for more than a week or so, don't you think?'

I agreed, but it was said with caution. I think Rachel and

I both knew it might end in tears, and that Sally would never be quite right: but she could be better. And stability would help. One thing was for sure, Rachel was too good and too special to devote her life to Sally and her aging father. I'd always thought the church would claim her one day, and maybe it would. But not yet. Not until her father had died. James would be pleased with her plans, I thought. I got up and busied myself, wiping down the draining board, knowing she didn't like too much attention. Now I knew the truth, I understood why James had felt such guilt about Rachel: why he always went so quiet at the mention of her name. So thoughtful. She'd been left holding the baby. Quite literally.

'She's the eldest, darling, and unmarried, so why not?' I'd once said, to which he'd replied, 'Yes, but I'm the man.'

I hadn't understood. I did now. We'd both help Rachel to get away. If not to Leith art school, then somewhere else. Out to France. Painting holidays. Sally, too, if she'd come, but maybe not together. Separately, to give Rachel a break.

'When are you going to break it to your father about Heather? That she's not an old mate from school?'

'Oh, I already have. Last night. When he'd had a couple of cognacs.'

'What did he say?'

'He said – you mean that rather fine-looking woman with the strapping thighs? Does it include a goodnight kiss?'

'Oh, God! Poor Heather.'

'Oh, don't worry.' Rachel grinned. 'She'll cope. Comes from a long line of demanding Geordie men, she tells me.

She won't take any nonsense.' She gave me a long, clear look as I leaned against the draining board. 'And you, Flora? You found some peace out here?'

Amelia came storming into the kitchen, dragging her case, fuming about the use of a sodding boyfriend who couldn't even pack his own *things*.

'Oh, yes.' I smiled. 'I've found some peace. I've found a great deal, actually.'

'Would you like some 'elp with that, Amélie?'

Étienne appeared in a pink T-shirt and putty-coloured shorts. Really rather tailored ones.

'Oh, gosh, thanks so much, Étienne. That would be super,' simpered my daughter, in textbook Fulham, pausing to flick back her hair. She had lipstick on, something I hadn't seen her wear for ages, not since she'd embraced a more earthy way of life. Also, a pretty top of Tara's.

'And Amelia? Has she found her more feminine side?' murmured Rachel as we watched her follow Étienne out to the car, swinging her handbag.

'Perhaps.' I smiled again. 'Perhaps.'

On the ferry, the long drive behind us, we sat up on deck in gloriously warm evening sunshine, gliding gently over the calmest sea I'd ever seen, skimming smoothly over a glittering English Channel. James and I were offered a *Daily Mail* by the couple beside us, who were getting up to go inside, and James took it with thanks. Behind us, in the second row of chairs, were Toby and Rory and, across the way, Amelia and Tara faced due south to get the last of the rays, both in shorts, both listening to the same iPod, an earpiece each.

Tara, I noticed, was reading the magazine she'd found abandoned on her chair, the one in French. She was so quick. And her French wasn't bad anyway. She'd pick it up in no time. Amelia's, if anything, was better. I tried not to let my imagination run away with me, tried not to let it gallop off to a long trestle table in daisy-strewn grass under the trees, a gingham cloth covering it. Both girls were jabbering away in perfect French to a table full of friends and relations: good-looking twentysomething boys, middle-aged couples – new friends of ours – and Lizzie, too. JC was coming out of the stone farmhouse with a huge platter of seafood to tremendous applause, Mum beaming proudly. I shook my head, banishing the vision, knowing I couldn't get too far ahead of myself. James had yet to resign. Had yet to tell the hospital what they could do with their Monday-morning list of bunions. I sighed and narrowed my eyes to the sun. Earlier, Rory had popped his head over to ask if we'd like a drink, and he returned now, with a tray of gin and tonics. As I poured my tonic into the wobbly plastic glass, James harrumphed beside me.

'What?' I asked.

'Look at this.'

He held the paper out in front of me. Page three of the *Daily Mail* had a colour photo of Camille, in a full-length emerald gown, on the arm of a handsome blond man in a dinner jacket. It was clearly some sort of a gala opening. I read the headline: 'CAMILLE DE BOUVOIR ATTENDS THE PREMIERE OF *DER ROSENKAVALIER* WITH SASHA RAIMONDI.'

'Who is he?' I peered at the photo.

'Some famous Italian conductor, apparently. Never heard of him.'

'Me neither.'

'No doubt poised to inject a little spice into her life.'

'Said with bitterness?'

'No, not at all. Relief. I was a fool.'

'No more than I was. And, actually, James, what we did discover was that our lives did indeed need an injection of spice. It was time. We were both just looking in the wrong places.'

He smiled. We toasted each other with our eyes and then our gins. And then we kissed briefly on the lips, before taking a sip each. As I swallowed happily, I caught the girls' eyes, their heads turned towards us. They rolled their eyes at one another before going back to their magazines. I smiled and lifted my face to the sun. A dazzling whelm of blue sky and sunshine made me squint, and I lowered the sunglasses perched on my head to my eyes, then regarded the glittering sea below. As the ship skimmed ever onwards on its stately bows, I had a feeling, as I gazed down at the water dividing two worlds, of having never been closer to the life I really wanted, with the people I most loved.

WISH YOU WERE HERE

Reading Group Questions

1. One of the great sources of humour in *Wish You Were Here* is Flora's disquiet over her mother's love life. Do you think it is always an uncomfortable scenario, seeing a parent embark on new romantic adventures?

2. Similarly, Flora also has her own teenage daughters – and their boyfriends – on holiday with her. Do you think witnessing her children and her mother appearing to have a more exciting love life than her own contributes to the temporary problems Flora's own marriage faces in the novel?

3. Flora comes across as a real home-maker, trying her best to make everybody feel welcome and have a great holiday. Do you think she spends enough time focussed on her own needs?

4. It's very heartening to see Flora's marriage come out even stronger after it's been rocked. Obviously, so often it can go the other way – how common do you think it is for marriages to fail that with a little more time or patience could have had the potential to re-blossom and fully recover?

5. Flora's ex-boyfriend, Max, turns up during the holiday and causes utter havoc. Do you think most people would be rattled by seeing an old flame many years later? Or does it depend on how vulnerable you are at the time? Do we ever fully lose the intensity of the feelings we once had for someone?

6. James's family went through such tough times all those years ago. Do you think the effect this had on them all was inevitable, or can tragedy leave no lasting scar in the right circumstances?

7. A holiday with extended family sounds wonderful. But in reality it is so often the cause of tension, rows and skeletons coming out of the closet. Do you think a large family being together for a long period of time would always be tension-ridden? Does it depend on the family or is it inevitable no matter how close you are?

8. Catherine Alliott writes with such humour about Flora's temporary mid-life crisis. Do you think the female mid-life crisis is a rising phenomenon? Do we expect too much from life?

Catching up with

Catherine

We donned our wellies and
trudged through the mud to catch up
with Catherine about reading,
writing and life in the country . . .

Chatting with

Catherine

Q: **It's been twenty years since your first book was published. What changes over the years have affected your stories since then?**

A: Over the years my books have included a wider age group of characters: I'm writing about grannies, mothers, teenagers – all sorts!

Q: **Which book have you found most challenging to write?**

A: *One Day in May* was probably the most challenging to write. I knew very little about the Bosnian war and had to do quite a lot of research, which was pretty harrowing. I had no idea . . .

Q: **How have your protagonists changed and developed since you started writing?**

A: Since I started writing twenty-three years ago my protagonists have definitely got older! Perhaps a little less scatty, but then again, perhaps not.

Q: **How do you choose your characters' names?**

A: I'm going so fast I just chuck anything in and think – I'll change that later. Unfortunately by the end I can't think of Mavis as anything other than Mavis, so it sticks.

Q: **What book are you reading right now?**

A: I found a John le Carré in my son's room; it's called *Our Kind of Traitor*. V. good. I read anything that's lying around.

Q: **If you couldn't be a writer, what would you like to be?**

A: A painter – as in artist, not decorator.

Q: **When you need to escape from your everyday routine, what do you do?**

A: Light the fire, watch daytime TV and eat chocolate.

Q: **What is your favourite food?**

A: In – macaroni cheese. Out – Dover sole.

Q: What would your super power be?

A: I'd like to be able to imagine supper – and there it is, on the table. Oh, and all cleared away, too.

Q: What is your idea of perfect happiness?

A: So corny. All my children plus boyfriends, girlfriends, any other friends and of course my husband, eating around the same table. Or actually, a table somewhere hot, on holiday, abroad, i.e. without me having to cook. Oh – and grandparents too.

Q: What is the trait you most deplore in others?

A: Deplore. Golly. Quite strong. Well, I'm not mad about bad manners, which come in many guises.

Q: When did you last cry and why?

A: Two weeks ago, at Badminton Horse Trials, watching a great friend's daughter jump round the cross-country course. Amazing. I've known her since she was seven.

Q: What has been your most embarrassing moment?

A: I suppose it has to be when I fell in the freezer in Safeway on the King's Road many years ago, a scene which later featured in *The Old-Girl Network*.

Q: What single thing would improve the quality of your life?

A: Training our Border Terrier not to fight other dogs and not to chase deer. I sound like a fishwife in the woods.

Q: What do you consider your greatest achievement?

A: Training our last Border Terrier. (Up to a point. She really did hate poodles.)

Q: What is under your bed?

A: So much embarrassing rubbish. Old sofa cushions, bags of material I intend to make into things and never do, loads of old clothes, a broken lamp, stacks of paperbacks I've run out of space for on the shelves, the odd mousetrap . . . I could go on.

Q: What is the most important lesson life has taught you?

A: Try to laugh it off.

Discover Catherine's other books . . .

The Old-Girl Network

Finding true love's a piece of cake – as long as you're looking for someone else's true love . . .

Polly McLaren is young, scatty and impossibly romantic. She works for an arrogant and demanding boss, and has a gorgeous if never-there-when-you-need-him boyfriend. But the day a handsome stranger recognizes her old school scarf, her life is knocked completely off kilter.

Adam is American, new to the country and begs Polly's help in finding his missing fiancée. Over dinner at the Savoy, she agrees – the girls of St Gertrude's look out for one another. However, the old-girl network turns out to be a spider's web of complications and deceit in which everyone and everything Polly cares about is soon hopelessly entangled.

The course of true love never did run smooth. But no one said anything about ruining your life over it. And it's not even Polly's true love . . .

Going Too Far

'You've gone all fat and complacent because you've got your man, haven't you?'

Polly Penhalligan is outraged at the suggestion that, since getting married to Nick and settling into their beautiful manor farmhouse in Cornwall, she has let herself go. But watching a lot of telly, gorging on biscuits, not getting dressed until lunchtime and waiting for pregnancy to strike are not the signs of someone living an active and fulfilled life.

So Polly does something rash. She allows her home to be used as a location for a TV advert. Having a glamorous film crew around will certainly put a bomb under the idyllic, rural life. Only perhaps she should have consulted Nick first.

Because before the cameras have even started to roll – and complete chaos descends on the farm – Polly's marriage has been turned upside down. This time she really has gone too far . . .

The Real Thing

Every girl's got one – that old boyfriend they never quite fell out of love with . . .

Tessa Hamilton's thirty, with a lovely husband and home, two adorable kids, and not a care in the world. Sure, her husband ogles the nanny more than she should allow. And keeping up with the Joneses is a full-time occupation. But she's settled and happy. No seven-year itch for Tessa.

Except at the back of her mind is Patrick Cameron. Gorgeous, moody, rebellious, he's the boy she met when she was seventeen. The boy her vicar-father told her she couldn't see and who left to go to Italy to paint. The boy she's not heard from in twelve long years.

And now he's back.

Questioning every choice, every decision she's made since Patrick left, Tessa is about to risk her family and everything she has become to find out whether she did the right thing first time round . . .

Rosie Meadows Regrets . . .

'Tell me, Alice, how does a girl go about getting a divorce these days?'

Three years ago Rosie walked blindly into marriage with Harry. They have precisely nothing in common except perhaps their little boy, Ivo. Not that Harry pays him much attention, preferring to spend his time with his braying upper-class friends.

But the night that Harry drunkenly does something unspeakable, Rosie decides he's got to go. In between fantasizing about how she might bump him off, she takes the much more practical step of divorcing this blight on her and Ivo's lives.

However, when reality catches up with her darkest fantasies, Rosie realizes, at long last, that it is time she took charge of her life. There'll be no more regrets – and time, perhaps, for a little love.

Olivia's Luck

'I don't care what colour you paint the sodding hall. I'm leaving.'

When her husband Johnny suddenly walks out on ten years of marriage, their ten-year-old daughter and the crumbling house they're up to their eyeballs renovating, Olivia is, at first, totally devastated. How could he? How could she not have noticed his unhappiness?

But she's not one to weep for long.

Not when she's got three builders camped in her back garden, a neighbour with a never-ending supply of cast-off men she thinks Olivia would be drawn to and a daughter with her own firm views on . . . well, just about everything.

Will Johnny ever come back? And if he doesn't, will Olivia's luck ever change for the better?

A Married Man

'What could be nicer than living in the country?'

Lucy Fellowes is in a bind. She's a widow living in a pokey London flat with two small boys and an erratic income. But, when her mother-in-law offers her a converted barn on the family's estate, she knows it's a brilliant opportunity for her and the kids.

But there's a problem. The estate is a shrine to Lucy's dead husband, Ned. The whole family has been unable to get over his death. If she's honest, the whole family is far from normal. And if Lucy is to accept this offer she'll be putting herself completely in their incapable hands.

Which leads to Lucy's other problem. Charlie – the only man since Ned who she's had any feelings for – lives nearby. The problem? He's already married . . .

The Wedding Day

Annie O'Harran is getting married . . . all over again.

A divorced, single mum, Annie is about to tie the knot with David. But there's a long summer to get through first. A summer where she's retreating to a lonely house in Cornwall, where she's going to finish her book, spend time with her teenage daughter Flora and make any last-minute wedding plans.

She should be so lucky.

For almost as soon as Annie arrives, her competitive sister and her wild brood fetch up. Meanwhile, Annie's louche ex-husband and his latest squeeze are holidaying nearby and insist on dropping in. Plus there's the surprise American house guest who can't help sharing his heartbreak.

Suddenly, Annie's big day seems a long, long way off – and if she's not careful it might never happen . . .

Not That Kind of Girl

A girl can get into all kinds of trouble just by going back to work . . .

Henrietta Tate gave up everything for her husband Marcus and their kids. But now that the children are away at school and she's rattling round their large country house all day she's feeling more than a little lost.

So when a friend puts her in touch with Laurie, a historian in need of a PA, Henrietta heads for London. Quickly, she throws herself into the job. Marcus is – of course – jealous of her spending so much time with her charming new boss. And soon enough her absence causes cracks in their marriage that just can't be papered over.

Then Rupert, a very old flame, reappears, and Henrietta suddenly finds herself torn between three men. How did this happen? She's not that kind of girl . . . *is she?*

A Crowded Marriage

There isn't room in a marriage for three . . .

Painter Imogen is happily married to Alex, and together they have a son. But when their finances hit rock bottom, they're forced to accept Eleanor Latimer's offer of a rent-free cottage on her large country estate. If it was anyone else, Imogen would be beaming with gratitude. Unfortunately, Eleanor just happens to be Alex's beautiful, rich and flirtatious ex.

From the moment she steps inside Shepherd's Cottage, Imogen's life is in chaos. In between coping with murderous chickens, mountains of manure and visits from the infuriating vet, she has to face Eleanor, now a fixture at Alex's side.

Is Imogen losing Alex? Will her precious family be torn apart? And whose fault is it really – Eleanor's, Alex's or Imogen's?

The Secret Life of Evie Hamilton

Evie Hamilton has a secret. One she doesn't even know about – yet . . .

Evie's an Oxfordshire wife and mum whose biggest worry in life is whether or not she can fit in a manicure on her way to fetch her daughter from clarinet lessons. But she's blissfully unaware that her charmed and happy life is about to be turned upside down.

For one sunny morning a letter lands on Evie's immaculate doormat. It's a bombshell, knocking her carefully arranged and managed world completely askew and threatening to sabotage all she holds dear.

What will be left and what will change for ever? Is Evie strong enough to fight for what she loves? Can her entire world really be as fragile as her best china?

One Day in May

May is the month for falling in love . . .

Hattie Carrington's first love was as unusual as it was out of reach – Dominic Forbes was a married MP, and she was his assistant. She has never told anyone about it. And never really got over it.

But years later with a flourishing antiques business and enjoying a fling with a sexy, younger man, she thinks her past is finally well and truly behind her.

Until work takes her to Little Crandon, home of Dominic's widow and his gorgeous younger brother, Hal. There Hattie's world is turned upside down. She learns that if she's to truly fall in love again she needs to stop hiding from the truth. Can she ever admit what really happened back then? And, if so, is she ready for the consequences?

A Rural Affair

'If I'm being totally honest I had fantasized about Phil dying.'

When Poppy Shilling's bike-besotted, Lycra-clad husband is killed in a freak accident, she can't help feeling a guilty sense of relief. For at long last she's released from a controlling and loveless marriage.

Throwing herself wholeheartedly into village life, she's determined to start over. And sure enough, everyone from Luke the sexy church-organist to Bob the resident oddball, is taking note.

But just as she's ready to dip her toes in the water, the discovery of a dark secret about her late husband shatters Poppy's confidence. Does she really have the courage to risk her heart again? Because Poppy wants a lot more than just a rural affair . . .

My Husband Next Door

For better or worse . . .

Ella was nineteen and madly in love when she married dashing young artist Sebastian Montclair. But that was a long time ago. Now Ella and the kids live in a ramshackle farmhouse while Sebastian and his paintings inhabit the outhouse next door – a family separated in every way but distance. Is it a marvellously modern relationship – or a disaster waiting to happen?

So when charming gardener Ludo arrives on the scene and Sebastian makes a sudden and surprising decision, Ella sees a chance at a fresh start.

Yet with two teenagers and her parents on the verge of their own late-life crisis, will Ella be allowed to choose her own path? And how long can she hide from the truth which haunts her broken marriage?